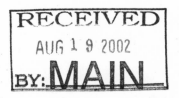

ALSO BY GUY JOHNSON

Standing at the Scratch Line

ECHOES
OF
A DISTANT
SUMMER

ECHOES OF

A DISTANT SUMMER

A NOVEL

Guy Johnson

RANDOM HOUSE · NEW YORK

Library of Congress Cataloging-in-Publication Data

Johnson, Guy
Echoes of a distant summer: a novel / Guy Johnson.
p.   cm.
Sequel to: Standing at the scratch line.
ISBN 0-375-50567-9
1. African American criminals—Fiction.   2. African American families—Fiction.   3. African American men—Fiction.   4. Oakland (Calif.)—Fiction.
5. Assassination—Fiction.   6. Grandfathers—Fiction.   7. Aged men—Fiction.
8. Mexico—Fiction.   I. Title.
PS3560.O3778 E28 2002   813'.54—dc21   2001048978

Random House website address: www.atrandom.com
Printed in the United States of America on acid-free paper

9 8 7 6 5 4 3 2

FIRST EDITION

Book design by Joseph Rutt

This book is dedicated to Caylin Nicole Johnson and Brandon Bailey Johnson, my grandchildren. Their lives lie before them, winding into the mists of the unknown. May future suns shine down upon them as gently as the ones that I have felt, and may the mountains they climb provide vistas that reach deep into their souls and cause them to be creative beings. Sweet children of the morrow, you have my heart. I hope only to have paved a small part of the path you will travel.

ACKNOWLEDGMENTS

As with any work that stretches into thousands of words, there are many people who must be thanked. Chief among them is my wife, Stephanie Floyd-Johnson, reader of a million versions and edits; sometimes impatient, but always loving and supportive. Then there are my friends and family: the village without whom there would be no one to ricochet against, no sounding board, and no harmonics with which to tune the personal melody. First, my mother: the artist in full stride, who has reached heights that I can only dream about. My cousin, Rosa Johnson, the artist in waiting. Then my irascible, independent-thinking friends. I mention the readers only: Amelia Parker, Ron Merritt, Janice Jones, Ernie Carpenter, Kate Hogdon, Lora Condon, Geoff Wood, Calvin Sharpe, Steve Turer, Sharon Brown, Al Nellum, Jim and Cynthia Hill, Leigh and Leland Brown, Norman Jayo, Elliot Daum, and Paul Schabracq. Paul deserves particular mention because he was the one who in 1982 suggested that I put pen to paper and write down some of the stories about my grandfather. From such simple beginnings came *Standing at the Scratch Line* and this book. Finally, I would thank my agent, Helen Brann, who has supported my work from the early years and represented me so ably.

Sunday, June 6, 1982

Sampson Davis was thinking about death when the hired black Cadillac stopped on the corner of Eddy and Fillmore streets in what had once been the heart of the black community in San Francisco. He was eighty-five years old and dying of lung cancer, yet he was not thinking of his own death. He was pondering why such a vital neighborhood as the Fillmore was in its death throes; it was a pale relic of what once had been. He remembered how it was in the forties and fifties: the streets filled with shiny new cars; storefront barbershops with gambling and numbers rooms behind them; bakeries; Russian delicatessens; five-and-dimes; restaurants; diners and chop suey houses; movie theaters; hole-in-the-wall blues and jazz joints; and always the streets filled with people in their many shades of black and brown. It was the death of vibrancy that haunted his thoughts.

Sampson looked at his watch. It was seven-thirty in the evening and despite the new high-rise apartment buildings and the modern facades on the Fillmore corridor businesses, the streets were relatively quiet. There were still some black people on the street, but they did not look affluent. They were not the ones living in the new apartments. They probably came from the towering, ugly, pink Section Eight apartments over on Buchanan Street, the last remnants of Fillmore's heyday. Sampson saw whites and a sprinkling of Asians going in and out of the new apartment buildings and grimaced. Asians he could understand. The northern part of the Fillmore had once been the heart of the Japanese neighborhood, until World War II policies had taken their properties and placed them all in prison camps. It broke Sampson's heart to see so many whites nonchalantly walking down streets that they had feared to tread in the fifties unless they were the police.

He was overcome by a bout of coughing, which caused his eyes to water. He was getting more things caught in his throat all the time and it was getting harder to catch his breath after each bout of coughing. If he could just last until this assignment was finished, death would come easily. He took a moment to take slow, measured breaths until it seemed that he was back to normal, whatever normal was for an eighty-five-year-old. The driver opened the door for him and he received un-requested assistance to his feet. A quarter of a block off Fillmore on Eddy Street was one of the few remaining black businesses. It was Eze-kiel J. Tree's Billiard Parlor. This was Sampson's destination. He scrib-bled a quick note on the small pad that he carried and handed it along with a hundred-dollar bill to the driver.

The note read: *I am going into that pool hall. If I do not come out within two hours, call the police.*

The driver, who was Hispanic, nodded and said, "I'll park somewhere close. If you look to your left when you come out, I'll be parked down the street."

Sampson shook his head. He wrote: *I don't want the car seen. You must wait until I have walked to the end of the block.*

The driver read his note and frowned. He asked, "Are you sure you can make it that far?"

Sampson nodded and smiled. He tapped his chest, checking to see if he still had the envelope in his interior breast pocket. He heard the crinkle of paper and felt reassured. Taking his time, he crossed Fillmore and walked slowly toward the billiard parlor. He moved fairly easily for a man of his age. Other than his cancer, the only time he had ever been ill in his life was when he had been made mute by a blow on the head, and really it was the terrible beating that he had received after that which had jeopardized his life.

When he pushed open the door of the pool hall, he knew that there was a very good chance that he might not come out alive, but that didn't cause him to hesitate one moment. In the thirty years that his wife, Wichita Kincaid, had been dead, living had become decidedly more unpleasant. Death was not nearly as frightening as the changes that he saw going on around him. This new, modern world was sicken-ing. Therefore, when he had been informed that he had lung cancer and that a regimen of surgery and chemotherapy could prolong his life, he had refused it.

He stepped into the establishment and saw that it was an extremely large room with a video arcade in the front which was being used by boys of different races from about ten years of age to those in their late teens, and behind that were pool tables lined up three across and five rows deep. Along the right wall was a long wooden bar which served beer, wine, and soft drinks, and cheap packaged snacks. The bar also doubled as the place where the pool balls were rented.

Sampson walked over to the bar and pointed to the draft-beer sign. He sat down on a stool at the end of the bar as far away from the front door as possible and surveyed the hall. The place was doing good business for a Sunday evening. There was an unwritten rule in pool halls like Tree's: The front tables were for walk-ins, people off the street, and casual players. The middle tables were reserved for the petty criminals and gang members, and the rear tables were for the real pool players and high rollers who bet their money under the table. True to this design the front tables were full with blacks, whites, and Asians, all recreational players. The middle tables, which were directly in front of him, were all occupied by young black street toughs and their girlfriends. They were all swaggering and talking loud, wearing lots of gold rings and chains, which they took special pains to show off. At the table closest to him, Sampson saw a young black man suddenly spin on his girlfriend and slap her hard across the face. "Listen, bitch!" the young man snarled. "You don't tell me what to do! If you want to keep those teeth in your mouth, you better shut the fuck up!" The young man looked around challengingly, daring anyone to take notice of his act. The girl sat silently and made no effort to protest.

The young man saw Sampson looking at him and challenged, "What the fuck you lookin' at? You got a problem?" Sampson merely shook his head and turned back to the bar. Behind him the young man continued, "That's right, you old motherfucker! You better turn around! I'll kick your ass too!"

Sampson took a deep breath and thought, This is what has happened to the black community. It has lost its respect for its women and elders. This young fool doesn't know, less than thirty years ago, how hard black men struggled to have their women respected, how the black woman was at the very bottom next to the Indian in taking shit from everyone, how black women had held together families torn apart by racism and poverty, how black people died of the simplest things because the nearest hospitals wouldn't give them medical attention. This fool doesn't know his history, because if he did he wouldn't dare treat his woman in such a profane manner.

Sampson began writing on his tablet and when he finished he tore the sheet off.

The bartender, a squat brown-skinned man with a broken nose and a missing front tooth, came over and asked, "You all right, old-timer?"

Sampson nodded and slid the written note across the bar. The bartender glanced at the note and a look of suspicion crossed his face as he asked, "Why do you want to see Mr. Tree?"

Sampson wrote another note and pushed it toward the bartender. The bartender asked, "Can't you talk?" Sampson shook his head and with a gesture indicated that he couldn't speak. The bartender read the second note and questioned, "You have some information about King Tremain? Who the hell is that? Why would Mr. Tree be interested in him?"

Sampson took the note back and wrote at the bottom: *Just tell Zeke Tree. He knows who King Tremain is. He'll remember the father of the man who gave him his scar.*

The bartender shook his head after he read Sampson's addendum. He leaned forward and whispered, "A word of advice, old-timer, Mr. Tree doesn't like being called Zeke. His closest friends call him John, but everyone else calls him Mr. Tree. And nobody who likes their health talks about his scar. I'm going to do you a favor and tear up this note. You can write another asking to see Mr. Tree." He tore the note in pieces and dropped it behind the bar.

Sampson nodded his thanks and wrote another note, which he handed to the bartender. The man took the note and went to a phone by the cash register. Sampson watched him as he talked. The bartender's demeanor was one of deference. Whoever was on the phone was of some importance. When he hung up the phone, the bartender returned the note and said, "Somebody'll be out soon. I hope you know what you're doing, old-timer. These are serious people you're messing with." He turned and went down the bar to serve some other customers.

Sampson did not have long to wait. Two black men came out of the back and made their way to the bar. One was a large, hulking man with a flattened nose and short, kinky hair, while the other was of medium build and was sporting a Jheri Curl hairstyle. They both appeared to be somewhere in their twenties. The hulking man was chewing on a cheap, pungent meat stick as he followed his smaller companion.

The smaller man stepped up to the bar and asked the bartender as he pointed to Sampson, "Conway, is this the guy who wanted to see Mr. Tree?" Conway nodded and hurried to occupy himself at the far end of the bar.

The man stalked over to Sampson, his Jheri Curls swaying sickeningly back and forth, and demanded, "What's your business with Mr. Tree?"

Sampson started to write a note in response when the larger of the two men stepped forward and slapped the side of his head. "My brother Frank asked you a question! Answer him, goddamn it, or I'll really give you something to worry about!" The big man had the face of a boxer who had, without proper preparation, stepped up in class too many times. He continued to bite off big chunks of his meat stick as he watched Sampson.

Sampson looked back at the man who had hit him. He was not afraid; if he was to die, so be it. It would be better than dying alone in a hospital. His only regret was that he had not met this particular fool even twenty years earlier. He would've enjoyed killing him. Sampson simply gestured to his mouth to indicate that he couldn't speak.

"What the fuck does that mean?" the big man demanded, pulling back his arm to slap Sampson again. "I told you to answer my brother!"

Conway, the bartender, came over and volunteered, "The guy's a mute, Jesse. He can't talk. That's why he's trying to write an answer."

Jesse nodded his head as this information sank in. "He can't talk, huh? Why the fuck didn't he say that?"

Frank turned to his brother. "Don't show what a dumb-ass you are, Jesse. The old coot can't talk! That's why he didn't say nothing!"

Jesse didn't like the fact that he had once again publicly displayed his dullness, and he held Sampson responsible. He grabbed Sampson's jaw in a tight grip and squeezed. "How we know he ain't jivin' us? He could be tryin' to run a game on us!"

Sampson made no move to struggle or get away, even though he was getting short of breath. If he lived he hoped that this man would be among those who would come after him. These men without history, rootless men, moving like tumbleweeds across the landscape. The earth would not miss them.

An older man in his fifties wearing rimless glasses appeared and he ordered, "Get your hands off of him! Can't you see there are people watching you? Are you two absolute fools? I told you, check the man out till I get off the phone with the boss. I didn't tell you to rough him up. Especially out here in front of witnesses."

Frank began to explain, "He ain't hurt, Mr. Gilmore. Jesse was just trying to make sure he knew we meant business. That's all."

"Yeah, that's right," Jesse confirmed. "I was gettin' him ready for you."

"Get the hell out of my sight and let me talk to the man!" Frank and Jesse backed away respectfully and walked down to the end of the bar. Gilmore turned to Sampson. "Who are you?"

Sampson wrote: *Sampson Davis. I used to work for King Tremain back in Oklahoma. I managed his general store after he left.*

"What do you want with Mr. Tree?"

I have information that he may find very valuable. Maybe even willing to pay for.

"What information?"

It's information for Mr. Tree's eyes only. If he thinks it's worth anything, he can reach me tonight at the Golden Gateway Hotel at Sixth and Howard streets.

After Sampson finished writing his note, he took the envelope out of his pocket and placed it on the bar.

Gilmore read the note quickly and picked up the envelope. He felt the envelope between his fingers, trying to determine if there was only paper in it. After he satisfied himself he said, "Okay, you delivered your message and we know how to contact you. Anything else?" Sampson shook his head. Gilmore gestured toward the door with his hand and said, "All right, you can go. If we need to contact you, we'll reach you at the Golden Gateway Hotel."

Sampson got up from the stool and walked slowly toward the door. He wasn't sure he could move his jaw. There was considerable pain when he attempted to open his mouth. It didn't really matter, he wasn't planning on eating again anyway. He stopped concentrating on his mouth and focused on his breathing. He didn't want a coughing fit in here. He had to get away before someone read what was enclosed in the envelope. He walked through the arcade, pushed open the door, and stepped out into the darkness of the street. He turned to his left and it did look like a long walk to the corner. He couldn't even *see* the corner; his night vision wasn't what it used to be. He kept moving, step after step, toward Fillmore. Once he reached the corner, the black Cadillac pulled out of a parking space and drove up alongside him. The driver jumped out and ran to open the door for him.

He sat back in the plush upholstery of the backseat and could not concentrate on anything but his wife, Wichita Kincaid, and the thought that he would soon be joining her. He just wanted to hear her laugh again, watch the way she moved her head when she was trying to make a point, taste some of her smothered chicken and dumplings again. It was hard for him not to daydream about her. She had opened his eyes to the world with her far-ranging interests and she had introduced him to literature. King Tremain had taught him to read, but all that King had ever read was newspapers and occasionally the Bible. Sampson had no idea that novels even existed until Wichita brought home Richard Wright's *Native Son*. From then on he read with a rabid frenzy. She introduced him to a world where his still tongue was irrelevant, a world where he could commune with philosophers and kings and dialogue with rogues and roustabouts. He was captured by the lyricism, the imagery, and the ideas expressed in the written word. He was stimulated and touched in ways he had never imagined possible. He actually gobbled up books, then he and Wichita would stay up late into the night discussing the questions the books raised, or pretended to answer. The seventeen years they were married were the best years in Sampson's life. She changed him from a virtual illiterate into a man who thirsted for knowledge. Then she died because the nearest hospital didn't treat Negroes.

He was embittered after her passing because she had died needlessly. Her appendicitis could have been easily treated. Nor did it make it more palatable to know that famous people like Bessie Smith and Robert Johnson had died in similar circumstances fifteen to twenty years earlier. Sampson felt that his life had been violated, that the one person he valued most had been stolen from him by the ignorance and hatred of whites. There were only two people he had ever met with whom he could spend unlimited time in harmony. The first was King Tremain and the second was Wichita Kincaid. He had never been a social being anyway, but after she died, Sampson lost the desire to travel far from home. King, who had come to the funeral, had visited him a few times after that, but otherwise they had kept their friendship alive through letters and assisted phone calls. Wichita's death had left Sampson with an abiding intolerance of his surrounding society, and over time he became a recluse.

The Cadillac pulled up in front of the hotel, which was a dilapidated three-story affair with a large pink neon sign. The sidewalk was alive with the south-of-Market nightlife. There were homeless people, leather queens, dope dealers, cross-dressers, sailors, drug addicts, narcs, people trying to sell a cheap trick and others trying to buy a cheaper one all wandering the street as if they had lost the way to where they really wanted to go, but were nonetheless in a hurry to get there.

Sampson passed the driver a note. The driver read it then turned back to him and asked, "Are you sure you want to go through with this? El Negro said that you could change your mind and it wouldn't be a problem."

Sampson nodded his head and held out his hand for the bag. The driver held back reluctantly then handed over a shopping bag.

The driver explained, "It's just like the one you practiced on in Mexico City. It's already wrapped in a dirty T-shirt. I suggest you pour the bottle of urine that's included on it and that will prevent people from picking it up."

Sampson wrote another note and handed it to the driver. The driver stared at him then conceded with a shrug. "You want the poison too? Okay, but if you take it too soon, you'll be dead before our friends come calling. Once you take it, you only have five minutes max, and given your age it might be much less. Are you absolutely sure you want to do this?"

Sampson merely nodded. There was no doubt in his mind. This night, God willing, he would join his cherished Wichita and put an end to the pain of his mortal flesh. His eyes had seen too much, his heart was weighted down by unresolved grievances, and he could not let loose the anger and indignation he felt boiling inside of him. He did not want to live in a world where history dictated everything yet meant nothing.

The driver handed him a small vial. "There are three pills in there in case you drop one or two. You only need one; if you take all three you may not have as much time as I originally indicated. Good luck to you. I hope this evening goes as planned."

Sampson smiled and nodded his thanks. He got out of the car and walked through the hotel's front door and went over to the registration desk, where he wrote a note and pushed it in front of the desk clerk.

The desk clerk, a thin, pale white man with stringy, dark hair and a sunken chest, looked over the note as he popped his chewing gum. After he finished reading he looked up at Sampson and said, "Sure! Sure, we'll call you if you get any visitors. That's hotel policy. We ain't going to treat you any different than our other patrons."

Sampson took two hundred-dollar bills out of his billfold and tore them in half. He gave two halves to the clerk and wrote on the bottom of the note he had previously written. He now had the clerk's full attention. The man's whole demeanor changed as he read the note.

"Mr. Davis, you don't have to worry. Your money talks! I'll make sure that everyone who works the desk and the switchboard knows that you want to be called the moment your visitors arrive."

Sampson turned and headed for his room, which was situated on the old mezzanine floor at the back of the hotel. There were only two other rooms on the mezzanine floor, which was part of the original hotel that had burned down in the forties. The rest of the hotel was newer, but it certainly wasn't visible to the eye. Like most flophouses that served the local down-on-their-luck stiffs, prostitutes, and small-time criminals, it was covered with the scum of years. Dim lighting in the halls and rooms helped hide the filth, but the smell could not be ignored. As he started up the stairs, he saw a white woman in a very short shift and fishnet stockings coming down with a muscular, black john. He recognized her. She had the room down at the end of the hall. The woman, whose makeup was so garish that she looked like a circus performer, gave him a professional smile as she passed. The john shouldered roughly past him, bumping him into the wall without a word of apology.

Sampson continued on up and entered his room at the top of the stairs. He set immediately to preparing the bomb. He lifted it out of the shopping bag, pulled back the T-shirt, connected the leads to their appropriate terminals, and took the bomb out into the hall. He placed it on the floor in the corner by his door then poured the strong-smelling urine on the shirt. Using the shopping bag to protect his hand, he reached up and broke the lightbulb at the top of the stairs and sprinkled the pieces on the floor in front of his door. When he went back inside his room, he pulled a rickety chair close to the door, moved the phone within easy reach, got himself a glass of water, which he set on the floor by the chair, then sat down to wait with the remote in his hand.

He did not feel even a twinge of regret that he planned to kill the men from Tree's before he himself entered the ether. They were men without history, tumbleweed men who raised only dust with their passage. This new, modern world seemed populated by such men. Sampson had read somewhere that an Uncle Tom had been appointed to some high panel over California's college system and that the fool had espoused getting rid of all affirmative action programs, as if racism no longer existed. Whoever he was, he definitely didn't know his history. Sampson wondered where was this man when the whites rioted in Tulsa in 1921 and burned down the black community, killing more than five hundred black people, many of whom were women and children; where was this man in the forties, when the water was diverted from the black-owned farms surrounding Bodie Wells and the land was squeezed dry. Where was he in the fifties and sixties, when only white farmers could get agricultural loans from the government? Where was this man when sad-eyed black people were driven by hunger and bank foreclosures off the farms on which their ancestors were buried? Where was this man and others like him when Wichita died in a pickup truck after being bumped around on rutted roads on the way to the closest hospital that would serve blacks?

Sampson sat for nearly two hours in his chair mulling over questions that only God and the fates could answer before the phone rang. He picked it up and was informed that three men were coming up to see him. No one else but King's men and the people at Tree's knew he was here, and King's men wouldn't visit him now. He returned the phone to its cradle and smiled. He opened the vial and put all three pills in his mouth. He picked up the glass of water and waited to hear footsteps outside his door. What did it matter that these three men would accompany him? Fate was a strange and twisted thing; there was no logic to it, no system by which it could be understood.

He heard the sound of broken glass being crunched outside his door and simultaneously drank his water and pushed the button on the remote. *I'm coming, Wichita. I'm coming.*

BOOK I

The Awakening of Jackson St. Clair Tremain

Tuesday, June 8, 1982

There are ominous events that occur in the sea of life, that rise above all other activities and happenings like a shark's fin above the liquid surface of a rolling wave. And so it was for Jackson Tremain when he received a call from his grandmother informing him of the death of Sampson Davis. After the call he attempted to concentrate on his daily duties, keeping a measured stroke, swimming through the passing minutes, but the meaning and importance of the call began to circle in a tightening spiral around his consciousness. He could ill afford such diversions. He had the tasks and responsibilities of a deputy city manager. Other areas that needed his full attention. He had fallen increasingly out of favor with the city manager, not for quantity nor quality of work but for things far more serious, differences in philosophy and style. Thus he had other predators in sight, ones that ate more than simple flesh.

Perhaps his response to the call might have been different if his whole morning had not begun in an unpleasant manner. Jackson had just arrived in his office when the phone began to ring. He glanced at his watch. It was seven-thirty. He put down his coffee and his cinnamon roll and picked up the receiver. The mayor's voice came bawling out in a blistering tirade. As a deputy city manager, Jackson had listened quietly to many such tirades; it was part of his job. He held the telephone between chin and shoulder and continued to drink his coffee, eat his cinnamon roll, and take notes all while being absolutely attentive.

The mayor's angry voice growled into the phone, "We need a Community Police Review Commission resolution to adopt during tonight's city council meeting concerning this matter. Goddamn it, this is an election year!"

Jackson listened quietly while Mayor Garrison Broadnax ranted on through the telephone receiver. He recognized that the mayor had every reason to be upset. The night before, two white police officers wearing masks while on duty in a patrol car had cruised the Chinese district of the city shouting words like *gook, Chink,* and *slope* to people on the street. The two patrolmen pulled a Chinese businessman from his truck and beat him after he cursed them for calling him racial epithets. They opened a five-inch gash in his forehead, locked him out of his truck, and left him lying in the street. They did not report the incident to police dispatch, but several scores of witnesses did. Jackson had received a call concerning the matter from one of his connections in the police department before he had come in to work that morning.

"What do you have to tell me, Tremain?" the mayor barked.

Jackson replied, "I may not have all the information. But as far as I know, the two officers in question have been placed on administrative leave pending an investigation into the allegations. It's only fair to say that they are denying everything and claiming that the Police Officer's Bill of Rights has been violated by putting them on administrative leave. They have requested a closed hearing in front of the Civil Service Commission to challenge any disciplinary action that may be forthcoming."

"I don't give a damn what those assholes say," growled the mayor. "The Civil Service Commission will deny any claims they have."

"I hate to remind you, Mr. Mayor, but you haven't had a quorum on the commission in three months. Only five of the nine seats are filled. You still need to appoint four commissioners."

"Damn!" the mayor exclaimed, and then there were several seconds of silence. "All right, I'll appoint at least two Asians; that'll fix their butts! What's the ethnic breakdown of the commission now?"

"Let me check the file." Jackson got up and went over to his filing cabinet, pulled a manila folder, and returned to his desk. "Two blacks, two whites, and a Hispanic."

"Hmmm, I need to give the Hispanic community another appointment and I've got to give that white woman from the Oakland Hills area something too. . . . All right! All right! I'll announce the commission appointments tonight at the council meeting. I want that Police Review Commission resolution you're preparing on my desk by three-thirty this afternoon!"

Jackson exhaled slowly, gathered his thoughts, then spoke calmly into the phone, "Mr. Mayor, the city manager has assigned me the responsibility of preparing the agenda for the executive session for this afternoon at four. I can't possibly poll all the council members for their agenda items, prepare the revisions, if any, to the executive session agenda, attend the executive session, and prepare this resolution."

"Listen, Tremain, Bedrosian didn't want to hire you. As the first black mayor of this city, I pressed him into hiring you. He was going to hire that white girl who had come here as an administrative intern three years ago over you even though you had three times her experience.

"And one of the important reasons I supported your appointment was that I wanted to be sure I could get at least some of the inside information on the legislation that he prepares for council. You know he was here before me and he thinks he's going to be here after me. But he doesn't know me. I've been dealing with white boys like him all my life. I'm going to get this boy treed, then I'll be looking forward to seeing the back of him!"

"That's pretty strong, Mr. Mayor," Jackson chided, thinking he couldn't risk being openly disloyal to his immediate supervisor. After all, the mayor was a politician and everything was salable if the right issue arose. "I mean, some of your electorate is white."

"You know what I mean and don't waste my time with naive remarks. There's people who happen to be white and there's white people. Now get me my goddamned resolution before three-thirty! Remember who helped you get where you are."

"I understand, Mr. Mayor," Jackson replied with resignation. The mayor played this card whenever Jackson showed any reluctance to perform some extra chore for him, and whenever he played it, Jackson responded appropriately. He assured the mayor, "The resolution will be on your desk by three-thirty." No reason to make an enemy of his principal advocate.

"Jackson, my boy, I knew you'd find the time for something like this." The mayor's voice now took on a honeyed tone. "I knew you came in early to work, that's why I called before eight. This resolution doesn't have to be a three-page monster with twenty *whereas*es either. Just something simple and to the point."

Knowing the answer, Jackson asked, "Shall I inform the city manager of this item at today's agenda luncheon?"

"Don't tell that fool Bedrosian a damn thing! All he'll do is find some pretext to delay. You know he's in bed with the police department on this matter. He and Chief Walker would love to see me defeated in this next election. Once I approve the resolution, I want you to send it directly over to the city clerk's office. She'll be waiting for it."

"You realize when you direct me to do something like this, it appears to my boss, Bedrosian, that I'm not following the chain of command. He'll know that I prepared this resolution, because I'll have to go to the agenda secretary for a number."

"As long as I'm here, you don't have to worry about him. Get it to the city clerk, I'll get her to get a number, okay?"

"Whatever you say, Mr. Mayor," Jackson replied, shaking his head. Bedrosian would still know that he prepared the resolution. As a result, Jackson knew that another confrontation with the city manager loomed. At least he had a job until the next election.

After he got off the phone with the mayor, Jackson called his administrative analyst into his office for a quick closed-door session. Corazon Benin was a short, good-looking woman in her mid-thirties who wore her lush, dark hair rolled into an attractive bun.

"What's up, boss?" she asked as she sat down with a yellow tablet and a pen.

"The mayor wants something and I can't report it at the agenda luncheon."

She laughed. "Again? He certainly doesn't mind putting you on the spot. What is it this time?"

"He wants a resolution for a Police Review Commission prepared for adoption by tonight."

Before Corazon could respond, the phone on Jackson's desk jangled loudly. It was the switchboard line. He complained, "What is this? I told the secretaries to hold calls before eight-thirty!"

"I'll go see," Corazon volunteered as she stood up and went out the door. The phone continued to ring and was still ringing when Corazon reappeared.

"Carol says it's your grandmother and she says it's urgent."

"What the hell can she want?"

"You told me she was dead," Corazon observed. "So it must be pretty important for her to call from the grave."

"She *is* dead, been dead for years, she just hasn't realized it," Jackson answered. "Why don't you let me take this call, and while I'm on it, would you make a copy of the resolutions that were recently adopted for the Parks Commission and the Civil Service Commission? Maybe we can lift some of the language right off of those two." Corazon nodded and left the office.

Jackson took a deep breath, picked up the phone, and said, "Good morning, city manager's office."

"Jackson, is that you?" A raspy, impatient tone.

"May I help you?" he asked, refusing to recognize the voice.

"This is your grandmother!" The voice was now imperious.

"What a surprise," Jackson replied without enthusiasm. "I'm sure that we could find something to talk about if we really searched ourselves, but frankly, I'm extremely busy right now."

"There is no need for rudeness! I shall overlook it this time for I have important news."

Jackson smirked. "You have important news? I'm sorry, but I really am busy. Perhaps we can talk when I'm not so harried."

"I said this was important!" The tone was now emphatic.

"To whom? You certainly don't have anything important to say to me. Now, I'd like to hang up. Can we agree to end this call?"

"Did you read this morning's paper? Sampson Davis, along with three other men, was killed two nights ago by a bomb in one of those south-of-Market fleabag hotels!"

"No, Grandmother. I don't have time to skim the paper for sensational news."

"Sampson Davis was one of your grandfather's closest and oldest friends. He hasn't been to the Bay Area since your grandfather went to Mexico, and he wouldn't come here unless your grandfather sent him."

"So?"

"This is your grandfather sending some kind of a message. Something is wrong! We need to know what's going on. He may be dying."

"So? I'm surprised it's a matter of concern to you."

"You and Franklin must go down and see him before he dies. I'm sure he wants to see you."

"He spoke to you? He asked to see Franklin?"

"No, but his lawyers called me from Mexico a couple of weeks ago about some real estate documents. That, combined with this piece of news, makes me think he's trying to get his things in order. I think it's a good idea if you and Franklin go down and check things out, to represent the family's interest."

"Send Franklin. I'm not flying down to Mexico City to see my grand-father, even if he is dying. Good-bye, Grandmother. Talk to you in an-other ten years. It has been ten years, hasn't it, since we last talked?"

"This is no time to go over our differences! Your grandfather may be dying, but he still has enemies. You need to talk to him. All our lives may hang in the balance."

"Thanks for the melodrama, Grandmother. If you're really that wor-ried, send Franklin. He's your boy. You and I have nothing further to say. Good-bye!" Jackson did not wait for her response, but set the re-ceiver down on its cradle.

The rest of the day was a kaleidoscope of actions and images. Jack-son gobbled a cold meatloaf sandwich during the city manager's agenda luncheon and along with the other deputies gave a basic status report of his agenda item assignments and reports. He made no mention of his task for the mayor. Thanks to Corazon, he delivered the requested res-olution by three-thirty and had the executive session agenda duplicated and ready by four. The executive session was hot and feisty, as the po-lice chief had to appear to explain to the council members what actions his department had taken as a result of the investigation into the previ-ous day's incident in the Chinese community.

Chief Torvil Walker was a florid-faced, potbellied man with white hair and pale gray eyes. He had the splotched and purple nose of a drinker. He was a good old boy who had come up through the ranks, who due to his mediocrity and caution had not made the enemies that many of his more talented rivals had, and thus had been appointed to the department's top position. Chief Walker began his presentation with a recommendation that a reprimand be placed in each officer's file. However, after an hour of merciless questioning by council members, he recanted and agreed that stronger action must be taken. Several of the council members were close to asking for his resignation.

The city council meeting didn't convene until seven in the evening and, of course, many minority community leaders appeared to speak on the incident in Chinatown. Waiting for a break in the line of speakers, the mayor dramatically pulled out his resolution to establish a Police Review Commission. Despite the police chief's and the city manager's objections, it was unanimously adopted to resounding cheers from the audience. The council then proceeded on to other city business.

It was nearly midnight before the city council was adjourned. As Jackson walked out, he saw City Manager Bedrosian staring at him with displeasure. It wasn't the first time and it probably wasn't going to be the last. He crossed the street to the four-story parking lot and sought to wash all thoughts of work from his mind.

At one o'clock in the morning Jackson Tremain stood out on the deck of his house overlooking the glittering lights of downtown Oakland. He could not go to sleep. There were too many memories flooding across his consciousness, washing up emotional driftwood. He sought to lose himself in the tranquillity of early morning silence. The night sky had been swept free of clouds by a persistent, gusting wind. The stars glistened with promise on the dark, blue velvet dome of night. There was a lonely, wavering train whistle from freight chugging its way through Jack London Square. He stared at the patterns of lights from the Bay Bridge, stretching in long arcing loops across the bay. The bridge itself could not be seen, but faded into the darkness that extended over the water. That same darkness seemed to reach right into his heart.

After the phone call with his grandmother, he had successfully suppressed all thought of her and his grandfather. Unfortunately, the loneliness of night reawakened the specter of his grandfather. He saw himself once more, just out of high school, kneeling in the shadows of a building in rural Mexico, a hand grenade and a rifle in his hands while explosions and gunfire echoed around him. After nearly twenty years, Jackson could still hear keening voices rising and falling with the wind from that last summer with his grandfather.

When the moon began to rise above the dark horizon, he went back into the house, thinking that he would simply ignore his grandmother's phone call. He would not let his grandparents pull him back into their conflicts. He would rise above their predatory distractions. He went to bed hoping for dreamless sleep.

Wednesday, June 9, 1982

Mclvey's was a bar located on the Embarcadero, along the old Jack London waterfront area, not far from Oakland's City Center. The bar was across the street from a vacant pavilion which blocked the view

of the bay and the estuary that ran between Oakland and Alameda.
Across the street in front of the vacant pavilion, Jesse Tuggle and
Fletcher Gilmore sat in a car and watched Jackson Tremain lock his car
and walk into the bar. Jesse was slouched over the steering wheel,
chomping on a pungent beef stick. He chewed and smacked uncon-
cernedly with his mouth open. His companion, sitting with a derby hat
in his lap, quietly cleaned his rimless glasses.

"You sure that's him?" Jesse asked, smacking loudly on his beef stick
in between his words.

The older man sniffed, "I couldn't miss him in a crowd. Except for his
color, he's the spitting image of his grandfather. Like he was reincarnated after burning in hell."

"He one of the guys who killed Frank? You want me to get him,
boss?" Jesse asked with an angry frown. He turned toward Gilmore, a
piece of beef hanging out of his mouth.

The older man averted his face from the smell and replied, "The way
you and Frank manhandled that old man is what got him killed. The old
guy would never have blown up that bomb if you two hadn't scared the
shit out of him."

Jesse didn't say anything. He and Frank had both been raked over
the coals by their uncle, John Tree, before Frank and two others had
been sent out to bring the old man back for further questioning. Their
subsequent deaths had only increased his uncle's rage.

Gilmore asked, "Is there a back door to that bar?"

"Yeah, but it lets out onto a little alley that only exits onto this
street," Jesse answered, his words slightly slurred by his chewing. He
laughed humorlessly and turned toward Gilmore. "That's sort of funny,
huh? The back door lets out by the front door."

Gilmore averted his face again and rasped irritably, "Why can't you
chew gum? I can't stand the smell of that stuff!" He did not share in
Jesse's humor. There was a great deal of money at stake, a fortune, in
fact. Although Jesse did not know it, many lives had already been lost
in the thirty-year battle with the man to whom this fortune belonged.

"We'll just wait for him to leave and follow him," Gilmore said as he
adjusted his clothes and flicked a piece of lint off his derby. He was fas-
tidious in his dress and manner. He exhaled slowly in an effort to relax
and prepared himself for a long wait.

Inside the bar, Jackson Tremain paused to get his bearings. It was happy hour and the bar was crowded. He was a tall, broad-shouldered man in his late thirties. His skin was a reddish-brown color, the genetic gift of his African and Choctaw ancestors. He was handsome, dressed in a fashionably cut double-breasted suit, and he received several admiring looks from women as he made his way farther into the bar. He heard himself being hailed over the rhythm-and-blues tune that blared from a jukebox in the rear.

"Jackson! Jackson Tremain! We're back here!"

Jackson turned and saw several men waving at him. He made his way through the crowd to their table. It was four of his friends, conducting their usual Wednesday evening male-bonding ceremony. A chair was being passed overhead to him. He took it and sat down.

His friends were drinking top-shelf margaritas and hotly discussing the pros and cons of working in the public versus the private sector. There was a full pitcher of margaritas in the center of the table along with several shot glasses of Grand Marnier and an empty pitcher. It was obvious they had started without him and were feeling no pain. The men, Presenio Cordero, Wesley Hunter, Dan Strong, and Lincoln Shue, had been his friends since childhood and they were all roughly the same age.

Pres Cordero reached over and jabbed Jackson in the arm. "Haven't seen you all week. Didn't think you were going to make it." Pres was a good-looking, brown-skinned man with an easy smile and twinkling eyes. He had straight black hair which he wore artistically long and a thick black mustache. He looked as if he could have been the product of any one of a dozen different ethnic groups, but he hailed from the Philippines. Pres jabbed Jackson in the arm again and said in a teasing tone, "Don't you value our time? We've been getting drunk waiting for you."

Before Jackson could answer, Dan Strong pushed a margarita toward him. "Drink up! We're tired of waiting for your sad, middle-aged ass." Dan was a big bear of a man. He had played on the offensive line for Howard University, and even though many years had passed and he was getting soft, the size of his arms and shoulders still reflected thousands of hours of pumping iron. Dan raised his glass. "Here's to working in the municipal public sector where the people still have access to their public officials. Also, I would like to drink to Romance, Liberty, Equality, Brotherhood, and pâté de foie gras!"

Lincoln Shue smirked and said, "And God bless Roy Rogers. I'm surprised you didn't include truffles." Lincoln was a graceful man of medium build with the pale skin and broad, flat face of his Chinese
ancestors. He wore his black hair cut in a neat, professional manner and
almost always had a trace of a sardonic grin on his face. He raised his
glass, "Nonetheless, I'll join you in drinking to some of mankind's loftier
goals."

"Liberty? Equality? Fraternity?" Wesley Hunter challenged. "Those
aren't societal goals, those are just words! The only thing that society
respects is power. And the way you achieve power today is through the
pursuit of money!" He was a dark-skinned man who wore his kinky hair
cut in a short, stylish flat top. When he smiled, even, white teeth were
exposed. He raised his glass to Dan. "But I too will drink to the mythi-
cal ideals."

Dan gestured at Lincoln and Wesley and said sourly, "You two
clown-butts have ruined the intent of my toast." Dan turned to Pres and
prodded, "You come up with a toast. See if they give you shit."

"I want to follow up on what Wesley said," Pres replied, sipping from
his glass. "I think Wesley is right. There is no societal reward for ethical
behavior or moral stature. Money is the only indicator of success. And
we wonder why our culture is falling apart."

Dan looked at Jackson. "You're mighty quiet."

Wesley interjected, "What about the brilliant point that Pres and I
just made? No response?"

Dan made a gesture of dismissal. "You're preaching to the choir.
There's nothing further to say, so we've changed directions." He
pointed to Jackson. "We're talking about him now." Dan put a look of
sincerity on his face and asked Jackson, "What's up, Ace? You look like
you heard that the woman you were going out with last year just died
of a dormant venereal disease."

Lincoln shook his head and said, "That was in poor taste."

Wesley shrugged. "The existence of dormant venereal disease would
make me sort of quiet. I love fucking and I haven't yet met all the
women I intend to fuck."

Dan waved a hand of dismissal in Lincoln and Wesley's direction.
"I'm trying to find out about Jax. He hasn't said two words since he got
here. What's up, Jax?"

Jackson shook his head. "You guys don't need my input. You're doing
fine without me."

Dan gave Jackson an evaluative look. "Are you having an emotional breakdown?"

Lincoln protested, "Why should he expose himself to your casual observation? He has a right to keep his sickness to himself."

Wesley agreed. "Some dysfunctions are best kept behind closed doors."

Pres waved his hand to quiet the liquored tongues. "Just ignore the peanut gallery, Jax, and tell us what's going on. You do look damn serious."

Jackson Tremain looked at the expectant faces around him and asked, "Do you think people are born evil, so evil that everything they touch turns evil?"

Dan boomed, "Whoa! How dysfunctional are we going to get here?"

Jackson took a deep breath. "We're going to the far side. I got a call from my grandmother on Tuesday. First time I've spoken to her in ten years." Jackson took a drink and then summarized his conversation with his grandmother.

Wesley questioned, "Your grandfather would do that? Send a close friend on a suicide mission? Just to send a message?"

Dan sipped his drink and said, "In his heyday, Jax's grandfather was a pretty bad dude. You have to remember, he removed a lot of people from the gene pool."

Wesley was incredulous. "But would he send a friend to his death?"

Lincoln interjected, "What does your grandmother think?"

Jackson shrugged. "She thinks he sent a message and that I ought to go down to Mexico with my cousin Franklin and see him." Jackson took a long drink from his glass. No one spoke and although there were voices and music in the background, there was silence at the table.

Finally, Wesley asked, "You're not that close to your grandfather, are you? Did you ever love him?"

"In sequence to the questions asked," Jackson replied, "no. And I hated him! I think he's evil incarnate."

Pres argued, "No human can embody evil. It's too big and complex a force. It's like entropy. Plus, humans are the products of their experiences. They're not innately anything."

There was a moment of silence then Lincoln asked Jackson, "You hated him back then; do you hate him now?"

Pres offered, "He hated him then, he loved him then. He hates him now and he loves him now."

Dan responded, "Thank you, Pres, for clarifying absolutely nothing."

"Some things are too complex to be clarified," Pres answered with a shrug.

Lincoln asked, "What are you going to do, Jax?"

Dan chimed in, "It seems to me you got to go down and see the old guy and make your peace."

"That's just like him," Pres exclaimed while pointing at Dan. "There can be serious issues or questions under discussion and Dan will attempt to provide all the answers himself, like no one else really needs to be there!"

Dan looked at Pres questioningly. "Are your biorhythms fluctuating off the scale? Is your rising sign in Haiti or Biafra? Are you on the rag?"

This time Pres had to shake his head. "That last was truly a politically backward statement."

Dan pointed a big, beefy hand at Pres. "Don't give me that politically correct fascism! I'm going to keep saying shit that I think is funny."

"All right! All right! You assholes don't care," Jackson interrupted. "I'm spilling my guts and you turkeys are busy capping on one another. Some friends."

Lincoln answered, "We've been drinking! What do you expect? If you want serious analysis, get here on time, not when we're on the second pitcher of margaritas."

Pres urged, "If you think he really is close to death, you have to go visit him before he dies. You have to forget about what has gone before and make amends. It's the only way you'll ever be totally free of the way his memory affects you."

Dan pointed at Pres and declared, "See! He's saying the exact same thing as me."

Wesley began to sing "Go Down, Moses," substituting the words, "Go down, Jackson. Way down in Mexico."

Lincoln stood up. "On that note, I think it's time to go." Wesley and Dan rose as well.

Jackson remained seated. "Well, thanks, you schmucks, for listening to all of my concerns about this matter. Shit, you didn't even let me discuss the details."

Dan put a restraining hand on Jackson's shoulder. "When you get to our level, details obscure the panorama."

Lincoln put on his coat, straightened his collar, and gestured to Dan with a nod of his head. "Come on, don't get caught up." He turned to Jackson. "If this is really something you want to talk about, let's schedule some time without alcohol and we'll brainstorm."

"Linc's right," Dan agreed as he picked up his briefcase and stood. He towered over both Lincoln and Wesley. Dan waved his briefcase in Jackson's direction. "Let's schedule another time to discuss your details. Otherwise, we could be here till midnight listening to you. Call me tomorrow in the A.M. See the rest of you turkey-butts later."

Lincoln waved at Jackson and Pres, both of whom had remained seated. "I'll be in the office tomorrow morning too, Jax. Call if you want to set up a talk."

"Wait a minute. I'm going to be out of town a couple of days," Wesley said. "Are we still going shooting at the range on Saturday?"

Dan pivoted and faced him. "Yeah, I need to get out to the range a few times before deer-hunting season opens. Make sure my sights are on target."

Jackson carped, "You and Lincoln still killing harmless animals?"

Dan shrugged. "The meat fills the freezer and I don't notice you turning it down when I barbecue." He turned to Wesley. "Be at my house by eight-thirty on Saturday morning."

Lincoln chimed in, "I have to clean my rifles, but I'll be there. I'm looking forward to hunting season."

"What about you, Jax? And you, Pres? You guys coming?" Wesley asked.

"I'm really not into it, thanks," Jackson answered without enthusiasm.

"He spoke for me too," Pres added.

"Okay, but you guys are missing a lot of fun. We're not killing anything at the range and shooting is close to ejaculation!" Wesley declaimed with a broad smile.

Jackson acknowledged without sarcasm, "That's high praise coming from you."

"I'm a straight shooter in both worlds," Wesley replied with a laugh. He nodded to Jackson and Pres. "Well, I'm walking out with them. I'll see you at the karate dojo on Thursday, Jax. Later, Pres."

The three men made their way out of the bar and into the night. Pres and Jackson sat for a moment in silence and finished their drinks. For the first time since he had entered the bar, Jackson noticed the music playing over the sound system. It was a slow, rocking blues number by

B. B. King. Although he could not honestly say he was sad, the music seemed to match his mood perfectly. He felt something skirting his consciousness. He told himself that it was only a feeling, a malaise, a form of emotional fatigue. Names, faces, and events came swirling to the surface of his mind like debris in some muddy pool that had been disturbed. For several minutes he lost himself in the past, feeling the sun and the winds of his youth and the terrible, brooding presence of his grandfather.

Pres brought him back with "Want another drink?"

Still within the well of his thoughts Jackson gave a shake of his head. He had made a conscious choice to walk away from all that his grandfather stood for prior to his freshman year in college and he had been successful. Except in the nocturnal world of dreams, he did not even acknowledge the old man's existence. However, the phone call had opened the vault and now the old memories came crowding into the forefront of his awareness.

Pres pushed his long, straight black hair out of his eyes. "You really are preoccupied. We've been here nearly ten minutes and you haven't said a thing to me. What am I? Performance art?"

"If you are, you aren't subtle," Jackson answered mildly. After a moment's pause, he said, "I'll tell you something." He leaned forward over the table and dropped his voice. "Since I received my grandmother's call, I feel like I'm moving out of step with the world around me. Everything seems unstable. I feel life as I know it is about to fall apart. The warp and weave of my life is on the verge of shredding, like there's a rip in the social fabric somewhere." A trickle of sweat dripped down Jackson's face.

Pres stared at him a moment then asked, "Are you sure you're not feeling all this because of the stress at work? You are serious, right? You're not putting me on?"

"I'm dead serious. This is no joke."

Pres nodded his head. "Well, in a way that makes sense. You've got a lot of unfinished business with your grandfather. He had a hell of a grip on your adolescence. But I don't get this 'Life as I know it is about to fall apart'! Isn't that a little dramatic?"

"This is just a sense that I have and I feel it strongly. The past and the present seem to be overlapping. Believe me, I've done my best to suppress all thought of my grandparents. But last night my dreams were filled with memories of my grandfather and Mexico. And I don't mean vague remembrances. I mean those dreams that I used to have in which I relive whole summers. Last night I relived the night my father was killed. This was real! Like I was transported back in time. When I woke this morning, I was actually sore and exhausted."

"Why do you think this is happening?"

"It's my grandfather. Ever since I talked to my grandmother yesterday I've felt him, felt the menace of him. This morning I awoke to the smell of blood and cigars. It was the smell of his hunting lodge."

"If it's really distressing you that much, have you considered getting some counseling? You may need to talk with a therapist."

"Why? These feelings are more real than a therapist could ever be. It's like I feel like my grandfather is calling me. That he's trying to reach out to me."

"What makes you say that?"

"I don't really know. It's just a feeling." Jackson chuckled. "He used to say that I should always trust my feelings. Well, this is strong. I can't rid myself of it." Jackson ran his hand over his short, kinky hair and discovered that it was wet with perspiration. "Let's get out of here," he suggested. "I'm cooking in this heat."

A few minutes later they were standing under a streetlight by Jackson's car. The wind was gusting through the Embarcadero corridor, causing occasional swirls of paper trash along the street. The moon had not yet risen, and the stars had faded against the backdrop of city lights.

Jackson looked up at the night sky and mused, "Sometimes we forget how good it is to be alive." Then he shrugged and looked at Pres. "What's going on with you? Still having trouble at the job?"

"Unfortunately." Pres pulled his coat collar around his neck. "There's a lot of crap happening at the radio station. This new director is trying to take money out of my training program to pay for the redecoration of her office and boardroom. She's a disgrace to National Public Radio."

"Isn't the station's new director a black woman? She should see the necessity for the training program. After all, you are training minorities and women for positions in radio production."

"She doesn't care about that. The only thing black about her is the color of her skin; everything else is ambition. She has no loyalties that can't be purchased."

"Sounds like you have a battle there," Jackson acknowledged. "Better walk carefully. You don't want to jeopardize your program."

"You don't have to intend harm for it to happen," Pres stated philo-sophically. "Look at you and your grandfather."

Jackson gave Pres a look of disbelief. "It would take an astral projec-tion to get from your problems at the radio station to the totally unre-lated subject of my grandfather."

Pres inhaled the salt air off the bay and put his hand on Jackson's arm. "He never meant to harm you. He was just trying to teach you to be like him. You didn't talk to him for nearly twenty years because of that. Yet, you didn't mean him any harm either. You were just taking care of your-self. And now, you're planning not to go see him before he dies." Pres paused a moment and looked up into Jackson's eyes. "There's a whole lot of harm been caused and now you are going to perpetuate it."

"How the hell can you say that?" Jackson sputtered angrily. "You must have forgotten what I had to do for that man. I don't owe him a goddamn thing. My debts are paid!"

"Remember, it was me who picked you up at the airport eighteen, nineteen years ago from the last trip you made to Mexico." Pres thumped his chest for emphasis. "I haven't forgotten! But I've watched this thing eat at you for all that time. It's rotting your insides. Now you have a chance to wipe the slate clean. Wipe it clean! Do the right thing! Get on with your life!"

"You think that by simply going down there, I'll wipe the slate clean?" The sarcasm was heavy in Jackson's voice. "I wish it was so easy!"

"It's a start, that's for damn sure! You sure won't make matters any bet-ter if you don't see him before he dies. The man's on the brink of meet-ing God or the devil. What the hell else can you do for him or to him, except forgive him?"

"I don't see what's so earthshaking about forgiving him!"

"How do you expect to build emotional bridges if you can't forgive those that love you? Plus, you're not forgiving him for himself, but for *yourself*. You are letting go of the anger and the resentment."

Another gust swept up from the estuary and Pres pulled his collar tighter around his neck. "Why do we always have to be outside before we talk?" As the two men shook hands Pres said, "If I didn't love you, I wouldn't even stick my nose into this. It's easier not to argue with you, but I can't help myself. I love you, man. You're my friend and brother."

Jesse Tuggle and Fletcher Gilmore watched Jackson and his friend get into their respective cars. "Want me to follow him, boss?" Jesse asked, pointing to Jackson's car.

"Of course, follow him!" the older man snapped with exasperation. "Just let me write down his friend's license number. And if you have to call me something, call me Mr. Gilmore." He was tired of Jesse. Jesse was a fidgeter and an incessant talker, the worst two crimes for surveillance professionals as far as Gilmore was concerned. The essence of watching was unobtrusiveness, and inherent in that concept was stillness and silence.

"If he goes home, do we have to wait around all night?" Jesse was not enthusiastic about the prospect of spending the evening in the car.

"Just follow the car," Fletcher answered tiredly.

Friday, June 11, 1982

Dr. William DuMont Braxton turned away from the balcony that jutted out from his hotel suite and waved to the three men at the table in his sitting room. He sipped his Bloody Mary and said, "We all have our drinks. Let's begin." He paused a moment to be sure he had their attention, then continued. "Let me bring you up to date on what has transpired since we last met."

One of the men, John Tree, elbowed the small, dark-skinned man to his left and asked, "You sure you don't want nothing stronger than that soda pop?" It was not an act of politeness, it was more a taunt designed to increase the smaller man's uneasiness. Tree was a big, barrel-shaped, brown-skinned man with thick, muscular arms, and when he grinned, gold-capped teeth glinted in his mouth. He had a mean-looking scar that angled from his right ear through the corner of his mouth down across his chin, which, in the process of healing, had tightened and pulled his lips and his eyebrows slightly to the right; it gave his face a sad smirk. But few were ever fooled by his expression, for he had the bearing of a large, dangerous animal.

Delbert Witherspoon shook his head nervously and edged away from his tormentor.

Tree elbowed Delbert more roughly and growled, "I thought a little drinky might calm you, huh?"

Braxton suppressed a look of disdain and said, "Gentlemen. Gentlemen. Shall we go on and review the information that we have?" He passed thin manila folders to both Tree and Witherspoon as well as the third man, Paul DiMarco. Braxton took out his glasses from a soft leather case and placed them gingerly on his face. "The one piece of information that is not contained in your folders is that King Tremain is seriously ill and may be close to death."

"One of our people finally got to him?" DiMarco asked, suddenly alert. He was a short, powerfully built, compact white man in his early forties.

"No, it appears to be natural causes," Braxton answered as he sat down at the table.

"Damn!" DiMarco sputtered angrily. "That bastard doesn't deserve to die of natural causes! All the pain he's caused my family."

Tree leaned forward and put his elbows on the table. He was looking at Braxton but he was talking to DiMarco when he said snidely, "You shoulda sent somebody to Mexico who knew how to do the job right."

DiMarco challenged, "Who? You?" He laughed derisively. His intense, pale blue eyes stared directly at Tree and there was no fear in them. The contempt was strong in his voice when he continued, "You're small-time. You don't have the organization or know-how to mount an international operation."

Tree scowled. He pointed a finger at DiMarco and threatened, "You better watch what you saying."

Braxton felt like he was watching two dogs sniffing each other before a fight. He interceded, "Do you gentlemen realize that our business today may possibly involve as much as fifty million dollars?" He paused to let DiMarco comprehend that information. He had already talked to Tree about not revealing the contents of the envelope that Sampson had left. Braxton had no intention of sharing all the money with DiMarco. He continued, "This is business. If we focus on what we must do, we'll see that success depends upon how well we all work together. Can I get an amen?"

DiMarco nodded his head in agreement and said, "It's business."

Tree gave DiMarco a gleaming and twisted smile. "It's cool! It's business."

Witherspoon stood up and put on his fedora. "I don't believe I should be here. I don't care about whatever business you're doing! Just leave T and W Construction out of it. All I want is the construction company."

"Your father was a partner in our business. You don't have a construction company without us," DiMarco said through gritted teeth.

"I do construction. My work is legal," Witherspoon tried to explain. "I don't want to know what you're doing. I don't care what my father used to do with you. He's been dead nearly a year. I just want to continue to run my construction company and I want you to launder your money somewhere else."

DiMarco hit the table with his fist. "My family has shed blood for the money this construction company was built with. There's no way you're going to walk away with ownership of this company. Not today, not ever!"

Witherspoon sat down and stared at the table.

"Gentlemen, gentlemen," Braxton reminded his visitors, "we're all on the same team. Let's keep up a professional front, shall we? Will you open the folders in front of you? Then we can review the facts available to us." He picked up the top sheet from the small stack within the folder. "This is a brief history of where we stand, starting in 1953 when King Tremain intercepted some money from one of our transactions. The following year he intercepted an even greater amount of money—"

"And killed five members of my family!" DiMarco interjected angrily.

"Yes, he killed a great many other people as well," Braxton agreed.

"He ain't the only one who's got a blood debt," Tree said, indicating DiMarco with a quick nod of his head. "I lost two brothers and his son gave me this." Tree pointed to the scar on his face. "And just last week, I lost a nephew! I got plenty to settle with King Tremain."

"The best way to settle with him," Braxton continued, trying to get the conversation back on track, "is to take everything he's worked so hard to build—to dismember his empire. So let's get on with the historical review. The money he took was never found. All the information that we've uncovered over the years seems to indicate that he invested the money in a land management corporation. We have narrowed it down to four different firms which, in the past, have done a lot of business in the Western Addition. Two of them have out-of-state papers. The other two were incorporated in California. One of the local firms owns the majority of the property management business that his wife still runs. One of the out-of-state firms actually owns the corporation that owns the T and W Construction company. Unfortunately, the incorporation papers for that particular firm are in Switzerland. This is the one I think is most likely to be the corporation that Tremain set up."

DiMarco spoke, "You've been saying this for years and we still don't have any real proof that's what he did with the money. Even Delbert's father didn't know what he did with the money and he was part owner in the construction company years before King ever hit a money shipment. Plus, it doesn't make sense. I don't see how an uneducated black could set up a complex system of corporations like this." DiMarco questioned, "And even if he did set it up, what good is it to us?"

"Yeah, a corporation like this? That ain't like King Tremain." Tree's voiced grumbled doubtfully, "He was a loner. He never kept no paper records. It was all in his head. I'd bet he has hid that money away somewhere."

"That's a mistake too many people have made about Tremain," Braxton interposed smoothly. "Just because he was uneducated does not mean that he was stupid. And believe me, if he owns any one of these corporations, we're talking about in excess of fifty million dollars in land and assets. If we move swiftly and carefully when his papers surface, we can set ourselves up quite well. The advantages for money laundering are obvious."

"You guys are crazy!" Witherspoon exclaimed. "You're going to take over a legitimate business? You think you're going to get away with that? I won't have any part of it!"

Tree turned on Witherspoon and drew back his fist.

"That won't be necessary, John," Braxton said quietly. "Delbert understands that he will do whatever we deem necessary. Since his father died, he's having trouble dealing with this aspect of the business. Isn't that right?"

Witherspoon looked around at the faces at the table and found no sympathy. He struggled to hold his position. "Just because you've laundered some money through my company doesn't give you the right to make me do anything."

DiMarco growled at Witherspoon, "It's not your company! Get that through your head!"

"Oh, Delbert," Braxton said sweetly. "It will be John Tree here who will make sure you do what we want. Don't you have a wife, a son, and two sisters?"

Tree smiled a crooked smile and put his big hand on Witherspoon's shoulder.

Witherspoon gave a hurried glance at Tree, then looked down at his hands clasped in his lap.

DiMarco looked at Braxton and said, "You still haven't talked about exactly how we can take control of his corporation. That's the critical piece of information."

Braxton put his thumbs under his suspenders and said smugly, "Well, I have it on good authority that when King was forced to go to Mexico in 1954, he had to sell everything with his name on it, otherwise it would have been seized by the police. He sold everything to a corporation that he had set up. The one failure in his plan was that no one's name was ever put on the corporation's founding papers because he was never able to come back to San Francisco and get the papers officially transferred to someone he trusted. Those papers are still hidden somewhere in San Francisco's Western Addition. We find them, we take control of a cool fifty million."

DiMarco leaned forward with interest and asked, "What's your strategy?"

"One of his grandsons is the key. Now, we know that when Tremain went to Mexico in 1954, the only person he had regular contact with was one grandson." Braxton looked down at his notes to refresh his memory. "Hmmm, yes, Jackson Tremain—"

"We know where he is," Tree interrupted enthusiastically. "I got two men watching him. Why don't we just pick him up and find out what he knows?"

"Because he doesn't know anything, yet." Braxton answered as he took off his glasses and cleaned them. "He stopped having anything to do with his grandfather when he was eighteen; that was in 1964. What makes this grandson key is that he is the only one in the whole family that King Tremain cared about. So, if he leaves a will, this fellow Jackson will figure pretty prominently in it." Braxton let the information sink in while he carefully adjusted his glasses. He didn't like wearing them but they were necessary for reading.

"How are we going to know if Tremain contacts this Jackson?" DiMarco asked.

"Well, you've got to think like Tremain," Braxton said contemplatively. "He wouldn't send a stranger, because the grandson probably wouldn't have anything to do with someone he didn't know. . . ." Braxton paused in thought then continued, "I think he'll contact the grandson directly and they'll meet face-to-face before he dies."

"Then we should have this Jackson under twenty-four-hour surveillance!" DiMarco suggested. "So we can give King Tremain the send-off he deserves!"

"We've already taken care of that." Braxton gestured to Tree.

"We on 'im, like white on rice," Tree confirmed. "We got him followed wherever he goes. I got one of my best men on him. It's Fletcher Gil—"

"John!" Braxton interrupted testily. "We agreed not to use the names of people assigned to surveillance activities."

"What's the big deal?" Tree complained. "It's just us and we know everybody!"

Braxton explained, "Precautions are necessary. We may not always be in a secure room."

DiMarco chuckled cynically, "He's too stupid to understand that."

Braxton caught Tree's eye and discreetly gestured to him not to respond. "Let's get on with our prospective assignments, shall we?" No one said anything. DiMarco was smirking and Tree was glaring at him. Witherspoon continued to sit quietly, looking down into his lap. "John, I want you to continue to keep this Jackson Tremain under surveillance. Learn everything about him. If he's got a girlfriend, find out where she lives and works. I want his friends' names and addresses. I want to know all his regular stops."

"I got it!" Tree answered gruffly. "He gon' be locked down tighter'n a drum."

"Good. Paul, you still have people down in Mexico City?"

DiMarco nodded his head affirmatively.

"Good," Braxton smiled. "I want you to put them on notice. If the grandson goes down there to visit him, we want him followed. Maybe he'll lead us right to his grandfather, and then we'll be able to resolve everything right then and there."

DiMarco said, "I'll have a man staked out at the Mexico City airport, once we know he's headed down that way."

"That's all the news on that front. Now to our local business transactions. Delbert, are you still with us?" Braxton spoke softly. Witherspoon raised his eyes and looked at Braxton, his face wooden with resignation. "We need to ship some money through the construction company. I want you to alert the accountant. The money will come from a bank in Canada. I want half the payment to go through the same subcontractor in Nassau that we used before, and the other half to the Bahamas account. Anybody else need a pass through?"

DiMarco nodded. "Yeah. I'm transferring money from my restaurant. I want the money sent to my Bahamas account."

Braxton looked at Witherspoon. "Got that?"

Witherspoon stared at Braxton without a word. His face was expressionless.

Tree leaned over and smacked the back of his head with a powerful forehand swipe. "You heard the man. Answer him!"

The blow knocked Witherspoon's hat onto the table. Witherspoon trembled as he spoke. "I got it."

"Good," said Braxton as he sought to bring the meeting to a close. "We should meet for a status report in one week at the Embassy Suites in Napa. Different place, same time. After that, it may be too dangerous to meet again as a group."

Braxton stood up as a signal of dismissal, but before anyone else could move, Tree said in a malevolent voice, "You ought to send somebody who knows what they doin' to Mexico this time." He indicated DiMarco with a hand gesture. "These greasy motherfuckers haven't been able to find nothin' in twenty years. Ain't no reason to think they gon' change now."

DiMarco bent over as if he were pulling up his socks when he began his snide retort. "I heard that you had more than a couple of opportunities to stand up to the man." He kept his eyes on Tree as he spoke. "The way I heard it, you ran away faster than everybody. Too bad it wasn't an Olympic year, you might have gotten a medal, except they don't give 'em for yellow streaks." DiMarco leaned back in his chair and laughed tauntingly.

Tree pushed back his chair and stood up. He leaned over the table and pointed at DiMarco, who remained seated. "I ain't gon' let no stubby-assed cracker talk to me that way!" He stepped behind Witherspoon's chair as he began to make his way to DiMarco.

DiMarco displayed a 9mm pistol, which he had pulled from an ankle holster, and set it on the table. "Come on! Come on!" he taunted, daring Tree to continue.

Braxton walked over and stood between the two men. "Gentlemen, we're here about business." He glanced back and forth between the two like a school monitor, intervening between miscreants. "Business," he emphasized again. Braxton watched Tree make his way truculently back to his seat and thought, *In a very short while you will have outlived your usefulness.*

"No more meetings," DiMarco stated coldly as he shoved the pistol in the waistband of his pants. He stood up and buttoned his jacket. He said to Braxton, "You have other ways of contacting me."

Tree began to taunt him, "You's a coward! And one day I'm gon' make you eat that little gun."

DiMarco turned toward him and said, "After this is over, I'm going to squash you like a bug!"

"You don't scare me," Tree answered triumphantly. "I know where your family lives. Where your little girl goes to school. What time she gets picked up by the chauffeur. I even know about your mother in New Jersey."

"You dare to threaten my family?! You dare to threaten—" DiMarco reached under his coat for his pistol.

Once more, Braxton stepped between the men. "No fireworks in here or the whole plan is finished."

DiMarco looked over Braxton's shoulder at the still-seated Tree and snarled, "You're a dead man; it's just a question of when! But you're a dead man!"

Tree laughed evilly. "You jes' better watch who you threatening!" He laughed a big belly laugh. He had succeeded in upsetting DiMarco and that was enough for him.

Braxton ushered DiMarco from the room, speaking to him in hushed undertones, but to no avail. At the door DiMarco pulled his arm roughly out of Braxton's grasp. "We'll go forward as planned," he said, adjusting the collar of his coat. "But if I see that fool again, I'll kill him and everyone who's with him!" DiMarco gave Braxton a long look then turned and walked down the hall.

Witherspoon came to the door and waited for Braxton to move so he could leave. His hat was in his hands. There was a pleading look on his long, narrow face and his mouth twitched with unspoken words. Braxton stepped out of his way and watched Witherspoon dart past him and scurry down the hall.

As Braxton reentered the sitting room, Tree was pouring himself a large brandy. Braxton sat down in one of the overstuffed chairs behind him and asked, "What is on your mind that you would want to antagonize DiMarco?"

"He ain't nothing," Tree responded, slopping his brandy as he dropped into a chair across from Braxton. "I liked it that you didn't let on about the real amount of money we's after. You think land and everything, King got more'n a hundred million?"

"Yes I do, but let me caution you. DiMarco is a dangerous man. When I asked you to get that information on his family, I never intended that he should know about it. It was for us to use in case of emergency."

Disgustedly, Braxton rose up and went over to stand in front of the window. The fog was lifting. He could now see the sailboats moored in the water and behind them, the shadowy presence of Strawberry Point still partially obscured by fog. He took a moment to control his irritation over Tree's stupidity. Once he gathered himself, he turned and said, "Now, we have a problem."

"What's that?" Tree asked.

"We knew before that DiMarco might not want to share the business with us, but now there's no doubt. He'll try to kill us once everything is in hand. We've got to be ready before that happens." Braxton poured himself a brandy and continued. "I want you to keep tabs on his family. I think he'll try to move them before he moves on us. That'll be our signal."

"I can do that," Tree said as he finished his drink. He got to his feet. "Anything else?"

"Three things." Braxton walked over to him. "It might be a good idea to lay low for a while on the drug business. DiMarco is well connected in the police department. You wouldn't want to get arrested now."

Tree protested, "I'd be walking away from an easy thirty thousand a week. And you'd be giving up your cut too."

"That's chump change compared to the potential we can reap from our project." Braxton forced himself to maintain an advisory tone. "Remember, it would be easy for him to get someone to take you down in jail. And we don't want that, do we?"

"Okay, I'll be cool," Tree acknowledged. "What's the second thing?"

"Don't ride Witherspoon so hard. If we don't handle him gently, he may crumble. He could even end up going to the police. He's already scared. We've got to make him think that there's nothing to worry about as long as he does what we say. If he feels that it doesn't matter what he does, that he'll be hurt anyway, we'll lose control of him."

"Okay, I'll be cool on that too. What's the last thing?"

"I want you to pick up one of the grandson's friends. For discussion purposes only. I don't want another botched job like the one with that Davis fellow. Tell your people not to use too much rough stuff."

"Okay, okay," Tree conceded grudgingly. "But who gon' pay for killin' my nephew? I don't want his death to go without no answer!"

"The man who killed Frank is dead!"

"But maybe he weren't actin' alone! The police say that bomb was pretty sophisticated."

"We'll sort that out later! Right now, we want to talk! No rough stuff! Maybe with the right incentive, if it's handled correctly, we can make a deal with one of his buddies. People can always use more money."

"Gotcha!" Tree strode to the door. "I got me another appointment. We gon' meet in Napa?"

Braxton thought a moment. "I doubt it, but I'll contact you. One way or the other."

With a wave of his hand, Tree opened the door and was gone. Braxton went back out onto the balcony and stared out at the finger of the bay that separated Sausalito from Strawberry Point. It was a beautiful view, an oriental water color captured in greens and browns and fading to gray where the fog had not yet lifted. But it was not the view which preoccupied his thinking. He wondered at the number of great ideas that were conceptualized but never realized because the men delegated to carry them out didn't have the focus to work together. It was a problem that had plagued him since 1940. He could never seem to find thinking, rational men to work for him who could also handle a little blood. Perhaps the two traits didn't commonly reside in the same body. But Braxton had known men who had possessed these traits. DiMarco's uncle, for example, had been a clever man who might have risen to national prominence within his organization if he had not underestimated King Tremain. All it took was one false step. One small miscalculation.

Braxton was a man who was used to success. In his youth, he had been a medical doctor, among the more prominent in San Francisco's black community. He also started the second black-owned San Francisco newspaper, publishing the *Bay City Gazette*. He recently had retired from his medical duties and now devoted himself entirely to his publishing business and his investments. Although he was in his late sixties, he had aged well. His hair was silver gray and went well with his light brown skin. On the surface he had a lot to live for. Yet he carried in his heart scars from his encounters with King Tremain.

He turned back into his hotel room and pulled an attaché case from beneath his bed. He removed a manila envelope from the case and sat down at the table to review its contents. It was the same envelope that John Tree had brought him the night after Sampson Davis had killed himself along with three of Tree's men. There were only two pieces of paper in the envelope. The first was a letter written to King Tremain from his attorneys in New York, and the second was a piece of a map. Braxton read the letter for perhaps the twentieth time.

May 20, 1982

Mr. LeRoi Bordeaux Tremain
1717 Embarcadero Blvd.
San Diego, California

Dear Mr. Tremain,

We were extremely sorry to hear of your serious illness and your subsequent hospitalization. It is our hope that sound medical intervention will assist you in regaining your health so that we may continue our long professional relationship.

We received your written, notarized request regarding the disposition of your estate upon your death. For the most part, your desires are fairly clear and easy to implement. There are, however, a few concerns. These concerns relate to your grandson, Jackson Tremain, inheriting all of your estate. At this time, there is no problem with the transition of land and fixed assets into his name, but there are some problems concerning the unsigned stock certificates which represent the bulk of your estate. According to our records these stock certificates amount to nearly a hundred million dollars. Since these certificates are unsigned and are not currently in your possession, there will be considerable problems with your grandson assuming control and ownership over them. We'll have to establish a chain of possession and ensure that these certificates have not been sold. Still, we may be open to challenges by parties as yet unknown. Clearly, it is in your best interest to find these certificates and have them in your possession at the time of your death. We also acknowledge your request that any transfer of possession of these certificates to parties other than your grandson can only be accomplished if he appears in person at the Central Bank of San Francisco and notarizes the transaction.

We further understand that it is your wish, should your grandson meet an untimely death before he inherits your estate, that everything you own shall be

donated to charities related to the care and maintenance of children. While we
may experience similar problems as those outlined in the preceding paragraph with
the transfer of the unsigned certificates, it should be less of an obstacle in that there
is no specific party of interest.

We await news of your recovery and are here to assist you in any way
possible. Please contact us, if we have misunderstood any part of your bequest, or
if you've regained possession of the certificates.

Sincerely,
Noah Goldbaum
Goldbaum & Goldbaum
3932 Fifth Avenue
New York City, NY

The other paper in the envelope was a torn-off piece of a map. It looked like a schematic of the San Francisco sewer system. He shook his head. What could those fools down at Tree's have been thinking about? How could they have mishandled this gift? Here in his hand was part of the key to breaking up King Tremain's estate.

The phone rang. It sounded harsh and discordant in Braxton's ears. It disturbed his reverie, and since he was not expecting any calls, he considered not answering it. However, after the fourth ring, it entered his mind that it could be one of his co-conspirators, so he picked up the receiver.

A familiar voice with a raspy, southern Louisiana accent asked, "Was the meetin' successful, William?" There was no warmth in the tone; at best it was businesslike.

"Uncle Pug? Is that you?" Braxton inquired with surprise.

"Co'se it's me, William! Who else know about this meetin'? You sho' put in some work in keepin' it secret, din't ya! You certainly din't try to call me and tell me about it! I got to say, after I found out I was some surprised. Yesiree! What with you conductin' secret meetings and all, a suspicious person might think that you was tryin' to get independent action goin'! But I knew better! I knew you remembered how we deal with traitors down here. I knew you'd remember—"

Braxton interrupted, "Uncle Pug, this really isn't necessary! I—"

"Don't interrupt me ag'in!" The voice had turned cold and authoritarian. "As I was sayin', I knew you'd remember the summer of 1954, the summer you spent with us when we opened that man's veins and staked him out in the swamp for the fish to feed on! I knew you wasn't fool enough to try anythin' at the expense of yo' family! Because, if you did, I just don't know how we'd deal with the disappointment! Get my drift?!"

Braxton quelled his anger and replied in a resigned tone, "I understand you."

"Now, was the meetin' successful?"

"Yes, I have assigned people to watch the key grandson and establish his social circle. The DiMarcos will use their Mexico City connection to follow him if he travels down to see King Tremain. I've also arranged for the next to the last payment of your money to be sent to your Nassau bank. If you please, Uncle Pug, I didn't know I had to check in with you to clear my every move. I thought I was serving you well by using my own initiative. That's the way we've been operating for the last few years."

"This be a new day! All debts is due now! We gon' take over this operation! You'll take your orders directly from me or my grandson, Deleon! You ain't got no say in this! We have some debts to settle and we don't want no bunglin'! One of us will be to Frisco in a couple of weeks. You hold your horses 'til we get there!"

"DiMarco isn't too receptive to direction," Braxton offered, trying to mount a diplomatic argument as to the drawbacks of his uncle's plan.

"We'll use him as far as he's useful, after that he's swamp food. As a matter fact, all the men you's met with gon' be swamp food after this is over. You should take care that you don't end up the same. You's a distant relative, yo' DuMont blood ain't that thick." The phone went dead.

Braxton exhaled and returned the receiver to its cradle. He spent a few moments breathing deeply. The intrusion of his mother's family was about the last thing he needed. Although he had gone to them when he had needed money for medical school and also years later when he needed capital to buy the Bay City Gazette, he didn't like spending too much time with them. The summer he had spent in Louisiana had been enough for him. He saw them as the epitome of an inbred, unsophisticated backwoods family. Nonetheless, he was not foolish enough to cross them. He knew they would track him across three continents to exact their revenge.

He was beginning to regret that he had discussed Sampson Davis's death and the letter with his uncle. He had thought his uncle would be satisfied with his taking the lead in the matter as he had done for years, but that was obviously not the case. Once the old man heard about the possibility that King was seriously ill, he got extremely excited, spouting far-fetched plans as soon as they came into his head. His outburst exemplified what Braxton feared most about the DuMonts. They were a primal, frightening, and passionate people, more interested in displays of courage than caution. A folk who after spilling the blood of their enemies would drink, dance, and carouse until exhaustion and excess took them. They relied less on organized planning than spur of the moment, impromptu actions, which often led to messy results, like witnesses, clues, and fingerprints. Given the DuMonts' overriding mania in all matters regarding King, Braxton was concerned that their impulsive brutishness might be directed at him should he show reluctance to perform some poorly thought-out directive.

A pain lanced across Braxton's back as the tension in his body reached critical mass. He needed to relax. Braxton went to the phone and made a call. A woman's voice answered. Braxton said, "I'm ready, come now." He returned the phone to its cradle and went out on the deck. His only option to keep control of the situation was to bring it to resolution before his relatives arrived.

There was one major, nagging unknown: the grandson, Jackson Tremain. If Jackson was anything like his cousin Franklin, there would be no problem. But if this grandson had more of King's skills, everything might unravel. Braxton simply did not know with whom he was dealing and yet he had already set actions in progress involving that person. This broke a cardinal rule of his, which was never to take an offensive move without a clear understanding of your opponent.

There was a knock at the door. Braxton had a moment's hesitation before answering it, thinking it might be DiMarco's men, but he put that thought out of his mind. He knew DiMarco would wait until the job was finished, or nearly finished. Braxton opened the door and a tall, stylishly dressed, golden-brown-skinned woman walked in and gave him a peck on the cheek. Her hair was in a full natural and she wore large, colorful hand-crafted earrings. She smiled at him, showing white teeth and sparkling eyes. She took off her coat and Braxton admired the curves of her body underneath her dress. As he ushered her to the bar his last business thought was, Who the hell *are* you, Jackson Tremain?

Deleon DuMont, a lean, whipcord-wiry man wearing an olive double-breasted suit, a white silk T-shirt, and loafers without socks sat at the bar and watched John Tree walk out the front door of the Miramar Vista. He sipped his drink slowly and turned to watch himself in the mirror. He was a brown-skinned man with high cheekbones and a triangular face who, no matter how well he shaved, always had a visible five o'clock shadow. Nonetheless, he thought he presented a striking image. He had tailored his look after that of the black detective on *Miami Vice*. He liked to wear silk T-shirts under his suit jackets and he liked the way his thick black hair was pomaded into waves. He pulled a pack of imported cigarettes from his jacket pocket and lit one of its dark brown cylinders of tobacco. There was a faint perfume in the smell of its burning ash. By the time he had finished his cigarette and watched a bit of a baseball game that was on the bar's TV, he saw the young woman with golden-brown skin and large, colorful earrings stop by the entrance to the bar. She did not enter, but merely nodded to him then continued on her way.

Deleon paid his bill and went into a phone booth, where he made a long-distance call. The phone rang several times then a male voice with a raspy, southern Louisiana accent answered the phone: "It's yo' dime!"

Deleon spoke into the phone, "The girl just went to his room, Grand-père. He's going to be there the night. It isn't likely he's going to leave before tomorrow morning."

The voice was querulous: "Any of 'em make you?"

"No, Grand-père. I was discreet, as you requested. No one saw me. I was simply calling to report in. There doesn't appear to be much else to do here. Unless you wish me to go upstairs and chastise him for his disobedience, perhaps show him how sharp my blade is?"

There was a moment of silence, then, "Naw, keep yo' knife sheathed. We don't want him to know you's already on the scene no way. You just keep an eye on him and that Tree feller. You done good, Deleon. Look like you gon' get some help on this here particular assignment. Some of our Mexican friends want a piece of the action. Frankie San Vicente will be arrivin' tomorrow. He'll be stayin' at the Hilton by the airport. Pick him up tomorrow night."

April 3, 1954

Jackson was eight years old when his father was killed and for him it marked the end of innocence. His life preceding that event was beyond the horizon of memory; it had fallen off the edge of the earth into darkness. His father was killed on a Friday night in April 1954 and the memory of that afternoon and evening remained unfaded by the years. The day had been cold and overcast, punctuated by numerous showers. The streets were wet and shiny like someone had covered them with sparkling cellophane. Jackson had hurried home after school, stepping over puddles in which he saw a dark and distorted world reflecting off the surface of the water. He was looking forward to the hot chocolate made by old Papa Butterball Brown. When he arrived, he was salivating with anticipation of the hot, sweet liquid.

Jackson was living in his grandparents' house at the time. His father had decided to move back in with his parents on Fulton Street after Jackson's mother had been killed in a car wreck in 1951. The house was a large, rambling Victorian with fourteen-foot ceilings and long, vertical windows which stretched nine feet from bottom to top. It was always cold because of its high ceilings, and despite its numerous windows, it had the dark, brooding character of its presiding matron. Although the family was ruled by his savage, iron-fisted grandfather, his grandmother ran the house on her own rigid, loveless terms. And as long as Jackson lived in its dank, shadowy gloom, it was a place without joy, without hope, and its darkness was filled with a haunting and lonely silence.

An hour before dinner, on the night of his father's death, Jackson's cousins, Franklin and his sister, Samantha, came over with their mother, Lisette. Franklin, at ten years old, was two years older than Jackson and slightly bigger. He liked to take advantage of their size difference and bully his younger cousin. Franklin was envious that Jackson lived in their grandmother's sprawling house and his envy manifested itself in a hectoring hostility. Jackson had tried numerous times to befriend Franklin, but his efforts were consistently spurned. Yet Franklin's sister, Samantha, just a few months younger than Jackson, was always friendly.

For dinner that night his grandmother cooked pork chops smothered in thick, dark gravy along with mashed potatoes, candied carrots, and big cat-head biscuits steaming hot from the oven. The children ate at the smaller table in the kitchen with Papa Brown while the other adults ate at the main table in the dining room and talked business. After dinner, Jackson wandered in to where the adults were sitting. The conversation paused when he entered the room, but his father beckoned him over. Jackson went to his father's chair and leaned against him. Seated around the table were his father, his grandmother and grandfather, along with his aunt Lisette.

His grandmother asked, "Where's LaValle?" LaValle was his father's older brother and Franklin and Samantha's father.

His grandfather, a large, broad-shouldered, light-skinned man seated at the head of the table, answered in his gruff manner, "He ain't taking care of business for me."

Franklin came and stood at the door, waiting for permission to enter, but his grandfather waved him back, saying, "Go on back where you came from. We got enough children in here!"

Franklin pointed to Jackson and began, "He's in here—"

His grandfather cut him off with a look. Franklin backed out of the room without another word.

The phone rang. His grandfather gestured to his son. "Jacques, see who it is."

Jacques put his arm around Jackson and whispered into his ear that he should go back into the kitchen with his cousins. Jackson obediently went into the other room as his father answered the phone. That was the last time he saw his father.

As soon as Jackson entered the back room where his cousins were playing, Franklin began to taunt and bait him, building up to making a physical assault. Jackson attempted to ignore him, but when Franklin said, "You're just a black nigger like your mother!" Jackson lunged at him. Jackson's charge caught Franklin off balance, but Franklin's superior strength soon made the difference. After a few minutes of wrestling, he sat astride Jackson, pinning his arms and punching him. When he could not make him cry with the first few punches, Franklin punched harder. But Jackson would not cry; his anger blocked his tears. When Franklin bloodied his nose, Samantha ran from the room and returned with Papa Butterball.

Papa Butterball was a man in his late sixties who despite his portliness was still a spry but not an intimidating figure. For nearly twenty years he had been a top chef in one of King's better restaurants. He had no family so when he desired to retire, King offered him a room in the Fulton Street house. King always repaid loyalty. Papa Butterball pulled Franklin off Jackson and said in his guttural voice, "Whatchoo doing, boy? That's yo' own blood you beating on! You better stop if'en you don't want yo' grandmother in here!"

Franklin sputtered as Papa Butterball grabbed him by the shirt collar, "He called my mother a name! And I don't take that!"

"He's lying," Samantha said matter-of-factly. "Frankie started it."

Papa Butterball said, "I don't care who started it." When Jackson scrambled to his feet, Papa Butterball pushed him toward the door and said, "Go clean yourself up, boy!"

As Jackson left the room, he heard Franklin threaten, "If you tell, I'm really going to kick your butt!"

After Jackson had washed his face and his nosebleed had subsided, he made his way to his secret place, behind the couch in his grandfather's sitting room. Although there was a large fireplace in the sitting room, there was also a gas heater installed in the wall next to the couch. Normally heat dissipated rapidly in the cavernous room, but it was always cozy behind the couch due to the wall heater. Jackson lay down on a couple of pillows and cried. The tears welled up and streamed down his face. He felt a sadness and a sense of loss that he could not express.

Franklin had touched on a sore point when he had mentioned Jackson's mother. Although he could not remember his mother's image, from the pictures in the photo album Jackson could see that she was a very dark-skinned woman with large eyes and full lips. His father often said that she was a beautiful woman and Jackson wanted to believe it, but he was confused. He had heard too many contradictory statements from other people in his family. Everyone else in his family except his mother and he was light-skinned, and he realized without being told specifically that light skin was better than dark. He didn't like being, as his aunt Lisette had often called him, "the black sheep of the family." Only his father had stood between him and the slurs and ridicule of the rest of the family. His grandfather never said anything; he merely watched to see how Jackson handled himself.

Jackson eventually fell asleep, pitying himself and wondering whether he would ever be happy like other people were. Hours later he was awakened by his grandmother's concerned voice: "What's happened? What's happened?"

His grandfather answered, "It was a trap! Jacques was killed!"

His grandmother's voice quavered, "Are you sure that Jacques is dead?" Jackson heard her sit down heavily in an overstuffed chair.

His grandfather dumped out something on the table that sounded like marbles. "If he hadn't been dead, I wouldn't have left him at Thompson's Funeral Home!" The grandfather's tone was matter-of-fact. His grandmother said nothing. Jackson could hear her breathing. His grandfather continued to move quickly around the room. Jackson heard some heavy metal objects being placed on the table. He knew they were his grandfather's guns.

"Are you sure?" his grandmother asked, her voice cracking. "Jacques is dead?"

His grandfather took a deep breath and said, "He was shot twice in the back with bullets from a high-caliber handgun. He's dead!"

"Oh, my God!" His grandmother's voice broke. Jackson heard the sound of a glass or an ashtray falling and shattering on the floor. Then there was another long silence, broken only by the sound of his grandfather loading his guns.

Several minutes passed before his grandmother demanded, "That's your answer, King: kill somebody?" His grandmother's voice conveyed her incredulity. "Like your killing people didn't pave the way for Jacques's death?" Her voice was getting shrill.

"Keep your voice down and don't get righteous with me, woman! You think my heart ain't broke? The only son of mine I got to raise, layin' cold in a funeral home?"

Serena hissed, "He died paying for your sins!"

King shook his head. "We both know this is still part of yo' stuff! We're gettin' to the last part of Sister Bornais's curse! Don't pretend that you forgot yo' part in this!"

"How can you separate your business from Jacques's death?" his grandmother demanded. "Your enemies killed him. Our son is dead and your business is the reason. The business that I begged you to quit. And you're telling me not to get righteous!"

"Seems to me you forgettin' that for more than thirty years, you been living pretty good off these here wages of sin, woman. You complain about it, but you use the money. How you think all these rich white families that you admire so much got started? Money don't grow on trees. Anyway, this ain't no time for arguin'. I want to find out who set this trap and I think I know just the person to ask."

Seeing the evil look on King's face, Serena asked, "Where's LaValle? Was he hurt?"

"I know you care about him, no matter how many others have died," his grandfather replied, and paused before he continued. "He'll live, but he's the reason that Jacques is dead. Once I find out who worked with who to set up this trap, we gon' have a little talk. LaValle's gon' be looking over his shoulder as long as he lives. Don't worry, I ain't gon' kill him. I'm just gon' break a piece off him every time I see him."

There was a long period of silence then his grandfather asked in his dangerously calm voice, "Don't tell me you want to coddle the weakling who caused Jacques's death, do you?"

Even from his hiding place behind the couch, Jackson could feel the tension.

His grandfather continued in a casual tone, "Has he called you yet?"

"You're planning to hurt our remaining son and you expect me to tell you whether he called or not?" His grandmother's voice seemed to be on the edge of a shriek. "How convenient that you can turn off your heart. It's so simple for you!"

His grandfather answered without inflection, "Don't get it twisted. LaValle's responsible for Jacques's death. He has information that I need, then he's fresh meat."

Serena paused for a breath and then shouted, "You promised me he'd be under your protection as long as you have the strength to provide it! We are talking about your remaining son!"

His grandfather's tone turned colder as he growled, "You know that white man's boy ain't my son. Never was. Because of you I only had one son. I would've had two, maybe three sons but we know that story, don't we? It don't matter either way, Serena. You know he's weak and rotten through to his core. We both know it, don't we?"

"What kind of father are you? You agreed to give him your name! You agreed to treat him the same as Jacques!"

His grandfather answered grudgingly, "He was yo' child. You wouldn't let me treat him the same as Jacques. You wouldn't let me have a hand rearin' him. You wouldn't let me make him my son. And the way you done raised him wouldn't do him justice even if he wore a skirt. Still, I won't go back on my word. I won't kill him, but I won't let a coward and a traitor go unpunished either. He gon' receive an ass-whipping every time I see him."

"You're going to sit in judgment on your own son? Damn, if that isn't audacity. You're responsible for the death of one son, now you're planning to maim the other! Who's sitting in judgment on you?"

"Who's sittin' in judgment on you, Serena? How many of yo' own people have you killed for this boy? I know you ain't lifted a hand in violence, but it's like you pulled the trigger. Let's talk about Della's miscarriages, the death of Tini and her baby. Let's talk about yo' brother Amos and yo' two sisters and why nobody else in yo' family got any chil'ren."

"Must you always bring up this subject?"

"Only when you forget Sister Bornais's curse."

"LaValle has a weak constitution. You can't measure him by the same standard."

"As usual, you's defendin' him without knowin' nothin' about what happened."

"I don't know anything about what happened tonight, but I do know about a boy struggling for his father's smile but not getting it, and all the while the attention going to his younger brother. I know about that!"

"Seems to me, I just reminded you of yo' part in that struggle. You didn't think manhood had to be earned. You thought it was automatic. Well, LaValle is a testament that if a boy don't get the right trainin', he just get older and bigger. He don't ever turn into a man."

"All right! All right! I made mistakes. Are you satisfied? I've owned up. LaValle shouldn't have to pay for my mistakes. It was my fault, not his."

"You talkin' like some white-bread head-shrink who's mo' interested in justifyin' weakness than in helpin' somebody be strong." The sarcasm was heavy in his grandfather's voice. "Life is all about dealin' with pressure and responsibility, and makin' hard decisions. You don't help nobody tellin' 'em they can run away from somethin', 'specially when you know they can't run away from nothin' important. You got to show them how to deal with things, how to find the courage inside."

"LaValle had a weak constitution! From birth—"

"That justifies him turnin' traitor to the people that raised him? His weakness?" King's sarcasm was sharp and jagged like the corroded edge of a razor. "Bullshit! The boy can't cut it; never could, never will. He ain't nothin' but a mama's boy, just sly and sneaky with no backbone. Thank God, Sister Bornais said he don't have too long to live now, otherwise . . ." His grandfather left the room and headed for the back of the house. His grandmother stifled a sob and then exhaled loudly several times before she too stood up and headed toward the rear of the house.

Jackson crawled out from behind the couch and went to stand in front of the fireplace. He did not know what to think. He leaned against the brick of the fireplace, hoping that his grandfather had made a mistake.

His cousin Franklin entered the room behind him. He began to taunt Jackson, "Pitch-black tar baby! Pitch-black tar baby! Your daddy's dead! Now you ain't got nobody to protect you! I'm gonna kick your butt every day till you die! Ha, ha! Your daddy's dead!"

Without warning Jackson picked up a poker from beside the fireplace and swung wildly. The poker glanced off the side of Franklin's head. Franklin cried out with shock and pain. Blood dripped down the side of his face where the poker had lacerated his skin. He started toward Jackson, shouting, "I'm going to get you for—" He didn't complete his sentence because the poker caught him across the forearm, snapping it with the force of the blow. Franklin screamed but Jackson wasn't finished. He swung again, catching Franklin on the shoulder and then on the back as Franklin fell to the floor, trying to escape the barrage. Jackson would have continued beating him if his grandfather had not entered the room and snatched the poker from his grasp.

"What's going on here?" he demanded.

Franklin bawled, tears running down his face. "He hit me with that thing and now my arm hurts so bad!"

"I'd do it again," Jackson proclaimed with tears also running down his cheeks. "He teased me about my father being dead and how he was going to beat me up every day till I die. I'm not afraid of him! I'll fight him every day till I'm dead!"

His grandfather looked down at Jackson and said with admiration, "That's my blood speakin'." He grabbed Jackson and held him so tightly that the boy could barely breathe.

"What about me? He hit me!" Franklin whined, slowly rising to his feet, holding his arm.

"You's a bully and you got what you deserved." King took a step toward Franklin and poked him in the chest hard with a forefinger, forcing the ten-year-old backward. "You lucky I didn't hear you. I'd have whipped your ass till the cows came home!"

Franklin's mother rushed into the room, along with Serena. When

Lisette saw Franklin holding his arm and the blood flowing down his face, she wailed, "What are you doing to my baby?"

"He made fun of Jackson being fatherless. He picked on the wrong Tremain and got his butt whipped," King answered. He slapped Jackson roughly on the shoulder and walked out.

Those were Jackson's images of the night his father died. He could recall voices and phrases; the timing of entrances; the smell of food, cigars, and dampness; the way the tobacco smoke hung about four feet off the ground in the dining room—but he did not recall anyone talking to him specifically about the death of his father. As a matter of fact, no one ever spoke to him directly about his father's death. In the months that followed, Jackson often wanted to ask someone how his father had died, but the mood in the house wasn't conducive to questions. His grandmother did not even speak to him, unless necessity or common courtesy required it, and his grandfather drifted in at odd hours during the night, only to depart by first light. Jackson saw him once when he got up in the middle of the night to use the bathroom. His grandfather was sitting at the big oak dining room table, puffing on a cigar; the smoke billowed around his head with each puff. To Jackson it looked like his grandfather was breathing fire. His grandfather beckoned Jackson to come to him. Jackson wanted to hold his breath when he smelled the pungent odor of the cigar, but he forced himself to breathe, to appear calm.

His grandfather saw the fear in his eyes. He pulled Jackson into a bear hug and held him for a long minute. He pushed the boy back and held him at arm's length. "You realize, you's my blood. I'ma take care of everythin' for you. You ain't gon' want for nothin', food nor housing! And I'm gon' to get everyone who had anything to do with your daddy's death. We gon' fill up a section of a graveyard 'fore it's over. These people don't know who they messed with. We gon' show 'em, boy. We gon' show 'em!"

For a moment his grandfather appeared to be lost in thought, but he gave Jackson a long look, as if he were trying to memorize his features. "Listen, I may have to go away for a while. But don't you worry, I ain't gon' to be that far away. I'm gon' always be close enough to do for you.

"Now, it's going to be hard here for you. You don't fit her mold, boy." His grandfather nodded toward his wife's bedroom. "And you remind her of your father. That's two strikes against you, boy. So, she ain't gon' be in yo' corner. You gon' have to tough it out. Remember, bein' tough ain't about winning every fight; it's about getting up off the floor with the same vinegar you had when you hit it. It's gon' be hard, but you got it in you. You my blood! And remember, I'm always gon' be there for you, one hundred and fifty percent." He shook Jackson for emphasis. "You my blood. I see my blood flowing in you. Out of this whole family, there is only you. So, just know, I'm watching out for you." Jackson returned to his room slightly dazed; that was the longest his grandfather had ever spoken to him.

Occasionally, in the mornings before school, Jackson would find Papa Brown at the table sucking his teeth at the news in the paper. Sometimes he would look up at Jackson and wink and then whisper, "Looks like yo' granddaddy done set someone else to right." Papa Brown whispered because he didn't want Serena to hear him. Jackson would stare over Papa Brown's shoulder at the article and accompanying photograph. The article always began, "Negroes Run Wild in the Fillmore" or "Another Senseless Mob Killing in North Beach." The victims were always black or Italian men and they were either strangled with a rope or kicked to death. According to Papa Brown, these were the two methods his grandfather favored most with people he really disliked. Jackson lost count of the victims after the sixth article.

Although it was impossible to believe, the icy atmosphere in his grandmother's Victorian grew even colder when LaValle was found shot to death outside of one of King's apartment buildings. He was killed three months after his brother. He had a closed-coffin funeral because he had been dispatched by a blaze of machine-gun fire and his body was beyond the reconstructive art of the mortician. Jackson's grandmother moved like a silent robot through the house and would brook no noise or conversation that was not absolutely necessary. Living with her was like living in a mausoleum.

These were images of his father's death. Images called to the surface by his grandmother's phone call. It had taken him years to bury these pictures and even longer to discover that an important part of his being was invested in the crypt that he had constructed to bury his memories.

Tuesday, June 15, 1982

Deleon DuMont made his way up the front stairs of his rented house as the barking of San Vicente's two Dobermans announced his arrival. The dogs' presence annoyed him. San Vicente had presumptuously come to San Francisco with a retinue of henchmen and canines and had expected Deleon to defer leadership to him. Deleon had immediately corrected San Vicente's misconceptions, but in doing so had engendered a coldness from San Vicente and his underlings. The dog handler had even allowed one of the Dobermans to threaten him, but Deleon had ended that situation by producing a cocked revolver and pointing it at the dog. There was now an underlying feeling of distrust in all his interchanges with San Vicente. Deleon was fairly sure that his Mexican colleague had no intention of sharing the bounty of King's wealth with the DuMonts. He knew he had to be on his toes. He had only two men with him; paid men, not ones he could really trust if things went awry. They would risk their lives up to a point, but that didn't extend to facing down a larger, committed force.

He opened the front door, which was a solid, wooden affair that swung inward with a loud creaking noise, and stepped into a long, dark hall. The living room door on his right opened and a man stuck his head out to see who had come in; it was Javier Gomez, one of San Vicente's men. Gomez nodded as he recognized Deleon and then ducked back into the room and slammed the door. There was no indication of welcome or friendship; Gomez was merely performing a duty.

Gomez was a Cuban of European descent, as were the rest of San Vicente's team. The Cubans were the offspring of fugitives who had fled the rise of Castro's regime. From what Deleon understood, most of them had undergone some sort of CIA training as part of a grand scheme to unseat the despot, but Castro's seeming invincibility over the years had caused them to look for other avenues of employment. The one thing that was clear to Deleon was their racist attitudes toward anyone of African descent. Their smirks and jokes told in Spanish revealed their prejudice without doubt. Although he didn't speak the language, Deleon heard the word *negro* numerous times before their raucous laughter spilled out like burning acid. Things came to a head within the first few days when Case Hardigrew, Deleon's man, pulled a gun on two of the Cubans. San Vicente stepped forward and calmed tempers all around. The Cubans' jokes ceased and they became cold and polite in the company of Deleon and his men.

Deleon had noticed that San Vicente's men functioned like a team. There were six altogether, including San Vicente and the dog handler. One of his men was always on guard. Every four hours or so one of his men would walk the perimeter. They even slept in shifts. Deleon passed two more doors and opened the one at the end of the hall which led into the dining room. A large gas heater roared in the hollow of a long-dead fireplace. Francisco San Vicente and Luis Martinez, his second in command, were playing draw poker with Case Hardigrew.

Hardigrew looked up, the brown skin of his shaved head reflecting the ceiling lights with a sheen. He waved. "How do? Want to sit in for a hand?" Hardigrew was a chain-smoking ex-cop who ten years ago had served as a bodyguard for Deleon's grandfather before going freelance. As far as Deleon was concerned, he was a big, beefy man who put too much reliance on his size as a physical advantage.

Deleon put a smile on his face and shook his head. "No, thanks."

Inviting San Vicente had been one of Deleon's grandfather's ideas. He had wanted to get man power out to the coast without paying for it. Now they would pay for it big-time. For all intents and purposes Deleon was operating by himself. Although Deleon's other man, Nolan Brown, was proficient at stealing cars, which was what he was out doing at that very moment, Hardigrew and Brown were just window dressing. Deleon would have to stay alert and watch for San Vicente's first move. He went upstairs to his room to clean his rifle. Once inside his room, he unlocked a heavy wooden chest and took out a 30.06 sniper rifle with a floating barrel. He began cleaning the rifle and thinking about his conversation with his grandfather.

One of the reasons he had left the house was to call on a secure line. He didn't know what San Vicente's men might have rigged up with the house phones. He had ridden the Muni down to the post office on Seventh Street and walked through the building and then had taken another bus down to the main Muni bus terminal. He always used public transportation when he thought he was being followed, but no one appeared to be tailing him. He had gone to a bank of public phone booths. Once inside, he closed the door and dropped some coins in the slot and dialed his grandfather's number. The first voice he heard was Zenia's. He smiled. "How's it going, Zee?"

"Is that you, Deleon, honey? Are you all right? Your grandfather's been chewing on nails to talk with you. I think your father's got his dander up over some foolishness. You know how your father is. Let me get your grandfather for you. Remember, take care of yourself."

As Deleon waited for his grandfather to pick up, he thought about Zenia Archambeaux. She was a pretty, tall, chocolate brown–skinned woman with a great body. She had been his grandfather's longtime nurse, until he had married her over a decade ago. She had always been tremendously friendly with Deleon and seemed dedicated to his grandfather's welfare. She was a lot of woman for the old man, but she tended his every care and, as a result, he seemed to have a new lease on life.

The receiver on the other side of the line picked up and a raspy voice said, "It's yo' dime."

"It's me, Grand-père. I'm calling to check in."

"Good, I been waitin' to talk with you. How's it goin' with Frankie and his boys?"

"Not good. Francisco wants to take over and the two guys you sent out are worse than useless. San Vicente brought dogs and a dog handler and a four-man team of Cubans who are always on guard. They act like they know there's something big at stake; maybe they even know about the stock certificates. They're watching us. No way I'm going to surprise them with Hardigrew and Brown. I need some seasoned professionals who know how to carry out a military engagement. Otherwise, we'll be blindsided by San Vicente and his boys."

"Damn it! The best men I got is in Nassau launderin' the money that Braxton sent. You just hold on, I'll send 'em out in a couple of weeks. Maybe what we need to do is take out both of Tremain's grandsons. To hell with the money! That'll send them Cubans packin'. Ain't no reason for 'em to stay if both Tremain's grandsons is dead. That's it! Just make sure you kill the one that King liked first."

"You sure that you want to do that, Grand-père? That letter Braxton mentioned states that if the one grandson is killed, the money all goes to charity. That's throwing away a lot of money, Grand-père."

"Damn! Well, we'll hold off killin' 'em until we get them certificates, but if things start to go south, you off 'em! You really think them Mexes know about them certificates?"

"I don't know what they know. They're pretty tight-lipped."

"Don't volunteer nothin' to 'em. Just keep an eye on Braxton's boys, in particular Tree's men. They do all the legwork for Braxton. That Braxton, he gettin' sort of slippery. We may have to do him too. And

watch out what you include them Mexes in. We don't want them takin'
over the show."

"No problem, I'll keep them at a distance."

"Don't be too obvious; give them somethin'. Just make sure that
whatever it is don't lead to Frankie gettin' ideas that we's tryin' to cut
him out. Do yo' business on the sly. We'll deal with him later on our
own time."

"Okay, Grand-père. I'll take care of it. I'm thinking about renting another place, in case there's a fallout with San Vicente, someplace secure
so I don't have to come down to the bus station to call you. It's got to be
across town from where I am—"

"Damn, you just reminded me of somethin'! Yo' stupid-ass daddy is
gon' cut off yo' credit cards and the money goin' to yo' bank account."

"That bastard! Why?"

"He say he don't want you takin' part in gettin' revenge on them
Tremains. He say you come into the office and work things out with
him. I ain't told him you's out in Frisco workin', 'cause then he'd have a
shit-fit! He say you can have a better life if you stay clear of settin'
things to right. He don't care that the Tremains killed yo' mama. He say
he want everythin' legit now. He say we should forget the dead, that
seekin' vengeance is out of date." Pug DuMont's raspy voice had risen
until he was croaking. He stopped to catch his breath.

The anger welled up in Deleon. "We'll see what he has to say when I
kill him!"

"Time enough for that once them Tremains is done. Don't get distracted. Set you up a new account and I'll have money transferred to
you from one of my banks." A fit of coughing overcame him. It was several minutes before it subsided. Just before he hung up, Pug gasped into
the phone, "If you decide to kill both them grandsons, you won't hear
no complaint from me. We can look for them certificates later."

On the bus ride home, Deleon's mood had been dominated by
thoughts of his father. He stared out at the parade of people along
Market Street with unseeing eyes. He was remembering his father's
drunken rages, the nights his mother screamed for help, of being awakened from sleep by the heavy, angry hand of his father, and the sad,
early morning light which showed the bruises and gashes that he and
his mother both bore. When he was fourteen he had come home from
school one day and had discovered his father beating his mother with a

broomstick. Deleon had gone to his room and gotten his baseball bat. He snuck up behind his father and tried to kill him. Unfortunately, he was only able to break an arm and a couple of ribs before his father got to his guns. Deleon had run out of the house with bullets whistling past him. He never returned to his father's house after that. From then on until he was eighteen he split his time between juvenile hall and the streets of Desire, which he called his home.

He had dropped out of school immediately after running away and had let himself be swallowed by the world of homeless children and all the gut-twisting experiences that street life entailed. As he grew older he became a hustler and a small-time thug. He ran errands for petty criminals and drug dealers until he and two friends were arrested for the murder of a pimp. The case was cut-and-dried. There were witnesses to the crime and, given his past juvenile record, it looked as if he were going to do many years of hard time in an adult detention facility. Then his grandfather had stepped in.

Deleon looked back on those times and realized that his grandfather had thrown him a life preserver when he had not even known he was drowning. He had unknowingly wandered out into deep water, where the large predators dwelt and the undercurrents were strong. He now understood that the old man's intervention had saved his life, that he owed a debt that he would never be able to repay. And that was the basis of his loyalty to his grandfather.

Additionally, Deleon and his grandfather had an agreement. It was an agreement to which Deleon was committed, for upon satisfactory completion of his duties he would be allowed to do what he had been waiting to do. He would, with his grandfather's blessing, kill his own father.

Saturday, June 19, 1982

The voice wavered over the loudspeaker as the class student body president read his speech in the plaza between the school buildings. The parents and family members sat quietly in rows of folding chairs and listened as the young man spoke of dreams and responsibility. The sun was out, but the sky was partially overcast for the St. Mary's High School graduation ceremony, and as a brisk wind swirled through the rows, people could be seen donning their coats.

Near the back periphery of the audience Jackson stood in front of his cousin Franklin and his grandmother, Serena Tremain. "Let me understand this, Frank," Jackson said without warmth. "You want to meet with me and make arrangements to go to Mexico with me?" Jackson paused and looked back and forth between his grandmother and his cousin. "Why should I want to do that?"

"It's really quite simple," Franklin answered in a condescending tone. "We need to be there to ensure that the will addresses the family's needs." Franklin was a light-skinned man with wavy brown hair. He rubbed his mustache with thumb and forefinger and affected the cavalier air of a man who cared for nothing too greatly.

"If it's that simple, then you go and take care of it. I'm sure you'll receive a hell of a welcome." Jackson smiled. "That's solved. Is there anything else to discuss?"

"I believe there is," Serena Baddeaux Tremain said. She was seventy-nine years old. The beauty that had once enamored men and devastated women was still in evidence, though faded. Her hair was totally white and her once creamy, light-brown skin was now mottled with age and spotted by freckles. Still, the years had not dulled the clarity of her gaze or the sharpness of her mind.

"Your facetiousness is not appreciated. There is a substantial fortune in the balance. The family's interests must be protected!" She looked at him sternly. "You may think that by isolating yourself these last few years you are relieved of responsibility, but you are not."

"Let me ask you, Grandmother, are you concerned about safeguarding my welfare? Because that would be news to me. That would be a first! Are you concerned about Samantha's welfare? Or is this just a ruse to make sure you've got Grandfather's blood money in your clutches?"

"How dare you!" Franklin exclaimed.

Jackson looked Franklin in the eye and warned, "Watch yourself, Frankie. You don't want to tangle with me." Jackson was bigger and more muscular than his cousin.

"I'll sue you for every penny you've got if you ever put another hand on me!" Franklin looked around. "I've got witnesses."

Jackson faced his grandmother. "Well, Grandmother, I think you have a picture of how well me and Frankie, the weasel, work together. So, the answer is no. I don't want to go anywhere with him. You want the money, send the weasel by himself. The results might even make the local papers."

Franklin sputtered, "You won't get away with it. We'll tie the estate up in the courts for years. You won't ever have it all to yourself!"

"Tie the estate up in legal battles, see if I care," Jackson retorted. "I don't want his money, you do! And we both know, if you were the last person in the world, he wouldn't leave you a cent."

Franklin started to protest, but Serena cut him off. "I believe there is nothing else to say at this time. Rhasan is at the microphone. Let us return to our seats."

Jackson watched them walk away and noticed that the valedictory address had begun. The address was being given by Jackson's nephew, Rhasan Tremain. Jackson stood at the back of the assembled crowd and listened to his speech.

Rhasan's voice sounded slightly tinny on the school's no-frills public address system. He spoke warmly and affectionately of his four years at St. Mary's High School. Then he addressed the charge that he and his graduating class had to shoulder. And after a rousing speech he closed with, "As I stand here before you, I cannot claim that my dedication or fortitude is as great as JFK, Malcolm X, or Dr. King, but I do understand that education is the first major step in creating the foundations for brotherhood and in eliminating ignorance. I am committed to continuing the struggle. Thank you, St. Mary's, for bringing me into the light."

Rhasan sat down amid applause. The dean returned to the podium and the ceremony continued. Jackson searched for his cousin Samantha. He found her near the front of the stage with a camera in hand. Samantha Tremain was an attractive, solidly built, light-skinned woman who wore her wavy, red-brown hair cut short and combed straight back. Both her hairstyle and the cut of her pantsuit were decidedly masculine. She saw him and her eyes lit up. She quickly closed the gap between them and gave him a tight hug.

"How's the proud mother doing?" Jackson asked, returning her hug.

"I'm filled to capacity with joy." She pushed back and looked up into Jackson's face. "My son, the valedictorian of the graduating class!" Suddenly tears streamed down her face. She made no effort to wipe her eyes. "It's been such a long road with so many terrible twists and turns; I don't know how I made it."

"You made it with faith and a loving heart," Jackson said, putting his arms around her and holding her close. "You met him more than half-way and you never gave up."

"Oh, I had help. I had you. I had my pastor and my church. But, really, it was your willingness to come pick him up whenever that crazy masculine energy took ahold of him—"

"Remember, that female energy can get pretty crazy too. Look at our grandmother!"

"Who can forget the Queen of Rigor Mortis? Speaking of the old witch, she's here." Samantha gestured toward the far side of the seats. "She's here along with my greasy brother and his pretentious wife, Vaseline, who's overdressed as usual. She's wearing a full-length mink coat!"

"I know, they cornered me on the way in. There haven't been this many Tremains in one place since the last funeral."

"Are they wearing your ear off about Grandfather's will? My brother thinks that the majority of the estate should go to him because he's the only one trying to build the family business."

"I wonder where that selfless idea originated?" Jackson mused.

"I don't know what Rhasan sees in his great-grandmother, but they seemed to have developed a pretty friendly relationship."

"We shouldn't begrudge him a relationship that wasn't available to us, or, rather, I should say to me," Jackson said. "You would have been fine with her if, years ago, you hadn't declared that you were a lesbian at the top of your lungs at one of her political fund-raisers."

"Rhasan was five years old then. I couldn't lie to him. It was the time to come out of the closet with everybody. It was time to be myself."

The loudspeaker blared that the names of the graduating seniors would be called to receive their diplomas. This news wiped away any frown from Samantha's face that their discussion had raised. She was beaming again. Frantically, she began to prepare her camera.

"Relax," advised Jackson. "They're calling the names alphabetically. It'll be some time before they get to Tremain."

"Jax, I'm out of film," she gasped. "I have to get back to my bag."

"Go on, Sam. I'll see you after they call his name." Jackson waved her away. She sprinted past a row of seats and disappeared in the rising crowd of adults with cameras.

When Rhasan received his diploma, he waved it over his head in triumph. His mortarboard sat at a jaunty angle on his head, his teeth flashed a bright smile, and his caramel-brown skin seemed to glisten in the pale sunlight. He rushed off the stage into the waiting arms of his mother. When Jackson arrived Rhasan was giving his great-grandmother a big hug.

"What did you think, Grandma Tee? Wasn't it fine? Did you see the applause I got for my speech? Isn't this a great day?" Rhasan was exuberant and his questions followed one right after another like railroad cars on a steep, descending track.

Although Serena enjoyed her great-grandson's warmth, she was uncomfortable with it. As Rhasan hugged her, she pushed against the clasp of his arms and cleared her throat several times. When he had released her, she said, "It was a good ceremony and you were acknowledged well for your valedictorian address. But you must not get carried away; this is only the first hurdle."

"I can't stop, Grandma Tee," Rhasan said as he pivoted quickly on one foot. "The world is spinning! In three months, I'll be at Morehouse!" Rhasan saw Jackson and a big smile spread across his face. "Did you see it, Uncle Jax?" Rhasan walked toward Jackson with his hand raised for a high five.

Jackson smacked Rhasan's open palm with his own. "It was a great speech!" he said, hugging his nephew. "Full of substance and imagery. How does it feel to be a high school graduate?"

Rhasan pulled away, a big smile on his face, and spun around again. "Like I've been released from prison. I'm on my way to college! Free at last! Great God, free at last!"

Jackson laughed at his nephew's exuberance and said, "Well, you got the grades, so I'll follow through on our deal. You can use my BMW for your graduation party and your girlfriend's birthday."

"Uncle Jax, you're the man! Thank you!"

"Since I'll be working late on a lot of budget revisions this month and next, I'll leave a set of keys in that paint can I showed you on the shelf in the garage. You can have the car for the weekend both times. But I want it returned in the same condition you took it, clean inside and out with the gas tank filled."

"No sweat, Uncle Jax! I'm on it! It'll be pristine!"

The smile on his nephew's face said everything. Jackson just patted him on the shoulder and said, "All right. We have a deal."

Rhasan waved to another graduate and said excitedly, "Uncle Jax, there's Wayman." Wayman made his way through the crowd, followed by a tall, dark-skinned woman in her early thirties. Wayman introduced her as his godmother and then gave Jackson a solid hug.

Jackson returned Wayman's hug and then held him at arm's length while he looked into his handsome brown face. "Congratulations on graduating," Jackson said with a smile. "You're looking damn good in that robe, Wayman. I know all your girlfriends will want pictures."

"Watch how you say that, Uncle Jax!" Wayman warned. "There could be somebody close!"

Unable to keep her hands off her son, Samantha wiped sweat from Rhasan's brow. "Yeah, it's hot in this robe," Rhasan acknowledged, pulling the robe over his head.

Wayman stood on his toes, looking over the heads in the crowd. "They're here!" he said excitedly to Rhasan. "And they're looking good!"

"Hold this stuff for me, Mom," Rhasan said hurriedly, shoving his mortarboard and robe into Samantha's arms. "Laura's here! That's my lady and you know I've got to go talk to her!"

"Whoa!" Jackson interjected. "You are going to leave your mother holding your stuff while you go romancing? That doesn't sound like the orator who made the valedictorian address."

"I knew it! I knew it!" Rhasan complained. "That address is going to haunt me! I'm not even going to be allowed a transition period!"

Samantha smiled. "Go ahead, lover boy, my transitional man. Just don't forget these are rented and they must be returned. Wayman, do you want to leave yours too?"

"No, thank you, Ms. Tremain," Wayman said, still scanning the far edge of the crowd. Samantha gave Rhasan a nod of her head

"Thanks, Mom," Rhasan said, then he and Wayman were gone.

Samantha looked down at the bundle of mortarboard and gown in her arms and the camera and case in her hands and said, "I think I'll go back to our seats and drop this off. I want to get a picture of Rhasan and his girlfriend."

After Samantha departed, Jackson was left standing alongside Wayman's godmother. He noticed that she was very good-looking. She had smooth skin, so dark there were purple tints in it, large eyes, and full lips. When she smiled, exposing her white teeth and opening her large, dark eyes, she had a vivacity in her look that was hard to deny. He did not want to stare, so he looked away, but even as his vision took in the meandering crowds of students and their extended families, he was thinking about the trace of a dimple in her cheek.

After standing a few moments with her in silence Jackson said, "Once again, the well-wishers are left to their own devices. . . . Your name is Elizabeth, right?"

She nodded and said in a husky contralto, "And I know your name."

Jackson was pleased. "You meet so many people at these events. Their names turn into a blur. I'm glad you remembered mine."

"Oh, I've heard about you." Her tone was filled with insinuation and her eyes were teasing. "I wouldn't forget your name."

"Is that because I have made a good impression somewhere or is this the result of some more character assassination material that has been prepared through the worldwide conspiracy of my enemies?"

She gave him an appraising look and replied, "I have my sources and from what I hear you're more than a well-wisher."

Her husky voice tingled in Jackson's ears. It made him look at her directly. A faint mischievous look skirted her large, brown eyes.

"How did you hear all that?" Jackson asked, studying her face.

"You're the great Jackson Tremain, Big Brother of the year! Surrogate father nonpareil!"

"That's only one of the ways I would describe myself, if given the chance," Jackson answered. Both her smile and tone had an enigmatic quality. He could not distinguish whether her intent was teasing or veiled hostility.

She moved closer to Jackson, picked a piece of lint off his lapel and said, "That's the way you were described by someone who respects and cares for you." She looked off in the direction that the boys had gone and then turned to face him again. "How would you describe yourself, if given a chance?" Her face was only a foot away from his, but suddenly it seemed to Jackson as if they were rubbing noses. The rich darkness of her skin made him want to touch her. Fighting against the unbidden urges, he stepped back and said, "First, let me say that you are quite beautiful. I'm a little stunned by it."

Her answer was glib. She tossed it off as if she had said it a thousand times. "Lots of people have said that and on the surface I am thankful that I look appealing, but on a deeper level I am reluctant to be placed upon a pedestal for such a transient thing as beauty."

"Only the beautiful can afford such a rationale," Jackson countered.

She gave him a bright smile then said, "Why walk a path that is well paved? Break new ground. Let's turn it around. Describe yourself."

"The physical profile is easy: six foot three inches, two hundred thirty pounds, reasonably athletic." He paused, unsure of what to say next. The woman's face was very mobile. She had a quick, mischievous smile that intrigued him and her eyes had a quality that made it difficult to look away. His body began tingling as if he was receiving an electrical message that his mind could only partially decode. They spent a moment looking at each other but when she put her hands on her hips, he realized that she was waiting for the elaboration or conclusion of his statement. He began, "The persona is more difficult. . . ." He did not want to continue. If he was going to give a description of himself to this woman, he wanted to work from a prepared statement. He wanted to make the best impression.

Elizabeth shifted her weight to one side, folded her arms, and said with a trace of impatience, "Go on! That's what I'm interested in: the persona. I can see you. You're not totally unpleasing to the eye. Provide all the personal detail that you dare."

Jackson was a bit cautious as he said, "Okay. I am a man who's interested in the pursuit of excellence and doing what's right. I attempt to avoid hurting people; sometimes through negligence, ignorance, or stupidity, I cause someone pain. If I do, I try to remedy it. I value niceness. I know some people think that's weak, but they don't understand how valuable niceness is. I believe in investing energy and time in our young people. Since I never had a normal family, I know the value of one."

"That's confusing to me," she said. "I've met several members of your family here today. They appear quite normal."

"Ah, they are masters of camouflage and deception. For short periods of time they may appear almost like regular humans, yet under the surface they constitute a major dysfunctional unit. I have often thought that my family should run a blood bank because we are so good at squeezing the blood out of everything we touch."

A frown flashed across her face and was replaced by a contemplative look. "That's a grisly metaphor but it leads us back to your description. I take it that you don't consider yourself a causal factor in this situation."

"It began long before I was born." Jackson smiled sadly. "I'm just a spoke in this wheel of pain, trying to stand as straight as I can." He gestured toward his grandmother, who was making her way slowly in his direction. "Here comes one of the primordial hubs from which we spring. Ask her why the wheel is bent."

Elizabeth cocked her head to the side as she looked at him and asked, "Are you always so morbid? Particularly with strange women?"

"Only when they bring up the subject of my family. Anyway, I don't know you well enough yet to classify you as strange," Jackson replied quickly, then after a moment's thought shrugged. "I might just be saying this because my family gives me terrible gas pains."

Serena stood patiently a few feet away, waiting to be recognized. Her magisterial presence could not be ignored.

Jackson asked, "Did you want something, Grandmother?"

"Yes, if you have a moment, I'd like you to walk me to my car."

"Surely, Grandmother," Jackson answered with resignation.

"I don't believe I've met your young lady."

Jackson mumbled awkwardly, "She's not my . . . uh. She's a—"

"We've met, Mrs. Tremain," Elizabeth said, rescuing Jackson from the need to explain. "You were with your other grandson on the far side of the stage. I'm Elizabeth Carlson, Wayman's godmother."

"You're right, Miss Carlson. Please forgive me, but when you get to be my age, the mind gets a little fuzzy with facts. Do you mind if I steal my grandson briefly?"

"No problem, Mrs. Tremain." Elizabeth flashed her a quick smile. "I should go and find Wayman. It's getting late." Elizabeth stuck out her hand. "It was nice meeting you, Jackson Tremain."

Jackson shook her hand and spoke into her ear, filling his nose with the smell of her body and her perfume. He whispered, "I'd like to see you again."

Elizabeth smiled at him and said, "Good." She turned and walked into the milling mass of people.

Jackson was surprised at how fragile his grandmother had grown. She leaned on him steadily as they made their way across the plaza to her car. They were halfway across before any words were spoken.

"Is it your intent to spend the rest of your life hating me?" His grandmother's voice was raspy from exertion.

"I don't hate you, Grandmother, I just don't love you." For reasons that he never understood there were never any moments of laughter or gentleness shared between them.

Serena Tremain paused for a moment and stared at her grandson.

When she started walking again, she said, "Word games make poor answers to serious questions. If you don't hate me, can we call a truce in the war between us?"

"How can you call a truce when your ally has sworn to outflank me?"

"I want peace! I have had two sons killed in the prime of life, watched my husband turn into a bloodthirsty killer, and had my dreams destroyed as I watched. I have paid dearly for my mistakes. Now, my time is growing short. I wish to set aside the hostilities and the anger. I wish to do what is best for what is left of my family. This is why I have come to ask you to represent the family's interests. Don't let your grandfather give the wealth that has been accumulated over the years to strangers. Our family has shed blood for all that he owns."

"Although you seemed to have developed manipulation to the level of an art, I won't be your instrument," Jackson said, shaking his head slowly. "I'm not old enough to set aside my memories and forget. I guess I'm not close enough to meeting my Maker, nor am I attempting to atone for a life of cruelty."

"Is that how you truly see me?"

"I don't pretend that I can truly see you. You image has always been distorted. The person that I see when I look at you may, in truth, be gone now. I say, who cares? The person you were is still alive and breathing to me.

"Let's be clear, I don't want anything to do with my grandfather either. I don't want his blood money and I don't care who he gives it to. That's final."

"If that is to be your final decision, let me warn you—"

"Ah, the threat; the other shoe drops." He shook his head as he helped his grandmother down the steps of the plaza. "This is what I have been waiting for. Your return to character."

"It is not me who threatens you," his grandmother chided him. "It is the life that your grandfather lived that threatens us all. He has made many enemies and though none would dare to stand face-to-face with him in his youth, they crowd around like jackals and hyenas at the death of an old lion. They seek not only his death, but all the territory that he controlled as well."

"Let them have it! The old lion lived by the law of the jungle; it is only fitting that he should die by it."

"Hmm," his grandmother said, stopping to stare at Jackson. "That is a coldhearted assessment. Your grandfather taught you well."

"I learned coldness from you, Grandmother. Grandfather taught me anger."

"Touché," she said, suddenly looking older. She leaned heavily on Jackson as they continued down the stairs. "Suppose we take the metaphor further," she posed in her raspy voice. "The jackals know that they can never truly possess all that the old lion controls without first eliminating his offspring. Even if you do not go down to Mexico, they will come for you and Franklin. And after you two are gone, they will come for the rest of us."

"Why should they? That doesn't make sense. All they should care about is his business and his money. What more is there?"

They were now standing beside his grandmother's car. Her driver opened the door for her and assisted her in entering. "The answers lie in Mexico," she said from the interior of the car and motioned for the door to be closed.

Jackson felt a coldness seep into his heart that he had not felt in nearly twenty years. It was a feeling that he had known well in his youth. It was fear, and he could not force it back into the vault from which it sprang.

"Congratulations, Rhasan," he said to no one in particular as his grandmother's car drove off. "What kind of world did we bring you into?"

July 1954

The air was thick with dust. It seemed to rise up and form shapes while floating on the warm gusts of air. Eight-year-old Jackson stood in the shadows of the bus depot, watching the hot afternoon sun desiccate everything in its path. His grandmother, dressed in black, stood silently a few feet away. They were waiting for his grandfather.

Jackson was in a storm of confusion and pain. His father was in the grave barely three months, the victim of a violent crime. Jackson's whole world had exploded and imploded at the same time. He had no conception or words for the emotions that he was feeling. He was a frightened little boy, yet no one reached out to calm his fears or explain what was expected of him. He was left to struggle through his heart-rending confusion by himself. Jackson kept brushing his face to keep what seemed to be millions of flies from landing on his eyes and mouth.

His grandmother was luckier; she had a black veil which she had pulled tightly over her face before they left the house in San Francisco and had kept it down for the full duration of their trip. It was an unnecessary barrier, for she had always been a forbidding figure. He had no relationship with her. If his grandmother had smiled at him, he would have rushed to her side, but she did not even talk to him unless circumstances required it.

Tecate was a smudge of a town ten miles south of the California–Mexico border. Most of the buildings were single-story wood-frame constructions. Other than the huge brewery on the edge of town, there may have been two buildings in the whole community which were three stories tall. Tecate lay nestled in the arms of two hills which opened to the eastward breeze. A film of red dust covered everything in sight. Up the street from the depot, there was a neon taco sign flashing in green and red over a small, dingy restaurant that had an old, dented pickup parked out front. Across the street, a small-time concessionaire sold chalupas from a wooden cart. Jackson was hungry but he didn't dare say anything.

Sweat dripped down his face. Even in the shadows of the depot, the heat was oppressive. It was worse inside, where the air was as still as a tomb and the flies sounded like jets zooming over a control tower. When they had first arrived, Jackson's grandmother had parked her rented car and had attempted to wait inside the depot. However, after twenty minutes in the ovenlike atmosphere she had to abandon it for the porch. Since everything outside was covered with dust, she found no acceptable place to sit, so she chose to stand. Jackson quietly followed her example. A half hour passed without a word being exchanged. Eventually, Jackson sat down on his suitcase.

There was no movement in the shimmering heat of the street, except for a couple of timid mongrels who paused hungrily for a few cautious sniffs. Another fifteen minutes passed and Jackson's grandmother began to pace methodically back and forth. She was wearing high heels and the prolonged standing was beginning to hurt her feet. She looked at the rented car but realized that waiting in it in this heat would be unbearable. She continued to pace.

Jackson did not remember when he first noticed that a man was standing in an alley down the street from the depot, staring at him. The man was dressed in a red shirt and jeans underneath a dirty serape. He wore a black, high-domed hat with a wide, flat brim and had a black-tipped white feather stuck in its band. The man started walking slowly toward the depot, casting glances both right and left. As he came closer, Jackson saw that the man had shoulder-length straight black hair, a brown face, and glinting black eyes. When he reached the stairs leading up to the depot, he stopped and said, *"Hola, señora."*

Jackson's grandmother watched the man silently. She was not in the habit of talking to strangers.

He said in halting English, "We have come for the boy."

"Where is King?" she asked evenly.

"He no come, many enemies. Send me to get boy."

"If King didn't come then we've wasted a trip down here. Tell King to arrange to come in person. Then he can have the boy." His grandmother turned with an air of dismissal and said, "Come, Jackson."

The man mounted the steps quickly, stepping in between Jackson and his grandmother. "Boy stays!" he said emphatically.

Jackson's grandmother put her hand in her purse and answered in a calm, steady voice, "If you try to stop me, you'll need a priest."

The man saw her hand grasp something in her purse. He raised his hand in a motion of surrender then pulled an envelope from his pocket and started toward her. "El Negro said to give you this."

His grandmother took two quick steps backward. "Put it down on the floor and step back."

The man placed the envelope on the floor and stepped respectfully backward.

"Jackson!" his grandmother said in firm voice. "Bring that envelope to me."

Jackson did as he was told and then waited while his grandmother ripped open the envelope and read it contents. She crumpled the papers in an unusual show of anger. Through gritted teeth she asked, "It says there are two of you; where's the other one?"

The man gestured off into the distance with his hand. "With the truck."

She nodded her head as she registered this information. She took the keys to her rented car from her purse and said, "You tell King to bring him back to San Diego. I won't cross the border again." With that she turned and walked away. There was no word of good-bye. Jackson was left standing with a man he did not know.

The man stepped out into the street and waved his hat over his head. A pickup truck which had been parked outside the dingy restaurant started up and came rolling toward them. Jackson realized that the truck had been there the whole time he and his grandmother had been waiting. Jackson's bag was thrown in the back and he was ushered into the center seat.

The man who was driving looked like a younger version of the man in the hat. He was handsome, in his early twenties, and his brown face had not yet become wrinkled and weathered like his older companion's. The driver greeted Jackson with a smile, the first he had received since leaving San Francisco. The truck rocked back and forth as it was driven on the rutted dirt roads which led south on the Baja California peninsula. The two men carried on a sparse conversation in Spanish. Jackson sat in the middle and said nothing.

They had been in the truck for about an hour when the driver broke out a canteen of water and had a drink. He offered the canteen to Jackson, who had not had anything to drink for a couple of hours. Jackson accepted the canteen and promptly drained half of it. He would have finished it had the older man in the hat not taken the canteen from him. After about three hours of steady driving, the truck abruptly pulled off the road.

The sun was low in the western sky and there were long shadows cast across the land by the San Pedro Martir Mountains, which formed the backbone of the northern part of the Baja California landmass. The landscape was dotted with saguaro, stunted madrona, and sagebrush. The two men got out and urinated on the side of the road. Jackson reluctantly followed their lead. He didn't know where he was and he didn't want to stray too far away from the truck. The older man in the hat squatted beside the truck and rolled himself a cigarette. It was still warm but the heat had dissipated considerably. Jackson leaned against the truck and thought about hamburgers and fries. He had not eaten since the morning and now he was hungrier than he could ever remember.

On the other side of the truck, the driver was chewing on some jerky. Jackson tried not to look but his hunger overcame his willpower.

He unconsciously began to stare. The driver noticed him. He averted his eyes. The driver walked around the truck and offered him a big piece of the jerky. Jackson thanked him and grabbed the offered food. The dried meat was tough and chewy, but it made his tongue spring to life. Jackson finished the jerky so fast the driver laughed and called out in Spanish to the man in the hat. The man in the hat came over to the truck and asked Jackson, "You hungry?"

The desire to eat overcame Jackson's fears and self-restraint. He nodded his head vigorously. He could not remember ever going all day without eating. He had no real awareness that there were many places in the world where people routinely did not eat every day. All he knew was that the refrigerator was always stocked and he could help himself at any time. He watched the man in the hat go to the back of the truck and rummage through various bundles.

The driver tapped his chest and said, "Carlos." He tapped Jackson's chest and made a questioning gesture.

Jackson understood him and said, "Jackson."

Carlos pointed to the man in the hat and said, "El Indio."

Jackson repeated Carlos's and El Indio's names and received a smile of approval from Carlos.

El Indio gave Jackson a dried fish and a couple of tortillas. Jackson accepted it gingerly. He wasn't used to eating food while its eyes stared at him. Seeing his bewilderment, El Indio cut the head off and showed him how to skin it. The fish and the tortillas were gone in minutes. As Jackson was loaded back into the truck, the two men laughed briefly about the boy's appetite. Carlos even made a joke in Spanish about Jackson's mouth being open as wide as a fledgling's.

Two and a half more hours in the truck and they drove into a small town lying on the edge of the Sea of Cortez. Jackson had fallen asleep on Carlos's shoulder. He was shaken awake by Carlos, who watched him try to slough off the bonds of sleep by peering at everything with wide-eyed looks. The sun had set and there was just a band of purple above the dark outline of the mountain ridges to the west. The lights of the little town shimmered off the waters of the sea. El Indio parked the truck and several minutes were spent collecting Jackson's suitcase and various bundles from the back of the truck and then the three of them walked down to the docks. The sound of music and the smell of grilled fish greeted them.

There was a waterfront honky-tonk blaring Ray Charles songs out over the water. It was a one-story, white stucco building with a flickering yellow neon sign written in cursive that read *Mary's Bar*. Next to the honky-tonk there was a small store that sold cigarettes, sodas, candy, and related items. Both buildings were part of a pier. In front of the store there was a man grilling fish. El Indio and Carlos spoke rapidly in Spanish, then El Indio took the bags from the truck and headed off into the night.

Jackson had identified the store and the source of the food smells the moment they stepped onto the docks. He headed toward the store, ready to slake his thirst and eat his fill. He had ten dollars in his pocket and he was hungry. The man grilling the fish was old and wizened and had the stump of a cigarette smoldering between his lips. Jackson watched him expertly flip a whole fish from spot to spot with his tongs. His hair was tied in a handkerchief and his pants were rolled up to his knees. He looked like a figure out of a Japanese samurai movie. Jackson pointed to the fish and the man answered him in a flood of Spanish. Jackson pulled out his ten dollars. The old man shook his head and repeated a word followed by *pesos* several times.

Behind him Jackson heard a male voice with an American accent say, "What have we here, Jimmy?"

Another male voice answered, bemused, "I don't rightly know, but he's waving enough money to drink all night."

Jackson turned and saw two young white men staring at him. They were wearing cowboy hats, T-shirts, and jeans. He had been taught to be suspicious of whites but not to fear them. "Do you have change for ten dollars?" he asked, his hunger impelling him forward.

The slimmer, taller man said, "Jimmy, you got all the Mex money."

Jimmy, the shorter, more muscular of the two men, said, "Sure, little buddy, I can help you." He reached into his pockets and pulled out a wad of money made up of bills from both the United States and Mexico. He counted out a wad of Mexican currency and handed it to Jackson.

Jackson accepted the money questioningly. "How much is this?"

Jimmy snatched the ten dollars from his hand and said, "Don't worry about it, you got enough to get a couple of fish!" The men turned to walk away.

Jimmy's friend laughed. "Easy money, Jimmy. You ought to go into banking!"

Jackson, concerned that he was being cheated, said, "Wait a minute! This isn't ten dollars!"

Jimmy turned and gave Jackson a hard look. "Better shut your mouth, pickaninny. You're lucky I didn't jes' take your money."

"I want my ten dollars back," Jackson demanded, his voice rising in volume.

Jimmy crossed the few feet that separated him and Jackson and poked the boy hard in the chest with his index finger. "I told you to shut—" Jimmy didn't get to say anything else. Carlos struck him hard on the side of the head with the butt of a large knife. The blow knocked Jimmy off his feet. He fell in a heap on the wooden planks of the pier. His friend started to come to his aid, but the cocking of a shotgun stopped him. El Indio was standing behind him with the weapon aimed in his direction. There was a short, swarthy, balding man with El Indio. When Jimmy's friend saw him, he paled noticeably and stuttered, "We didn't know, Señor Ramirez. We didn't know he was a friend of yours!"

Señor Ramirez ignored Jimmy's friend and went right to Jackson. He knelt in front of the boy and asked with a thick Mexican accent, "Did he hurt you?"

Jackson shook his head to indicate that he wasn't hurt. He mumbled, "He took my ten dollars and gave me this." He opened his hand to show Señor Ramirez the wad of five-peso notes.

Señor Ramirez glanced at the money briefly and asked, "Did he touch you?"

Jackson nodded affirmatively and rubbed his chest where the man had poked him.

"Which hand?" asked Señor Ramirez.

Jackson indicated his right.

Señor Ramirez stood up and walked over to Jimmy, who was still sprawled on the ground, woozy from the blow he had received. Señor Ramirez said something to Carlos, who quickly knelt and held Jimmy's right arm. Señor Ramirez stomped Jimmy's immobilized hand. Jimmy's scream shredded the night as his knuckles popped like popcorn. The foot raised and stomped again. Jimmy screamed again and then suddenly stopped.

People started to pile out of the bar. Someone even said, "That's Jimmy." But the sight of the shotgun quelled any thoughts of heroics. There were hostile rumblings from the bar's clientele when an older man pushed his way to the front. He had the air of a man who was used

to being obeyed. When he saw Señor Ramirez his posture changed
from commanding to solicitous. "Sorry to bother you, Señor Ramirez,"
he said with a quick, respectful nod of his head. "Everyone back in the
bar! This is not our business. Back in the bar!" There was a brief milling
and mumbling as the patrons filed back into Mary's. The door to the bar
closed with a slam and curtains were drawn across the windows.

Señor Ramirez turned to look at Jimmy's companion, who was shivering with fear. "What am I going to do with you?" Señor Ramirez
asked as he walked toward the man.

"Please, señor," the man begged. "It was an honest mistake! We didn't
know this kid had anything to do with you! Honest!"

Señor Ramirez gestured to El Indio, who swiftly stepped up and
smashed the butt of the shotgun behind the man's knee. The man crumpled with a wail: "I didn't even touch the kid! Please!"

"Show me your money!" Señor Ramirez demanded.

The man emptied his pockets. A jingling sound rang out as change
and keys fell on the wooden planks. He offered his paper money to
Señor Ramirez, who then counted the money swiftly and threw down
some bills. "There is money to buy gas or catch the southbound bus to
Santa Rosalia. It leaves from the plaza at ten-thirty tonight. If you are
here in the morning, you will be treated in the manner that you deserve." Señor Ramirez walked over and said something to Carlos. Carlos knelt down and began rifling through Jimmy's pockets. Jimmy was
delirious with pain and not yet fully conscious. He began to moan. Carlos took the money out of Jimmy's pockets and gave it to Señor
Ramirez, who spit on Jimmy then threw a few bills on his supine body.
Señor Ramirez went to the old man who was grilling fish and spoke
quickly, then he gave him some bills. The old man accepted the money
gladly and began wrapping all his cooked fish. Señor Ramirez turned to
Jackson and offered him the remaining money, which was considerably
more than the amount Jackson had originally been given. He took the
money with trepidation. He was frightened by the decisive violence of
the man and by the deference showed him by the people in the bar. He
nodded his head and said respectfully, "Thank you."

Señor Ramirez nodded his head as well and a big smile broke out on
his face. He patted Jackson warmly on the shoulder and said, "El Negro's grandson. I have not seen you since you were christened, but I
have heard much about you!" As he turned to walk away, El Indio fell in

step with him. Jackson started to follow the two men off the pier when the old man with the fish caught his attention. The old man gestured that he should take the bundle of fish. Jackson's expression lit up. Forgotten were the two men who still lay crumpled on the pier. He rushed over, almost losing his money trying to take the bulky package of fish.

El Indio said something in Spanish to Señor Ramirez that made everyone, including the old fishmonger, laugh. Bewildered, Jackson followed the two into the darkness. Still chuckling, Carlos appeared at his side and took the bundle of fish from him. Jackson looked up at Carlos with a quizzical expression.

"Do you want to know what my uncle is saying?" Carlos asked without a hint of an accent.

"You speak English?" Jackson asked, surprised.

"Second-year business major at San Diego State College," Carlos answered with a laugh. As they stepped out onto the floating dock, he explained, "I went to high school in Imperial Beach."

"Why did everyone laugh back there?"

"My uncle was talking about you. He said, 'The wolf cub has the appetite and spirit of a wolf, but is still a wolf cub.' "

They climbed onto a large, shiny motorboat. Big lights on the roof of the top cabin illuminated the deck. Provisions and fuel were being loaded by several barebacked men. Jackson had never been on a boat so large. Keeping out of the way of the stevedores, he began exploring. There was a large cabin on top of the boat with a steering wheel and a lot of electrical instruments. In front of the cabin, there were several chairs with seatbelts that were bolted to the deck. Jackson noticed little windows on the side of the hull and assumed there must be several cabins below, but he did not venture there because of the bustling traffic. Señor Ramirez was moving about the deck, barking orders and directing men. El Indio, apparently having stashed his shotgun, joined the work crews and pitched in like a veteran. Jackson looked for somewhere to sit that would be out of the way. He saw Carlos waving to him from a seat on the main deck. Jackson made his way carefully to him. Carlos had been assigned to keep an eye on him by Señor Ramirez to ensure there would be no further problems.

From the security of his seat Jackson watched Señor Ramirez get his boat ready for the open sea. Carlos handed him a large, orange life jacket and helped him strap it on. It was bulky, but Jackson liked the feel of it. He felt the boat's powerful engines roar to life and was excited by the muffled throb of their forceful presence. When the boat pulled out of the little harbor, Jackson could contain himself no longer, and rushed to the stern to watch the lights of the little town diminish in the darkness. The bright spotlights were turned off and the deck was left in the semidarkness of the boat's running lights. To Jackson, the stars had never been so bright before. He stared up into the moonless night sky and it appeared almost three dimensional, as if he could reach out and touch any one of the millions of points of light.

The trip took three hours and Jackson loved every minute of it. He liked the rumble of the powerful engines and the rocking motion of a becalmed sea. He saw the lights of other boats pass in the darkness, the inky outlines of small islands, and finally the moon. It made its dramatic entrance about halfway through the trip. It was not quite full but had a bright beige image which reflected off the darkening water. Carlos called him. They were breaking out the fish. Someone brought out a stack of warm tortillas and salsa. The men drank beer, while Jackson was given a Coke. It was the best meal Jackson had had in a very long time. After they finished eating, Señor Ramirez brought him up to the captain's cabin and showed him how to steer the boat. In the darkness, they passed a large landmass with lights on it called Tiburón Island. When the boat finally pulled into Bahia Kino, it was nearly midnight. Jackson was sorry that the trip was over.

As an adult, when he recalled this initial summer with his grandfather he saw it in terms of Greek mythology: He viewed his boat passage as the crossing of the River Styx; Jimmy and his companion symbolized the two-headed Cerberus, the dog that guarded the gates of Hades; Ramirez was Charon, who ferried dead souls to the netherworld; and his grandfather was Pluto himself.

However, as an eight-year-old he could not complicate his thinking with symbolism. He knew only that he had left the land of the known, the world of routines and cold interchanges, when he and his grandmother got out of the rented car in Tecate. This was more than the recognition that Mexico was a nation different from the United States. He realized on an unspoken level that he had entered a world in which men lived by dint of their wit, the courage in their hearts, and the force in their fists.

Señor Ramirez called for the lights to be turned on again so that the process of unloading the boat could begin. Men appeared out of no-where and began carrying bundles off the boat. Jackson found his suit-case and began making his way to the gangplank. When he stepped onshore he saw his grandfather standing in the shadows of an old build-ing, watching him.

Monday, June 21, 1982

The bag swung back and forth slowly. It was a ten-inch-long leather oval which had an elastic cord attached to each end. One end of the cord was attached to the ceiling, the other to the floor. Jackson, dripping with sweat, stared at the bag intently. It was the elusive, chest-high object that he had been keeping in motion with his kicks. He wasn't interested in simple repetition; every time he kicked the bag, he tried for power, to drive his foot through its leather casing. Each time he began his assault on the bag, he thought of his grandmother's part-ing words at Rhasan's graduation: "Even if you do not go down to Mex-ico, they will come for you. . . ."

He was tired, but he had twenty more kicks with his left leg before he finished his routine. The bag was an adversary to be battered and driven back. He took a forward stance and swung his foot up quickly and forcefully in a front kick, which struck the bag squarely and sent it swinging in rapid patterns that he could not follow.

"It looks like your timing is way off," Wesley said as he came over to watch Jackson. "It's the same principle as a punching bag: You attack it from the same angle and get into a rhythm."

"Doing side kicks is like playing solitaire," Jackson grunted as he be-gan his kicks again. "You can be in a room by yourself and some weird-butt will come over and tell you to put the red queen on the black king." He missed his last three kicks by wide margins and stopped to catch his breath.

"As far I am concerned you have two red queens and two exposed black kings. You obviously need help," Wesley said as he poised him-self, then kicked the bag lightly four times in rapid succession.

Jackson snatched a towel from Wesley's shoulder and began wiping off. "If you wanted to help, why didn't you loan me your towel? I'm the one who's sweating. All you did was show off for a few seconds."

"I worked out hard last night. The only reason I came back here with you tonight was to stretch. Now I'm ready to go. Let's hit the showers."

In a sparring ring on the other side of the dojo, two men were working out. From the sounds of the blows landed, it was full contact. Jackson and Wesley paused on their way to the showers to watch the match.

"That's not kempo."

"No, it's kick boxing," Wesley answered. "Their gym got closed down and Sensei Matsuo has allowed them to work out here." As Wesley finished speaking, one of the combatants delivered a spinning back kick. It was delivered with such force that even though it was partially blocked, it still knocked his opponent to the canvas.

"Damn! That was a hell of a kick!" Jackson said as they entered the locker room.

Jackson took off his T-shirt, turned from his locker, and asked, "Have you ever been driven by something? Propelled by some all-consuming passion?"

Wesley paused before he answered. "I don't know . . . I mean, I like money and I'm reasonably ambitious, but all-consuming? No, I don't think so. Not unless you include my twenty-four-hour pursuit of pussy. Why?"

Jackson gave Wesley a long look. "Don't you ever worry that you're devaluing women when you think of them as pussies?"

"No! I want to connect with them on that primal level. I'm into that caveman shit! While you're fucking and sweaty, being a dick or a pussy is reaching into the essence of it all. That's the real reason mankind is a successful species. Despite his brain, he has to fuck."

Jackson laughed. "Thank you for another neo-Freudian interpretation of human history. So what happens when you run across a woman who doesn't feel that way?"

"We only fuck once."

"That sure is simple."

Wesley held up his hand. "Wherever you're going with this, I give up. You win! You can have the moral high ground. Okay? Now, we started off talking about you. Where was that going?"

"Well, sometimes I worry that I don't have the capacity to really care about something. I don't have any life goals which require me to dedicate myself. I sometimes think that I've lived my whole life by default and that I don't exert any consistent control over where my life is going. For example, I work at the City of Oakland because I came out high in the selection process. I didn't even start off wanting to work in the East Bay." Jackson grabbed a dry towel and headed into the showers with Wesley. "It's more than that, really, more than being driven. I have never really had an all-consuming desire for anything. It's scary, like I'm drifting through my life."

Before he disappeared in the steam of the showers, Wesley jibed, "Thank you for sharing the fact that you're suffering from attention deficit disorder."

Jackson smiled. What did he expect? This was one of his macho male friends; there could be no intimate exchange without some derision. He had unthinkingly just done the same thing to Wesley. That was part of the game. There were too many games. Too many rules. Too many things to worry about. He stood under the shower, wanting the hot water to wash all thoughts from his mind with its cleansing heat. He wanted to lose himself in the pounding heat of the streams of water. Yet he could not find even momentary peace. He began to see metaphors in the shower. He was part of an eternal human flow, a fluid of countless faces. Funneled through the vast sprinkler head of birth to different destinations, some to be stopped by objects in midflight, others to hit the wall, while still others evaporated into the very air that was breathed by all. As he walked out of the shower, Jackson wondered which stream his grandfather had passed through, and at what destination he would soon arrive.

Wesley was almost dressed when Jackson got back to his locker. He gave Jackson a questioning look and said, "Damn, man, I thought you drowned. What were you doing in there, masturbating?"

"Thinking," Jackson answered as he began to dress.

"Thinking?" Wesley challenged. "About what?"

"Life, my grandfather; the whole ball of wax."

"That's it? That's all you thought about during a two-hour shower?"

"Lifetimes have been spent in resolving issues smaller than these."

"Suppose you tell me in plain English what the hell we're talking about."

"My grandfather may be dying. He was a man who took many lives, who was addicted to the drama of violence. If there is a soul that exists after death, is there some grand scheme of poetic justice that exacts payment for negative deeds?"

"You're talking about heaven and hell," Wesley said, fixing his tie. "If you're a Christian, you've already bought into some alternative of this scenario. But ain't nobody but the dead really got answers to these questions. It's a riddle that can't be answered. I say, let's go get a drink."

"I don't think I'm up for it," Jackson said, buttoning his shirt. "I've got a lot of things to think about."

"Give me a break! Like you're going to find answers to this tonight?" Wesley picked up his gym bag. "Aren't you ready to go yet?"

Jackson pulled on his slacks and sat down to put on his socks and shoes. "Something my grandmother said keeps running through my mind," he said as he slammed his locker shut and picked up his bag.

"It's only seven-thirty!" Wesley grumbled as they walked out of the dojo. They were greeted by a brisk wind coursing up the Broadway corridor, chilling their scalps, which were still wet from the shower.

Suddenly, a drink in a nice, warm establishment didn't seem that bad an idea to Jackson. "Okay," he conceded. "Let's go to Justin's." There was nothing awaiting him at his house except work and convoluted memories.

Justin's was one of three black-owned bars in the Jack London Square area. It catered primarily to black professionals, but there was a smattering of Asians and whites who also frequented the establishment. The walls were gray but the furnishings were done in pink and black. There was a pink neon light encased in Plexiglas which ran the length of the wall behind the bar. The bar itself was a long, narrow, angular black Formica construction which thrust out into the room. There were a series of high black Formica tables scattered throughout the main room around the bar. Each table had its accompaniment of tall, pink stools. The decor was hard to ignore, but generally Justin's was so crowded one did not notice its interior colors. However, after seven in the evening on a Monday night, the bar crowd had begun to dissipate; there were even a couple of unoccupied tables when Jackson and Wesley entered. They stepped aside for two women who were leaving and then made their way to a vacant table.

Wesley craned his neck to give the departing women a last appraising look. "Looks like we missed some meat on the hoof."

"Watch yourself!" Jackson retorted as he looked around for the waitress. "This is the Bay Area. If some woman hears you talk like that, you could find yourself being stomped by a frenzied mob of indignant *Mother Jones* feminists."

"If they've got that much hostility, do you think they're getting any?" Wesley asked with pretended interest.

"I'm sure you can ask them while they're trying to remove the top of your skull with steel-tipped Reeboks."

A waitress came over and took their orders. Wesley watched her depart. "That's a fine heifer. Look at those powerful hocks. Damn! That's butt made in Africa!"

"Yeah, you marry that and in five years it turns into a continental shelf," Jackson commented dryly.

"Now who's being a sexist dog?" Wesley prodded. "I do believe my politically correct brother has fucked up!"

"Your labeling me is characteristic of the type of thinking that hinders philosophical inquiry."

"That's one opinion," Wesley conceded with a nod of his head. "Say, speaking of philosophical inquiry, what did your grandmother say to you the other day to get you so disturbed?"

"That's a hell of a segue." Jackson chuckled.

"You brought it up when we were leaving the dojo. I was just following up."

"She told me that my grandfather's enemies would come for me after he was dead."

"Come for you? Come for you how?"

"I guess they would come to kill me."

"For what? What's your connection with all this?"

"I'm not quite sure, but I think it has something to do with my grandfather's estate."

"She said that they would come to kill you? She said that?"

"Not exactly, but that was the clear implication."

"That would disturb the shit out of me too! What are you going to do?"

"I'm not sure. I don't know how real the threat is; there are just too many unknowns to make a decision."

"How does your grandmother know about this?"

"Damned if I know. She and I aren't close. We don't chat, if you get what I mean." The waitress returned with their drinks and the conversation halted briefly while Jackson paid her.

"Why did she tell you this, then?" Wesley continued after taking a long sip of his drink.

"She wants me to represent her interests in Mexico. She expects me to go down before my grandfather dies."

"Would she lie or manipulate the truth in order—"

"No, she wouldn't lie. She might not tell me the whole truth, but she wouldn't lie."

"How old is your grandfather?"

"Eighty-three or -four. He was born before the turn of the century."

"How old are his enemies? If we're talking about some doddering old guys, I wouldn't be so worried."

"I don't know, but I imagine some of them could be my age."

Wesley sat up with surprise. "How do you know that? This could be some serious shit!"

"I don't know anything. I'm just guessing. I'd have to go to Mexico if I really wanted to find out what's going on—" Jackson paused suddenly, realizing that he was reluctantly considering the decision to go to Mexico. As he continued speaking, a trace of a smile played across his face. "It looks like, whether I like it or not, the old man is going to drag me into his world. He spent all those years training me, now I'm being called to duty. Another soldier in the undeclared war, following in my father's footsteps to an early grave."

"What happened to your father? He was dead a couple of years by the time I met you."

"My father was gunned down in one of my grandfather's business deals when I was eight." Jackson's words were matter-of-fact, as if he had been over the subject many times.

"This is the same grandfather you used to spend your summers with?"

Jackson exhaled slowly. "To be exact, seven memorable summers."

"We were talking about being driven before. Was your grandfather a driven man?"

"No more than your routine serial killer."

Wesley exhaled quickly. "Whew. It looks as if you have as much unfinished business with your grandfather as I had with my father."

"It would take several lifetimes to finish all the business I have with my grandfather."

"I might have needed more than one lifetime to resolve things with my dad too." Wesley paused and reflected with a smile, "I loved him but I didn't understand him. He was so tight with money, my older brothers and I hated him when we were kids. But in hindsight, I see it was his frugality that allowed us to buy that house on Fulton Street. I might never have met you if he hadn't bought that house three blocks from your grandmother. And he did it on the salary of a custodian. You remember, after college, when I went to the hospital to see him and we finally really talked as men? By then he was dying of cancer. It was only after that I discovered he was a guy I would have liked."

"No fear of that with me and my grandfather," Jackson answered, leaving two dollars on the table for a tip. "You ready to go?"

Wesley stood up and stretched. "Yeah, I'm ready. Why don't you tell me when you plan to go down to Mexico; maybe I'll go down with you. Give you some company."

"If I ever decide to go, it's a possibility," Jackson replied.

"Let me just leave a big tip for this foxy waitress, so she'll remember me."

Jackson turned and said, "The woman with tremendous hocks, as you call them, has swallowed bigger tips than you'll ever give her without a smile."

Wesley leaned his head to one side in a questioning manner. "Do you know something I don't know? Was that a play on words? Speaking of hocks, what's happening on the woman front for you?"

"Nothing particular, but I did meet a new woman! She has skin so black she reminds me of a summer plum, one of those purplish-black ones. She looked so good and succulent I just wanted to bite her right there and then. She made me think of Langston Hughes's poem 'Harlem Sweeties.' "

"A really black sister, huh? They say the blacker the berry, the sweeter the juice. You going to see her again?"

"I'd like to; there was something about her, and it wasn't just the way she looks. I felt something, something inside. It was eerie. If our paths cross again, I'll certainly follow up on speaking with her."

"What do you mean if, huh? You better help fate out. Good pussy waits for no man!"

"Wes, I'm not a womanizer like you. I can't chase after women. I don't have the time or the inclination for it, and I don't want to play any of the games associated with pursuit."

"Damn! It's the pursuit that makes my dick hard!"

The wind greeted them as they came out into the night air. Wesley stopped, transfixed for a minute, staring across the street. Jackson turned and asked, "What is it?"

"There's an old brown Cadillac that looks just like the one my father owned," Wesley said as he pointed across the street. Jackson's gaze followed the direction of his hand as they headed toward the corner. Wesley continued, "Same shit-brown color."

Neither Wesley nor Jackson really looked at the interior of the car or they might have seen the shadows of Jesse and Gilmore slumped down in the front seat.

Tuesday, June 22, 1982

Franklin LaValle Tremain sat at his huge polished teak desk and stared absentmindedly at his distorted sepia reflection on the desk's surface. His financial security was in danger. He pulled a pen out of a drawer and began to doodle aimlessly on a sheet of paper. He was not used to feelings of insecurity and doubt. He looked at the various marketing charts around his office. The charts were an indication of his image as a successful businessman and real estate speculator. He didn't want anything to taint or discredit that image. Normally, he liked coming to work early in the morning before the rest of the staff; it gave him a chance to think and develop a strategy for his day. But this morning was different; he could not enjoy the solitude.

At thirty-eight he had done quite well for himself. He was the chief executive officer for King, Inc., a real estate management firm that in the previous year had exceeded a million and a half dollars in revenue. Through some borderline deals, done outside his firm, he had finagled himself a small mansion in Pacific Heights. He and his wife were fixtures in black society. If there was an event at which it was worth being seen, Franklin and Victoreen were there. Yet, there were changes in the wind. His grandfather was dying. This, in itself, did not greatly disturb Franklin; he never had much of a relationship with the man, but the potential ramifications of his death were very upsetting.

His private line rang five times before Franklin answered the phone. It was nearly seven-thirty in the morning. He had considered letting the phone ring, but thought better of it. Many a good business deal had occurred at the beginning of the day.

Franklin had wavy black hair and a café au lait skin color that had considerably more milk than coffee. In certain lights he was occasionally mistaken for Caucasian. His nostrils were perhaps a shade too wide and his lips a touch too full for that particular mistake to happen in full daylight. He wore a thin black mustache, which he felt required an ascot to be fully appreciated.

The voice on the other end of the phone asked, "Franklin, is that you? This is Bill Braxton."

"Bill, how are you doing? Long time no see." Franklin was immediately cautious. Braxton had been a longtime friend and occasional business partner of his grandmother's, a sort of financier or venture capitalist. Franklin had seen him at numerous family gatherings over the years, but there had never been any meaningful exchanges between them and there had been little contact in the last ten or fifteen years. Although nothing was said directly, Franklin had deduced that his grandmother and Braxton had had a falling-out. He wondered what Braxton had on his mind.

As if reading his thoughts, Braxton said, "I called because I was wondering how you're doing."

"Another day, another dollar," Franklin answered. What does he want? What's he fishing for? Questions zipped through Franklin's mind like tracer bullets.

"I hear your grandfather is very ill. . . ." Braxton let his voice die, trying to prompt Franklin into speaking.

"The only two things we really have to do is stay black and die," Franklin said. "And my grandfather is doing both of those."

"I guess you're not concerned that the execution of your grandfather's will may cause changes in the management of your firm?"

"What do you mean?" Franklin asked, maintaining a casual tone. But Braxton had hit a nerve. The majority share of the company, seventy percent, could be bequeathed to Jackson Tremain and that prospect was extremely irritating.

"It's likely that your grandfather will leave everything to your cousin. Since you don't get along with him, where does that leave you?"

Franklin knew exactly where that left him: out in the cold. But he said, "It's hard to predict what will happen at the reading of the will. There may even be some legal challenges to various aspects of the will. So, it's hard to say where that will leave me."

Braxton continued in a congenial tone, as if he were speaking to his best friend, "Do you really believe that you'll be able to successfully appeal any section of your grandfather's will? After all, you're an estranged family member. You haven't seen him since you were ten or twelve years old."

"What's the purpose of this call?" Franklin didn't have the patience to wait until Braxton's agenda revealed itself. Further, he was concerned about how Braxton had gathered his information. It was unlike his grandmother to share this level of information with anyone.

"Well, I thought that perhaps we might have similar goals," Braxton began conversationally.

"How are you involved?" Franklin didn't think he had anything in common with Braxton.

"Well, you may or may not know this, but many years ago your grandfather took a lot of money from some people here in San Francisco. . . ." Braxton let his words die once again, hoping that Franklin would volunteer something, but he said nothing. With an internal sigh, Braxton continued, "These people haven't forgotten. They still want their money."

Franklin felt a cold sensation moving down his spine. Did these people want to try to take over the real estate management firm? That possibility was actually worse than Jackson inheriting his grandfather's seventy percent. Even in his worst-case scenarios, Franklin had always calculated that at the very minimum, he would get the lion's share of his grandmother's thirty percent. "How long ago was this? How much money was taken?" His questions were delivered in a calm voice, but his heart was pounding. His grandfather had stolen from the Mob. If they were to collect, there was a possibility that he could be totally ruined. Wiped out. Without his job and the little kickbacks that he had arranged along the way, he might even lose the house in Pacific Heights. His hand shook as he held the receiver.

"It was a lot of money at the time. They think he either buried it or invested it." Braxton cursed himself for not arranging to have this meeting in person. He needed to see Franklin's face as he received this information.

"What's this got to do with me?" Franklin asked, barely able to stop himself from stammering.

"Well, it seems they feel some of the money was invested in your company."

"They feel? What the hell does that mean? Do they have proof?"

Braxton answered firmly, "When people like the ones I'm referring to feel something, they don't need proof." There it was, the implied threat. The fire was heating up; now, the art lay in shaping the metal. Braxton gave an experimental tap with a question: "You do understand what I'm saying?"

"What are you, their front man?" There was a trace of indignation in Franklin's voice. "I seem to remember you as being a friend of the family; now you're speaking for people who want to take our business away?"

Braxton laughed smoothly. "I come in peace. I come as a friend. These people came to me. I—"

"Who are 'these people'?" Franklin interjected.

Braxton cautioned, "It wouldn't be healthy to know that."

"So, you expect me to give up my company because 'these people,' sight unseen, think my grandfather invested some of their stolen money in it? You must be insane!"

"I never indicated or even suggested that you give up your company," Braxton corrected evenly. He decided to take a different tack. "As a matter of fact, I was in the process of making you a proposal that would allow you to keep the firm. A proposal which might prevent the inheritance of your grandfather's share by someone else other than you."

"What do you mean?" Thoughts raced through Franklin's mind. Was Braxton implying that Jackson would be killed? *If something happens to Jackson am I, as a result of this conversation, an accessory before the fact?* Franklin looked at the phone and saw an instrument of entrapment. The phone call could be in the process of being recorded. Franklin rushed to clear himself of any implication. "I don't know what you're talking about and I certainly don't want to be a party to anything illegal."

Braxton scoffed, "Who's mentioning anything illegal?" He quelled his anger. Franklin appeared to be just another idiot who was unable to decipher the art of inference and had no understanding of subtlety. Braxton reached down and adjusted his tape recorder. He would review the taped call at his leisure and try to figure out where he had gone wrong.

"Then what did you mean?" Franklin asked as he struggled with the limits of the phone cord, trying to reach his own tape recorder, but for totally different reasons. He thought that having a taped copy of the conversation might provide evidence of his innocence should something happen to his cousin. With a final lunge, he switched it on and attempted to cover the sound of its operation with "Let me change phones. I'm going to switch to the cordless." He picked up the cordless from its base, which was adjacent to the tape recorder. "So what did you mean?"

Braxton stated expansively, "We live in a world created by negotiation and renegotiation. I'm a negotiator. I think I can negotiate something that will benefit you as well as me."

"We also live in a world created by negotiations that didn't work out," Franklin responded cynically. "Before you tell what you can do for me, tell me what you're getting out of all this . . . this negotiating."

Braxton explained patiently, "I am being asked to facilitate an understanding by old friends. Personally, I have nothing to gain, no matter how it ends."

His initial fears had subsided, and Franklin now felt more in possession of his faculties. He was beginning to analyze and tabulate information when he asked, "When did my grandfather allegedly steal all this money anyway?"

Braxton paused, assessing how valuable the information was, then decided that the less Franklin knew, the better. "It happened a long time ago. As I understand it, a number of people were killed in the process. The deaths of those innocent people changed it from being merely a business situation to a blood feud."

"What year was this?" Franklin was impatient. He thought he saw a way out.

"It was nineteen fifty-four. Twenty-eight years ago."

"How much money was taken?"

"I wish it was that simple," Braxton answered, presuming that he knew the direction of Franklin's questions.

"Just tell me how much money was supposedly stolen." Franklin was getting insistent.

Braxton didn't like his tone and he didn't like Franklin. He had been around Franklin off and on from the time Franklin was a youngster, and in all that time Braxton had never seen anything to indicate that Franklin was particularly intelligent, insightful, or brave. Braxton thought of him as a slick, glib pretty boy who chased anything in skirts when his wife's back was turned. He wasn't particularly astute in business and he certainly didn't have his grandmother's gift for land speculation. Braxton had hoped to appeal to Franklin's greed and thereby enlist him to do several tasks. But Franklin was either too smart or too stupid to take the bait. "The amount of the money doesn't matter; these people want to be paid back with interest. I wanted to offer you a simple proposal that might leave you in sole possession of King, Inc., after the reading of the will."

"Okay, what's the proposal?" Franklin asked, attempting to suppress his enthusiasm.

Braxton heard the eagerness in Franklin's voice. Perhaps Franklin would be a worthy foil after all. Braxton surmised that Franklin's only concern about an illegal act was whether he would be made the fall guy. The telephone was not the appropriate medium to discuss such important details, so Braxton said, "Why don't we get together at Julius Castle on the edge of North Beach this Friday. I'm free all afternoon."

"That sounds fine with me," Franklin agreed.

After determining the details of their impending meeting and exchanging a few pro forma pleasantries, Braxton hung up and Franklin was left with his thoughts. This could be it, he thought. This could be the answer to all of his problems with Jackson; this could be the way to offset a lifetime of humiliation and defeat. The problem was how much of the estate would be left after Braxton's friends had taken what they wanted. Franklin fidgeted nervously for several minutes as he attempted to think his way through the labyrinth of alternatives. The difficulty was that he didn't know if Braxton was really representing the Mob. Perhaps his grandmother could shed some light on Braxton's friends. Franklin decided that he would stop by her house on his way home.

It did not occur to him that he might be simply a pawn in someone else's scheme. Although Franklin was thirty-eight years old, he had not forgotten the terrible beating he had received at Jackson's hands when he was twenty. It was an embarrassment that he sorely wanted erased from his memory. Even now it caused anger to swell in his breast. If Braxton was truly able to give him the vengeance he so richly deserved, as well as King, Inc., Franklin would be standing on top of the world. He decided that this apparent turn in his fortunes deserved a hearty breakfast. There was a diner just down the street that opened before eight. When he turned out the lights and walked out of the door of his office, there was a lightness in his step that had not been there for many years.

Tuesday, June 22, 1982

Jackson arrived at work slightly rumpled from a sleepless night. During the night, in those brief moments when he'd had the good fortune to doze off, his sleep had been disrupted by old memories of summers with his grandfather. He was happy to awake to the pale light of morning. Strong coffee and a hot shower had given him some semblance of awareness, but he still felt disconnected from the world around him, as if he had been placed in an unfamiliar body and had to reacquaint himself with its sensations and movements.

When he walked into his office, he checked his daily calendar and discovered that one of the secretaries had written in that he was to meet with his boss, the city manager, later that morning at nine-thirty. An unscheduled morning meeting with his boss did not bode well for a pleasant start to the day. He began shuffling through his in basket when the phone rang. The first call of the morning.

He picked up the phone. Both fatigue and resignation were in his voice as he answered, "City manager's office, Jackson Tremain."

The voice that answered was husky and heavily accented. "Is that you, Diablito?"

Images came swirling out of the ether. Jackson had not been called Diablito since his teenage days in Mexico.

"Who is this?" he asked brusquely.

"It's Cisco, an old friend."

Jackson was on guard immediately. Cisco and Pancho were the nicknames for two brothers, Reuben and Julio Ramirez, who Jackson had known in Mexico. The older brother, Reuben, was wiry and slick in his ways, while the younger brother was slightly overweight, slower of speech, and looked like a country bumpkin, even in a suit. Their nicknames were based on the *Cisco Kid* radio and television programs. Their father used to work with Jackson's grandfather. Reuben's call opened a seam in Jackson's world, and through it he could see the past. He now hesitated to step through the seam.

"Diablito?" the voice questioned.

"How is it with your brother?" Jackson asked cautiously. He had to be sure with whom he was speaking.

"Pancho is here."

Julio's voice, farther away from the phone, called, "Hey, Diablito, remember Señora Ruelas's enchiladas? How about fried grunion on the beach in Baja?"

Reuben's voice dropped an octave. "I know you remember our night at the Blue Fox!"

Experiences which had lain collapsed in some subterranean vault within his mind miraculously sprang inflated to life with attendant colors and smells. He could almost taste the señora's enchiladas. "It's been a long time," Jackson observed.

"Time passes too quickly," Reuben acknowledged. "I am sorry to say that I am calling with difficult news." Reuben paused for a moment to let his words sink in, then continued speaking: "Your grandfather is gravely ill. He may not live much longer. He has asked to see you."

"I know. I heard," Jackson replied, hesitating briefly before revealing his true thoughts. He realized that he felt ashamed to expose his lack of love for his dying grandfather to Reuben. Realizing that he had no other option, Jackson continued, "But since he and I have chosen to lead different lives, I didn't think my presence would be good for either one of us. I thought it best that I stay here."

"Diablito, you are his only heir and his dying wish is that you come." There was no emotion in Reuben's statement. It was a straightforward declaration.

Despite his best efforts, Jackson's explanation sounded defensive. "I can't come now even if I wanted to. I have a number of important assignments to complete. If I fail in any one of them, I risk losing my job. Tell him to select someone else as his heir. I don't want his money."

"You know he will not do that. You are his heir, whether you come or not, and he is leaving you sufficient money that you need not work unless you choose to do so."

"I don't want his money!"

"His enemies are still numerous, Diablito, and it is very sure they will come for you after he dies. Because you are the key."

"I don't see why. Especially if I pass up the inheritance. They're only interested in the money. They'll understand that I'm living a different life, that I have had nothing to do with him. No involvement whatsoever."

"If it were that simple, Diablito, I would tell you to go ahead, but it isn't. You, even after all these years, don't believe the words you've just said. They will come because they want more than the money. Plus, they will have to come through you to get to any of the estate; your grandfather set it up that way. Whether you like it or not, they will come. Money aside, after he dies, they'll want your blood."

"I don't have any choice in this?"

"I wish you did, because I know that you have made a different life for yourself. I know that you've walked away from him. That will not matter to his enemies. Perhaps if you come down, he will listen to you and make different arrangements. I don't know."

Anger bubbled up inside of Jackson. It seemed his grandfather still had the capacity to drag him into things in which he had no desire to participate. He took a deep breath and asked, "Let's make this clear: You're saying that my life will be in danger after my grandfather dies?"

"Yes, but if you come down we can help you prepare to deal with them. It's the only choice you have. . . ." There was a long pause, then, ". . . if you want to live until next year."

Jackson felt like an animal in a trap and his frustration level rose like a temperature gauge in a boiling pot. He felt like killing his grandfather himself. But anger aside, he had been warned, and only a fool would ignore such a warning. With reluctance Jackson said, "I will make arrangements—"

Reuben interrupted. "Let us make the travel arrangements for you. I shall call you and tell you where you can pick up the tickets. Is this a secure line?"

"Basically, but there are extensions."

"Oh." There was a pause while Reuben considered the problem. He asked simply, "When can you come?"

"This weekend."

"How long can you stay?"

"Let's leave it open."

"Claro! I look forward to seeing you." A tone of adjournment was in his voice.

Jackson took his cue and said, "It will be good to see you again." He heard Julio's voice, with a remote echo, say, *"Suerte, Diablito. Suerte!"*

Jackson put the phone back on its receiver and turned his attention to reviewing his work notes on his various projects, but his mind was still entangled with thoughts of his family. Without ever having reached a voluntary decision, he had agreed to go to Mexico. He stared around at the familiar furnishings of his office and felt even more dislocated. When the secretary came in and announced that the city manager was waiting for him, Jackson's mood had degenerated into anger and resentment.

Each summer but one, from the time he was eight until he was eighteen, he had spent in Mexico with his grandfather. At first, he didn't think anything could be worse than sharing a dark, drafty Victorian with his cold, aloof grandmother, but he was mistaken. He came to dread the coming of summer and the annual forays to the backwater villages and towns along the coast of the Sea of Cortez.

July 1954

There is a dry, desert heat in parts of Mexico that wraps around the flesh like a tight-fitting suit, a heat that emanates from an unblinking sun that pounds the desiccated earth. It seeks to enter every pore and burn the lungs with every breath. It even reaches into the shade and presses water from the body. Eight-year-old Jackson was not used to such heat. Sweat streamed down his body, stinging his sunburned skin. He had not yet learned the secret of wearing heavy clothing as protection against the sun. He wore only a short-sleeved shirt, shorts, and sneakers.

He stood in the shade outside his grandfather's four-room cottage on the outskirts of a small village. He was hungry again. It was a new sensation for him and one he could not escape. There was no food in the house and his grandfather had taken away his money. He lived from

one mealtime to the next. Every morning at seven, his grandfather prepared a small breakfast of cornmeal mush for the two of them. Then his
grandfather left for the day without explanation and sometimes did not
return until well after dark. Generally, when his grandfather came home
in the evenings, he brought small-game animals like jackrabbits, squir-
rels, quail, and wild duck, which had to be skinned, plucked, and
cleaned before they could be cooked. Sometimes, after twelve hours
without food, Jackson thought he would die before the evening meal
was put on the table. At first, Jackson's impatience caused him to get underfoot as his grandfather prepared the food, but a backhand that sent
him to the floor taught him to stay clear. Dinner was the only meal at
which he got seconds. He was not allowed thirds because his grandfather told him he was too fat and soft. The meat was strange tasting
and gamey, but Jackson ate every bit that was put on his plate. When he
tried to speak to his grandfather about his desire for lunch and snacks,
his grandfather laughed humorlessly and said, "A man should only have
to eat once a day. If'en he has to eat more than that, he can't control
himself."

It was the most unhappy time in Jackson's short life. At least at his
grandmother's house, no one tried to starve him. Sometimes during the
long, hot day in between his dreams of hamburgers and eclairs, he
would cry for no reason. It was too hot to stay in the cottage and too
hot to stay in the sun, so he would sit outside in the shade of the cottage and cry for hours. He missed his father terribly.

Although he had been living in the cottage for nearly a week, Jackson had not made friends with any of the village children. They did not
speak English and he did not speak Spanish, plus they seemed to shy
away from him. After a while it didn't matter, for he was too hungry to
play games.

He had three constant companions: hunger, heat, and boredom. At
first, he attempted to devise ways to distract his mind from the thought
of food, but there was nothing around the house but cacti, scorpions,
and lizards. He soon grew tired of trying to divert his attention from
hunger and spent days sitting in the shade with his back to the cottage
wall, writing in the dust. Finally, in his second week of residence, his
stomach drove him out of the shade of the cottage. Hunger caused him
to be bold. He went to the village store.

There was only one store in the village, and like most stores of its
kind it sold a wide variety of goods, from foodstuffs to clothing to hard-

ware. Jorge Olazabal owned the store and, like every small-time merchant, he knew every item in his inventory by heart. He was one of the leading men in his village, so he had heard the rumors and stories about Jackson's grandfather being a criminal on the run from the authorities in the United States. It was reputed that he was a dangerous man, but Jorge always scoffed when he heard these unsubstantiated comments. "No man is tougher," he was wont to say, "than a man who knows what is rightfully his." He also knew that Jackson had been left to his own devices for days at a time. He had heard about how the boy stared hungrily at anyone eating food.

Jorge knew it was a question of time before the boy came into his store to steal. Jorge was ready for him. He would make an example of the boy and show the village who was tough. The day Jackson came into the store, business was slow, so Jorge had ample opportunity to observe the boy. The boy moved furtively along the aisle closest to the door, obviously seeking something he could take and dash away with. He was typical of all the hungry children Jorge had seen and he felt no sympathy whatsoever. Jorge, like millions of merchants who preceded him, kept his valuable items and meat products near the counter where bills were paid. Pretending to ignore the boy, Jorge kept him in view out of the corner of his eye.

Jackson probably would not have had the courage to steal anything had not Jorge's attention been distracted by the store phone. The phone was one of Jorge's prize possessions. It was one of two phones in the whole village. It was unheard of to have the phone ring and not pick it up. The phone was by the door to the back room. Jorge hustled his chubby body over to the instrument and picked up the receiver. It was his brother-in-law calling to find out if Jorge could get a good price on tires. Jorge could no longer see the boy from where he stood, but he saw a string of cooked sausage disappear from the line hanging over the counter. Jorge screamed, "No!" and dropped the phone. The boy had already escaped the store. Jorge ran back to the phone and told his brother-in-law that he would call him back.

As Jorge walked to King's cottage, he called out to the villagers to come and watch how he dealt with a thief. By the time he reached the door of the cottage, half the village was with him. He banged on the door forcefully. There was no answer. As with most doors in small villages, this one was built for privacy, not to stop forcible entry. Jorge put his weight against the door and broke it open.

Jackson had barely eaten one sausage. It had not occurred to him that anyone would dare to break down his grandfather's door. Jorge dragged him struggling and kicking from the house and knocked him to the ground with his fist.

When the blow landed next to Jackson's right eye, he saw red and yellow lights. There was no pain, only a loss of sensation. He felt himself being pulled to his feet. Another blow was aimed at his head but he ducked in time so that it glanced off his forehead. He pulled free of the grip that Jorge had on him and ran pell-mell through the crowd of villagers as they laughed at him. He ran until he couldn't catch his breath, until the village was out of sight.

Jorge went into King's house and reclaimed his remaining sausages, vowing that now they were unworthy to sell, that he would feed them to his dogs. He fooled no one. Everyone knew that the sausages would be washed off and rehung on the line over the counter. Jorge also declared that he would return the next morning and finish administering the beating that the boy deserved.

Jackson had never been so far away from the village. He could no longer see the buildings themselves, only the smoke from various cooking fires. The sun now restated its presence by burning him every time he stopped to get his breath. In the distance, he saw a small arroyo lined with scrub and stunted trees. He sought safety from the sun in the shade of the shrubbery. In the middle of the arroyo was a small stream of cool water. Jackson threw himself facedown in the water and soaked himself. His head was throbbing and his chest hurt from running full speed. He stood up and heard the warning rattle of a sidewinder. He watched the snake writhe out of view under a thicket of sagebrush.

Jackson did not return home until he saw his grandfather drive up to the cottage that evening. When he walked in, his grandfather was examining the door. Jackson was so exhausted and hungry that he could barely talk. Nonetheless, his grandfather interrogated him while he prepared the evening meal. Jackson told him everything, except that he had stolen sausages from the store. His grandfather examined his eye, which now had a large, dark bruise around it, and saw that he was slightly feverish from too much sun. Jackson was so spent, he could not finish his dinner. He fell asleep at the table. His grandfather put him to bed and had to rise several times during the night to place cold compresses on his body.

Jackson was awakened before dawn by his grandfather. He was told to get dressed. There was no breakfast cooked. They left the cottage as soon as Jackson was dressed and went to Jorge's house. There were no lights on when they arrived. Jackson was told to wait outside. His grandfather drew an ivory-handled pistol from a holster and kicked the door open.

Jorge had gone to sleep with his rifle at the foot of his bed as a precaution, although he didn't expect any trouble. He was awakened by the sound of his door splintering, but he had trouble coming to full consciousness because he had been in a deep slumber. By the time he had his wits about him, King was in his bedroom. At first, Jorge was indignant. He was about to give King a piece of his mind when King picked up his rifle and smashed the butt into his chest. The blow knocked the air out of Jorge and stunned him. His wife began screaming for help as King pulled Jorge by the hair from his bed. She tried to intercede and help her husband, but King knocked her down and she did not get up.

Jorge was dragged outside of his house and dropped in the dirt. King pulled out both his pistols and fired several rounds into the store to wake the village. He then proceeded to beat and kick Jorge senseless, taking his time with every blow and kick, repeating in Spanish, "You will never lay a hand on my grandson again, even if he comes for your mother!"

Before he passed out, Jorge begged his fellow villagers for help. No one came to his aid. King continued to kick him even after he was unconscious. Finally, an old lady yelled that Jorge had been only trying to protect his business and that King's grandson had stolen meat from the store.

King turned to his grandson; there was fire in his eyes. "Did you lie to me? Did you steal from this man?"

Jackson nodded his head in admission.

King went and pulled a wire coat hanger off a nearby clothesline and opened it. He wrapped part of the wire around his hand and advanced upon his grandson, who was now quivering with fear. King commenced to whip his grandson with the wire until the boy's legs were bloody with welts while the whole village watched. When he finished, he said in Spanish for all to hear, "I will kill the next person who lays a hand on my grandson. I have whipped him so that you will see we do not coddle thieves and liars in my family. If you have a problem with him, come to me. I will see that justice is done."

Jackson remained in the house for the next three days with the shades pulled down. He was too embarrassed to show his face to the villagers. He had been humiliated twice in front of them. When his grandfather came home in the evenings, Jackson stayed out of his way and kept silent. He never initiated another conversation. He would rather do without than ask his grandfather for anything. The seedlings of hate and resentment had been sown and they would be fed and watered regularly over the years by his grandfather's stern code.

When Jackson did leave the cottage, he avoided the village and went to the arroyo with the little stream. As the days passed, he wandered farther afield. He went upstream and discovered a series of steep ravines, which he explored. Once again, his hunger made him bold, and he attempted to eat anything that he saw animals eat. Unfortunately, he did not realize that some animals were able to metabolize certain foods which were toxic to man. So, when he attempted to make a meal of red berries which he saw both birds and kangaroo rats eating, he did not expect to get sick. In less than an hour after eating as many of the bitter berries as he could stand, his stomach began to hurt. In fact, the pain doubled him up so that he could not walk. He dragged himself to a shady spot by the stream and passed out.

When he awoke, he heard the mournful howl of a coyote. The stars were out in all their brilliance. A quarter moon smiled down upon him. The ravine looked strange and ominous in the dim moonlight. The terrain was unrecognizable. He didn't know which direction was the way home. He forced himself to his feet and discovered he could barely walk due to the pain. The temperature had dropped nearly fifty degrees and he was shivering with cold and sweating at the same time. He sat back down, dizzy and exhausted. He fell back in a stupor which lasted for hours.

In the early morning before dawn, the sound of men's voices awakened him. He did not have the strength to call out. He attempted to drag himself closer, but he was too weak and stiff to move. He lay back and waited for discovery or death; he no longer cared. His grandfather's voice brought him out of his delirium. Jackson heard him say, "Where the hell is that boy?" There was unmistakable anger in his voice. If Jackson had had the strength he would have crawled deeper into the thickets of madrona and manzanita to avoid discovery. He did not want to face the anger of his grandfather again.

A flashlight passed over his foot, then steadied on him. "I've found him!" he heard a familiar voice say. There were sounds of running feet. Hands reached underneath him and propped him up. Someone poured cool water down his throat. A flashlight shined in his face. He heard his grandfather ask, "What happened, boy? Are you all right?"

Jackson raised his hand in front of his face defensively and pleaded weakly, "Please don't whip me. Please don't whip me."

Strong arms lifted him up and held him close. He could smell his grandfather's cigars and cologne as he was carried back to a waiting jeep.

The next morning, Jackson had vague memories of men in white coats putting tubes down his throat, making him throw up. He turned over in his bed, hoping to fall asleep again, but a tantalizing smell brushed away the cobwebs of sleep. It was the smell of frying bacon. He threw back his blankets and swung his legs slowly out of bed. An occasional pain lanced through his stomach. He sat on the side of the bed for several minutes, trying to marshal his strength.

His grandfather appeared at the door and watched him silently. When Jackson saw that his grandfather was watching him, he grew frightened. "I'm sorry I didn't get up earlier," he mumbled. He tried to push himself to his feet and his legs collapsed under him. He fell back on the bed heavily. His grandfather was by his side in an instant. Jackson felt cool hands touch his brow and then his legs were lifted back in bed. He fell asleep again despite his desire to see if bacon really was cooking.

When Jackson awakened, there was a woman sitting in the room knitting. He did not recognize her, but she seemed friendly enough, for she smiled at him when she saw him stir. She washed his face with a damp towel and gestured with her hand, asking him if he wanted to eat. Jackson was famished. He nodded his head so enthusiastically, it made her laugh. She brought in a big plate of scrambled eggs, bacon, and tortillas. Jackson's eyes grew big when he saw the food. He wasn't sure it was all for him, but she indicated that it was. He cleaned the plate and would have asked for more, but the memory of his grandfather made him keep his desires to himself.

Later that afternoon, Carlos walked into his room. Jackson greeted him with a big smile.

"How's the wolf cub?" Carlos asked lightly.

"I'm fine," Jackson answered. "What are you doing here?"

"I'm here to teach you how to hunt, fish, and forage for food," Carlos answered. "El Negro says that all your problems have originated with your desire to eat. So, he says, it's time for you to learn what's safe to eat and what's not."

"How am I going to hunt?"

"Well," said Carlos, reaching underneath Jackson's bed. He pulled out a soft rifle case and handed it to Jackson. "I'm going to teach you how to use this."

Jackson couldn't believe his eyes. He opened the case slowly and pulled out a Marlin twenty-two-caliber rifle with a small scope. "This is mine?" he asked incredulously.

"It used to be your grandfather's but he's had your name carved into the stock."

Jackson turned over the rifle and saw that his name was indeed carved deeply in the rich wooden luster of the rifle stock. "Gosh" was all he managed to say.

For the next seven weeks, Jackson spent nearly every day with Carlos, sometimes leaving the house early in the morning before his grandfather departed and returning late at night. Each morning, the woman who had brought him the breakfast while he was recuperating came in to cook a hearty meal. His first week was spent learning to use and care for his rifle. Shooting came easily to Jackson. He practiced target shooting on cans and small rodents. He was taught to field-strip and clean his rifle. Next, he learned to set traps for rabbits, quail, roadrunners, and armadillos. He was taught to find evidence of different kinds of animals by checking the feces and their tracks. During the fourth week, he learned to build a smokeless fire, and how to skin and gut small game in the field. He also learned what seasonings grew wild and what type of vegetable matter could be digested by man.

At the end of the summer, Jackson's skin was tanned and sun hardened. He had grown leaner from physical exertion. He and Carlos explored the area throughout the nearby foothills and ravines surrounding the cottage. Sometimes they hiked as far as twenty-five miles from the village. They took only salt, tortillas, and canteens of water with them. They lived off the land, eating only that which they could forage, catch, or kill. It was one of the most thrilling experiences that eight-year-old Jackson could imagine: walking the desolate land with a knife in his belt and a rifle in his hands. He was an avid learner and he sucked in the information that Carlos gave him.

On the last day that Carlos was to spend with him, they were sitting around a small fire, roasting a rabbit which Jackson had shot and cleaned. An old mesquite provided partial shade from the omnipresent sun. To the north and east of them lay the dry, red, furrowed foothills which were the beginning of the southern branch of the Sierras. To the south lay the blue-green ravines and arroyos leading to the village, the colors supplied by sagebrush and desert shrubbery. And fifteen miles to the west was the shimmering presence of the Sea of Cortez. It was some of the most beautiful country Jackson had ever seen.

Carlos prodded him with a foot and nodded his head toward the rabbit, indicating that it needed to be turned on the makeshift spit. Jackson responded quickly, adjusting the rabbit so that the backside cooked.

"You have learned much, Wolf Cub," Carlos observed, watching his young companion.

Jackson nodded his head appreciatively. He very much wanted to earn Carlos's respect and affection. No one since his father had treated him as well.

"Next week, you'll return to San Francisco and civilization," Carlos commented, still watching him. "How do you feel about that?"

"I don't know," Jackson answered slowly, nudging a large beetle with his foot. The insect climbed on top of his shoe and stopped to take stock of its whereabouts, waving its antennae. Jackson put his hand down and let the beetle crawl up on his finger. He held his finger in front of his face to inspect the insect more closely. "This has been the best and the worst summer of my life."

Carlos nodded understandingly. He did not intrude further. He looked at the shadows on the hills and figured it was about one in the afternoon. "You know, about fifty years ago, this area was the home of some of the most notorious banditos that ever lived."

"Really?" Jackson asked with interest, flicking the beetle off his finger.

"Yes," Carlos confirmed. "A band of men could hide in these hills and ravines for years and never be found. There are endless canyons and arroyos around here and many of them have water."

"Really?" Jackson asked again. "How did you find me when I was sick? How did you know where to look?"

"We didn't. Your grandfather threatened to burn down the whole village if we didn't find you. So, we had a lot of volunteers. Your tracks were discovered by the creek. We just spread out from there, checking every ravine and canyon in the area."

"I thought that he would be happy to get rid of me," Jackson said, pulling his knife from its sheath. He began sharpening it with his whetstone as he had been taught.

Carlos shook his head. "You are the most important person in El Negro's life." Carlos smiled wryly. "He would have hung the owner of the store and burned the village to the ground if you had not been found." Jackson said nothing. He continued to sharpen his knife. Carlos realized that Jackson did not believe him. "Your grandfather is a hard man who grew up in hard times. He does not express affection well, but he is one of the best friends that a man can have. He will wade into a pack of wolves for you, if he takes you as his friend."

Jackson heard Carlos's words but did not respond. All he remembered was the beating that he had received in front of the whole village. The physical pain was insignificant compared with the humiliation which he felt. He knew that he would never forget, and forgiveness was an act far beyond his eight-year-old consciousness.

Tuesday, June 22, 1982

Creighton Bedrosian was a round-faced, pink-skinned, chunky man of average height. His brown hair and mustache were peppered with gray. He wore rimless glasses over his pale blue eyes, which gave his face a quaint appearance. But there was nothing quaint about Creighton Bedrosian. He was a man with agendas. He had been the city manager for the City of Oakland for nearly five years and he was now ready to move on. He was under consideration for two different city managerships in larger municipalities.

He began rifling through the papers on his desk, looking for the materials that he would need for the meeting. The list of council resolutions was incomplete. There were several city council subcommittee meetings scheduled for six that evening. Creighton detested late council work; it reflected badly on him as the administrator of the city council agenda. He gritted his teeth. Someone was going to get his butt kicked. Then, of course, there was that little matter of the mayor's surprise resolution on a Citizen Review Commission Over Police Activities. Yes, someone was definitely going to get his butt kicked. He gathered up the printouts and left his office for the conference room. Creighton seated himself at the head of the conference table and began reviewing his notes. He was working on his strategy to deal with Jackson when Howard Gomes entered the room.

Howard sat down at the table next to Creighton with a smile and a quick nod of his head. He was a tall, angular man with straight black hair, prominent cheekbones, and a beak for a nose. His small brown eyes were set deep in his face, giving him a ferretlike appearance. There was a trace of a New York City accent when he spoke.

"How's it going, boss?" Howard asked, dropping his file onto the table in front of him. He wore an expensive designer suit with casual arrogance.

Creighton looked him up and down intently. "New suit?"

"No, I bought it last year," Howard said, fingering the lapel. "The tie is new. I got it last night."

Creighton picked up a sheaf of papers and tapped them on the table, attempting to align the sides. "You spend too much money on clothes. Watch out, or I'll think you're going ethnic on me."

"Hell, I'm as ethnic as a burrito and beans, a bar mitzvah, or a pizza."

Bedrosian warned, "Just don't let it get to chitterlings and collard greens."

"No worries!" Howard chuckled in response then asked, "Did you ever come to a decision about who you want to fill the graffiti-abatement position?"

Bedrosian looked up. "No, why?"

"Why don't you let Elsa handle it?" Howard paused, searching for the right words. "She's in between project assignments and it would result in a significant salary savings. You could put her up in Montclair."

"Not in this political climate! You obviously didn't listen to council testimony. The position has to start work on East Fourteenth. What's a nice Protestant girl from Minnesota going to do with a bunch of community activists from Little Soweto in east Oakland?"

"Her legs will dazzle them. She has one fine pair of legs."

"I guess you've seen them up close and personal?"

Howard answered with a wide grin.

Bedrosian shook his head with a rueful smile. "I'm always coming to bail you out."

"Hey, if you want to bail me out of something, transfer this municipal classification study to someone else. This is a thousand-headed monster. You're damned if you do and damned if you don't."

"What did you offer to shut the union up?"

"I told them if this study isn't complete by 1988, we would pay retroactive pay for every day after that until the study was complete, if the reclassification resulted in an increase in pay. And, I also agreed that the union would have approval agreement over all their specific job classifications."

"Damn! Howard, are you a fool? That could take years!"

"You said to come out of the meeting without a strike. I had to give up something. Otherwise, the big two would have gone out on strike."

"Damn!" Bedrosian shook his head grudgingly. "Who do you think would want this assignment?"

"I don't know. Give it to Superboy." Howard gestured to Jackson, who was just opening the door.

"Good morning," Jackson said as he pulled out a chair and sat down at the table. He hadn't heard Howard's comment. He stated, "I didn't know the purpose of this meeting, so I brought papers related to the progress of all my assignments."

Bedrosian nodded at him then asked Howard, "I believe your administrative assistant was responsible this week for assembling the list of council resolutions for subcommittee review?"

Howard stared at the table as he spoke. "She couldn't complete the assignment because three resolutions weren't available."

Bedrosian demanded, "What do you mean three resolutions weren't available?"

Howard looked at Jackson apologetically. "I couldn't find Jackson's three resolutions on the new recreational facility, the municipal bond sale, and the Canalea Development contract. I checked with Martha and she hadn't received them. I even checked on his computer for the resolutions. No luck."

Bedrosian looked at Jackson and had a difficult time keeping a smile

off his face as he said, "Those are about the three most important resolutions on the agenda."

Howard interjected smoothly, "Since we couldn't find your resolutions," he nodded to Jackson, "I was concerned about making tonight's
subcommittee meeting agenda. So, I helped Elsa draft up some new
ones. We brought them for your review." Howard slid a sheaf of papers
across the table to Jackson.

Jackson said nothing. He was furious. This was the third time in recent weeks that an unusual problem had cropped up in one of his critical assignments.

"Well?" Bedrosian asked, waiting for an explanation. He was hoping
that Jackson was actually late in the three assignments, but it occurred
to him that Jackson might well have completed the resolutions and that
Howard had done something to erase them. Bedrosian prodded Jackson, "What do you have to say?"

The faint smile on Bedrosian's face further infuriated Jackson. He
knew that the city manager would not be unhappy if there was an assignment over which he could take Jackson to task. He had implied
several times in the past that Jackson needed to be taken down a couple
of notches. When Jackson spoke, he contained himself. "That assignment was complete before I left work Thursday evening," he said
evenly. He flipped through the pages that Howard had passed to him.
"But before I produce proof, I want to direct a question to Mr. Gomes."

"This is not a court of law; let's dispense with the inquisition,"
Bedrosian said with a listless laugh. "Does the copy in front of you contain all the necessary elements?"

Jackson wondered how his grandfather would respond in his place
and then he felt something snap within him as he turned to Bedrosian.
"This is important to me." Although he had not raised his voice, there
was an edge in his tone which cut across everyone's consciousness. "I
want to clear myself of any inferences that I have not performed my duties in a timely manner. I think it is imperative that it be revealed that
Mr. Gomes and his assistant are liars. And not very good ones."

Bedrosian was shocked. In the four years that Jackson had been a
deputy he had never once caused a social breach like this. There was no
way Bedrosian could avoid entangling himself in this unpleasant situation. Jackson had made a statement which could not be ignored. Plus,
there was a dangerous hostility in Jackson's voice which caused Bedro-

sian to unconsciously distance himself from it. He sputtered, "Ah, ah, I'm sure that your words were a little strong and that you would be open to offering an apology to Howard, now wouldn't you?"

Howard said with false graciousness, "Let's drop it. I'm sure it's all a mix-up. I know Jackson wouldn't mess up on an assignment that was this important."

"You're right!" Jackson confirmed with a grim smile. "I gave the completed resolutions to Angelica Winston. She entered them in the resolution log and distributed them to the members of the development services subcommittee, parks and rec council, and the council budget committee." Angelica was the office manager and the matriarch of the clerical staff. She was the city manager's right hand and a stickler for perfection. If she had entered it into the log, it was unquestioned that the resolutions were submitted on time.

Howard said weakly, "You didn't follow procedure. You're supposed to give the original copy for resolutions to Martha. . . ." His voice trailed off. He recognized the futility of continuing.

"I did," Jackson said. "But it seems that you and your colleague devised a way to erase their existence."

"This is absurd!" Howard snarled. "No one has time to involve themselves in your affairs." Howard looked to Bedrosian for assistance. "Do I have to put up with this nonsense?"

Bedrosian stood up for emphasis and addressed Jackson. "I think you better apologize to Howard for these unsupported remarks, don't you?"

Jackson could not contain himself. He stood up as well and stated clearly, "I think not. An investigation would support my contentions."

Bedrosian was now astounded. Nobody, particularly a black person, had ever confronted him as Jackson was now doing. "You refuse to apologize?" he questioned incredulously.

Jackson answered, "I have no reason to apologize and since you're defending Howie and his intern's actions, let me make it clear: I am prepared to take this to the mat and get legal representation. You don't intimidate me."

Bedrosian sat down and swallowed his anger. He had to remain focused. He couldn't afford to have a problem arise that had any hint of racism. It could jeopardize his career advancement. He coughed into his hand. "Let's get on with the meeting."

Jackson sat down as well, but the smile he gave Howard had no warmth in it.

The meeting proceeded as if there had been no confrontation, except no one was fooled. Subsequent topic discussions were brief and inconclusive. Before adjourning the meeting Bedrosian recapped the budget committee decisions and stated emphatically that a rotation of assignments would be coming in the next month. From his tone it was clear that the conflict with Jackson was not over.

Jackson asked, "Does that mean all assignments, or just departmental assignments?"

"I will assign or reassign projects and departments as I see fit," Bedrosian answered brusquely.

Jackson stared at Bedrosian and said, "I would not be happy to receive the municipal classification study as a transferred assignment after Howie here has messed it up."

"This is really absurd!" Howard said. "You don't supervise me! You have no right to malign my work!"

"Aren't you lucky that I don't supervise you?" Jackson retorted.

"Are you saying that you would refuse an assignment that I have every right to assign to you on a rotational basis?" Now there was an edge in Bedrosian's voice.

"No, I wouldn't refuse it, but I would document in writing all the major errors that have been made, errors that I have consistently argued against in staff meetings. And I'm sure that my report would find its way into the correct hands."

"What do you mean?" Bedrosian growled. His patience was vanishing rapidly. Was Jackson threatening him with the mayor?

"Hell, there's so much wrong with this classification study, it would take a week to bring it all to light."

"And you are planning to, as you say, bring this to light?" Bedrosian's voice was even, but he was nearly choking with anger.

"Only if you try to set me up with this assignment. It's about to explode and I won't be your fall guy. Let Howie go down with his own stupid decisions."

Bedrosian realized that the ramifications were too serious to allow himself to give voice to his anger, so he stood up with an air of dismissal. "Is there anything for the good of the order?"

"Yes," Jackson responded.

Bedrosian waited silently for him to continue.

"I would like to request time off. A member of my immediate family is seriously ill."

"We'll discuss it later," Bedrosian answered as he gathered his papers. "After we've had a chance to seriously evaluate the status of your work."

"Oh," Jackson began casually. "So you plan to treat me differently than Howie here? Who you let take off, I might point out, in the middle of putting together last year's budget narrative. And that was for Howie's stepfather's third cousin, I believe. Or was it his dog?"

"Now, listen here, goddamn it!" Bedrosian was beside himself. He walked over to Jackson and pointed his finger in his face. "Don't you ever fucking talk to me—"

Jackson grabbed his finger and bent it sharply backward before releasing it. Bedrosian gave a little yelp and held his injured appendage. Jackson stood up, towering over Bedrosian. "If you have anything to say to me, it can be accomplished without vulgarity and putting your finger in my face, can't it?" Jackson awaited an answer but there was only silence. Both Howard and Bedrosian were in shock. Jackson was displaying a side of himself that no one had seen before. Indeed, if Jackson had thought about it, he himself would have been confounded to explain his actions. But he was not thinking, he was reacting. "Now, let me make it clear: I am requesting family death leave. If I am to be denied, I want to know on what basis, so that I may take the necessary legal actions."

Bedrosian left the room without speaking. Howard gave Jackson a panicky look and followed Bedrosian. Jackson caught Howard's eye as he was leaving the room. "I'll be seeing you, Howie," he said to Howard's retreating back.

Jackson gathered his papers and returned them to their respective folders. He suppressed a sardonic chuckle. He had been right about a rip in the social fabric. What he didn't know was that he was going to tear the hole himself. Fourteen years thrown away for twenty seconds of righteous indignation. Could he truthfully say that it was worth it? He knew as soon as he started in on Howard that he was committing professional suicide.

By the time he returned to his office, Jackson's thoughts were filled with his grandfather. He recalled his grandfather saying that the only things a man truly possessed were his courage and the spirit with which he employed it. The old man contended that without courage, none of the other virtues could be accessed consistently. A man was supposed to stand up to fear. He didn't have to like it, but fear should not deter him from practicing the virtues that were in his heart.

Jackson looked out his second-story window at Fifteenth Street and all the little shops which operated across the street from city hall. The sunlight was pale through a screen of clouds, and a brisk breeze swirled debris at intervals. At the moment the street was deserted except for a shabbily dressed black man, who was probably a homeless person. The man had a ragged blanket wrapped around his shoulders and was making his way slowly into the intersection. A lone car pulled up and stopped for the light. When the man in the blanket saw that the car was an expensive foreign model, driven by a young white man, he changed his walk to an arrogant swagger. The light changed as the man was mid-street; the driver, impatient to be on his way, honked. The man exaggerated his swagger and took his time getting to the curb. The car zoomed past; the man watched it and then turned to continue on his way. Jackson watched the manner in which the man's shoulders slowly drooped and his swagger disappeared, and Jackson understood the change in the man's demeanor. The man had attitude and perhaps it was the only thing separating him from the depths, but it wasn't the same as courage and spirit. Attitude was a temporary thing: donned or doffed like a piece of clothing depending upon the weather. But as his grandfather had told him so many times, courage and spirit were what made a man continue to get off the floor with the same vinegar he had when he hit it, regardless of climate or circumstance.

Tuesday, June 22, 1982

DiMarco's Seafood Restaurant was located at the end of Hyde Street in San Francisco, right on the edge of the marina. The restaurant was built on a pier which jutted out over the bay. In its grander days, in the early fifties, the restaurant was crammed with diners from opening to closing. The menu had consisted of a variety of fish, shrimp, and crab drawn that same day from the seemingly endless wealth of the sea. DiMarco's was known for its tangy red sauces, pesto, and food served in man-sized portions. Unfortunately, for Paul DiMarco, by the 1980s the restaurant no longer enjoyed its earlier popularity. In fact, it just barely survived on the tourists who frequented the waterfront and

who generally did not know the difference between an alfredo and a
marinara sauce, or polenta and pesto. The restaurant, had it been run
with a loving hand, could have been a success, for it was in a good site
and possessed a panoramic view of the bay and the Golden Gate
Bridge. But Paul was not disposed to invest his heart and soul in the
clank of pans and the clatter of dishes. He was intimately familiar with
the complexities of running a food service operation, yet he did not
care for it. It was just a means of survival until something better came
along.

The restaurant was about half full, which was not particularly good
for a sunny-day, summertime lunch crowd. Paul stood with his maître d',
Dominique Asti, and watched the waiters and waitresses scurry back
and forth from the kitchen to their assigned tables.

"We should have more people in here," Dominique said, giving Paul
a steady look. She was a lean, athletic woman with dark brown hair.
"We need a strong promotional campaign. I think you need to have
some posters made like I suggested, and get them passed around to local businesses and perhaps hire an advertising agency to develop some
local radio and television spots."

There was something about her tone that Paul didn't like, a borderline haughtiness, as if she were directing him. It irked Paul that someone would have the audacity to speak to him like that in his own
restaurant. Nonetheless, he kept his own counsel. She had been re-
ferred to him by one of the Chicago families, after he fired his last
maître d'. Even then, he would not have hired her had not Joe Bones
asked him to do so as a personal favor.

"Why don't you go ahead with that idea, if you think it will bring
in business," Paul said evenly, showing no evidence of his displeasure.
Dominique gave him a quick nod of her head and walked off toward
the entrance, where there was a couple waiting to be seated.

Paul watched her walk away with a sour taste in his mouth. She was
an enigma to him. It had seemed strange that Bones would take such a
strong interest in the placement of a restaurant employee, so he had put
out a few feelers. The rumor on the circuit was that she was a high-paid
assassin who needed a place to cool out until things calmed down. He
knew better than to inquire too deeply about such things, so he gave
her wide berth. The amazing thing was that she was a damn good
maître d'. Both the food and the service had improved since she started.

The thought had occurred to him on more than one occasion that she had been sent to keep an eye on him. In that regard, he had been careful to keep all his nonrestaurant-related business on the sly, which was why he was standing near the kitchen door, next to a large window: He was expecting visitors. From his vantage point, he could see the crowds of people walking along the pier. He saw a heavyset man and a tall, thin man standing near the edge of the pavement leading up to Ghirardelli Square. It was the Lenzini brothers. DiMarco gave them an acknowledging wave. He retrieved his briefcase from his office, then went over and told Dominique that he was going out for a short while. She nodded and gave both him and the briefcase a look, but said nothing.

The air was brisk as the wind blew off the bay. DiMarco walked across the cable car turnaround at Hyde Street and went into O'Hare's Irish Pub, which was crowded. This irked DiMarco, since he knew their food wasn't as good as his. He made his way slowly through the crowd. He saw the Lenzinis sitting in a booth by the window.

Victor, the taller of the two brothers, stood respectfully as DiMarco approached and stuck out his hand. DiMarco shook his hand and sat down opposite the two men. Victor's tone was solicitous as he said, "Me and Tony came as soon as we got your call, Mr. DiMarco. You got something for us?"

A waitress appeared and slid a plate with a double-decker sandwich in front of Tony and then set down two drinks. She turned to DiMarco. "Would you like something, sir?"

"Give me a latte," DiMarco replied. After the waitress had departed, he turned his attention to the two men across the table. Tony, who was pudgy and balding, had already wolfed down half his sandwich and had an obnoxious habit of chewing his food with his mouth open. DiMarco hid his distaste and directed his attention to Tony's gray-haired older brother. Paul leaned across the table and said in a low voice, "I want you to pick up somebody. I need to question him. He can't be hurt too bad. You get me?"

Victor Lenzini was the oldest of his four brothers and served as their unofficial leader. He was a saturnine man who rarely laughed. He was the only one of all his siblings who still remembered when the Lenzini family had shared control with the DiMarcos of all the seafood sales made on the San Francisco docks. Victor nodded. "Is this one of the guys we been followin'? One of the friends of that eggplant?"

"Yeah, I want that you should pick up that little gook that works at the radio station in Berkeley. He shouldn't be no trouble. Maybe he don't know nothing, but he'll serve as a hostage. I got to move fast on this. I don't want nobody beatin' me to the punch on this. And no gunplay! The whole West Coast'll come down on us if any of this gets into the papers. There's an election comin' up." A rumpled black man in a plastic, opaque raincoat brushed past Paul. Paul swiveled and watched him find a seat farther down at the bar before turning back to the Lenzinis. He tapped the table with his index finger. "My uncle's running for mayor. This has got to be done cool-like. Get me? *Real* cool."

"You want us to take him down to the old warehouse south of Market?" Victor asked before he downed his drink in one gulp.

"That's good. Yeah. Pick him up as soon as you can. The sooner the better."

Victor fixed his cold eyes on DiMarco and asked, "We get wartime pay? Everything got to be done hush-hush. We can't use no guns. Gets more dangerous that way. Takes more plannin'."

DiMarco paused before he answered. He reminded himself that he needed the Lenzinis' loyalty and it was easier to pay for it upfront than after the fact. "Sure! I'll pay double. Expenses too." He opened his briefcase and took out a slim file. He pushed it across the table to Victor. "Everything you need is in there, includin' picture, home and work addresses, and ten thousand dollars. You'll get ten thousand more when I see him at the warehouse." DiMarco grabbed his briefcase and slid out of the booth as the waitress brought his coffee latte. He threw a ten-dollar bill on the table and walked out of O'Hare's.

A cool, refreshing breeze swept across the marina and DiMarco took a deep, invigorating breath of it as he walked back down Hyde Street.

He smiled as he entered his restaurant. He was on a path to outmaneuver Braxton and the rest of his niggers. Once he was in possession of King's empire, his whole image would change. People would have to pay him the respect that he deserved. He would be recognized as a separate entity from the rest of the DiMarcos. He would be special. As he walked into his office whistling, he saw Dominique Asti staring at him.

Half an hour after DiMarco met with the Lenzinis, Braxton was on the phone to John Tree. "I tell you, DiMarco is up to something!" Braxton declared angrily as he paced back and forth, keeping in range of his desk so that the receiver's cord wouldn't pull the phone off it. "He wouldn't meet with the Lenzinis if he *wasn't* up to something. He's bold too. He met them right across from his own restaurant. Goddamn his impatience! He's forcing our hand. It's too soon to come out in the open. But that witless fool doesn't know it."

"How you know he met them?" Tree asked suspiciously. "Maybe it was somebody else."

"My man walked right by all three of them. He couldn't be mistaken."

"You got people followin' them? You didn't tell me that."

"I needed somebody independent. Somebody he didn't know. I need to think; hold the line a minute." Braxton set the phone down on the desk and paced the floor. He was searching his mind trying to figure out DiMarco's plan of action. The Lenzinis were thugs. They weren't hired to follow people. They did strong-arm work. The only mission they could be sent on was to hurt someone or to make a snatch. A light went on in Braxton's skull. They were going to make a snatch. The question was who? The main grandson was too dangerous a target. Snatching him would alert King, then all hell might break loose. DiMarco couldn't be that stupid. No, he probably intended to pick up one of Jackson's friends and hold him for safekeeping. It was the same as Braxton's strategy. One such hostage could provide insight into the grandson's life as well as a bit of collateral when the time came. It was a safe move. King would hardly be concerned about his grandson's friends.

Braxton walked back over to the desk and picked up the phone. "You there?"

"I's here," Tree replied.

"Put a fire under Jesse and Fletcher and have them pick up that friend of Jackson Tremain right away. The one he went drinking with the other night. I want the man in good health too. Make sure that they know that."

"Can do. Uh, who you got followin' DiMarco?"

"Just an independent. Of no consequence. When this is all over, you can eliminate him. Right now, I want to keep him anonymous." Braxton had no intention of telling Tree anything that he didn't need to know. One could never tell when Tree himself might become expendable.

After he had hung up, Braxton continued to pace the floor. This was one of the things that he had feared: the moment when either Tree or DiMarco would take matters into his own hands, forsaking all of Brax-

ton's carefully planned-out strategy for an impulse. A rumbling vibra-
tion, attended by a deep mechanical hum, rolled through his office. It
was the sound of the printing press gearing up to print the next day's ads
and comics. Normally, it was a sound that had a calming effect upon
him, but today it was simply another distracting noise. He couldn't stop
worrying. His only hope was that King really was close to death and
there wouldn't be any retribution. Even this possibility brought no
peace for Braxton. Thoughts and fears clashed against one another like
billiard balls shot by a person of great strength but poor aim. For the
first time in many years Braxton was truly frightened.

Wednesday, June 23, 1982

Wesley Hunter parked his Porsche in his spot in the main garage,
grabbed his briefcase, and caught the elevator to the fifteenth
floor. He walked down the hall to his apartment and unlocked the door.
He was greeted by the view of his floor-to-ceiling windows, which
looked out over the north bay toward Richmond and San Rafael. The
last stray beams of sunlight were reflected through the haze off the rippling yellow surface of the bay as the sun gradually sank behind the
dark green hills of Marin County. Alcatraz and Angel Island looked as if
they were floating in a sea of molten gold. Wesley smiled. He loved his
view.

He hung his jacket in the closet and poured himself a shot of Stoli
from the bottle he kept in the freezer. After dropping a couple of olives
in his glass, he sat down on his leather sofa in front of the view and admired what nature could do with polluted air. Within ten minutes, the
sky had begun to glow with colors ranging from pinkish red to purple.
Wesley liked to end his day with a drink and a silent sunset. It was the
meditative way that he made the transition from the hectic pressures of
the corporate routine. Not that he minded the daily pressures. He understood that any position which carried the rank and salary that he desired came with pressure and competition. He had worked his whole
adult life to reach the level he had attained. He looked around at his

spacious apartment with its expensive furniture and art collection and thought smugly, I have earned this. Then a strange, disquieting thought occurred to him: What would his father have thought of his achievements: the job, the Porsche, the apartment, the expensive clothes and furniture?

Wesley knew the answer before the question was fully formed. His father had been a simple man of the church. He had raised three boys in Hunter's Point's cement-block projects and later in the Fillmore on a custodian's salary and the unshakable faith in the Almighty. He saw success not in terms of material possessions, but in relationship to one's standing in one's community. If you weren't doing God's work, or working to improve the lot of your fellow Negro, you were just a carpetbagger, as far as he was concerned, living off the gifts of a gracious God.

Wesley's father was not a particularly humorous or outgoing man, but he was liked and well respected in the neighborhood and church community. Wesley remembered his father's funeral and how surprised he was at the number of people in attendance. At the time it was hard for him to accept that so many people would come out to pay respect to a man who had never attained a position higher than a custodian. The passing years had made him regret that he had not understood all the qualities that his father had possessed.

A small reminder alarm beeped in his jacket in the closet. He downed his drink and set his glass down on a custom-made glass-top table and went to the closet for his electronic scheduler. He took the beeping device out of his jacket and popped it open. Its small display reminded him that he had scheduled a tryst with a married woman in half an hour. She was the deputy vice president of marketing for his firm. The woman regularly booked a room at one of the hotels near the airport for their meetings; however, this evening's meeting was a rescheduling of a prior appointment that he had been unable to make due to his interest in another woman. It would not bode well for him, careerwise, to miss another appointment or even be late. He had half an hour in rush-hour traffic to make it.

Wesley swiftly performed his toilet and changed clothes. Fifteen minutes had passed when he walked out the door. He was busy checking for his keys and identification, or he would have noticed someone following him into the garage. A large brown-skinned man came out the doorway that led to the laundry room, but Wesley was oblivious. He walked swiftly down the ramp to the level on which his car was parked. When he neared his spot he saw that there was a slim brown-skinned man, in his late fifties, leaning on his Porsche. The man wasn't a panhandler, for he was dressed in an expensive topcoat and derby hat.

"What the hell are you doing?" Wesley demanded, rounding the back bumper of his car to confront the man.

"Watch your mouth and you'll be told everything you need to know." The man's tone was curt and confident. His rimless glasses reflected the glare of the garage's lights and prevented Wesley from seeing his eyes.

"Like hell I will. Get away from my car!" He pushed the man away from the Porsche. As he did so, the man reached in his pocket. Wesley didn't wait to see what the man had in his pocket—he attacked. He hit the man twice solidly before the man fell heavily between the cars.

The man that had followed him from the laundry room threatened, "You shouldn't have done that," as he lumbered toward Wesley. "Now, I'm gon' have to kick yo' ass good fo' Mr. Fletcher!"

Wesley said nothing, but turned into a spinning back kick, which caught the big man unprepared as he was coming in. The impact of the kick snapped the man's head around and caused him to fall against an adjacent car. Wesley did not wait for him to recuperate but pressed his own attack and kicked his opponent between the legs. The man doubled over like a flower wilting in the heat. Wesley stepped to his right and side-kicked his opponent in the head. The man stumbled sideways, barely maintaining his balance. Wesley pressed his advantage and that was his undoing. Had he left at that moment and taken his car, the first man that he knocked down wouldn't have had the opportunity to recover. But such are the vagaries of the human psyche. Wesley forgot himself and his appointment, and let indignation overwhelm him.

His antagonist had finally fallen to one knee. Blood was running from the side of his face and mouth. Wesley was preparing to deliver another kick when a voice from behind him warned, "You better stop it, asshole! I've got a gun on you!" Wesley turned to face the speaker. The first man with the rimless glasses was pointing a small-caliber pistol at him. The man's nose was bleeding, his glasses were bent and sitting atilt on the bridge of his nose, and his derby was gone. "You all right, Jesse?" the man called to his companion.

Jesse struggled to his feet—an act of great determination, for he had taken a considerable beating from Wesley—and mumbled, "I'm gon' kill you fo' that! I'm gon' kill you!" He stumbled toward Wesley, who timed his approach and met him with another spinning back kick. This time the kick landed flush on his mouth and Jesse fell backward onto the cement floor.

"I said stop it, goddamn it! I swear to God, I'll shoot!"

Wesley turned and faced the first man. "What the hell do you people want?"

The man picked up his derby hat and set it on his head. He straightened his glasses and said evenly, "You should have thought about that before you started showing how tough you think you are."

Wesley watched the gun. It did not waver as it pointed directly at his torso. He was afraid but he saw no value in showing it. "Cut to the chase!" he demanded. "What is it you want?"

"Some important people want to talk with you about something."

"They should make an appointment. They can call my office anytime. I'm busy tonight," Wesley rejoined.

"You don't realize how important these people are. The only reason you aren't dead right now is that they want to talk to you."

"Oh, so you haven't been given permission to kill me? I guess I should just go on to my meeting." Wesley didn't think it would work but he decided to try the ploy anyway.

"You ain't going nowhere, fool!" the man warned, waving the gun. The shadows cast by the bare bulbs of the parking lot gave a stark and ominous look to the man's visage. Wesley was momentarily paralyzed by the threatening gun. The man called out to the man behind Wesley, "Get up, Jesse. I need you to drive while I keep an eye on our friend. Jesse, you all right?"

Wesley could hear Jesse behind him gradually getting to his feet, but he also heard the high-pitched sound of several female voices coming from the direction of the elevator. He realized quickly that this might be his only opportunity to escape. He spoke in a loud voice to the man in front of him, "You still planning to shoot me even if there are witnesses present? Or will you kill them too? How many people do you plan to kill?" He started edging toward his car. He heard Jesse coming up behind him. He raised his voice further, confident of his escape: "Do you still expect to shoot—"

Wesley never got to finish his thought. Jesse shoved a six-inch

switchblade into his back, through his kidney and liver. Wesley turned
to face his attacker with a surprised look on his face. He felt a tremendous heat as he sank unwillingly to his knees. The lights around him
grew dim gradually, as if everything he saw was blackened by the invisible flame which scorched deep in his back. There was no sound except
the pumping of his heart. Then there was a tremendous roar and he
felt the firestorm burning across his scalp. He tried to speak, to call out
to the women whose voices he had heard, but no sound issued from his
throat. He tried to raise his arm to no avail, and despite his efforts to remain on his knees, he slumped against the car and continued his decline
until he was facedown against the cement. Suddenly, he realized that
he was going to die, and a strange, wild panic gripped him, but it was
unable to manifest itself for he was helpless. As his last thoughts flitted
across his consciousness, he wondered if many people would come to
his funeral. Then blackness swallowed his vision and all was silent.

The sound of more voices issued from the door leading into the garage. "You dumb-ass fool! We weren't supposed to kill him!" Fletcher
hissed at Jesse. "You're going to have to explain this on your own. Now,
we got to get out of here. Duck down! Stay out of sight!"

"It was self-defense," Jesse said defiantly, wiping his hand across his
forehead and smearing blood across his face. "Ain't nobody ever give
me a beatin' and lived. Anyway, this motherfucker is one of them that
killed Frank."

"Get down, you fool! We don't have time for your talking and ex-
cuses. You can work out the details with your uncle."

"You gon' back me, ain't you?" Jessed demanded as he knelt down beside Fletcher. "You's a witness!"

"Hurry up and let's crawl down to our car. We don't want to be found
next to this body or we'll both be suspects in custody."

"Damn, he bleedin' a lot!" Jesse grunted as he crawled after Fletcher.
"Must have got him in the heart."

They were about four car lengths away from Wesley, crawling in the
narrow space between the bumpers of parked cars and the wall, as a
party of four white women appeared from the direction of the elevator.
They were wearing warm-up suits and carrying tennis rackets and gym
bags. The women's conversation echoed throughout the garage, and as
they disappeared around a corner, the trill of their voices and laughter
still resounded off its barren gray walls. As soon as the women were out
of sight Fletcher and Jesse scuttled to their car and jumped in. Jesse

turned on the ignition and pumped the accelerator, and the car's engine roared to life. He backed out of the parking place with a screech of rubber against cement and headed to the exit.

Wednesday, June 23, 1982

Deleon's day began as it had so often, with a dream. It was a sharp-edged dream that had haunted him from the early days of his youth. It was one of the blades that helped sculpt the man he had become. As he grew older, the keenness of its edge dulled and it became instead a psychological weight that he dragged through his nights, a ball and chain that prevented him from ever climbing out of the pit of his past.

The thick leather strap came whistling out of the darkness and fell upon his legs and back with flashes of burning pain. It struck him again and again, times beyond count. He writhed and struggled to avoid the belt but he could not escape. His father had a viselike grip on his arm and swung him around into the path of the belt so that he could continue whipping him. At first Deleon had tried not to cry, but the pain from the belt was relentless. His eyes filled with tears and still the belt fell upon him. His will came to an end, then he began to wail, to scream, to beg for mercy. It had no effect on his father, who continued to beat him.

Deleon's mother came running into the room and threw herself into the path of the belt. She tried to hug Deleon and hold him close to her. She screamed at her husband to stop beating their twelve-year-old son. His father let go of him then turned and punched his wife in the face, knocking her down. As soon as his father let go, Deleon burst for the door. Before he left the room, he saw his mother's bloody face as she lay crumpled on the floor.

As he left the house, he heard his father shout at his mother, "Goddamn it, bitch! You let the little bastard get away!" The last thing Deleon heard as he ran to a neighbor's house was his mother's screams.

Deleon pulled himself out of bed with his mother's voice still ringing in his ears. He was not rejuvenated by his hours in bed; he was fatigued. The first light of dawn was gleaming behind the closed shades of his windows. He went through his morning rituals with a modicum of effort. A dull headache pulsed above his eyebrows. By the time he descended the stairs to the kitchen, San Vicente and two of his men were sitting around the kitchen table drinking small cups of thick, black, sugary Cuban coffee. Their conversation stopped as he entered the room. Deleon gave them a perfunctory nod and walked over to the stove. He was disgusted that the men his grandfather had sent were still in bed despite the fact he had discussed with them the need for alertness and the necessity of rising at the same time as their Cuban associates. He poured himself a cup of the syrupy coffee and drank it down in two gulps. The coffee was hot and nearly scalded his throat, but he gave no indication of his discomfort.

He walked out of the kitchen and went to the closet for his jacket. As he was putting it on, San Vicente came out of the kitchen.

"You have business this early?" San Vicente asked.

Deleon hesitated briefly before he answered. He was pondering whether or not to inform San Vicente of his plans, but since he only planned to follow Fletcher and Jesse, and they were both bumbling fools, he thought no harm could come of it. He informed San Vicente of his intentions and San Vicente surprised him by asking if he could come along. "These are just some peripheral thugs," Deleon explained. "They aren't important enough for you to invest your time."

"Oh," San Vicente replied, rubbing his chin. "Then maybe I should send one of my men along with you."

Deleon gave San Vicente a long look then said, "I don't like the attitudes of your men. There might be trouble if you send one of them along with me."

"Then please let me join you. Perhaps we can get to know each other better. Our interests are the same, no?"

Deleon nodded but he knew that he and San Vicente would eventually be enemies and he cursed himself for divulging his plans. He had been stalling him with the line that nothing would be done until his grandfather arrived. Now he had no choice but to invite San Vicente along. He put a smile on his face and said, "Sure, come with me. Two heads are better than one."

"What you say is true," agreed San Vicente. "Perhaps my men can assist your men today as well."

Deleon kept his smile, but he said, "As I said before, your men's attitudes are a problem. I think it's better that they stay here."

"Whatever you think," San Vicente conceded with noticeable reluctance. "But you need not worry, my men are soldiers. They will do as I tell them."

San Vicente had meant his words to be calming, but all that Deleon could see was that the situation was highly flammable. He had a sudden thought; it was pure intuition, but he knew it to be true. San Vicente was having his men followed. Fortunately, Deleon had given them relatively simple assignments such as stealing getaway cars, checking the routes to be taken in emergencies, and identifying motels along the path of the projected departure. San Vicente's men would not learn much, but in the future Deleon would have to increase his vigilance.

Deleon suggested, "Let's leave them here for now and go on. When my grandfather gets here, there will be important work for every able-bodied man."

"Whatever you say," San Vicente replied. He had a smile on his face, but his displeasure was nonetheless evident.

Deleon suggested, "If you are carrying a gun, you should leave it here. We won't need it today and there's always the possibility we may be stopped and questioned by the police. We'll be doing a lot of sitting in the car as we maintain surveillance on our friends. Sometimes that can draw the attention of a patrolman."

"Don't worry, I never carry a handgun. I have only this." San Vicente pulled a ten-inch knife blade from a sheath beneath his jacket. "If I am close, it is as good as a gun."

After a brief discussion of logistics, the two men agreed to meet in twenty minutes in the garage. Deleon aroused Hardigrew and Brown and informed them of his concerns, then gave them assignments which would take them out of the city for the day. As he walked down to the garage he hoped that Jesse and Fletcher's schedule wasn't going to be critical to the overall operation. The less San Vicente knew, the better. The only reason Deleon was following them was that he knew that their employers, John Tree and Braxton, used them to perform all their legwork. Once they were in the car, joining the traffic leaving the Potrero Hill area, where Deleon had rented his house, he asked San Vicente, "Is this your first time in California?"

"No. I graduated from UC Irvine. I've spent a lot of time here. That's why my English is so good."

"Have you been to the Bay Area before?"

"No," San Vicente responded quickly, and turned the question back on Deleon. "Have you?"

Deleon lied. "No, this is my first time."

"Hmm." San Vicente grunted with a trace of incredulity.

It was a regular San Francisco commuter weekday morning. The rush-hour traffic impeded their progress out to the Westlake District. There was a heavy silence in the car, similar to the quiet in a high-stakes card game where neither player knows the other's hold card. Deleon recognized that their day together would be tremendously ar-duous if neither he nor San Vicente was willing to build a bridge. He searched for a subject which wouldn't seem like small talk. Finally, he determined there was no better subject than the core of their associa-tion. He said in his best conversational tone, "This is a beautiful city. I wish I had the opportunity to see it like a tourist, but that won't happen this time. I'm here because my grandfather sent me. He wants to kill the last of the Tremains. My family has been at war with the Tremains for over a hundred and fifty years. I'm just here to make sure that when my grandfather arrives, we can end this thing once and for all."

San Vicente growled in response, "There will be no doubt. We will make sure that all the Tremains are dead before we leave!"

The emphasis with which San Vicente spoke was not lost on Deleon. He reacted with surprise. "Oh, you know the Tremains? I thought you were simply paying my grandfather back for a past favor."

"He told you that?" San Vicente's tone contained both disbelief and anger.

Deleon explained with a chuckle, "No, man, I just thought—hell! Why else would you be coming all the way up here? I mean, what's in it for you?"

There was a cold determination in San Vicente's words when he re-sponded, "I will kill the grandsons of the man who killed both my grandfather and my father. Then I'll take their heads and their hearts back to Mexico and bury them beside the graves of my father and grandfather."

Despite himself, Deleon was surprised at the visceral intensity of San Vicente's answer. His words were spoken with the same fervor that Deleon's grandfather used when he talked about the blood debt be-tween the Tremains and the DuMonts. It appeared that his grandfather and San Vicente felt a similar bond of kinship to their respective fami-lies. For them family was something tangible and real; something they experienced and participated in; something for which they would risk their lives. Deleon had little comprehension of that type of familial bond and he was doomed never to experience it, for he would not ever give his heart and soul to another person, nor to any cause. To him the concept of family and loyalty was a hoax that was foisted upon the trusting to make sure that rebellion and anarchy seemed less inviting. His whole life experience, from his father's house to incarceration in adult institutions, had introduced him to all the creatures and ill intentions that used love as a cover, and when the cover was removed there was always a stench beneath it.

So what was family to him? Ever since he could remember, he had wanted to kill his own father, and while he had wanted to save his mother from his father's abuse, she had done little to engender in him a love for her. The truth was that he had stopped loving her because she had stayed. Despite all that passed, she had continued to live with his father. At the time he could not imagine what was going through her mind. Did she actually love that bully? Love him more than her own son? They had lived, for weeks sometimes, in abject fear of the man, fear of the times he would actually catch them while his rage was upon him. Obviously, the fact that her only child was in living hell was a point of no substance. Deleon had been in jail when he was informed that his mother had been beaten to death by an unknown assailant. The news did not surprise him, nor did it occupy his mind for any length of time. He had said good-bye to her many years before. He had no blood relative to whom he felt any positive emotional connection.

After Deleon's mother was killed, his father had become a successful businessman, a pillar in the community, a born-again Christian who swore that he had forsaken the path of anger, that he had been made anew. Deleon didn't buy any of it. He felt only hate toward the man.

As he drove along Ocean Boulevard, Deleon found himself wondering was it simply hate which motivated his grandfather and San Vicente or love for their families. And whether it mattered in the grand karmic scheme if one was motivated by love or hate. It was idle musing, for the answer didn't matter, his path would be the same. He would complete this assignment and then kill his father; that was his agreement with his grandfather. This was the last in a long line of tasks; after this he could exact his payment. He wondered how the sound of his father's whimpers would make him feel; would those sounds drown out the din of his nightmare? With that one death would his own demons be exorcized?

Deleon pulled his gray sedan into a parking space facing downhill,
up the block from Fletcher's house, and turned the engine off. He
looked out the window and saw below him lines of little two-story,
square houses stacked against one another like boxes on the sides of the
hills. The only things that broke the monotonous lines of the houses
were occasional small trees which grew at the edge of the curbs, next to
the street.

Deleon and San Vicente sat in silence. Twenty minutes passed before
they saw Jesse's lumbering walk as he climbed the hill to Fletcher's
house. Fletcher's garage door opened as soon as Jesse rang the bell.
Jesse waited for the door to rise, then stepped under it and went inside.
The brown Cadillac backed out of the garage almost immediately following Jesse's entrance. When it took off down the hill, Deleon followed. Deleon tailed the brown Cadillac throughout the day. When
Fletcher and Jesse headed across the Bay Bridge, Deleon was several
cars behind them. Consequently, he and San Vicente watched the assault on Wesley Hunter from inside the parking structure.

Five minutes after Fletcher and Jesse drove off, Deleon and San Vicente came out of the shadows and walked across the silent garage to
where Wesley lay next to his vehicle. Deleon knelt down and put his
hand on Wesley's throat. He discovered a weak but still distinguishable
pulse. He shook his head at his companion and whispered, "The
damned fools! They left the man alive! Damn, don't they have any
brains?"

San Vicente, who was a short, stocky man, nudged Wesley with his
foot and said with his barely discernible Mexican accent, "Looks like he
just needs a little help and then he won't be testifying. I help people like
this all the time."

Deleon responded, "But this was unnecessary. If these fools keep operating like this, they can bring down a whole lot of heat on everybody."

"Maybe, maybe not," San Vicente mused while Deleon then went
through Wesley's pockets and removed his car keys. "What's another
dead black? From what I understand, they are found dead on the streets
all the time."

Deleon said nothing, but he didn't like San Vicente's remark. He
opened the trunk of Wesley's car and removed the tire, then with San
Vicente's help stuffed Wesley's body into the cramped space. He said,
"We'll leave the car with the keys in it in Emeryville by those movie

theaters. Some asshole will come out and take the car. Then the body'll be their problem."

San Vicente nodded and replied, "Good idea, but *primero . . .*" He pulled out his long-bladed knife and slit Wesley's throat with one savage cut, then slammed the trunk shut. It took several tries to close the trunk, but he finally succeeded. As he wiped his knife on some tissues, he turned to Deleon with a trace of a smile. "I'll follow you."

Deleon was not pleased by San Vicente's actions. The man had already been mortally injured and was not likely to regain consciousness. He knew that San Vicente was sending him a message. Deleon chose not to show any reaction. He returned San Vicente's smile and got into Wesley's car.

Wednesday, June 23, 1982

The day following his altercation with Bedrosian, Jackson completed a hard workout at the dojo and joined his friends at Justin's. It was slightly after seven, so the press of the happy hour crowd had thinned. Jackson saw his friends seated around a table in the back. They were loudly discussing his exploits of the day before. Both Dan and Lincoln worked for the city as well, and the news had made it through the grapevine. As he neared his friends, Dan jumped up. "All hail the Gladiator from Crete!"

"Why Crete?" Jackson asked as he sat down. "Why not Africa, Songhai? Mali? Carthage?"

Dan paused, searching for the answer. "I know Greek mythology better than African. It was the king of Crete who had the Minotaur in his labyrinth, wasn't it?"

"A labyrinth where young maidens were sacrificed," Lincoln confirmed with a nod of his head.

"That's it," Dan agreed. "And the Minotaur was half man and half bull, right?"

"What the hell you guys talking about?" Jackson asked while trying to get the waitress's attention.

"It's Greek to me," Pres said with a shrug, taking a long sip from his drink.

"I'm throwing pearls before swine," Dan complained to no one in particular.

"We know what you're doing," Pres interjected. "Tell us what happened at the office, Jax?"

The group quieted and let Jackson tell the events firsthand. When he finished they began to clamor for explanations.

"Why did you choose this time to stand up to Bedrosian?" Pres asked.

Before Jackson could answer, Dan jumped to his feet, his big body swaying above them, and said in a booming voice, "Service! Service! I wish to buy a round of drinks in honor of my wild and madcap brother!"

"Oh, yes," Lincoln rejoined in his most cynical tone, "let us drink to our friend, fourteen years before the mast and now he has struck an officer. Let us drink to the grimness of his fate!"

"Lincoln's right," Pres agreed before sipping his drink. "Jackson's going to have to get his résumé out. There's no way he can stay at the City now." His friends all knew how much Jackson wanted to be a city manager and that his recent actions would only serve to hinder his chances. Pres continued his thought, "But that doesn't necessarily have to be a negative proposition. He wasn't happy working for Bedrosian. This forces him to give all his options a serious look."

"Is that a euphemism for the want ads?" Lincoln asked.

Pres waved him off. "Seriously, this might be just the change that Jackson needs. He knew this was coming. He told me about it last Wednesday."

"He knew he would bend back Bedrosian's finger?" Lincoln challenged.

"No, he said there was a rip in the social fabric someplace, and life for him was about to change."

The waitress took this moment to make her entrance and it was like a circus coming to a small town: There were colors and points of interest everywhere. She was a big brown-skinned woman, beginning to fill out in the middle, but it was obvious that she had once been a show-stopper. She wore a short orange leather skirt over an iridescent yellow bodysuit. Her makeup and her hair were heavy with application. Everything she wore clashed with the bar's gray, black, and pink interior. But the look she gave Dan was the pièce de résistance. It said, *Come on, asshole. I've met so many assholes like you that one more will not make a difference.*

"May I have your order, please?" she asked in a professional tone.

Dan took one look at her expression and her outfit and said in his most conciliatory manner, "Dear Handmaiden of Zeus, we'll have one more round."

After she left the table with the orders, Pres looked at Dan and questioned, "Handmaiden of Zeus? You're a very sick puppy."

"She's a goddess or a demon," Dan explained. "Her makeup looked like it was done by Picasso while he was on a binge. The only thing that saves her is she's got a helluva butt and a nice long pair of legs."

"That statement was backward and sexist and you know better than that," Pres said, shaking his head.

"Give me a break from this fascism of the politically correct," Dan answered. "If I can't be me with my friends and say what I want, then what the hell use are they?"

Lincoln asked Jackson, "Where's Wesley? He said he would be coming with you from the dojo."

Jackson shrugged. "I didn't see him. He's probably chasing after some nubile maiden."

"A man after my own heart," Dan declared. "He appreciates the value of long legs and a fine behind!" He gave Pres a leer.

Pres ignored Dan and asked Jackson, "I want you to answer my question. Why did you decide to stand up to Bedrosian now?" He noticed that Jackson was not listening to him but instead was looking over his shoulder at some object behind him. Pres turned to see what caused Jackson to be so distracted. He saw a tall dark-skinned woman wearing a stylishly cut suit heading for the rest rooms.

Jackson spoke in low tones, "I met this woman briefly at Rhasan's graduation. As they say in the Old Country, she is a stone fox! She's simply beautiful!" His gaze followed her as she walked away from the bar. When she had first risen from her barstool, their eyes had met and held for a long instant. The connection was broken when he smiled. She continued on her way. Something in that brief shared look stirred Jackson; a sense of ease and familiarity, an understanding of the unspoken. In that moment he thought he saw beyond her eyes, into her intention. He stood up and stepped back from the table.

Observing him, Lincoln said, "Periscope up. Target sighted. Load forward tubes."

Dan added, "The quarry may be too elusive. He may have to call in the fleet for assistance."

Jackson leaned over and said quietly, "Would you people be cool? I would really like to talk to this woman."

"Why are you whispering?" Dan boomed.

"Please, brothers, be cool," Jackson urged.

"At least we've moved from 'you people' to 'brothers,' " Pres acknowledged.

Dan said with a big smile, "Bring her over. I'm sure we'd all like to meet her."

Jackson laughed but did not attempt to respond. He simply headed to a spot where he could intercept her upon her return. He waited several minutes at the doorway of the hall leading out of the ladies' room, trying to think of something imaginative to say. But when she exited the rest room all that he could muster was "Hello, Elizabeth, do you remember me?"

"How could I forget? You're the Big Brother of the year," she said in her husky contralto. Her big eyes took him in slowly. There was a trace of a smile on her lips.

Jackson felt giddy for a moment as he wondered whether she was being sarcastic. He asked, "Are you accessible to polite approaches? When we met you indicated that it would be all right if I called you. Has something changed?"

She put a hand on her hip and surveyed him coolly. "Only the circumstances. I am with a few friends. Another time would be more appropriate."

Jackson retreated back a step and replied, "Whatever you say. I hope to talk with you when it is appropriate." He bowed his head briefly. "Pardon me for bothering you."

"My, that was formal," Elizabeth observed, then an impish smile spread across her face. "Are you thin-skinned?"

Jackson replied, "Not really, but in parting, I'd like to reconfirm that I'm very interested in seeing you when it's appropriate. Have a good evening." With those words he turned and walked back to the table with a calm demeanor, but his heart was thumping loudly in his chest.

His friends greeted him with a few derisive comments concerning his lack of commitment to them, his inability to establish sound relationships with women in general, and whatever else they could think to say.

Jackson took the hazing in stride. These were his best friends, his in-

ner circle. The years had proven that there was a strong love bond between the men. Theirs was a tight circle formed when the men were
still boys, when trust was a simple concept, when sharing meant "everything that was in your pockets." They called themselves the Alamo
Square Rangers because they all lived around Alamo Square Park. Five
boys, including Wesley, from diverse cultural backgrounds, who re-
tained their bonds of brotherhood for over a quarter of a century. It was
a relationship that grew and stretched and changed as its members
grew and were metamorphosed by time, but the bonds that connected
them never weakened. It was Jackson's real family. The brothers that he
never had. The folks that would always be on his side. Thus, there was
no rancor for the ribbing he was taking. When one is being teased out
of love, it is easy to abide.

The conversation turned to why people suddenly decide, after years
of acquiescing, to stand up for their rights.

Lincoln said, "I think it's indignation, but it's an indignation fed by a
high level of social anger and unhappiness. Patience gets used up, stub-
bornness sets in. It's like adding more sugar to water that is already sat-
urated with it. When you reach a critical mass, everything crystallizes."

"You're off base. All people yearn to be free!" Dan countered. "It's in-
trinsic to human nature. Liberty, equality, brotherhood, these concepts
are the basis of every holy book. Indignation is just a passing emotion.
The desire for freedom is a constant."

Pres turned to Jackson and asked with a smile, "Was it as simple as indignation, or was it your innate desire for freedom that stirred you to
rise up?"

Jackson was in another world. He had been basking like an alliga-
tor underneath the warm, bantering conversation of his friends, intermittently rising to the surface to voice his opinion on the issues under
discussion, but otherwise sipping his drink and lying submerged in
meditative thought. A couple times during the discussion he had
caught Elizabeth staring at him, but she averted her eyes. When Pres
asked his question Jackson was once again exchanging looks with Elizabeth. This time she did not look away but held his eye for more than
ten seconds. It was incomprehensible, yet energy seemed to be rico-
cheting between them. Jackson did not know whether it was good or
bad. He was drawn to her like an iron filing to a magnet or a lemming
to the sea; he didn't know which, nor did he care.

"Earth to Jackson! Earth to Jackson!" Pres prodded, trying to get Jackson's attention.

Regretfully breaking eye contact, Jackson turned toward Pres and said sarcastically, "Yes, my celestial fundament, how can I help you pursue the greater truth?"

Pres hesitated for a second then asked, "What does *fundament* mean?"

"It means ass or anus," Dan volunteered.

"That's a shame," Lincoln chimed in. "It doesn't appear that our Third World brother knows his fundament from a hole in the ground." Everyone laughed.

Repressing his desire to join in the laughter of the others, Pres declared, "You fools are lucky that I know you need me. Otherwise, I'd have hit the trail long ago. I get all the abuse I need from the station where I work."

The rest of Pres's words were lost on Jackson; he had made eye contact again. Elizabeth was looking at him while idly sipping her drink. He was attracted by the smooth, dark, bittersweet-chocolate color of her skin, the dimples at the corners of her mouth, the large, dark eyes with the mischievous gleam. She lifted one hand and beckoned him with a finger. Initially, he was hesitant, but he decided to make another effort to talk to her. He stood up. The comments began again but Jackson ignored them and made his way over to Elizabeth and her friends. She was sitting with two other women. Her friends were engrossed in an intense conversation while she was left to her own devices. She watched him without a change of expression. When he arrived he said, "May I buy you and your friends a drink?"

Elizabeth said nothing, merely looked him up and down approvingly. She held up her glass. "Chilled Stoli with two olives, no ice."

"A friend of mine drinks that," Jackson said and caught the eye of the waitress and waved her over. One of Elizabeth's friends turned and faced Jackson. There was a trail of tears down her brown face. Her eyes were still red and angry from crying. Jackson nodded to her out of politeness.

She demanded angrily, "What are you looking at? Why are you over here bothering us? Can't you see that we want to be left alone?"

Surprised, Jackson mumbled, "Sorry to disturb you. I was just buying Elizabeth a drink. No harm meant."

"Leave now!" the woman ordered in a loud voice. "You're so damn arrogant. You think women want to meet you? Well, they don't! We just want to have a drink in peace!" At this point the woman broke down in tears and turned away.

The waitress came up and asked bluntly, "You bothering these ladies?"

Jackson denied responsibility. "No, ma'am, it was all a misunderstanding. I'm returning to my table now, but I'd be happy to buy all these ladies a round of drinks should they desire it." As he gave Elizabeth one long last look he saw her make a discreet calming gesture to him with one of her hands. He nodded in acknowledgment and returned to his table.

This time there were no teasing remarks. The woman's outburst had been overheard and his friends understood Jackson's disappointment. Lincoln put a brotherly hand on his shoulder as he sat down.

Dan raised his glass and made a toast: "To our brother, who yesterday stood up for freedom." Then the conversation began anew and centered once again on why Jackson had chosen to confront Bedrosian. Pres pressed the subject. It was almost anticlimactic that after being placed in the spotlight, Jackson had no explanation. All he could think of was his grandfather and how the old man had always spoken his mind without concern for the consequences. He related his thoughts to his friends and Dan reacted immediately.

"The spirit of your grandfather must be speaking to you or through you," he said emphatically, as if no other possibility existed.

"That's an interesting thought," Pres mused. "Do you really believe his grandfather has the ability to project his intentions?"

Jackson interjected, "That depends upon whether or not you think he is an instrument of evil."

Dan responded, "I don't know about that, but I'll bet he's part of the reason you reacted like you did yesterday."

"Perhaps it's the angst created by my memories of him," Jackson replied. "He's been strong on my mind these last few days. I've been reliving the summers that I spent with him. He had a lot of qualities that I now value. Qualities that I ignored because I let my hatred for him block out some of the good lessons he had to teach."

There was silence at the table for several seconds. Jackson's words had changed the mood. A breeze had swept the table, driving the light repartee before it like so many clouds.

"You had to grow up before you could really examine your relationship with your grandfather," Pres said. "And finding out which lessons are the valuable ones can take some people their whole lives."

Lincoln spoke, and there was no hint of sarcasm or cynicism in his words: "When we were kids, I envied you, Jax, because you had no parents. You see, I hated the store my family owned. It seemed to me that I spent the majority of my adolescent life in that damn store. My father and mother never wanted to modernize; they wanted to do business exactly as it was done in China. My father and I used to fight over my going to school. There were days when he wanted me to cut school to work in the store and I wouldn't. School was one of my major links with the world outside the store. Yes, for a long time I particularly hated my father."

"That's not true!" Dan challenged. "I remember you cried at your dad's funeral. How old were you then, seventeen?"

"I was seventeen, but I cried for different reasons than you think," Lincoln answered.

"I remember that day because we got there late," Pres mused. "Wesley's rundown 'fifty-seven Chevy stalled."

"We've heard this story a hundred times," interjected Lincoln.

"It's closer to a million," Jackson corrected. He turned to Lincoln. "I'm interested in hearing why you envied me, Linc. I didn't know your father well, but I thought your mother was pretty nice."

"Yeah," Dan said. "I want to hear the reasons you cried since you say they're different than I think."

"My folks were born in mainland China. They came here to Gold Mountain to make money and eventually return to China as conquering heroes. All my father wanted me to do is learn enough English to run the store. I didn't want that. I wanted to be an American. I wanted to wear jeans and sneakers and drink Cokes and root beer floats and hang out with the Rangers. My father didn't like me to spend time with you guys. He used to beat me for hanging out with you guys. He told me that I was trying to run away from my responsibilities. I didn't see myself that way. My membership in the Rangers was an important element in my perception of myself. You remember when I was sixteen and I had that big fight with my father?"

"Yeah, I remember. You broke his arm with a lead pipe," Dan confirmed.

"After that, he threw me out. My mother begged her brother to take me in and he did. My uncle was good to me. He was more modern-thinking than my father. He understood the value of education. When my father died, I hadn't spoken to him since our fight. But I knew his death meant my return to that damned store. That's why I cried. I knew my mother would need me. While my father was alive, I had escaped."

"Oh, but we had some damn good times in that store," Dan said.

"Yeah, Jackson practically lived there during our senior year," Pres recalled. "Wasn't that where he got dressed for the senior prom?"

"And tore his pants on the pork rind rack." Dan began laughing.

"Do you ever wish that you had cleared up the problems between you and your father?" Jackson asked.

"No!" Lincoln's answer was short and clipped. "His death was the best thing for our family. My sisters, my younger brother, and I all have professional careers. We never would have had that if my father had lived. He would have had us working in that damn store."

A presence had entered the ring of conversation and caused it to lapse. Elizabeth had come to their table. Jackson rose immediately and greeted her.

"Hello." Jackson extended his hand. Elizabeth let him take her hand and returned his brief squeeze with one of her own.

"Are these your friends?" she asked. Her contralto seemed to wrap itself around him. She smiled and looked around the table.

"No," Dan blurted out. "We were all cellmates at Q."

"Forgive him his friends," Pres attempted to explain to Elizabeth. "Jackson is not as weird as they would have you believe."

"I quite agree," Lincoln said with mock seriousness. "The papers he received when he was released from that maximum-care facility indicated he was quite sane."

"Would you like to step away from the table and talk?" Jackson asked, hoping to speak to her without the raillery of his friends.

"I don't have time now," she said as she looked Jackson directly in the eye. There was only a trace of a smile, but the look in her eyes, a look that was directed solely to him, conveyed her desire for more time to examine their differences and meetings. Without a change of expression, she explained, "My friends want to leave now. I just wanted to come over and apologize for Diane's going off on you. She's very upset." Elizabeth paused and gave Jackson another impish look then said,

"It might be fun to see you without your squad of Musketeers." She pressed a card into his hand. "Call me."

Lincoln said to Elizabeth without a hint of sarcasm, "You've made a good choice. He's a good friend and brother."

"He's my brother too," Dan chimed in. "But we have different mothers."

"Don't listen to them," Pres interjected. "We've all been friends since the fourth grade."

Elizabeth laughed and said to Jackson, "You have quite a rooting section."

Jackson smiled. "Sorry for the promotion, but they're my friends. They're good people."

"Don't be sorry for the promotion," Elizabeth returned. "Unsolicited, it says something about you, something good."

"Either that, or we're in a cult," Lincoln observed.

"All right! Before you guys begin again," Elizabeth declared, raising her hands to hold off the potential flood of badinage, "good night, gentlemen." She turned to go and Dan lumbered to his feet.

He walked with her a few steps as he said, "If you still have any reservations about being alone with this man, I am available as an escort. However, I prefer dinner dates."

Later, sipping a cognac in the darkness of his house, Jackson felt as if he had pulled out of a small, placid tributary to join the floodwaters of a rapidly changing river of events. Already, in his inner ear, he could hear the rumble of the rapids. He felt no regret, only puzzlement as to the direction his life would take as a result of the forces that had been unleashed.

His thoughts drifted to Elizabeth. It was strange to have a woman enter his life at this time, for it was a time of upheaval, a time for hardening the heart, not opening it. Yet there was something about her he could not deny; her voice had an echo in it, an echo that he remembered in moments of solitude. It wasn't logical: They had not spent more than twenty minutes together, yet he knew this was serious. He pulled out her card and discovered that she had written her home number on it. Jackson decided on impulse to call her.

As he dialed her number, Jackson wondered what it would have been like to have had someone to love him without reservation; to have had someone sincerely concerned about his welfare; someone with whom he could confide his deepest secrets; someone who would never judge him too harshly. It was a fantasy and he knew it. The phone began to ring.

The ringing stopped and a woman's husky contralto said, "Good evening."

Thursday, June 24, 1982

It was seven-thirty in the morning. Serena Baddeaux Tremain looked at her grandson Franklin and was not pleased. She stood behind a newly reupholstered 1930s vintage couch. Her grandson, sitting in an overstuffed chair of the same period, was sipping on what appeared to be a healthily poured drink. Serena wrinkled her nose; she did not like men who needed to drink alcohol in the morning just because they were confronted with problems. She walked slowly around the couch to the coffee table and picked up a polished brass bell, which she rang several times.

Franklin was unable to contain his impatience. He had spent several uncomfortable days worrying. He asked, "What do you think? Who's he representing? Do you know?"

A middle-aged, brown-skinned woman entered the room in answer to the bell. "Yes, madam?" She spoke with a Hispanic accent. Her straight black hair was pinned up in a neat bun. She was the majordomo of the house staff and ensured that the organization functioned like clockwork. She had an attitude of quiet competence.

"Mrs. Marquez, may I please have a cup of chamomile tea? Very hot, please." Serena always addressed everyone she employed by their last name and expected the same. She felt it gave them due respect and prevented any unnecessary crossing of social lines.

Mrs. Marquez nodded her head in understanding, and asked Franklin, "Mr. Tremain, would you care for something?"

Franklin waved his drink at her. "I'm fine, thanks." He turned to face his grandmother. "Why are you making this a mystery?"

His grandmother waited until Mrs. Marquez left the sitting room

before she said, "Some topics are best discussed in privacy." She took a
moment to seat herself comfortably on the couch. It irked her that Franklin did not have sufficient insight to see that Braxton was just using him.

"You realize that Braxton hated your grandfather, hated everything
about him?"

"Who didn't? Hell, I hated the man myself! I thought you hated him
too."

Serena took a deep breath. She had spent the better part of her life
letting her emotions rather than reality dictate her actions. The irony
of what she was about to say to Franklin was not lost on her. "Put aside
your feelings for a moment and think of what is best for the family.
Doesn't that make you wonder about his motives? You don't really think
that if you helped him that would in any way mean that he would keep
his word, do you?"

"We're talking business. I scratch his back, he scratches mine. Anyway, I thought this guy was a friend of yours. You used to invite him
over a lot."

"That was many years ago. Many things have changed since then. I
know more now than I did then."

"What's that supposed to mean? Why don't you just tell me who he's
representing instead of beating around the bush."

Serena saw that her grandson was not interested in reasoning out the
problems confronting him. All he wanted was an answer that would
make the decision that he had already made appear correct. In the end
she would probably have to intervene anyway. Life was so frustrating;
she had wanted to be the mother of a new order, to start a dynasty, and
all the material she had left to work with was Franklin. It was frightening the way dreams went astray over the years.

As stated in her separation agreement with King in the early fifties,
Serena had taken over management of the properties that they had accumulated in the Bay Area. She had a gift for real estate speculation and
an understanding of when neighborhoods were on the brink of change.
Money came easy to her hand. There was never any discussion of di-
vorce. Serena and King had both grown up in a time when people remained married for better or for worse. Despite their separation, he
remained very much in her life.

For many years after they parted, King reached out from Mexico and
caused people to disappear. He never forgave those involved in the killing of Jacques. Serena knew that King employed a vast system of spies

to keep tabs on the whereabouts of his enemies and their families. Sometimes, he would materialize in person without warning, to lie low for several days in preparation for taking some action against his various enemies. Even though King had worked out a deal establishing the "noncombatant" status of his wife and family, it was extremely nerve-wracking for Serena during those early years. Finally, on the condition that King restrict his activities to Southern California, Serena ceded him seventy percent of their real estate management firm. King's thirst for blood was never quenched, but it did not disrupt her life as much.

Serena wondered whether an understanding of all this history would help Franklin appreciate that he did not possess the skills to become a player in this game. Serena was certain the first time he was seriously threatened that Franklin would come scuttling back to hide behind her skirts. However, if the faceless "they" decided to take action without warning, Franklin could lose his life. He was the only one of her three grandchildren who had not traveled off some side road and the only one who had continued to obey her rules and requirements in order to get the favors she had to give. She was compelled to protect him.

Franklin was studying his grandmother over the top of his glass. What is this old, judgmental bitch thinking about now? he wondered. His relationship with his grandmother had never been more than cordial. It seemed they never had a conversation that didn't have some element of reproof. It seemed he had never quite lived up to her expectations, but he was sure that even the character Sidney Poitier had played in *Guess Who's Coming to Dinner?* would have fallen short as well.

Serena broke the silence. "Be very careful of Bill Braxton. He is not acting as a friend of this family." She said no more.

Franklin exploded. "What's going on? You invited him to family picnics and birthdays for years—"

"Keep your voice down!" Serena commanded.

"Are you going to tell me what's going on?" Franklin demanded, enunciating each word.

"There is nothing that you should know," Serena said evenly. "All you need to do is stay away from Braxton and his friends. You don't have to worry about anything. I'll take care of it. Just refer all calls from Braxton to me."

Franklin was amazed. "You're not planning to tell me anything?" he sputtered. "I'm the head of the company and you're not going to tell me? This is ridiculous!"

"Watch your tone!" she warned. "You didn't act like the head of the company. You didn't handle this problem. You kicked it up to me. So I will handle it. That's that."

"What did you expect me to do," Franklin challenged, "agree to Jackson's murder over the phone?" Franklin was really exasperated by the conversation with his grandmother. It seemed to typify their whole relationship.

Mrs. Marquez brought in the tea on a tray right at the end of Franklin's outburst. Serena gave him a quick, disapproving look. Mrs. Marquez set the tea tray on the coffee table and excused herself.

Franklin wanted to say more, but he was no fool. He knew that Serena held the reins of control over the company as long as the stock was in her name. The only power he possessed was that which she delegated to him. He had hoped, given the circumstances, for her immediate support and that she would willingly share her information with him. However, once again, she had shown herself unpredictable. He decided that if she wasn't going to tell him anything, he was wasting his time meeting with her. Why should I tell her that I'm having lunch with Braxton? he thought. Hell, I'll probably cut my own deal and leave her totally out of the picture. He swallowed his drink and stood up. "Okay, you've got it handled. I'll bow out," he said.

Serena sipped her tea and watched him pick up his coat. How like a child he is, she thought. So impatient, so unable to just sit, listen, and analyze. Franklin didn't give his mind a chance to catch up with his mouth. She watched him walk to the door and knew that this boy, this man, did not possess the essence of King's seed. He was simply not built on the scale of King Tremain.

"Good-bye, Gran," Franklin said and walked out the door without waiting for a response.

Serena thought about what she could have told Franklin that might have satisfied him. She knew she couldn't tell him the truth. She didn't think that he would bear up well under such a burden. He was not like the other one, his cousin, who was a direct descendant of King. The hot tea felt soothing as it flowed down her throat. She suppressed the thought of her other grandson. He was not her worry. His life had always flowed through wild country beyond the scope of her protection.

Thursday, June 24, 1982

The sky was partly overcast with meandering gray clouds that the sun was gradually burning away. A cold mist sprayed across its bow as the Angel Island ferry made its way across the choppy surface of the bay. There was a steady breeze blowing off the Pacific as Jackson and Elizabeth stood on the upstairs pilot deck, watching the sailboats in the bay heel to the wind. The water was a deep, deep blue, and small white-caps appeared as the wind hurried the waves to their destination. The green fingers of the Tiburon and San Quentin peninsulas stretched out into the bay and, despite being dotted with buildings, gave a sense of the pristine beauty the bay must have had at the turn of the century.

The wind was blowing in Elizabeth's hair, which was braided into numerous thin strands that she wore shoulder length. Jackson wondered why he had not noticed that her hair was braided before.

Elizabeth saw that he was watching her. "I needed to get out and smell some fresh air." She nodded her head at the Golden Gate Bridge. "This was a good idea. What a wonderful view." The bridge's two burnt-orange towers rose out of the whitecapped, blue-green waves of the bay and seemed to touch the sky as their tops were lost in mist. On the left, San Francisco's neighborhoods climbed in tiers above its down-town skyline. On the right, the Marin peninsula looked green and inviting, promising pastoral relief from the urban pressures of life on the other side of the bridge.

"It's a view that not many see," Jackson replied, "looking straight out the Golden Gate." He turned to her and said, "I was happily surprised that you agreed to come with me."

"I was a little surprised myself, but if we didn't do it today, we might have had to wait several weeks. I have a trial starting next week and you say you might be going away this weekend. This was our window."

"Perhaps the one or two isolated incidences," Jackson chuckled, "that we will be granted to see into each other's interior. It's like we're two boats passing each other in a narrow canal. Even as we meet we draw farther apart, pulled by our individual life forces."

"What is the most valuable thing to learn about you in the time I have?"

"That depends upon your interests," Jackson said quietly, watching the trace of a smile play across the smooth, dark skin of her face.

"For the sake of time, I'll tell you what I know about you. Wayman's mother said some very good things about the work you've done with her son. And you did all this without ever once hitting on her. That sounded to me like the actions of a decent man. So I wanted to meet you. Decency is important. It serves as the basis for a constructive relationship. I'm at a point in my life where that is the only type of relationship that I want. Is that clear?"

Jackson cocked his eyebrow and said, "Crystal. You're checking me out to determine whether I'm worth an emotional investment." He smiled and continued, "If you discover that I am, I proceed to the greatest hurdle of all: whether you can love me."

"I'm so happy that you've thought our relationship out and have it summarized. I did notice that in true masculine style, you did not mention your feelings once."

The ferry horn blared as the vessel neared the island's pier. Passengers began making their way below to the exit. Jackson shouldered a knapsack and turned to follow the crowd, but Elizabeth grabbed his arm and demanded, "No response?"

Jackson replied as he guided her in front of him on the way down the stairs, "Who was it that said, 'The measure of a man is what he feels about what he thinks and the measure of a woman is what she thinks about what she feels'?"

Elizabeth waited until they had descended the stairs before she turned to him and scoffed, "That is such absolute bullshit! Only a man could have thought up such a weak oversimplification. The measure of a woman is greater than the man's, for she has to have courage, resolve, willpower, discipline, intelligence the same as a man, as well as love, nurturing, compassion, understanding—"

"All right! All right! I'll concede that the measures are equal, with some small differences. Now, let's get off this boat."

Elizabeth allowed herself to be ushered down to the ramp, but she said, "I still want to continue this conversation."

"What's the issue?" Jackson asked as their forward movement was halted by the crush of people moving onto the docks. He was standing directly behind Elizabeth. He could smell the fresh, lightly scented shampoo in her hair. He looked down and saw the voluptuous curve of her buttocks. She turned and caught him staring down at her butt and immediately he had an embarrassed look on his face.

"Drop something?" she asked sarcastically.

"I wouldn't say that it has dropped yet," he said, looking down at her behind again.

"And it won't in your lifetime," she snapped as they walked down the gangplank.

"Good," Jackson answered with a smile. "Because I'm an admirer of the African American behind. Yours is a particularly spectacular representation."

"I know, it has quite a following," Elizabeth replied with a toss of her head. "Let's get back to our original line of discussion."

"What was the outstanding question?"

"The question is you didn't mention anything about your feelings in your synopsis of our potential relationship."

Jackson answered in a bantering tone as he stepped off the gangplank, "You're a district attorney. You know that wasn't a question. It was an observation on your part which in no way solicited a response from me. Plus, how can I talk about feelings that have yet to evolve?"

Elizabeth raised her eyebrows. "I had no idea I had a hostile witness. I'll be clearer in my phrasing from now on."

"I am not hostile," Jackson protested.

"Recalcitrant, then."

"Those are the only two choices I have?"

"Until you respond clearly as to why you didn't mention your likely emotional investment while you were outlining mine."

"Ahh, another nonquestion." Jackson touched her arm. "Let's head to the other side of the island."

The path that they followed lay between the small sandy cove facing the Tiburon peninsula and the rolling green sward of lawn and picnic benches that fronted the two-story Victorian ranger station. Behind the ranger station the island rose to a peak four hundred feet above sea level. The path soon left the grassy valley and passed under some weathered oak, bay, eucalyptus, pine, and madrona trees as it ascended the island's steep incline. Then the path turned to gravel and flattened out as it curved around the side of the island. They walked in silence. But it was not a hostile silence. The view required no words and the air was filled with the twittering songs of different birds, the buzzing sounds of flying insects, and the erratic rustling of leaves as gusting winds rushed through the trees. Their pace had been fast but not hurried when they reached the rough wooden stairs which led up to the paved road that circled the upper part of the island.

After they climbed the stairs, Jackson directed Elizabeth to a bench that provided a view that looked straight out onto the turbulent blue of the Sausalito Straits. Jackson took off his pack and sat down next to her. He began to speak. "The reason I didn't mention my feelings is because I'm better at suppressing my emotions than recognizing them."

"Why did you call me? Was it simply the way I look?"

"That sounds like the type of segue used in lie detector tests."

"Answer! Don't avoid."

Jackson looked into her eyes for a moment then shrugged. "Okay, I felt something when I looked into your eyes and heard your voice. It was internal. It made me think that I had a connection with you and that it might be mutual."

"That's good. Is there more?"

"The fact you're beautiful didn't make the decision harder either. Now you have a totally honest answer. What are you fishing for?"

Elizabeth smiled impishly. "Total honesty can be refreshing in a crude sort of way. Please continue."

Jackson shook his head. "I said what I had to say. Did you expect a speech?"

"Have you ever been in love?" Jackson started to protest, but Elizabeth pressed the fingers of her right hand gently against his lips and requested, "Just answer, please. Pretty please with cherries and whipped cream on top."

Jackson relented and said, "I think so, but that was a long time ago. Infatuation is the closest I've come since then."

With an expression of mock-seriousness Elizabeth observed, "That's a very sad commentary on your life. To have only loved once. To what do you attribute this?"

"I owe it all to my grandmother, who you met. She has the warmth of a frozen trout and she taught me all that she knew."

A trace of a frown hovered over Elizabeth's eyebrows. "Aren't you a little old to still be blaming things on the people who raised you?"

"Some scars are too deep for one ever to obtain the full range of emotion. But you're right, who I am today is my responsibility, not my grandmother's. Maybe it's because I have never found the right person."

"What can you offer me?"

Now it was Jackson's turn to frown as he retorted, "I had no idea that we needed to establish the type of emotional buffet I can offer on our first date. What about companionship and friendship? Are those meaningless? And, Counselor, this interrogation is getting old."

Elizabeth moved closer to him and whispered, "Don't get indignant." She traced the line of his jaw lightly with a finger. "I want to get to know you and I don't want to waste time."

Her words and actions took all the heat out of Jackson's response. He exhaled and said, "I thought that the protocol was to establish whether we had sufficient things in common and then determine whether we'll proceed."

"There's no protocol except what we agree upon." Elizabeth took a barrette out of her purse and gathered her thin braids into a ponytail. "I want us to know each other better by the end of this day, and as long as we both agree, we don't have to follow any preordained route to achieve that. I knew when we first met that we had something in common. I felt it. It surprised me. It made me feel at home with you, like I'd known you a long time. I feel the same thing now, or I wouldn't even be talking to you like this. Thus, I want to know all I can before your boat passes out of sight." Elizabeth stood up. "Let's continue walking."

"Look!" Jackson pointed beyond the shoals of the island to a flock of low-flying pelicans that were skimming the waves through a school of fish. They watched the birds complete their pass and then beat their way back into the sky to repeat the cycle once more.

Elizabeth nodded. "That's great. Let's go."

Jackson grabbed her arm and asked, "Will you sit down for minute?"

"Why? I'm ready to go. Let's walk and talk."

"Please, sit down," Jackson said a bit more forcefully.

Elizabeth gave him a long look then sat down with obvious reluctance. "What's going on?" she asked.

Jackson paused and said in a sober tone, "I don't want to make a big thing out of this, but I feel it's necessary to sit here for a few minutes longer."

"Why?"

Jackson sighed and said, "It may be nothing, but it seems like this big, beefy guy in the brown shirt coming up the stairs has been following us. I noticed him on the ferry."

"So did I. I didn't like the way he was staring at me."

"Let's just sit here," Jackson advised. "And see which way he goes now."

The man was big-shouldered, with skin the color of wet cardboard. There was a bandage across his nose, bruises on his left cheek and chin, and gashes over both eyes. He looked like he'd been in a hell of a fight. His black, kinky hair was cut short and he had a sizable gut, but it was evident that he was still physically quite strong.

"Do you have a reason that someone should be following you?" Elizabeth asked before she turned sideways on the bench so that she too could watch the man.

"Following me? How do you know he's not following you? It's probably someone you prosecuted unfairly."

"I've never prosecuted anyone unfairly. I may have requested unusually high bail every now and then just to keep the court thinking expansively. . . . Hmmm, this guy is big and he's by himself. He really doesn't look like the nature type."

"Well, if he's not, he's a damn poor surveillance professional. He doesn't look like he's in great shape and he's got some great walking shoes," Jackson commented sarcastically. "Those loafers look like some endangered species. He's probably just a mugger who doesn't know how to vacation."

"I'm not worried," Elizabeth said. "It looks like he only mugs people who can fight back."

"I don't want it to get that far. I just want to outthink him."

"As long as the effort doesn't involve your emotions, I'm sure you'll come up with the correct course," she said with a sly smile.

Jackson gave her a quizzical look. "Do you ever stop?"

Elizabeth chuckled and said, "Not with you; you seem to bring out the worst in me." She paused a moment as she held his gaze then said, "What do you think about when you make love?"

Jackson shook his head then asked, "How did sex get included? We've had our little give-and-take over feelings and emotions, but we certainly haven't covered the big S word."

"I'm not talking about sex. That's for animals," Elizabeth corrected. "I'm talking about making love. Making love requires emotions and feelings."

Jackson challenged, "Where does intelligence and lust fit into this?"

"I was hoping you were too old to be looking for something lustful. I was hoping you were more interested in sensual, romantic, interactive lovemaking than just mere sex."

"How do you know I'm not? I haven't heard anything that approximates a voir dire on this subject. And by the way, does your concept of romantic, interactive lovemaking include good, old-fashioned jungle fucking?"

Elizabeth was distracted. She said through gritted teeth, "He's definitely staring at us! And I don't like the way he's looking at me!"

"If I have to confront him, it might as well be now," Jackson said with resignation as he pushed off the bench and got to his feet. "This guy may have a gun. If he pulls one out, I want you—"

"If he pulls it out, I'll blow his nuts off," Elizabeth said, patting her purse.

"You carry a gun?" Jackson asked incredulously.

"I'm an ex-policewoman and now I'm a district attorney with a case-load of violent felonies. Of course I'm carrying a gun. I have a license and I never go anywhere without it. I've been attacked twice. Don't tell me you're one of those anti-handgun nuts?"

"I grew up around guns. I favor registration, but I'm not for banning handguns."

Jackson turned and saw that the man was standing indecisively fifty feet away. He said with a derisive laugh, "This appears to be a problem beyond his ability."

"Why don't I just show him my gun and badge so we can go on?" Elizabeth suggested. "I don't want this fool to ruin our day. I'm enjoying myself."

Still watching the man, Jackson asked, "Why did you quit being a police officer?"

"They claimed I used excessive force, but I still left in good standing."

Keeping the man in his peripheral vision Jackson suggested, "Let's sit tight for a minute or two and let him decide what he's going to do. It may be that he is simply a habitual sex offender who has the good taste to fixate on you."

"Only that, huh? Well, Mr. Tremain, you sure seem to know how to charm a girl."

"Anything for a laugh," Jackson retorted. "Look, he's headed back along the pavement toward the ranger station."

"Let's go in the other direction."

"Why don't we make it hard for this guy?" Jackson suggested. "Why don't we run him a bit?"

"Run him? I run three miles four times a week and I hate it, but I do that for my body. This is a mental health day. I'd rather confront him than run anywhere."

Jackson smiled but he questioned, "Are you serious? Anything might happen."

"Do you know something I don't?" Elizabeth pulled on his shirt as Jackson was pulling on his pack and cinching it tight.

"Well, there's a slight possibility this may have something to do with my grandfather, but they are professionals. This guy is obviously an amateur."

"What have you gotten me into?" Elizabeth asked, standing up next to Jackson.

"I'm not sure that I've gotten you into anything yet. This may be just a random event."

"Tell me why someone might be following you."

"Listen, I promise to answer all your questions, but let's leave this clown in the dust. He's in terrible shape. We'll wear him out in less than a mile."

"I'm not thrilled with the idea of running. We only defer an inevitable confrontation."

"If this guy works for my grandfather's enemies, he is not too bright and he won't know shit. If, on the other hand, he's just a fool looking for trouble, we avoid all that by leaving his lard-ass behind."

"Okay, but do you promise to tell me everything about your grandfather?"

"As much as I know," Jackson agreed.

"Let's go."

Jackson and Elizabeth set out at an easy pace, jogging in unison, occasionally looking back over their shoulders for the man. He appeared after they had gone about a quarter of a mile. When he saw that they were running away, he followed, lurching back and forth in a heavy trotting gait. After a mile they came to the steep descent to the west garrison. Jackson directed Elizabeth to the path which followed the slope down under a large stand of eucalyptus. Neither of them was winded when they reached the path.

"Be careful," Jackson cautioned. "The ground is hard and it's covered with all these little eucalyptus seeds, which makes the footing a little tricky." He went down the path, sliding on masses of the seeds. Elizabeth followed and slid into his arms at the bottom of the hill. Jackson caught her easily and guided her to solid ground. Holding her hand, he led her across an open meadow then behind a row of vacant, boarded-up old houses, where they waited for the man to appear on the far side of the meadow.

When Jesse got to the path under the eucalyptus that Jackson and Elizabeth had taken, he was out of breath and panting. There was a pain in his side which lanced across his abdomen each time he took a deep breath. He couldn't remember the last time he had run so far. This was not turning out the way he planned. He was told to follow the john and his girlfriend and take pictures of anyone they met, but they must have identified him after the ferry. When they started running, he knew he was in trouble. He hated this stupid assignment. It was impossible to follow someone in a park without being seen.

Jesse's legs were still trembling when he started down the hill. He stepped on what he thought was solid earth, but it turned out to be a patch of dried grass and eucalyptus seeds. His leg shot out from underneath him and he fell heavily to the ground and rolled to the bottom of the hill. He lay supine for several minutes before he attempted to move. He got to his feet slowly, wincing from a searing pain. His right hip had taken the brunt of his fall and now it was painful to stand. He dusted himself off, but it was a lost cause. His clothes were ruined.

He looked around quickly to see if anyone had witnessed his humiliation. Fortunately, there appeared to be no one in the immediate vicinity. He was intensely ashamed, but anger soon displaced his feelings of embarrassment. When he walked out from underneath the eucalyptus into the meadow, he discovered that his hip hurt so badly that he could not walk without an obvious limp.

Looking through the shrubbery of Texas privets beside a vacant house, Jackson said, "I feel better. He's walking like he's got a stick up his ass. Now we can go and finish our talk. I don't think he'll be able to keep up with us or find us."

"Are dates with you always like this?"

"Only when the woman carries a gun," Jackson said as he led the way through bushes behind the row of houses to a narrow dirt path which climbed steadily up a heavily wooded hill.

"That's very funny," Elizabeth said lightly. "At this point I am trying to figure out why I am unfazed by the fact you have some clown following you."

"How do we know he's not following you?"

"I prosecute serious, violent felons. They don't follow me to state parks while I'm with a man, they attack me at night when I'm alone on the streets of Oakland. They don't act like fools; they're scary. This guy is a buffoon and I'm certain I've never seen him before."

Jackson scrambled up a particularly steep section of the path and then turned and offered his hand to her.

"Step back and give me room," she advised him as she climbed up on her own.

The path leveled at the top of the hill and ended at the base of two large cement structures which had an unobstructed view of the Golden Gate. To the left of the bridge, in the distance, the multicolored haziness of San Francisco's buildings rose above the blue of the bay as if rendered with an impressionist's brush. There was a steady breeze flowing through the mouth of the Gate, blowing past Angel Island. Bunches of white calla lilies growing at the base of the cement structures danced back and forth on their slender green stalks from the force of the wind.

"Oh, look!" Elizabeth exclaimed, pointing to the lilies. "This is one of my favorite flowers. Look at those perfect ivory flutes filled with those orange stamens. It is both simple and elegant."

Jackson nodded in acknowledgment. "They are pretty. It's time to climb." He began to climb the outside of one of the structures. The top of the structure was only fifteen feet above the ground and it was an easy climb, with both handholds and footholds all along its side. Elizabeth followed without difficulty.

"I had no idea that you were going to turn this date into an athletic event," she said, following him down into a deep, circular depression in the top of the structure. "What is this thing we're on?"

"It's one of the gun emplacements that was used to guard the entrance to the bay in World War Two."

"What are we doing here?" Elizabeth demanded.

"This is where I propose we talk. Come on and sit down out of the wind in the cavity left by the turret. I brought a picnic blanket and something to nosh on. Are you hungry?" Jackson asked, opening his backpack and pulling out the blanket.

Elizabeth helped spread the blanket then said, "Food sounds good, but what about our friend?"

Jackson knelt down on the blanket and gestured for her to join him. "I don't think he'll find us. Unless he knows to look up here, and I doubt that." He took out two baguettes he had cut to fit into his pack, as well as a large slice of Brie, a slab of pâté, apples, a bunch of green grapes, a bottle of wine, and a half-gallon container of water.

Elizabeth rearranged everything that Jackson set out and when he gave her a questioning look she said, "See how well we work together?"

"As long as I don't argue with your decisions," Jackson surmised.

"You learn fast," Elizabeth said as she picked up and examined the wine bottle. The label had come off. "What kind of wine is this?"

"Sonoma Chardonnay," Jackson answered. "By the way, what was up with your friend last night? She really seemed to have a wild hair up her ass. Is she always like that?"

"A wild hair? I thought I explained that over the phone."

"All you said was that she was emotionally unstrung," Jackson replied as he took out a corkscrew and opened the wine.

"I guess you'd have a wild hair or two if you discovered that the person you'd been sleeping with for two years had been sleeping around the whole time."

Jackson conceded with a nod of his head, "Maybe I would." He handed her a napkin and a knife and gave her a long look.

Elizabeth returned his look then asked, "Have you brought other women here?"

"You're full of questions."

Elizabeth threw a grape and it hit him on the chest. "So answer."

"Nobody worth anything."

"That's romantic."

"It wasn't meant to be; it was just meant to be true."

"I love it when you get basic," Elizabeth said as she put a branch of grapes in front of him. She looked up at him and asked with a mischievous smile, "So, am I worth something?"

"I'm trying to find out, but all I've been doing is answering questions."

"Okay, here's your chance. Fire away. What do you want to know?"

Jackson thought a minute and asked, "Are you from the Bay Area?"

"No, from Chicago."

"What caused you to move out here?"

"I moved out here to join the police force after my father died. My uncle Elroy told me that several Bay Area police departments were looking for qualified women."

"Oh, you have family here?"

"Not really. Uncle Elroy was a friend of my father's when I was a child. My father was a police officer in the early fifties in Chicago, and Uncle Elroy was an officer with the San Francisco PD, and they met at a conference for black military police and became close friends. Our families would spend vacations together."

Jackson shrugged and said, "Couldn't have been too many blacks working for local police departments in the fifties. Let's eat."

"Your questions were rather pedestrian," Elizabeth observed with a teasing smile. "But did you determine if I'm worth something?"

"You are relentless!"

Elizabeth hiked up a shoulder to emphasize that she was still waiting for an answer.

Jackson threw up his hands and conceded, "All right. All I know is that I feel something with you that I haven't felt in years."

"Are we back on the unfamiliar ground of your emotions?" She raised an eyebrow. "Or just in the dark generally?"

"If you want to be snide—"

"I'm sorry. I forgot you were sensitive."

Jackson gave her a long, steady look. "I don't have to be sensitive; there are other options."

Elizabeth raised her hand in surrender. "I don't like the sound of that. I like it when you're sensitive, okay? Can we change the subject and talk about your grandfather? Do you have wineglasses?"

"In the left side of the pack. What do you want to know?"

"Why would someone be following you?" Elizabeth asked as she removed the glasses.

"I really don't know," Jackson said as he poured the wine. "All I really know is that my grandfather has enemies and that he has amassed a substantial financial empire. I have had nothing to do with him since I was eighteen."

"Why?"

"That's a long story, deserving a whole evening."

"On the phone you said you were going to Mexico to see him. Why are you doing that, if you've had nothing to do with him since you were eighteen?"

Jackson paused before answering, "He asked me to come."

"What kind of business was he in?"

"He was a gangster. He dealt in everything except drugs and he didn't mind sending his enemies into the void."

"Sounds like he was a real community-spirited guy. What's his name? I must have heard of him. I've been a police officer and a DA in Oakland for nearly thirteen years."

"I doubt that you'd know him. His heyday was in the forties and fifties. He went to Mexico in 1954."

"Why would he still have enemies nearly thirty years later?"

"I don't know, but I do know that he carried on a war for over ten years after he went to Mexico and he produced more than his share of corpses."

"Why do you think he's sent for you?"

"I'm his heir. He spent ten years training me, now he's calling in his chips. He wants me to carry on where he left off."

"Is that what you want?"

"Be serious! I don't want any part of his life, including his money. Everything he owns was purchased with blood."

Jackson's words were spoken with an unusual intensity. They revealed a jagged edge in an otherwise smooth exterior. Elizabeth didn't know what to say. They ate in silence for several minutes before Jackson began to speak again. "If I thought someone was following me, I would have never involved you. This is new to me as well, that is, if this guy really is following me and not you!"

Elizabeth reached across and lightly picked some crumbs off his shirt. "When I was a cop, I was addicted to the adrenaline rush of the job. Today, I got a twinge of the old feeling. I liked it. In the past, it's caused me to have relationships with men with whom I have had little else in common. All of that led to disappointment. But with you, I think I'm on the right track. I just hope you won't try to find a thug to follow us on all our dates."

"Listen, the guy who is following us may be a buffoon, but he's the only one. These people are serious and dangerous. We're talking about organized crime."

Elizabeth stopped sipping her wine and her expression turned serious. "Are you going to stand up to them?"

Jackson shrugged. "It may not be that simple."

"I know it won't be simple, but I want to know whether you're planning to resist the intentions of the men who sent the buffoon or are you going to fold?"

"That's tough talk, but I'm not sure that it applies to this situation. I don't want to continue my grandfather's war. I don't want to risk my life for an inheritance built upon blood. What is there for me to stand up for?"

Elizabeth set down her wineglass. She looked Jackson directly in the eye and asked, "Will you stand up to *them?*"

Jackson gave her a questioning look and asked, "Why is this one particular component of this much larger, complex problem so important to you?"

"Because there is a possibility that you will be important to me and I want to know how you'll react. My father was killed by organized crime. Part of the reason I joined the police was to follow in my father's footsteps. Another reason was to take as many of these people off the streets as possible."

Jackson put down his bread and paused a moment to gather his thoughts. "I don't have such a clear sense of right and wrong, or even whether I wish to take a side. You see, my grandfather would have been one of those you would have wanted taken off the streets, and his enemies aren't necessarily good people either."

"If you decide to stand up to them, I may want to help you. If we work together, we may be able to incarcerate all of them."

"That's a little premature at this point. But I'll tell you one thing: If I stand up to these people, I may have to kill some of them. Are you ready to help with that?"

Friday, June 25, 1982

Julius Castle Restaurant sat high on the precipice of a hill above San Francisco's Embarcadero. It catered to a select clientele that was prepared to pay top dollar for exquisitely prepared dishes, top-notch service, and a beautiful view of the bay. Julius Castle was popular during the lunch hour. The main dining room was usually full, but there were various alcoves which could be reserved if the customer was known to tip well.

This was where Braxton had chosen to meet Franklin and he was pleased with his decision. The alcove he had chosen had only one table and a large picture window which looked northeast, past Richmond and Mare Island, toward the mouth of the Sacramento River. The Bay Bridge and Treasure Island framed the right side of the view, and a rich, dark purple curtain, which fell in ripples from a valance of the same color, framed the other side. Only people passing by the door could see who occupied the alcove. It was public enough, yet it afforded privacy. A waiter appeared noiselessly and after a quick review of the wine list, Braxton ordered a bottle of champagne. He settled back to wait for his guest.

From the moment Franklin entered Julius Castle, he was impressed. From the thick, padded carpets and the quiet clink of glassware to the large pictures hung in ornate frames, the restaurant emanated an ambience of money and opulence, the two things of which he was always in pursuit. The waiter led him to the alcove in which Braxton was waiting.

Braxton waved him expansively to a chair. "Glad you could make it."

"If it's business, I'm there. If it's in the ballpark, I want to play," Franklin answered as he sat down.

"What if it's out of the ballpark, do you still want to go on?"

Franklin stared at Braxton before answering, trying to determine exactly what Braxton was referring to, or whether he was just making conversation. Franklin didn't like trick questions and his tone indicated that when he said, "I don't join losing sides and I don't play losing hands."

Braxton smiled at Franklin's cocky indignation. Franklin reminded him of a bantam rooster who owned the barnyard at sunrise but, when the dogs came out, was quiet and still. "Have a glass of champagne," Braxton suggested, offering to pour some into Franklin's glass. "Sometimes," he continued with a philosophical tone, "you have to play the hand you're dealt, even if it has no face cards." He filled Franklin's glass and set the bottle back in the bucket.

"Maybe it's a question of tactics," Franklin countered. "Maybe it's a question of bidding four low, like in whist." Franklin felt he was participating in some sort of competition that he had to keep up at all costs.

"There's a limit to the number of four low bids you can make over the span of a lifetime."

"I don't know about that," Franklin answered, searching for a counterargument. He took a drink of his champagne and then continued, "I've had some pretty good runs myself and I've been lucky so far."

Braxton spoke without enthusiasm, "Then let's toast to your good fortune, and may it continue."

Franklin stopped with his glass midway to his mouth. He hesitated briefly, trying to determine if there was any innuendo in Braxton's words. He took a long sip of champagne and set his glass down gently. He looked at Braxton and asked, "What are you talking about?"

"I was merely toasting to your luck." Braxton raised his glass. "It doesn't last forever; that's why they call it luck."

"Then that applies to you too!" Franklin retorted with irritation. As far as he was concerned, the conversation had taken on a threatening tone.

"Yes," Braxton replied. "But a wise man always seeks to supplement his luck by making wise decisions. I have supplemented my luck many times over. I'm prepared for most eventualities."

"What are we meeting about, Braxton? I mean, really?"

"We're talking about you getting control of King, Inc."

"And suppose I don't go along with the way you want to make this happen?"

The waiter appeared and asked for their lunch orders. Franklin ordered the most expensive item on the menu just to spite Braxton. He didn't like the tenor of the conversation and he didn't like Braxton. Franklin waited for an answer to his question.

Braxton poured more champagne for both of them. When he set the bottle down, he said, "That depends on whether you make yourself an obstacle or not."

"What do you mean, 'an obstacle'?"

"That's really quite a good question. An obstacle would be anyone who thwarts or hinders the people that I represent from getting their just due."

"After thirty years, it's kind of hard figuring out exactly what is their just due."

"You don't need to worry about that. You'll have the controlling interest of King, Inc. That's more than you could have expected, if we weren't involved. Isn't that true?"

"Just how are you going to get my cousin to give up his claim?"

"That won't be any concern of yours, as long as you have King, Inc."

"It's a concern of mine, especially if I'm going to be on the likely-suspects list." Franklin rubbed his thin mustache. "You know, if anything happens to him."

"In the unlikely event that something should happen to your cousin, I assure you that it will be of an accidental nature and as a result, there will be no suspects."

Braxton said the words so calmly that it chilled Franklin to his core. If it was going to be so easy for them to remove Jackson from the scene, why wouldn't they come after him as well? Franklin drained his glass and the waiter refilled it. He suddenly realized that he was over his head. He was totally unprepared to negotiate with people who were prepared to kill to get what they wanted. "What guarantees do you offer?" he asked quietly, continuing to rub his mustache meditatively with the tips of his fingers. "How do I know that I won't be next after Jackson?"

Braxton smiled broadly; it was obvious Franklin was frightened and the heart had gone out of him. "Mr. Tremain, do you think that we are barbarians? That we force our will on innocent people? I only mention the remote possibility of your cousin having an accident should he desire to prevent the acquisition by the rightful owners."

"I still don't know what makes your people the rightful owners," Franklin said querulously. He was beginning to feel the effects of no breakfast and two large glasses of champagne. "Why didn't they collect earlier when my grandfather was still walking the streets?" Franklin drank down the rest of his champagne. He was afraid, but he felt compelled to say something. "I guess they were scared of him?" Franklin glared at Braxton and said nastily, "I bet you were too, huh? I bet you would never have climbed out from under your rock if the old man was still walking around."

Braxton contained himself and kept his smile as he said, "Your grandfather has many enemies who are still living and in good health; you should be careful that you don't get too closely associated with him. You might become the object of their attention." Franklin's eyes widened in response, but he said nothing.

The food arrived steaming on heavy silver trays. Braxton ate with gusto and kept up a conversational banter that centered on the respective failure and success of the Giants and 49ers. Franklin ate mechanically, barely tasting the stuffed lobster. He kept up his end of the conversation with monosyllabic answers and grunts. When lunch was finished, Franklin mumbled his good-bye and walked away hurriedly, leaving Braxton still sipping his champagne.

The meeting was a success for Braxton. He had determined beyond a reasonable doubt that Franklin posed no threat and that he could be immobilized by either his greed or his fear. As long as ownership of King, Inc., was waved in front of him, he would probably behave. Of course, the threat of the mailed fist must be consistently and clearly implied to extinguish any potential sparks of disobedience. Another benefit derived from the meeting was that Braxton now had the necessary link within the Tremain family that he would need in order to facilitate his assumption of control over King's financial assets. Although the money meant little to him, he had decided that he would have his fair share of it despite the threat posed by the DuMonts and DiMarco. All he needed was a bit more information.

There remained questions concerning the other grandson. Was he like his cousin? Was he a calculating coward, or did he have fire burning in his belly? Was he truly King's heir, or would someone else crawl out of the woodwork? The next few weeks would reveal all. The truth was that Braxton did not really expect effective resistance from Jackson; it was only his sense of caution that caused him not to be, well, positively confident. The likelihood was that he wouldn't present much more of a challenge than Franklin.

Braxton smiled and lit a cigar. All he had to do was wait for King to die. If he couldn't find the certificates, he would persuade his relatives to snatch the two grandsons. They would conduct their ghoulish form of questioning and find out exactly where the certificates were hidden. Then, if things went according to plan, DiMarco would be eliminated along with Tree. After obtaining the necessary signatures to transfer ownership of the certificates, both Jackson and Franklin along with other family members would follow King into the grave. Braxton knew his own relatives would be sloppy and leave a lot of clues, while his fingerprints would be on nothing. A few discreet, well-placed leaks to the authorities would remove them from the scene or at least get them on the run. He would put a huge contract out on their heads, which eventually would leave him in control of everything. Then and only then would Braxton have his vengeance. He would have wiped out King's descendants, assumed control over his empire, and rid himself of the yoke of the DuMonts. He tapped the ashes off his cigar and drew in a breath of the sweet, acrid-tasting smoke and then exhaled slowly. He sipped his champagne and thought, Life is really going to be wonderful.

July 1956

I n the hot afternoon sun a yellow, mange-ridden dog walked slowly across the empty square and found a cool resting place in the shadows of a two-story stucco building. Across the square, a stout, black-haired woman with reddish-brown skin opened the rickety shutters of her second-story apartment and screamed, *"Miguel! Miguel, venga aquí!"*

Miguel did not answer, and except for the irritating drone of the flies, all was quiet. The doors and shuttered windows of the businesses and apartments that faced the square were closed. There were no people on the street. The old yellow dog was the square's sole occupant.

On the roof of the building adjacent to the woman's apartment, ten-year-old Jackson sat. His brown skin was covered and protected from the blazing sun by a heavy woven serape. A straw sombrero covered his kinky hair. He sat very still in accordance with the instructions he had received. His duty was to signal the coming of the strangers. In an alley off to his right stood four men waiting for his signal. He did not turn, nor acknowledge their presence. He had been taught to wait in absolute stillness. The scolds and slaps of previous summers had developed his control to perfection. He did not even move to wipe away the sweat which was running into his eyes.

From the corner, down the street to his left, he heard voices: raucous, drunken male voices, laughing and carousing. Three men appeared. As they drew nearer, it was obvious to Jackson from their accents that they were American.

The woman came to the window again. This time there was panic in her eyes. She looked up at Jackson, but he did nothing to acknowledge her presence. She peered down the street at the approaching men and many expressions crossed her face, the first of which was painful resignation, as if she realized that it was too late to call again, but the last and most enduring expression was hatred. It was the mask she wore when she closed her shutters on the passing men.

When the men were abreast of him, Jackson stood up. He took off his sombrero and waved it at the men, saying, *"Hola, señores!"*

The men, caught off guard, looked up at him simultaneously, their pale faces reddened by the sun. One of the men shaded his glance with a hand. To Jackson it looked like a sloppy military salute. The man and his companions never had an opportunity for another reaction. They

did not even see the men rushing from the alley until the first was in
their midst. A savage fight broke out. It was three against four, and the
four had machetes in scabbards which they wielded like clubs. The
fight was over in minutes. The three men were subdued then their arms
were tied tightly behind their backs. Once again the square was silent.
No one had opened a door or come to the aid of the men.

Jackson left the roof to join the attackers. When he got to the street,
the three men were being led down an alley away from the square by
their attackers. As he started to follow the group, his grandfather, still
carrying his machete, turned and cut him off.

"Where do you think you're going?"

"I was going with you, Grandfather," Jackson responded with surprise.

"You's too young for this part! You done what I wanted, now git!"

"Can't I wait for you, Grandfather?"

"Boy, didn't you hear me say *git*?"

"Yes, Grandfather," Jackson answered obediently.

His grandfather turned away without another word and walked rapidly down the alley to join his comrades.

Jackson stood watching the thick, muscular torso of his grandfather
dwindle in the distance. When the men were out of sight, he was left
standing in the square alone. He knew better than to disobey his grandfather, but he had no place that he wanted to go. He stood until the sun
forced him to move. By the time he crossed the square, the small stores
and shops began opening their doors. The owners nodded at him respectfully as he passed and continued his way along the sun-baked cobblestone streets.

He did not concern himself with the fate of the three *norteamericanos*.
All he knew was that the Chavez family had been avenged and that
these three men would never rape anyone else's teenage daughter.

Friday, June 25, 1982

A steady breeze came off the Alameda estuary, blowing leaves and scraps of paper eastward, the detritus of anonymous lives. The charcoal sky was filled with large, dark cumulus clouds that rolled before the wind like huge dumplings boiling in a pale gray fluid. The surface of Lake Merritt was covered with ripples, moving in ranks like liquid soldiers, marching west to east to die upon the banks of Lakeside Park. Elizabeth Carlson was not concentrating on the weather. She was focusing on getting a full breath and coordinating the movements of her arms with her legs. She was in the last quarter of a mile of her three-mile run around the lake. She was turning the corner onto Lakeshore Drive and she had been gradually increasing her pace as she neared the end of her run. She kept her knees high and lengthened her stride. Her heart was pumping. Her chest was heaving. Her arms were swinging back and forth. Sweat ran down her face. She was running nearly at full speed and was now concentrating solely on her footing and her breathing. Her running companion and friend, Diane Holloway, was just behind her. It had been Elizabeth's intent to leave Diane behind, but Diane would not accommodate her. She could hear Diane's footsteps right behind her. A pain was beginning in Elizabeth's chest. Her breathing was getting labored. Still she kept up the pressure. She squeezed out a little extra speed. She began to pull away from Diane. All she had to do was to run to the stop signal at the intersection of Brooklyn and Lakeshore. She forced herself, despite the pain, to run the remaining distance at top speed.

She was leaning against a lamppost when Diane caught up to her, waving her finger at Elizabeth and mouthing words she was unable to say because she was out of breath. Elizabeth wanted to laugh, but she was too busy concentrating on catching her own breath. She bent over and rested her hands on her knees. After a few moments of deep breathing, Elizabeth had recuperated. She leaned down slowly and touched her toes with her knuckles, stretching her back and hamstrings. She stood up and said to Diane, "I see your new manless regime hasn't made you any faster."

"Maybe not, but I'm a lot healthier," Diane replied as she checked her makeup in a small mirror which she had taken out of her fanny pack. After making what small corrections she could, she snapped the mirror shut and looked up. "Hey, let's catch this light!" Both women scurried across Lakeshore before the light turned red and walked up half a block to Diane's apartment building, which had a broad lakefront view. As they rode the elevator up to her third-floor apartment Diane asked, "Did you finish submitting all that paperwork for the apartment upstairs?"

"Yes. That's what I meant to tell you over the phone. I've got it. The manager called me this morning."

Diane rushed to hug her. "That's great! Now I'll have me a running buddy as a neighbor. Since neither of us has the burden of men in our lives, we can get together for drinks and dinner on a regular basis now."

"I don't know about that," Elizabeth demurred as they entered Diane's apartment. "I met somebody. A real man."

"Are you talking about that slick pretty boy who tried to force his attentions on us in the bar the other night? Damn! Can't you learn from my mistakes? He's probably nothing more than facade anyway!" Diane was stripping off her Spandex jogging suit. She stopped and faced Elizabeth and declared, "They are all sleazes! Why do you think black American women writers never have strong, positive black male characters in their work? There aren't any, that's why!"

Elizabeth sat down and untied her shoes then replied, "I don't know that that's true. I haven't read every black woman writer—"

"I'm talking about the major ones! Naylor, Morrison, McMillan, Walker," Diane interrupted as she stepped out of her panties. "Can you point to just one positive male character?"

"I don't consider myself to be well read enough to give a knowledgeable answer to that question."

"Think about it while I'm in the shower," Diane said, picking up her workout clothes and heading into the bathroom.

Elizabeth went over to the stereo, turned the radio on, and tuned the station to KJAZ. The sounds of a quintet with a mellow lead alto saxophone floated out of the speakers. She walked over to the living room windows, which looked out upon the lake, and studied the view. She wondered if there wasn't a grain of truth in Diane's words. Perhaps Jackson wasn't what he appeared to be, but the possibility that he was real was too great an opportunity for her to pass up. Certainly there was something between them. She had never felt such an attraction to anyone before. She had even noticed it when they first met at Wayman's graduation ceremony. At first she had sought to discount her feelings as simply the response of a woman who had not been intimate with a man for over a year, but there was more to it than that and she knew it. This was a totally new feeling, a sensation of excitement.

Strange as it was, she was not distressed by the man who had followed them the day before on Angel Island, nor was she put off by Jackson's explanation of his grandfather's world. What she remembered most was the ease with which she bantered with him, how there seemed to be no obstacles in saying what was on her mind, how comfortable she had felt in his presence and the wonderful anticipation that she felt when they were parting at the end of the day. When he had walked her to her door there was an undeniable tension between them as she waited for him to decide whether he was going to kiss her. He had not kissed her and she, although she was reluctant to admit it at the time, was disappointed. She thought of his last words before he turned and went back to his car. He had stepped close to her and looked directly into her eyes and said, "It seems to me that this is no ordinary first date. I feel something for you, Miss Carlson, that I have no right to feel. It compels me to want to see you again. Is there a possibility you feel the same way?"

Despite her better judgment, she had grabbed the lapel of his jacket and pulled him closer until his dark brown eyes were inches from hers, then replied, "Anything is possible. Why don't you call me and we'll see?" He had smiled, his even white teeth gleaming in the afternoon light, then he touched her cheek softly with his hand before turning away and walking down the steps to his car. She had followed him with her eyes, the skin of her face still tingling from his caress. She had known right then that he was the one who was meant for her.

Diane entered the living room wearing a robe. "The shower's yours," she said as she got a large bottle of juice out of the refrigerator. "I put out towels on the toilet seat."

When she got out of the shower, Elizabeth went into Diane's bedroom and found her friend half dressed in front of a floor-to-ceiling mirror, checking out the fit of her skirt over her behind. She said, "That looks great on you, Diane. What are you doing?"

"I just want to make sure it still falls like it's supposed to," Diane answered as she turned in front of the mirror. "I want to make sure that the thousand leg lifts I do monthly are keeping me in trim."

"No fear," Elizabeth said as she began to get dressed. "You've got the body of a twenty-five-year-old!"

Diane frowned. "I look that bad?"

"That's good!" Elizabeth countered. "To have the body of someone who's a decade or more younger."

"Honey, as hard as I work to keep in shape, I want the body of a teenager! Did you think about my question? Could you come up with a positive, strong black male character in any novel you've read? I mean, one who's alive at the end!"

"Truthfully, I didn't give it much thought."

"You ought to. There's a lesson there. As far as I'm concerned there's only two reasons to have a man in your life: one, the dick is so good you want to give up TV; or two, he can give you expensive gifts and do something for you financially."

"That's very cynical," Elizabeth observed with a laugh. "What about love?"

"Love is just a concept that some men thought up to mess with women's heads."

Elizabeth declared, "I don't believe that. I know my mother loved my father and I know that he loved her. He was a good man and although I didn't get along with him, I loved him. I'm seeking what they had. I know it's still possible."

Diane finished off her glass of juice then said, "Damn, girl, orient yourself to the times. This is 1982! Women have been liberated. Your parents lived at a time when people stayed married because they had to. They had to put up with shit and work out their differences. People today can get to stepping!"

"But where does that leave you?" Elizabeth countered. "Particularly when you know that everything of value takes work. And to have something of value, you must risk."

"Okay. Okay. I can see that something serious has bit you in the ass. What makes this guy you've only seen twice so damned important? You haven't even spent an hour together!"

"Oh, yes, we have," Elizabeth declared as she put on her jacket. "I went to Angel Island yesterday with him and it was wonderful. It was the best time I've ever had with a man."

"So that's why you took off from work! Well, you better tell me about him, since I may see him once or twice before you scuttle him."

"Don't bet on it! It was like something out of a fantasy. I'll tell you about it as we ride back to work. I have to be in court at two o'clock. Are you ready?" Diane nodded as she got her purse and turned off the stereo. The two women took the elevator down to the garage and got into Diane's car. As they drove back to the district attorney's office, Elizabeth recounted the events of the previous day.

When Diane pulled into her parking spot she was flabbergasted. "I can't believe you slashed the tires of a stranger's car! You're supposed to uphold the law, not break it!"

"Jackson recognized this brown Cadillac and when the man in it started to follow us, we knew he was the partner of the guy we left on Angel Island. We didn't want him following us. So while Jackson went and got us a couple of ice cream cones I doubled back and slit the guy's tires. It's really not that much different from the time you put sugar in that public defender's gas tank. I think he had to get a new engine after that. All this guy had to do was change a couple of tires."

Diane put a hand on her friend's shoulder and her voice softened when she said, "I've known you since you were a police officer in San Francisco. I was the one who encouraged you to go to law school. I know how much you sacrificed to get your law degree and pass the bar. It took five years of your life. Even though you spent a wonderful day with this man, you really don't know who he is. You don't want to jeopardize your career for what could be a flash in the pan. He could be involved in drugs, organized crime, you don't know!"

"Oh, come on, Diane! That's a leap! He's a deputy city manager!"

"No more a leap than Mayor Broadnax's son. You heard how they found a hundred thousand in cash in the trunk of his car and how he pretended he didn't know where it came from. There's no way he wasn't involved in drug dealing."

"Leo Broadnax is sleazy. There's a great deal of difference between him and Jackson Tremain."

"You say that now, but you don't really know. I didn't know that Carl was seeing white women behind my back and I went out with him for nearly two years."

Elizabeth looked at her watch and discovered it was twenty to two. "I've got to get back to the office and pick up my files before court."

As they got out of the car, Diane persisted, "Don't try to change the subject. You don't know this man." She and Elizabeth began to walk toward the exit of the parking garage.

Elizabeth said, "I love you and I care for you, but you and I don't always share the same perspective on men."

"That may be true. Unlike most women, I admit where I'm coming from. I intend to use men and get what I can. Most intelligent women come to the same conclusion. But let's put that aside. You're worrying me, and as a friend, I want to caution you. Don't get your feelings involved until you've had a chance to see him over time. Anybody with a little cunning can act like something different for a little while. Time reveals everything. Hold up!" Diane stopped before the exit and pulled a mirror from her purse to check that her makeup and hair were properly done.

Two men dressed in suits entered the garage in deep discussion. One man was black, the other was white, and as they passed Elizabeth and Diane, the black man nodded to them. Diane ignored the greeting and stuck her arm in Elizabeth's and kept on walking out the exit.

As they waited at the crosswalk for the signal to change, Diane said, "I heard from Marcie down in municipal court that the man we just passed is hung like a horse, but he uses it like a shovel. He just wants to dig-dig-dig. He knows nothing about giving a woman pleasure. Marcie said she couldn't walk right for a week after bedding him."

The signal turned to green. Elizabeth asked, "Who are we talking about?"

"That Negro who just walked by! You know Marcie wouldn't be giving a white boy none. You know, if we could open a school that taught men how to be romantic and how to give pleasure to women, we could be millionaires within the year. Damn, if they could just learn to be romantic!"

"Sometimes, Diane, I think you actually hate men."

"Girl, the only reason I don't become a lesbian is that I don't want to feel about women the way I feel about men. Plus, I'd have to have a partner who'd strap on one of those big plastic dildos. Because licking just don't get it."

"Diane, you really are crazy!" Elizabeth said with a laugh and soon both women were laughing. Once they were inside the courthouse, Diane saw a superior court clerk she needed to speak with. Elizabeth went on alone to her office to collect her files. When she opened the door, she saw on her desk a vase filled with calla lilies. Beside the vase was a brown bag containing a pastrami sandwich and a card. Elizabeth opened the card and read:

Ms. Carlson,

You said that today was going to be hectic and that you wouldn't have time to pick up lunch. I bring these gifts as a small token of the pleasure and the delight that I experienced with you yesterday. I hope they evoke my image in your thoughts as your image lives in mine. I want to say more, but my thoughts are unruly; they stray from the task and center on you.

I look forward to seeing you again. I will wait a suitable period and then call you.

> *With all my good thoughts,*
> *Jackson Tremain*

"Oh, this man is truly slick," Diane said as she stepped into the room. "He sent you flowers, did he? Is that his card?"

Elizabeth nodded and handed her the card. She was a bit breathless. With this small act, Jackson had done something that resonated within her. It filled her with anticipation of their next meeting.

"Hmm! I wonder how many times he's written these words?" Diane asked sarcastically. "I think you're going to need my help to keep this one at bay."

Elizabeth frowned. She went over and took the card out of her friend's hands and said, "I love you, but I don't need any help. I'll see you later." She ushered Diane to the door.

"Damn, this is serious!" Diane declared as she went reluctantly through the door. "Girl, this is deep water. You have to remember that the current goes straight out to sea. No land in sight!"

Elizabeth pushed her friend out the door and closed it. She held the card to her chest a moment as she leaned against the door. A strange excitement suffused her. Her cheek tingled where Jackson had touched her. She went over to the desk and took a big bite out of the sandwich. Diane was right about being cautious. Still, Elizabeth had to take Diane's advice with a grain of salt. Diane had no idea how to establish a constructive relationship with a man, nor did she have room in her life for one who was any more than a sugar daddy or a sex object.

Elizabeth finished her sandwich, picked up her files, and headed out of her office to the courtroom. She discovered she couldn't keep the smile off her face.

Friday, June 25, 1982

The phone rang four times before Jackson picked up the receiver. "Good morning, city manager's office."

"May I speak to Mr. Tremain?" It was a male voice with a slight Mexican accent.

"Speaking," Jackson answered.

"Diablito? That you?"

"It's me, Cisco."

"Can you talk?

"Sure, what's up?"

"We've made arrangements for you to leave tonight. Are you ready?"

"Not really, but if that's when you arranged it, I'll do it. I've scheduled the time off."

There was a pause then Reuben said in a quiet voice, "Nobody knows for sure if your grandfather will make it beyond the weekend. We've got your travel plans scheduled to the last detail. Nobody will be able to follow you."

"Hey, there's already somebody following me. Do you know who it is?"

"I don't know. Maybe your grandfather knows. If not, others will know."

"Before I go I have to have a number where I can receive faxes down there because I have some work due Monday morning. My assistant is coming in tomorrow morning and Sunday morning to finish the reports. I need to see finished copies before they go to the subcommittee."

"Your people work on Sunday?"

"What can I tell you, one of the reports is on which solid waste management company should get the contract with the city."

"Garbage is always political," Reuben said knowingly.

The conversation was over as soon as Jackson got the number from Reuben. Jackson felt a strange anxiety. He felt the vortex of his grandfather's world slowly pulling him down into its spinning center.

Friday, June 25, 1982

"Serena, what a surprise to hear your voice. I haven't spoken with you in years and yet I still remember your wonderful elocution."

"Let's not waste each other's time with useless flattery, Bill. My grandson, Franklin, came over here right after his lunch with you."

"Oh, and what did the young man have to say for himself?"

"He said that you threatened him."

"That just goes to show how perspectives may differ," Braxton said easily. "I don't recall that at all. I remember discussing options that involved his having total control of King, Inc."

"Just how would you propose to do that when you have no legal financial investment in this company? I hope you don't think that you have everyone in this family intimidated." Serena's words were clipped and pointed like pieces of tin cut by heavy shears.

"I'm a negotiator." Braxton was all oil and Vaseline. "I discuss alternatives. I'd be happy to meet with you and talk over the options I discussed with Franklin, but I don't think that's necessary. I think that you already know the bottom line. Everyone knows that King is dying. He can no longer strike fear into people's hearts. All debts are now due."

"And what if we don't cooperate with the payment of these alleged debts?"

"Life is so unpredictable. Did you realize that the insurance industry's actuarial reports indicate that black people are far more prone to have accidents and be victims of violent crimes than whites? These statistics were collected for both men and women."

There were a few seconds of silence before Serena asked quietly, "That's your answer?"

"That's my answer."

"Given the statistics, how could anyone be assured that cooperation would result in a longer life?"

"Well, I don't think that anyone can forestall the action of natural causes, but I think that we can rule out certain types of accidents and perhaps limit the potentiality of being victims of certain violent crimes."

"So, you can point the finger at people and cause their demise?"

"Serena, Serena, you attribute to me too much power. I am a negotiator who'd be happy to present any proposal you have to the right people."

"I had assumed that you contacted my grandson because you were seeking some specific help. I didn't know that I was to come up with something."

"I see; of course that makes sense." Braxton coughed lightly and said, "The subject matter is rather sensitive and warrants a face-to-face meeting, don't you think?"

"No." Serena's voice was cold. "If there are any options that are acceptable to me, they must be found during this conversation." She would not further soil herself by meeting with him in person.

"Let's get directly to business, then."

"Let's," Serena agreed in a sarcastic tone.

"Well, Serena, your other grandson seems to be headed to Mexico. It would be extremely helpful to know exactly where he was going and how he could be reached."

Serena knew they were hunting for King and that they would kill both King and Jackson if they could find them. Then they would force Franklin to accept whatever crumbs they decided to throw him.

"What guarantees can you give me if I give you the information you want? It all rests upon guarantees."

"Well, if your assistance helps to achieve their ultimate goal, I think that Franklin can look forward to being head of King, Inc."

"For how long?"

"For as long as he lives."

There was no reason for further discussion. Serena realized that Braxton had spoken the most honest words of the whole conversation. The real issue was how long Franklin would live. "Why don't you let me get back to you. I may be able to get the information you want."

"I'm always happy to hear from you, Serena. Call me anytime. We can talk about old times."

Serena hung up the phone and poured herself another cup of tea. There had been a time when she could have counted upon Braxton's affections to sway him, but those times were long gone. He had once been deeply in love with her. She knew that he would've given up all his worldly possessions to have her love in return, yet she did not commit to him. She could not. She was married to King Tremain. She had given Braxton his chance after LaValle's bullet-ridden body had been brought to her. Braxton was working with the police at the time to set up a trap for King. She had taken one of King's guns and had given it to Braxton to plant at a crime scene. The trap had failed and King had escaped to Mexico. Since Serena could never remarry as long as King was alive, Braxton was doomed to the sad monotony of settling for another. The marching years had fermented and soured the sweetness of his love until it was like a wine that had turned to vinegar. Now, he was fronting for King's enemies and impervious to her machinations.

Her thoughts drifted to King Tremain and anger filled her. She muttered grimly in a barely audible tone, "You bastard! You're dying and you're going to drag the whole family with you!" Yet as she sat in her chair and pondered the matter, she came to a totally different line of thought. King would have considered the eventuality of revenge upon his family. He knew very well that some of his enemies were prepared to wait until his death before they exacted their due. King would have left some mechanism to protect his family. Of course, King's concept of family probably didn't extend to include either her or LaValle's children, but he would definitely protect Jackson. He might even have a team of men assigned to him. Thus her problem boiled down to the method she would use to get Jackson concerned with saving the rest of the family.

A lone tear dripped down Serena's face. She had achieved a measure of wealth and comfort. She was surrounded by valuable things that she had purchased, but other than a small clay ashtray made by one of her grandchildren, there was not one object given to her out of love. In all the brocaded, embroidered, bejeweled, carved, chiseled, hammered, woven, upholstered, painted, smelted, and baked things that accounted for her riches, not one had any real sentimental value. She felt as if she could walk out the door of the house in which she had lived twenty years with only her coat and miss only the habit of living there. It was with true sadness that Serena understood it was her actions more than fifty years earlier that had set in motion the forces to tear her family asunder.

Yet neither the knowledge nor the weight of her misdeeds caused her to hesitate at bargaining away Jackson's life. There was no question in her mind as to whom she would try to protect: It was Franklin. Like his father before him, he was the child that had come running to find safety and solace in her skirts. He sought her protection while his cousin stood off at a distance, watching her with his large, accusing eyes. Serena had desperately wanted things to be different, but she could no more change her basic approach than a cable car could climb a hill while off its tracks.

She picked up the phone and dialed a number. The phone rang and then a voice answered, "Good afternoon, Oakland city manager's office."

"Hello," Serena said. "This is Jackson Tremain's grandmother, Serena Tremain. I wanted to check if he has gone to Mexico yet, to visit his grandfather who is seriously ill. Unfortunately, I appear to have misplaced the number where he can be reached. I was wondering if you could help me. . . ."

The voice on the other end of the phone line said, "I sorry, ma'am, but we don't give out such numbers to callers."

"Is there someone else I may talk to? This is extremely urgent." Serena was transferred and then transferred again. She finally spoke with the acting assistant city manager, Howard Gomes, who assured her that if Jackson should call, her message would be relayed. She left her number and hung up. She realized that when she gave Jackson's number to Braxton, she would be placing one of her own blood in jeopardy, but she nonetheless felt it was a wise decision. Strangely, Serena felt that if there was any hope for the family, it lay with Jackson. It was time to see if King did indeed have a master plan and whether his grandson had the will and the grit to carve a place for himself in the new landscape. If he was to be the savior of the family, he had to survive the dangers. Even the dangers created by betrayal.

Saturday, June 26, 1982

Deleon leaned against one of the supporting poles while the M Taravel streetcar clattered across another line's tracks as it headed toward downtown San Francisco. He casually allowed himself a sweeping glance out the back window. Yes, the beige Ford Galaxy was still following. It was the second time in as many days that he had discovered someone following him. He knew it was San Vicente sending him a not-so-subtle message indicating his distrust. Further, the fact that the men tailing him had done little to conceal themselves was nothing less than an insult, and Deleon knew that also was intended. Well, he had had about enough. He had decided to send his own not-too-subtle message. To that end, he had left his car at Nineteenth and Sloat and caught the streetcar to downtown. He wanted to get his followers on foot, to take them into the heart of the city.

Two elderly women got on at one of the stops and once the streetcar started moving they needed assistance. Deleon stepped forward and helped each of them to their seats and returned to his pole. His action did not arise out of generosity. It would not serve him to have one of the old ladies injured and the streetcar delayed on its rounds. He had taken the M Taravel to split up his followers. He knew that at least one of them would get on the M before the tunnel which issued out onto upper Market. He could deal with one man or a two-man team, but three men was stretching it. Two men might be stretching it if they were good professionals and they attacked him simultaneously. He smiled to himself. He would make sure to avoid such a turn of events. There would be no loss of focus. No loss of attentiveness. His eyes swept over the other passengers then confirmed that the Galaxy was still following. Yes, his message would be written as he desired to write it.

Streets clattered by with a slow and grinding regularity. Deleon watched the changing neighborhoods and allowed himself to relax, only giving particular attention to people boarding and exiting. He was preparing himself, clearing the decks for action. It was a method he had learned in prison. It allowed him to stay relaxed during the long waiting periods before the violence began. Staring out the window at the passing street scene, he saw a young Asian couple waiting at a sheltered bus stop. They were holding hands and staring into each other's eyes. There was no other description for the expressions on their faces but rapt, their minds captured as if by some secret enchantment that wrapped itself around only them.

Deleon smirked because he thought of the couple as dupes, gullible people who had bought the complete fraudulent bill of goods on love. He had always considered people like that as sheep, the herd animals, the abundant and necessary chaff to fill in the spaces between the predators. The streetcar jerked and rocked as it turned and crossed another line's tracks. Despite his intention to avert his eyes, he watched the Asian couple until they were lost from view. His cynicism aside, there was a trace of uneasiness in him, and perhaps a touch of envy. He wondered what it would be like to share feelings of such trust and affection that you would be willing to commit yourself to that one person, and come what may, the future would be shared together. Deleon knew that such commitment existed. He had seen it in prison. He had seen men willing to kill or die to save their partners from threatening situations. He had never experienced such emotions himself. Deleon placed his bets with the smart money. The smart money said every time you allowed yourself to care for something or someone too much, you raised your level of vulnerability by a factor of ten. Invulnerability was based on caring for nothing too greatly.

Deleon did not believe in happiness; the best one could do was to limit the amount of pain experienced. Prison had honed and shaped Deleon's understanding of this reality, spinning him on its lathe of days and nights until his comprehension was chiseled smooth and seamless. The truth was, the first time he had ever heard the word *love* used in connection with himself was in prison. Of course, that was generally during or just after someone had rammed their penis into his rectum. *Love* took on a very different meaning when someone held a knife to your throat so tightly that the blade cut the skin and blood dripped down your chest, and all the while they're thrusting it in you. They really didn't care if you were alive or not; the only difference was if you were conscious, they could fuck you standing up. In the first year alone, he was gang-raped four times. There were a couple of times after which he didn't know if he would be able to take a normal shit again. How could he ever go to a romance movie and believe it? Nobility, like morality, was a myth.

Fortunately, after his first year of incarceration he was accepted into a gang. One of its leaders, Butch Austen, was a lifer who had already spent twenty-five years behind bars. He took the nineteen-year-old Deleon beneath his wing. For a price, of course: bimonthly rectal access. The lifer taught Deleon many things, but the greatest was a love of books and reading. Deleon could barely read when he was first incarcerated, but by the time he was released five years later, he possessed his GED and had read all the American and British classics, in addition to uncounted volumes of pulp fiction. It was reading that saved his sanity in the jungle world of prison life. Books introduced him to worlds that he sensed existed but had never seen. The written page gave him an awareness of lives not lived in the moil and toil, or in the stinginess of the life he knew. Further, his reading provided the images that he painted and sketched. During his years in prison he became quite accomplished with pen and ink, and he truly appreciated the rare times he was able to obtain both canvas and paints. Drawing and painting allowed him to rise above the grimness of his surroundings.

The streetcar lurched to a stop with a mechanical squeal of its brakes in a small neighborhood commercial district, the last stop before the tunnel. A number of passengers stood up and made their way toward the exits. Deleon drifted to the rear of the vehicle and sat down in a seat next to the rear door. There was a crowd of people boarding at this last stop. Sure enough, two of San Vicente's men boarded the streetcar and sat down behind the driver. Although Deleon never looked directly at them, he recognized them. It was German Diaz and the card playing, pockmarked Martinez.

Deleon shook his head. Fate was a strange thing. He had just come to the decision that he would simply kill the grandsons and let others fight over the whereabouts of the certificates. If he didn't take matters into his own hands Jesse and Fletcher were going to make a serious mistake. With the death of the grandsons, he would've fulfilled his obligation to his grandfather and he would be free to return to New Orleans. But now San Vicente had forced him to take action against him. He smiled to himself as the streetcar started rumbling into the darkness of the tunnel. San Vicente's men would die before they realized how good he was. Technique, stamina, and speed were weapons that could never be found wanting, and Deleon had all in good measure; their possession was the basis of his confidence. He decided he would kill Martinez first.

BOOK II

The Immersion

Saturday, June 26, 1982

On Saturday afternoon Carlos Zarate watched through the tinted windows of the terminal as the small private jet swerved in the cloudless blue sky and took bearings on its landing course. It was a ten-passenger Lear, the third private plane that had landed in the last thirty minutes. As directed, the plane pulled all the way into a hangar that jutted out from the main building, before disembarking its passengers. Carlos peeled himself off the wall against which he was leaning and walked down the gangway, through the baggage claim, and across a breezeway into a small customs office. Lieutenant Juan Flores, a chubby, round-faced man in a sweat-stained, khaki uniform, looked up from the pile of documents he was studying and asked, "Qué pasa?"

Carlos merely pointed through the wall, in the direction of the hangar into which the plane had entered.

Lieutenant Flores pulled himself erect, sucked his stomach in, adjusted his uniform, dusted off his cap, placed it firmly on his head, and straightened his back in his best imitation of military bearing, before leading the way out of the office. They crossed another breezeway and followed a long corridor which led directly to the back entrance of the hangar. Jackson was standing next to his luggage by the wing of the jet when they entered. Lieutenant Flores walked ahead of Carlos and introduced himself in English to Jackson and, for the next several minutes, asked the necessary customs-related questions to clear Jackson for entrance into Mexico. Jackson's passport was stamped with a flourish by Lieutenant Flores and he marked up Jackson's luggage with a gaudy signature in yellow chalk.

All the time he was interacting with Lieutenant Flores, Jackson kept looking over the lieutenant's shoulder at Carlos. Jackson thought it was Carlos, but the man in his memory was so different from the man in front of him. The customs process was completed so quickly that Jackson was pleasantly surprised. He walked over to Carlos, who stood watching him with a smile. "Carlos?" he asked.

"Diablito?" Carlos asked in response.

Jackson studied Carlos's face and saw that the years had left crow's-feet around his eyes. There were many streaks of gray in his hair. Carlos now looked like his uncle, El Indio, had when Jackson first met him.

Carlos smiled slowly and asked, "How was your trip down here?"

Jackson nodded his head and answered, "Cloak-and-dagger, but fine. It was sort of interesting getting off Amtrak at an unscheduled stop and being whisked away by a waiting car. And I've never flown out of a private airport before."

"It was the best way to lose the men who were following you. But you'll get a full debriefing at the house."

Jackson gave Carlos a quizzical look. "A debriefing?"

"All in good time." Carlos paused and commented, "You look good." He patted Jackson's arms and chest, assessing their musculature. He grunted in approval and held out his hand.

Jackson not only shook Carlos's hand but gave him a hug, which was returned. Carlos insisted on carrying Jackson's bags. As they walked out of the hangar, Jackson asked, "You're still working for my grandfather?"

"I'm a security consultant. I have my own business." Carlos directed Jackson toward an exit. When they walked out of the dark, air-conditioned environment into the bright, sweltering sunlight, it seemed to Jackson that someone had turned a halogen lamp on his face. He was temporarily blinded. Carlos pointed out a nearby limousine with tinted glass windows.

Once they were settled in the dark coolness of the limo, Carlos said, "You look like your grandfather."

"You look like El Indio," Jackson said in response and instantly regretted it. The eighteen years that had passed since El Indio's death could not sufficiently cushion the mention of his name.

Carlos seemed to feel none of Jackson's angst, for he smiled broadly and said, "Yes, I do look like my uncle."

Jackson said nothing. El Indio had been killed because of him, because he had hesitated in pulling a trigger.

Several minutes passed in silence before Carlos spoke again and he seemed to be speaking from a place deep within himself. "The old people say there are only a few souls in the world and that these souls are reincarnated again and again. I would be happy to be the one chosen to carry my uncle's soul forward."

There was a quiet, forceful sincerity in his words that caused Jackson to remember how Carlos had held his dying uncle in his arms as his blood trickled into the dust of the arid earth.

More minutes passed, then Jackson said, "I'm sorry, Carlos. . . ." His words dissolved into his confusion. It was another of the haunting memories from the last summer spent with his grandfather.

Carlos reached across and touched his shoulder. "It is good to see that your heart has not changed, Diablito."

Jackson grabbed Carlos's arm and said earnestly, "I owe you, Carlos, and I'll never forget that." Carlos smiled in acknowledgment and sat back in his seat. Jackson's words appeared to have put a seal on the moment, but his emotions were volcanic. He had not been in Mexico for half an hour and already he felt his heart losing its shape, shifting like molten magma within his chest. Under pressure more memories spewed up, racing past his consciousness at almost light speed, blurring the colors and sounds like the sights seen during a roller-coaster ride. Even in the air-conditioned cool of the limo, sweat began to drip down his face.

The driver asked Carlos something in Spanish that brought Jackson back to the present. Carlos turned to Jackson and said, "We are going to the house first. El Negro is being moved to a private clinic. You'll be able to see him at six o'clock this evening."

Jackson's shirt was damp. He wanted to wash his face. He actually wanted to delay seeing his grandfather, but now that the decision had been made for him, he perversely wanted to see the old man right away. "Why is he being moved?" he asked.

"He requested that he be moved off all life support systems when you arrived."

"What?" Jackson asked incredulously. "Why?"

"He is ready to die. He just wanted to see you first."

The old bastard knew I was coming all along, before I had even made the decision myself, thought Jackson. It was this byzantine level of planning that seemed to imbue his grandfather with almost supernatural qualities. On the edge of death, he's still outguessing me, Jackson marveled. He asked, "What kind of condition is he in?"

"Heart and kidney failure," Carlos answered. "Been getting dialysis to stay alive."

Jackson merely nodded. It was eerily surprising that the old man was mortal, that his body was giving out, that his desire to live was gone. If anyone had the spirit to live forever, it was his grandfather. He asked, "What's the projected time after he gets off the life support equipment?"

"Who knows?" Carlos shrugged. "Three days, a week at the outside."

Jackson sat quietly with his own thoughts as the limo crawled through the busy afternoon traffic. He turned to Carlos. "I was surprised to see you. You're a college graduate. I thought you would have severed ties with my grandfather by now."

"Federico Ramirez, El Indio, and your grandfather were family to me. These three men took me in when I was thirteen. They fed me, clothed me, and took responsibility for training and educating me. What I did with you when you were eight was done for me when I was fourteen. Everything that I've ever taught you was based upon a foundation laid down by those three men.

"Your grandfather treated me like a son and he did the same for Rico's boys. After their father was killed, he took them in, provided shelter, trained and educated them, then, when they were ready and capable of protecting themselves, handed over their father's share of the business. And the only thing he ever asked in payment was that we treat you as he treated us. He is a true man of honor. With his passing, I will lose one of the most important members of my family."

Jackson snorted. "You make him sound like Robin Hood."

"He is a sort of Robin Hood. He stood up to forces that other people would have laid down for. He fought back and he made a living taking money from rich and arrogant criminals."

"True, but he didn't give to the poor!"

"That's not exactly true. He didn't donate money to organizations, but he did things like—Do you remember that first village you stayed in when you were eight years old? Where I first taught you to hunt?" Jackson nodded. Carlos continued, "Your grandfather built a school there on his own land and paid the salary of the teacher for years until they incorporated into a larger school district. He did this predominantly because he wanted to build a good relationship among the villagers, but also he let it be known that if anyone in the village was caught participating in an attack against him, the school would be shut down. He regularly donated to the local church and the village's festivals. He was very generous. The medical clinic where he is staying is another example of that. He bought that building for the doctor who for years had been providing us with discreet medical services for bullet and knife wounds. The doctor wanted his own clinic and he was willing to direct a good percentage of his services to the poor. I negotiated the deal. It was just one of your grandfather's ways of protecting himself from treachery and keeping in the good graces of the local people. Almost every place he lived, he was liked as well as respected, because of what he put into the community. His approach was and still is good business."

The limo turned into a walled, white stucco compound and heavy iron gates swung shut behind it. Inside the courtyard there was a circular drive which arced underneath the overhanging second story of the house. Two men dressed in suits walked out of the front door as the limo rolled to a stop. Jackson got out and greeted the Ramirez brothers. The older brother, Reuben "Cisco" Ramirez, had grown into a handsome, brown-skinned man of average height. He had the Rudolph Valentino good looks that women so often admired: his straight, black hair combed back; flashing dark eyes under arched, black eyebrows. He had inherited his father's swarthy coloring, while his younger brother, Julio "Pancho" Ramirez, was much lighter skinned and had light brown hair, but he shared a strong family resemblance with his older sibling. They had many of the same features—the same hairline, eyebrows, and eyes—yet the results were significantly different. Julio was a bigger man with a broader face, so that the features which made Reuben look dashing were strangely coarse and unfinished on his brother.

"How was your flight?" Reuben asked, extending his hand. The greetings were exchanged between the three men. Jackson was escorted inside as Carlos took care of his bags and gave directions to the limo driver.

Jackson was guided to the chair behind the desk in his grandfather's den. It was a room he associated with smells of Scotch whisky, gun-cleaning oils, cigars, and aftershave. The room seemed the same: floor-to-ceiling bookshelves along one wall; on the opposing wall a bar with a mirror behind it; in the center of the room a large, circular green felt–covered card table surrounded by solid wooden chairs; and at the far end, the big wooden desk in front of high, arching windows, which allowed natural light to cascade over half the length of the room. He looked across the wooden expanse of the desk and remembered the

countless times he had stood in front of it pleading his case to an uncaring judge. Jackson was deep in his recollections when Reuben began
laying out various legal papers, and it was only then that Jackson realized that Julio was talking to him.

Julio was providing a quick sketch of the last two decades. The
Ramirez brothers had been serving as his grandfather's attorneys for all
the South American and West Coast business from the time each had
passed the bar in California. Julio began listing a number of businesses
which were among King's assets and went on to discuss Jackson's grandfather's considerable real estate holdings in both Mexico and in California. The brothers explained how, in an effort to avoid inheritance taxes,
part of the estate had been transferred to another corporation in Jackson's name. However, the bulk of his grandfather's estate remained in
stock certificates.

The discussion of money made Jackson feel uncomfortable. He
looked at his watch. Almost two hours had passed and there were still
two hours yet to pass before he could see his grandfather at six. He
needed to wash up and relax, and wander around the old house. He
asked to be excused. The Ramirez brothers arranged to meet Jackson
the next day to discuss the legal aspects of the will. Jackson did not reveal his reluctance to get involved with his grandfather's affairs. He was
surrounded by loyal men who expected him to pick up his grandfather's
mantle. He decided that he would first see his grandfather before he
aired any of his intentions.

Julio picked up a weathered valise and placed it on the table. Jackson
gave him a questioning look. Julio said simply, "It's a list of names along
with some reading material. El Negro will explain it."

Jackson did not inquire further. He figured that the valise contained
information concerning his grandfather's enemies. He hoped in reading
its contents that he would discover the key to disengaging himself from
the conflict. He smiled at the Ramirez brothers. "Has my grandfather
taken care of you for your years of service?"

"He's treated us like family," Reuben replied. "He has taken care of us
extremely well. He has given us control over all our father's old businesses and paid us well too. If anything, we are in your grandfather's
debt."

"I'm glad to hear that." Jackson smiled again and said, "I want my
blood brothers taken care of."

"You still remember that oath we all took together?" Julio asked with surprise.

"I remember it and still honor it."

"Good," Reuben asserted. "We may still have need to rely upon one another."

Julio offered to introduce him to the people who maintained his grandfather's house. On the way out to the kitchen, Jackson asked about the facsimile machine for which he had been given the number and when he might be able to check for the receipt of documents. Reuben informed him that he would check with his friend who was a manager in the multinational corporation that had the fax machine. If documents had already been sent, Reuben would call him.

After a brief introduction to the three house-staff members, Jackson was left to his own devices. The limo was scheduled to take him to the clinic at a quarter to six. He walked through the house, reacquainting himself with its shadows and doorways. As the cool darkness enveloped him, Jackson could hear echoes of long-dead conversations, the scuff of leather boots on the cold tile floors, and the gruff sound of his grandfather's voice.

He walked into the kitchen and interrupted the hushed conversation of the house staff. There was a gray-haired man named Mario who stood up immediately, ready to be of service. His comrades, two women, stood up more slowly. Jackson assured them in broken Spanish and hand gestures that he was just looking around. He went upstairs and discovered that his bags had been placed in the master bedroom, his grandfather's bedroom. He went down the hall and pushed open the door leading into his old bedroom. Nothing seemed changed from the last time he had slept in it. It touched him that his grandfather had maintained the room as he had left it.

On the far wall of the room, between his bed and the window, there was a painting of a beautiful young Mexican woman. Her name was Maria. Jackson's heart ached at the sight of her picture. She had been his first real foray into the minefield of love. Their relationship had been quick, intense, and heartrending. He had never opened himself to anyone like he had with her, and she had given him sexual pleasures that had never been rivaled. It had seemed a match made in heaven, but shortly after their meeting she was carried away in a tide of bloodshed and death.

On his return to the master bedroom, he saw his grandfather's majestic gun case. It was a huge chifforobe made of dark red wood. He reached up and took the key from its hiding place atop the chifforobe and unlocked the main cabinet. The guns gleamed in the light from the hallway. There were ten to fifteen rifles and shotguns stacked upright in neat rows. The pistols lay flat, crowded into ten narrow drawers. The smell of the cleaning fluid on the guns stirred even more memories.

In the back, hanging above the rifles, he saw the wire coat hanger that his grandfather had used on him that first summer. He had never forgotten that whipping. Anger flushed his face. Roaming through the old house that he had known since he was a child was like digging through scar tissue; wounds that he thought had long since healed were reopened. He could feel the pain of the welts again on the backs of his legs. Suddenly, it seemed too warm in the house. He decided to go outside. Descending the stairs he heard the yapping of a small dog. It came from the kennel that his grandfather had maintained for his hunting and fighting dogs. Jackson went to investigate.

The kennel was at the back of the house and consisted of four caged runs, each with a covered shelter built against the outer wall of the compound. One of the women Jackson had seen in the kitchen was attempting to feed the kennel's sole occupant, a bullterrier puppy, which was more interested in escape than the food she was providing. It was also obvious that she was not used to dealing with the puppy, for she kept waving a broom at it every time it came near. The puppy, nearly six weeks old, was fearless; it bit the broom several times trying to defend itself. The woman and the puppy were battling for position by the door of the run.

The scene brought laughter to Jackson's lips. He entered the run behind the woman and indicated that she could go. The puppy stopped to consider its new antagonist. Jackson sat down in the run with his back to the door and waited. The puppy, with its big head and feet, came over cautiously to examine Jackson. As it was snuffling him, Jackson began to pet it. It was a black-coated young male with the broad white chest mark of the fighting Staffordshire bullterriers. The puppy was happy to receive attention. It tried to lick Jackson's face and his hands. It began to wag its tail so furiously that its whole body bent back and forth. It was a healthy young dog. Its nose was cold and damp, and its coat was thick and shiny. Jackson spent half an hour in the kennel with the puppy. Jackson knew that in his prime, his grandfather would have had this puppy trained for the pit, to fight and perhaps die amid the shouting and laughter of uncaring voices.

When Jackson went upstairs to wash up, he let the puppy come with him. Because he knew that terrier puppies liked to chew on various objects, he stopped by the kitchen and got a bone. The staff were surprised to see that the puppy was following him. It appeared that the puppy had been in desperate need of affection, and now that it had received a little, it was not going to let the bestower of that affection out of its sight. Its curiosity would cause it to venture off, but it soon came scampering back.

The phone rang several times before Jackson picked it up. It was Reuben calling to inform him that he had received several faxes marked *urgent* and that they would be delivered shortly. Jackson would be able to send his responses any time after six o'clock until midnight. After he finished speaking with Reuben, Jackson immediately called Corazon at home and inquired as to what had transpired in his absence.

Corazon's tone was concerned when she said, "You really lit a fire under Bedrosian. He has contacted every one of your council subcommittees looking for mistakes or somebody with a grudge, and it seems he found someone. He convened an emergency meeting of the waste management subcommittee Friday night."

"On what basis? The chairwoman was out of town. Did he get a quorum?"

"Just barely. He had allegations of toxic dumping that weren't included in your report. But we've outsmarted him this time. I've sent you his report so that you can cut and paste it into yours."

"As soon as I get it, I'll work on it. Mexico City is two hours ahead. I'll have it faxed off tonight before midnight. It'll be there waiting for you tomorrow morning."

Corazon sighed. "I can't guarantee that I'll be the first one in there in the morning. You better make sure that you send it tonight and I'll go into the office around nine-thirty this evening and stay until ten waiting for it."

"Corazon, you are a sweetheart and a lifesaver! I really appreciate this. Your husband doesn't know how lucky he is."

"He knows. I don't let him forget it. Just remember, my mother is coming from Manila in two weeks and I'll need time off."

"If I'm still employed, you got it." After he hung up the phone, Jackson slid down on the floor and petted the puppy's wiggling body as it tried to lick his face. Once it saw that he wasn't going anywhere, the puppy slumped against him and lay down on the floor next to him. Jackson continued to run his hand along the puppy's side as he let himself ruminate over his future in the city manager's office.

Ten minutes after Jackson had hung up the phone, the limo driver brought the fax documents that Corazon had sent. There was a brief note from her indicating that she didn't think he should change his recommendations because lengthy police surveillance had not confirmed any of the allegations. He sat down at the table in the dining room and studied the faxes. In twenty minutes he had made the necessary corrections and had written the new wording for his report. This part of the work came easy for him. In fact, he enjoyed preparing reports and resolutions for council review and approval. But for Bedrosian, Jackson would have loved his job. He would deflect this particular attack, but his long-term problem was that he was down the slope from Bedrosian and shit would continue rolling in his direction until he got tired of dodging or was covered with it. Jackson set his jaw grimly. He would possibly consider a severance package if it was the right amount and it was offered without any attempt at character assassination. Otherwise, he would not go quietly.

Jackson went into his bedroom to get ready to see his grandfather. He washed up and changed shirts while the puppy alternately prowled underfoot or attacked its bone with furious little growls. There was a knock at the bedroom door. The puppy was at the door in an instant, growling threateningly. It was Mario. He informed Jackson that the limo was ready. Jackson picked up his leather jacket and his edited report then headed downstairs. On the way out, he put the puppy back in the kennel. He heard its disappointed yelps until he closed the front door.

Carlos was in the car waiting for him. As the limo pulled out of the gate, Jackson asked him to have the driver take his report and get it faxed back to his office. Carlos nodded and they sat back and watched the traffic of early evening thicken with daily commuters. The clinic was located in a well-to-do suburb on the western outskirts of Mexico City. All the houses along the street which led up to the clinic were mansions set well back on large, manicured lawns behind wrought-iron gates. The clinic, which had originally been a private school, was constructed on a hill overlooking the surrounding environs. There was a small guardhouse at the entrance gate. The limo was waved through without scrutiny and continued up the driveway, which arced in front of the main building.

The inside was cool and pale under the fluorescent lights. There was a thick carpet and numerous overstuffed chairs and couches placed throughout the lobby, which appeared to be crowded with both patients and visitors. Carlos ushered Jackson upstairs to his grandfather's room without checking at the desk. They walked up two flights and turned down a corridor which seemed to lead to an unoccupied wing of the clinic. Carlos gestured to a door that had no number or other visible insignia on it. Jackson opened the door and stepped into the room. Immediately, a short, stocky man emerged from behind the door with his hand under his jacket. He saw Carlos behind Jackson and stepped back. Carlos gestured for the man to leave with him, and Jackson was left alone in the room with his grandfather.

The old man had the back of his bed raised slightly and was looking directly at him. No words passed between them as they stared at each other for several minutes. Two men connected by blood, but separated by nearly fifty years. Jackson was shocked at how the changes wrought by age had affected his grandfather. Where once there had been a big, broad-shouldered man, there was now a shrunken husk. Wrinkles hid the face that had once struck fear in so many hearts. Only the eyes gave a hint of the man within the atrophying flesh. Jackson broke the silence with "Hello, Grandfather."

The old man gave him a final once-over then smiled. When he spoke, his voice had a slight hiss from his weakened condition. "You look good, boy. Told 'em you'd come."

"You were right, Grandfather."

"You done growed into a man," the old man acknowledged. "Look a lot like yo' daddy."

"Maybe I look like he would have looked had he grown this old." As soon as the words were out of his mouth, Jackson regretted them. He was not here to air his issues with his grandfather. He was here to get information and to pay his last respects. He had to stay focused. He sat down in a chair at the foot of the bed.

"Something grinding you, boy?" His grandfather pronounced the word *boy* as "bwaah."

"No, Grandfather."

"Blame me for yo' daddy's death, boy?"

The direct question was too much of an intro for Jackson to ignore, but he contained himself. "You don't want to discuss that subject."

"Why not?" the old man wheezed challengingly. "Ain't got much time left, might as well spend it on somethin' important. Floor's open. Whatever you got to say." A fit of shallow coughing racked his body. Jackson stood up, prepared to take whatever action necessary. The old man waved him back to his seat. "Sit down. Sit down. I ain't ready to go jes' yet." The old man could barely raise his head, but his spirit was strong.

"Can I get you something?" Jackson asked as the coughing subsided.

"Jes' speak your piece. Let me hear yo' straight-from-the-gut thoughts. Do you blame me for yo' daddy's death?"

"Yes."

"Yo' daddy was killed by treachery, treachery that was intended to kill us all. Yo' daddy was the only son I got to raise." The old man paused, regaining his breath. "That's why I dedicated my life to getting those who gunned him down."

Tell me anything, Jackson thought. He knew that his grandfather had spent a lifetime getting even. The death of his youngest son may have added to his zeal, but it did not preempt his own blood lust. There seemed to be nothing for Jackson to say. Why argue with the old man? History could not be changed. His father could not be resurrected.

"That's part of the reason that I wanted to see you." The old man chuckled humorlessly.

"To discuss my father's death?" Jackson was having trouble keeping the barbs out of his delivery.

"Yes and no." His grandfather paused and gave him a penetrating look. "You can't hurt me with resentment, boy. Life has done more to me than you could ever do. So, if you finished whinin', I'll get on to the important things that I want to cover with you."

His grandfather's tone of dismissal was more than Jackson was prepared to handle without retort. "You're dying and you're still the same self-centered old bastard that you were twenty years ago! You think you can dismiss my feelings with a wave of your hand! Only the issues that you are concerned with are important! To hell with everybody else!"

If he physically could have, his grandfather would have sat up in his bed. He struggled for a moment then resigned himself to turning his baleful glance on Jackson. In his mind's eye, Jackson saw the manner in which his grandfather would have turned twenty or even ten years ago on an antagonist: eyes glinting evilly, gliding as close as possible before beginning his attack. There were no rules. There was no mercy, only death and maiming for the vanquished.

"You finished?" There was a petulance in the old man's tone, as if there had been enough time wasted on foolish talk.

Jackson got himself back on track. "Yes, I'm finished, Grandfather. But I think we need to clear something up first. I came down here to see you. I will be happy to assist you in settling your affairs and to generally help in any way that I can." Before he said these words, Jackson had had no intention of having any involvement with his grandfather's activities. Yet, once he said them, they seemed right so he thought he would go with it. He continued speaking without a break. "But I'm not down here to be insulted. I don't want you to dismiss my feelings or my resentment—"

"You talkin' like a white boy. Everybody got pain. Everybody got feelings. What makes you special? Whole damn world's hurtin'!" The old man had a spasm of pain, which he stifled with a grimace. He looked out the window and sucked in a long breath. "I ain't got time to spend arguin'. I got something to tell you, a little family history; something you gotta know 'cause you inheritin' everythin'."

"I don't want your money. Give it to Franklin. He wants it."

The old man laughed; this time it was a real laugh. The coughing began again. It racked his whole body. Jackson again stood, ready to come to his aid or call a nurse, but his grandfather waved him back to his seat.

"Franklin wouldn't live to see his bank statement. Anyway, he ain't my blood and I never did take a liking to that boy. Reminded me of his father."

"I've heard you say this before. What do you mean, Franklin's not your blood?"

"His father wasn't from me. Was a white man's child. Ain't my blood. Ask yo' grandmother if LaValle was my son."

It was too much to assimilate. It was the type of information that Jackson felt should have been disclosed years ago. "Did you kill him?" Jackson blurted out. Why not put at least one mystery to rest, he thought. The old man was at the gates; he'd tell the truth.

"Who? LaValle?" The old man's eyes opened wide with inquiry.

"Yeah." Jackson nodded his head.

"No. His mouth and his greed killed him. Would have done 'em, but I promised yo' grandmother that I'd let him alone."

"You're a piece of work, Grandfather. You would've killed your own son?"

"Wasn't my son! He was a white man's son! And he was a traitor to the family that raised him!" the old man answered righteously. "A man who ain't got no loyalty is just a mercenary, don't deserve a Christian burial."

Jackson shook his head and wondered what kind of man it took to be facing death, having committed all the crimes that his grandfather had committed, and still be unrepentant.

His grandfather was peering at him. "You think I'm heartless? Well, ever since yo' so-called uncle got yo' mama killed—"

Jackson sat up quickly as if he'd received an electrical shock.

"Got your attention, huh?" His grandfather nodded knowingly. "Well. I tell you about it. LaValle was drinking that night and he had lost a lot of money. Had a problem that way. He was always overdoing it, whether it was alcohol, gambling, or women. Never seemed to know when to stop. . . ." His grandfather's words fell into a rhythm, his soft voice rising and falling with his changes in inflection. Jackson sat back in his chair and let the old man's words pour over him like warm syrup as he re-created with his descriptions the sights and sounds of that fateful night.

Friday, August 18, 1951

In the semidarkness of the Blue Mirror, Jacques (known as Jack in the Bay Area) Tremain discreetly adjusted his forty-five automatic in its holster then pulled his jacket closed. He stood at the back of a crowd that was listening to Sugar Ray Robinson slug it out with Bobo Olson on the radio. The polished wooden radio sat in a prominent place behind the bar and its volume was turned all the way up. The patrons lining the bar as well as those seated at the various tables were intent on the fight. As the announcer's voice excitedly described each flurry of punches in staccato bursts, he drew cheers or moans from the bar's occupants. It was a fast-paced fight with each boxer taking his turn in pummeling the other. No one among the listeners thought that the bout would go the distance. In between rounds, people would order more drinks or shout to friends across the room as the fast-talking announcer provided his unrequested analysis. Jack, without making any noticeable effort, was watching the egress and ingress of traffic. He was trying to identify potential problems.

His let his eyes follow the shapely, long-legged form of Verna French, who was waiting tables. She was an attractive, light-skinned, red-haired woman who had become an institution at the Blue Mirror during her five-year tenure. Jack watched her weave in and out between tables, professionally serving drinks and bantering easily with customers. She brooked no advances and was generally a no-nonsense type. The only problem, as far as Jack was concerned, was that she was one of his brother's early conquests.

Occasionally, he would catch the eye of the heavyset bartender, Doke Browner, and with a glance point out a particular individual for his assessment. So far, no one had entered who caused Doke any concern. But Jack was worried; it was going to be a lively evening. He could feel it in the air.

It was Friday night in postwar Fillmore. It was payday and the eagle had flown. Folks had on their best threads and were parading the street. It was eleven o'clock at night and Fillmore was still clogged with cars slowly cruising up and down. Often the street was blocked by people double-parked in their vehicles, shooting the breeze with their friends. Despite the lateness of the hour, the sidewalks were still crowded with promenading pedestrians as people made their way to bars, restaurants, and the late-showing movies located along the Fillmore corridor.

The Blue Mirror Lounge, owned by the Tremain family, was located on Fillmore Street between Fulton and McAllister. It was a large establishment consisting of four rooms. The main room had a long wooden bar running along the right wall as customers entered. Behind the wooden bar was a huge blue-tinted mirror, which gave the establishment its name. Two of the back rooms were used for dice and cards, respectively, and the third served as a small office. The Blue Mirror was a popular place and Friday night was no exception. It was considered one of the nicer cocktail lounges where a colored man or a woman could go without fear of being hustled or assaulted. And for those who wished to challenge fortune, the games in the back rooms were honest.

Jack Tremain was riding shotgun on the games under way in the back rooms. There was big money on the tables. More than thirty thousand dollars would change hands this night. Several merchant marines and sleeping-car porters were in town to gamble their hard-earned cash. Periodically, Jack would make his rounds through the back rooms as well as the bar. He was a little over six feet tall, lean of build and light-skinned. His hair was black and wavy. He had the hairline, the straight black eyebrows, and square jaw of his father's people and his mother's large eyes and full lips. Jack was a good-looking man, but not the looker that his older brother was. He had other qualities that his brother did not. As evidence of this fact, Jack had been the one selected to assist in his father's business. LaValle had been passed over. A fact that LaValle resented in silence around his father, but complained about loudly in Jack's presence.

Doke signaled to Jack that he was wanted in the dice room. Jack detached himself from the crowd that was engrossed in the fight and made his way to the back. He was buzzed in by Doke, who had a button behind the bar. Once inside, he walked swiftly down a dim hallway lit with one low-wattage bulb to the dice room at the end of the hall. He knocked twice and entered. One of the security staff, Joey, a big, dark-skinned man in a rumpled suit, stood up and informed him of the situation. There were three dice tables in the room, but everyone was crowded around one table. A longtime customer, a large, sweating fat man named Mr. Trotman, was holding the dice and he'd had quite a good run. There was nearly four thousand dollars wagered on the table, more than three times the amount that many of those who were standing around watching would earn in a year. They were waiting for Jack to approve the bet. He nodded to the croupier, who then called out the bet. There was a gasp from the crowd around the table; more than ten thousand dollars lay in the next roll of the dice. As Jack left the room, he heard Mr. Trotman say, "The Tremains run a classy place. They don't mind a run of luck." It was exactly what Jack wanted to hear. It was good business to have people win occasionally.

In the bar, the radio had been turned off; the fight was over. People were discussing the decision. One man declared Sugar Ray Robinson to be the best boxer who ever lived and that Olson was given the title because he was white. Another man asserted that Henry Armstrong was the best. Another protested that Joe Louis was the best. The discussion dissolved into Friday-night camaraderie. Doke beckoned Jack over and whispered in his ear that Mr. Trotman had lost on his next roll.

It looked like it was going to be a pretty good evening, until LaValle came into the bar at midnight.

LaValle was drunk again. As soon as he came staggering into the bar, Doke got Jack's attention. They both knew it meant trouble. LaValle was a mean drunk who, because of his father and his brother's reputation, would bully people. But basically, he was a pretty boy who liked to make time with other people's women. Either way, he was a troublemaker. Jack intercepted him as he made his way to the bar. "LaValle, you know Dad said for you not to come into any of the family places when you're drunk."

"You ain't going to tell him, are you, little brother?" LaValle slurred his words, looking over Jack's shoulder to see who was in the bar. He saw Verna and waved.

"I can't let you in, Val," Jack advised, standing in front of his brother.

LaValle knew he could neither bully nor manipulate his brother. He swayed drunkenly back and forth, on the verge of losing his balance. "I got a couple of problems. . . ." He hiccuped and fell silent. There was a pleading look on his face.

"What sort of problems, Val?" Jack asked tiredly. He had been the foil for every ploy that his brother had ever thought up and he knew him well. Nonetheless, Jack loved his brother and that connection always made him act generously on his behalf.

The nature of LaValle's problem walked through the door. It was John Tree, the youngest of the three Tree brothers. He was accompanied by two of his ruffian friends and when he saw LaValle, his eyes lit up.

Doke had been watching the interchange between LaValle and Jack from behind the bar, but when he saw Tree enter with his friends, he picked up the shotgun and walked to the end of the bar. Everyone in the Fillmore knew the Tree brothers and that John was trying to build a reputation as a tough guy. Doke waited with the shotgun hidden behind the fold in his apron.

LaValle saw Tree and turned to face him. A smile broke across his face. "This is one of them, little brother, but I didn't think that he was fool enough to follow me in here."

Tree walked up to the two brothers with a frown on his face. He didn't quite know what he was going to do, but he wanted to show everyone that he was fearless. He figured if he just threatened LaValle in his father's place, it would be all over the Fillmore in hours. "I come to get my money and satisfaction from the punk that likes to hit on women!" he said in a loud, demanding tone.

Jack knew that Tree had only entered the bar to start trouble. Jack opened his jacket, showing his gun, and said quietly, "I got your money and your satisfaction right here. Why don't you come and take it."

The sight of the gun along with what he knew of Jack's reputation made John pause. There was no doubt in his mind that Jack would shoot him if provoked. It was unfortunate for John Tree that he was an ambitious man, for it was his ambition that drove him forward. He taunted, "I heard that the Tremains were supposed to be tough and they always paid their debts. Yet, I got to come after a damn coward who beats on women and lets his mouth take him where his wallet can't go!" His two backups chuckled encouragingly.

Jack took a step toward Tree. "If you don't keep your voice down, you won't be able to finish this conversation."

There was a moment of silence as Tree saw Joey take a position off to his left. "Whatchoo gon' do, shoot me?" he challenged. "You gon' shoot me 'cause I come to collect my money from yo' punk-ass brother?"

The lounge grew suddenly quiet as patrons turned their attention to the drama unfolding near the entrance.

"Let's take him the next time he talks!" Jack ordered. Doke cocked the shotgun. Joey pulled out another shotgun and cocked it. There was absolute silence in the lounge: Coincidentally, the jukebox was in between records. Everyone heard Jack's words. People were edging away from the bar. Reputations were important. The Tremains commanded a sprawling real estate empire along the Fillmore corridor consisting of apartment buildings, movies, restaurants, and shoe parlor card rooms. It was the Tremain reputation which kept these businesses operating smoothly, without fear of extortion from other criminals. The police, of course, received their cut on a monthly basis.

The tension between the men at the door was broken momentarily when an attractive, young, dark-skinned woman with a pixie haircut walked through the front door. She walked between Tree's two men and made her way to Jack's side. It was Jack's wife. Without taking his eyes off Tree, Jack pushed her away. "Go stand behind the bar, Eartha. Call an ambulance." She followed his directions and went behind the bar. Jack goaded Tree, "Open your mouth now! We've got the whole bar's attention. Come on! Let's do it!"

The jukebox was now playing Billie Holiday's "Don't Explain" and that was the only sound in the room.

Tree knew that his bluff had been called. He raised his hands and laughed nervously. He wasn't a fool. He was outnumbered and out-gunned. He knew that if he was to live beyond this night he would have to back down. Tree started to speak and fell silent when he saw Jack's raised gun pointed directly at his head. He gestured with his hands, indicating he wanted to say something.

Jack ordered, "Apologize for disturbing our patrons!" He kept the gun aimed at Tree's head. "If you say anything else, I'll kill you where you stand!"

"Sorry," Tree said begrudgingly.

"Louder!" Jack ordered.

The taste was extremely bitter in Tree's mouth. "I's sorry."

Jack lowered the gun, but he kept it pointing in Tree's direction. "How much do you say my brother owes?"

"Over eight hundred dollars."

"Is it true?" Jack asked his brother, but still keeping an eye on Tree. It was just like Val to do something stupid like this. The whole community would be talking about it for weeks. This was exactly the kind of foolishness that really pissed off their father.

"Yeah, I lost a few games," LaValle admitted cavalierly. "Eight hundred seems about right."

"Eartha, please get the money out of the till and bring it here." Jack shook his head at his brother. It was always the same thing. Val over-rated himself in every game that he played. Against amateurs he seemed like a professional, but against professionals, he was just a good amateur.

LaValle saw Jack's disapproval and said, "A run of bad luck. I musta dropped my wallet. The check's in the mail. What the hell's the difference?"

Eartha gave Jack the money and Jack threw it on the floor at Tree's feet. "You got what you came for, now get out of here!"

Tree stooped and picked up the money. The bile was rising in his throat. He stuffed the money in his pocket next to his switchblade. As he turned to leave he growled, "We ain't through with this, not by a long shot!"

LaValle, always one to rub in a victory, stepped forward and slapped Tree on the back. "That's a good boy," he said cheerily. "Tell your brothers they can find me here too."

Tree spun without thinking and slashed LaValle across the face with his switchblade. LaValle fell backward with a wail. Jack had begun to move as soon as Tree started to turn. He arrived just after the knife sliced through LaValle's face. He swung the butt of his gun hard and felt it crunch against Tree's temple. Tree fell over a table and sprawled on the floor. Tree's two companions, who were headed out the door, were caught by surprise. Both men were met with Joey's shotgun when they turned around to see Tree fall to the floor. Jack pointed his gun at the semiconscious Tree and pondered killing him. A few minutes earlier, he would have shot him without a second thought. At that time, he had been posing a threat to the establishment. Now, he was lying on the floor at Jack's mercy. It didn't seem fair that Tree should pay with his life for LaValle's stupidity. Tree was just doing his job, just as Jack was doing his. He put his gun in his holster and kicked Tree in the head to make sure that he stayed down, then bent quickly and removed the knife from Tree's hand and checked his body for other weapons. Jack pulled a revolver from beneath Tree's jacket. He signaled Joey to lock the front door.

Jackson turned to survey the situation in the bar. People had come forward from among the onlookers and were assisting with towels, trying to stop the flow of blood from LaValle's face. Even if he had killed Tree, Jack knew that it was highly unlikely that anyone would go to the police. In the Fillmore, black people did not view the police as friends. Besides, John Tree was a rising young thug who was known to strong-arm regular people for their hard-earned cash. He was not popular. Jack's father, King, on the other hand, had stature; he may not have been liked, but he was respected. The people that he killed were mostly crooks and criminals. He generally left the common man alone. So the police were not the concern. It was the possibility that a gang war would break out with the Trees that had the customers upset, although it was clear that some of the folks looked upon this as an opportunity to align themselves with the legend of the Tremain family.

LaValle was moaning and sobbing, but he was in no danger. Eartha had called a family doctor. From the sounds his brother was making, Jack surmised that he was lamenting the cosmetic consequences of his injury. Jack didn't feel sorry for his brother. The whole evening had disintegrated because of his stupidity.

Joey brought Tree's companions over to the bar at gunpoint. Jack decided that Tree and his pals should be held in the office until his father arrived. After all, Tree did have two older brothers in the business. If any real harm came to him, it could trigger acts of retaliation. Tree was still unconscious from the blows to his head. After assuring himself that they were disarmed, Jack made Tree's two companions drag his unconscious body back to the office.

LaValle was seated near the bar with his head back. He was being attended to by two women, but he pushed them out of the way when Tree was being dragged past. He screamed, "You cut my face, you bastard! You cut my face!" His voice was laden with despair. Before anyone could stop him, LaValle swayed to his feet and snatched an empty beer bottle from a nearby table and broke it across Tree's unconscious face. His two companions, now duly intimidated, dropped Tree's arms and stepped back. LaValle bent down, took the broken neck of the bottle, and slashed it across Tree's face and neck. "You cut me, you bastard! You cut me!"

Jack came up from behind and clubbed his brother to the floor. "What the hell are you doing? Do you want to start a war?" There seemed to be no limit to LaValle's idiocy. Jack knelt to check Tree's injury, but the blood was pulsing out at such a rate that he could not discern just how serious the injury was. Jack gave orders that towels should be brought to staunch the flow of blood from Tree's face and neck, and that a long folding table should be brought to carry Tree into the back.

There was a smell of fear in the room. People realized that they had witnessed something that might jeopardize their lives. If Tree died from LaValle's savage attack, the Trees would have to respond in kind and they would probably brutalize witnesses for information and as punishment for patronizing a Tremain-owned establishment.

As LaValle was helped to his feet, he shouted at his brother, "You giving him all the attention! What about me? He cut me for no reason! Don't you care about that?"

Jack stood up and turned to face his brother, who was looking at him with accusing eyes. Jack walked over to LaValle and hissed through tense lips, "I don't want to hear your whining shit! You brought all of this on yourself!" Jack stood up and said loudly, "Doke, I need someone to take LaValle to Doc Wilburn's. We'll let whoever's already been called attend to Tree in the back. And let's get this floor cleaned up." He also directed that security should staff the rear entrance to the lounge to close that off as well. Jack was now marshaling the area and policing the cleanup. He looked at Eartha, who was standing behind the bar. She looked shaken. Jack went up to her and put his arm around her. "You all right?" he inquired. The question was rhetorical; he could tell by her expression that she was unnerved. She was not used to violence.

She nodded her head to indicate that she was fine, then pressed her face into his shoulder. They stood together silently while the activity continued on around them for several minutes. Finally, she pushed away from him to study his expression. The curls of her pixie haircut outlining the smooth, dark brown skin of her face, and her large, brown eyes glistening with tears staring up into his affected him. It made him want to protect her and shelter her from the harsh ways of the business. The reality was that she wanted more than mere protection, she wanted freedom from the anxiety of late-night calls, freedom from the rigors of wrapping bloody wounds. She wanted to escape the smell of cordite forever. Jack had already agreed to give her what she wanted.

"It's all right, honey. It's over," he said as he sought to calm her down, but his words had a programmed, automatic quality which glanced off her.

"I thought I was going to have to watch you blow the top of that man's head off! I never want to have a memory of you killing anybody!" Tears streamed down her face. "I couldn't stand it if I saw someone hold a gun to your head like you did to that man!"

"I know, honey. I know," he said soothingly. "Next week, we'll be headed to Texas and I'll be finished with the business."

"I wish it was tonight," she said with tearful sincerity.

"It's over now, honey. Why don't you go home. I'll be there as soon as I've closed up here."

Doke caught Jack's eye and interrupted their discussion. "If I send someone to take LaValle to the doctor, I'll have to take someone out of one of the back rooms. Oh, by the way," Doke dropped his voice and leaned forward, "several people asked if they could leave."

Jack tapped his head with an open hand. "Should have thought of that." He paused and thought for a moment. "Tell them, sure. Just make sure we get some contact information from them; verify it with ID. Tell anyone who wants to stay that drinks are on the house till we open up again."

Eartha pulled on his sleeve. "I can drop LaValle by Dr. Wilburn's. I'd like to get out of here anyway."

"Are you sure you're up to it, honey?"

"Yeah, I've phoned Lisette and told her to meet him at Doc Wilburn's. I'll just stay until she comes." She took a deep breath and gave him a weak smile. It was a sincere but feeble attempt to put on a game face. It made Jack laugh. He pulled his wife to him and hugged her tight.

She put her hands on his cheek and said, "I love you, but I'm afraid of all of this. I'm afraid of losing you. If only we could go away and leave all this tonight."

"Don't worry, Eartha," Jack assured her. "Nobody's going to take me away from you. My dad and I have just a few things to wrap up before I go."

"No more guns, please," she begged.

Doke gestured to Jack across the bar. "Young Dr. Broadhead is here."

"Have him look at Tree," Jack suggested. "We'll take LaValle to old Doc Wilburn. The old guy is better at sewing up cuts and slashes."

Doke nodded and made his way back through the crowd to the rear of the bar. People had come out of the gaming rooms and were talking with others who had been in the bar during the altercation. They moved respectfully out of Jack and Eartha's way as the couple walked to the front door of the lounge. Eartha had parked the car on Fillmore. Jack asked her to pull the car around back to the alley entrance of the building. He gave her a final hug and assisted her in buttoning her coat. She kissed his hand and he kissed hers in return. "Don't worry, honey," Jack said, studying her face as he unlocked the door. "I'm not going to let things get out of hand again like they did tonight. This is the last time. Just drop that stupid brother of mine off at Wilburn's and I'll see you at the house."

Eartha nodded and squeezed his hand and walked out the door. Her heart was pounding in her chest. She felt a strange, nervous energy, as if she had somehow been connected with the flickering neon signs that gave the Fillmore corridor its night colors. Everything seemed to have an unusual clarity and brightness. The sounds of car horns and shouted conversations lanced through her consciousness. Even her four-door sedan, which reflected the distorted, surreal shapes of passing traffic, seemed unusually shiny. She turned on the ignition and as she pulled out into traffic, she wondered why she could not quell the fear within her. She exerted all her effort to breathe calmly.

LaValle and the waitress, Verna, got into the backseat when Eartha pulled up to the rear entrance. LaValle lay back in the seat and Verna held a towel to his face.

Although Eartha did not like LaValle, she felt that she should at least advise Verna of a potentially awkward situation. "Excuse me, Verna," Eartha began gingerly. "I thought you should know that Val's wife is going to meet him at the doctor's."

"Who called her, you?" Verna's voice was hard and brassy.

"I did what family is supposed to do," Eartha answered, feeling strangely defensive.

"Well, honey," Verna said snidely, "are you going to hold the towel to his head *and* drive? Do you want blood all over your upholstery?"

"I just thought you should know. I was just trying to be polite," Eartha explained.

"You done your duty, thanks."

They drove on in silence. The night was clear and stars could still be seen even against the brightness of the city lights. Eartha headed west on Fell Street, intending to follow the panhandle of Golden Gate Park to Lincoln. It was a fifteen-minute ride to the doctor's. Dr. Wilburn maintained an all-night office for particular clients that was located on the edge of the Westlake District. His clients paid him well and he returned the favor by providing first-class medical services in a discreet setting. Eartha heard a sound of scuffling in the rear seat. She heard LaValle say, "Get off me, woman!" Then she saw his head, swathed in towels, briefly in her rearview mirror.

"Where are we?" LaValle asked, peering through an opening in the towel.

"We're crossing Divisadero on Fell Street, heading for the panhandle," Eartha answered, happy to concentrate on something neutral like geographical locations.

LaValle directed, "Turn right on Divisadero."

"That's not the way to Doc Wilburn's," she protested.

"I don't care. I told you to turn! Now, turn!" LaValle's tone was filled with impatience.

"I'm not chauffeuring you around," Eartha answered evenly. "I'm only going to drive to the doctor's office, then I'm finished. Your wife will meet you there. You can get her to drive you anywhere you want." She wasn't generally so uncooperative, but LaValle had made several passes at her before and after she was married. The last time he had been particularly aggressive, but fortunately for her King had walked in while she was fighting him off. She didn't know what transpired after she left the room, but LaValle never bothered her again.

LaValle declared, "I need something to drink bad! Just drive me by Mike's Liquor on the corner of Golden Gate and Baker."

Eartha knew that Mike's was a place where the crowd was cruder and the honesty of the house was on a much lower scale than that of the Blue Mirror. Knifings and shootings were common in and around Mike's. It was not a place that Eartha would have ever chosen to go, yet her loyalty to her husband, who loved his brother, caused her to attempt to be generous. "If we go by Mike's, I'm not waiting if you're inside longer than five minutes." If LaValle didn't care about his injury being treated immediately, that was his responsibility.

"Damn! Aren't you a little dictator!" LaValle said sarcastically. "Give me a break. I may need ten minutes."

"I'm waiting five minutes!" Eartha responded, wishing that she hadn't volunteered to take LaValle anywhere.

"Okay, okay. You win." LaValle agreed with obvious distaste. He was offended that Eartha would even attempt to enforce some time limit on him. Once inside of Mike's he would stretch it. He knew that she was not likely to drive off without him.

Mike's was a two-story brick building located one block off Divisadero. The liquor store took up the whole ground floor. The gaming rooms were reached by a door to an enclosed stairway on the side of the building. As per usual, until closing time, there were a number of colored men loitering around the entrance. When LaValle exited the car after Eartha parked in front, there were several exclamations from the men as they recognized him. LaValle didn't go into the liquor store. He went straight to the side door. Even with the windows up, the loitering men could be heard talking about LaValle. Verna rolled down her window and called one of the men over.

"What's going on, Chet?" she asked.

"That you, Verna?" the man inquired as he came up to the car.

"It's me, Chet," Verna confirmed. "What's all the yammering about?"

"Ain't you heard?" Chet asked incredulously.

Verna was impatient. "Heard what? If I'd heard, I wouldn't be wasting my time with your sorry ass!"

"If'en it was me, I wouldn't be riding around with LaValle Tremain jes' right about now." Chet mouthed his words as if they were unusually profound.

"Goddamn it, Chet. I've been good to you, loaned you money and given you free drinks. If this is the way you're going to repay my—"

Chet interrupted her. "You ain't got to get all mad and everything. I'll tell you what's happening. Two of the Tree brothers came by here twenty minutes ago, looking for LaValle. Ben Tree, he say that LaValle snuck out of his gambling joint owing big money. And the word on the street is when Ben's wife tried to stop him from leaving, LaValle cold-cocked her. Ben say that when he find him, he gon' let his blood flow. And he offered five hundred dollars for anybody who knows where LaValle is." This last sentence was said in a manner that implied that lots of people were interested in collecting the reward.

"Thanks, Chet. I owe you." Verna rolled up her window and got her bag. "Damn! LaValle's been a busy little beaver tonight!"

"Are you going to go in and warn LaValle?" Eartha asked Verna. The fear was back. She could feel it in her chest.

"I bet somebody here's already on the phone to the Trees. This is where I get out, honey," Verna retorted in her cold, professional voice. "He's cute and I like him, but I'm not dying for him or with him!"

Eartha was shocked. "You've got to go in and warn LaValle," she urged. "Is this all that friendship means to you?"

"He ain't my friend," Verna snapped. "If he was my friend, he would have treated me better. And for that matter, he ain't your friend either. If you had any brains at all, you'd be driving out of here right now. That fool has started a war!"

"I can't leave Val," Eartha answered. "He's family. His brother would never forgive me."

"You probably right," Verna acknowledged as she opened the car door. "But that's your problem, not mine. Val had plenty chances to make me family and he didn't. I'm out of here!" She got out and slammed the car door shut. The men around the liquor store made several crude comments about her body and what they would do to it if given the chance. The men didn't bother Verna. She was used to attracting male attention. She knew how to deal with it. But she was bothered by Eartha's words. In fact, Verna felt guilty. She briefly considered going in and warning LaValle until she saw a large, late-model car pull up across the street and turn off its lights. The men in its interior did not get out. They were waiting. She figured there must have been a stampede to collect the reward when LaValle appeared at Mike's. Verna's survival mechanism kicked into high gear and she stepped on down the street without looking back.

LaValle came out several minutes later with a bottle of scotch in his hand. He opened the back door and got in. "Where's Verna?" he asked.

"She left when she found out that the Tree brothers are looking for you for beating up Ben's wife." Eartha was barely able to force the words out. She felt soiled by his presence. She had no doubt that LaValle had punched someone's wife. She started the car and pulled out of her parking space. Unseen by Eartha, the large, late-model car followed her car into the crosstown traffic.

"Oh, you heard about that, huh?" LaValle asked, taking a long drink out of the bottle of scotch. He belched and said, "Ain't no big thing. She liked it."

Suddenly, her heart began to pound so loudly that she scarcely thought she could hear. There appeared to be no level to which her brother-in-law would not sink. She turned off Portola onto a small street that wound above St. Francis Woods and led eventually to Ocean Avenue. It was then that she noticed that they were being followed. For the first time, she was frightened for herself. If indeed the car behind her was following her, it was because of LaValle. If she was found with him, she would receive a fate similar to his. The thought caused chills to run up and down her spine. She resolved in that moment that she would not let herself be forced off the road and under no circumstances would she stop. Eartha pressed down on the gas and felt the big Packard reassuringly surge forward.

LaValle, sitting in the back, nearly lost his balance as the vehicle began climbing the hill along the narrow, winding street. It was obvious to him that she was speeding. "Slow down, damn it!" he growled. "What's the damn hurry?"

"We're being followed," Eartha said simply as she watched in the rearview mirror the car behind her increase its speed.

After he turned and looked, LaValle gasped, "They're right behind us!" As he spoke, the following car swerved out into the oncoming lane and tried to draw alongside the Packard, but Eartha accelerated and blocked the car. The street dipped sharply to the right and then continued to ascend. Eartha careened off of several cars fighting for control over the Packard, which lost traction on every sharp turn.

LaValle cried, "Be careful or it'll be you who kills us!"

"What's the difference?" Eartha asked in a monotone. She was concentrating on driving the car, yet she felt somehow distant from herself, as if she were watching herself in a dream sequence. The street continued to climb but straightened out into a long, flat curve. Along the outside of the curve, the hill dropped away steeply. The following car sought to pass once more, this time more aggressively. It was only the momentary narrowing of the street that prevented it from drawing even with the Packard. Both cars were now maintaining speeds in excess of sixty miles an hour on a street built for twenty-mile-per-hour traffic. The car behind surged forward and crashed into the rear of the Packard. The Packard skidded sideways, precipitously close to the edge, before the wheels caught traction and pulled the car out of danger.

"We should pull over," LaValle shouted over the roar of the engine. "I don't think they'll do much. They don't want to go to war with my father."

"I don't intend to find out," Eartha answered as she negotiated the crest of the hill and the street began to descend in sharp turns. The Packard sideswiped three cars as Eartha struggled to keep the speeding car on the street.

"Pull over, bitch!" LaValle shouted. "I'd rather take my chances with them than die with you."

Eartha heard LaValle's words, but they did not penetrate her consciousness. She was consumed with steering the car. She had given up trying to avoid parked vehicles, and she was glancing off them left and right. The sound of the Packard's engine, the screeching of its tires, the metal-on-metal collisions with parked cars all turned into one long, distended sound, and it was the sound of bedlam. Houses were flashing past. They blurred into a continuous wall that was broken only by the occasional street. Every little movement of the steering wheel caused the car to change direction. All her energy was focused on keeping the car on the street.

"Let me out!" shouted LaValle.

Eartha spoke between bouts of wrestling with the car's inertia. "The only way you'll get out of this car is if you jump!" The street descended steeply and veered to the right around a bank of apartments. Along the length of the right side of the street, a metal barrier guarded the edge of an embankment which dropped steeply to another street below. Eartha swung the Packard around to follow the curve of the street as the following car rammed them from behind. The Packard fishtailed out of her control and went into a spin. Every time the car swung around, she saw the apartments coming nearer and nearer. It looked like the Packard was going to skid right into the supporting pillars of the apartments, but the car slammed into a fire hydrant on the passenger's side and ended up facing uphill. The hydrant was knocked off its seating and water gushed upward before falling on the Packard. The other vehicle, located farther up the street, had run through a fence on the uphill side of the street and was now attempting to back out. Eartha, slightly dazed and bruised but uninjured, turned the Packard around and accelerated down the street. The other car pulled free from the wreckage of the fence and roared after her. On her right, she could see another street rising to intersect the one on which she now drove. However, before the intersection, there was another sharp turn to the left as the street followed the curve of the hill. She knew she was going too fast to make the turn. She attempted to apply her brakes, but the car started to skid toward the edge of the embankment. The pursuing car rammed the Packard again, sending it hurtling through the metal barrier. The car was briefly airborne as it tore off the top of a stop sign and then nosedived into the street, crashing amid sparks and the tortured sounds of twisting metal. It ricocheted off the pavement, went flying, bounced off a pickup truck, and landed on its side, where it skidded briefly before falling heavily upside down on its roof.

LaValle, who had been trying to get out of the car after it crashed into the hydrant, had his door open when the car went airborne. He was thrown clear when the Packard nosedived onto the pavement. He landed in a hedge that broke his fall and saved his life. He lay partially on the hedge with one leg touching the ground for several minutes as he fought his way to consciousness. In the background he heard sirens and people's voices as the neighborhood awakened. He rolled out of the hedge and fell heavily to the ground. The pain caused him to pass

out. LaValle lay unconscious a few minutes then awakened groggily
and forced himself to sit up. He discovered when he attempted to brace
himself with his left hand that a splitting pain shot up his arm and
clanged in his brain. Holding his left arm carefully, LaValle got un-
steadily to his feet. His back and his arms were terribly lacerated and
bruised, but it appeared only his left arm was broken. He stood in the
shadows of the bushes surrounding him, watching the spectacle in the
street.

He heard someone say, "Stay back, this car is leaking gasoline!" He
heard a woman's voice: "There's someone in the car." Suddenly the car
caught fire. LaValle could see the black silhouettes of the bystanders as
the leaking gasoline caught flame. Far below, he heard an explosion and
looked down the hill. There was another car burning in the rear parlor
of a house on the next street below. Their pursuers had not escaped un-
scathed. The sound of high-pitched screaming interrupted his thoughts.
He realized the sound was coming from the Packard. Staying in the
shadows, LaValle gingerly made his way down the hill until he could no
longer hear the sound of Eartha's screams.

Saturday, June 26, 1982

The M Taravel issued out of the darkness of the tunnel at upper Market and returned to daylight. The sun shone wanly between large,
wind-shredded clouds that whisked their way eastward. Deleon sat on
the edge of his seat watching the crowd of passengers that boarded the
streetcar. Most of the people were under thirty. A number of them were
dressed in punk black with their hair dyed different shades of red, purple, and green. None of the other boarders stood out, particularly as a
possible addition to the existing two-man team. Deleon did not discount the possibility that San Vicente might have men on the scene
that he didn't know about. He needed to take some divergent action,
but it couldn't be too elusive. He had no desire to lose his followers,
merely to identify them. He had made up his mind that he would
switch to one of the bus lines crossing Market then would transfer to

another bus which would take him to the central bus station at First and Mission. No one who had a legitimate business or personal errand would follow the circuitous path he intended to take. He saw the 54 Van Ness bus waiting to cross Market Street. As he used the pole to swing erect he thought, It won't be long now.

The streetcar screeched to a stop and the doors opened. Deleon exited quickly and ran across the tracks to board the bus. He showed his transfer and took a seat in the back, facing the door. Only the two men he had recognized earlier boarded the bus from the streetcar. The bus lurched forward and began the long, slow grind up Van Ness to California. Deleon looked at his watch and smiled: It was ten-fifteen in the morning. If things went according to plan their bodies would be cold by noon. He relaxed himself with the thought that when his debts were paid he would be free. He owed only two men on the whole planet: his grandfather, who had provided the ladder by which Deleon had climbed out of the pit of poverty, despair, and ignorance; and his father, who had been the one to put him in the pit in the first place. Life in prison had taught Deleon very clearly that all debts had to be paid, in one form or another; and when messages had to be sent, they were best understood when they were written in blood.

The first time Deleon ever really talked to his grandfather was just before his trial as an adult. Deleon had been eighteen years old at the time and was facing twenty to life for participating in the murder of a pimp. His grandfather had worn a colorful, short-sleeved shirt with a floral print, a panama hat, and had a cigar sticking out of his mouth. There was no word of greeting shared between them. They sat across the table from each other in a small blue-walled room for nearly five minutes without saying a thing. They had simply stared at each other. Finally, Deleon had gotten impatient. He stood up and called for the transport deputy. Then his grandfather had asked, "Is this all you wants from life, or is you lookin' to be somebody's girlfriend? 'Cause you sho' ain't tough enough to avoid that when you gets sent up!"

The truth of his grandfather's words stopped him. It was only luck and timing that had prevented him from being raped while in juvenile hall. He was well aware that he wasn't the toughest kid around. He had sat back down at the table, then his grandfather had continued, "I got lawyers that can get yo' time reduced. Maybe down to five years, but I needs yo' oath that you gon' pay yo' debt to me." Deleon had started to babble some inane promises, but his grandfather had held up his hand. "Don't say shit you don't mean! I ain't doin' this 'cause I want to be nice. I's doin' it 'cause you's blood and we got a war on our hands. I needs to know whether you's ready to do yo' part."

Deleon was confused. He sputtered, "What war? I don't want anything to do with some crazy war!"

"Why not? You's throwin' yo' life away, ain't you? Why not help yo' family? Shit, boy, we can do more for you than you can do for yo'self. You ain't exactly made a success out of livin' in the streets."

"What family are you talking about? I don't want anything to do with my father. I hate him!"

"Ain't nobody talkin' 'bout yo' jive-ass father. He ain't in the mix. We's talkin' 'bout the DuMont name, boy! We talkin' 'bout you standin' up fo' yo' family name!"

Deleon had thought for a minute then asked, "What do I have to do?"

"Let's talk 'bout what kind of life you wants first: like, do you wants some money in yo' pocket? You wants a nice car? Nice clothes? I heard you used a knife on that pimp. Do you wants to learn how to really use a knife? How to fight and defend yo'self? How to be one of the baddest motherfuckers around?"

Deleon was incredulous. "You can do all that? You'd do that for me?"

His grandfather had nodded. "I can do it, but I ain't doin' it for you. I's doin' it for the DuMont name. For the family. But I ain't gon' throw money away. You got to come on with the program heart and soul! First, you got to get yo' GED whiles you in prison. Then when you gets out, you got to make a commitment to go to college and get you a degree in business."

"College?" Deleon couldn't believe what he was hearing. "How long that take?"

"I'on know. Fo', five years, I guess. It don't matter how long it take. You got to get you a BA degree."

"How come I got to get a degree? I mean, four or five years! Damn!" Four years sounded like forever.

His grandfather nodded his head. "Yessiree bob! That's it! You gon' need book learnin' to win this battle. If we win, you gon' need the smarts to hold on to what we get. Anyway, it gon' take that long to train you and to see that you got the grit to do the job."

"What job is this?"

His grandfather leaned forward, his face grim, and hit the table emphatically with his fist. "We got to set things aright with them Tremains! We got us a blood debt that got to be paid!"

Deleon smiled as he remembered how he had promised everything that his grandfather wanted to hear without having any intention of following through on his agreement. He would've said anything to get his sentence reduced. The memory of his first year in prison was almost too painful to bear. Prison was the only place where men did not kill time; instead it killed them. Boredom was as deadly as a knife, it merely took longer. All the shucking and jiving he had done on the streets was useless in prison. He soon learned that death was in the balance every hour of every day. Even after he had been accepted as a soldier into one of the prison's most vicious gangs, his days were still dominated by fear and boredom. There was a continuous pattern of violence between the top four gangs in the struggle to control the drug trade. Rival gang members were killed whenever the opportunity arose. It was only through the escape provided by his reading and his painting that Deleon had maintained his sanity.

The bus wheezed to a stop at Geary Street and Deleon saw the 55 Geary bus coming toward him a block away. He pulled the exit cord to alert the driver he wanted to get off and the rear door swung open. Deleon got off and walked over to the Geary bus stop. There was a bookstore right behind the bus shelter and Deleon peered in the window, concentrating on the reflections. Once again, only the two men he had recognized got off the Van Ness bus. Not yet wanting to confront his followers, Deleon continued to look in the bookstore window. Surprisingly, he saw an edition of *The Wretched of the Earth* for sale. It was a touch of kismet, after all the years that had passed, that he saw a copy of Fanon's book. Butch Austen, with whom he'd bunked his last four years in prison, had discussed this book with him at considerable length. It had been an awakening for Deleon and had helped him focus on his desire to throw off the shackles of ignorance. After he was released from prison he got his bachelor's degree, then went on and got a master's in fine arts, and his grandfather, true to his word, had paid for everything.

Deleon boarded the 55 Geary and went to the back of the bus. His followers sat in the middle, where they could keep an eye on him.

Deleon was beginning to get excited. The Cubans were so smug. Soon they would see what he had learned about handling a knife, what his six-month, eight-hour-a-day stint in Hong Kong had taught him.

The ride to the central bus station at First and Mission was short despite the traffic. Deleon disembarked with the rest of the passengers. He wandered through several small diners and eateries then hurried out to where the commuter buses were loading. He stood in line to board a bus bound for Gilroy and caused consternation in his two followers. Martinez hurriedly sent Diaz to buy tickets for Gilroy. Deleon waited for Diaz to return with the tickets before he stepped out of line and wandered back into the main hall of the bus station. He saw Martinez go to one of the phone booths. Deleon didn't want that. He then trotted out toward the loading area again. When he was sure Martinez and Diaz were following him, he took a detour down to the terminal's lower level, to a little-used bathroom at the far end of a poorly lit hall.

He was exultant when he entered the bathroom and found it empty. Deleon unsheathed the seven-inch blade of his knife and pulled some paper towels from the rack to cover it. He had just turned on the water in one of the sinks when Martinez entered the bathroom. Diaz remained at the door, keeping a lookout. The expression on Martinez's face gave a clear picture of his frustration and anger as he walked toward Deleon. It was obvious that he intended to punish Deleon for leading them on a wild goose chase. Deleon, pretending to be wiping his hands on the paper towels, started forward to meet Martinez, a smile on his face.

Martinez was in no mood to play. He growled in his thick Cuban accent, "What you t'ink you doin', you stupid fuck? You t'ink we got time to play with your fucking ass?"

"It's a beautiful day to ride public transportation," Deleon replied, maintaining the smile on his face as he kept the knife hidden in the paper towels.

Martinez said, "You need a lesson, punk, and I goin' to give it to you!" He dropped down into a crouch, ready to kick or punch depending upon the opening. He feinted quickly with his left hand, and Deleon the fool moved directly into the path of his right. Martinez smiled; this was almost too easy. His right hand snaked out, driving for the throat. He was surprised when Deleon ducked under it and even more surprised to see that Deleon wanted to close with him. Martinez was still going forward; his momentum wouldn't allow him to stop. He tried to adjust and turn as Deleon moved to his right. He didn't even see the knife until the last moment, just before it sliced through his neck. There was a searing pain and a whistling noise. He tried to call out to Diaz, but there was no sound. Then he saw the floor rushing up at his face.

Deleon did not hesitate after he slit Martinez's throat, nor did he hurry. He continued walking right past Martinez toward the door, where Diaz stood. The smile was still on his face. He even waved to Diaz as Diaz stood watching him with a questioning look. It wasn't until Martinez fell to the floor that Diaz became alarmed. He just barely had time to raise his arm to defend himself from Deleon's attack. Unfortunately for him, he never had time to raise his other arm. Deleon sprang forward with such speed and force that he had driven his knife up to the hilt into Diaz's heart before Diaz could mount a defense. Diaz was dead before he hit the floor.

Deleon never stopped moving. He wiped his knife on the paper towels and threw them in a nearby trash bin. He checked his clothes for stains and allowed himself to smile. The art of using a knife was not only in killing your foe, but in not getting any blood on your clothes.

He walked outside the bus station and hailed a taxi. He gave the driver directions and sat back to think. There was no distress or regret for the lives he had just taken. Instead he was thinking of his future life, a life that was so close he could almost taste it. It was a world far different from the one he had known, a world filled with vibrant colors and blank canvases. He wanted to try his hand at pastels, oils, and acrylics, and he thought that he would spend a couple of years studying composition in Haiti, Jamaica, Trinidad, or Martinique. Deleon thought about the first picture he would paint. He had not formulated its subject or shape yet, but he particularly liked the thought of a canvas covered with a bright, transcendent color. Perhaps it would be a fitting memorial to the end of a way of life, a painting dominated with the color of fresh blood.

Saturday, June 26, 1982

Presenio Cordero was extremely angry as he walked down the corridor of KFRE Public Radio to the employees' lounge. The lounge
consisted of a long, narrow, unpainted room with a dingy, broken-
down couch, a candy machine and a drink machine, a tired little refrigerator which was barely able to maintain fifty degrees, and two Formica
dining room tables accompanied by an assortment of uncomfortable
folding chairs.

Pres looked around the room and thought, I'm giving up my middle
age for this? I could be making money and driving a new car! Instead I
work for peanuts, watch executive directors mismanage the funds that I
raised, and endure tedious board meetings in which the board members
don't even read their agendas or program packets, and for what? Why
am I sacrificing?"

He knew the answer by heart and it was a good answer: to bring more
people of color and women into the radio broadcasting environment, to
provide the trainees in his program with the necessary technical training
to enable them to compete for jobs in the production and broadcasting
ends of radio operations. He had committed himself to giving back to
the community in an attempt to atone for the lives he had taken and the
harm he had caused during his military service in Vietnam. If he hadn't
had to deal with the financial mismanagement of the station's director,
the job would have been a dream; as it was, it was a nightmare.

He put two quarters in the drink machine and pressed a button.
Nothing happened. He flicked the coin-return lever and nothing happened. In a fit of pique, Pres hit the machine with his fist and a can of
soda rolled down the chute.

"We have to pay for any damage to lounge dispensers," a prim voice
chided him. It belonged to Gwen Hewlitt, the executive director of
KFRE, a trim, brown-skinned woman in her mid-thirties. She wore her
short, black hair in a strange perm that had her hair standing straight up
on her head.

"Give me a break!" Pres said, still angry from her presentation to the
board. "If you used the employee lounge, you'd know these machines
don't work half the time!"

"The board has finished their executive session. They're ready for
you to come back in," Gwen informed him with a steady look. "Your

threat to get a lawyer and challenge the manner in which I've dispersed funds did not go over well. If you don't tone down your approach, your continued employment here could come into question."

"The board can do what it wants," Pres said with resignation as he opened his soda. "I can take this trainee project anywhere."

There was a moment of stunned silence, then Gwen sputtered, "You can't do that. You raised money under the auspices of KFRE!"

"As a matter of fact, I never mentioned KFRE in any of my written proposals or grant requests. I even mentioned KQET in San Francisco and KPSM in San Mateo as possible alternative sites in all the grants."

"Your position is paid for by KFRE. So, in effect, we're partially funding this program."

"I am not paid to be the director of the training program. I started that on my own. I'm paid to produce twenty-five hours of programming a week, ten hours more than anyone else who's making my salary. In addition, through this training program, I provide support for another thirty additional hours of programming. This training program is an asset to this radio station. And I won't have the salaries of my trainees cut to pay the costs of overruns elsewhere in station operations!"

"That means someone else won't get paid," Gwen concluded.

"Oh, please, don't give me that crap! It was poor planning like that that causes you to be over budget every year. I can't let the trainee program suffer because of your incompetence."

"Well!" Gwen said haughtily. "I came in here to work something out with you and what do I get? More accusations!"

Pres took a sip of his soda then said, "I have worked here for over ten years. Eight years before you came here! The only reason that I stayed here was this trainee program. And I won't stand by and see it destroyed by mismanagement and illegal acts. You have my resignation, effective immediately!"

Pres turned to walk out the door of the lounge and said to Gwen, "You better get someone to staff the ten hours of radio production assignments that the trainees are scheduled to provide tomorrow."

He walked out the door and down the hall. He entered his crowded office, which he shared with two other people, and began to clean out his old wooden desk. He had three boxes of trainee files, which he set on his desk. In a fourth box he put tapes of the best shows he had produced and all the grant and fund-raising paperwork.

With two boxes of files and papers in his arms Pres descended the stairs slowly, wondering whether he had allowed his ego to interfere with finding a reasonable solution. After a few moments' thought, he discarded that as a possibility; the only solution was that the trainees should continue getting paid as they were promised at the outset of the program.

KFRE was located above a good but inexpensive Cambodian restaurant. The restaurant had long served as a meeting place for KFRE staff and people associated with Public Radio. Tonight the trainees had taken over the lower floor of the restaurant next to the entrance and were awaiting Pres's arrival.

Pres heard someone tapping on the restaurant window as he walked out the door of KFRE. Since his car was parked right in front of the restaurant, he just nodded. His burden seemed to increase in weight with each step. He fumbled for his keys and had just opened the car door when two men came up on either side of him.

One man was of medium height and muscular with sandy blond hair, and the other was short and fat with a receding hairline, which he sought to cover by combing his hair from one side of his head to the other. They were both wearing dark suits. Pres gave them an angry, questioning look. He was in no mood for any shit.

"Just put your stuff in the car and come with us," the blond man hissed.

Pres noticed that the man's face was terribly pockmarked and he had a chipped tooth. "Why should I go anywhere with you?" he demanded.

"Because of this, asshole." The fat man showed Pres a gun in his holster.

"Piss off!" Pres said. "You've got the wrong person. And I've had a terrible day!" Before he could react the fat man clipped him with the butt of his gun. Pres staggered and fell against his car. Blood dripped down his face.

"What's going on here?" a woman's voice shouted. "Pres, are you all right?"

"Mind your own business!" the blond man commanded as he unlocked the door of a black sedan parked directly in front of Pres's car.

The woman, wearing her hair in long dreads, was short and dark-skinned. She retorted hostilely, "He *is* my business, you big shithead!" She then opened the door of the restaurant and shouted, "Hey, two guys are out here beating up Pres!" She turned and held the door open defiantly.

In moments the sidewalk was filled with twenty people. Jamal Henderson and Tito Camacho stepped forward.

"You guys came here to start trouble with Pres?" Jamal asked with a smile. "In front of KFRE? You have got to be stupid!"

Tito threatened, "We might have to tear you a new asshole for this mistake."

The fat man pulled his gun from the holster and let his arm hang at his side. "I wouldn't get too bold if I were you."

When the crowd saw the gun, there was a sudden fear; some people even stepped backward, but others staunchly maintained their ground. Someone yelled, "He ain't gon' shoot all of us!"

"We're police!" the blond man claimed, walking back to where his companion was standing with Pres. "We're taking this man in for questioning!"

One of the women yelled, "Let's see your badges!"

Someone in the crowd said, "They ain't got to show us no fuckin' badges!"

The blond man returned to the black sedan and opened the door. He had his hand on his gun as he reiterated, "This is police business."

"Good," said a woman in the back. "'Cause I just called them and they're sending a couple of black-and-whites to investigate you."

The fat man hurriedly pushed Pres toward the open door of the black sedan. The blond man went around to the driver's side and exclaimed, "Oh, shit!"

"You're not going far in that car," someone shouted. "I already slit those tires."

Police sirens wailed in the background.

"The real police are coming now," a woman shouted. "What are you going to do?"

"We'll take his car!" the fat man said as he pushed Pres back toward his vehicle. There were more angry rumblings in the crowd and they began to press closer. The fat man jammed his gun under Pres's chin and said, "You better stay back or he's a dead man!"

"Get his keys!" the blond man said hurriedly.

The fat man yelled to the crowd, "Stay back or I'll shoot!" He jammed the gun further into Pres's chin. "Where are your keys?"

"You aren't the police!" a woman yelled.

Someone else shouted, "If they were police, they would have shot somebody by now!"

Two police cars pulled up with their lights flashing. As the officers got out of their cars, the fat man and the tall man placed their guns on top of the cars and raised their hands. "We have permits to carry guns," the blond man said loudly.

As soon as the fat man raised his hands, Pres kneed him in the crotch. Air whooshed out of the man's mouth as he bent over.

"What's going on here?" said a policeman as he pushed his way through the crowd. Someone stepped out from the throng and kicked the fat man in the head as he started to straighten up. "That's for Pres!" The fat man staggered back against the car and snarled, "Oh, fuck, no!" He spun and reached for his gun, but Pres intercepted him.

"Can't let you do that," Pres grunted as he wrestled with the fat man, who outweighed him by seventy pounds.

The crowd came immediately to Pres's aid. In no time the fat man was being pulled away. Pres saw him go down in the center of a swarm of bodies. People crowded in front of him; he couldn't see what was happening. A woman came to his side and grabbed his arm supportively and led him away.

"Get back! Get back!" a policeman ordered as he and two other officers shoved people out of the way to reach the fat man, who was now being pummeled on the ground. "Get back, goddamn it!"

Someone brought a damp towel and began gently wiping the blood off Pres's face. A chair was brought out of the restaurant for him. People crowded around him asking if he was all right. Many of the faces he recognized as trainees, but there were others he didn't know at all.

A stockily built female officer pushed through the crowd and said to Pres, "I guess you're the victim, Pres Cordero. Now, why don't you tell me what happened." Pres recounted step-by-step the course of events as he remembered them. The officer, a woman with pale skin and a broad Slavic face, asked occasional questions as she wrote down his statement. She turned to the circle of onlookers and asked for names and addresses of witnesses and practically the whole crowd volunteered.

"Are you all friends of his?" she asked with a trace of humor. There was a predominance of affirmatives and nodding heads.

One man came forward and said, "I don't know this guy," he indicated Pres with a nod of his head, "but those two goons you got locked up in the squad car started it. I saw the whole thing."

The officer turned to Pres. "Do you wish to file a complaint?"

"Definitely! To the fullest extent of the law!" Pres asserted, his whole forehead aching.

As the officer turned to go, she said, "You're a pretty lucky guy. You got a lot of support from these people; without them, who knows what would have happened."

"Friendship and community spirit are the real treasures and riches of life," Pres said sincerely. "You're right, I am very lucky."

Saturday, June 26, 1982

There was no sound in the hospital room after Jackson's grandfather finished speaking. Muffled movement and voices could be heard through the closed door, but there was only an intense quiet between Jackson and his grandfather. Thirty-one years of silence had been broken and Jackson was speechless. He sat and pondered why he had to wait so long to hear how his mother had died. He wondered what his grandmother and grandfather had gained from their long silence. Was there some purpose behind it?

His grandfather interrupted his thoughts. "Took me nearly three years to collect this information and interview everybody connected with the happenin's of that night. By that time, yo' daddy was dead and I was raising hell!" His grandfather shook his head sadly. "Yo' daddy was some man! Bad luck you never got to know him." With these words, his grandfather seemed to sink farther down into the bed. Jackson looked at his watch and discovered that he had been in the room nearly two hours. His grandfather was obviously tired, but the old man's eyes were alert. He watched Jackson, assessing his reactions.

"You all right?" Jackson asked.

The old man nodded his head. "Now you here—it's all right!"

"What's so important about me coming down here, Grandfather?"

The old man spoke quietly and Jackson had to pull his chair closer to hear him. The old man's voice had a feathery quality. "Never lost track of you, boy. You my blood. The last of the line. The fire's in you."

"What fire are you talking about, Grandfather?" Jackson asked suspiciously.

"Flame of life, boy! Flame that burns in the belly! Makes a man stand tall for his family and what he believes in! You got to take care of the last few that had a hand in yo' daddy's death!"

He stared at his grandfather incredulously. The old man was watching him, waiting for him to speak. Jackson said, "Grandfather, I'll be happy to assist you in handling any legal issues, or executing your will, but I'm not killing anyone or causing anyone to die. That's not my world, Grandfather. That's your world."

"These last men got yo' father's blood on they hands!" The old man coughed and rasped out his words with as much anger as his exhausted condition would allow. He was fading, his strength was ebbing as Jackson watched. Jackson realized suddenly that he was alarmed for his grandfather. He stood up ready to find a nurse, but his grandfather waved him to his seat, protesting. "It's all right. Jes' sit down. Did you hear what I said before?" the old man asked querulously. "There's a blood debt still to pay!"

"I'm sure that you've let enough blood flow to more than repay that debt," Jackson answered with a touch of sarcasm.

"They gon' come after you! What you got to say to that?" Jackson shook his head unbelievingly. The old man lifted his head briefly in consternation. "You's a warrior, boy! You tryin' not to accept it, but you's a warrior. You been one since you was pint size. I know what's in yo' heart better'n you do. You's a strong, courageous man. I know what you think about me and the things I've done. I'm tellin' you, put that aside and look at the facts. A man who fights just to protect his life and his family ain't no killer. That's all I'm asking you to do. They gon' come after you, so fight to protect yo' life and yo' family!"

"Give it a rest, Grandfather," Jackson suggested. "I'm not picking up weapons to continue your feuds. But I want as much information as I can get about these people who are following me."

"They on to you, huh? They must figure that Franklin don't amount to much."

"They could be following both of us, I really don't know," Jackson answered. "All I care about is who are they and what they want with me."

"Jes' because I'm dying don't mean it's over. I wiped out a pretty good section of the DuMonts and the DiMarcos. Them folk ain't forgot nothin'! They want payback. Second, they want the corporate papers and certificates for my management company."

"Who would want to carry on a thirty-year-old feud? What's the purpose?"

"Feud was old in 1916 and the purpose was and still is revenge."

"You mean to tell me that the men who were following me are descendants of someone killed in 1916? That doesn't even sound believable!"

"Better say joe, 'cause you sho' don't know. There ain't many left, I took care of that, but there's one or two DuMonts left and maybe a couple of DiMarco's boys still in the business. It was their fathers and uncles we had to deal with when you was eighteen, only they was workin' with the Jaguar at the time. You ain't got to worry about the main family of the DiMarcos. I hear they've gone legit. Movin' into the political arena. They got too much to lose now to play this game. People following you is probably jes' hired hands and paid guns. They in it for the money, but the DuMonts and some of the renegade DiMarcos want blood. And they won't be satisfied with anything less than Tremain blood. I got a list of people for you to talk to and they gon' give you the rundown on everything."

"The DuMonts? DiMarcos? Who the hell are they? I don't remember these names!"

"DuMonts is yo' blood enemies. They been blood enemies to the Tremains since my granddaddy's time."

"What can we do to end it? This is why you haven't seen me in all this time."

His grandfather rasped out a hoarse laugh. "Ain't no end to it as long as someone with will and grit remembers. It's all about blood. They think it's safe now. Then there's others who just want the corporation's papers and certificates, and them bonds."

"What corporation certificates and bonds?"

"Jumped a couple money shipments back in the early fifties from the Mob. Money made from heroin sales in the Fillmore. Wasn't about to let some white boys move in on my turf and sell that shit! They didn't know who they was messing with. Anyway, I invested the money shipments in real estate and bought some twenty-five-year government bonds. Them bonds alone is probably worth ten million dollars now.

The rest of the money I invested in real estate through a dummy management company. Company is based in Switzerland and it owns all my properties, including the ones in San Francisco, and seventy percent of King, Inc. I owns property all over the United States and South America."

"If these bonds and certificates are registered in your name, and they are part of your estate, why are there other people interested in them?"

His grandfather answered, "My name ain't on nothing, boy. You remember I had to leave the States in 'fifty-four? If I had anything in my name, the IRS would have taken it. I knew they was after me so a couple of years before things hit the fan, I sold all my holdings to this company I had set up in Switzerland."

"What's the problem? You have the company in Switzerland."

"Problem is, there ain't nothing with my name on it. The papers and documents is buried under a new housing project in San Francisco."

For the first time since he entered the room, Jackson laughed out loud. "So, what's the problem? It's out of everybody's reach. Why don't you tell them where it is and let them fight it out among themselves?"

"Rather be bit in the ass by a snaggle-tooth mule and be dragged all the way to Mississippi!" The old man looked as if he was going to have another bout of coughing, but it subsided. "I'm gon' leave you everything, whether you want it or not. Read the papers I had put together for you. Make up yo' own mind what to do." He started to cough again, his body shaking with the effort.

"Take it easy, Gramps," Jackson advised. "Don't upset yourself."

His grandfather looked at him and said, "First time you ever called me Gramps."

"You weren't ready for it earlier," Jackson retorted.

"Don't know if I's ready for it now." The old man put his head back on the pillow and his voice dropped audibly as he said, "Gramps is what you's called when you gets really old."

Jackson studied his grandfather's face then mused aloud, "You must be tired. I was wondering should I come back later tonight or tomorrow?"

"Come back tomorrow, late afternoon. Gettin' dialysis in the morning. I likes to sleep after that."

"What exactly is your medical situation, Grandfather?"

"Look here, boy." His grandfather stared him in the eye. "I's ready to die. They done everything that I want them to. Hell, I'd rather die hard, shot in the gut, than die piece by piece, lyin' in bed like this. Tomorrow is the last dialysis I'll do. The last anything."

Jackson looked at his grandfather and shook his head. Most people would choose a natural death at an old age over one due to violence, yet his grandfather preferred a bullet.

He asked, "Can I bring you anything when I come tomorrow, Grandfather?"

"I want carnitas!"

"Are you sure that's allowed on your diet?"

"What's it gon' do, kill me?"

Jackson laughed. "I'll bring you carnitas. About four-thirty or five in the afternoon?" He rose and went to stand by the bed.

His grandfather grabbed his hand and his voice trembled with feeling when he spoke. "Thank you for comin' down. Means more to me than you know. I just needed to lay my eyes on you, to see you as a man. I can let loose now. Thank you, boy."

Jackson held his grandfather's hand in his for several minutes. He was overcome by a sudden flood of emotion that was filled with heartache and loss. For a moment he was almost close to tears. He bowed his head and pressed the back of his grandfather's hand to his forehead. He remained in this position until his grandfather said, "You my blood, boy. I knows I took you down a hard road, but you the one gon' lead this family to right."

Jackson didn't bother to argue. He stood up and helped adjust the position of the pillows so that his grandfather was comfortable. When he left the room, the man who had been on guard got up from a couch across the hall and returned to the room. He gave Jackson a perfunctory nod as he passed. Carlos and the limo were waiting for him outside. Jackson looked at his watch: It was nearly eight-thirty in the evening. The sky was dark and overcast. He was too full of turmoil and sadness to speak, so he sat silently gazing through the tinted windows of the limo and watched the lights of Mexico City pass. There seemed to be many more tall buildings than he recalled, but the traffic seemed as chaotic as he remembered. The perpetual honking of car horns sounded briefly like a riff from a straight-ahead jazz tune, a plangent salutation to the wild cacophony of life.

At last, the heavy iron gate swung open and the limo pulled into his grandfather's courtyard. Jackson watched as the gate rolled closed with a clang behind the car. He invited Carlos in, but Carlos declined, indicating that he had some errands to run. When Jackson walked through the front door, Mario informed him that hot food was available. Jackson attempted a reply in Spanish, but soon gave it up. He asked that the food be brought to the dining room.

Jackson went immediately to the kennel and freed the puppy, who was delirious with gratitude. The puppy's tail was whipping back and forth as they made their way back into the dining room. The possession of dogs was a fundamental element in his grandfather's concept of home security, and because he transacted much of his business at the dining table, his principal dog had a place of comfort in the room. His grandfather always had one or sometimes two dogs that he prized over all others. These would be his house dogs. He always had his terriers trained to fight in the pit; that way they could fight off other dogs who had graduated from the pit. Sure enough, in the corner of the dining room there was a large cushion and a place for food and water.

After supper, Jackson went into the den and poured himself a healthy shot from a bottle of Small Batch Bourbon and sat down at the desk. As he sipped the liquor he wondered how it was possible that after all the time that had passed, his grandfather could affect him so strongly. He admired the old man's courage in allowing his failing body its rightful death. Jackson hoped that whenever his own end came upon him he would be as resolute.

That night Jackson slept in his grandfather's bed and it seemed to him that it was a rite of passage, belonging with the first time his feet touched the floor when he sat at the dinner table, or the first time he rode a bike, or the first time that he drove a car. He had clearly passed one of the demarcations separating the different age periods of his life. Jackson slept a dreamless night for the first time in weeks and awoke in the morning feeling refreshed.

The puppy came running as soon as Jackson's feet hit the floor beside the bed, greeting him with absolute joy. Its tail was whipping back, its ears were flopping. It leaned against his legs as it waited to receive affection. He reached down and petted it and it began to wag its tail even more violently. The puppy brought a smile to Jackson's face. He played with it while he washed and got dressed. Breakfast and an English-language newspaper were on the table waiting for him when he entered the dining room. He and the puppy ate alone. After glancing though the paper, he took the puppy out for a short walk then returned to examine the papers in the valise. He spent the rest of the morning going through his grandfather's documents. There was nothing to break his concentration but the puppy. The house was empty and the silence was broken only by the distant murmurings of the hired staff, who moved like ghosts through the halls. Whenever Jackson came upon them they fell respectfully silent then moved on to perform chores in other rooms. The puppy's friskiness and playful antics made the emptiness more bearable. Without forethought, Jackson was becoming attached to the dog.

It didn't feel like a Sunday to him even though he could hear the church bells pealing as they called the devout to afternoon Mass. The morning had rushed by for him. He took the puppy for another walk, then upon his return, changed into workout sweats. Next to the garage, his grandfather had built a small gym. There was a set of free weights, a speed bag and a heavy punching bag, jump ropes, and assorted other equipment used by prizefighters to stay in shape. Jackson worked out hard, finishing with five sets of two-minute sessions on both the speed and heavy bags. After Jackson's shower, Reuben called to schedule a meeting.

Reuben and Julio arrived at two-thirty. The two brothers brought several accordion files full of paper documents. Without being asked they began laying out various forms and documents on the dining room table. The puppy growled threateningly from its corner at the two strange men and advanced on the table, but Jackson quieted him with a few strokes and soft words.

Julio and Reuben saw the puppy and nodded their heads in approval. Julio said with a smile, "This dog is a direct descendant of the first Diablito. He is but a puppy, but already we can see his heart."

Jackson looked at the puppy with new respect. The puppy saw his look and thumped his tail. Jackson laughed to himself. His grandfather was too smart. He knew that Jackson would be unable to resist the puppy, particularly when he knew it was from the line of Diablito. He and the puppy were both distant sons of true warriors and he did not need to be told that the puppy would serve him well. The thought of his grandfather reminded him that the old man had requested carnitas. "Speaking of my grandfather, he wants some carnitas. Where's a good place to go?"

Julio answered, "We'll have Sanchez, the limo driver, pick up some for you when you go to the hospital today."

"Thanks, Julio. He'll appreciate it." Jackson smiled. "Looks like you brought part of the Brazilian rain forest with you." He indicated the piles of paper with his hand.

Reuben began, "These papers reflect all your grandfather's holdings in the United States, Mexico, and South America. The books are ledgers indicating the revenue generated over the years and how that money was invested."

"But we also brought you some papers that were faxed to you," Julio interjected. "It looks like your work wants to keep you busy."

Jackson took the file of faxes and set it aside on the table. "I wish that was what they truly wanted, but they spend more time trying to sabotage people outside of their circle than getting things done."

"People are the same the world over, no matter what language they speak," Reuben said with a shake of his head. "Do you wish to work on that now, or shall we proceed with your grandfather's will and property holdings?" He gestured to a stack of papers Julio had placed on the table.

"Let's go through the will." Jackson picked up a thick sheaf of stapled papers and began to read. The documents were the incorporation papers of a holding company. "My grandfather really established a holding company?" Jackson asked with disbelief. It seemed antithetical to his perception of his grandfather; gambling and financial planning originated from opposite poles.

"El Negro had some problem with the IRS and he had to sell all his property or risk losing it," Julio answered. "He gave the family house to your grandmother then sold seventy percent of the rest of the San Francisco property along with all his other properties to this holding company in Switzerland."

The puppy, who had been checking out the two strange men to satisfy himself that they were not dangerous, came over and sat down heavily on Jackson's foot. He smiled and reached down and rubbed the puppy's head fondly. "Who runs this holding company?" Jackson asked.

"A law firm in New York has been doing it, but you run it now. However, to take full control you must get the corporation's certificates and papers." Reuben stepped forward in his smartly tailored Italian suit. "This company's holdings are worth more than one hundred million dollars. You're a rich man, Diablito, and this does not include the government bonds that your grandfather says are hidden with the certificates in San Francisco."

"How can I run a company without any proof of my possessing it?"

"Your grandfather named you executive director of the board when he founded the company in 1954. For the last ten years we have been paying about one hundred fifty thousand a year into a trust fund that you get once you agree to the terms of stewardship, then you can take your time and find the hidden documents."

"A million and a half dollars? Give me a moment to think," Jackson said. It was an astounding amount of money. Jackson was a little awed by the prospect of having access to that amount of wealth. But he also knew that if he accepted the money he was duty-bound to carry on his grandfather's feud.

The puppy went to the closed door leading to the kitchen and began snuffling. Moments later, there was a knock at the door and Mario entered with cups and an urn of steaming coffee. Jackson remembered his grandfather always drank coffee during the day when he was transacting his business. Jackson gestured to Mario to place the coffee on the uncluttered end of the table. Mario poured coffee for everyone then left the room.

Julio and Reuben went over all the papers on the table with Jackson, explaining the purpose of the various forms and the nature of documents written in Spanish. It was nearly four in the afternoon before they finished reviewing all the papers. It was clear that his inheritance, should he accept it, would make him a financially independent man.

Julio looked over at Jackson and said, "I was happy that you remembered our oath to be blood brothers. We need to be able to trust and rely on one another. The next two or three months will be very dangerous for us all."

"Why?" Jackson asked, perplexed. "Do you have the same enemies as my grandfather?"

Reuben answered, "You have to remember that both your grandfather and our father fought the drug traffic for many years before it was recognized as a national problem."

"That was what your father did; how does that affect you?" Jackson asked.

"They both made numerous enemies among the criminal element as well as among government officials. Our father has been dead nearly seventeen years and we are still dealing with the fallout from his actions."

Stuffing his shirttails into his pants, Julio added, "There are many who would like to make use of our connections and facilities that we have scattered throughout Mexico and California."

Jackson mused, "I'm surprised that it would still be a problem. Aren't you guys legit now?"

"It is not good manners to ask such a question. You know that, Diablito," Reuben chided him gently. "But for your information only, we still run several different gambling facilities. We provide our big spenders with female escorts, and there is still a little smuggling going on."

After the Ramirez brothers left, Jackson sat out in the sun of the courtyard with the puppy and made the final changes to the faxed report. Afterward he read through some more of the files which laid out his grandfather's holdings and considered the amazing twist his life was taking. He had often dreamed what he would do philanthropically if he had money. He now had the opportunity. All he had to do was kill an unspecified number of human beings. He laughed cynically. That's not too much to ask in order to fund a philanthropic desire.

Carlos and the limo came for Jackson at four-thirty in the afternoon. Jackson went to the refrigerator and took out four cold beers. He returned the puppy to the kennel, despite its yelping protests. Then he and Carlos got into the limousine and drove off into the haze of the afternoon. The limo pulled up to a large, ten-story glass building with a wide cement plaza in front of it. Carlos offered to go up and take his revised work to be faxed and Jackson nodded gratefully. He knew that his Spanish wasn't up to the task. He sat for a few minutes in the darkness of the car, watching the people walk across the plaza, but after ten minutes the car began to feel too stuffy and confining. Jackson got out of the car and walked across the plaza to a large, ornate fountain. He was staring into the water, lost in thought, when Carlos returned.

Fate is a strange and twisted fiber that runs through the material of human lives, and is in part responsible for weaving the patterns by which those lives are lived. Although some small control can be exerted over the racing shuttle of passing days that affects the larger warp and woof of the marching years, often it is fate's pattern in another's life which totally changes the design in one's own. When Corazon placed the paper with Jackson's Mexico City fax number on the corner of her blotter Friday afternoon, she had no idea that there would be any reason for someone to be at her desk. Bedrosian had arranged for Martha and Howard to meet him on that morning to correct the same report that Jackson was in the process of rewriting. Martha sat at Corazon's desk because she was making a long-distance call to her sister in Iowa and she didn't want the call on her own phone line. When she finished the call to her sister, she saw Jackson's name and underneath it "Mexico City," along with the number. Martha recalled that Bedrosian had announced in a late-Friday-evening meeting of his management team that anyone with contact information for Jackson in Mexico City should forward it to the city manager's desk. Martha copied the phone number on a slip of paper and took it to Bedrosian.

Bedrosian was only too happy to call Serena with the number. He had decided that he would take some sort of disciplinary action against Jackson, but first he wanted to do something that showed he was a caring supervisor. Bedrosian saw his calling Jackson's grandmother on Saturday as an act of showing concern for his subordinate. It would not have stayed his hand had he known that he was actually jeopardizing Jackson's life. Bedrosian, after all, never forgot a slight or a challenge to his authority.

Serena, upon receiving the information, called Braxton. Braxton forwarded his information to DiMarco, who communicated with his people in Mexico. With their connections and a little money, his agents soon had the name and address of the building in which Jackson was picking up his fax. But even that would not have been enough if Jackson had remained in the limo while Carlos took the faxes into the building. It was not until Jackson exited the limousine that DiMarco's men identified him. From that point on, he was followed, and unknowingly, he provided them all the information they needed.

The limo stopped at a small restaurant to pick up the carnitas-filled burritos for his grandfather, then continued on to the clinic. The enticing smell of carnitas filled the car and made Jackson's mouth water. The drive seemed to take longer than the day before. At first, Jackson thought it was the tantalizing aroma of the food, but then he realized that he was just anxious to see his grandfather.

When Jackson walked into his grandfather's room, the guard rose and left. His grandfather had his bed raised in the same position as the day before. The old man watched him. His eyes noted every movement that Jackson made. As Jackson returned his grandfather's gaze, he thought, These are not the eyes of a dying man. "How are you today, Gramps?" Jackson asked.

The old man merely nodded his head; he was looking at the package that Jackson held in his hands.

Jackson went over to the bed. "Would you like to eat now, Grandfather?"

His grandfather smiled. It seemed as if it was the first time the old man had smiled since Jackson had seen him. There was an adjustable-height hospital table next to the bed. Jackson raised the table so that it was close to his grandfather and began unwrapping the package. There were two full dinners with rice and beans. Jackson could see the old man smacking his lips in anticipation. The scene made Jackson smile. He arranged a towel, to serve as a bib, around his grandfather's neck and got the old man a fork and found a sheathed bone-handled hunting knife in a drawer in the bedside bureau. He washed it and placed it along with the Styrofoam food container on the adjustable serving table. He rolled the table into position so that the food was in front of his grandfather then went to deposit the beers he had brought into the little refrigerator by the washbasin. When Jackson returned to the bed, he observed that there were several pieces of meat on the floor while the fork lay in his grandfather's quivering hand. It took a moment, but Jackson finally figured that the old man didn't have enough strength to serve himself and was embarrassed by his weakness.

Jackson saw the serrated blade of the hunting knife lying in the folds of the blanket under the serving table. He picked it up and cut the burrito in bite-sized pieces. He stabbed a small piece of pork with the fork and offered it to his grandfather. The old man's eyes searched his warily, looking for pity.

"Come on, Gramps, this is what you want," Jackson urged.

His grandfather accepted his assistance without further scrutiny and opened his mouth. Jackson fed his grandfather for nearly twenty minutes. Finally, the old man waved away the food. He wanted something to drink. Jackson went over and took two beers out of the refrigerator and his grandfather's eyes lit up. Jackson opened a bottle and offered him a choice: "Bottle or glass?"

The old man wanted the bottle. Jackson held it for him while he took two long gulps. His grandfather burped loudly then had another long drink of beer. He raised a trembling hand, indicating that he had had enough. They sat in silence for several minutes before his grandfather spoke. "Wanna hear how your daddy died?"

"Are you up to telling another story, Gramps?"

"If'en I wasn't, I wouldn't ask," the old man snapped impatiently. "'Fore I get started, I want me some more beer tonight with the rest of my dinner."

"I have two more bottles in the fridge."

"No, I'll give those to my men who keep watch. I want a couple of six-packs."

"Sure enough. I'll either bring them back myself or I'll send the driver," Jackson said as he rose to clear away the food from the table.

"Leave it be, boy, and sit down there," his grandfather said. "'Cause this here is the reason you got to pay the blood debt."

Sunday, June 27, 1982

When DiMarco walked into the bar, he could tell by the looks on the Lenzini brothers' faces that something was amiss. As a matter of fact, Tony, the fat one, looked like he had been dropped in a meat grinder. His face was black and blue with bruises and his nose was covered with bandages. DiMarco slid into the seat across from them, placing his briefcase on the seat beside him, and asked, "What's the news?"

Victor, the older brother, spoke: "Last night Tony and Mickey Vazzi went to pick up that little gook you wanted and all hell broke loose. It seemed like everybody and his mother climbed out of the sewer to save him."

"To save him?" DiMarco questioned sharply, his impatience just beneath the surface. "I don't understand. Do you have the guy or not?"

A tall, thin waitress came over and asked for their order. The Lenzinis asked for scotches. Paul ordered a caffe latte and waited for her to leave. As a second thought, Tony ordered a sandwich. The waitress took the order and quickly disappeared among the milling crowd.

"That's what I'm trying to explain," Victor continued earnestly. "It was a simple pickup, but all these people came out of a nearby restaurant and jumped Mickey and Tony. Hell, look at Tony's face. He was mobbed. Even though he got arrested, he's lucky the police showed up, otherwise the crowd would have torn him apart."

DiMarco exploded, but he kept his voice down. "Got arrested?

Damn it! Is everybody an imbecile? I can't get nobody to do things right!"

"You told us not to use no guns," Tony protested, his voice filled with tones of injured dignity, and then he lied adroitly, "If I could have used my gun, we'd have that little slant under lock and key right now. How were we supposed to know that everyone on that block was willing to fight for him? I was lucky the police came!" Tony nervously took out a comb and combed his hair across his bald spot.

"I told you I wanted this handled low-key! Goddamn it!" DiMarco tapped the table for emphasis. "You guys owe me. I've turned a lot of business your way in the past and I've lent you money when you needed it. I thought I'd give you a chance to get even board, but maybe I chose the wrong men for the job. Maybe you guys just don't have it anymore."

Victor argued, "Tony was arrested in the East Bay, not in San Francisco! It won't even make the papers here. We just had a small problem. We'll take care of it this evening. You don't have to worry."

"No, I can't afford to waste time with small fry any longer. I need to go after the main guy. I want Jackson Tremain." DiMarco looked from one to the other of the Lenzinis. "Can you handle it?"

Both Tony and Victor nodded. "No problem," Tony said. "I got me a score to settle with this crowd anyway!"

"Don't let your temper make you foolish," DiMarco warned. "I've got a line on him in Mexico, but if he gets away from my men down there I want you to pick him up when he returns here."

"You got men in Mexico?" Tony asked in a tone of surprise and respect.

"Yeah, I got people wherever I need 'em," DiMarco replied nonchalantly. "Now, the problem is that I need him alive and he can't be too roughed up."

"Suppose we have to beat him up a little to make him cooperative?" Victor asked, nudging his brother conspiratorially.

"Yeah, suppose we have to smack him around?" Tony challenged angrily, agreeing with his brother's implication.

DiMarco smiled. "He can be smacked, but nothing serious. I need information from him and I may need to take him to a public place, so no marks on his face. After I get what I want, you can have him."

"Okay, you got a file on him?" Victor inquired.

"It's all here," DiMarco said, sliding the briefcase off the seat and onto the floor. He pushed the case across to Victor with his foot.

"When do you want him?" Tony asked eagerly.

"If he gets away from my men in Mexico, as soon as he returns," DiMarco replied. "If he don't get caught down there, I'm sure he'll be back in a couple of days. I've given you his home address. If you have to tail him, use a minimum of two cars. He's crafty. I heard he was pretty slick in giving some other guys the slip when he was heading south of the border. I'm telling you, I want this guy bad! You get him and the money will be good. Real good, get me? You fuck this up and the big boys will be on your ass! You get me? The eggplant's got to go to ground sooner or later. I figure two, three days, maybe a week at the outside, we'll have 'em! Do this right and I'll call us even."

"That's very generous," Victor said, nodding his head. "Ain't it generous, Tony?"

"It's real generous," Tony concurred.

DiMarco nodded and decided that he had spent sufficient time with the Lenzini brothers. He said his good-byes and made his way to the door and out onto the street. As he walked back to his restaurant, he hoped that the Lenzinis would be more successful than they had been in their most recent job.

When DiMarco entered the restaurant, Dominique was at the door thanking some customers who were leaving. As he passed her she asked, "Leave your briefcase somewhere?"

"It's in my car," he said lamely, furious that she had the audacity to be watching and questioning him. She raised an eyebrow and walked into the kitchen without another word. The thought that she had been placed to keep an eye on his activities reoccurred to him. There was even a possibility that she might have been planted to take him out, if he became a liability to the election campaign. DiMarco promised himself that if his plans went awry, he would make sure to kill her first; that way he wouldn't waste time looking over his shoulder and wondering. Until such time, he would maintain his professional relationship with her and suppress his anger. Her time was coming. He forced himself to smile.

Thursday, April 2, 1954

On Sunday night, a few days before Jack was killed, the Tremain family sat down to dinner. King, as usual, was at the head of the table and Serena sat at the other end. Jackson and his father sat on one side of the table. On the other sat LaValle, his wife, Lisette, and their two children, Franklin and Samantha. There was no conversation at the table other than what was necessary to pass the food or correct the children's table manners. The atmosphere was dense with resentment and unresolved anger.

Jack helped his son cut his thick slice of ham and then watched him stuff a forkful into his mouth. Every once in a while Jack would see Eartha in the boy's face, in a fleeting expression or a turn of the head. Jack heard his mother sharply chastise his son for placing his elbows on the table. Jack turned and looked at her and there was no warmth in his look. It had finally dawned on him that she was unable to contain her dislike for Jackson. His mother saw his look, then concentrated on her food.

Jack had made a mistake moving back to his parents' house and had begun to look for a home of his own. After a thorough search and through lucky accident, he had finally discovered a house that was suitable for both him and his son. He had decided to move in the coming month. His mother had not received the news well, but Jack did not care how she received the news. After the death of his wife, Jack had changed. There was a hardness about him, except where his son was concerned. He no longer desired to quit his father's business, and where he had been merciful before, he had become merciless. If anything, he confirmed the family's reputation and its legend, a legend which continued to grow when both of the elder Tree brothers were found hanging in their own garages.

Jack had also become estranged from his brother, LaValle, blaming him for Eartha's death. In fact, he could not bear to be in LaValle's presence. He only tolerated it at the weekly Sunday dinners, which were made more unpleasant by the cowed and fearful reactions of LaValle's wife and children. Jack looked across the table and noticed that Lisette had another bruise on her cheek. He shook his head. Sometimes even the children had bruises.

LaValle ate his food in silence. He hated coming to dinner at his parents' house. He had become bitter since receiving the disfiguring scar;

he was no longer the handsome, carefree man about town. He also no longer enjoyed the status that a son of King Tremain warranted. He had been disowned by his family. Only his mother remembered her responsibility to him. LaValle put down his fork and looked around. The tension in the room made the food tasteless. LaValle only came to these dinners to hit his mother up for money. He resented the fact that his brother and his father had cut him out of the family business, and since the death of Eartha, he had even been banned from going into any of his father's establishments. He had no job skills and as a result, he was forced to live off handouts from his mother. Lisette had been forced to get a job waitressing in one of his father's restaurants. It was not the way a man of his station should live. LaValle knew he deserved better and blamed his father for playing favorites and loving his younger brother more. He put his hand up to his face. He had developed a nervous reflex of running his index finger along the line of the scar that ran from his jawbone across the bridge of his nose. Dr. Wilburn had done pretty well, given that LaValle didn't get to him until midafternoon the following day. He said that if LaValle had arrived the night of the injury, it would have healed invisibly. LaValle didn't believe him. LaValle knew that life was just tougher for him than it was for most people.

After dinner King, Jack, and Jackson excused themselves and went downstairs into King's office and closed the door. The men drank scotches neat, smoked cigars, and chalked their cues to play nine-ball while Jackson drank a Coke and played on the floor with his Erector set. The office was a large carpeted room that had a full-size bar and pool table at one end, a big rolltop desk in an alcove, and a green felt card table surrounded by chairs at the other end.

"Did you see that bruise on her face?" Jack asked his father as he racked the balls. King nodded but said nothing. Jack continued, "He's beating that woman like she's a slave and then coming up here all bold, not caring whether we see the evidence of his weakness! It's sickening. Your break, Dad."

King gave his cue an extra bit of chalk and broke the rack. The four-ball fell. He missed the next shot because he was snookered behind the seven. King got himself another drink. He offered one to Jack, but he declined. Jack proceeded to run the table. King's thoughts turned to LaValle. It was a terrible thing to watch someone with the Tremain name compromise his manhood with cowardice and stupidity, to see him go off the path with no way to retrieve him. King understood not only that LaValle was weak and easy prey to temptation, but further, that he had no internal compass, and therefore could not control his direction. King's understanding did not make him sympathetic. He expected adults to carry their own weight. All adults. He knew about giving an occasional helping hand. He knew nothing about the long-term bolstering and nurturing of fallen campaigners, even if they were his children.

There was a knock on the door at the top of the stairs. King looked at Jack and shook his head with displeasure. They both knew who desired to enter. Only one person would ignore the implied statement of the closed door. King said, "Come in."

The door opened and LaValle walked down the stairs with a big smile. "Can I join you for a game of pool?"

"What do you want?" King asked bluntly.

"I, er . . . I . . . I wanted to talk with you and I kinda thought . . . ," LaValle paused, uncertain of his father's reaction. He gathered his wits and continued. ". . . maybe it would be good to do it while we played a game of pool."

"What do you want?" King demanded. "I'm not going to ask you again." King turned and walked over to the rolltop desk, where he kept his cigars and guns.

LaValle saw his direction and shuddered. "Please, I came to ask a favor."

There was silence in the room as King relit his cigar then pulled a revolver from the drawer and laid it on the desk. "Ask," he said simply.

"I want to work for the family." LaValle spoke as if he had memorized his words. "I'm ready to handle my share of the responsibility. I'm read—"

"How can you say that bullshit?" Jack interrupted. He was standing across the pool table from LaValle.

"Don't get jealous, little brother. You ain't the only son."

"You give men responsibilities," Jack retorted. "You're not a man. You don't care about your family. You bring your wife to dinner with bruises on her face!"

"At least my wife's alive," LaValle countered.

Jack would have attacked his brother had not his father stepped between them. Jack looked his father in the eye and said, "You're right, Dad. I shouldn't let myself get provoked." Jack started to turn away, but the anger returned. He pivoted and faced his brother again. "You're the reason my wife is dead! I can't stand you! I used to love you, but now I can't stand you! You have no pride! You brutalize your wife like she was an animal! Where's your manhood? Don't you have any self-respect left?"

"I don't know what you're talking about," LaValle retorted haughtily.

"That's the real problem. You have no standards, so you can't understand what I'm talking about."

"Don't fool yourself, you ain't nothing but a nigger with a couple of suits! Everything you own was given to you by Papa! You just jealous because I'm trying to get my share."

"Damn, LaValle, you're more fool than I thought!" Jack shook his head indignantly and tapped his chest. "Because I'm your brother, I've always wanted you to succeed. I loved you. I've been there for you. But you lost it with Eartha and you're still sinking. You're beginning to act like common scum. You beat your woman. You gamble away the handouts that you get and you blame your problems on other people. And what's worst of all is that you're a coward. A goddamn coward!" Jack leaned forward to give his last statement the necessary emphasis.

King stepped out of the way and looked at LaValle, waiting to see what he would do. King didn't expect LaValle to pick up his brother's challenge, so when he stepped out of the way of his sons, he was merely proving that LaValle was indeed a coward.

LaValle looked from his father to his brother. He saw the set in their jaws and the look in their eyes and he knew that he had somehow failed again. He didn't want to fight Jack. He just wanted to get through with his request and take whatever scraps his father threw and leave. "I just want to work for the family," LaValle began weakly. He looked at his father. "I'm your son too. Don't I have a right to something? The family's got money. All I'm asking is something to take care of my family with."

It was a pathetic plea that had no chance of being answered. In a family that valued strength, LaValle had none. The lack of that one trait alone would have made him an outcast, but added to his other failings, it doomed him to banishment. Jack turned away. Even though he detested him, he couldn't watch his brother abase himself.

"For yo' information," King said in an even tone, "I have only one son and his name is Jack Tremain. You don't look like me and you don't act like nobody I know. Nobody who has the name Tremain should be treated the way you treat yo' wife and children. If yo' wife is stupid enough to stay with you, that's her business, but I don't have to watch you bring any more shame on the name of Tremain. I've been a witness and ain't said a thing. So, let me say it now." King picked up the revolver then walked over and stood in front of LaValle. "You don't have a share of anythin'! Yo' wife and children will always have money for food and clothing, but I ain't givin' you a damn thing! You ain't even welcome in my presence. If I see you on the street, I want you to go the other way. If I come into a place where you are, I want you to leave. The only time that I want to see you is at Sunday dinner. And when you come, don't bring that woman here with bruises on her face!"

"I'm your son. You're going to disown me like that?" LaValle protested. "I've got no money. I have some big debts. I—"

"Then get a job!" King said coldly. He raised the revolver and pointed it at LaValle. "If you're still here sixty seconds from now, I'm gon' to shoot you in one of yo' legs. See if I don't."

"Sometimes I can't believe you, Pa!" Jack said as he stepped in front of his father's gun. "You're not going to spill blood in here!" He turned and with a wave of his hand said, "Get out of here now, LaValle!"

LaValle began to back rapidly up the stairs toward the door. When he reached the door, King stopped him with "Oh, LaValle." LaValle turned, hoping for a change of heart. King continued, "Don't ever come down here again."

King saw LaValle once during that next week, when he brought King a message from his enemies. They wanted to set up a meeting. The Fillmore District was in transition. There was a new force on the street. It was created with money gleaned from the sale of heroin. The people behind the source were Italian and well connected. They were trying to extend their organization into the Fillmore. The Tree brothers had been their agents. King stood against them not only because he didn't like heroin, but because he saw them as encroaching on his power. So far, he had held them off pretty well. There were a few skirmishes. They shot up one of his bars. He blew up their office building in North Beach. They raided his headquarters on Sutter. He allowed them to set his building ablaze, then killed almost all of their men when they unsuspectingly returned to their cars. Next, he dynamited their warehouse. He had learned a lot about demolitions in World War I.

The local newspaper reported that the Mob bosses were fighting it out. The editor surmised in his column which families might be involved in the war. Not once did he mention a black family. That was fine with King; he had no need of notoriety. His business functioned best when it operated in the shadows. He had all his people on alert, waiting for a counterstrike. Three days after King had told LaValle not to come down to the office, Serena came down and told him that LaValle had a message for him from the people at 2325 Filbert Street; that was the address in North Beach of the DiMarcos' headquarters, a building that King had destroyed. When King went up the stairs and saw the smiling face of LaValle, he truly considered killing him.

LaValle, on the other hand, was happy with himself. In one brilliant stroke, he had forced his father to forsake all that he had said about not wanting to be in the same place as him. His father now had to talk to him, whether he liked it or not. LaValle wanted to go into the sitting room to convey his message, but his father refused. King made him stand in the hall by the stairs, where their voices echoed through the house. The conversation progressed rapidly, because King responded in monosyllables. The DiMarcos wanted an interim truce until a meeting could be convened. King could choose the site. King could come with two escorts; that was all Marcello DiMarco would bring.

King operated under the assumption that anyone who brought news of a deal with the enemy had to be in bed with them. Why else would the enemy approach LaValle to carry a message? The question in King's mind was, who set LaValle up to be the intermediary? LaValle didn't know the DiMarcos. One possibility was that they could have bought his outstanding markers and approached him through his debt. No, he seemed too smug for that; LaValle had the air of a man who had a sweetheart deal. To get a sweetheart deal, you had to have something of value, or give something of value. King's mind was rapidly sifting through the potential options. What did LaValle have that they would want? King looked at the triumphant, smiling face of LaValle and asked, "What do you get out of all this?" He was trying to determine whether LaValle was a traitor or just a dupe.

LaValle looked down at his nails, which had been recently manicured, before he spoke. "I'm performing a service." He looked his father in the eye and continued. "I'm getting paid to perform a service."

"You's here representin' our enemies? And you take money for this?" King was incredulous.

"I ain't with the family," LaValle explained with a slight trace of anger. "You told me to get out. I had to do for my own family."

"Yo' family?" King challenged. "You don't know the meaning of fam-

ily! You take money to bring me a deal that smells of double cross."
King took a bat out of the closet under the stairs and took several slow
steps toward LaValle. He smacked the bat in his palm and said with a
quiet malevolence, "I don't think that I want to see you again. I don't
even want you to come to this house while I'm here."

LaValle, his eyes wide with fear, was backing away toward the front
door when Serena floated down the stairs dressed in her overcoat. It
was obvious that she had been listening over the banister. "Are you
ready to go, LaValle?" she asked as she tied a plastic rain scarf over her
hair.

LaValle blurted out gratefully, "Yes, Mama. I'm ready to go!" King
threw back his head and laughed at LaValle's fear. He returned the bat
to the closet and stood with his arms crossed, watching. LaValle was
breathing a sigh of relief. His mother's appearance may have saved his
life or, at the very least, saved him from some broken bones. He waited
gratefully for her by the door.

On her way out the door with LaValle, Serena said to King in a low
tone, "You can't stop my children from coming here. You gave me this
house. If my children can't visit me here, I'll move somewhere else."

"It's yo' house, woman," King conceded. "Just be careful who you invite; they may look like somebody you know, but it may turn out that
you don't know them at all."

King didn't see LaValle again until the night Jack was killed; however, he had him followed. The evening before Jack's death, LaValle
was trailed to a bathhouse on Market Street, where he met with some
men. Parked across the street, watching the traffic move in and out of
the bathhouse, was John Tree. He had been in hiding nearly a year. The
men King chose to follow LaValle wouldn't have seen Tree sitting
across the street in an old Ford pickup if he hadn't lit a cigarette. In the
brief flare of the match, Tree's distorted smile was clearly visible. One
of the men followed LaValle into the bathhouse, the other waited outside. In the steam and poor lighting of the sauna, only two of the men
that LaValle was meeting were identified. The third escaped detection.
One man was Charles Witherspoon, the general contractor for King's
construction company, and the other was muscle for the DiMarcos.

As far as King was concerned, the unknown third man was the key.
He was the one who brought LaValle, Witherspoon, and the DiMarcos
together. King laughed to himself. He would take odds that LaValle

didn't know about Tree, but that Tree knew about him. LaValle would probably be Tree's prize after whatever they were planning was completed. The question was, who was this third man and what was being planned?

On the night of Jack's death, after the dinner dishes had been cleared away, the family sat around the dining room table. Jack and King were talking. Jackson was leaning against his father and playing with a rubber band. Serena and Lisette were discussing which was the better actor, Victor Mature or Richard Conte. All conversation stopped when the phone rang. Jack sent his son back into the kitchen and went to answer the phone. When he returned his face was grave. He excused himself from the table and went down to the office. King joined him a few minutes later and discovered him laying out guns and ammunition on the pool table.

"They've got LaValle," Jack said, glancing up at his father as he continued to load bullets into magazines.

King stared at Jack and asked, "What makes that important?"

"Pa, I talked to LaValle," Jack explained, his voice hoarse with tension. "They cut off one of his fingers while he was talking to me. They're going to kill him if we don't meet them in three hours at the old Genaro warehouse near pier fourteen on South Embarcadero."

"Why is that important?" King asked again, looking his son directly in the eye. "And why you gettin' ready to do somethin' about it?"

"Pa, it's different for you than it is for me. LaValle's my brother and I can't forget that. I just can't forget that. I grew up with him. He's been part of my world my whole life. Even though he's a dog, I don't intend to stand by and let somebody kill him. I've got to do something."

"It's a goddamn trap, boy!" King exploded. "LaValle got himself into this mess, just like he had a hand in Eartha's death!"

"You're right on both counts, Pa, but that doesn't change a thing for me."

"LaValle ain't worth dying for! He wouldn't even be in this spot if he hadn't turned traitor on his family. You committin' suicide!"

"I don't intend to commit suicide, but I'm going. Are you with me?" Jack looked at his father. "I've been with you every time that you needed me. Now, I need you. Are you with me?"

There was a long silence while King considered his options. He would have preferred to let them kill LaValle then wreak his vengeance later. LaValle was a liability and would continue to bring shame on the family for as long as he lived. What could be more ideal than to have someone else kill him? If Sister Bornais had not specifically warned King against killing LaValle, he would have done it himself long ago. King looked at his son and said, "You my blood. I'm with you." He had a bad feeling about meeting the DiMarcos on the ground of their choosing. Now, he was risking his life to save the fool in order to protect the son he cared for. King closed off his thoughts and commented as he picked up his shotgun, "In a warehouse, we can probably use tear gas. Did you pack some?"

"That's a good idea, Pa," Jack acknowledged with a smile. "I'll get some masks too."

The two men began strapping on holsters and ammunition belts. King packed several bundles of stick dynamite along with detonator caps in a small canvas bag. He also packed a Thompson machine gun with a collapsible stock and loaded magazines, and put the bag by the stairs. Jack placed a larger bag next to King's.

"I think a team of seven can do it if we enter from the roof," Jack suggested. "I've been to Ciachetti's, which is right next to that building at pier fourteen. Both buildings were built at the same time. I think that they are identical. We'll have to take out their sentries on the roof, then we can cross with two fifteen-foot ladders between Ciachetti's building and theirs. We leave two men on the roof to take care of our exit. The top floor is administrative offices; we leave two men there to cover the hallway. Three of us will go down to ground level."

King mused, "For this to work, everybody got to use silencers and every shot got to count, because surprise is our only advantage."

"I have silencers for everything but the shotguns."

"If we got to use the shotguns," King observed, "we won't worry about surprisin' them." The two men chuckled humorlessly as they commenced working out the details of their plan. They identified and contacted the men they wanted on the team. Two of the men were directed to steal two vans. The team convened at a vacant apartment in a building that King owned in Hunter's Point. The men all knew one another, having worked together on various assignments in the past. There was Doke and Joey from the Blue Mirror. For the sharpshooter, they had chosen Herbert Broadhead, a tall, angular man with a gaunt, brown-skinned face. Broadhead could hit a letter-size piece of paper at two hundred yards, ten out of ten times. He had served with Jack in

World War II in the 761st Colored Tank Battalion and had proven his marksmanship many times in life-and-death situations. The remaining two men were friends of King's from Mexico. One was a stocky, swarthy man named Rico Ramirez and the other was a wiry, taciturn man called El Indio.

The Port of San Francisco functioned nearly twenty-four hours a day loading and unloading cargo and large passenger liners. Piers 14 and 16 were centers of activity. Under the glare of bright lights, there were the grinding sounds of engines, the mechanical squeal of large cranes and hoists, and the shouts of men as heavy crates and equipment swung from ship to shore and back again. Genaro's and Ciachetti's warehouses were on the street side of pier 14, but were blocked off from view of the Embarcadero by a long, three-story office building which was dark and vacant during the night hours. One van was left three blocks from Genaro's warehouse. It would provide a second means of escape, should the first van be recognized during the raid. The remaining van, with two fifteen-foot ladders and two twelve-foot lengths of thick pine protruding from the rear, was driven into the shadows of Ciachetti's warehouse, on the opposite side from Genaro's. The van pulled to a stop underneath the outside fire escape. Standing on top of the van, Jack and Herbert caught the lower rung of the fire escape and ascended to the roof. They both had 3.08-caliber rifles with silencers and sniper scopes. The principal source of lighting came from the dockside pier, which possessed a bank of high-wattage lamps to allow for around-the-clock loading and unloading of freight and passenger shipping. Once atop the roof, they easily spotted the first sentry; he was making regular circuits of the roof, occasionally peering down at the street for signs of movement. The other sentry had placed himself in the shadows and would not have been seen except that the barrel of his rifle reflected the pier's lights. Herbert directed Jack's attention to the man's movement in the shadows. Only the top of his head and his legs were visible. Herbert took careful aim and Jack signaled when the other sentry was on the other side of the roof. Herbert squeezed off a shot that made a soft popping noise and the man's head disappeared. The sound of his gun hitting the roof brought the other sentry at a run. Jack caught him in the chest with a shot from his rifle and saw his body jerk backward as if pulled by some invisible wire. Herbert put another bullet into him as he fell.

Communicating by military walkie-talkie, Jack informed the men below that the roof was cleared for entry. The two fifteen-foot ladders were lifted to the roof and the pieces of pine were tied tightly to the ladders to reinforce their strength. The men assembled to discuss the crossing. With Doke and Joey holding each ladder upright and Jack and Rico holding ropes fastened to the topmost ends, each ladder was gently lowered across the ten-foot span that separated the buildings. The ladders were laid side by side. Carrying lead ropes Jack and Herbert walked across the ladders, balancing themselves on the pine boards. They fastened the lead ropes to metal stanchions projecting from the roof and the other men crossed with benefit of the guide ropes.

King crossed the ladders without any overt evidence of concern, but as he looked down at the ground thirty feet below, he thought, Gettin' too old for this. We gon' to have to leave by the front door. Upon reaching the other side, he spurned Jack's hand and jumped down to the roof without assistance. He watched as Jack assigned the men to various tasks. Herbert would take the roof. El Indio would be the first man inside, and his job was to take out anyone patrolling the balcony and hallway, then he was to search the upstairs offices. Joey and Doke would hold the second floor hallway and balcony. Jack, King, and Rico would descend to ground level, where Jack figured LaValle was being held. Silently, King admired the way his son commanded respect. The men listened attentively as Jack laid out the plan once more. He explained that there were only gas masks for five men. If the gas was used, two of the team would have to exit through the roof and go across the ladders again.

It was nine-thirty, approximately half an hour before the scheduled meeting. Guns were checked, everyone was ready to go. King handed Herbert his shotgun and a belt of shells. "If a car pulls up with reinforcements, fire that through its ceiling. It's loaded with shotgun slugs."

El Indio cracked the door leading down to the second story balcony and went down the stairs cautiously. Joey and Doke followed him. Jack, Rico, and King descended the stairs after them in time to see a brief scuffle, which was ended when Doke broke the man's neck. The team had safely entered and no alarms had been set off. A quick glance over the rail revealed a haphazard arrangement of stacked wooden crates lit by several banks of fluorescent lights that hung twenty feet above the floor.

There was a loud banging on the door of the warehouse. Voices emanated from a large stack of crates set against the far wall away from the stairs. King heard the voices and pressed himself into the shadows. He looked at the balcony and he saw Joey sitting on the stairs, out of sight of the door. Joey was motioning at something on the ceiling above King's head. King looked up and saw a foot briefly swing into view. The DiMarcos had placed someone in the roof scaffolding on a square of plywood. The view between the square of plywood and the balcony was obstructed by several large ceiling fans. Obviously, the man had been placed there to protect the entrance, not the balcony.

King heard a heavy door swing open and then the growls of dogs. He had to give them credit, they were smarter than he thought: They'd sweep the place with dogs first, to ensure that the site hadn't been breached. King pulled one of the matched pair of Colt .45 pistols that he carried from a holster and awaited the dogs. He heard the heavy door swing shut.

A voice called up to the balcony, "Hey, Turo!" There was silence. The voice again, with impatience, "This ain't no time to play, Turo! Turo! Danny! Answer me, one of you guys!"

Joey answered, trying to speak with a New York accent, "Yeah, I heard you!"

There was a pause, then the voice spoke again, this time with fear. "That ain't either one of them guys' voices! The niggers are here! Let them dogs—" The man did not finish his sentence; Jack shot him through the throat. The dog handler fought to release his animals, but a forty-five slug in his heart ended conscious thought. Over his body, there were four rottweilers snarling and struggling to be free. Jack killed two of the dogs while they fought to release themselves from the tangles of their leashes. The other two pulled free and disappeared into the labyrinth of crates.

King fired a full magazine from his pistol into the floor of the plywood square and watched a body fall heavily onto the crates. He was changing magazines when a rottweiler rounded the corner and began approaching him. The dog's head was low and the growl that issued from its throat was spine-tingling. King pushed a new magazine into his pistol, but it didn't catch. The dog broke into a run, charging him. King pulled out his other pistol and shot the dog three times before its dead body collapsed against his legs.

Rico Ramirez was not so lucky. His back was turned when the remaining dog discovered him. Its charge caught him by surprise, knocking him off his feet and causing his gun to fall from his hands. Things might have gone badly for him had not Jack come to his aid. The dog was on top of Rico and had sunk its fangs into his left shoulder and was trying to shift the grip to his neck when Jack shot it. It took two bullets to bring down the enraged dog.

There was complete silence in the warehouse. Jack checked Rico's wound. There were deep lacerations and punctures, but no bones were broken and no major blood vessels were cut. Rico had some difficulty moving his left shoulder, but he waved Jack off and picked up his gun.

A voice cried out, "King Tremain? King Tremain, are you out there?" King answered back, "I'm here."

"We got your son. You wanna talk to him?" King did not answer. There were sounds of a number of voices in angry conversation. Then LaValle screamed, "No, not another finger! Please! Plea—EEEEEEEE!" LaValle's words turned to a shriek and then to a whimpering moan.

The voice spoke again. "We're going to chop him up piece by piece until you come out and talk like a man!"

Jack ran, hunched over, back up the stairs. He retrieved the bag with tear gas and masks. He left two masks on the second landing and descended to ground level to find his father.

Herbert Broadhead liked sentry duty and he did it like he was still in the military. When he heard a car door slam he rushed to the side from which the sound emanated. Peering over the edge of the roof, he saw a balding, blond-haired man in a long coat leave his limousine and go into an unmarked door in the side of the building. Herbert picked up the shotgun and sighted the roof on the driver's side of the limo. He waited for a hoist's engine to rev up, then he squeezed off two shots through the roof, hardly audible above its mechanical roar. A limo door squeaked. A man on the front passenger side of the limo pushed open his door and ran for the building. He didn't make it. The shotgun slug nearly separated him in two before he reached the door. Herbert fired several more shots into the limo's engine to ensure that it would not operate.

Jack knelt on the floor as he passed out gas masks to his father and Rico. They had determined where LaValle was being held. There was a large stack of crates set against the far wall behind the stairs. Jack wanted to lob tear gas over in front of the stack, but King thought that would give the DiMarcos a chance to disperse under cover of the clouds of gas. The three men edged stealthily closer until they could see the opening leading into the stack. Jack removed the launcher from the bag and affixed a tear gas canister to it. King took out his machine gun and snapped the stock to its full extension. Jack caught Joey's eye and pointed to the stack of crates, then gestured with his pistol. Joey nodded his head in understanding. Jack launched two canisters into the opening of the stack and King laced the opening with machine-gun fire. Doke and Joey also pumped round after round into the opening.

LaValle was lying on the floor in a haze of pain when the first canister landed in the darkened interior of the room formed by the crates. The second canister actually hit one of his captors in the head before it fell in front of LaValle's face. A whiff of the acrid odor brought him back to the world. He sat upright, partially dizzy from the pain and the gas. In the darkened room there was pandemonium, particularly when the bullets started sending splinters flying. Someone fell over his feet, another stepped on his still-intact left hand, someone else kneed him in the head. LaValle staggered to his feet, driven by a desire to get a fresh breath of air. The narrow beam of a flashlight lanced through the darkness. Someone had opened the outside door. There was a brief silhouette of a man in a long coat, standing in the doorway, then the man rushed out to get into the limo and was met with an explosion. No one else followed him.

In the confusion, LaValle appeared to have been forgotten. He threw himself on his stomach and the pain of breaking his fall with the remains of his right hand caused him to crumple up on the cold cement floor. Spurred on by his desire to survive, he crawled out underneath the fire that his rescuers were concentrating on the stack of crates. One of his captors, attempting to escape the discomfort of the gas, ran into the line of fire. A hail of bullets hit his body, and he fell within three feet of LaValle. It was too much for LaValle. He had endured all the pain and suffering he could stand. Escape was all that he could think of. His mind blanked out; animal panic controlled him. He struggled to his feet and ran to the corner of the next aisle before a bullet fired by his captors shattered his right shoulder. The impact carried him face-first into the crates in front of him. He crashed into the hard, wooden surface and slumped to the floor.

Jack leapt to his feet and had to be forcibly restrained by Rico and King. "He's lying in their line of fire," King warned, gripping Jack roughly. "You go after him and you'll both be dead meat. I heard from Herbert on the walkie-talkie that there's an outside door leading into those crates. Let me send Doke around to fire a few shots through that door to spark 'em."

A tear gas canister was thrown out into the aisle where LaValle lay crumpled. The gas billowed up from the canister like an evil genie. Jack pulled himself free of his father's grasp and said, "There's my cover. I'm going to get him!" Jack ducked down along the sides of the crates and made his way to within five feet of LaValle's unconscious form. LaValle's body was lying in full view of the DiMarcos. In the background, Jack heard the front door slide open. He looked back at his father, who signaled that Doke had gone outside. Jack did not want to wait. He was sure that once the DiMarcos discovered that they were cornered, they would make sure that LaValle was dead by firing more bullets into his body.

But he was momentarily stymied as to what he should do. Sweat dripped down his face. The goggles of the mask were beginning to fog over from his body heat.

Jack heard footsteps behind him; it was Joey with a shotgun. Joey mumbled through his gas mask, "Let me fire a couple of rounds of buckshot in there, then you might have a chance."

"Do it!" Jack replied and readied himself to make a dash for his brother.

Joey stood up and fired three quick shots from his shotgun into the entrance. Jack started to move on the first shot and reached his brother by the third, but by the time he had a grip on LaValle, a man ran out of the stack of crates, firing a machine gun. The bullets swept in front of Jack, forcing him to retreat to cover. Joey caught the man with a blast of his shotgun that lifted the man off his feet and propelled his body backward into a wall of crates. Jack ran out and grabbed his brother underneath his arms and began to pull him to safety. Joey saw movement on top of the crates. Two men were frantically struggling to climb out of a narrow opening about fifteen feet above ground level. Crates blocked the two men from Rico's and King's view and partially blocked a clear shot of them from where Joey stood as well. The first man who freed himself saw Joey and swung his gun up. But Joey reacted more quickly and fired off another blast from his shotgun, which knocked the man down.

Jack stepped over his brother's body so that he was facing where he was going, and dragged his brother between his legs. The second man scrambled free. Again Joey pumped his shotgun, but the chamber was empty. The man smiled as he pulled the trigger of his .357 Magnum and shot Joey in the heart.

Jack was nearly to safety when the bullets tore through his back and ripped through his abdomen. He fell with his brother in his arms and landed heavily on top of him.

When King saw Joey jerk backward from the force of a bullet then fell in a heap, he started running for a vantage point from which he could either kill or pin down the shooter. King's heart was pumping. He saw that Jack had not yet reached the cover of the next aisle. King was in a full run, pushing his fifty-six-year-old body to its limits. He saw a man standing on a stack of crates peer around the corner and aim his weapon at what King assumed to be Jack's retreating back. King desperately drew his gun and fired up in the man's direction to distract his aim. King's shots went wide and the man calmly took his time and pulled his trigger twice. King tore off his gas mask, came to a full stop, and aimed. His next three bullets destroyed the man's chest cavity. The man slumped back against a crate, then fell ten feet to the cement below with a thud.

King saw Doke come through the entrance of the stack of crates. When Doke saw King, he waved. "It's over. They're all done!"

King merely nodded; he was no longer concentrating on anything that Doke was saying. He walked rapidly to where Jack should be. He rounded a stack of crates and saw Rico kneeling on the cement floor, holding Jack in his arms. From the blood spilling out on the floor from underneath Jack's shirt, the pasty color of his face, and the distant, glazed look in his eyes, King knew that his son would die before they left the warehouse. Jack saw him and recognition lit up his face. Jack put his hands on LaValle, who was lying unconscious beside him, and said, "He's alive." Jack smiled weakly then died.

Jack's head fell backward on Rico's chest and his eyes slowly closed. LaValle moaned and stirred briefly before falling back into the well of unconsciousness. King walked over to LaValle and drew his other Colt pistol and pointed both his guns at his head.

From where he sat with Jack's body still in his arms, Rico said, "Don't, my friend. One son is already dead. Please."

King allowed his arms to fall to his sides. His rage was so great that his body trembled. He struggled to contain his desire to kill LaValle. It was too much. Joey and Jack both dead because of this worthless piece of trash lying at his feet. His oldest son, someone else's child, a child of a million disappointments. King raised the guns again with determination in his eye.

Rico spoke again. "We have already lost two of our own tonight. If you kill him, you make their deaths meaningless. Show restraint, please."

King looked at Rico and said, "You right." King holstered his guns. "He has some information that I want anyway." King directed Doke and El Indio to bring back both vans. Both Joey and Jack's bodies were placed in the van that King was driving. While King and El Indio were carrying Jack's body out, Rico and Doke saved LaValle's life. They carried LaValle to the second van. Then Doke called Lisette and told her LaValle would be dropped off at Doc Wilburn's.

The two vans were more than ten blocks away when the dynamite in the Genaro warehouse exploded, totally destroying the building and its inventory. Of the thirteen bodies found at the scene, only three could be identified via dental records.

Sunday, June 27, 1982

After he had left the clinic and returned to the house, Jackson's thoughts swirled around the morbid tale of his father's demise. He went and sat in the darkened living room. It was a terrible injustice for his grandparents to have kept their silence for so long and he had expressed this sentiment in no uncertain terms to his grandfather before he left.

At first his grandfather had merely shrugged and said, "I did what I knew to do at that time. Didn't have no words to explain to a child that his daddy was dead. You wouldn't have understood the why of it. And no words was gon' make you feel any better with both yo' parents gone." His grandfather had paused, trying to find a better position on his pillow, then continued. "I wanted you with me, but I was a man on the run for a while. I had to set up a base and an organization in Mexico. I couldn't put you in danger like that. Then after LaValle was killed, Serena would only let you come down in the summers."

Jackson had exclaimed, "Why? She didn't care about me!"

"She wanted you as a hostage. To make sure that I would still protect the family in San Francisco."

"She sure made me feel like a hostage."

"I's probably part of the reason for that. I told her not to lay no hands on you and not to mess you up with her thinkin'."

"What do you mean, 'her thinking'?"

"Give you an example. Yo' mama was a dark and pretty gal. The only reason Serena didn't like her was the color of her skin. Serena wanted yo' daddy to marry somebody high yellow like she was. That was more important to her than his happiness. Serena was full of puffed-up, snooty stuff like that. So, I told her if she couldn't say nothin' nice to you, not to say nothin'!"

"Well, Grandfather, she didn't say anything for years. I guess you could say she kept her word."

"You done lived a tough life, boy, and I know I'm part responsible for that. I ain't askin' you to excuse me or forgive me. Just know I did the best I knew to do. I was just tryin' to make you tough enough to deal with the world. To stand tall among men, I knew you had to be strong and have yo' own mind."

"You were preparing me for war, Grandfather."

"It's true, the world I was preparin' you for done changed a bit. But them lessons you learned still apply: Them that's got write the history while the weak ones fade."

"I didn't have a problem learning to be strong. It was all the violence and bloodshed."

"It was what I knew. I growed up in a violent world, in a white man's world. Every time a colored man stood up or tried to act like democracy applied to him, them whites would riot. They'd lynch and burn. There was major riots in Tulsa, east St. Louis, Rosewood, Louisiana, Chicago, and New York, just to name a few, and in each one hundreds and hundreds was killed and most of them was colored folks. They ain't never wrote what it was like to have the drunkest, no-good white man be able to spit in yo' face and put his hands on yo' wife and daughter. If you tried to live within the law, you swallowed yo' pride and you turned away when it happened to others. But it made you feel sick like you ate some bad fish. I never wanted that feeling. I was prepared to die rather than eat shit off somebody's boots. Passing time done made the in-yo'-face racism go undercover. Who could see that all that was gon' happen? But don't get it twisted, the color problem ain't that far under-cover. It's just a question of time. As soon as things get hard, it'll be back out in the open."

Jackson had countered, "It may rise up again, but it will be changed. The way things are going, whites will be the minority in this country soon."

"Don't get it twisted, boy. Money is power. The whites is gon' keep control here just like in South Africa. But as far as the rest of the world goes, their day is done. This next century gon' be Chinese. They gon' run the world like the whites did before 'em. Only one thing gon' be the same: racism. Just be a different color on top."

Jackson had commented, "That's a pretty cynical outlook, don't you think?"

"I been to mainland China a couple times, boy. Them people done come out of the Stone Age in less than fifty years. They got a way to go but they pushin' hard."

The subsequent discussion had meandered through world politics and the Cold War. Jackson was surprised at how knowledgeable his grandfather was about current events. The conversation came to a close when his grandfather began to get exhausted. Before Jackson left the clinic, the old man pulled him close to the bed and whispered, "I know you got to do what's in yo' heart. I ain't askin' you to fight just to fight. I'm askin' you to look at the facts real hard and make yo' move based on the facts. If it looks like you can walk away without a fight, do it. Just be realistic."

Later, Jackson realized that he had just had his first man-to-man dis-cussion with his grandfather. He felt good about it and that surprised him. It also surprised him that the old man had changed his tack in ask-ing him to pick up the gauntlet and carry on the fight. He had left the final decision in Jackson's hands. That change in strategy alone caused Jackson to be more receptive to him and his advice. Again Jackson began to feel the sense of loss his grandfather's passing would cause him, and his thoughts were wrapped in melancholy. He let the puppy out and walked through the darkened house.

There were faxes waiting on the dining room table for him. He reviewed them, but found no cause to make changes in the finished report that Corazon had prepared from his revisions. He called her at home and thanked her for all her extra effort. He was in the process of complimenting her on the quality and thoroughness of her work when she interrupted him.

"Jax! There's a note here that says your grandmother was called and given the fax number in Mexico yesterday. Did you call and give someone the approval to do that?"

"No! How would they have gotten it?"

"It was written on my ink blotter."

"But who would have done that? She's not on my emergency call list. She must've called for it. Why would she want the number?"

"She's your grandmother, you ought to know. All I can tell you is this looks like Martha's handwriting. Bedrosian must've directed some people to work this weekend."

The malaise of his mood deepened after he hung up the telephone. What was his grandmother up to? Why would she want the number? Thoughts too numerous to mention swirled around him like wisps of vapor, leaving trace elements of guilt at every turn. At around nine-thirty in the evening, he had to get out of the house. He took a walk with the puppy along the outskirts of the cemetery which lay behind his grandfather's house. It was the beginning of the new moon, there was only a sliver visible in the sky. The stars appeared dim and indistinct as if they were behind a sheet of opaque material. The only light that illumined the darkness came from an occasional streetlight.

Jackson entered the cemetery through the Montecido Street gate. He had no fear of the cemetery. He had often played among the crypts and mausoleums as a child and his grandfather had placed more than a few bodies there himself. Jackson was headed to a knoll which overlooked the cemetery and had the city skyline in the background. He wanted to think about Elizabeth—what she was doing, what she was wearing—but he could not put the fact out of his mind that his grandmother had the fax number in Mexico. Why would she want it? She definitely wouldn't send Franklin down to Mexico alone. It was too dangerous. Then a terrible thought dawned on him. What if she was working with the men who had followed him? What if she was passing on information to his grandfather's enemies? The very thought brought the taste of bile to his mouth, but it had the ring of truth. She and Franklin both stood to benefit if Jackson and his grandfather were killed.

The puppy distracted him. The young dog was happily straining at the leash to investigate various things in the darkness, yet every once in while he would stop and look back the way they had come and his ears would prick up. At first, Jackson paid no attention, but the third or fourth time the puppy looked back Jackson knew there was something or someone behind him. When he reached the top of the knoll, he stood in the shadows of the old Bustamante family mausoleum. The Bustamantes had built themselves an edifice for the ages. It was a huge stone building that towered above all the others. It was topped with a dome and had large columns lining its entrance.

Jackson knew from his childhood that the shadows in the mausoleum's entrance would hide him from view. He knelt with the puppy behind one of the mausoleum's columns and waited. Within five minutes, against the pale background of tombstones, a dark form could be seen moving deliberately in Jackson's direction. From the path his follower was taking, it looked as if he would pass within twenty feet of the mausoleum. The puppy growled at the stalking form in the darkness. Jackson immediately grabbed the dog's muzzle and held it firmly, but the stalker had heard the growl and was now casting about for its source.

Jackson had no weapon, but he was sure that whoever was following him had one. He quickly considered his options. His only real chance was surprise. He tied the puppy to the pillar and dropped to his hands and knees and crawled out of the shadows behind some shrubs that lined the walkways. He stood up as soon as he was away from the mausoleum and moved into the shadow of an adjacent crypt. His intent was to flank his follower and attack from the side. The puppy whined a few times after Jackson left, then commenced growling again as the form drew nearer. The man was within ten feet of him and Jackson could see the glint of a weapon in his hand. Jackson waited for the distance to shorten and prepared himself to spring. He was mentally kicking himself for being so foolish in taking the dangers of his grandfather's world lightly. He held his breath and moved to the balls of his feet. He had to put everything in his leap to catch the man by surprise. Otherwise, he would die in the attempt.

"Diablito?" the form asked cautiously.

It sounded like Carlos. The man had the shape and size of Carlos. But Jackson had no intention of revealing himself until he was sure that it was Carlos.

"I am only doing what your grandfather requested," the form continued. "I see that you have tied the little dog, but where are you?"

"Right here, Carlos," Jackson responded, emerging from the shadows.

"That was very good," Carlos commented, shaking his head appreciatively.

"Thanks," Jackson acknowledged. "How long have you been following me?"

"Since you left the house. When I came from the clinic, you were sitting in the dark thinking, so I camped out in the kitchen and got something to eat. When you left, I followed."

"All part of the security consulting biz, hey?" Jackson said in a friendly, teasing manner. The puppy whined, reminding Jackson that he had been left tied to a column. As he untied the dog, he asked, "How was my grandfather doing when you left?"

"Not too well," Carlos replied. "He's having some problems with his heart. He needs to rest quietly and he doesn't know how to rest."

"Well, I want to see him again," Jackson said, feeling a sudden urgency. "I have to tell him something. Do you think that it would be a problem if we went to the hospital now?"

"No, it's not a problem." Carlos smiled. "Your grandfather and the Ramirez brothers own the clinic. Many of the doctors and nurses who work there had their education paid for by El Negro and Señor Ramirez."

"It's the clinic mentioned in the property papers that my grandfather donated to that doctor," Jackson commented as they walked back to the house.

"Yes, I mentioned it in the car when you first arrived," Carlos answered.

Despite the lateness of the hour, there was still vehicular traffic clogging the streets. As they sat in the limo waiting for the traffic to crawl forward, Jackson asked Carlos, "Did you know my father?"

"Yes, but he was killed before I got to know him well. We first met on one of your grandfather's annual hunting trips when I was about fifteen or sixteen. He was nine years older so we weren't friends, but he was nice to me."

"I don't know anything about your family, Carlos. You've never mentioned your mother or your father."

Carlos shrugged. "My father's dead. My mother lives in Chiapas. There's no reason to bring them up in conversation."

"Is it that you don't want to talk about them?"

"I was born of poor Indian folk living in a village in rural Chiapas. My father died when I was little. We were dirt poor and always close to starvation. It's a monster being poor and a pure-blood Indian in Mexico.

"El Indio saved me from the streets. He was my mother's cousin and he visited us on my thirteenth birthday. When El Indio left he took me with him."

"How's your mother doing now?"

"She's alive and well. I bought her a house when I was twenty-one. I put all my brothers and sisters through college. One of them is a doctor. Another is a teacher. One is an artist. And I was able to do that because your grandfather helped me."

"Hell of a story!" Jackson said with a shake of his head.

"The world is filled with stories," Carlos replied. "Most don't end as well as mine. Look, there's a break in the traffic!" Carlos pointed to a broad side street. He spoke in Spanish to the driver, who turned and took the detour as directed.

When the limo arrived at the clinic, the gate was shut, but as soon as the guard saw the limousine he hurried to open the gate. The front doors were unlocked by another guard. As Jackson ascended the stairs he heard a siren. When he entered the hall, he saw nurses and doctors running to the far end of the hall. Jackson headed toward his grandfather's room, which was in the opposite direction.

Thinking that his grandfather might be asleep, Jackson entered the room quietly. As he opened the door he saw a man in a white coat leaning over the bed. Over the man's shoulder he could see his grandfather's thin arms flailing away frantically.

"What going on here?" Jackson demanded.

The man turned and Jackson saw blood on his hands. The man held something shiny and he flicked it with a snap of his wrist in Jackson's direction. Jackson had started toward the man, but he stumbled over the legs of a body sprawled on the floor. As Jackson lost his balance and fell against the foot of the bed, the knife intended for him flew past his shoulder and stuck in the wall. His attacker followed his knife throw with several kicks aimed at Jackson's groin and solar plexus. Jackson barely had time to block the attack before he regained his balance.

Once he was squared up to the man, Jackson saw that he had a considerable size and weight advantage. The man was thin and wiry, but his body was rip-cord strong. He had dirty blond hair that occasionally fell into his face and squinting eyes. There were no words spoken. Jackson knew that he was in a fight to the death. He was letting the years in the dojo control his actions and reactions. After blocking the man's initial attacks, Jackson even began to feel confident, parrying and attacking, often grazing the man, coming closer every time. Jackson was just getting into a rhythm when the man pulled a large knife from his belt and slashed it in the direction of Jackson's neck. Jackson barely eluded the tip of the knife as its sharp blade sliced through the arm of his shirt, nicking his skin.

Now it was the man who parried every attack and forced the fight with his slashing blade. Jackson, backed up against the wall, picked up a chair and held it over his head. The man smiled and tossed the knife from hand to hand. He was showing off. Jackson timed his charge for the moment that the knife was airborne and then ran straight at his attacker, driving him backward against the wall with a crash. One of the legs of the chair hit him in the stomach, a second pinned his knife arm briefly, but he pulled it free and slashed at Jackson's face. Jackson dodged backward, barely avoiding the knife, and then rammed the chair forcefully into the man's body again. This time Jackson felt the satisfying crunch of broken bones as the man's ribcage caved in slightly. The man's knife hand was caught underneath one the chair legs. As he fought to free it, Jackson looked around for some sort of weapon to end the fight. Next to him on a hospital cart was his grandfather's bone-handled hunting knife. Jackson flung off its sheath and jammed it deep into the man's chest.

The next moment, the man freed his arm and slashed again at Jackson, this time slicing his arm. Jackson fell back, dropping the chair in the process. The man took a few steps toward Jackson then fell on his face. Not wanting to get caught by a ruse, Jackson tipped the hospital cart over on the man for a reaction. There was none. He stepped on the man's arm and removed the knife from his hand. Holding it at the man's throat, he quickly frisked him for other weapons. Finding none, he checked for a pulse; the man was dead. Grateful that he had stabbed the man in a vital place, Jackson stood up and went over to check on his grandfather. The old man was bleeding from a deep stomach wound.

Jackson snarled bitterly, "Goddamn my grandmother! She sold us out! She sold us out, Gramps!"

His grandfather said nothing. His eyes were glazing over, but when he saw Jackson, he actually smiled and mumbled something softly that Jackson couldn't hear. Jackson turned away to get medical assistance, but his grandfather restrained him with a surprisingly strong grip. Jackson saw that the old man wanted to say something. Jackson leaned over to hear his grandfather's words. The old man whispered, "You's my blood."

"Let me get help, Grandfather," Jackson urged, peeling the old man's fingers off his arm. His grandfather shook his head and whispered, "Time to go. You ready now."

"Ready, Grandfather?" Jackson questioned. "No, I still need you. Grandmother sold us to the enemy. I need your help."

"You ready, boy! Tell Serena—tell Serena . . ." The old man fell silent.

"Tell her what, Grandfather? Tell her what?"

In a soft, hissing voice the old man whispered, "Tell her—tell her thank you!"

Jackson demanded, "For what? For sending this assassin?" There was no answer; he was talking to a dead man. The old man had died with his eyes open and a slight smile on his face. Gently, Jackson closed his grandfather's staring eyes. An overwhelming sadness settled upon him. He realized that he loved his grandfather and, more important than that, he knew that the old man had loved him, perhaps not in the way most civilized people could appreciate, but it had been love. Tears began to trickle down his face. It was uncanny that the years of professed hatred could be pushed aside so easily. The love that Jackson thought had withered had merely lain buried under his indignation. It now pushed through to the surface and there was no denying it.

The door opened behind him and Jackson whirled, ready to face another antagonist, but it was Carlos who entered. He hustled Jackson down to the car, explaining that there were two other assassins still in the building. He told Jackson to go home and be careful, that he would take care of all the paperwork regarding the old man's death and the body of his assassin.

When Jackson entered the dark, still house, he was on the alert. The driver had returned to the clinic to assist Carlos, but before he left he had given Jackson an old British service revolver. It was an unwieldy Webley .455. Jackson hoped there would be no reason to fire it: The gun looked as if its frame would blow apart with the first shot. He did not have to worry. Mario came out of the dark, carrying a shotgun. In the candlelight of the kitchen, Jackson saw that both the women were present. The younger woman, who was somewhat stocky and in her early thirties, had even armed herself with a hammer, which she carried stuck in the strings of her apron. Combined with her no-nonsense attitude, she looked like a formidable opponent. With the thought that nothing increased security like a dog, Jackson went and released the puppy.

When he returned to the kitchen, it was obvious that Mario and the two women were upset. Carlos had called from the clinic and had informed them of King's passing. They repeatedly offered their condolences to Jackson on the death of his grandfather. The older woman, her hair streaked with gray, wanted Jackson to know that his grandfather had been very good to her, that she was loyal and was prepared to stay if Jackson needed. Jackson was touched. Through Mario, he told them all that their loyalty was unquestioned, but that he would prefer they return to their own homes rather than risk potential injury. He said he did not know if the house would be attacked. The older woman called her son to come and pick her up. Mario refused to leave; he had his pride.

The younger woman, whose name was Theresa, had no other home. She had worked for King nearly eleven years. He had taken her out of a brothel in Chihuahua when she was nineteen. From the texture of her hair and the shape of her nose and lips, Jackson could see that she had African ancestors in her lineage.

Jackson informed both Mario and Theresa that they should remain on alert until Carlos arrived. He went to his grandfather's gun cabinet and took out the matched pair of forty-five-caliber Colt pistols. The custom ivory grips made the guns feel comfortable in his hands. They had been his grandfather's prize possessions: Series 70 National Match

Gold Cup, single-action pistols. Jackson donned a double-holster harness, attached custom-made silencers to the guns, checked their operation before chambering a bullet in each weapon. As he put the guns into his holsters he wondered what Elizabeth would think of him. He situated Mario at the back door near the kennel and Theresa in the foyer. Jackson and the puppy made regular rounds of the house, but otherwise they were based on the balcony, overlooking the courtyard.

Within the hour Carlos arrived with the Ramirez brothers, along with two prisoners. Jackson had no time to ponder his grandfather's passing or the fact that he himself had taken a human life. It was not that these events meant nothing, but rather they loomed so large on his horizon that he was only capable of seeing that portion which was closest to him. He put the puppy in the kennel and went to see the two men who had helped murder his grandfather. When he walked out the front door, they were kneeling in the courtyard with their mouths taped shut and their hands tied behind their backs. Their faces were bloody. It was obvious that they had undergone some rather brutal questioning.

Jackson looked at the men and felt no remorse. "Who are they?" he asked Julio, who was standing next to him.

"They work for the same organization that killed my father!" Julio said as he delivered a powerful kick to the abdomen of the man kneeling closest to him. The victim gasped and fell over on his side, moaning.

Reuben stepped forward and said, "We do not have much time. Their superiors know about this house."

"How did they find out? How did they find where my grandfather was?"

"They got a tip that you would be faxing and receiving information at the Data-Max Corporation and they saw you get out of the limousine yesterday. From that time on, you were followed. By tomorrow morning, you must be out of here or you will be in grave danger."

"I don't know if I can leave that soon," Jackson said absentmindedly. He was preoccupied with the knowledge that his grandmother was assisting the enemy. "I want to bury my grandfather first."

"El Negro did not want to be buried," Julio advised. "He wanted to be cremated and have half his ashes spread on the Sea of Cortez and the other half in San Francisco Bay."

"Well, I want to do both," Jackson stated simply.

"We'll send the urn to you," Reuben suggested. "If you stay here, you'll stick out like a sore thumb."

Julio said, "They'll try to kidnap you or kill you." He gestured to one of the kneeling prisoners. "At least, that's what we learned from our friends here."

"What purpose would be served by kidnapping me?" Jackson asked with surprise.

"They didn't know that," Reuben answered. "All they knew was, it was better to capture you alive than kill you and it was better to kill you than let you escape."

"What purpose could I serve as their prisoner? Why is it valuable to have me dead?" Jackson shook his head with concern. "There's some factors missing out of this equation."

"It might have something to do with the bonds or possession of the corporate certificates in the Swiss Algiers Company," Reuben offered.

From the kitchen, there was the sound of a scream. Jackson started toward the house, but Carlos came to the door and explained that Theresa's brother had been the man assigned to guard Jackson's grandfather on the graveyard shift. It was his body that Jackson had stumbled over in the hospital room.

Jackson turned to face the Ramirez brothers. "I could leave tomorrow, but I want to take many things from this house with me, including the dog."

Reuben said, "Label them, we'll ship them to you. You'll have them next week, including the dog."

"Next week?" Jackson questioned. "That soon?"

"Did you forget that we're in the import-export business?" Julio asked with a sad smile.

Carlos, Mario, and Theresa came out of the house. Theresa walked over and stared angrily at the two prisoners, her face still shiny from the tears she had shed. One man still lay on his side while the other remained on his knees.

Reuben said to Jackson, "We thought it might be a good idea if you had someone watching your back for a while. Carlos has offered to return with you and perhaps stay with you for about six months. There is much he can teach you about living in danger."

"Sounds like a good idea," Jackson agreed. He looked at Carlos. "Can you leave your business for that long?"

"That's no problem," Carlos responded. "But before I can do that, I need to resolve another problem." Carlos gestured to Theresa. "Theresa's brother was killed tonight. She's got no other family and with El Negro's death, she's got no job." Carlos turned to Jackson. "Your grandfather made me promise that I would look after her when he passed on and he didn't mean give her money."

Reuben affirmed, "You're right, Carlos. El Negro would want some provision to be made for her if she wants to stay with the family. It isn't a question of money."

Julio asked Jackson, "Do you need a cook or a maid?"

"This is kind of sudden." Jackson scratched his head. "I don't think I need a live-in cook or a maid."

"If you move back in the old Fulton Street house you'll need one," Carlos suggested.

Jackson looked at Carlos questioningly and then asked Reuben, "Why isn't it a question of money?"

"Your grandfather left her sufficient funds to live comfortably, but she has no family now that her brother was killed," Reuben answered. "El Negro always took care of the loyal people who worked for him."

"What does that mean?" Jackson asked.

"Give her a job," Julio suggested. "She wants to work for you. And you've got the money to employ her."

To Jackson it seemed as if a decision was being pushed down his throat, that he was required to do something that would have never oc-curred to him to do. He looked around at the expectant faces and sud-denly realized that this was his first test. He would be judged on the basis of this decision. Jackson looked at Theresa. Carlos had been translating the conversation for her. Jackson saw her mouth the words *Estados Unidos* and saw the worry in her eyes and thought, What the hell! "Okay. Sure, she's got a job with me." As soon as he said the words, there was a sudden release in tension. Theresa caught Jackson's eye and nodded her head several times in gratitude, as tears ran down her cheeks.

Jackson looked at his watch. It was nearly two-thirty in the morning. "What are we going to do about these two?" He gestured in the direc-tion of the prisoners.

Reuben came forward and handed Jackson a pistol with a silencer. He said simply, "These are the men who helped kill your grandfather."

Jackson took the gun and once again he looked at the faces around him. They were expectant, a mosaic of glinting eyes and taut lips. They waited for him, the one linked by blood, to take final action. It was part of the ritual of revenge and it could not be resolved without the death of these two men. Jackson examined the gun Reuben had given him. It was a Browning nine-millimeter automatic. A good weapon, but it did not feel comfortable in his hand. Jackson handed the gun back to Reuben.

Somewhere deep inside, Jackson heard a voice screaming. The voice was muffled as if it originated from behind a closed door and yet, it had the quality of an echo. It was not until he pulled an ivory-handled pistol from its holster and pointed it at the head of one of the prisoners that he heard the words clearly. It was his own voice yelling over and over again, *I won't ever kill for you again, Grandfather! I won't ever kill for you again!*

Sunday, June 27, 1982

First, there were waves on a darkened shore. Serena was standing up to her waist in the warm surf. Water washed up around her body, only to run back into the changing shadows of the breakers. The sky was black. There was neither moon nor stars. The beach faded into darkness on either side of her. Beyond the beach behind her there was the dark line of a dense tropical forest. Only the white foam on the surging black swells of water had visible movement. There was a regular, hypnotic quality about them, a lulling, comfortable pattern of sound and image. She was not frightened. There was no undertow as the water caressed her.

She could not tell when the footsteps began because they were obscured by the sounds of the surf, but she knew she heard them somewhere near the bottom of the stairs of her old Fulton Street house. She saw herself sleeping upstairs in her old bedroom. The actual footfalls themselves could not be heard because of the carpet runner that extended all the way up to the second floor, but each step on the old staircase had its own creaking sound, a changing melody depending upon ascent or descent. From the sequence of the sounds pressed from the tired wood, there was no doubt someone was coming up the stairs, someone large.

An immediate, ominous undercurrent of something dark and drear flooded her senses, sucking at her legs, pulling her off balance deeper into the heavy, pounding surf. The water suddenly turned cold and gripped her. She tried to wade to shore, but the force of the riptide was powerful and relentless. Her struggles to gain the shore were weak in comparison. Serena knew she should wake up, but she was several levels down in her mind, asleep in her old Fulton Street house. Either the waves or being asleep in her old house was a dream, but she couldn't tell which. The steps were coming closer, reaching the top of the stairs. She did not question how she could be caught in a dangerous surf while at the same time asleep in her bed. She was too busy trying to survive. Her fear became acute as she felt the force of the breakers pulling her deeper, below the roaring darkness of the waves, to a place where there was only the sound of the approaching footsteps. Despite the fear, she could not bring herself to wakefulness. She felt an invisible film of warmth begin to creep up her leg, numbing her body with its passage. Strangers, people whose faces were not visible to her, were trying to lift the bed upon which she was sleeping, so that she could be tipped into the gaping darkness of a large trapdoor in the floor. Serena became truly afraid because she recognized that the trapdoor led to a cellar deep in the labyrinth of her sleeping mind, and there was no escaping from that labyrinth. The faceless people had lifted the bed and were starting to tip it. She scrambled to shift her weight and get ahold of the side of the bed, but she was only able to move slowly; her body was not fully under her control.

All the while the footsteps were drawing closer. Even as she struggled to stay on the bed she could hear them. Each footfall was now separate and identifiable. She knew that she did not want to be asleep whenever those footsteps entered her room. She had to wake up, but suddenly she could not move. Her body wouldn't respond or open its eyes. She tried to scream but couldn't open her mouth. She was a prisoner in her own body, at the mercy of whoever came upon her. The footsteps entered her bedroom. The faceless ones who had been trying to dump her through the trapdoor dropped the bed and scurried into the shadows. The trapdoor slammed shut and disappeared. She was now alone as the footsteps drew near the bed. She heard his breathing as he stood and watched her sleeping body. She felt his hand upon her shoulder.

Serena Baddeaux Tremain sat bolt upright in her bed and stared into the piercing eyes of King Tremain. There was a cold and evil smile upon his face. He glowered at her. "Ain't you gon' get up and greet me, Serena? How can you sleep so sound after all you done?"

"What do you mean, coming into my bedroom like this?" she demanded indignantly. Other people may have feared King Tremain, but she did not. "We aren't husband and wife! We aren't partners and we aren't friends!"

"Tain't friendship what brung me," King answered with a smile. He produced a folded piece of paper from an inner coat pocket and unfolded it with care and deliberation. "I come because of this here oath you done signed many a long year ago. You swore to do right by my grandson and you done signed this here paper in yo' blood to seal yo' vow."

"What has this got to do with storming into my room in the middle of the night and awakening me? You have no rights here! If you want to talk about this, come back during the day and please make an appointment first! Have some decency!"

King smiled more broadly, but there was no humor in his face when he said, "This can't wait. Don't have to wait. You see, you done broke that vow and now there's hell to pay. I'm here to see you pay it."

"What do you mean? I've taken care of him. I fed him and I clothed him. I gave him a roof over his head. What more do you want?"

"At his christenin' you signed this here piece a paper and it don't have no date when the vow is up. It's for life! Personally, I's happy you gave Braxton the number in Mexico. Matter of fact, I came to thank you for sending them killers, but you broke the vow to the boy. It's yo' butt now, woman. You gon' pay in blood."

Serena gave King a long, slow look. "You think I'm afraid of death? Kill me! I have been ready to meet my Maker for decades. The weight I've carried these last few years has tired me out. I'm ready to die!"

"That's just it, you ain't gon' die. You just gon' live a long, lonely life. With yo' action you done ensured that Franklin and his kids gon' die within the next few years. You might've done Samantha and her chile too. Can't tell that yet. Yesiree, you got a long, lonely life filled with aches and pains to look forward to. And the prize is, I get to come and go as I like. So, I'll be back every now and again to see how you likin' things."

"You won't be back, you'll die first."

"Who's sayin' I ain't already dead?" King stared at her in silence for a moment. It was only then she saw the fleshless skull behind his eyes. "I'll be back regular and often." He turned and walked out of the room. The sound of his steps echoed in the hall and ebbed as he reached the bottom of the stairs.

When Serena awakened the next morning she had a throbbing headache. It seemed to peak with each beat of her pulse. Flashes of pain washed across her forehead. She was exhausted. Her seventy-nine-year-old body was stiff and sore. She felt as if she hadn't slept at all. Her night had been filled with fear and restlessness due to the dream, and it was still very much with her. When she sat up, her body was still numb and it seemed to weigh much more than it had the night before. She had to concentrate just to get to her feet. She made her way into the bathroom and took a couple of pills for the headache. She was unsteady. She stumbled as she left the bathroom and fell against a highboy filled with knickknacks. A hand-painted clay ashtray toppled off the shelf by her shoulder. Serena turned to catch it but lost her balance again. She had to grab on to the dresser to keep from falling. The ashtray hit the floor and shattered. Serena surveyed the damage and recognized that the ashtray had been made by Franklin when he was in elementary school. *Is that a sign?* she wondered as she stepped over the pieces and returned to her bed.

The day passed slowly for Serena. She took her afternoon tea in the front sitting room and opened Saturday's mail. Most of the envelopes were bills, but there was one letter from New Orleans and it was lightly scented with lavender. She hadn't received a letter from Louisiana for many years. She pushed all the business correspondence off to the side and placed the letter directly in front of her. She rang for more tea. She studied the letter's envelope. She did not recognize the name, Mr. and Mrs. Chauncey Ford. Nor did their address bring anything to mind. The envelope was gray and embossed with a faint silver weave design. It was personalized stationery. The faint scent of lavender spoke of breeding and class. Serena waited until Mrs. Marquez brought in a new urn filled with hot tea. Serena poured her tea first then proceeded to open the letter. Inside was a funeral announcement for her younger brother, Amos Baddeaux. The announcement indicated that he had died after a long, painful illness. The service was scheduled for Wednesday, June 30, at Pine Knoll Baptist Church.

Serena put down the announcement and put her head in her hands. Her head was throbbing again. The angst and turmoil of the dream returned to the forefront of her consciousness. There was much pain where Amos and Della were concerned. She and her brother and sister had been estranged after he had been paralyzed. They had blamed her for his paralysis. They had blamed her for their youngest sister's, Tini's, death. They blamed her for all of Della's miscarriages. All because Serena had not heeded Sister Bornais's warnings. Bornais's image haunted her, like a will-o'-the-wisp, moving just on the edge of her vision, and the words she had uttered in 1927 in the room at the Hotel Toussant echoed in Serena's ears.

It seemed to Serena that her life was like a spiderweb: Every major spoke of her existence ran through a core dominated by her one meeting with Sister Bornais. All the rest of her important moments revolved like strands around that one event, an ever-growing spiral outward, entwining and ensnaring everything she touched, including her family. A glistening trap of her own making. Now that she was near the end of her life she had no fear of death; in fact she yearned for it. She often wished that King had killed her when he had found out about his son. Death would have alleviated the pain of living for her and left King with regret lying heavy on his soul. She wanted him to share some of her unhappiness. It was never to be. Death had given him release from the significance and the insignificance of life. She now knew that the entity waiting on the edge of the web was not death, but fate. Its venom was far more painful and its appetite was much more rapacious. It would not let her rest until all her vital juices had been sucked dry.

In truth, Serena's problems had not begun with Sister Bornais, but six years earlier, in 1921, in a black township called Bodie Wells in southeastern Oklahoma. She and King had left Louisiana to escape the relentless sheriff of New Orleans, and they bought a general store in a black-run township at the feet of the Ouachita Mountains. It was one of the few black towns that King could find in the nearby states that had electricity. He did not want to give up the comforts that came with electricity.

In 1921 Bodie Wells was a town of six hundred souls, not even a postage stamp on the vast, flat envelope of Oklahoma. It was a town in which the citizens daily girded themselves for battles against forces over which they had no control, yet its people felt a certain pride. Although many worked in the city of Clairborne, where they were brought face-to-face with their second-class citizenship, each day they returned home, they returned like victors, for they lived in a town where their voice and their vote mattered. The town's existence itself was a victory. In those days victories were judged against the worst that could happen rather than the best. There was no pretense in 1921 that the "Land of the Free" was meant to include black people. Racism and gravity were two certainties. The people of Bodie Wells were tough and hard. They struggled through twelve-hour days to wrest a crop from the temperamental earth and then went home to drink or gamble until they passed out. If they were temperance people, after they worked their twelve hours they went to one of the churches and spent hours on their knees praying. Subtlety and moderation had as little to do with their lives as justice and fairness. It was a town struggling to hold on to land that had been hard won with sweat and tears. At night shotguns were loaded and leaned against front doors, in case the Klan should come calling. The people had dug in to fight. There was no place to run; the windswept plains lay to the west, and to the east lay the cold, inhospitable ridges and crests of the Ouachitas.

Serena knew well hard work. She had been raised on a sharecropping farm where there was never enough money to lift the family out of the muck and mire. She had seen her mother work herself to death just to keep the family clothed and fed. Serena knew the torpor, the stupor, the exhaustion that came from day after day of long hours of muscle-tearing, back-wrenching work. There was a tyranny in that life which pressed the joy out of living, a tyranny so complete that most never escaped its oppressive clutches. She had seen them on Sunday at the clapboard church, people so tired and beaten that their bodies could not hold a laugh and their faces could not frame a smile. They were shackled by hopeless exhaustion. They were inhabitants of a world where there was no beauty. Sunrises, sunsets, full moons were merely nature's alarm clock signaling the passage of time. Beauty was an abstraction having nothing to do with their lives—lives in which days turned into centuries, and finally the meaningless death following the meaningless life, with never once any true hope of escape.

She wanted to escape that world. She wanted to leave it entirely behind. She wanted to live in a real city, someplace that had an indoor toilet and electricity. King had been her ticket out. He had given her a chance to dream, to hope, to see what was possible. With him she had intended to craft a new and different life. She saw herself becoming a grand lady presiding over a dynasty of her own children, children who would succeed in the world because prejudice was not heavy enough to keep them down or stop them from dreaming and becoming. It was true that it was King's money, money derived from his gambling and bootlegging businesses, that bought her the standard of living the likes of which she had only fantasized. And his willingness to use violence ensured that they would keep what they possessed and would always have money. In the back of her mind, she had thought that she would eventually wean him away from his guns and in time they would lead the lives of honest, breadwinning people. She had begun working on her dream within a month of arriving in Bodie Wells, when she persuaded King to buy one of the two general stores in town. She planned to craft a life that had none of the meanness and sordidness of poverty in it. Her family would be joyful. There would be laughter around her hearth.

Bodie Wells allowed her to shape her dream in the relative safety of a small pond. Running the general store gave her a position of respect and also an opportunity to establish herself as one of the town's important women. Buying merchandise, doing the inventory and the accounting, and keeping the store books all helped give her a real understanding of operating a business. She worked on her manners and her diction. She read books on etiquette. She was prepared to work to improve herself. It was a small pond, but during her six-year stay she became one of its big frogs.

The letter had come a week after Thanksgiving in 1921. King was away in Mexico at the time. The snow had been falling steadily for several days in thick, powdery flakes that covered everything, including Main Street, which was the only paved street in town. King had been away nearly a month dealing with his bootleg business. Their marriage was still new, only a few months old. It was her first time being alone. She had never, ever spent a holiday by herself, but both Thanksgiving and Christmas passed and there was no word from King. It was hard to remember what she hated more, the wind or the silence. The wind populated the passing hours with haunting voices borne of desolate plains, while the silence confirmed in its own empty way that she was alone. Some nights before she went to sleep she wondered whether King ever planned to return to her.

When Christmas passed, Serena could no longer wait. She opened the letter. There were actually two letters in the envelope. The first one was from Captain Mack, a white man who was like an uncle to King. It read:

> *. . . I don't know if this is one of my brother's tricks or not, but a woman came here named Mamie. She had a little boy with her who she claimed was your son. I didn't tell her nothing, but she gave me a letter to send to you. She told me that you told her we was about the only family that you had. I can't tell you how good that made me and Martha feel, boy. We told her we didn't know where you was, but if we got a chance we would forward her letter. I hope you and your new wife is doing good. No matter what you thinking, don't come back here! My brother, the sheriff, has people all over the place looking for you. You done shot his leg off and now he's madder than an alligator with eggs.*
>
> *If you decide to come back, don't come to the mill! Corlis has got people watching us.*
>
> *Go to Poindexter's and he'll contact me. We'll still find a way to help you just like when you was seventeen and needed money and a horse.*
>
> *You take care of yourself, boy. You all we got.*

For Serena the next letter had been even more difficult to read, but she could not put it down. Her hands and eyes would not obey her. In her mind she was screaming, shouting at herself, *Drop the letter! Don't read it!* Yet her eyes followed each line of the letter to its horrible conclusion. It read:

> *Hello King,*
>
> *I can't tell you how much I've missed you in the eighteen months since you've been gone. You're one of a kind. I never had a chance to tell you how grateful I was that you appointed me manager of the Rockland Palace. A regular paying job is on the path to happiness. Smitty or one of the guys stop by every once in a while to make sure things are running well. The Palace is one of the most popular places in New York City and we regularly take in a profit. Life is so crazy; now that I don't need the money I get from singing, I have more offers for work than I can*

handle. I have an offer to be part of a traveling revue. I really want to do it. I want to see where my singing career will go if I put time in it. But I have a problem and it's not the Palace. Vince knows the ropes better than I do.

I don't know how to tell you this, but six months after you left, our son was born. Yes, I knew I was pregnant before you left, but I didn't want you to stay if that was your only reason for staying. If you stayed, I wanted it to be because you loved me. It was hard for me to accept then, but I realize now that you didn't know how to love.

I came looking for you to find out whether you had learned how in the time that you've been gone. I hoped that there still might be a future for us. Even if we can't get together, I thought you would like to see your wonderful son. He reminds me so much of you. He is not even a year old and he's already walking. He is tough and fearless. Nothing scares him. I was hoping that I could leave him with you while I travel with the revue.

I have been talking with your lawyer friend Goldbaum and he's the one who told me you were in New Orleans. I have been here two weeks and no one knows where you are. Please contact me as soon as you get this. I'm staying at the Tri-Color Hotel on the edge of Storyville. I really love the music that's being played in some of the clubs down here.

Oh, by the way, a friend of yours invited me out to his farm next week. He wants to see your son. The man's name is Alfred DuMont. He says he's known you all your life. I'm really looking forward to some home cooking.

Your loving Mamie

Serena didn't remember what had happened after she finished reading the second letter. All she knew then was that her world had come crashing down around her ears. All because of some floozie who couldn't keep her pants on. She didn't know this woman, but she knew her. The woman was coming to contaminate the world that Serena was creating, bringing the sordidness of unmarried sex and children out of wedlock. Mamie was a woman of easy laughter and easy liaisons. She wasn't planning ahead, trying to build a future like Serena. What right had this woman to come looking for King? He had left her once. Wasn't that enough? But underneath Serena's indignation was fear, fear that she couldn't escape the life that she had lived on the farm, fear that she wasn't entitled to success and happiness.

She did not know what to do, but of one thing she was certain: Her concept of dynasty did not include having another woman's whelp preside over her children. She would fight that all the way. She did not stop and think for a minute that King should have a choice in the matter. It was her dream. It was her decision. When King arrived the day before New Year's, Serena told him nothing of the letter. After all, if that woman was going to visit the DuMonts, perhaps the problem would take care of itself.

Things were wonderful between King and Serena for a month, then the second letter had arrived. It was delivered to King directly. Serena only got to read it after King had left to return to Louisiana. With no response to the first letter, Serena had sincerely hoped that there would be no more news of the woman and her child, that they would sink back into whatever swamp they had crawled out of. The look on King's face after he read the letter revealed to Serena that she had driven a wedge between them by her silence. This was the point at which Serena first noticed that her life was divided. She could see herself from a distance, as if she were walking parallel on the opposite side of a small creek. This wasn't a problem initially; but over time the creek grew to a stream, and the stream to a river, and the river to a sea, and the sea became the wide, vast ocean. It took years, but eventually she lost sight of herself. The second letter had effectively driven the nails into the coffin of her dreams.

January 15, 1921

Dear Bordeaux,

I'm really surprised that I haven't heard from you since I wrote you the first letter in December. I just hope that you and your new wife are all right. I'm sorry to be writing you with this news. The woman from New York, who said she was the mother of your child, was found last week in the swamp. She was out of her head delirious. Her body looked like it had been tortured and violated. It looks like the DuMonts took advantage of her and passed her around. The woman's people are coming to get her in the next few days to carry her home. I hope she regains her senses. There was no sign of the baby.

I have put out feelers, trying to find out if anybody knows about the child, and had no success. Corlis sent me a message to mind my own business. So, it looks like once again, he and the DuMonts are working together. If you decide to come back, you best be on your toes. There's a trap waiting to slam shut on you. I'll keep on searching for the child, but the baby may be already dead. It would be foolish for you to hope for anything different.

I know nothing will stop you from coming now, but it's very dangerous. You got to be very careful. Remember, Corlis has people watching us. Go to Poindexter's hunting cabin or Baptiste's fishing dock. They'll tell me when you arrive.

Martha and me, we pray for you, son.

King had left Bodie Wells directly after reading the letter. He was gone within two hours of opening it. Serena was left surrounded by the silent distance of hired help. Six weeks passed and no word from King. She had no idea what had happened to him, nor what to think. Doubt gnawed at her like a rat nibbling cheese, and the passage of each day left another tooth mark on her heart. Within two weeks of his departure she realized that she could not keep the general store without King's money and support. The store was earning money, but not enough to maintain their standard of living. If there was just one bad harvest and a stretch of bad times fell upon the citizens of Bodie Wells, the store would be out of business. Another problem was that men were not used to dealing with a woman. They tried all sorts of tricks to cheat her. The traveling hawkers and salesmen did not accord her the same deference and respect as when King stood behind her. People were even beginning to shoplift merchandise. Her success was tied to King's presence. Without him the pursuit of her dream would fail, and the prospect of failure frightened Serena: It meant returning to the farm in Louisiana. She could clearly hear that world calling her, welcoming her back to the morning sadness and the evening fatigue. She wanted desperately for King to return. She was prepared to do anything to keep him. Anything. In the second month she received a letter from New Orleans. It was about King. He and another man had been arrested by Sheriff Corlis Mack's deputies. Serena was almost happy to find out that King had been caught by the sheriff of New Orleans: At least he hadn't left her to live with that other woman. There was a reason he had not returned. It gave her the chance to prove herself to him, show him that she was sorry for her mistake. Serena resolved that she would help him escape no matter the cost.

She arranged to meet some of King's men in Algiers, across the river from New Orleans. Her dreams drove her forward. She took charge of the rescue effort. King had a number of good men working for him, trustworthy and fearless. Her determination to rescue King, manifested in her face and words, impressed all who came in contact with her. The men deferred to her forcefulness. There was a confidence and certainty about her that was reminiscent of King himself. She was a methodical and tireless worker in the achievement of her goal. Within two days she had developed a plan from the information available. The sheriff, Corlis Mack, a fat spider of a man, was still in the hospital recuperating from the amputation of his leg, which King had caused when he shot it off. Corlis Mack had delegated the responsibility of running his department to Captain LeGrande. The sheriff and his executive staff always met at the Lafayette Social Club. Serena got herself a job at the Lafayette and, due to some staff absences, had the opportunity to serve LeGrande.

This is the point where Serena released the details of her memory; like a school of fish from an overturned net, the specifics wiggled away into the encroaching darkness. She preferred the obscuring haze of time, preferred to let the curve of the earth block her sight. It was all too horrible to recount. Suffice it to say, she allowed LeGrande to force himself upon her, to violate her, all in order to discover where King was imprisoned. In the end it was one of the colored waiters who revealed that King was locked away in a basement room of the Lafayette. King and his friend were rescued, but many people died in the escape. She remembered the smell of blood, then immediately after that the smell of gasoline as King's men doused the room where King and his friend had been imprisoned with the contents of five-gallon drums.

There was one memory she could not forget. After King had been carried out and LeGrande had been shackled to the wall in King's very same chains, LeGrande began to beg for his life. King's men had left the room to get more gasoline and lay fuses for the dynamite. LeGrande had babbled, panic in his eyes, babbled that he knew where the baby was. It was in an orphanage in southeast Texas. He pleaded that if she let him go, he would tell her exactly where it was. Serena nearly laughed in his face. The man did not know to whom he was speaking. As she raised her revolver and pulled the trigger, she remembered thinking, I let you rape me, but I will not let you do it to my family! She emptied her gun into his chest, then watched as gasoline was dumped on his dead body. She had to kill him. She had to make sure he never told anyone else. She still had no intention of letting the ghost of another woman walk through her house on a daily basis. Serena had paid with her body for the right to bear all of King's children. She never intended to ever mention the baby to him again. It was as dead a subject as LeGrande.

When Serena and King returned to Bodie Wells, Serena had thought that they could leave all the bad experiences behind them, that they could start anew, building their lives together. She tended King night and day while he recuperated and regained his strength. She understood intuitively that King would honor her sacrifice, that he would put aside his anger and resentment because she had risked her life on his behalf. His code of conduct would let him do no less. She slipped into a schedule of letting her staff open the store in the morning while she was tending to King. After several hours in the store she would return to check on her husband. She often spent the afternoon with him. She was happy and almost blissful until she discovered that she was pregnant with LeGrande's child. She didn't dare tell King. She thought she could get rid of the fetus without him knowing. Serena never doubted that King would hate his enemy's child.

The five weeks of imprisonment had destroyed something inside of King. The mechanism that created smiles and laughter appeared irreversibly broken. There seemed no room for anything in his psyche but hatred. He was like a lantern in which the wick had been withdrawn down into the body of the lamp, so that it wouldn't light, but nonetheless always had the potential to explode. Shortly after he had recuperated fully from his injuries, King went back to New Orleans. He said he would not return until the sheriff was in his grave. Serena used his absence as an opportunity to try and abort the baby. She nearly killed herself with the potions that she took. She was in a coma on the edge of death when King returned from his successful mission of murder.

LaValle Baddeaux Tremain was born premature, weak, and colicky. Once she had the child in her arms, Serena wondered what could have made her want to kill her own baby. How could she have tried to take the life of this gift from God? This sweet, little miraculous boy, how could she? There was a terrible weight on her heart. She felt great guilt because she thought the potions she had taken had adversely affected her infant son. She was immediately overprotective and doting with him. The first few years were touch-and-go, and he was in need of her constant care. She was committed to tending his every need and she was to remain so throughout his life. She never trusted King to be fair or just with LaValle. Why should she expect King to react differently to LeGrande's child than she had to Mamie's spawn?

With the birth of Jacques Bordeaux Tremain, LaValle's weakness became even more apparent. Jacques, better known as Jack, was rough-and-tumble from the moment he was born. He was his father's son and King took him everywhere with him. Lavalle was always more thin-skinned and cried more easily than his younger brother. Serena blamed herself for his weakness; he was her firstborn, a child who clung on to life despite his mother's depredations. He came into the world needing more care than his younger brother.

It was predestined that Lavalle would be jealous of Jack, for Jack was everything he was not. Jack had a likeable manner and made friends without difficulty. He was good with animals, had the patience of a hunter, the steadiness of a person far beyond his years, and most of all he was fearless. LaValle could never compare. He was always the odd man out and often remained on the sidelines while his younger brother was chosen for games. He suffered the further indignity of being one of those unfortunate people who could not disguise his true feelings or intentions. It was obvious to all that he treated Jack unfairly, but Jack, to his credit, took all that LaValle dished out and kept moving on. The end result was that everyone disliked LaValle and loved Jack.

It pulled at her heart to see her oldest boy in such misery. She did everything she could to shelter him from the rancor of others and the unfairness of life, but she was unable to control the world in which he lived, and she hadn't known then that his success depended upon his changing his reactions to that world. King was always suggesting to her that he take LaValle along on his trips with Jack. Serena never said yes to those suggestions. She didn't trust King. At best he tolerated the boy. Jack was the child in whom King invested and Jack ate it up. He got tougher while LaValle stayed behind her skirts. Serena knew something was wrong, but she didn't know what it was. There was very little laughter around her hearth, and joy seemed a thing of the past.

In 1927, when LaValle was five and Jack was three, Serena and King decided to move out to California. Serena went to New Orleans to see her sisters and pick up her fifteen-year-old brother, Amos, who had run away from the family farm because of their father's cruelty. King would only allow her to take LaValle; he took Jack with him to Oakland and found a house and set things up for her arrival. As fate would have it, LaValle developed a bad cough and it had the possibility of turning into something serious. Serena was concerned for him. Sister Bornais, a medicine woman, knocked on her hotel room door unsolicited late one night and gave LaValle potions that had him sleeping soundly for the first time in days. Serena was so thankful to see her tired, little son snoring in deep slumber she nearly wept. But to her misfortune, Serena learned that the medicine woman was not through with her.

Sister Bornais was known far and wide as a practitioner of voodoo. Her name, spoken anywhere in southern Louisiana, was mentioned with awe and respect. She was not a charlatan. She could read bones, tea leaves, palms, and faces. She was an expert on ghosts and haints. Her spells, potions, and cures continued to come with the highest recommendations. She was the one called in when the midwife had done all within her power and the doctor had thrown up his hands. Some people said she had the hands of God, others thought it was the devil's gift, but none doubted her power. Yet Serena chose to disregard her advice.

It began when Sister Bornais took her hand. Sister Bornais's yellow satin head tie seemed to reflect the lamplight and the numerous gleaming gold bangles on her wrists tinkled like the bells of a miniature carousel. She looked Serena directly in the eye and said: "You's King's wife, but this ain't his son. I see from yo' hand that King got two sons, but this chile here sho' ain't one of them. I see three boys, two related through their father and two related through their mother. The sign say that you and King only had one chile together.

"I didn't ask for this, it come to me. I just see things, kinda 'round the corner; sometime it be days, sometime it be years; sometime it's a vision, sometime it's a feelin, and sometime I just know, like I been there and witnessed it. And with you, I is witnessing. I is tellin' the buck-naked truth! There ain't no mistake!

"What I see is this: If'en you want to help this here chile, you got to help his older brother. The problem with this here chile is there is a spirit that be hangin' over him like a dark cloud. Only way to get rid of that spirit is to do right by the oldest. I's beginnin' to see it now. You got the power to change it all for the better, but for some reason you won't.

"I got a clear vision of what's gon' happen if'en you don't do right.

This here sleepin' chile gon' be a mama's boy all his life, which ain't gon be that long, really, and mo' than that, he gon' be the cause of death of his youngest brother. You don't follow what I say, you gon' be left with no sons at all! No chil'ren! King's oldest boy gon' be all right no matter what you do, he just won't ever know his daddy. If'en you keeps to the path you's travelin', you ain't gon' have no chil'ren and the only decent grandchil'ren you gon' have is gon' hate you. You done messed with a powerful and vengeful spirit! That boy was s'posed to be with his daddy from the git. You done stuck yo' finger in destiny's business and less'n you right it, you's got an unhappy life ahead. If you don't take care of it right, I see unhappiness spreadin' to yo' family members, to yo' sisters and yo' brother; stopping yo' kin's seed from flourishing, makin' you the only chile from yo' family that bears chil'ren. You best take heed and pay the price to make that spirit move on! Do right by the oldest boy! I can't say it no clearer. What will be will be."

Intuitively, Serena knew exactly what Sister Bornais meant when she said "Do right by the oldest boy!" It meant take him into her home, the place where her own, younger children slept. On the way to California, Serena had made an effort to do right. She found the orphanage in southeastern Texas where the boy had been placed. She even stopped in Port Arthur and visited the orphanage. She had vague intentions of bringing the boy to San Francisco with her, yet when she saw King's son she could not make herself take him into her home. She recognized the boy. He looked like his father. She felt an immediate fear for LaValle. He would lose his position as the oldest and then he would have nothing. He would be smothered by King's two sons. He would be pushed even further to the periphery. She had to protect him from that. It wasn't his fault that he was born into such a world. She determined that a voodoo woman's words wouldn't frighten her from doing the best thing for her oldest child. She left the orphanage without taking the boy, Elroy Fontenot, with her. Serena sent five hundred dollars a year to the orphanage from then on, hoping that would appease the evil spirit.

Over time it was revealed that everything Sister Bornais had predicted had come to pass. Serena was the only one of her siblings ever to have children. Her two sons were dead and in their graves before they were thirty and one grandson, the one most like King, did indeed hate her. Her family consisted of Franklin and his family. She had practically no relationship with her granddaughter, Samantha, although Serena was beginning to talk with her great-grandson, Rhasan. He was the only great-grandchild who called her and came to visit her regularly. Her siblings in New Orleans would not speak with her. Her telegrams and letters were returned unanswered. After he was paralyzed, Amos had informed everyone that she had ignored Sister Bornais's advice. She was not aware until years after the fact that Amos had known from the very beginning that she had failed to take the medicine woman's advice. Now King was dead and Serena was doomed to live on into her fading years. It was totally unfair. He had more blood on his hands than she, yet he was allowed to escape the haunting memories, the feelings of dissatisfaction and regret, and the echoes of what might have been. The grand dream of Serena's youth was in total carnage and she had been living in its wreckage for years. Her life was a husk, an empty shell, a casing that enclosed a seed that never germinated. She had longed to escape her origins, but after nearly eighty years of living she discovered she had brought all its meanness and sordidness with her. Her body might die in her huge, silent Victorian house on Fulton Street, but her essence would lie in one of those dank and dimly lit cabins that dotted the exhausted soil of the lowlands around Lake Pontchartrain.

Serena took a sip of her tea and discovered that it was cold. She rang the bell for Mrs. Marquez, then picked up the scented envelope. There was a contact number beneath the name and address. On the spur of the moment, Serena decided to call. She picked up the phone and dialed the number.

A woman's voice answered after several rings. The soft, muted tones of a New Orleans drawl drifted across the wires. "Ford residence. May I help you?"

Serena was momentarily taken aback upon hearing the long-forgotten inflections of her place of birth. She cleared her throat and replied, "This is Serena Tremain. I'm calling in regards to a funeral announcement that I received. The funeral is for my brother, Amos Baddeaux."

There was a pause on the other end of the line, then the woman's excited voice: "Aunt Serena, is that you? Is it really you? My sister and I didn't know if you would respond to our letter. What a blessing!"

"Are we related?" Serena asked with an imperious tone.

"Yes! Yes, Aunt Serena! We've never met, but I'm Della Baddeaux Thompson's daughter. My sister and I thought that Uncle Amos's funeral was the perfect event to bring all the family together, to put aside old arguments and celebrate Uncle Amos's life. We want us to be one family again."

The woman's words shocked Serena. "You're Della's daughter?" she questioned with disbelief.

"Yes, ma'am. My sister, Tini, and I want to bring the family back together."

Serena was speechless. After all these years, was it possible? Could Sister Bornais have been wrong? Could she have made a mistake? Obviously, she had. The proof was on the other end of the line. Della had daughters, one of whom was named after Serena's other long-dead sister.

"Aunt Serena, are you still there?"

"Yes, child," Serena replied in a gentler tone. She was still mulling over the news. If Sister Bornais had been wrong about this, she could be wrong about other things. Perhaps her supernatural vision wasn't twenty-twenty and there was a limit to her power. Serena was beginning to smile. She felt as if a dark, dense cloud was being lifted from her heart and it was being replaced by fresh breezes.

"Do you think you'll be able to come for the service, Aunt Serena? We realize it's short notice, but we had no choice. Uncle Amos wanted Chester Broadfoot's Ragtime Band to lead his casket through Storyville with second liners and all. It was the only day we could get him."

"I'll be there, honey. Tell your mother I'm coming. I'll make my arrangements today."

"Auntie, let's let it be a surprise."

"Whatever you think, honey," Serena agreed. "By the way, what is your name? The announcement says Mr. and Mrs. Chauncey Ford."

"I'm Rebecca. I'm named after my maternal grandmother."

"It's a beautiful name, a name with biblical history behind it. I look forward to seeing you in person, my dear." After the phone was returned to its cradle, Serena sat pondering the call. There was, after all, a light at the end of the tunnel. The clouds did indeed have a silver lining. The rainbow was real. Her family had not been destroyed because of her decisions. Children had been born to one of her siblings. The curse was not all-encompassing. It was finite. Sister Bornais had proved to be mortal, and as a mortal had make a mistake.

This was just the kind of news that would put a limit on the number and regularity of King's nighttime visits. There would be less power in his presence. Yes, she might even be free of him. Serena sipped her tea and actually laughed out loud.

Sunday, June 27, 1982

There was no wind. The sun was clear and bright overhead, but a haze had settled over downtown San Francisco and the bay. From Potrero Heights the Oakland hills looked fuzzy and indistinct in the distance. Deleon sat at his bedroom window and stared out as the lateness of the sun's red advance brought out the pinks and lavenders in the polluting haze. The dark green hills across the bay took on a purple tinge while the bay itself became mauve. It looked like a scene out of one of Monet's paintings. Deleon took a deep breath and listened to the muffled sound of angry exchanges in Spanish coming from downstairs in the living room.

San Vicente's men were obviously upset because Martinez and Diaz had not returned. It sounded like they wanted to take matters into their own hands and interrogate Deleon. Deleon smiled. That was one of the problems with hiring mercenaries: They had a greater loyalty to one another than they had to their employer. Unless you paid for the very best, they always had second thoughts about their assignment when they sustained losses in personnel. The argument below had actually begun last night, when it was obvious that the two men were not returning. Deleon wasn't worried; he had made preparations. He had informed both Hardigrew and Brown of the situation and told them to sleep with their guns at the ready. For his own safety he had set up a shotgun at his bedroom door, so that if it was opened unexpectedly, the gun would discharge into whoever was unfortunate enough to be standing there.

Deleon heard his name shouted in the rooms below and smiled again. He had hoped to cause some disruption to the well-oiled precision of San Vicente's team, but the result was better than his expectation. Despite their regimen, their unity was in disarray. They had realized that Martinez and Diaz were in the hands of an adversary or were dead, which were essentially the same in end result. Deleon guessed the Cubans were now worrying about their individual welfare. Martinez had been the leader of the other three men. They functioned as a four-man team; they took their direction from him, not San Vicente. Thus, Deleon had cut the team's spinal cord when he killed Martinez. To San Vicente, the remaining two Cubans were like legs he couldn't control.

Deleon didn't have to speak their language to know exactly what was going through their minds. Now they would be worrying over the prospect of whether or not he had an unknown number of additional soldiers in the surrounding community. Escape routes would soon be a topic of conversation. San Vicente, if he was truly gifted, might be able to rally the remaining two. Adolfo Arce, the dog handler, was a Colombian and he had been with San Vicente for fifteen years; his first loyalty was to San Vicente.

Twenty minutes passed. The angry voices died down. Then Deleon heard footsteps on the stairs leading up to his bedroom. He moved to the side of the door and waited. The shotgun was rigged to fire when the door was opened. The steps halted outside. There was a moment of silence then San Vicente's muffled voice issued through the closed door.

"Deleon, this is Francisco. May I have a moment of your time?"

Deleon made no effort to move or open the door. He merely inquired, "What's up, Frank?"

"Oh, just a few questions. A couple of my men think that you may have had something to do with the disappearance of Martinez and Diaz. I told them that was silly, that we were allies, but they need to hear it from you."

"Your men will believe me?" Deleon almost laughed, it was so absurd. "If they don't believe you, why should they believe me?"

"Who can explain human suspicion? There is no logic to feelings. Will you not come down so that we may talk this out? After all, there is still Tremain to think about."

"My door's always open to talk," Deleon said as he checked his pistol's magazine. He pushed the magazine home and continued. "But I'm thinking, if you don't have control over your men, a discussion could get messy and distracting."

"May I come in so that we may both lay our cards on the table?"

"Sure, just let me finish dressing." Deleon slipped the trigger string off the door handle and picked up the shotgun, then he moved the chair against which the shotgun had been propped so that there was no sign of his hastily rigged booby trap. He picked up a cloth and sat down with the shotgun. "Come in," he said as he pretended to be cleaning the shotgun with the cloth.

San Vicente pushed open the door and stepped into the room. He smiled when he saw Deleon's shotgun pointing in his general direction. "It's good to see someone taking care of his weapons."

"Yeah," Deleon replied dryly. "Firearm maintenance is very important. What do you want to talk about?"

"We have a problem."

"We?"

San Vicente nodded his head. "Yes, my friend, we have a problem. It appears that two of my men don't think that you have their best interests at heart."

"Why?"

San Vicente gave Deleon a long look then asked, "Did you not see Martinez and Diaz yesterday on the streetcar?" Deleon shrugged as if to indicate that if he'd seen the two men, it hadn't stood out in his mind.

San Vicente shook his head with disappointment. "Why must we play games with each other? I know you either have these men or you killed them. If you didn't do it yourself, you had someone else do it. Can we not put aside our feelings of distrust so that we can fully participate in this venture as allies?"

"How can I trust men who hate me because of the color of my skin?"

"Is there nothing we can do to repair the damage? We have a greater chance of success against Tremain's organization if we combine our efforts."

"There is one thing that may help," Deleon ventured quietly. Although he evinced an outward calm, San Vicente's words had him in turmoil. Tremain had an organization? An organization that one of the grandsons could potentially head? If indeed there was such an organization, Deleon would have to contact his grandfather and discuss a change in strategy.

San Vicente prodded. "There is one thing that can help? What is it?"

"Send your Cubans back to Miami."

"Ohh, I'm sorry, my friend, but I cannot do that. I cannot send them home without some sacrifice on your part. I'd never be able to hire again from their network if I don't give them a chance to avenge their loss. Give me one of your men to assuage their anger. You have killed two of mine. One for two. After that they will go home. It is not a bad deal, then we'll both have one, eh? What do you say?"

Deleon thought for a minute. He realized that San Vicente's back was up against a wall because he had to show loyalty to his hired men. Deleon deduced that if he didn't take his offer, a pitched battle would be fought in the house. Under those circumstances, the casualties would not be limited. It was cleaner just to give up a man. Deleon nodded and then, despite knowing the answer, he asked, "Which one do you want?"

San Vicente smiled. "You are a wise man. Give us Hardigrew."

"Okay, but he can't be killed here. It has to be out somewhere."

"No problem. Once he is dead, the two men will catch the next flight back to Florida. Then we can get back to the real work."

"Before you go, I'd like to know how much you know about Tremain's organization. Do you think it will survive the old man's death and can either of his grandsons lead it?"

"El Negro's organization is well known in Mexico. He has many men and for some years he made a living stealing from drug dealers, but that time has passed. His organization can no longer compete. He cannot afford to pay the bribes that a drug lord can pay. He cannot pay the big money to his soldiers. He worked by the old system of loyalty. It is much harder to establish than greed. Almost all of his soldiers are old men. It is the end of an era. When he dies, his organization will die with him."

"Then you are not worried about either of the grandsons mounting a resistance?"

San Vicente scoffed, "They are both soft American boys! They have not been battle tested! What do they know about pain? About sacrifice? About leading men in dangerous situations? What they know about bloodshed, they learned from the movies. Believe me, their hearts will come easily out of their chests. It will not even be a challenge. We only wait for the old man to die, then we will collect his grandsons like sheep in a corral."

After San Vicente had returned downstairs, Deleon sat by the window, musing over their conversation. Giving up Hardigrew had been the easiest part. Deleon had decided to send him out to steal cars in the Westlake District later that evening. That would give the Cubans plenty of opportunity to take him down. The issue which kept troubling Deleon was not losing a man, but whether San Vicente was underestimating the grandsons. There was a good chance of it; after all he had underestimated Deleon. Deleon shook his head in tired resignation. As far as he was concerned, the whole situation was becoming too complicated. He had begun to feel a growing sense of uneasiness about the way things were proceeding beginning with the arrival of San Vicente. This feeling was heightened when Jesse and Fletcher unnecessarily assaulted the man in the parking lot. Their stupidity was bound to be the source of trouble.

He reasoned it would be easier to kill both grandsons now and forestall any possibility that one would assume leadership of the organization. Let others hunt down the certificates later. The longer he thought about it, the more certain he became that his earlier decision to kill the grandsons was the best course of action.

He looked out the window toward the bay and saw that the colors had deepened. The bay was now a bluish fuchsia before the dark, burgundy-green horizon of Oakland's undulating hills. The pink triangular sails of small boats reflecting the last light of western skies drifted on the windless bay. Monet could only have dreamed of painting something so beautiful.

As the view faded into differing shades of navy blue, Deleon turned his thoughts back to his problem. Even if San Vicente was right and the grandsons really were soft, things were not over. There was still San Vicente to consider. He did not doubt that he and Francisco were headed toward a final conflict and he intended to show Francisco that the underestimation of one's rivals had mortal consequences.

Deleon pulled the curtains over the window and permitted himself to hope. Just a few more tasks and he might be sketching and painting in the Caribbean long before he planned.

July 1958

Twelve-year-old Jackson moved through the mesquite and manzanita, attempting to avoid the prickly branches which snagged his clothing or caught on his backpack. The morning sun was already hot. He could feel its intensity on his skin and it had not yet reached its zenith. He was beginning to perspire. He pulled a well-used handkerchief from his pocket, lifted his sombrero, and wiped his face. Jackson stepped around one of the many barrel cacti which dotted the landscape and looked up at the red sandstone cliffs in front of him, their serrated peaks jutting into the eggshell-blue sky. Behind the peaks in the distance towered the green and rust colors of the San Pedro Martir Mountains.

To his right a covey of blue quail started and took to the air, veering away from him. Jackson chambered a round into his rifle. He knew that the upland terrain was not the usual habitat of the peccaries, but he also knew that the vicious little pigs ranged wherever there was food. After a minute or so, he relaxed. The flock appeared to have taken flight because of him. Up above, to his left, he could see his grandfather making his way to an angular ledge which ran horizontally across the cliff wall. The ledge slanted slightly upward toward a patch of green, which looked like a break in the rock.

Jackson hoped that this was the pass that led to the fertile canyons on the other side of the ridge. His grandfather had spent the better part of the morning searching for this gateway. At least this break in the sandstone appeared to be an easier climb than the next two possibilities. He leaned his rifle against a cactus, removed his backpack, and checked his canteen. It was still three-quarters full. He took a small sip. He wanted more, but he knew better. His grandfather had told him that the water in his canteen might have to last him all day. Jackson turned and looked back on the lowlands whence they had come. It was a view of a broken and rough land with sharp rock outcroppings jutting up from the sun-baked clay. They had climbed between two and three thousand feet since seven that morning. The valley in which they had left their jeep was lost in the distant haze.

They were hunting the small bands of bighorn sheep that frequented the high bluffs above the desert sagebrush and manzanita and the mountains beyond. He remembered from the night before how his grandfather had complained that the bighorns were vanishing from the Baja Peninsula. Jackson knew that the hunting trip could last up to five days if they were unable make an early kill. There was only a couple of pounds of jerked beef and dried fruit between them, but they could live off the land. Small game was plentiful. During the morning, Jackson had seen sage hen, quail, and lots of jackrabbits. His grandfather and Carlos had shown him many times how to cook fresh game with sage, wild onions, piñon, and sego lily bulbs.

Jackson was perspiring continuously. He pushed his sombrero back off his forehead and wiped his brow again with his handkerchief. When he reached for his rifle, he misjudged it and knocked it into a yellowing patch of vetch. As he stooped to pick it up, he heard the warning sound of a big rattler hidden in a thicket of weeds. The snake had obviously retreated to the safety of the shaded thicket to avoid the killing heat of direct sunlight. Perhaps it was the movement of the rifle glinting in the sun, or the sweating presence of the boy so close, for the snake struck as Jackson pulled his rifle to his side.

As the snake launched, Jackson leaped backward into the barrel cactus. The snake missed him by a good six inches, but Jackson landed squarely on the long spines of the cactus. The stiff bristles penetrated his clothing like the tines of a fork in a tender steak, stabbing deep into his right arm and lower back. He dropped to his knees in pain as the snake slithered off.

He picked up his rifle. He had no intention of shooting the snake, because he had been taught that a gun was only fired to kill game or to deal with emergencies. In his grandfather's hierarchy, snakes were not an emergency. He knew that he should have let the snake leave unmolested, but he was angry. He wanted to retaliate for the pain he felt. He popped out the rifle's magazine and removed the shell from the chamber. He then followed the snake through the brush, looking for an unobstructed shot at its head. When the snake wriggled across an open space of ground, Jackson brought the butt of his rifle down on the snake's head. He struck the snake until it no longer moved. When he was sure that it was dead, he stopped to view his handiwork. It was a big diamondback rattler, perhaps five or six feet long.

Jackson was happy with his kill. He had never skinned a snake before and he decided that this would be his first. He reached down to pull its body further into the clearing of brush. As his hands closed around its

thick body, the snake's head snapped back and its fangs stabbed deep
into the fleshy part of his forearm. Jackson stumbled backward in pain
and surprise. Without hesitation, he popped the magazine back into
the gun and chambered a bullet. He emptied his magazine into the
snake, obliterating its head. He looked down at his wound. There was
blood dripping from it and it had already begun to burn. He shivered in
fear. This was a mistake that could end in death.

Jackson knew he had to conserve energy and limit his movement,
otherwise he would assist the poison that was coursing through his
body. He opened his pack and took out a white T-shirt, which he tore
into strips. He tied a few of the strips to the highest branch of the
mesquite that he could reach. The white material would show his
grandfather his location.

He knelt to clear himself a space underneath the mesquite. He
turned over several nearby rocks to see if there were any other unwel-
come visitors, and a yellow and orange millipede scuttled off to the
darkness of its burrow. He sat down and began to tie a series of tourni-
quets above the bite. His whole arm had begun to swell and sweat trickled down his face. He lay back in the shelter of the bush and waited for
his grandfather to come.

When Jackson awoke, he was in a hospital, or what served as a hospital for a small village. There was one doctor and two nurses. All other
medical attention was provided by nuns, who moved quietly from room
to room whispering novenas and psalms of condolence. He was informed by the doctor that when his grandfather had brought him in
three days before, he had been suffering from a raging fever and they
had not thought he would live. He learned that his grandfather had sat
with him until the fever broke and then he had disappeared.

Jackson rested in the hospital three more days. At first, he was a little
woozy when he walked, but each day brought renewed strength and
energy. And, of course, his appetite was raging. When the nuns saw
how much food he was able to eat, several of them wondered out loud
as to how soon his grandfather would return for him. On the evening of
the third day, his grandfather appeared. When he came into Jackson's
room, he had a package under his arm wrapped in brown paper. He set
it on the bed and waited for Jackson to open it. Jackson opened the
package and saw that it contained a new rifle: a 30.06 with a scope.

His grandfather said, "I saw me a big ram up there with horns yea big."

He gestured with his arms to indicate the size. "He got your name on him!" His grandfather went to the closet and retrieved Jackson's clothes, which he threw on the bed. "If you got the vinegar, let's go get him."

Monday, June 28, 1982

It was three o'clock on Monday afternoon. Paul DiMarco was standing in the kitchen of his restaurant, chopping piles of fresh garlic and parsley. He had given his prep cook, Mickey Vazzi, an assignment to get the addresses of Jackson Tremain's friends. Paul minced the garlic quickly and efficiently. He was an old hand with the cleaver and had spent many hours in his youth working as second cook. He had just finished tasting the minestrone soup for flavor when Dominique entered the kitchen and told him that his cousin Edward was in the front, waiting to talk with him. Paul wiped his hands tiredly and went out to meet his cousin.

Edward DiMarco was tall and debonair. His thick brown hair was layered in a razor cut, his tailored Armani suit fell without a wrinkle, and his soft white hands had never done a day's manual labor. There was a slight family resemblance between him and Paul, but after that initial likeness, they were worlds apart.

Edward was swishing some Chianti around in a goblet, taking occasional sips when Paul appeared.

"How's it going, Ed?" Paul asked amiably, even though he was thinking that his cousin was a pretentious bastard.

"I'm all right, Paul," Edward answered in measured tones. "How's your family?"

"The family's fine, Ed. But you didn't come down here to ask about my family. We both know you don't give a shit about my family."

Edward sighed. "There's no reason for hostility, Paul. I had hoped that we could complete our discussion without resorting to diatribe and anger."

"Dia-who?" Paul asked sarcastically as he went behind the bar and poured himself a tumbler of grappa.

Edward followed him to the bar and sat on a barstool. "We have to talk. We might as well keep it pleasant."

"Do we now?" Paul challenged as he took a long drink from his glass. "The only time you ever come down here is to hassle me. You're not family! You didn't come to my son's wedding or my daughter's First Communion! So what do you want, Mr. Big Shot?"

Edward contained himself and smiled. "All right, Paul. Let's get down to business."

"Let's," Paul answered, swishing the grappa in his tumbler, scornfully parodying Edward and his Chianti.

"I spoke to Joe Bones in Las Vegas recently," Edward began. With the mention of Joe Bones's name, he noticed that he had Paul's undivided attention. "He told me that a month ago you had asked for some help in Mexico City from some people in his international organization. He said he gave it to you because of your father." There was silence as Edward waited for an explanation.

Paul took a long look at his cousin and said, "So?"

"Well, it appears that the men assigned to help you have disappeared and last night one of Joe's buildings in Mexico City was destroyed by a bomb." Edward swished his Chianti and watched Paul for a reaction.

Outwardly, Paul remained calm, but he was stunned. The last he heard was that King Tremain and his grandson had been located. With the plans he had set in place, he had been confident that it was only a matter of time before King was killed and his grandson was in hand. He could not imagine what could have gone wrong. He wondered briefly whether old Joe Bones had assigned professional-caliber men; not that Paul would dare ask, but it was a concern. He returned Edward's rather sardonic look with one of his own. "What's all this got to do with me?"

"Joe asked me to come over and get an explanation." Edward spoke casually, finishing his Chianti. "He wants to know what you're doing and who's involved."

"Why didn't he call me if he had questions?" Paul snapped. He resented having to explain anything to his egghead cousin.

Refusing to get embroiled in Paul's anger, Edward answered as if he were speaking to a child. "He doesn't want you to call him again. He has honored your father's memory with a favor. That's the end of it. If you need more favors, you come through me."

"Through you?" Paul exploded. "Who the fuck do you think you are? What makes you think that I would waste my time with you?"

"I'm your only link to Joe Bones," Edward said with a smile. He was enjoying himself.

"We'll see about that!" Paul declared as he came from behind the bar. "I'll call him myself!"

"Do that," Edward said, setting his glass on the bar and standing up. "Then you can come to my office and give me the details of your current enterprise." Edward straightened his jacket and pulled his shirtsleeve cuffs down to the prescribed quarter inch of visibility. He gave Paul one last smile and said as an afterthought, "Oh, by the way, before you come to my office, make sure you have an appointment."

"I'll be goddamned if I'm going to come to your office and tell you anything!"

Edward gave Paul a toothy grin and said, "That's fine with me. I'm sure Joe Bones will love it." Edward turned to leave.

Paul, unable to believe that his cousin had such high stature, demanded, "How'd you get to be Bones's pet, huh?"

Edward turned and looked at his cousin questioningly. "Is that really all you see? You think that Joe is just playing favorites?" Edward shook his head sadly.

"Why don't you explain it to me, Ed?" Paul said, pulling out a chair at a nearby table for Edward. Paul sat down on the opposite side of the table and waited for his cousin to join him. Normally, Paul would not have wasted his time with Edward, but it had occurred to him that it was very likely that his cousin was telling the truth about representing Joe Bones. But why old Bones had chosen his white-bread cousin as his point man was beyond Paul's understanding. It was worth it to him to listen to what Edward might say.

Edward pulled out the chair that had been offered, still watching his cousin questioningly. "If you're serious, I'll give you a rundown of what's happening, but I don't want to deal with a lot of interruptions or spend time arguing with you." It was business necessity that caused Edward to sit down and talk with his Neanderthal cousin. As of this moment, Paul was at worst a nuisance. Edward hoped that his explanation would prevent his cousin from becoming a full-time problem. He pointed a finger at Paul and said, "No interruptions!" Paul exhaled disgustedly, but nodded his head.

Edward took a moment to compose himself. The DiMarco family had some big plans, beginning with the mayorship, and with the right business deals substantial wealth could be secured for the family's future generations. If the mayorship was achieved, then without doubt there'd be a political future for Edward as well. But these plans could brook no smudge, no hint of criminal doings or connections. Everything had to be squeaky clean. He began expansively, hoping that his historical references would broaden Paul's perspective. "In less than seventy years, this family has evolved from being illiterate immigrants to being a political force in the Bay Area."

"Save the Horatio Alger shit for your public appearances," Paul interjected impatiently. "I know family history as well as you."

Edward started to get up, but his mission was more important than doing battle with his cousin. "You may be familiar with family history," Edward retorted, unable to totally suppress his displeasure, "but you don't appear to have a grasp of the family's future direction and long-term objectives."

"Well, you're going to run it down for me, aren't you?" Paul asked snidely, mocking Edward's use of words.

Edward's patience was eroding rapidly. "You were given an offer late last year that would have invested considerable money in your restaurant business in return for your ceasing your criminal activities. Do you remember?"

Paul laughed sarcastically. "Yeah, I remember." He pointed his finger at Edward and sneered, "It was an insult to my family, part of a long line of insults. You throw us scraps while you take the prime cuts. Of course I refused it!"

Edward decided that it was time to take the gloves off. "The deal wouldn't have paid the costs of your Chinese mistress on Grant Street, or your ex-stewardess on California, or even your coke connection on Powell, or your gambling debts, but your family would have lived well and, more importantly, would have been positioned to participate in anything the DiMarco family may undertake in the future."

Paul was furious. The spineless punk had been spying on him and was now trying to muscle him with the information he had gained. "I didn't know you were a Peeping Tom," Paul said with a smirk. "But I guess it's typical of the gutless wonder you've become."

Now it was Edward's turn to smile. His cousin was so predictable: Push the right button, you got the desired response. "The DiMarco family no longer depends upon criminal enterprises for income," Edward spoke, staring straight at Paul. "We've diversified. We have trucking, unions, toxic waste disposal, the junk-bond market.

"Now, with our Republican connections in Texas, we're ready to get into the savings and loans business. If this election is successful, we're looking at putting someone in a statewide office. The opportunities that will be available through an elective office are too numerous to count. There will be enough for everybody. You're the lone liability, still involved with illegal activities. It's a pity you didn't take the deal, because we're going to have to close your drug operations down."

Paul stood up, his face red with rage. "Who the hell do you think you are? Close me down? I'll cut your balls off and stuff them in your mouth first!"

"And what will you say to Joe Bones when you try to explain to him that you assaulted his representative?" Edward asked, smiling. "Joe likes the proposal for this branch of the family to go legit. We've done it with his blessing and help. He understands that elected officials can be very valuable in a lot of different projects."

Paul's eyes were slits as he tried to comprehend the totality of what Edward was saying. Was Edward in business with Joe Bones? What kind of arrangement did they have?

"You made two and a half million dollars last year in your drug dealings. Maybe another quarter of a million from your extortion racket," Edward recounted, still smiling. He waved to a passing waitress and requested a scotch. He turned back to Paul and saw his cousin studying him. "A million dollars of this money you laundered through a construction company. The remaining money you passed through your restaurant." Edward spoke casually. He knew the facts by heart.

"Your books and ledgers read like loony tunes. You cannot account for the money you have passed through this restaurant, nor can you reconcile it with your annual tax statement. In short, cousin, you're a disaster waiting to happen. The family cannot afford to be in the political limelight while you are running a sloppy, unsophisticated operation. We'll have enough of a struggle without you giving our opponents ammunition."

Paul was steaming but said nothing. Again Edward smiled. He was confident that he had revealed sufficient information to cause Paul to reconsider his course of action. The waitress delivered his scotch and Edward raised his glass to Paul before drinking.

"So what do you want from me?" Paul asked through gritted teeth.

"I need to know what's happening in Mexico. Joe was not pleased to lose a ten-story office building as part of what he thinks is a retaliatory raid. Particularly when he hadn't done anything to provoke such action except let you use one of his strike teams."

"Okay, that's one. What else do you want?" Paul asked angrily.

"Take the deal we offered last year," Edward urged. "We'll guarantee a certain dollar figure of business annually and it will be well above what is needed to break even."

"So, I become a caterer while you become a politician, is that correct?" Paul demanded. He wanted to spit in Edward's eye. "Does that sound fair to you? I need to know."

"Well," Edward pondered a moment before continuing then said, "you're not much of a politician."

Paul had had enough. He stood up and leaned over the table. "Fuck you! I'd rather be dead."

Edward knocked back his drink and stood up. "That can be arranged."

"You threatening me?" Paul started around the table, but before he got to Edward a large shape loomed in the corner of his eye. He turned to face the threat and was shocked to find it was Vince Rosetti coming to Edward's aid. "Vince?" Paul asked in surprise as he looked into the weathered face of the assassin. "What are you doing here?"

"Joe said I should come and help Eddie explain things to you," Vince said in his thick, gravelly New York accent.

It was now obvious that Edward was fronting the party line, not his own agenda. Paul was shocked to think that Bones would send a killer to help Edward explain. It was a statement from the organization, clear and simple. Desperately, Paul needed time to think. They had him in a box. The only escape was to get hold of King's fortune. He needed to play for time.

"Why don't I come down to your office tomorrow and I'll bring everything that pertains to the Mexico project?" Paul suggested to Edward.

Edward said nothing. He merely looked at Vince and nodded his head at Paul.

Vince stepped forward and said, "I think you should talk now, 'cause Joe wants to know now." Vince's throat had been cut early in his career so his voice sounded like a cement mixer filled with aggregate. "Let's go in the back," Vince suggested.

Paul signaled to Dominique that he would be meeting in the office and informed her that the prep cook assignments had not been completed. As Paul walked back to his office, he promised himself that one day soon he would be standing on Edward's grave.

Tuesday, June 29, 1982

Jackson was sitting at a kitchen table, wiping his sweating face with a towel as he looked out the window and saw tatters of early-morning gray fog drifting through the trees of the park across the street. As a precaution, he had moved into one of his grandfather's San Francisco safe houses. He had informed no one of his return and would not until he had familiarized himself with all the materials he had received from his grandfather. He exhaled slowly then took a deep breath. He and Carlos had just completed a rigorous workout together. Carlos was intent on teaching Jackson knife technique, and they had been working on attack and parry patterns. As they sat across from each other at the table and recuperated from their physical exertion, they discussed their plans for the day. Carlos had several errands to run and Jackson had committed to finish reading the files that he had received from the Ramirez brothers. Theresa came out of the laundry room, picked a coffee urn up off the stove, and poured both Carlos and Jackson mugs of the thick, black steaming liquid then went back to buzzing around the kitchen. She was moving so fast that it hurt Jackson's eyes to focus on her. The potent aroma of strong coffee now filled his nostrils. He lifted the mug to his lips, took a sip, and grimaced. The aroma had not misled him. It was his grandfather's coffee, a black mixture of coffee grounds and boiled water, something that could've been cooked over a campfire. Jackson pushed the mug away.

"Don't have to guess who taught her to make coffee," Jackson said softly to Carlos.

Carlos smiled. "You don't like the coffee again?"

Jackson retorted, "This is something you drink only when one foot is gangrenous and you still have to walk fifteen miles in the snow without shoes. Otherwise you avoid it because it's bad for your kidneys!"

A burst of angry Spanish erupted from the kitchen and pots and pans began to clang. Jackson turned toward the kitchen door and then looked back toward Carlos, who was now laughing. Theresa continued her loud tirade without breaking for breath. Jackson looked questioningly at Carlos.

Carlos chuckled. "She is angry. She says no one told her how you like your coffee. She says she would do it the way you want if somebody tells her how that is. She wants to please you, not anger you."

"I'll get some Peet's coffee and show her how to use a drip carafe."

Carlos held up two manila folders labeled PAUL DIMARCO and JOHN TREE and then slid them across the table to Jackson. "Did you review the copies of these two files that I left in your room last night?"

"I read them. Not exactly bedtime reading. Both these guys are serious killers."

"These are just two of your known enemies. We're still searching for the third man. He's the one who brings these two thugs together."

Jackson picked up one of the folders and leafed through it. "Your men really put together thorough reports. How did they find out Di-Marco is laundering drug money through his restaurant?"

"I use people who specialize in information collection. They don't reveal their sources, but they guarantee the report's accuracy. If any of their reports have a critical inaccuracy, they will refund triple the fee paid, and that's quite hefty."

"I've been hoping that your information collectors would come across something that might give these people pause, perhaps consider reaching a negotiated settlement."

Carlos shook his head. "No way! Too much money at stake." He stood up. "Right now, I'm going to leave you to the rest of your reading. I need to contact some people I've got working in the field on other assignments and I've got to prepare for my trip to Mexico on Friday. I'll be back some time this afternoon."

"Before you go, tell me what's happening with the puppy. Is he going to be sent up here soon?"

"I thought it would be better if we held off the dog until you've settled things with your enemies first."

"I'm going to leave two men with you while I'm in Mexico. I want you to continue your knife practice with them. I don't want you to miss a day."

Jackson frowned. "This is getting more onerous than a job!"

"You need the blade work until you've memorized all the patterns of attack and defense. You need to keep to a daily two-hour workout schedule. My job is to prepare you to deal with whatever physical threat comes your way. We cannot rule out assassins, can we?"

"Whatever you say," Jackson agreed with a tired wave of his hand.

He was left alone in the dining room after Carlos departed. He could hear Theresa moving through parts of the house, cleaning, but the sounds were muffled. He had read for almost an hour before he came across a file marked ELROY FONTENOT. There were several inches of papers contained in the file. After going through it once, he set it down and wiped his forehead. It was confusing. The deeper he got into his grandfather's affairs and papers, the stranger the reality became. He had been reading a detective agency case folder and final report on the search for Elroy Fontenot, completed in 1952. Apparently, his grandfather had a son by a woman before he ever met Serena and this son, as a result of DuMont treachery, was left in an orphanage in south Texas in 1923. Serena knew of the whereabouts of the child from the very beginning but had never told King. She'd left the child to grow up in the orphanage. If that wasn't weird enough, King spent thousands of dollars and nearly thirty years searching for Elroy, and when he found him, he never once approached him. Elroy had actually been living right in San Francisco in the years after World War II. He was among the second group of black American officers hired by the San Francisco Police Department in 1951. King Tremain had known that Elroy was his son and had done nothing to inform him of their kinship.

It was all too strange. Jackson stood up and stared out the window, which looked upon the green meadows of Alamo Square Park. The park's grassy swards, dotted with stands of twisted pine, junipers, and oaks, rose gently to a peak which overlooked the Fulton Street corridor. He found comfort in the sight. The park was familiar ground. His grandmother's house was on the far side of the park. All his friends had lived around this same park and they had defended it against all comers.

He turned away from the window. His head was filled with questions. Why would his grandmother commit such cruelty to a child she didn't know? Although on some levels he saw her actions as consistent with the coldness she had displayed toward him, still there were other

questions. Why would King search for years for that same son and
then, upon finding him, not attempt to contact him? It was so strange
that Jackson could decipher neither intent nor motive from either of his
grandparents' actions. They were like icebergs whose visual surface
could not begin to indicate what lay beneath their dark waters. They
were moved by currents that ran far beneath the surface, to destinations
that could be neither predicted nor imagined.

Jackson exhaled. He had spent the last two days familiarizing himself with his grandfather's papers. The old man, in his craftiness, had
dictated his thoughts and memoirs for Jackson to read. There was no
other purpose; he wanted the papers burned after Jackson had read
them. The story of King Tremain's life, told in his own words, was a
strange and bleak saga of a man who saw life as a constant battle. The
only times there was ever a hint of warmth or affection in his narrative
was when he mentioned his son or grandson. He wasted no time or
words on regret. There was no remorse for the men he killed. He told
his story in a dry, humorless manner.

The papers clearly conveyed the tenor and mood of the Fillmore in
the early fifties. The words seemed to leap off the paper, molding themselves into audible tones, flowing with his grandfather's drawling inflection. For Jackson it was like listening to his grandfather tell his stories
aloud. Vaguely remembered names were brought to life, given motiva-
tions and woven into the fabric of the memoirs. This world took substance from the page and wrapped its arms around him, enfolding him
into its intrigues.

In order to better prepare himself, Jackson had requested that Carlos
pay some investigators to work up a portfolio of up-to-date information
on the DuMonts, the DiMarcos, and John Tree. Perhaps by sifting
through the collected information, he might discover a path through
the minefield. He picked up another sheaf of papers but returned them
to their box. He needed a break. He wanted to see Elizabeth. He
wanted to bathe himself in the contralto of her voice, hear her laugh,
be warmed by her smile. He went to the phone and dialed her number
at work. A secretary answered and informed him that Miss Carlson was
in trial and not expected back into the office until the late afternoon.
Jackson left a message that he would call back at four-thirty and returned to the desk. He poured himself a cup of the thick, black coffee
then picked up the DiMarco file again and began to read through it.

Every once in a while his mind would drift in an elemental tide back to the hospital room where his grandfather had died. He was unable to free himself from the gravitational pull of that memory. It acted upon the unorganized metallic fragments of his thoughts like a magnet. The death of his grandfather had filled him with a tremendous sense of loss. It pained him more than he thought possible. He had not forgotten that he had killed men, but their deaths did not weigh heavily on his heart. If he had any feelings of sorrow and penitence, the mere thought of his grandfather's murder erased them. Jackson had begun to realize that the most important thing to him was that he missed the old man. It did not seem to matter that in the last eighteen years they had only spent a few hours together. Jackson cherished those last hours and he was glad that he had been with his grandfather at the time of his death.

At five o'clock he reached Elizabeth at work. There was fatigue in her voice when she answered the phone, but it turned to warmth when she discovered it was him. Her reactions on the phone reassured him that she had missed him. He proposed to take her out to dinner that evening. Elizabeth demurred, saying that she had work to complete for a morning conference and that she had to be home that evening in case one of her investigators should call.

"What about take-out? You have to eat. I could bring it over," Jackson suggested. "Perhaps some Chinese? Fish and chips? Barbecue? Colonel chicken? Pizza? Anything you like."

Elizabeth laughed. "Sounds like you want to see me. Say, what happened with your grandfather? Is he all right?"

Jackson paused a moment as pangs of regret pulsed across his consciousness then said, "He's passed on to his reward, whatever that may be."

"Oh, I'm sorry. Did you get to spend time with him before he passed?"

"Yes, but more on that when I see you. What type of cuisine will you choose?"

"My place is a mess; it's in the transition of moving and I'm in the middle of a trial that's driving me crazy. No snide remarks."

"Deal."

"Okay, who would you go to for Chinese?"

"Probably Yang Sing on Broadway."

"The dim sum place in North Beach?"

"Yeah, one of my childhood friends introduced me to it when I was in junior high and I've been going there ever since. The food is always good. What do you want me to order?"

"Order your favorites. I'll judge you by your choices."

"Done! We'll have a fabulous meal. But if you're going to judge me, you should see my demons first."

Elizabeth laughed again. "I'm sure I'll see them long before I want to. Say, if you're willing to go all the way to North Beach, I'll buy. Can you come by my house and pick me up at six-thirty?"

"Why? You need to stay home. Your investigators—"

"They probably won't call until after eight. Anyway, you won't be able to park in North Beach, particularly on Broadway. You'll circle the block while I go in. It'll be easier and it means we'll eat earlier as well. What do you say?"

"I'll be there." Jackson hung up, pleased that he was going to see Elizabeth, but there was a strain of anxiety in his pleasure. He was not sure what her reaction would be when he told her that he had blood on his hands. He recognized there was a strong possibility that she would not continue seeing him if he could not disentangle himself. It never occurred to him that he had the option of being silent. Jackson wanted everything between them to be honorable, no shadows, no hidden agendas. The truth. Should Elizabeth choose not to go on, he would abide by her decision.

The fog had been blown away eastward by the winds off the Pacific and a late-afternoon blue sky was visible between gaps in the clouds. Elizabeth had a large flat in Noe Valley and she was standing out in front of it when Jackson drove up. She climbed in the car and gave him a light kiss on the lips and a brief smile. Jackson's radio was tuned to KJAZ, and the complete album of Miles Davis's *Sketches of Spain* was being played.

"Would you please turn the radio up?" Elizabeth asked. Jackson complied. She exhaled and settled back in her seat, staring out the window at the passing traffic. The melodic and haunting music of the trumpet filled the car's compartment as they drove through neighborhood after neighborhood.

Perhaps it was the music of Miles Davis, perhaps it was just two people who felt sufficiently comfortable with each other to relax in the warmth of silence; whatever it was, it allowed Jackson and Elizabeth to pick up the Chinese food and drive all the way back to her flat without saying a word. The aromas of the food wafted through the big sedan and entwined a sense of expectation in with their other feelings. Jackson parked across the sidewalk in front of her garage and they carried the food upstairs to her flat.

Once inside the door, Jackson noticed that there were taped-up boxes everywhere, there were almost no pictures on the wall, and there was nothing on the shelves. Everything was boxed in preparation for a move. Elizabeth led him through the chaos to her kitchen and directed him to set the food cartons on the table while she set out silverware and dishes.

As she was putting plates and napkins on the table, Jackson asked, "Moving far? Out of state?"

"Not hardly," she replied. "I've just got an apartment on Lake Merritt in Oakland. I've been on a waiting list for this building for nearly two years. The move to the East Bay will simplify the logistics of my life. And, I'll be closer to you."

"I wish. I just moved over to San Francisco. I'm living in one of my grandfather's old houses."

Elizabeth stopped selecting silverware and gave Jackson a long, pensive look. "Why? What's happened?"

Jackson took a deep breath and asked, "Do you want to talk about this right now?" She nodded. He continued, "The second day I was there I interrupted an assassination attempt on my grandfather. He died shortly thereafter from the wounds he received."

"My God! Your grandfather was murdered? What happened when you interrupted the assassin?" She put several serving spoons down by the food cartons and waited for him to answer.

Jackson sighed and replied, "I killed him and I killed his two assistants."

"What? You did what?"

"I killed the men who murdered my grandfather!"

"How?"

"I killed one with a knife. I shot the other two."

Elizabeth stared at him for several seconds then asked, "Was it self-defense? How did you explain it to the police?"

"It was self-defense and it was never reported to the police."

"What? How did you dispose of the bodies?"

"They were disposed of discreetly."

"Who disposed of them?"

"My grandfather's men."

Elizabeth sighed slowly. She asked, "Have you taken over for him? Are you the head of some sort of crime family? What's going on?"

Jackson shook his head. "I'm just looking for a way out of this mess."

"I thought you weren't interested in his business or his money."

"I'm not, but until I work something out, my grandfather's enemies are *my* enemies. I'm hoping that I'll be able to negotiate some kind of settlement with them. I have a lot of money at my disposal to sweeten the kitty. If I can't work it out, I'll have to fight them."

"You could leave the area. You could live somewhere else."

"Are you serious? And have these people track me down? No! These people killed both my father and my grandfather. If they don't want to settle, I'll fight them. I'm not going to spend the rest of my life looking over my shoulder."

Elizabeth sat down at the table. "What are you saying? When I asked were you going to stand up to them, this was not what I had in mind. I was thinking that we would use the law to put them away. Not gunning down people in the streets!"

"I'm trying to be honest with you because I value you. I want you to have all the information necessary to make the decisions that you feel are correct. Look, I think we have the possibility of having something really special, but I want you to understand what is happening in my life. I want you to know because of your legal position, as well as because it may be dangerous to be with me. I wouldn't want you to take a bullet meant for me."

Elizabeth gave him a long look then asked, "How do you know these people didn't follow you over here?"

"Because no one knows that I've returned but you. I haven't even contacted any of my friends. I would've had some concern about these people knowing where you lived if I had picked you up here rather than meeting you at the ferry for our trip to Angel Island. Since then I've been very careful to ensure that I'm not followed."

"Why haven't you contacted your friends?"

"I wanted to keep to myself until I've developed a strategy. You're the only person I had to see."

"What's your strategy?"

"I've got people investigating every aspect of this situation. I'm hoping to unearth something that these people don't want revealed. Maybe with a mixture of blackmail and money, I can diffuse their desires of revenge."

"And if you can't?"

"If I can't, there'll be war."

"Don't you realize you're compromising my position as a district attorney by informing me of felonies that you have yet to commit? My oath of office means something to me!" Elizabeth stood up abruptly and paced back and forth. "The first time I meet a halfway decent man in years, he turns into the Godfather while I'm getting to know him!" She turned to face him and pointed at him. "It hasn't even been a week since I saw you last and your words now have the authority to dispose of people. This is out of a movie or novel by Danielle Steel or Michael Crichton. This doesn't happen to real people!"

Jackson replied, "I wish! I don't have any control over this situation. This is a blood feud between my family and theirs."

Elizabeth was aghast. "A blood feud! It's 1982; that went out with the Hatfields and the McCoys!"

"You don't know how I wish that was true! But wishing doesn't change reality. If I don't find a way out of it, people will be killed."

"My God! You say those words so matter-of-factly, like you're talking about the weather."

"Would their meanings be changed if I said them dramatically with heartfelt regret? I have made the necessary accommodations to my circumstance. I am not happy about it, but how I feel doesn't matter a damn! I've got to prepare my mind and my strategy for dealing with the enemy. To do otherwise would be foolish."

Elizabeth sat back down at the table and looked Jackson in the eye. "You sat here and told me that you've killed three men! How do you feel about that? Or do you feel anything?"

"I killed the men who killed my grandfather. I don't feel good about it, but it had to be done. Be real! What do you think I should've done with these men? Let them go? They'd have been back in less than two hours with a death squad. This is not a game. These men were professional killers."

Elizabeth persisted: "Do you regret that you've taken lives?"

"Yes and no. I didn't enjoy killing them, but they murdered my grandfather. Despite all the bullshit I said about him, I discovered that I loved him. We had our first man-to-man talk the evening he was killed! I lost somebody important to me!" Jackson stood up tiredly. "May I use your bathroom before this inquisition goes on?"

"Sure." Elizabeth gestured with her hand. "First door on the right down the hall."

Upon his return Jackson passed a photograph sitting on an end table of three hatless black men in fifties police uniforms. What caught his eye was that one of the men looked like his grandfather: the shape of the head, the eyes, and the smile. Jackson went over and studied the photograph, then carried it into the kitchen.

"Who are these three men?"

Elizabeth took the photo and replied, "My older brother, my father, and my uncle Elroy. I told you about him when we were on Angel Island."

"Well, this is a hell of a coincidence. Your uncle Elroy is my uncle too. He is a Tremain!"

Elizabeth scoffed, "Your stories are getting more bizarre by the moment. My uncle's last name is—"

"Fontenot. He was stolen by the DuMonts when he was about a year old and raised in an orphanage in south Texas, an institution run by the Oblate Sisters outside of Port Arthur. He came out to California in 1947 with the military police, and when he mustered out, he got a job working in the colored section of the jail. He became a temporary police officer in 1951. He was hired on as a regular in 1952."

"How do you know all this?"

"He's my grandfather's oldest son."

"You're not making this up? You're serious? You think you're related?"

"I'm serious as a heart attack. I need to speak to him. Do you have his number?"

"Why? What could he possibly have to do with this?"

"If they know he's got Tremain blood, he could be a target. And there's always the chance that he would be interested in collecting some of his inheritance. It's legally his should he choose to opt for it."

"I'll have to call him and ask him if he wants you to have his number. You have to remember that he was a policeman for more than twenty years. He may have problems with your criminal activities."

"You act like I'm involved in the rackets."

"Killing people is about as bad as it gets."

"I didn't have a choice! Please call him now before you convict me of everything."

Elizabeth stood and went to the telephone. A short, muted conversation followed. She returned to the table and stood leaning against it. She said, "He wants me to bring you over tomorrow afternoon. He said he's been expecting you."

"Great! Let's eat this food before it gets too cold."

Elizabeth shook her head. "I can't. Why don't you take it with you? I've lost my appetite."

"What's wrong? Have I become so heinous that you can't eat with me?"

"No. It's just that I believe we're traveling on very different roads. I took an oath to enforce the law and I am committed to it. I'm interested in you, but I can't afford to throw my values and my career away."

Jackson stood. "I don't want the food. I'll go now if you wish."

Elizabeth put her hands on her hips. "That's all you have to say? Some stiff-necked gallantry? That's it?"

"What more is there to say? I want to get to know you better. I've already said that I thought we could have something very special."

"Special? What does that mean?" Elizabeth threw up her arms in frustration. "God! I want to argue with you! I don't want to argue with you! I want you to leave! I don't want you to leave! We've spent one day together and I feel like I know you, like we're old friends. It's like getting in the car with you tonight. I didn't have to tell you I didn't feel like talking. You knew it and complied. I just needed to be quiet and the ride in the car really calmed me down. I've needed a friend and partner for a long time, much more than I've ever needed a lover. I want you to be that friend. I don't want to stop seeing you, but I feel I have no choice."

Jackson rose and went around the table to where Elizabeth was standing. "I don't know what to say, but I think about you all the time. I thought about you in Mexico. I wanted to be with you tonight. I don't want to stop seeing you. Frankly, I was looking forward to you being the love affair of my life."

"Oh, Tremain! We seemed so right for each other!"

Jackson moved forward and took her in his arms and kissed her lips lightly, brushing his lips back and forth against hers. She did not resist, but lifted her face to his. After the kiss they stared into each other's eyes for several moments. Her arms moved around his waist and they kissed again, this time passion was more prominent as their bodies molded together. When their kiss subsided, they stood cheek to cheek in a tight embrace for several minutes.

Elizabeth said softly, "I can't tell you how long I've wanted to feel this."

"It does feel good," Jackson confirmed as he caressed the nape of her neck and then allowed his hand to trace the line of her spine.

When his hand touched her behind, Elizabeth pushed him away and took a deep breath. "Well, it's nice to know our connection isn't just platonic."

"You knew that before we ever touched."

"I definitely knew it when you put your hand on my butt."

Jackson laughed. "I tried to resist but there was an intense pull."

"Listen, Tremain, I don't want to be any more invested in you than I already am. I don't want sexual intimacy until we've figured this thing out. As long as you haven't committed any crimes in this country, we can go on. If you just stay and eat, will that present a problem to you?"

"No, as long as I know where your butt begins, and other such off-limits areas are identified with posters."

"If you make the right decisions and don't push your luck, you just might get enough answers eventually to satisfy your curiosity."

Jackson bowed in a courtly fashion and said, "Let's eat."

Tuesday, June 29, 1982

Elroy Fontenot put down the phone and chuckled cynically at the fate that had kept him from his blood family for sixty years. Now, when he was more aware of his death than his birth, when the fires had burned low within him, suddenly the forces were aligned and conducive to the meeting for which he had sorely yearned in his youth. His eagerness to meet the family that had abandoned him in his infancy had faded, and an abiding bitterness had taken its place. All the long years of wanting, desiring to be part of a family had eaten away at him, leaving caverns of disappointment that no future action could ever hope to fill.

Elroy was sixty-one years old and a retired policeman. He had long been divorced from the mother of his two sons. He bore his ex-wife no malice. She had not possessed the makeup of a policeman's wife. She hadn't been able to handle the long hours that he put in at the job or deal with the frustration that he often brought home from work. It had been extremely difficult for him, enduring for years the racism and injustice of the whites who didn't want Negro officers in their department, while on the opposite side having members of his own race call him everything from an Uncle Tom to the worst they could imagine. He had walked that tightrope for many years. He had taken umbrage from both sides and kept his course. But he took no one into his confidence. He was self-reliant and strong. No one could tell that he was going through hell.

Elroy looked around his apartment and saw nothing that indicated his life had been special. He possessed nice furniture and a few paintings, but nothing that couldn't be bought in any of the nicer furniture showrooms. His medals and awards were for fleeting moments, for actions taken many years in the past. His apartment, like his life, was empty of true valuables, absent of the objects that symbolized success, void of the emblems of romance and affection. It could have been a hotel suite, for all the meaning it had for him. He had no family life, no one to share the lonely moments of the day, no one to warm up the shadows of the night. One son was dead in Vietnam, the other was estranged and hadn't spoken to him in nearly five years. Thanksgiving and Christmas were ominous, terrible holidays that emphasized everything he didn't possess.

He hadn't realized how much his life in the orphanage had shaped his ability to love and be loved until his children were born. In the marching, metered, organized chaos of an institution run by women, none of whom were mothers, he had not learned how to nurture, how to express disapproval constructively, how to compromise without resentment, how to show love in little ways. By the time he came to understand what he did not know about love, a wedge had been driven in his marriage and his sons displayed only anger and rebellion in response to him. He saw himself as a negative force, the Midas touch in reverse, in all serious exchanges with his wife and sons. No matter what he intended, their communication ended either in unhealthy silence or in shouted words. He lacked the ability to communicate the hard lessons that experience had taught him. Elroy knew himself to be a failure as a father; his sons grew up in spite of him and in reaction to him, not because of him.

What could he say to this man who was coming tomorrow? Was there any reason to acknowledge a blood relationship after all this time? Elroy went to his refrigerator and got a can of beer. He popped the lid and felt the bubbling burn of the cold liquid flowing down his throat as he walked into his den. A desk, where he had finished so many police reports, stood in front of the window, along an adjacent wall was a leather sofa and against the opposite wall was his television. The bookshelves above the TV were lined with books about law enforcement administration and tactics. He had spent many lonely hours in this room, days of processing paper, nights spent studying for promotional examinations in which there was no chance of his appointment, wasted years watching forgotten TV programs. This room where he had spent so much of his life had the warmth of a padded cell. What did he have to say? Why had he agreed to let Elizabeth bring the young man over?

There would be no surprises. Elroy already knew the name of his family. He had done his own detective work. In 1960 he had taken two weeks off and researched the Port Arthur archives for the orphanage's records. He had unearthed the notes of the mother superior who in 1927 actually met with the woman who annually sent money to the orphanage in his name. Her name was Serena Tremain, which was consistent with the initials on the overcoat she had left behind. Elroy still possessed that coat. It took no great effort to discover the owner's whereabouts. He had known for over twenty years about the Tremains and his relationship to them. His close resemblance to King had often been brought to his attention by fellow officers. It didn't take a rocket scientist to put the facts together.

The main reason Elroy never contacted the Tremains himself was that during his time in Port Arthur he uncovered some disturbing and confusing information. From the records that he was able to piece together, he had been brought to the orphanage as an infant by a Captain LeGrande from the New Orleans Sheriff's Department. The captain had left certain instructions that the child in question should never under any circumstances be released to the custody of King Tremain. According to the captain, King Tremain would kill the baby if he ever got his hands on the child. If he was truly King's child, it didn't make sense, but there was much about his origins Elroy didn't understand. The other reason that Elroy never initiated contact was that King Tremain was a legendary crime figure in the corridors of the San Francisco Police Department. Special squads were assigned to put a stop to his operations. The city's law enforcement practically ignored the depredations of the Mafiosi while they were dedicating their resources to fighting King. The unspoken order was that administration wanted him dead, a feat they were never able to achieve. Elroy's only face-to-face meeting with King occurred before Elroy knew his relationship to him, but King had certainly known who he was. This was another confusing piece in the abstract, nonrepresentational puzzle of Elroy's life: Elroy had long since given up trying to fit the pieces together. He had accepted that the logic and progression of his life were beyond his reasoning, and that some pieces were doomed never to fit together. Perhaps, in the giant wheel of life, he was not meant to be happy, not meant to enjoy the precious gifts of family; perhaps he was meant to be among the broken and pulverized, who like aggregate lie crushed and faceless beneath the feet of human activity.

It would have been different, perhaps, if Elroy had never known the loving warmth of a family, if he had never known how a mother and father were supposed to act, or how a brother and sister knitted together for support, but he had tasted that life. For four short, wonderful years he had lived in the bosom of a family. He had been adopted two years after Serena had visited by a family that had lost a boy his age to the venom of a cottonmouth moccasin. Four short years, long enough to taste but not long enough to learn.

The Caldwells had a boy and a younger daughter. Their nine-year-old child had not been in the grave six months when they came to the orphanage. They were poor, God-fearing folk who had sufficient love and food to adopt another child. When they selected him, Elroy couldn't believe it. It made him think that there might really be a God hidden up in the sky, someone who really watched over the lost and forlorn. He left the orphanage with only the clothes he was wearing, but he felt like royalty. He was going to have what had been denied. He was going to be part of a family. The first year in the Caldwell household, he had gotten down on his knees every night and secretly thanked God for blessing him. Little did he know at the time that it was a blessing soon to be revoked.

Elroy crushed the beer can in his still-powerful hands. Just the thought of the Caldwells brought a sudden rage. He knew that the anger and bitterness he felt could not all be directed at the Tremains. It was fate, what the Hindus called karma, that was the true enemy. It had predestined him to a life of loss, a life in which the important lessons were learned at great personal cost. He opened the blinds of the window above the desk and stared out at the dark windows and aged brick facade of the building across the alley. He threw the crushed beer can into a wastebasket and closed the blinds. The view out the window was void of life and color. There was nothing memorable about it, yet it was etched in his mind from all the years he had looked out upon it; etched in his mind like the night his life with the Caldwells had ended. He could not stop his thoughts once he began thinking of that night.

It happened in 1933, during the Depression, when he was thirteen, during the early morning hours when he had gone eeling with his adoptive older brother and father. The evening had started off so well for Elroy's family. Dinner was hoecakes and mustard greens cooked with ham hocks followed by molasses pie, then Elroy's father had read from one of the two books that the family possessed. The first book was the Bible and the other was *Lyrics for the Hearthside* by Paul Laurence Dunbar. Most times his father read from the Bible, but this particular night, he chose to read Paul Dunbar.

Of course, Elroy's younger sister, Ruthie, wanted her father to read "Little Brown Baby" and Elroy remembered how his older brother, Judah, who had just turned sixteen, called out for "How Lucy Backslid" and there was a moment when his father had looked over the small book of poems with a stern expression, but then it changed into a smile. What made the evening so special is that none of the three children had to practice their "recitation." His father took time to read everyone's favorite poem and finished with the "Warrior's Prayer."

Elroy went to bed with a full stomach and stanzas of Dunbar's poetry dancing in his head. He was shaken from sleep early the next morning by Judah. He struggled into his clothes in the flickering darkness of candlelight. The sound of Ruthie's even breathing on the pallet next to him made him think about returning to the warmth of his blankets, but his mother offered him a steaming cup of black coffee and after the first few burning mouthfuls he was wide awake.

All the gear had been packed by the door so as to make their departure in the darkness easier. So, as they loaded up to walk down to their canoe his father asked, "Where's the bait I asked you to put out, Elroy?" Elroy was immediately ashamed for he had forgotten to do the task. There was a moment of silence before Judah spoke and said, "It's here, Pappy." Judah was holding up a pail full of live earthworms and minced meat. He winked at Elroy in the darkness and there was a brief flash of uneven white teeth. Elroy sighed with relief. His older brother had come through for him again. As he followed the dark silhouettes of his father and brother through the pines and palmettos along the half-mile trail that led down to the water, he waved to his mother standing in the dim light of the cabin's doorway. She was the one who truly understood how intensely important it was for him to have people he could call sister, brother, father, and mother. It was the happiest period in his young life. He had no idea that it was the last time he would see her alive.

In the distant trees Elroy could hear owls hooting to one another and the stars seemed bright overhead. The canoe was hidden in the underbrush above the high-water mark and covered with a piece of tarp. Judah and his father hefted it on their shoulders and waded into the water. Once everything was loaded, they pushed out onto the black surface of the water and paddled quietly through the shallows toward some small islands out in the bayou where the eels were known to spawn. The frogs and the cicadas created rhythms in the darkness with their mating calls.

Elroy's father lighted an old kerosene lantern and hooked it to the prow of the canoe and asked Judah, at the back of the canoe, to troll slowly while he threw little bits of bait into the water under the lantern. When his father started to see activity just under the surface, he told Elroy to throw out baited float lines, while he sat at the prow with a homemade net scooping for anything that came to the surface.

The fish weren't biting in the first spot so they paddled to another cove where the delta created shallow waterways. Along the way Elroy's father asked him, "You didn't put out that bait like I asked, did you?"

Elroy had no choice but to tell the truth. "No, I forgot, Papa."

"Yo' brother done yo' job for you again, huh?" he asked as he continued to paddle in the front of the canoe.

"Yes, sir," Elroy answered, shame bending his head. He stared at his father's carbine, which lay in the bottom of the canoe.

His father turned around and looked at both his sons with a smile.

"That's what brothers are for. Yo' brother did the right thing, but you, Elroy, got to stay on yo' job; that way yo' brother don't have to forget his to cover for you." His father paused as if to let his sons digest the content of his words and turned his attention to his rowing before he spoke again. He guided the canoe through a narrow channel which meandered between several small islands. He commented over his shoulder, "Judah, you ain't doin' too well on yo' readin' and writin'. When we finish buildin' the schoolhouse and the teacher arrives, I'll expect better from you. But you's learnin' the lessons about family that I wanted you to learn. You's learnin' about helpin'. You's both good sons. I pushes you, 'cause it's my job to prepare you to deal with the world these white folks have set up." His father had to turn and concentrate on paddling because the canoe was crossing an area in which there were a lot of submerged logs. He guided the canoe into a little, narrow canal. From the rise of a small island on their right, the red eyes of some fair-sized animals reflected the light of the lantern.

"You got yo' carbine, Pa? We got swamp deer right there!" Judah whispered.

"Sure! You got yo' sling?" his father rejoined. "If you want to go about chasin' wounded deer in the dead of night, might as well use that. I could hit him dead in the heart and he'd still run off thirty-five yards somewheres out there in the swamp." The deer took off at the first sound of their voices and splashed away in the night.

There was a late moon rising overhead; it was nearly full and tinged pale blue. It cast a soft light over the half-submerged landscape. "I ain't ever killed anything as big as a deer with my sling, Pa!" Judah mused.

"I was only funnin', son. We's after fish tonight. We got plenty meat smoked and put away."

The canoe continued slowly forward through the narrow shallows until there was plenty of activity under the lantern. They fished steadily for nearly two hours, removing hooked fish and placing fresh bait on the float lines. Both eels and catfish were biting in the new area. Their handwoven basket was nearly full of slithering eels and wiggling catfish when the first gunshots echoed across the water.

Judah looked up and there was a red brightness above the trees in the direction of their cabin. "Pa, it look like there's a fire somewhere near home!"

"Get them oars out!" commanded his father. "And start pulling hard.

We got a mess of distance to clear!" Elroy saw his father cut the trolling lines, leaving the store-bought hooks and floats to drift with the twine. He saw the muscles of his father's bare back flex in a pattern of ripples in the lantern's glow as he sent the prow of the canoe back toward the main channel.

"Help on the right!" Judah called out behind him and Elroy switched his paddle to the right side and dug deeply into the rippling surface.

They bent their backs to the task. Elroy could hear his heart drumming in his chest like the sound of an old mill saw. He focused on rowing, changing sides every two strokes like his father taught him. The canoe pushed through a narrow waterway where the thickets had grown dense on either side and several branches smacked Elroy across the face, then they were through into open water.

"Put your backs into it, boys!" his father commanded. As he finished speaking there was a barrage of gunfire.

A rider sitting astride his horse at the back of the group of twenty hooded riders watched as his uncle, the Grand Cyclops of the Den, yelled out to the cabin, "Come out, niggers! You was warned to get out of this parish! You was warned not to try buildin' no school! You was told there ain't no place for educated niggers down here! Now it's time to pay the piper! The Invisible Empire is here! Come out or we'll burn you out!" Several of the riders at the front of the group were carrying torches.

There was only a woman's voice in answer: "You ain't got no right! Our people done lived on this land since before the Civil War. This is our land!"

"Ain't that just like niggers?" the Grand Cyclops shouted over his shoulder to his followers. "The menfolk is too scared to come out of the pantry and talk, so they send a woman!"

"Let's burn 'em down!" shouted another voice from the front. "Teach 'em a lesson!"

The Grand Cyclops gestured to a couple of riders who were carrying torches and they spurred their horses forward. When they neared the cabin, rifle fire erupted from inside. One man fell from his horse and the other turned his horse away. Suddenly, there was pandemonium and confusion among the riders; no one had expected resistance. "Return fire!" ordered the Grand Cyclops, riding out of danger, and a hail of bullets splattered against the cabin, breaking the glass windows and punching holes in the walls and the door. A torch was thrown on the thatched roof and another through the broken window. The dry thatch caught immediately and the fire spread rapidly. The riders continued to fire their guns into the cabin despite the fact that there was no answer from inside the building.

Elroy's mother was already dead. She was killed in the first hail of bullets from the Night Riders. Her seven-year-old daughter lay on the floor crying by her mother's body until a piece of the burning roof fell on her. The child tried to put out the flames, but more burning thatch kept falling until finally both her dress and her newly oiled hair caught fire. The flames and the pain made her forget the men outside. She got up and ran from the cabin screaming. She stumbled off the front porch and fell in the dirt. She got up once and staggered blindly about until a shot from the Grand Cyclops's gun knocked her over backward.

The rider who had initially been at the back of the group now found himself next to his uncle. He had seen the child come running from the burning cabin with her clothes and hair ablaze. Her body was still smoldering in the dirt. The smell of burning flesh was now strong in the clearing in front of the cabin. The rider was sickened by the carnage. It was not what he expected. He had ridden along for fun, but not to kill children. He turned his horse and kicked it into a gallop and, by doing so, saved his own life.

The first bullet that Elroy's father fired hit the Grand Cyclops in the chest and knocked him off his horse. Elroy's father continued firing until he was out of bullets. Several more riders fell. Once again there was confusion among the Night Riders. About half of them took off, riding for their lives. Others returned fire, aiming their guns into the darkness, hoping to drive off their foes.

Elroy's father was out of bullets, but he couldn't stay out of sight. His daughter was lying in the front of the burning cabin and he had no idea where his wife was. He had to at least get to his daughter. Using the shrubs and underbrush as cover he made his way toward the cabin. His carbine was useless. He prepared himself to make a dash into the clearing to get his daughter. He waited behind a bush, looking for an opportunity.

The remaining riders were having difficulty maintaining control of their horses, who were boggling because of the loud discharges from the weapons. There was considerable dust being raised by the horses' hooves. After some shouted exchanges the remaining riders appeared to decide that it was best that they also depart, for they reined their horses and followed their comrades back along the road.

It was the moment Elroy's father had been waiting for. He rushed out into the clearing and knelt by his daughter's still-breathing body. The skin on her face and legs was burned black, and liquid from her wounds ran down his arms as he hoisted her to carry her to safety. He nearly made it out of the clearing when a shot rang out. The bullet hit Elroy's father in the shoulder and spun him around. Nonetheless, he did not drop his daughter, but staggered back into the bush. The sound of returning hoofbeats followed close behind. Before Elroy's father reached the cover of the oleander thickets another shot dropped him. He fell on top of the body of his daughter and lay still.

Elroy and Judah rushed to kneel by the bodies of their father and sister. Judah gently rolled his father's bloodstained body off his sister's and discovered they were both dead. Elroy was in shock. His gaze shifted back and forth from the flames of the burning cabin to the bodies of his father and sister, back and forth again and again. His mother was probably still in the house. If she had escaped, she would not have left Ruthie behind. Elroy couldn't believe what was happening. He was afraid to even touch the blistered body of his sister. She smelled like meat cooked over an open fire, like barbecue. Tears began to trickle down his face. The blessing that was his family was being destroyed before his eyes.

Three hooded riders warily reined their horses to a walk just before they entered the clearing. Judah jerked at Elroy's shirt, indicating it was time to escape into the thickets, but Elroy knelt as if he were frozen, heedless of his brother's urgency. Judah shook him again but more forcefully. "Come on," Judah hissed. "They gon' kill us too!"

Elroy allowed himself to be helped up by his brother and led into the bushes. He seemed to have lost his fear of death, for he walked as if he were in slow motion. With Elroy's arm over his shoulder, Judah half-carried, half-dragged him deeper into the protective cover of the underbrush. But not before they were seen.

"I see a live one, Lon!" a hooded rider shouted as he spurred his horse forward. "We still might have someone to hang yet!"

"Watch yourself, Shorty!" warned one of his companions. "They may still got some bullets!"

As soon as he heard the horse pounding toward them, Judah let El-roy slide to his knees and took out his sling. He reached into his pocket and found a particularly large stone in his collection and placed it in his sling. He started whirling the sling, getting the feel of his projectile, and waited for the rider who was almost upon them.

The horse and rider rounded into view and began to bear down on the two boys. The rider saw that his victims were not running and be-gan to slow his horse. When he realized that Judah had a sling in his hand, the rock was already in flight. It hit him in the forehead just above the nose and caused him to lose consciousness and slump back-ward off his horse.

Judah pulled Elroy to his feet and slapped him hard across the face. "If we gon' live, we need to be runnin'! I mean puttin' a foot in it!" Elroy seemed to come to his senses and began to jog through the thickets. "Faster! Faster!" shouted Judah.

One of the remaining riders pulled the hood from his head, revealing two watery-blue eyes and a pockmarked face. He pulled a Winchester rifle out of its scabbard and focused on the retreating backs of the two boys. Because of the darkness, he decided on the larger target and waited for his shot. The boys had nearly made it to a stand of magno-lias when they passed briefly into the open. The rider pushed a lock of corn-silk-blond hair out of his eyes and fired off two quick shots, then looked to see the result.

"Run, Elroy! Run!" Judah cried out.

After his brother shouted, Elroy heard the first bullet go hissing by his face and saw it knock a branch off a tree to his right. The fear which had strangely eluded him earlier was upon him now. It grabbed him like a hand and squeezed his heart. It spurred the pumping of his legs and drove him running pell-mell into the cover of the outlying foliage. He ran through thickets and bushes, heedless of the branches smacking his face. He ran until he could run no longer. Elroy tumbled to his knees, gasping for breath. He pulled himself underneath the branches of a dense-looking bush and lay back against its trunk. There was a large lime-green garden spider with a body the size of the first joint of his little finger devouring some hapless insect within two inches of his face. Elroy did not have the strength to move away. He lay there as daylight returned.

Elroy did not remember when he had gotten separated from his brother. He spent the next two weeks hiding in the swamps, stealing in at night to eat the partially burned meats from the Caldwells' smoke shed. It seemed to him that he was being punished by a cruel and merciless God. His desire for a family was filled then rudely snatched away. He did not leave the area until he overheard a neighboring colored family discuss the Caldwell family's fate. When he heard that everyone in the family had been killed, Elroy headed back to Port Arthur. He lived by stealing and rifling through garbage. He arrived at the door of the orphanage a month later, starving and in rags. The sisters took him in and once more the cacophony and the regimen of motherless children enfolded him. He did not speak for nearly six months and would not eat any meat that was smoked or grilled over an open fire. Elroy recuperated from his experience without visible scars, but his innards had been mangled and he grew into a man who rarely smiled.

Wednesday, June 30, 1982

Braxton's soundproof office at the *Bay City Gazette* was a large, rectangular affair with dark wainscotting halfway up the walls. Two of the walls had venetian-blind-covered windows above the wainscotting. The windows on one side looked out on a labyrinth of four-foot-high modular offices, where the six news and editorial staff members worked. The opposite wall of windows in his office looked out on a catwalk above the old printing press, which he had purchased in 1950.

It was a quarter of six, Braxton's favorite time of day at the paper. Most of the news and advertising staff had gone home and only the press operators were working, printing out the morning's edition. The din and the voices of the newsroom were replaced by the intermittent jangling of the Teletype and the grinding clatter of the press. Yet with his door closed the silence in his office was like the quiet experienced in the eye of a storm.

Unfortunately, at this very moment he was unable to appreciate the quietude and meditative value of silence, for he was involved in a serious phone call.

"What do you mean, disappeared?" Braxton exploded. He held the telephone in a trembling hand. His secretary came to the glass-paneled door and looked in with concern, but Braxton waved her away.

The voice of Paul DiMarco continued, "I don't know what happened. They disappeared after calling in to say that King was done—"

"How could they simply disappear?" Braxton questioned, keeping his voice lower but feeling an old familiar fear. "There was no message or word from anyone? How do we know they're not just celebrating a successful mission somewhere?"

"Because on Monday, the office building where they were headquartered was demolished by a bomb." DiMarco's voice was tired. It was obvious that this news had caused him some consternation as well. "It was a ten-story building and now there's nothing left but rubble."

"My God!" Braxton said. He was not concerned for the lives lost, but rather the implications of the bombing. It was too reminiscent of other attempts on King Tremain. A terrible thought occurred to him. "Do you think that they actually got him?"

"I received a confirmation call. It was correctly coded and there was no hint in my contact's voice of any problem. In fact, the man was ecstatic."

"This complicates things," Braxton mused, pondering this unexpected reality. Less than half an hour ago, he had been sitting comfortably in his office considering what he would do with the money from King's estate. The phone rang and against his better judgment, he answered it, and the subject of the call, like a rock thrown in a placid pool, caused his vision of the future to be disrupted by ripples. He had foolishly assumed that once he received the news of King's death, all his plans would automatically fall into place. Now, with this disturbing new information, everything had to be reexamined.

"Is this a secure line?" DiMarco asked.

"Of course," Braxton snapped. "I wouldn't have continued to talk with you so candidly if it wasn't."

"We need to pick that grandson up as soon as possible. I need to resolve this issue ASAP."

Braxton heard the urgency in DiMarco's voice and knew there was more to his request than a simple desire to complete the task. "I've already given directions for that to be done," Braxton said.

"I want him brought to my place in North Beach." It was not a question, it was an order.

"That idea could have some merit," Braxton commented, although he had no intention of turning the grandson over to DiMarco. "Why should he be brought to your place?"

DiMarco was losing his patience and it was reflected in his tone. "Because I—" DiMarco stopped himself and began again. "I've learned some techniques that make people talk. I think if you leave him with me for a day or so, I'll get all the information we'll need."

And I'm sure that you'll like making him talk too, Braxton thought distastefully. Braxton saw himself as a civilized man who had a taste for art, culture, and haute cuisine. Although he had directed others to take actions which occasionally resulted in someone's death, he had never spilled blood with his own hands. It was an important distinction for him. It was what separated him from animals like Tree and DiMarco. In addition, it required extra work to prove his connection, should the actions of his minions ever draw the eye of law enforcement. "Let me ask you," he began easily. "What do you propose to do with the information that you develop?"

"What do you mean?"

"If we have to get the corporate papers signed over, for example, we're going to need a live and healthy human being to appear before a notary in a bank. Not someone who has been tortured into a state that they cannot appear in public."

There was a silence on the other end of the line. Braxton surmised that DiMarco had not considered such an eventuality. It was even likely that he had planned to kill the grandson. Once again, Braxton felt he was saddled with an ally who couldn't think his way out of a paper bag. "I didn't hear your answer," he prodded gently.

"How were you planning to handle it?" DiMarco asked suspiciously.

"Oh, I thought we'd bring him to an isolated spot for a little show-and-tell. Evaluate him as an adversary. Rough him up a little so that he knows we mean business. Tell him what we want and then let him go."

"Let him go? Why, he'd go straight to the police!" DiMarco sputtered.

"I don't think so," Braxton retorted. "What's he going to do, tell the police about all the money that he has inherited from his grandfather, a felon wanted for murder who probably never paid taxes on half of what he owns? The only two men he'll be able to identify will be the ones who pick him up. I've already got jobs waiting for them in two different states. He won't know where he's been taken. All it will do is put him in the spotlight. I don't think that he wants that."

"What if he doesn't cave in?"

"We'll kidnap a couple of his friends and send him a few pieces of their bodies. He'll cave in. We're not dealing with King Tremain."

"How long do you think all this will take?"

"Why are you so pressed for time?" Braxton asked, expecting a lie.

"Well, if I don't have this resolved by next week, they'll contact you soon enough."

"Who?" asked Braxton, on the alert.

"The people from the organization that I got the strike team from."

"Why would they want to contact me?" Braxton asked, his mind quickly shuffling through the possibilities.

"They figure that I owe them at least three million dollars for the loss of their building and their men."

"What's that got to do with me?" Braxton questioned, afraid of the answer.

"We're partners, aren't we?" DiMarco demanded. "There's no reason I should take this loss by myself!"

"Who do you owe this money to?" Braxton asked, knowing the answer.

"Joe Bones in Las Vegas." There was fear in DiMarco's voice.

"Old Joe is still alive, huh?"

"You know him?" DiMarco asked, surprised.

"I know of him," Braxton lied smoothly. It was Joe Bones who had led the organization's retaliation efforts, attempting to burn down a large section of the Fillmore after King killed Marcello DiMarco and his family. Braxton had interceded for the community and had gone to Joe with a proposal. It was as a result of that proposal that King was framed for the murder of four white policemen, which in turn forced him to move the base of his operations to Mexico.

"Why don't I call you when the grandson is brought in?" Braxton suggested, hoping to end the conversation. He needed time to think.

"When do you think that will be?" The time issue was still of importance to DiMarco.

"Whenever we catch him," Braxton said, knowing that he would not call. "I'll have my secretary call you and tell you that the editor's meeting is on."

Braxton's answer seemed to please DiMarco, for he said, "Okay, I look forward to hearing from you soon."

There was no good-bye, the phone simply went dead. Braxton put the phone on its cradle and stood up. He walked to the inner windows of his office overlooking the printing press and watched as the two press operators prepared the old machinery to run the next weekly edition. It appeared they were trying to replace one of the smaller rollers and were having some difficulty aligning it. Braxton's mind drifted away from the scene in front of him and turned to address the problem with DiMarco.

Two days earlier, Braxton had attended a fund-raising effort to put a different mayor in power in the coming San Francisco election. The brain trust behind the fund-raising effort had dedicated the proceeds to Michael Giuseppe DiMarco as their candidate. Mike ran a prominent law office with his son, Edward, and his daughter, Sophia. Braxton had heard from his sources that the real money behind Mike's campaign came from Las Vegas. It didn't take much thinking to arrive at the conclusion that Joe Bones was financing Mike's electoral ambitions. It made sense. Obviously, the DiMarcos could do more for their friends with the mayoralty in their pocket.

At one point during the fund-raising event, both Mike and Braxton were standing at the sumptuous hors d'oeuvres table sampling the offerings. Braxton said to him, "Running for political office puts the whole family in the spotlight. You'll have to reduce your liabilities as much as possible. How do you expect to achieve that when some of your relations aren't always amenable to listening?"

Mike turned to face him. He was a tall, distinguished-looking man with a craggy face and dark hair and the silver sideburns of venerability. After giving a quick look around to see who else was nearby he asked, "Is this an interview that will appear in the *Bay City Gazette?*"

Braxton smiled. "You know that we have discussed many things that have never seen the light of day, much less appeared in the *Gazette.* This is for my information only."

"We know you're still doing business with my nephew. And we know how much you made last year from your, shall we say, import business. If you're asking will that business be able to continue, the answer is no. We can't afford it. The election is more important to us. We're closing everything down. Anyone who continues to carry on illegal activities will suffer the full weight and wrath of our legal system. And if they are too crafty to be caught by the law, we have other means at our disposal."

"I see," said Braxton, not really surprised. San Francisco was a small town as big cities go; all the movers and shakers knew one another's secrets.

Mike leaned toward him and said softly, "Write some positive editorials. If you can bring your people to the ballot box, there'll be other business opportunities you can invest in. The rewards may not be quite as great immediately, but over time they will be more and they will be legal." Several other people approached Mike and he turned to greet them with a flashing smile.

Braxton had mingled with the other guests and then after an appropriate period left the event after writing a ten-thousand-dollar check. He had gotten the information that he needed. He had been duly warned. The election was more than four months away. He had to divest himself and close down all the drug-related activities within the week.

Below him, the big motors of the printing press started up again. The muffled sound throbbed through the windows. Braxton watched the journey press operator, a woman, run to the collator assembly and start pulling levers. The press was turned off and both operators climbed on top of the collator assembly and removed the sheet-metal housing.

The problem, as Braxton saw it, was to neutralize Paul DiMarco long enough to let his own family deal with him, but that was not realistic. They wouldn't move against him soon enough to help Braxton. An additional problem was that Joe Bones would want a piece of the action now that Paul had told him what was afoot. After all, the property and the holding company had all been set up with money stolen from Marcello DiMarco's organization in 1954. First things first; he had to get the grandson in for a brief interview, then he would have a better sense of the total picture.

He watched the female press operator. Her name was Samantha Tremain. He had hired her almost fifteen years ago upon Serena's advice. Serena had said that Samantha was struggling to support her three-year-old son in a field in which there was considerable resistance against women. Braxton had noticed that Samantha had a very nice body, so he had said yes. He had not known at the time that she was a lesbian. He probably wouldn't have hired her had he known, but she turned out to be an excellent press operator. Braxton believed that homosexuality was an abomination and that it should not be tolerated; it was an indication of societal decadence. He did not apply this same standard to murder; that was a necessary evil. He wondered briefly if King's grandson cared about Samantha, whether she would serve as a suitable hostage, but he crushed that idea immediately. She was too close; someone might make the connection.

His secretary knocked on his door and entered the office holding a sheaf of papers. "Yes, Marta?" he said with a slight touch of impatience.

She was a petite brown-skinned woman who wore her hair long and straightened. "I brought the layout for the editorial page and several important phone messages. One is from Roy. He's trying to set up a meeting with you and City Cab."

"Thank you. Come back in fifteen minutes for the layout. Call Roy and tell him that Friday is good for me."

"All right." Marta spun on her heel and walked out, shutting the door behind her.

His thoughts drifted to Serena. What type of reward should she receive for the assistance she had provided? Perhaps she should receive King, Inc. It was a sticky question. Unfortunately, he was not able to live up to his verbal agreement with her and spare the life of Franklin. Both grandsons had to die. The one who went to Mexico would be first, then Franklin would have at best six months. It was Braxton's intent to kill all of King's male descendants. After the grandsons were gone, he would take his time. Taking perhaps one or two a year until there were none. He would have paid King in full and Serena would have tasted the pain that he had grown to know.

Braxton was a man of good standing in both his social and financial affairs, yet he felt that life had passed him by. He had successes in both his medical and his publishing practices, but those achievements did not sustain him. He was a man unfulfilled, because he had lived more than half his life with a broken heart. Braxton had once been a romantic man. Affairs of the heart had been serious business to him and he had given them his full attention. In his youth, he had dreamed that someday a woman would cross his path, a woman to whom he would give himself heart and soul. Such was the irony of fate that he got his wish. He fell in love with an older woman. Tragically, this woman was unable to return his love. She was married to someone else. She was King Tremain's wife; and because of that single fact, she had lived just beyond Braxton's reach for more than forty years. Nor could he forget that King had humiliated him in the late forties at a USO social for colored soldiers. Braxton had mistakenly not given full credence to the rumors about King's reputation and had allowed his infatuation with Serena to carry him away. He had presented her with a large bouquet of flowers from the stage and King had subsequently confronted him. When he attempted to laugh off King's anger, King had set upon him and slapped him around until he begged for mercy. When none of the witnesses would step forward and testify, Braxton knew that he would have to seek revenge clandestinely. He lived with the furtive looks and whispers from that one incident for years afterward.

Now, at seventy, his body chronicled each passing day with new aches and pains, and decreasing strength. He felt that his youth had been squandered on makeshift love affairs that pleased neither him nor the women he was with. And the final waste was his marriage. His wife was a good woman, but it was a drab relationship; there was no passion, only infrequent spasms of animal energy. And all this transpired in full sight of the woman he truly loved. He felt it in his bones; this was the love of which poets wrote. Each year without her was another turn on the torturous rack, until it seemed that he was stretched beyond the edge of sanity.

He wasn't threading the tightrope among the DuMonts, DiMarco, and Tree just for the money. He wanted revenge. No amount of money could make up for what he had suffered. He was organizing this effort to tear down the empire that his enemy had built and then to wipe his seed from the earth.

Wednesday, June 30, 1982

Serena walked out of the air-conditioned Hilton and was assaulted with the thick, moist, morning air of the Crescent City. She had forgotten the humidity of New Orleans that swathed itself around the body like a warm towel. It was too late to take her expensive black wool coat back to the room, plus it was part of her ensemble of black hat, dress, and shoes. She had judiciously chosen her clothing before her flight. It would take an emergency before she would break up a set wardrobe. She clearly wanted to present an image of wealth and class. The doorman whistled and a cab pulled up in front of the entrance. She pressed two dollars into his hand and was assisted into the cab. She gave the name of the cemetery to the driver and sank back in the seat to study the strange, new New Orleans that had risen up in the form of skyscrapers and overpasses since she had left over sixty years ago.

As the cab drove past unfamiliar buildings, Serena thought about her sister Della. She had no idea what she would say to her, or even how she would begin their conversation. She knew she wouldn't mention that Della had erred in blaming her for all the miscarriages, at least not immediately. The very existence of Della's daughters proved that Sister Bornais was fallible. And if the old medicine woman had made one error, maybe the rest of the things that had happened could be chalked up to coincidence too. Why couldn't the old woman be wrong about everything? It was a conversation that Serena had conducted many times in her mind but to no real resolution. All she could do was hold up Della's daughters as proof that the curse was not all-encompassing. She stared out the window and saw signs indicating that they were passing the western edge of Lake Pontchartrain toward what used to be Nellums' Crossing. Serena knew the Crossing wasn't there anymore. She had checked a map in the hotel. A housing development and mini-mall covered the area abutting Pine Knoll. The undeveloped rolling hills and lowlands were gone; buildings and houses had popped up everywhere she looked. Except for a few meadows and creek beds, there was construction everywhere. She shook her head. The place where she had grown up had been paved over. A new, slick neon landscape lay on top of the world she had known.

Della was the last person alive with whom Serena had experienced that other New Orleans, who remembered when horses and mules were the regular means of transportation owned by colored people, when outhouses were in common use, when no one colored outside of town had electricity, when only rich people had store-bought clothes. How would Della react when she first saw her? What would be her first words? It really didn't matter; it was Serena's intent to be generous and gracious. She would show what big-city class meant. Perhaps she would invite the family to the hotel for dinner one night for something *très cher*. She was going to turn their heads. Her nieces would be impressed with their newfound aunt. Perhaps she would invite them out to her home in San Francisco. Young ladies under her wing that she could mold and sculpt as she had been unable to do with her own children. King had always gotten in the way of her plans. Yes, she planned to be generous, to let bygones be bygones. It was a new day.

The cab pulled into a driveway which ran through a rusted iron fence. The old wrought-iron gate lay unhinged against one of the stone pillars which flanked the entrance. The cab bumped along a worn and rutted road as it chugged over a rise and pulled into a rough parking lot jam-packed with cars. Serena was surprised to see so many cars. For some reason, she thought the funeral would be small and intimate. The presence of all the vehicles made her think that Amos must have belonged to a very big church. Why else would so many people attend? She paid off the driver and made her way down a path that led to the Baddeaux family plot.

She passed through a stand of trees and saw a great crowd of people listening to a small jazz band that was playing on a raised platform. There were around two hundred people in attendance, many of whom were quite young, in their early twenties. A person with a white armband approached her and asked if she was a member of the family. She nodded and was led through the crowd to two rows of folding chairs which were facing the dais. They approached the chairs from the rear and she was seated in the second row next to a woman she did not know.

She studied the backs of the heads of the people in the first row, trying to identify Della, but the hats and veils worn by the women obstructed her view. Serena sat back and waited for the music to end. From her vantage point she could see that the members of the band were also quite young, which was surprising. She would've thought the musicians would have been older, perhaps even Amos's contemporaries. The music ended with a crescendo and received a rousing ovation from the attendees. A reverend climbed onto the platform and introduced the musicians. From his words Serena deduced that the band members had all been Amos's students, as had been many of the people in attendance. The reverend asked if any desired to say a few words and a line formed at the foot of the platform. A succession of faces, young and old, spoke touchingly of their relations with Amos. Apparently, Amos had risen to prominence as a teacher in a local music school and had touched many during his tenure. The mourners were there to acknowledge not only their respect but their gratitude.

It was not what Serena expected. She rather presumed that Amos had returned home a crippled and beaten man, that he had drowned himself in self-pity and resentment, and had led a reclusive life of inactivity. It was quite a shock to her to find that was not the case. A young man in dreadlocks addressed the crowd with an impassioned oration about Amos's impact on his life and when he finished, people rose to their feet and applauded. Serena shook her head in disbelief. She had never thought much of Amos other than in the context of him being her little brother. His unexpected prominence sort of threw her planned approach off track. She had projected that she would make a dramatic entrance to a sparsely attended service and she would make up with Della in front of an audience. She would be the grand lady over ne'er-do-well relatives.

The reverend called upon members of the family to speak. Serena was pleased to see two light-skinned women in their late thirties rise to the podium and say positive words about their uncle. Serena thought she could see the Baddeaux genes in their eyes and lips. They certainly had the family's light skin. Then Della was assisted up on the platform. Serena recognized her despite time's ravages. Her hair was gray, her face was lined with the passing years, and her body moved stiffly, but her eyes still had that sparkle that Serena remembered. Della spoke without notes about her brother's achievements. She mentioned his disability and how that had not stopped him from being a giving person. She revealed that she had been a teacher as well and had shared the heartbreak with him when he was unable to reach a particular student, or stimulate members of his class with his own love of music. Her voice was occasionally raspy as she was sometimes close to tears, but Della controlled her emotions and continued speaking. All the while she spoke, Serena studied her. Della's being a teacher explained why her clothes had a used and worn look. Obviously, she had not enjoyed financial success in her profession. Some of Serena's projections had been accurate.

She was not sure when Della's eyes fixed upon her, but Della fell silent midsentence for a few moments while she stared at Serena. Many of the people in attendance twisted to see what she was looking at before Della regained her composure, thanked all the attendees, and abruptly left the platform. The service ended with the lowering of the coffin into the earth as the band played "St. James Infirmary." Serena waited in her seat, expecting Della to come to her, but Della was occupied, surrounded by well-wishers. Serena stood and began to make her way slowly through the crowd toward her sister. Through a break in the mass of bodies, Serena thought she made eye contact with Della. She smiled and waved, but Della turned away and began moving toward the exit. Serena hastened to intercept her.

When she was within five feet of Della, Serena called out, "Della! Della Baddeaux, wait for your sister!" One of Della's daughters, a light-skinned woman who had spoken from the podium about her uncle Amos, was at Della's elbow. She saw Serena and smiled. Serena hurried over to stand in front of Della. She pulled back her veil and opened her arms to hug her sister, but was rebuffed.

Della looked at her malevolently and declared, "How dare you! How *dare* you!"

Serena, in surprise, explained, "Della, it's me, honey! Serena! Serena, your sister!"

There was no warmth in either her expression or words as Della snarled, "I know who you are! How could I forget you? You've marked my life! You've stolen from me treasures that cannot be counted! How could I forget you?"

Serena was completely taken aback. This reception was one that had not even entered her mind. "What—what are you talking about?" she sputtered.

Della growled, "You have the gall to ask me that question? How dare you! I had hoped you were dead, yet you have the gall to come here and defile Amos's service with your presence. You have no business here. You're not part of this family. You are dead to us. Get out! Get out now!"

Serena shook her head uncomprehendingly. "Della, I've come a long way! I've come to patch things up between us! How could you say these words to me? You don't mean this! I'm your sister!"

Della shrieked, "I've never meant anything more! You're not wanted here! Amos hated you as I hate you! He wouldn't want you here! And I don't want you here! Get out!"

People were beginning to stare as one of Della's daughters said, "Mama, you're getting upset. Try and calm down. Aunt Serena is here as a member of our family."

"You don't know what a snake she is, baby," Della declared loudly. "This woman has robbed this whole family of a future and she did it knowingly. She did it *knowingly!* She's no relative of mine. I don't even want to see her face!"

Serena's lips had begun to tremble. She could not believe what was happening. She stretched out a quivering hand. "Please, Della, don't do this! Please, I'm your sister! We're family!"

"How dare you claim me as family!" Della screamed as tears ran down her face. "You killed Tini! You crippled Amos! You've robbed me of the fruit of my womb! You killed my babies! *You killed my babies!*" Della swayed and her daughters took firmer grips on her arms.

Serena struggled for understanding. She pleaded, "How can you say that? You have daughters!"

With a final surge of strength, Della pulled free of the hands that held her and spit right in Serena's face then screamed, "I hate you! I *hate* you! You killed my babies!" Della collapsed in sobs and needed to be supported. She was led away by caring friends.

Serena was left standing alone with spittle on her face. She took a deep breath, gathered herself, then calmly took a tissue out of her purse. While she wiped away the last vestiges of Della's insult, she felt the numbing weight of unfriendly stares as people walked past her to their parked cars. She had made no arrangements for a ride back into town, nor was it a priority in her thinking. Her principal focus was to make it to the exit without collapsing or breaking down in tears. Della's words were ringing in her ears. She took another deep breath and followed the crowd on wooden legs up the path to the exit. Although she was walking among many people, she was alone. She felt the banishment conferred by the silent stares, eyes that furtively followed her movements as if she had been guilty of exposing some private part or urinating in public. She could not think of a time in which she had endured greater humiliation in full view of so many strangers.

Although she felt as if she had been stabbed and choked, on the surface she was unfazed. Serena's backbone was made of steel. It would not let her crumple, or let her surrender to her desire to scream. She put one foot in front of the other. And kept walking. Her heart and mind had been sent through the fan blades of a wind tunnel. Her feelings and thoughts were shredded and in confusion like swirling confetti caught in a dust devil. She felt strangely unstable, as if Della had somehow knocked down a vital pillar in the structure of her life. Serena had never realized the level of animosity her siblings harbored against her. The mere knowledge of it caused pains to go shooting across her forehead and chest. She was starting to have difficulty getting a deep breath.

"Aunt Serena! Aunt Serena! Wait up, Aunt Serena!"

Serena turned and saw one of Della's daughters hurrying toward her. Immediately, Serena began to straighten her clothes and compose her expression. She wouldn't let anyone see her broken.

"Aunt Serena, I'm so glad I caught up with you." A plump, light-brown-skinned face smiled, and a white-gloved hand shot out. "I'm Tini, the younger sister. Rebecca and I are so sorry about what happened. All we can say is that Mother has been under some considerable strain lately, Father having died last year and all. It's been a tough time for her, but I've never seen her react like that. She just wasn't herself today. I hope you'll forgive her."

"I was mortified by her outburst!" Serena said sadly as she started walking again. Tini fell in step with her as Serena continued, "We haven't talked for so many years. I thought this would be a good opportunity to patch things up."

"Maybe it's still not too late," Tini replied. "If you're going to be in town for a few days maybe Rebecca and I can work something out with Mama for some private time. Where are you staying?"

"The Hilton downtown."

"Do you have a car? May I give you a ride back to the hotel?"

"That would be very kind of you, if you would, please. I took a cab out here from town."

"It would be my pleasure. I'd be happy to help. Uncle King has been so good to us, we're in debt to you, Aunt Serena. All you have to do is ask."

"I beg your pardon? You know King? King Tremain?"

"Oh, yes, he used to come and visit Uncle Amos a lot. He was the one who donated the money to start Uncle Amos's music school. Back when Rebecca and I were little, we'd see him a couple of times a year, always bringing gifts and treats for us kids. And you know, of course, that he paid the total freight for Rebecca and my board and education at Spelman."

More astonishing news. Serena was speechless. She concentrated on keeping her balance and moving her feet. So, King had kept up the communication with her family and never told her. Irony of ironies: Della's daughters knew him, but not their blood aunt. Regret washed over her; nearly fifty years of silence and all she had to show for it was that she was a stranger in her own family. How had it happened? How had Della come to hate her? Serena mused out loud, "I don't know why Della said such things to me. She has two beautiful daughters and you look so much like your mother and grandmother too. I just don't understand."

Tini explained, "I'm sure it all had to do with the terrible miscarriages that she had before we came along which prevented her from having children of her own. She always gets very emotional about that. I remember once—"

"What did you say?" Serena demanded. Her face paled. She was reeling on the edge of an abyss. "What did you say?"

"About Mama's miscarriages?" Tini asked, her face filled with innocent concern. Had she been looking, Tini might have seen the terrible, intense look of Serena's face and halted herself, but she didn't so she continued on blithely, "The miscarriages were horrible. From what I understand they nearly drove Mama mad. She used to say that the only thing that kept her sane was me and Rebecca entering her life. I guess that's why she and Papa adopted us."

"You're—you're adopted? But-but-but you loo-look like . . ." Serena did not finish. She saw clearly now, there was no escape. Sister Bornais had not made a mistake. She now had no doubts that King was also right. He would be her escort as she descended into hell. For the first time, Serena shouldered the full weight of her actions and it was almost too much to bear. Her vision began to grow dark. She stumbled. All she remembered was that she had slipped over the edge and was falling into the abyss. She saw the sky and realized that she was actually falling over backward, then blackness.

Wednesday, June 30, 1982

Elizabeth hung her work suit in the closet and then checked the fit of her jeans over her behind in the mirror. They weren't too tight . . . yet. Despite all her recent trial work and long hours spent developing her case strategy, she was still holding shape. She turned to face the mirror and checked the tightness of the waistband. Not so good. She had to get out and run some miles pretty soon or she would begin to have midriff bulge. Sit-ups alone weren't enough. It was hard enough being a consistent shark in the courtroom while maintaining a caseload of serious felonies, including murder one, but it became a superhuman effort when she tried to keep all the elements of her feminine guile up as well. She adjusted the barrette that held her thin braids on top of her head. She thought if white women had hair like black women, the Western world would be different. On humid and rainy days concerts and theater activities would be canceled and restaurants wouldn't be open. She looked at her watch: Jackson was due in ten minutes, at six o'clock. She went into the kitchen to pour herself a glass of Chardonnay.

The thought of Jackson coming over made her heart flutter. Elizabeth took a quick look around her apartment to ensure everything was in order. She stood still for a moment and composed herself. She was not one to rush into things. She was thirty-four and had never been married. She had been waiting for the right man to come along and she would not be hurried. Many an impatient man had walked away because she would not be intimate before she was ready. There were no such obstacles with Jackson. He was the right man and every fiber of her being confirmed that decision. She had never enjoyed herself so much with anyone. Just thinking about the way he cocked his right eyebrow when he looked quizzical made her smile. There was a harmony between them that preempted conversation.

The right man had finally appeared, but not without grave complications. She was by law an officer of the court and a representative of law enforcement. She had signed an oath that she would uphold the laws and the Constitution of the United States and the state of California and she took the oath seriously. There had been occasions when she had crossed the line, but they had all been minor infractions. Jackson had admitted to her that he had killed, and that posed a real problem for her. She had spent a good part of her adult life apprehending and prosecuting people charged with attempting and committing violent crimes. What was she going to do? Murder was not something that could be overlooked. Was she just going to say good-bye to this man? A man to whom she was ready to give her heart? Should she risk everything? And what if it didn't work out between them? Would she still be able to go back to being a DA? Her heart told her one thing, but her mind said another.

The truth was that she was becoming pretty disenchanted with prosecution work. Her caseload was unending and required that she consistently put in long hours to stay current, but that wasn't the principal problem. The most troubling reality about her job was that the vast majority of the people she was sending to jail were men of color, men who had not had the same advantages in their youth as she and her white colleagues. Other than the drug dealers and the pimps, most of the men were poor, uneducated, and possessed no means of joining the mainstream. It wasn't that these men didn't deserve jail time for their crimes, but jail taught them nothing except how to become lower animals. What to do? Should she give up being a district attorney? Eight years of work in the wrong career direction? She was in line for the next chief position in the DA's office. There were no easy answers.

The doorbell rang. Elizabeth made final adjustments to her appearance in front of the hallway mirror before opening the door. Jackson stood there with a bottle of wine and a bunch of calla lilies. "Are those for me?" she asked, indicating the flowers with a nod of her head as she opened the door wider.

Jackson pressed past her and replied, "Of course. There's no one else I'd rather give them to."

He took a seat at the kitchen counter while she went behind it and squatted down to find a vase under the sink. Jackson leaned over the counter and said, "I thought about what you said last night after I left and I want you to know that if I could turn my back on this conflict, if I could walk away, I would do that to be with you. Even if it meant losing my grandfather's fortune."

Elizabeth looked up at him and there was a smile on her face as she said, "Well, I like that. I like that a lot." Her smile slowly vanished and was replaced by a serious expression. She continued, "You've come along at a very confusing time. I don't have a road map here like I've had in the earlier years of my life. But I am sure of some things. I don't want any part of a gang war and I don't want to be involved with anyone who commits violent felonies." She pulled out a vase and stood to arrange the lilies in it.

Jackson reached out and touched her, his hand caressing her cheek.

"I want to be a law-abiding citizen. Tell me how to escape this situation. Help me find a solution that doesn't have me looking over my shoulder."

Elizabeth took his hand in hers and studied him with her large brown eyes. "You could leave and go somewhere else. Use a different name."

Jackson kept eye contact and asked, "Where? How? Would you go with me? Even if we did, could we raise our children with confidence? Would you feel secure?"

A big smile spread across Elizabeth's face. She asked, "Children?"

Jackson nodded and pressed his point. "Would you feel secure?"

She thought a moment then shrugged. "Probably not."

"What good is your advice if you won't take it yourself?"

Elizabeth removed her hand from Jackson's. "Did you really just mention 'children'?"

"A normal concept for a heterosexual couple to discuss. Is there a problem?"

"Yes! You're just this side of being a gangster!"

"Bullshit! I'm looking for a way out! Perhaps I can arrange something."

"What kind of arrangement?" Elizabeth asked as she moved away to run water into the vase.

"I want to avoid a conflict if I can."

Elizabeth began arranging the lilies in the vase, concentrating on the position of each stalk. She spoke as if musing aloud to herself. "I've attempted to think things through in terms of various what-if scenarios, but no matter what decision I reach the only thing that seems to matter is what I feel. I have never had this happen before."

"I know what you mean," Jackson confirmed. "I felt it immediately when I met you. I was drawn to you. I couldn't help myself."

Elizabeth gave him a long look then said with a trace of a smile, "Don't cut it too thick, Tremain. You've shown amazing restraint for someone who couldn't help himself."

"I had to work my way through what was happening myself. Plus, if I had moved any faster, you would've run and you know it."

Elizabeth brought the lilies over to the counter and stared at Jackson. "Do you have any idea what I feel? How much I'm conflicted about you? What big changes this would mean in my life? How did you know I like calla lilies so much? This is the second time you've brought them."

"Which question do you want me to answer?"

"The lilies."

"You mentioned it when we were on Angel Island, then I saw you had two calla lily lamps and one of your upholstered chairs has a lily design on it."

"That's what makes you dangerous, you're observant. Are you this way with all your women?"

Jackson replied, "There's never been another woman that interests and intrigues me the way you do. Anyway, I would have to be blind to have missed all those cues."

"In your whole life? There's not been another woman of equal interest? Not one?"

"Maybe one, but it was young love. I was eighteen, but still a child. I have more control over my life direction now. I have a better understanding of what I really need."

She put a hand on her hip and a smile crept across her face. "How do you know I'm what you really need?"

"A trick question," Jackson replied with a chuckle. A serious look came into his eyes as he continued, "How about this: I have memorized the form of your lips when you smile, the liquid, creamy sound of your laughter, the shape and color of your eyes, the way your hips move when you walk, the soft darkness of your skin."

Jackson stood up and walked around the counter. He put his hand under her chin and lifted her face to his and then when they were looking into each other's eyes, he said, "More important than any physical attraction I feel for you is the sensation that I have when we're together. I feel connected when I am with you. I've never had this feeling before, and believe me, I don't want to lose it now."

"Don't be glib. Don't say things you don't mean," Elizabeth said as a serious look entered her eyes.

Jackson reached down and took both her hands in his. "My heart is behind everything I've said. And I never want to hurt you. I want to be your partner and protector. I want us to see and enjoy the sun and the stars as few have."

Elizabeth stood quietly trying to memorize the angles and color of his hands, the calluses on his knuckles, the veins beneath the skin, the lines which crisscrossed the joints. Were these the hands that would be holding her in her declining years? She felt emotion welling up within her. She realized that there was only a thin line of restraint holding her from rushing into his arms. She looked into his eyes and their gazes locked. They stood for several seconds in silence then Jackson cocked his right eyebrow and gave her that quizzical look. She could not help herself. She smiled. He had something nobody else had. He could touch her inside and make her laugh. She wanted to hug him, feel his arms around her, have his chest press against her. There was a roar in her inner ear, like the sound of a powerful current rushing through a confined space. She was on the verge of being swept away.

An alarm went off on top of the fridge and the mood was broken. Elizabeth pulled her hand free from his grasp and exhaled. "Time to go, Tremain. Uncle Elroy is expecting us."

"What is this 'Tremain' stuff? Don't you like my first name?"

"It's just a holdover from my days as a police officer," Elizabeth answered as she donned her coat. "Everyone was called by their last name. Jackson is an okay name, but it isn't what I want to call you. It's too formal for me. What's your full name?"

"My friends call me Jax."

"That's a guy name. What's your full name?"

"Jackson St. Clair Tremain."

"St. Clair? Oh, I like that. St. Clair Tremain. I'm going to call you St. Clair. Do you mind?"

"Only if I can do the same with you."

"Just don't call me Liz, Beth, Betty, or Eliza and you'll be okay."

"What's your full name?"

"Elizabeth Alexandra Carlson."

"Alexandra? Too long."

"Don't call me Sandy!"

"What about Alex? It's got a crossover quality."

Elizabeth nodded her head. "Alex, hmmm. Alex is good. I like that, but don't introduce me like that. That's a special name only for you."

"You have a hell of a lot of rules."

Elizabeth grabbed his arm and ushered him to the door. "You ain't seen nothing yet, Buster."

Elroy Fontenot stood on his balcony and watched the traffic whiz back and forth in a sunken roadway over which Ocean Boulevard passed. The fourplex which he owned was located in the Westlake District of San Francisco on a hill with a view over the City College campus and

Ocean Boulevard. He lived in the top apartment and when the fog rolled in like milk of magnesia billowing in water, and visibility ended at the street below his building, Elroy would go out on his balcony with a drink and stare into the gray nothingness. It gave him a sense of the supernatural. He often imagined that the entrances into both heaven and hell would be shrouded in swirling fog. For the most part, he was a pragmatic man who gave little thought to gods or demons. Elroy was an empiricist, who believed in cause and effect, action and reaction. There was a logic to life; one need only piece the facts together. He had little use for faith or prayer. He believed in solid things like hard work, property ownership, guns, flag and country, and an eye for an eye, and a tooth for a tooth.

The afternoon sky was free of clouds. The view from his balcony extended across the bay to the dark line of the East Bay hills. Elroy sipped his scotch and looked at his watch. He was awaiting the arrival of Elizabeth and King Tremain's grandson. He still did not know what there was to say, yet he felt that finally meeting some member of his long-lost family would bring to resolution some of the questions that used to haunt him. Who was LeGrande? Why was he left in an orphanage? Why had King never contacted him? Was Serena his mother? These questions no longer possessed the intensity to upset him, but if there were answers, he'd like to hear them.

He heard the sounds of footsteps climbing the stairs to his apartment and went to the front door. He opened the door as Elizabeth was poised to knock. He smiled and stood back for her and her companion to enter. Elroy was prepared to be formal and polite. After all, her companion had neither a hand in the injustice of leaving him in the orphanage, nor the ability to remedy the situation. At best, he would be a source of information. At worst, a brief nuisance. The man who followed her was tall and athletic, but it wasn't until Elroy stood face-to-face with him as they shook hands that Elroy saw something that shook him to his core.

"Hello, Mr. Fontenot. My name's Jackson Tremain. I'm glad to meet you."

"Nice to meet you" was all that Elroy could muster. Jackson Tremain looked like his oldest son, Denmark, the one who was killed in Vietnam. It was not that they could be confused with each other, but there was no doubt they were part of the same genetic stream. The eyebrows, the cheekbones, the shape of the head, the little smile which appeared at the corner of the lips: all were pieces of Elroy's dead son, pieces that were assembled differently, but recognizable nonetheless. Elroy had not expected anything like this. The resemblance was unsettling.

"I brought Grandfather's file on you." Jackson held up a fat accordion file. "Where would you like me to put it? I'm sure you will find it very interesting reading. I did."

"Take it to the kitchen table. We can sit and talk there." Elroy watched as Elizabeth led Jackson into the kitchen. He felt a shortness of breath and a hollowness in his chest cavity as if the air had been knocked out of him. All the unresolved issues that had existed between Elroy and his sons seemed to bubble to the surface of his consciousness. He had not even said good-bye to Denmark before he had shipped overseas for his tour of duty. He had not ever told the boy that he loved him. Neither of his sons had received much warmth from him, a fact that filled him with regret whenever he thought of them. Unknowingly, he had denied them the very same things he had been denied in the orphanage. A bad taste filled his mouth, but he suppressed his misgivings and followed his guests into the kitchen.

"We brought some wine to lubricate our palates and some barbecue to ease conversation," Elizabeth said with a smile. She went to a drawer and pulled out a corkscrew. "St. Clair, get three glasses out of that cabinet."

"I'm doing the higher-octane stuff, I'm already drinking scotch," Elroy interjected with a frown. "I don't need a glass. And I'm going to have to ask you to take that barbecue back to the car, because the smell of it makes me sick. Sorry about that."

There was a moment of silence then Jackson shrugged. "Sure thing; if we'd have known we would've brought something else. I'll be right back."

Jackson was gone several minutes and when he returned the wine was opened and poured. Elroy watched the interaction between Elizabeth and Jackson and saw them exchange a bantering conversation without words, consisting of facial expressions and hand signals. He saw her use her hip to nudge Jackson toward the table. Elroy mused that if she liked Jackson sufficiently to show this level of affection in front of him, then Jackson must have something. Elizabeth had high standards. He wondered how they had met. If Jackson was even thinking about carrying on his grandfather's business, they were from different worlds. Elroy sipped his scotch as he studied Jackson covertly. What was his story?

Jackson raised his wineglass for a toast and said, "To the end of a long search and the reestablishment of family ties." Elizabeth raised her glass in agreement and Elroy followed suit but with reservation. Jackson continued, "It's unfortunate that this meeting didn't happen while my grandfather was alive, but you'll see from the file papers, he kept up with the events in your life. Personally, I don't know why he never contacted you himself, but it's obvious he wanted me to talk to you, or he would've never left this file for me to read."

"How well did you know your grandfather?" Elroy took out a cigar and clipped the end before he lit it. He puffed it until it was glowing brightly. "Did you know he was one of the main crime bosses running the Fillmore back in the forties and early fifties?"

"I don't know details, but I know my grandfather was an Old World gangster. He started back in the prohibition era. Did you know him? He doesn't mention that you knew him."

Elroy examined the end of his cigar and replied, "I knew of him, through police reports. I only met him once."

"There's nothing in his papers that mentions you met him. You saw him face-to-face?"

"It was 1954. We were looking eye to eye. He saw me and I saw him. He knew who I was then, but at the time I didn't know who he was. He didn't say anything to me about our kinship then, so I don't understand this now."

"He's dead. I'm the one making the overture," Jackson answered, thumping his chest. "You have a right to your inheritance. You and I are related. We should know each other. I'm just trying to do the right thing now. I can't help what went before. In his papers he acknowledges you as his son. I want to respect that. After you were kidnapped, he spent thirty years looking for you. He had no idea that Serena knew where you were all along. By the time he tracked you down, you were already working for the police department."

"I was kidnapped?" Elroy scoffed. "By whom? From whom?"

"You and your mother were taken by the DuMonts and the sheriff of New Orleans. It's all in here." Jackson tapped the accordion file.

Elroy was silent for a while as he digested Jackson's words. He looked at Jackson and asked, "You know who my mother is and where she is?"

Jackson nodded. "Why don't you read the materials and we can talk when you're ready. It's better you have all the information first."

Elroy took another long puff on his cigar then gently tapped it out in the ashtray. He looked at Jackson and asked, "Why are you doing this? What's in it for you? If you don't have to cut me in, why do it?"

"Two reasons. First, it's the right thing to do. Second, your life may be in danger. The feud with the DuMonts is still going on and if King's enemies found out you were alive, they might come looking for you. You deserve a fighting chance."

Elroy picked up the file. "How do I know that the information contained in here is true?"

Jackson shrugged. "You don't, but you have to think what do I have to gain by misinforming you?"

"I'm not worried about you, I'm wondering if some old man who was close to death was trying to rewrite history, put his own spin on reality, make up for past weaknesses. Somebody trying to adjust his account."

"Read it and make your own decisions," Jackson suggested as he stood up. "We can talk in a couple of days if you like. Here's a number where you may reach me." Jackson handed Elroy a card.

Elroy studied Jackson then got to his feet slowly. "You believe what's in here is true, don't you?"

Jackson nodded. "My grandfather was a lot of things but he wasn't a liar. His word was his bond. I believe this information is true to the best of his knowledge." Jackson stuck out his hand. "Nice to meet you, Mr. Fontenot. I look forward to seeing you again."

Elroy shook Jackson's hand but kept a grip on it as he said, "I wouldn't like to hear of Elizabeth getting hurt behind some mobster activity. I hope you're not keeping anything from her and you've got the means to protect her if things get rough."

Jackson smiled. "She knows what I know and I plan on protecting her with every means at my disposal."

Elroy released Jackson's hand and stepped back from the table. Elizabeth rose and gave him a hug. He whispered in her ear as they walked to the door arm in arm that she should call him later. She nodded and gave him a quick kiss on the cheek and walked out the door with Jackson. Elroy watched them descend the stairs. He saw there was a bounce in Elizabeth's step and a sparkle in her eyes that was new. This Jackson Tremain was a serious contender. He was a cool customer too. Elroy reviewed their conversation. Jackson had revealed very little about his grandfather's business or his involvement in it.

Elroy refreshed his scotch, opened the windows, and went out onto the deck. He wanted to air out all smell of the barbecue. The night was clear. The lights of the city and the East Bay sparkled and twinkled in the distance, allowing the imagination to run to fantasy and illusion, yet the streets immediately below his building seemed windswept and wretched. Dim shadows of people in flapping coats appeared and disappeared under the sporadically placed streetlights. The lights of passing cars revealed a neighborhood without magic. Elroy took a large drink of his scotch and chuckled humorlessly. It was always easier to see mystery and pleasure in the distance.

Elroy thought about the file sitting on his kitchen table and experienced an unusual giddiness, as if he were about to take an important examination for which he had prepared for a long time. He felt both reluctance and excitement. Would the file answer all his questions? Could he really believe it, if it did? Did the answers really matter? He turned away from the view and walked back into his apartment. If the contents of the file affected him one-tenth the amount that Jackson had, he was in for quite a ride. It was like experiencing something out of the Twilight Zone, to see a man who looked so much like Denmark walk through his door. Elroy had read somewhere that people who made mistakes concerning important events were doomed to repeat their activities in a recurring cycle until they got things right. Was Jackson an augur of such a lesson? How else to explain the similarity in appearance to Denmark? How else to explain that Jackson had stirred something inside of him that gave him a trace sense of belonging, a genetic bridge linking past and future? Against his will and better judgment, he knew that he liked Jackson and wanted to see him again. If he couldn't be a father to his own sons, perhaps he could be an uncle, or distant cousin, to someone else's son. He sat down at the table and opened the file.

A few blocks away from Elroy's building Jackson pulled the car to the curb and turned off the engine. He stared into the lights of the passing traffic, seemingly lost in thought.

Elizabeth gazed at him with concern in her eyes. "Are you all right?"

He exhaled and turned to her. "This is a big night for my family. A son who has been lost has been found. I have made the first move in correcting a tragedy that has gone on for more than sixty years. I had no idea it would affect me emotionally. Elroy looks so much like my father and grandfather that it's eerie. I was actually getting choked up in his apartment."

Elizabeth commented, "I thought our departure was a little abrupt, but it wasn't apparent to me that you were upset." She put her hand on his shoulder and smiled. Her face was illuminated only intermittently by headlights, yet the warmth in her expression was obvious even in the semidarkness. "Why do you think you were affected so deeply?"

"I don't know. I just felt the floodgates weakening. Since my grandfather was killed I feel like I'm holding so much back, so many unresolved things that they're slopping over the dam I've built to keep them from overrunning my thoughts."

"What do you mean?"

"Oh, thoughts like I've wasted a lot of time resenting my dysfunctional family. The truth is I didn't even have it as bad as some others in my family. I wasn't abandoned in an orphanage. I didn't suffer that level of isolation. Then there's the realization of all that has been lost as a result of Elroy's absence and all that could've been had he been part of our family. My father and mother might both be alive. I've wasted so much time trying to understand my grandparents' intentions when they can't even explain their actions." Jackson shook his head resignedly. "There's been so much unnecessary pain and unpleasantness. And I've come too late to remedy this injustice. At best I'm putting a bandage on a wound that's scarred over but will never heal."

Jackson grimaced and rubbed his neck. "Damn! I've really got a crick in my neck. Hmmm, let me take you home." He started the ignition and pulled slowly out into the night traffic.

Elizabeth observed, "You sound like you could use a hot tub or a therapeutic massage. That's the therapy I use whenever my work or my life gets me uptight or depressed. I think some deep-tissue work might help you release tension and I know just the place on Judah and Ninth."

"It's not the deep-tissue work I had hoped you would offer me," Jackson replied with a sad smile. "But if you recommend it, let's do it."

It was a short, twenty-minute drive to the hot tub and massage parlor. Upon arriving at the parlor, Elizabeth went to the women's side while Jackson went to the men's. Due to the fact Elizabeth took time to wrap her hair in towels to protect it from the ambient moisture in the air, she did not get her massage immediately. While she waited in a terry-cloth robe for her masseuse to finish with another client, she thought about Jackson and the way he had stormed into her life. There was no denying that she was attracted to him. She liked everything that she had seen so far. And the more she saw of him, the more she liked him. He seemed to be perfect in all ways save one: He appeared to be a man caught in circumstances not of his making. Perhaps he was being naive, but he felt there was a possibility everything would end peacefully. She wanted to believe him and she felt optimistic that he would rid himself of all the entanglements.

Elizabeth realized that she was rationalizing, that she was intellectually removing the impediments that would prevent the two of them from getting together. She was risking being hurt and disappointed, yet she did not want to stop. She told herself that her heart was strong enough to deal with whatever consequences resulted. She had taken risks before and survived. Even though these palliatives offered no real comfort, she felt not fear but excitement when she thought of Jackson. The prospect of seeing him later thrilled her, made subtle tremors pulse through her body. As she waited to be called in for her massage, she even allowed herself to wonder what making love with him would be like, to be skin to skin with him, to open herself to him. The thought of intimacy with him filled her with expectation and tingling anticipation. The sound of her name being called broke her reverie.

Immersed in the room's soft light, the air scented with a trace of sandalwood incense, she let herself drift with the rhythms of the masseuse's hands and the soft tones of the Shankar raga playing on the PA system. Although it seemed to pass quickly Elizabeth was relaxed when her massage session was over. She slipped on her robe and felt better able to deal with the vicissitudes of her imperfect world. She went out into the common area expecting to find Jackson dressed and waiting but he was nowhere to be seen. She went to the counter and inquired of the young woman who was working behind it as to Jackson's whereabouts. She was informed that he was in room five in the hot tub section. Elizabeth tightened her robe and headed toward room five. She did not have a clear picture in her mind exactly what she would do when she entered the room, but there was a tartness in her mouth that made her tongue hurt.

She knocked on a solid wooden door that had a large brass "5" mounted upon it. There was no answer. She pushed the door open and entered into semidarkness as the blaring sounds of jazz fusion swept around her. The music was so loud that it had muffled both her knock and the closing of the door. Elizabeth slid the lock across the door and turned around. Jackson was sitting in a large oaken hot tub against the far wall with his head laid back. His arms were resting on the rim of the tub as he stared up at the ceiling. The muscles in his chest, shoulders, and arms were apparent even in the soft light of the wall sconces.

She did not know how long she stood there watching him, but suddenly she noticed that he was staring back at her. No words were spoken. They merely stared at each other for uncounted seconds. Old questions rushed past her, borne on an anxious breeze. Was this truly the man? The one to grow old with? What was truly in his heart? Then Jackson smiled and the wind changed. The questions were whisked away and certainty returned. She wanted this. She wanted to be with him.

Without taking her eyes off Jackson, Elizabeth untied the belt of her robe. She let the robe hang partially open, allowing her long, dark legs to be exposed, as she walked over to the hot tub. She felt his eyes follow her. Her skin was prickling and sensitive underneath the robe. She felt the rough nap of the terry cloth rubbing against her nipples, making them hard. Adjacent to the steps leading into the hot tub was a wide wooden bench with a large futon on it. Elizabeth let the robe slide off her shoulders. She stood still for a moment, allowing him to admire her naked beauty, until she saw the arousal in his eyes. As she climbed the steps to enter the hot tub, she knew that she had passed the point of no return.

Friday, July 2, 1982

The 1965 metallic green Mercury Cougar turned onto Tunnel Road and headed up the hill on the tortuous, winding street as it climbed high above the entrance to the Caldecott Tunnel and Highway 24. The sun had just recently set and there was still a line of lavender on the western horizon below a sky of deepening blue. On the highway below, the lights of the rush-hour traffic inched along slowly through the tunnel toward Contra Costa while the lights of the opposite-bound traffic whizzed westward. Inside the Cougar the radio was booming with the bass beat of hip-hop tunes.

Rhasan Tremain leaned forward from the backseat and tapped the driver, Fox Malone, on the shoulder. "Fox, we got to be cool with the sounds around my uncle's crib, man. I don't want his neighbors calling and complaining to him that me and a bunch of my friends came to his house playing loud music."

"It's all good, Dog," Fox replied. "I'll turn it down when we get near his house. Right now, we're just a bunch of niggers from the flats. People don't know who we're going to visit."

Wayman, who was sitting up in the front next to Fox, said, "I ain't no nigger. Shit! I'm going to college! I'm planning on kicking butt with the books to escape all that West Oakland nigger shit!"

Fox glanced at Wayman as he steered the car, negotiating the tight, twisting curves of the road as it climbed higher above the freeway. "Don't fool yourself, Dog. Soon as a white cop sees you, you ain't nothing but a nigger. It don't matter whether you got money or not, or whether you got an education. Everything is based on the color of your skin. Ain't that right, Deshawn?"

Deshawn Edwards, a dark-skinned, well-muscled young man who was sitting in the back next to Rhasan, said, "Goddamn straight! But I wish it was only the police that pulled that shit. Hell, I could be working in a nice job right now! But as soon as that white woman saw my black face walking through the door, my chances were shit."

Rhasan elbowed him. "Did you have your head tie on, Deshawn? Were you wearing your gang colors? Because you can scare anybody when you put your street stuff on."

Deshawn waved dismissively. "Man, I had on one of my church suits.

That bitch wasn't gon' give me a damn thing. When I walked out of there, I just wanted to slap the shit out of her!"

Wayman shook his head and said, "Knowing you, I bet you didn't hide your feelings either."

"Fuck no, man!" Deshawn confirmed. "Ain't no way I'm gon' smile when a door's slammed in my face. Didn't even give me a damn chance. If it keep on like this, I'm gon' end up working for Fox's brother."

"That's cool, we always got openings for strong young brothers!" Fox confirmed with a nod of his head. He looked in his rearview mirror and saw Rhasan shaking his head. "Don't say nothing, Rhasan! The drug biz is the only equal-opportunity employer that hires homeboys whether they graduate high school or not!"

"It's a dead end and it's hurting our people, man!" Rhasan protested. "We all know at least ten people who've been killed and twice that many who're in jail. And the money isn't good enough to change your life, or for you to escape Oakland."

Fox countered, "For most brothers, there ain't no other alternatives. Who the hell wants to work at one them fast food outlets? Come home smelling like greasy fries! Or being a goddamn janitor! Hell, ain't everybody got an uncle like you, willing to take off work and spend time with you. Willing to get you tutors and whatever. Willing to take you to Yosemite, Hawaii, and every damn place. Man, you is lucky you got him standing behind you. Ain't everybody got family like that."

Rhasan replied, "When he came to get us out of juvie, he made all four of us the same offer, the same promise. Only two of us took him up on it. At first, Fox, you went along with the program. You went to the after-school tutoring. You went to Hawaii with us, but then you dropped out. And Deshawn never—"

"Don't go there!" Deshawn interjected angrily. "You know I had an after-school job! You knew if I didn't work, me and my little sisters weren't gon' have a damn shirt or pair of pants to wear. If I didn't get home before the mail arrived, my mother was gon' cash her welfare check and spend it on cheap weed and liquor. I had responsibilities! I couldn't stay after school."

"My uncle offered to help you with—"

"Don't you get it? I was ashamed! Your family was willing to do everything for you, while mine wouldn't amount to a pile of shit on a busy street. I couldn't take charity, especially from somebody who wasn't family. I know I ain't got no money and no education, but I got pride. I'm gon' do for myself and I ain't afraid of hard work. All I need is a chance. Just let these white fucks give me a damn chance!" The intensity of Deshawn's words momentarily stifled the conversation and left only the sound of Grandmaster Flash and the Furious Five rapping to a funky beat.

Fox patted his steering wheel. "You see my ride." He waved his hand at the Mercury Cougar. "Ain't nobody who went to Berkeley High or Oakland Tech got a ride cherried out like this but drug dealers like me!"

Wayman challenged, "There were some white boys at Berkeley with classy rides."

"Ain't nobody talking about whites!" Fox retorted. "Shit, they start off with advantages! I'm talking about homies!"

Rhasan said, "My uncle Jax says if you're prepared to work and sacrifice, this is one of the few countries in the world where you can change your station in life."

Wayman interjected, "He says racism is like gravity, you just have to keep on pushing against it."

Fox gave Wayman a sideways glance then said, "It sounds like both you boys swallowed everything the man said and got it memorized. Damn!"

Deshawn added, "No disrespect to your uncle, but you can't change the most important thing: You still gon' be a nigger! No matter how much money you got. No matter what your achievements. You still a nigger, and a nigger ain't shit!"

Wayman couldn't contain himself. He turned to face Deshawn. "It's that 'a nigger ain't shit' attitude that's the problem! If you believe it, you can't be anything more. I'm not a nigger now and I don't ever plan on being one."

Fox laughed and gestured over his back to Rhasan and said, "That sounds like some more shit straight out of the mouth of Rhasan's Uncle Jax. I heard him say the very same damn thing!"

Rhasan asked, "Do you disagree? Do you think he's wrong?"

"Naw, Dog," Fox answered. "Your uncle is cool with me. Ain't no lie, he's a down brother and he ain't forgot where he came from. All Deshawn is saying is, the whites don't see shit else but the color of your skin and the kink in your hair!"

Wayman maintained, "Skin color and kink don't mean nigger!"

"Hey, Fox, we're coming to the turn before my uncle's house. We need to cut the music down. He's the second house on the right after this turn."

"I remember where it is!" Fox answered indignantly, turning the music down to a more reasonable level.

Deshawn mused, "Shit, I wish I had me an uncle that would lend me his BMW for the weekend."

Fox teased, "Dog, you wish you had an uncle who had something worth lending!"

"Here it is." Rhasan pointed across Deshawn's chest. "Just pull to the edge of the driveway and I'll get out."

Fox looked in the direction that Rhasan had pointed and said, "Your uncle's house is the only one on this curve of the hill. We can turn the music up as loud as we want."

Deshawn observed, "Ain't no lights. Don't look like he's home anyway."

"That's okay. I know where the key is. I'll be out in a few minutes." Rhasan opened the car door and stepped out into the night air. The gloaming was gone and the shadows of night had fallen. Rhasan walked quickly down the driveway toward the darkened house, and headed down some stairs located on the right side of the structure.

"Damn! He's even got a key to his uncle's house!" Deshawn said with a shade of awe. "That's some kind of trust. In my uncle's house you got to get a key to open the refrigerator and that's after you've shown some ID to get in the house."

"Hey! Look at that!" Fox interjected, pointing at the house. "There's some fat white guy following Rhasan down the driveway!"

Deshawn asked, "Is he a cop?"

"Don't think so," Fox replied, reaching under his dashboard. He pulled out a snub-nosed revolver. He flipped open the cylinder to check the ammunition. "Undercover cops are generally in pretty good shape. I don't know who that fat fuck is."

Wayman exclaimed, "Damn, Fox! Rhasan asked if you were carrying before we got in the car and you said no!"

"Rhasan was asking if I had any kind of dope in the car. He wasn't talking about guns. He knows I don't go nowhere without a nine or a Mag."

Wayman was aghast. "You're still carrying weapons in this car even after your last arrest?"

"Wouldn't leave home without it. This is my Oakland express card."

Deshawn hissed, "There's another white guy coming toward the car!"

"Fox, don't do anything crazy!" Wayman whispered warningly.

"It's all good," Fox replied with a smile. "I'll be cool." He put the gun down in his lap and watched the man come up to the driver's-side window.

"How we doin', boys?" the man said as he reached the car. He stooped down to see who was in the car. "It's dark in there! Why don't you boys smile so I can see how many of you there are."

"Who the fuck are you?" Fox demanded.

The man gave Fox a hard look then snarled, "It ain't for you to ask questions, nigger! You answer! Now, how many spear catchers you got in there?"

Fox's voice dropped as his smile froze on his face. "If you're a cop, show your badge, otherwise get the fuck out of my face!"

The man opened his jacket and revealed a holstered gun. "That's all the badge I need. You understand me now, nigger?"

Fox raised his revolver and pointed it directly in the man's face. "Let me show you my badge, motherfucker!" Fox cocked the hammer with his thumb. "Why don't you go for your goddamned badge!" he goaded the man. "Go ahead and I'll blow a hole in you that your fat-ass mother could walk through!"

The man dropped back a pace and held his hands up. "Wait a minute! Wait a minute! We don't want to get jumpy here! We're not here about you boys. We're just after the fellow who owns this house."

Fox growled, "Ain't no boys in this car, motherfucker! Deshawn, get my shotgun out of the trunk!"

"What's your buddy doing to Rhasan?" Wayman demanded.

The man waved his hands placatingly. "He's just asking him a few questions."

"A few questions?" Fox challenged. "It looks like we got some ass-kicking to do! Look under your seat, Wayman, there's a pistol wrapped in a towel."

The man sputtered, "Listen, we don't want any trouble with you! Why don't we all step back and call it a truce?"

Fox and Deshawn got out of the car. "Ain't no truce, motherfucker! You in for a penny, you in for the goddamn pound! Get his gun, Deshawn!"

"Hold on! You don't want to take my gun!"

"Oh, no? Stop us from taking it!" Fox prodded and leveled his gun at the man.

Deshawn approached the man from the side and lifted the man's gun out of its holster. He tossed the gun to Wayman, then without warning he hit the man on the side of the head. Deshawn put his whole power-fully built body into the punch and the man dropped to the ground dazed, as if he had been poleaxed. Deshawn looked down at the man's body and snarled angrily, "Call me a nigger, huh? Nigger this!" He kicked the man in the kidneys several times.

"Hey, what's going on up there?" Tony called from the top of the stairs as he pushed a bloody-faced Rhasan ahead of him. "Victor, are you all right?"

Fox replied, "No, Victor ain't all right! He done fucked with the wrong people!"

Wayman moved toward Rhasan. "Rhasan? Rhasan, are you all right?"

Tony warned Wayman, "Keep back, you black bastard! Keep back or I'll blow his brains all over this pavement! Where's my brother? Stand him up!"

"He ain't getting up, motherfucker!" Fox retorted. "'Cause I got my foot on his head!"

Tony pressed the barrel of his pistol into the nape of Rhasan's neck. He ordered, "Do as I say, goddamn it, or I'll kill your friend. Believe me, I'll kill him!"

Fox raised his revolver and pointed it at Tony. He warned, "Soon as you pull that trigger, you're a dead man and so's your brother! Deshawn, move around to the other side of the car so you can blast away with both barrels as soon as he pulls the trigger!" Deshawn moved to take up the position as directed.

"Hold on, Fox!" Wayman pleaded. "He's got Rhasan, man! Both their lives aren't worth his!"

"Listen to your buddy, punks! Listen to your buddy!" Tony advised, still pushing Rhasan forward. "I'll trade your pal for my brother!"

Fox nodded. "We'll trade, but you stand where you are and send Rhasan forward. We'll send you your brother!"

"You don't fool me! I'm not giving up my cover! I'll send him forward if you put down your guns."

Fox retorted, "You'll be a dead motherfucker before we put our fuck-ing guns down!"

Tony was beginning to sweat. This was another job gone bad. How did it happen? He went after the one little nigger that was trying to enter the house and when he returned, there were niggers everywhere with guns and Victor was nowhere to be seen. It wasn't good. If any shooting got started, it would be the end of the Lenzini family. Tony grabbed Rhasan by the collar and jerked him backward toward the darkness and the safety of the stairs.

"Don't take another step!" Fox warned.

Tony stopped momentarily. "We got us a Mexican standoff here! It's a no-win situation for everybody. Let me get back to the cover of the house and then we'll trade." Tony jerked Rhasan backward again. "Come on, boy. I don't have time for lazy nigger shit!"

Rhasan, who had initially resisted Tony's efforts, suddenly threw his body backward, causing Tony to also stumble backward, and even with Tony's grip on his collar, Rhasan fell hard on his behind. Tony again tried to drag him by his collar to the safety of the stairs, but Rhasan's shirt separated in his hands.

Tony ordered, "Get up or I'll kill you where you lay!"

"I'm not going anywhere with you!" Rhasan shouted. "I'm not going to let you pistol-whip me again! Kill me!"

Tony cocked the hammer of his pistol and pointed it at Rhasan's head. His face was contorted. "I'm going to count to three. If you don't get up . . ." The threat had been made. Maybe he could scare them. He couldn't afford to lose his hostage, not while they still had Victor. He started to count, hoping against hope that the boy would get up. "One!"

Fox called to Wayman, "Bring me that nine you got. I think I can hit that fat bastard from here!"

Tony jerked on the back of Rhasan's shirt, but he still wouldn't get up. Tony pressed the barrel of his pistol against Rhasan's head and growled, "Two . . ." He didn't want to start shooting, but he wasn't just going to let some niggers kill him either. He had to show them he meant business. After waiting a moment for a response, Tony reluctantly said, "Three!" and pulled the trigger.

Friday, July 2, 1982

The day had not started well for Pres Cordero. He had spent his third straight night sleeping in his car and he had awakened at 5 A.M. stiff and aching from the experience. Since he still had the keys to KFRE, he drove over to the station and took a shower in the director's newly refurbished office suite. He put on a suit and tie that he had hastily thrown into his garment bag before he left his apartment and finished his morning ablutions. He had scheduled another morning of interviews at various radio stations, still seeking a site for his trainee program. It was hard sledding, but he felt triumphant when he completed his last presentation at a PBS station and the director offered him a deal that he couldn't refuse. Pres accepted the offer contingent upon final contract language and left with his spirits high. Now that he had a prospective home for his program, he could turn his thoughts to his own housing situation.

He had been sleeping in his car because two days after the incident outside KFRE the police had called to inform him that the two men who had attempted to kidnap him were small-time hoods who worked for various figures involved in organized crime. Both men had extensive rap sheets for violent felonies. It had taken very little for Pres to realize that these men were in fact King Tremain's enemies and that they wanted him because he was a friend of Jackson's. And it wasn't too much of a leap to connect Wesley's death, which had been headlined in the East Bay papers earlier in the week, to the same cause. Pres had gotten on the phone immediately and called Dan and Lincoln so that they could safeguard their families. At first they both had reacted with skepticism, but by force of argument Pres got them to take heed. No one could get ahold of Jackson; as far as his job was concerned, he was still in Mexico and they could not provide a date for his return.

As soon as he had finished calling his friends, Pres had gotten out his military-issue M16 rifle and his forty-five pistol and cleaned both of them. It was the first time since he was discharged from the army that he had picked up either gun. When he felt their weight in his hands, unpleasant memories wavered in front of his eyes, distorted images created by heat and distance. He began to think unsettling thoughts. What if he had to kill someone? Even if it was to protect himself, how would that make him feel? If the war had taught him anything, it was that there was no pleasure in killing. By the end of his tour he had seen all the dead and dismembered bodies that he wanted. There was no honor in war. It was merely a question of surviving the tour of duty. If you were lucky, you killed from a distance; when things got funky, you fought hand-to-hand. There was no philosophical connection between killing North Vietnamese and fighting for the "Free World." War was only about death. Nothing else.

Pres decided that he didn't want to stay at his apartment in case some other goons wanted to try to nab him. Yet he couldn't go to the house of anyone he knew for fear of endangering their lives. His modest income didn't allow him to stay in even a cheap motel for more than a few days, thus his car had become his dwelling. In pondering his problem, there appeared to be only one viable solution: Contact Jackson and have him get the dogs called off. He wondered whether Jackson even knew that his grandfather's enemies were on the move. He hadn't called or made contact with anyone since he had left for Mexico. The grim possibility that he might already be dead passed through Pres's mind several times, but each time he suppressed it. All he could really do was hope for the best and await Jackson's call.

After his last presentation was completed, Pres decided that he would drive over to Jackson's house and leave him a note; that would ensure that Jackson would contact him as soon as he returned. The sun, unfettered by clouds, was streaming brightly over the bay, raising the temperature to shirtsleeve weather. During his trip back across the bridge to the East Bay, Pres found the sun's brightness in sharp contrast to the shadow that had fallen across the community of his friends.

He arrived at Jackson's house around two in the afternoon after stopping at a local deli for a take-out lunch. He quickly left a note, but when he returned to his car the view and the isolation were so nice that he pulled his car a little way up the hill and sat looking out at the south bay while he ate his lunch. The air had been swept clean by evening breezes. Across the bay the San Francisco peninsula could be seen in sparkling clarity. It was a truly beautiful day. Pres had a few documents from the PBS station that he had to review, so he took them out of his briefcase and began to read. Perhaps it was the warmth of the sun, perhaps it was the boring manner in which the documents were written, or more likely it was the fatigue that had dogged his steps since he had begun sleeping in his car that caused him to fall into a deep, sound sleep.

When he awoke it was dark. He looked at his watch; it was nearly seven o'clock. He looked out his car window and saw someone who looked like Jackson's nephew Rhasan walking down the driveway to the stairs on the side of the house. Pres was about to roll down his window and call him when he saw a heavyset white man get out of a car across the street from Jackson's house and follow Rhasan down the driveway. The fat man looked familiar. Pres suddenly recognized him as one of the men who had jumped him outside KFRE. As Pres watched, another white man got out of the same car and walked across the street to the car from which Rhasan must have exited.

Pres flicked a switch to prevent the interior light from coming on when he opened his door and quietly got out of his car. He crouched down and scuttled down the hill out of view of the street and made his way laterally across the steep incline to Jackson's house. He had to pay attention to his footing, not only because of the slope, but he was also moving through some tall, dry grass that was quite slippery. He made it safely to the shadows of the house and stood a moment under the overhang of the deck. He heard the timbers over his head creak suddenly as a body fell heavily to the deck. He heard Rhasan groan in pain then heard the fat man growl, "Goddamn it, nigger! You answer me! Where is he? Answer me or you'll feel the butt of this pistol again!"

Rhasan hissed, "I've told you already! I don't know, you fat bastard! I don't know where he is!"

As Pres sought to move around the house's supporting pillars to the deck's stairs he heard some soft thuds and then more groans from Rhasan.

The fat man threatened, "Don't get smart with me, punk! I'll kick in your goddamn chest! Now get up, or I'll give you some more of the same!"

"I'm getting up! I'm getting up!"

Pres heard footsteps moving across the deck. They moved down the deck's wooden steps and started up the cement walkway along the side of the house. By the time Pres made it around to the deck's steps, he could just see the dim shapes of the fat man and Rhasan climbing the cement steps to the driveway. Moving as silently as possible, Pres followed them. When he got to the top of the steps, he stood hidden behind the corner of the house and watched. He saw Rhasan's friends push the crumpled body of the fat man's colleague behind their car. One of Rhasan's friends was armed with a shotgun while another had a snub-nosed revolver. Pres listened while the fat man exchanged threats with them.

The fat man tried to drag Rhasan backward, but Rhasan fell in the driveway and refused to get up. Pres slipped from his hiding place and began to steal forward, hoping to catch the fat man unawares. One of Rhasan's friends called to another, "Bring me that nine you got. I think I can hit that fat bastard from here!"

The fat man jerked on the back of Rhasan's shirt, but he still wouldn't get up. The man pressed the barrel of his pistol against Rhasan's head and growled, "Two . . ." Then after waiting a moment for a response, the man said, "Three!" and pulled the trigger.

Pres had launched himself at the fat man and was airborne when the man pulled the trigger. He had hoped to intervene before the man had a chance to get off a shot, but he was too late. The hammer of the pistol fell upon the firing pin with a dull click.

When the weapon didn't discharge, Tony realized that he had forgotten to chamber a bullet. He scrambled to pull back the gun's slide, but Pres's hurtling body hit him from behind and sent him sprawling. He scraped his face on the pavement and landed hard on his stomach. The air was knocked out of him. Still, he tried to roll over and load a bullet into the chamber, but Pres was on him before he could get both hands on the pistol. Pres's elbow smashed into his face, cracking his head against the cement. Then Pres was on top of him, preventing him from getting a rejuvenating breath.

Pres kept smashing his elbow into the man's face. He was trying to catch the man's windpipe, but the man's double chin prevented him from getting the killing blow. Pres kept on pounding the man's face until he no longer moved. When he was sure that his adversary was unconscious, Pres rolled off him and pulled the gun from his hands. He got to his feet slowly.

Rhasan, his face bruised and bleeding from several contusions, staggered erect and recognized his savior. "Uncle Pres? Is that you? Man, am I glad to see you! You saved my life! Thank you! Thank you!" He stumbled toward Pres, arms outstretched.

Pres hugged him and responded, "Thank God you're alive, not me! Thank God! It's a miracle the gun misfired!"

"You're right, Uncle Pres. You're right!" Rhasan bowed his head and closed his eyes. He prayed silently.

Pres bowed his head as well, but he could not close his eyes. He stared at Tony's unconscious form. He could not erase from his mind that he had just tried to kill the man, that he had meant to kill him.

Wayman walked over and put a hand on Pres's shoulder. "Uncle Pres, that's the fastest I've ever seen you move. You really took him down!"

Pres shrugged. "Three and a half years of recon in front-line Vietnam. If you don't learn how to fight well, you die." Pres paused and looked down at Tony before he continued, "And you never forget how to kill. It's easy to learn but hard to forget."

Rhasan, who had finished his communion, put his arm around Pres. "I thought I was toast! I heard the hammer fall! Then you came flying out of the night! What are you doing here?"

Pres dusted off his clothes. "I was looking for your uncle Jax, but it looks like I'm not the only one."

"Yeah, he was trying to find out where Uncle Jax is too! Who the fuck is this guy?"

"He works for the Mob. I had a run-in with him three or four days ago myself."

Wayman asked Rhasan, "You all right, man?"

"Yeah. That fat fuck chipped a tooth when he was smacking me around with his gun, but other than that I'm fine. Uncle Pres says that this guy is working for the Mob."

"No shit? The Mob, huh?" Fox asked as he walked over and kicked Tony, who had just started coming to, between the legs. Tony groaned with pain and drew his legs up into a fetal position. Fox snarled, "You in Oakland now, motherfucker! And you ain't got no business here!" He kicked Tony again. "Bring that other one over here, Deshawn!"

Deshawn walked Victor down the driveway, prodding him in the back with the shotgun. He asked, "What we gon' do with them?"

Fox suggested, "We ought to send them straight on down the hill in their car! That'll teach them not to send assholes into Oakland!"

"Fox, that's your answer to everything!" Wayman retorted angrily. He gestured to Tony. "You were going to let him kill Rhasan!"

Fox denied the accusation vehemently. "That ain't true! I just let him know that if he killed Rhasan, he was a dead man! That's all, so he knows it's no option!"

Rhasan said, "Fox, you and I've been brothers since the third grade, but I thought you were throwing my life away too! Bracing him like that with my life on the line! He was going to kill me, man! The pistol misfired! That's the only reason I'm here!"

Pres interjected, "We don't have time for this. None of us is the enemy. The enemy is on the ground. We need to spend time on what we're going to do from here, not arguing with one another!"

Victor spoke for the first time since Deshawn had knocked him unconscious. His tone was conciliatory. "Listen to him. We should go our separate ways. Let bygones be bygones. We weren't after you."

Fox exclaimed, "Ain't this a bitch. Now every little motherfucker think he can join in the conversation!" He pointed his gun at Victor's face. "Motherfucker, I absolutely don't want to hear what you think! So keep your goddamned mouth shut!"

Deshawn asked, "If we ain't gon' send them down the hill in the car, what are we gon' do with them?"

Pres ventured, "Well, I have a few ideas that will discredit them to their organization. From what I understand from the detective who called me, the DiMarcos have an old association with some of the people within this organization and the media knows about it, but has had no reason to exploit the fact. It's old news, but we could give them a new reason!"

Tony groaned and pushed himself to a sitting position. He put his hand to his bloody face. "These fucking niggers have broken my nose! My goddamned nose! I'll kill them for this! Niggers did this!"

"Nigger this, motherfucker!" Deshawn growled as he stepped forward quickly and kicked Tony in the side. The force of it knocked Tony over on his side.

Tony wailed in agony, "You niggers don't know who you're messing with! We'll come back over here and kill all of you! You're fucking with the Mafia now! Oh, God, my side! You fucking niggers are going to get it!"

"Well, if we're all going to get it," Rhasan said through gritted teeth as he walked over to where Tony lay, "I might as well give you back what you gave!" He kicked Tony in the face as hard as he could. Tony partially blocked the kick, but the brunt of it landed on his cheek. Rhasan moved to a different angle and kicked at his face again. This time there was a satisfying crunch as his foot smacked against Tony's face. Tony screamed in pain.

"That's enough!" Pres advised. "His screams will carry up here. The police will be notified any minute now."

Victor stared down at his brother and growled, "You fuckers better run to the ends of the earth, because we're not going to forget this!"

"Oh, yeah! Then remember this too!" Fox whacked Victor on the side of his head with the butt of his pistol. Victor fell on top of his brother and lay still. Fox stood over the two brothers and snarled, "This is Oakland, motherfuckers! Guns 'R' Us! We'll be waiting for you!"

"Let's get on with my plan," Pres suggested. "Now, I saw a house under construction just down the hill. . . ."

Later that night when Pres was sitting alone in a booth at Edie's Restaurant in Berkeley, his thoughts were absorbed with the events of the night. He was wondering whether there was anything that Jackson could've done differently to avoid all that had happened. It was obvious that King's enemies wanted him badly. If they were willing to attack Jackson's friends and family to get to him, how much leeway did he have?

Not the least of Pres's considerations was his own involvement in the evening's earlier altercation. He had tried to kill the fat man when he first attacked him. It was only due to luck or fate that Pres had failed in his attempt. He was at once grateful and saddened: He was thankful that he hadn't killed, but he was shaken by how little it took to make him want to kill. The whole sickening experience had taken him back to his years in Vietnam, back to the dichotomy of fighting in a war that he knew was being fought for all the wrong reasons, back to killing merely to survive, back to the smell of blood and the sight of mutilated bodies. It was as if all the lessons he had learned from the war meant nothing, that the commitment he had made to invest his time and attention into his community to atone for the lives he had taken was merely veneer. All of it could be scraped off like a cheap polish and the animal within him laid bare.

His thoughts rendered the food in front of him tasteless. He pushed his plate away and stared out into the deepening gloom, at the pedestrians of the night, strangers treading paths which were probably no less unsavory than his own.

Saturday, July 3, 1982

High in the Oakland hills a chilly morning breeze wafted through the small valley in which the Chabot Gun Club was situated. The sun had not yet cleared the eucalyptus trees on the eastern hills and its light filtered through their rustling, crescent-shaped leaves and brought no warmth. The sky was cloudless and eggshell blue. Off to the west the low-lying flatlands of Oakland and San Leandro shimmered in an early-morning haze. The pastoral quality of the view was diminished only by the echo of intermittent gunfire through the valley.

Jackson and Elizabeth walked down the hill along a paved path that led to the shooting stalls of the handgun range. He was carrying two hard-sided handgun cases. Elizabeth was toting an equipment bag and an ammo can. There was only one other person occupying a stall on the far end of the row of stalls. Jackson and Elizabeth dumped their cases and gear on a table. He began opening the cases while she looked over his shoulder. Inside one case were six revolvers and in the other were five pistols.

"You've got quite an arsenal there," Elizabeth declared as Jackson handed her a set of ear baffles.

"Just a few instruments of American leisure time," Jackson replied as he slipped a pair of baffles around his neck. He took out two matching, ivory-handled pistols and locked the slides back in an open position. "Wouldn't be America without handguns. What do you want to shoot?"

"I like revolvers. Let me shoot that long-barreled .357 Magnum on the end."

Jackson picked up the gun, flicked open the cylinder to ensure that it was empty, then handed it to Elizabeth. As he watched her check the gun he asked, "Where do you think Elroy is?"

Elizabeth shook her head. "I don't know. I haven't heard from him since the night we went to his house."

"I really enjoyed what happened outside your apartment. I haven't made out in a car like that since I was in high school."

Elizabeth took a deep breath and replied, "What I remember most is waking up with you the next morning, waking up and not feeling regret."

Jackson put down the pistol he was checking and said, "These last few nights have shown that the physical is just one of the many places where we meet." He stepped over and kissed her lightly on the cheek, and murmured in her ear, "I really loved making love to you, but I loved holding you in my arms as we slept just as much."

Elizabeth pushed away and looked at him appraisingly. She asked, "Do you really want children?"

Jackson smiled and replied, "Yes, lots of them. At least four."

"Why have you waited so long? You'll be forty in a few years."

"And you'll be nearly forty," Jackson retorted.

"Answer my question!"

Jackson shrugged. "I haven't had children because the relationships were never right. I've paid for a couple of abortions, but that's as close as it got."

Elizabeth declared emphatically, "I'll never have an abortion! If I get pregnant, I want to carry the baby to term and raise it. I'll never want to kill my own child. I don't care whether I have to raise it by myself. I feel very strongly about this."

Jackson frowned at her and commented, "I didn't know you were a pro-lifer."

"I'm not. I'm for the woman's right to choose. This is my personal choice. I'm going to give birth to any baby that I conceive. Be fore-warned."

Jackson smiled. "That's okay with me. If you get pregnant with a baby of mine, I'll want us to raise it."

A horn blared and the tinny voice of the range master roared out on an aging public address system, "Cease firing! Cease firing! Remove all bullets from their chambers, secure your weapons, and step behind the safety line!" After receiving the all-clear from the monitors, the PA system blared, "Hang up your targets and return behind the safety line." Jackson and Elizabeth strolled out across the uneven, grassy meadow to set their targets on the wooden frames.

Jackson observed as he walked beside Elizabeth, "I like being with you."

She smiled and replied, "You don't think I introduce everyone to my uncle Elroy, do you?"

"Speaking of your uncle again, it doesn't look like anyone has been in his apartment in a couple of days. I thought he might have taken a trip somewhere and maybe you knew where."

Elizabeth gave Jackson a sidelong stare and said, "That sounds like you've been in his apartment, or sent someone in, is that right?"

Jackson nodded while he placed red dots in the bull's-eye and on the corners of his target.

"Are you serious? Breaking and entering? What are you thinking?"

Jackson slipped his arm under hers and walked back to the stalls. "Just entering, no breaking," he explained. "I had to see that the file I had given him was still secure. If that information fell into our enemies' hands, we would have to take action immediately to protect him."

"We!" Elizabeth demanded. They walked under the roof of the pistol stalls in silence. She followed him over the yellow line and demanded, "Who is this 'we'?"

"It's a form of speech."

She moved to face him and through gritted teeth said, "I want to know! I want to know everything!"

Jackson sighed. "I have access to my grandfather's organization. His head of security is like an older brother to me. I've been living with him since I got back."

The horn blew the all-clear and the public address system squawked, "You may cross the yellow line and commence firing!" The sound of intermittent gunfire began to echo across the valley.

Jackson slipped on his baffles and walked over to his stall. He clicked home the magazines into his pistols. He picked up one gun and took aim at his target.

Elizabeth was suffused with a sense of dread. She watched Jackson calmly take aim at his targets and fire off measured shots. She wondered for perhaps the thousandth time whether she had misjudged him. She looked down at the revolver she had chosen, but the pleasure that she usually derived from shooting seemed to have evaporated. She leaned over the partition which separated the shooting stalls and demanded, "Have you changed your mind about leaving your grandfather's business?"

Jackson put down his gun and looked at her. There was a trace of exasperation on his face when he responded, "No! Just because I have access to the organization doesn't mean that I'm hatching assassination plots and organizing hits. I'm using it to find out about my enemies. Nothing more!"

"You're not planning to pick up where your grandfather left off?"

"I thought I made it clear that this is not my war. I don't expect to pick up a gun or organize resistance unless I am attacked. Right now I'm engaged in collecting intelligence. That's it."

"What was the purpose of entering Uncle Elroy's apartment?"

"Just to ensure there was no foul play, that he hadn't been attacked or kidnapped."

Elizabeth studied Jackson for a moment. "If he was, would you be willing to take retaliatory action?"

"That's a hard question. If he has been taken, it would certainly narrow my range of options."

"What does that mean? Would you try to get the assistance of law enforcement?"

"If there was a probability of arrest and prosecution of all involved; otherwise the law couldn't provide protection for my family or me from these criminals and you know it!"

There was something awry in his words, but she couldn't put her finger on it. "Tell me again why all this sudden interest in Elroy. Why would you trust him with critical information? You don't even know who he is!"

"Oh, I know who he is. I know who he *really* is. I don't want him to get killed because he hasn't been brought up to speed on the situation. Plus, I didn't give him anything that wasn't his. My grandfather left directions that if I wanted to bring Elroy into the family, I should give him that file."

"Are things that serious that they would kill him? He's never been a Tremain!"

"He's always been a Tremain!" Jackson corrected. "The reason he was raised in an orphanage in the first place was because the DuMonts kidnapped him and his mother when he was an infant. But I cannot answer for what these people will do until I meet with them. Nonetheless, for your information, I still plan on following the strategy I outlined earlier: giving up my grandfather's estate if that will permanently end all hostilities." He handed her a set of goggles and adjusted his own. "Can we shoot now?"

Elizabeth was not completely mollified, but there appeared to be nothing further to say. She could not, however, simply turn away. She pointed to Jackson's target and asked, "What are those red dots for?"

"Just to give me something extra to aim at; twenty-five yards is really not that challenging," he replied, sighting down the barrel.

"Oh, really? You're a marksman, are you?" Elizabeth asked as she watched him nod his head. This new information did nothing to allay her concerns. She steadied herself, but she had an ominous feeling that things were slipping away. She said without enthusiasm, "I used to be a pretty good shot myself but that was in another life."

Jackson was intent on loading a magazine with bullets. He did not see her expression or notice her tone. He pointed back to the target. "You're a good shot, huh? Let's create a circle of bullet holes around the outside edge of the bull's-eye, on the line that separates it from the next, larger concentric circle. The most evenly spaced shots win."

Elizabeth was surprised. "Are you serious? You shoot that well?"

"I used to. During the summers in Mexico, I used to practice shooting nearly every day, and during the school year my grandfather used to have a man pick me up once a month to go shooting. I don't think I've lost too much." He began firing from a standing position. After he had emptied both guns one after another, he took out a scope and a tripod from the equipment bag and set it up. He sighted the scope on the target and smiled broadly. "Take a look for yourself. Hell, this a stationary target at twenty-five yards with no time pressures. It's just a matter of getting used to the guns. I should be able to shoot bull's-eyes with either hand."

"You are good!" Elizabeth said, looking into the scope. "Very good. Where did you get this matched pair of pistols?" She indicated the ivory-handled Colts he was reloading.

There was pride in Jackson's voice when he said, "These were my grandfather's Colt National Gold Cup Series 70 forty-five-caliber pistols. He swore by them. He said he used the same basic 1911 frame in World War One. He had a gunsmith retool these for even greater accuracy." He fell silent, intent on laying out more ammunition. He quickly reloaded spent magazines and inserted them into his pistols. His concentration on his pistols was unbroken. He never stopped and looked at her before he stood and took several practice shots. He had pistols in both hands as he fired on the target. He stopped to check the result through the scope. When he commenced firing again he took measured, relaxed shots, letting the sights of the pistols fall upon his target as he brought his arms down.

The blush was gone from the rose for Elizabeth. The warmth and joy of the last few days had somehow dissipated in the last half hour. She no longer felt optimistic. Nor was she pleased by Jackson's inability or unwillingness to recognize how their recent exchange had affected her.

She was searching her mind for a way to broach the subject without letting her growing disappointment wash over everything.

Jackson was staring through his scope when he began to speak to her. "After I've had a little more practice, my accuracy will improve." He looked up and gave her a quick smile. "Why don't you fire off a few rounds?"

She had no reason why she shouldn't shoot, so she picked up the revolver and began firing methodically at the target. They finished out the shooting period and were standing behind the safety line when Jackson was hailed by Dan Strong and Lincoln Shue. The two men were walking toward the pistol range down the path from the registration office. Jackson beckoned in response and awaited their arrival.

"Goddamn, you're alive! Thank God for that!" boomed Dan. "We were beginning to think the worst! Where the hell have you been?"

"We've all been trying to reach you," Lincoln added. "Pres tried to get ahold of you just last night. He wanted to stay with you, but he ended up staying in a motel."

Dan put his big slab of a hand around Jackson's shoulder and gave him a bear hug. There was a look of concern on his face when he asked, "Where have you been, Jax? You had us worried to death!"

Lincoln also gave Jackson a hug. "Man, it's good to see you! Good to see you in good health!"

Jackson was a little surprised with the fervor of his friends' words and affection. He asked, "What's all this? I mean, I'm happy to see you guys, but—"

"Then you haven't heard?" Dan asked. "All the shit that's been going on?"

"What shit?" Jackson inquired.

Lincoln ignored his question and asked Elizabeth, "What's your relationship in all of this?" His tone was polite, but his manner was all business.

Jackson interjected quickly, "What's that about? This is Elizabeth Carlson. You met her at Justin's!"

Lincoln nodded to Elizabeth. "We still have to know whether we can talk candidly."

"She's with me. Say what you have to say."

Lincoln grimaced then said, "Wesley has been murdered."

"Wesley's dead?" Jackson was flabbergasted. He sat back on the table where the gun cases lay. He felt as if he had been kicked in the stomach. "How? Why?"

Lincoln answered, "He was knifed in the back and then his throat was cut. We read about it in the newspaper. His body was found the Saturday after you left in a Dumpster in Emeryville."

"In a Dumpster? Damn!" Jackson exclaimed as he put his head in his hands and closed his eyes.

"Yeah," Lincoln said without inflection as he took a long-barreled Ruger revolver out of its case. "Dan and I went down to the morgue with his mother and arranged to have his body taken to the funeral home."

Dan declared with an angry glint in his eyes, "I never want that particular job again! Old Mrs. Hunter tried to be strong, but when she saw his body she broke down. We had to carry her out. It was terrible. It made me want to fuck somebody up."

Jackson couldn't contain himself. "Do the police know who did it?"

"No. They asked us if he was involved in drug dealing. But we think we know," Lincoln answered as he finished loading his revolver. "Because that's not all that's happened."

"There's more?" Jackson exclaimed. "What else?"

Dan said, "Two men tried to abduct Pres outside KFRE the same day Wesley's body was found. The trainees from his program stopped them and called the police."

An expression of shocked concern flashed across Jackson's face. He questioned, "Was Pres hurt?"

Lincoln answered, "He was smacked pretty good with the butt of a pistol. The side of his face was bruised and swollen for a couple of days, but he's all right."

Jackson scowled and asked, "Who were the guys who jumped Pres?"

Dan said, "After Pres filed charges against them, the police told him that the men were small-time Mafiosi."

Jackson looked at Elizabeth and asked, "Are these guys in jail?"

"Not hardly." Lincoln chuckled humorlessly. "They made bail the very next day."

Dan added, "No shit! Last night when Pres stopped by your house he saved Rhasan from being killed by one of the same guys who had attacked him outside KFRE."

Jackson's jaw dropped. "What? Rhasan? Is he all right?"

Dan replied, "They chipped a tooth and gave him some lumps, but other than that he's all right. They were going to kill him, but the gun misfired."

Jackson was incredulous. "Why? He's a kid!"

"They were trying to find you. Other than that, all we really know is they carry guns and they mean business," Lincoln answered. "We've had to take precautions to protect our families. Dan has half the Samoan population guarding his house. I've got my wife and kids staying at her mother's. Tell us what's going on!"

For a brief moment, Jackson felt the old hatred for his grandfather settle in his throat, but the feeling was quickly whisked away by the realization that his grandfather was murdered by these same people. When he began to speak he felt only an icy anger. "I wish I knew! I had no idea these bastards would attack my friends and family. Believe me, if I thought this was a possibility I would've contacted you as soon as I returned." He turned and looked at Elizabeth and said, "They must've been following me long before I realized."

Elizabeth returned his gaze and shook her head sadly. Her premonitions had been right. The conflict was heating up and Jackson was going to be pulled into it whether he liked it or not.

Dan put his hand on Jackson's shoulder. "You can see why we began to worry about you." He dropped his voice. "When I received that coded message from you to meet here today, I was so relieved."

Jackson sighed and stared down at the ground. He questioned, "Why would they kill Wesley? Why would they attempt to kill Rhasan? What have they to do with my grandfather? It doesn't make sense."

"It may not make sense, but this shit is scary to those of us who have families and children," Lincoln said with a grimace.

"I'll bet!" Jackson acknowledged. "Damn! I'm so sorry that this crap has come down on you. Understand, I had no idea things would develop this quickly. I thought they would contact me and present me with some demands before taking action. I just wish I understood the logic behind their attacking my friends. What's the connection? Why would they come after you guys? How can you help them?"

Elizabeth ventured, "Ransom. They probably feel they will be operating from a position of strength if they have a hostage you care about."

There was a snarl on Jackson's face when he replied, "They could not have struck deeper into my heart!"

Dan nodded and asked Jackson, "Will you go to the police about this?"

"I have nothing to tell them! I'm not even sure who all these people are. Nor do I have evidence as to who was involved in these crimes. And if I had something to tell the police, do you think that would make these people change their minds about attacking you, or sending more people after me? You said that Pres filed charges against his attackers; did that stop that same asshole who attacked him from being at my house?"

Dan conceded, "No, it didn't, but this seems to have escalated awfully fast." Then he gave Jackson a long and steady look and asked, "Have you killed someone, Jax?"

Jackson looked down at the ground then answered, "I killed the men in Mexico who murdered my grandfather."

The range master's amplified voice squawked, "Cease firing, secure your weapons, and step behind the yellow safety line!"

"My God," Lincoln exclaimed. "Your grandfather was murdered?"

A scowl flashed across Jackson's face then disappeared. "It was an assassination squad. They were after both of us."

Lincoln raised his hand. "Man, I'm so sorry. We were so caught up in our own stuff that we didn't even ask about him!"

"That's why I didn't contact you. I thought they might follow me to your homes and I didn't want to endanger you. If I had known what they were going to do, I wouldn't have delayed."

"We know that," Lincoln affirmed. "We know who you love. Right now, we just want to know what you know."

Jackson said through gritted teeth, "I promise that I'll share what information I possess and do everything I can to ensure your families are safe."

Dan asked, "You think you can get the thugs to back off? Can you tell them we're noncombatants?"

There was an angry glint in Jackson's eye when he said, "These assholes haven't even contacted me and it doesn't seem to me they're interested in talking much. Despite that, I'll initiate a dialogue as soon as possible."

The all-clear horn blared and the PA system echoed that it was safe to cross the safety line and begin firing. Jackson said, "I need a few moments to gather my thoughts." He crossed the safety line to his stall and picked up a pistol. The regular discharge of his gun betrayed no trace of preoccupation. He seemed to be concentrating solely on firing his weapon at the target.

Dan and Lincoln exchanged looks, then they stared at Jackson's back for a while. However, after a few minutes their gazes fell upon Elizabeth. She returned their stares, shifting back and forth between their faces. After a few moments, she asked, "What's the question?"

Lincoln answered, "How much do you know about this?"

Elizabeth answered, "Not enough to tell you anything. All I can say is that he had no idea that any of you were in danger. He was thinking that he would have some time to work out an arrangement." Elizabeth stuck out her hand and said, "By the way, we haven't really met formally. Elizabeth Carlson."

A sad smile crossed Dan's face. "Pardon our manners, I'm Dan Strong and this is Lincoln Shue." Dan extended his hand. "We're Jax's oldest friends. He's told us about you, so we're happy to meet you and welcome you into our community. Although this isn't the best of times."

"Glad to meet you both," Elizabeth said with a brief nod of her head.

Lincoln shook hands with Elizabeth and said, "You're the first woman he's been excited about in years. Too bad you have to come along now. I hope when this is over we'll be able to welcome you in a more appropriate manner. But right now, we don't want any more of our friends turning up in Dumpsters."

Dan tapped Lincoln on the shoulder and pointed in Jackson's direction. "Look at those pistols he's using. I'll bet you they were his grandfather's. Look at those ivory handles."

"You're right," Lincoln answered. "We haven't seen those before."

Elizabeth asked, "Does Jackson have a lot of guns?"

Dan shrugged. "Is thirty to forty a lot?"

"That's quite a few," Elizabeth acknowledged, shaking her head. Of course, it was consistent with her recent feelings. The puzzle was falling into place and the picture was rapidly becoming clearer. She now realized, whether he admitted it or not, that Jackson would never walk away from this conflict. He possessed all the skills and wherewithal to carry on this war to its bitter end. He was merely a warrior who needed to be awakened, and the events of the past few days were enough to bring him out of his slumber. She knew this to be true down in the pit of her stomach. It seemed so obvious now, she didn't understand why she hadn't seen it from the very beginning.

Jackson walked up to the table and opened a box of bullets and began loading magazines for his pistols. Jackson turned and faced his friends and said quietly, "This is not the place to talk about this. Let's go someplace where we can have a little privacy. I have a proposal to put to you concerning this situation."

As he strode across the open meadow to get his targets, Jackson realized with foreboding that he would have to take some proactive steps in order to deflect attention from his friends and family. His situation was complicated by the fact that Carlos was in Mexico and not available for consultation. Nor would his decision be made easier by the expression he had seen on Elizabeth's face. It was clear that his dangerous and winding path into the future would be traveled without her presence. He swallowed his sadness and tore the targets off their mounts. When he looked at the shreds of paper in his hands, he felt he was holding the ripped tatters of his heart.

BOOK III

The Resurrection

Sunday, July 4, 1982

Dominique Volante Asti stood at one of the large wooden cutting boards, expertly chopping zucchini into thin slices. Her knife flashed in the bright kitchen lights as it cut through the soft squash and hit against the cutting board in a rapid staccato. Dominique moved swiftly through the large bowl of zucchini. She did not let her anger affect her efficiency. It was nearly eleven-thirty, time to open the restaurant's doors for the lunch crowd. Simple vegetable preparation should have been completed by ten o'clock. She was furious at the lack of organization with which DiMarco ran his business. Once again Mickey Vazzi, the prep cook, had called in sick and DiMarco, who had the responsibility of setting up the cash drawer and assisting in lunch prep, was nowhere to be seen. In addition, Carlo Luna, the head chef, had not arrived. Consequently, she had to reassign the waitstaff to lunch preparation chores instead of letting them set up tables with linen and cutlery.

"Rosaria, bring me the bowl of red bell peppers and I'll chop those before I go out and open the restaurant's doors. Did you finish washing the lettuce and cutting the tomatoes?"

"Almost, Dominique," Rosaria answered. She was a short, plump woman with rosy cheeks and short brown hair. She bustled over with a large metal bowl. "Here's the red bell peppers. We won't have all the tables prepared by the time you open up. Do you want to hold off opening until twelve?"

"Can't run a restaurant business like that," Dominique said with a shake of her head. "We'll prepare the tables by the windows first and seat people at those until we finish with the rest." She began cleaning bell peppers while cursing DiMarco under her breath.

Carlo Luna staggered into the kitchen with a huge box and set it down on the counter. He stared at Rosaria and Dominique performing their chores and asked, "Where's Mickey? He was supposed to have that finished this morning."

"He called in sick again," Dominique answered without warmth. "Where were you? You were supposed to be here."

"I've been to the fish market. I told Paul that I could get some good prices on fresh calamari, crab, and shrimp from my brother. Paul told me to go ahead. He knew I was going to be late." Carlo took off his jacket and washed his hands. "Did somebody take out the sauces? Is the minestrone on the stove?"

"Only the minestrone," Dominique answered. "I didn't know what the specials were going to be today. We've got to work out better communication. Nobody told me you were coming in late and I don't know where the hell DiMarco is. If we are going to run a good restaurant I need to know what's going on!"

"I don't blame you," Carlo said as he began moving swiftly around the kitchen. "I'll make sure to tell you my ideas for the next day's menus before I close the kitchen at night. You can go and finish in the dining room. I've got the kitchen covered."

Dominique took off her apron and went out to assist with the work in the dining room. At a quarter of twelve, she opened the doors for customers. There were two men waiting at the door. She showed them to a table by the window and informed them that lunch entrées were a bit delayed, but if they would wait she would provide the wine free of charge. The men declined the wine and indicated that time was not a problem. Dominique returned to her chores and told the waitress to be attentive to the two men. Several other customers entered and Dominique seated them and made them the same offer as she had the first two.

Nearly all the tables were set with linen and cutlery when Jackson Tremain entered the restaurant and waited to be seated. Dominique grabbed a menu and went to greet him.

"Would you like lunch?" she asked with a smile.

He returned her smile and nodded his head. "A table by the window would be great."

"You're just ahead of the rush hour, so I think I can squeeze you in."

Jackson looked around at the nearly empty restaurant and said, "I certainly hope so. It looks like people really knock one another down to get in here."

Dominique was in no mood for sarcasm. "We're running a little late today, sir. Perhaps you'd rather choose another restaurant. I can recommend several that are close by."

"No, I've chosen correctly. Sorry if I offended you. I know the restaurant business takes considerable work and investment of energy."

Dominique was mollified by the apology and as she led Jackson to a table by the window she said, "I normally have more of a sense of humor, but on days when people don't show up for work, I get a little crazy. It makes it quite hectic for the remainder of the staff."

"I know what you mean," Jackson said, sitting down. "I ran a bar on the east coast of Spain that served food in the late sixties and early seventies."

"I spent a lot of time in Spain," Dominique said. "Where did you manage a bar?"

"In Sitges, about twenty-four clicks southwest of Barcelona."

"I've been to Sitges!" Dominique exclaimed. "I was there in 1969! What was the name of your bar?"

Jackson replied, "The Taverna, but everyone called it the American Bar. We used to sell hamburgers and fries from four to ten in the evening."

Dominique took a step backward and said, "I've been in that bar!" She looked closely at Jackson. "You were the black guy behind the bar. You used to put on Jimi Hendrix's 'All Along the Watchtower' at closing time. I remember you! You and your roommates had an apartment on the beach and used to give wild parties."

Jackson nodded. "That was me!"

"This is quite a coincidence! What's your name?"

"Jackson Tremain, and what's yours?" He extended his hand.

"Dominique Asti," she said, shaking his hand. "Everyone called you Jax and one of your partners in the bar was a short guy with a Spanish name, but he wasn't Spanish. . . . It was Pres something."

"Pres Cordero."

"That's it! I went with him to one of the private parties you guys gave up at Villa San Miguel! He was a really nice guy. What ever happened to him?"

"Pres lives in Oakland. He will be very interested to hear that I saw you. He was truly heartbroken when you disappeared. You got under his skin."

Dominique smiled. "I'd like to see him again. He sort of got under my skin too."

"Thirteen years and ten thousand miles away; what kismet to meet you here," Jackson mused. "You're not related to the DiMarcos, are you?"

The mention of DiMarco's name brought Dominique out of her reverie. There were some customers waiting by the door. "No, I just work here," she said with a sad smile. "Pardon me, there are people waiting to be seated." She whirled away and went to the door.

As she was seating the second party at a table near the bar, she saw Paul DiMarco and Mickey Vazzi enter the restaurant. DiMarco went straight to the bar and got himself a shot of scotch. Vazzi saw Dominique and his pockmarked face broke into a leer, then he continued on into the kitchen. Dominique went over to DiMarco as he was downing his second scotch.

"We almost didn't open for lunch," she said in a flat, toneless voice. "There was no prep cook this morning and Carlo didn't come in from the fish market until after eleven."

"So? We're open now, ain't we?" DiMarco replied in a surly tone.

Dominique looked at Ernie, the bartender, who upon seeing the look found something to do in the storeroom. "As maître d' I need to know when people are not going to be at work, especially if I'm going to be responsible for opening up!"

DiMarco growled, "I don't have time for this shit!" He stared at her and thought he didn't care whether she was a trained assassin or not. His life was already in jeopardy because of the Lenzinis. The local newspapers had been full of reports of how they had been found in a house under construction, stripped of their pants and underwear and tied together. They had been arrested because they were both carrying guns and neither had a valid license for concealed weapons. The only reason he was still alive was that they hadn't squealed on him yet, and they wouldn't, if he found them first. DiMarco and Vazzi had scoured the town looking for them, but no luck. They had gone into hiding after making their bail. However, the police were now looking for them also, since discovering that one of their guns had been used in an unsolved murder. He had to find them soon or it would be his ass. They would sell him out to save themselves. DiMarco set down his glass and saw that Dominique was still waiting as if she deserved an answer. He pointed a thick, stubby index finger at her and growled, "I own this goddamn restaurant! Get it? Not you! You work here! Now get the fuck out of my face!"

Dominique was so angry, she was speechless. She stood silently staring at DiMarco. DiMarco reached over the bar and poured himself another scotch then picked up his glass and returned her gaze with a smirk on his face.

Rosaria came over and stood waiting for DiMarco to acknowledge her. He broke off his visual duel with Dominique and turned to Rosaria. "What the hell do you want?" he snarled.

"Sorry to interrupt, Mr. DiMarco, but one of the customers wants to talk with you," she said politely.

"Who?"

Rosaria turned and pointed to Jackson sitting by the window. "The gentleman at table twenty-six."

"What the hell does that eggplant want?"

"I don't know, sir. He said to tell you his name was Jackson Tremain, that you'd know what he wants."

The look on DiMarco's face changed suddenly. The smirk was gone and it was replaced by a sly, cunning look. "Tell Mickey Vazzi to come out and join me in five minutes." He turned and walked toward table twenty-six without another word to Dominique.

Jackson watched the compact, muscular DiMarco walk toward him. Jackson smiled broadly and sipped some of his red wine.

DiMarco came up to the table and said in a gruff voice, "Come on, you, we can talk in my office."

"If we talk, we'll talk right here!" Jackson replied with a smile.

"Listen, asshole, I'll drag you back there if you don't come under your own power! I don't have time to play with niggers!"

"Tsk, tsk, tsk, such language," Jackson said, shaking his head. "One would think that you don't need to negotiate. Why don't you try and drag me back there, runt! You'll end up hanging from a rafter like the Lenzinis. Come on, let's see how good you are!"

The blood was rising in DiMarco's face. It was becoming mottled with red blotches. "What did you call me?" he demanded.

"How about Neanderthal runt? Your mother must've been a dwarf! Of course, your father couldn't have been much bigger!"

The blood now drained from DiMarco's face. He stared glassy-eyed at Jackson. DiMarco wanted to strangle him slowly, to cause him pain, but there was a warning signal going off in his brain. After all that had already happened, he knew Jackson wouldn't come into his lair unprepared. And for Jackson to sit in his restaurant and taunt him, he had to have backup. DiMarco looked around and saw two men in long coats sitting a few tables away. They were staring at him. It looked like they could have shotguns hidden under their coats. He was not frightened by the two men, but he realized that if he had an altercation in his restaurant after the Lenzini fiasco, he would be dead before Monday morning. His own family would kill him. He took a deep breath and forced a laugh.

"Okay, eggplant, what do you want to talk about?" He pulled up a chair and sat down at the table.

"I want to talk about your family, dipshit!" Jackson said with a smile. "I want to talk about how you and they will die if you make another move on me or my friends. Your son and his wife at Colorado State, your arthritic mother in Gilroy, your overweight wife, your little girl at the Urban School, and last but not least, you. You'll suffer the same fate as your friends in Mexico!"

DiMarco was having a very difficult time restraining himself. He stared at Jackson unbelievingly. "You—you're threatening my family?"

"Yes, and I'll burn down your restaurant too. It'll look like arson. Everyone knows the way you're running this place, you're losing money. Everything you've ever worked for will be gone."

DiMarco was apoplectic. He roared, "I'll kill you myself! I'll tear out your fucking lungs with my bare hands!" Diners at other tables turned to stare at the cause of the commotion.

Jackson said to two old ladies at a nearby table, whose mouths were agape with surprise and fear, "Hard to believe this is the owner, isn't it? I haven't gotten the food yet and he's already talking about the bill! Hell of a way to run a restaurant!" Jackson saw a man come out of the kitchen and head toward his table. "Here comes the calvary to save poor Paulie. I think you'll need more help than that, Paulie."

DiMarco stood up and knocked over his chair. The only thing holding him back was the knowledge that his family would find out if any rough stuff happened in his restaurant. He leaned on the table and growled, "You're a dead man! I'm going to take pleasure in killing you! You better keep looking behind you!"

Mickey Vazzi walked up to DiMarco and whispered in his ear. Whatever he told DiMarco caused a look of consternation on his face. He turned to walk away.

Jackson called out, "Hey, aren't you going to tell me today's specials?" Neither DiMarco nor Vazzi turned to acknowledge his remark, but continued on into the kitchen.

Dominique had gone to the phone as soon as DiMarco had walked over to speak to Jackson. She called and left a message on an answering service. Within two minutes the phone rang in DiMarco's office. Unfortunately, Mickey Vazzi was in the office changing into his work clothes. He answered the phone. After he found out who was on the line, he obediently went and got Dominique.

She went into DiMarco's office and picked up the receiver. "Dominique here."

"Domei? That you?" It was Bonifacio Unzo, better known as Joe Bones. He was calling her by her family nickname.

"Hello, Uncle Joe," Dominique answered. "I'm sorry to call you like this, but I've got to request a new placement. This DiMarco is a total crazy fool. He doesn't know the meaning of respect. He doesn't care if this place is a success or not, and he insulted me in front of the employees. Right now, he's out in the dining room threatening to kill a customer at the top of his lungs. If I stay here, I may end up doing something he will regret. I can't stand him!"

"The family needs you to stay where you are. We may need you to do just what you desire. I ask only that you be patient. All things will be clearer in time. We are trying to keep things quiet until after the election. You follow?"

"That's in November! That's five months away!"

"There are other things that will occupy your mind in the meantime. You must be careful. I am going to tell you something that I was ordered to keep to myself. I am breaking my word, but I owe it to your father and grandfather to tell you. Pascal Langella has received permission from people in Chicago to clear away all debts. He is coming for you. I argued against it, but could do nothing."

"What? Haven't I proven my value?" Dominique protested. "I have performed every assignment successfully. Why am I to be a victim of a feud that started before my father was born? Langella killed my brothers, isn't that enough? As I swore to you, I have never attempted revenge. You promised that if I carried out the assignments, I would be free of threats and further attacks!"

"Sicilians never forget or forgive. It will never be over. Pascal has made his bones. He is a fully qualified man now and he has gone through channels and received the okay. There is nothing I can do. The Minetti family in New York has called in many markers for this approval. Remember, you cannot take aggressive action, or they will know that I have told you. They know I'm your advocate. You follow?"

"You mean I have to stay and play target while he comes for me? Uncle Joe, this isn't right!"

"Your only chance is to wait until he strikes. No one will blame you for defending yourself, but even then there will be problems. It's best if he disappears without a trace after he has made an attempt on you, particularly if the evidence leads away from you. I will argue before the families that you have once again proven your worth, that you deserve recognition and more assignments. But you must remember, if you can be linked to the killing of a qualified man, you will have to die. It is the law. If you kill Pascal, you must set it up like a hit from one of his enemies. Furthermore, there can be no evidence and no body. The lack of a body will make the matter easier to overlook. Nothing must taint this election!"

Paul DiMarco walked into his office and saw Dominique sitting at his desk and talking on the phone as if it were her office. His anger bubbled over. He leaned on his desk and said through gritted teeth, "Get off my phone and get out of my office!"

Dominique gave DiMarco a cold look and said into the phone, "Uncle Joe, it's DiMarco. He's throwing me out of his office." She listened for a minute and then handed the phone to Paul. "He wants to talk to you." As DiMarco went to take the phone, she dropped it on the desk and then stood up and walked right past him.

DiMarco stared at her as she passed and snarled, "Bitch!" He picked up the receiver and said, "Joe Bones! Didn't expect to hear from you so soon!" Dominique left the office and slammed the door behind her.

"Don't bullshit me, Paul! I told you that everything had to be shut down until after the election!" The angry voice issued out of the beige, plastic earpiece like a snake crawling out of a hole and it slowly coiled itself around DiMarco's neck. Joe Bones was not finished. "Eddie told me that you were still going after that eggplant, but I thought he was saying that because he didn't like you. I didn't believe you'd be that stupid! Anyone who causes problems in this election campaign is completely expendable. You follow? What do you know about this shit with the Lenzinis?"

"I don't know nothing about them! They probably got involved in something freelance."

"Don't bullshit a bullshitter, goddamn it!"

"What are you talking about, Joe?" DiMarco protested. "I'm doing exactly as you said! I just got a couple of men in the field, but it wasn't the Lenzinis. And nothing that I'm doing is going to disrupt the election! I'm closing down, like you said!"

"The Lenzinis are dead men. Edward's got people looking for them now. We'll get to the bottom of this eventually. How's Dominique working out?"

DiMarco was only too happy to switch to a different subject. "I've got to tell you, you've saddled me with a witch and she's really becoming a pain in the ass when it comes to running my restaurant. You cut off my other businesses, I understand that; it's for the election. But this woman is taking the bread out of my family's mouth. She's ruining my restaurant!"

There was a pause in the conversation as Joe Bones had a coughing fit. When he cleared his throat he said, "Don't worry about her. She's going to be taken care of. This is strictly for your ears. Pascal Langella has finally received the approval he has been seeking. He understands the true delicacy of the situation and has promised she will just disappear."

DiMarco offered, "I could help him. He doesn't even have to come out here. I'll do everything!"

Joe Bones disagreed. "You leave her be. She's Pascal's responsibility. You follow?"

"Got you. I understand," DiMarco replied with some disappointment.

"I talked to your pal Braxton and he told me that you and he were just trying to take control of the construction company for money-laundering purposes. I thought to myself, Why is he lying? Then I figured this eggplant is the grandson of that nigger we chased to Mexico. Back in the fifties. We covered it up, but I remember he hit our bankroll shipment good a couple of times. He got between six and eight million dollars. I guess I'm going to have to come out there and take charge of this operation. Everyone will want to wet their beaks. There may be enough cash to finance a small war in South America!"

DiMarco's heart sank. Joe Bones would take all the spoils for himself. At most, DiMarco would receive a small percentage of the wealth that he already had begun to count as his own. "When do you think you'll come out this way?" he asked in a subdued voice.

"I've got a couple of errands to run first. My jet is in the shop for overhaul, so my schedule is a little unsure. Hey, do you still maintain that sixteen-passenger jet at Oakland airport?"

The cold, unpleasant iciness of surprise dripped down DiMarco's back. He had purchased that jet secretly with money skimmed from the drug trade. It was to serve as his escape hatch should things ever go awry. He did not dare ask how Joe Bones had found out about the aircraft; he merely said, "Sure do, Joe. Be happy to loan it to you. How long do you think you'll need it? I'll get the crew ready to travel."

"Loan?" Joe asked pointedly.

"A matter of speech," DiMarco answered with a forced chuckle. "Of course, everything I have is at your disposal!"

"I don't need your crew. I'll send my own to come out and get the plane in the next week or so. I should be out there within the month. I wouldn't like to find out that you've taken further action after I've spoken to you."

"No problem, Joe," DiMarco said into the receiver. "I'll wait till you arrive. Everything will be kept on ice."

DiMarco returned the receiver to its cradle and sat quietly in his office. There was good news and bad news, and the good did not offset the bad. The good news was that Dominique Asti would soon be out of his hair, but the bad was that Joe Bones would replace her. It was like trading termites for army ants: Both could destroy you but only one would eat you alive. If DiMarco was going to keep possession of Tremain's holdings, Joe Bones would have to swim with the fishes he so often mentioned. Bones had many powerful enemies; if he disappeared there would be many suspects given consideration before the attention turned to DiMarco. DiMarco would have to be careful; Bones had lived so long because he was a crafty old devil who trusted no one.

In the cold storage where the fresh pasta, sun-dried tomatoes, olives, polenta, and other such goods were kept, Dominique removed her earphone clip from the junction of DiMarco's office telephone line. She folded the earphones and placed them in her pants pocket. She now understood: She had been thrown to the wolves. Joe Bones was no advocate and had never been, he had merely used her to get rid of his enemies. He was an opportunist. If she was killed, he would take credit for handing her over; if she survived, he would use that to his advantage as well. She smiled coldly. Perhaps she could throw a wrench in their plans. She returned to the dining room and seated a party of four with a smile.

Las Vegas's afternoon sun shone brightly through the penthouse windows of Joe Bones's spacious rooftop apartment. He was lying barechested directly in the sun on a custom-made sofa. He liked to feel the sun on his aging skin, no matter what his doctor said. It was hard to believe that good, clean sunlight was bad for the skin. As the sun baked into him, creating a sense of warmth, he thought of his good fortune. It looked like the troublesome problem of Dominique Asti would soon be settled. Perhaps when he had heard that she had made her final Communion, he would stop looking over his shoulder for her. Bones knew that it was only luck that had prevented her from discovering that he had set up her father and brothers' demise.

The Volantes had grown powerful and rich in Las Vegas and had created envy in many hearts, not the least of which were the Minettis'. Bones had rocked the baby Dominique on his knee. But he had realized that if he was to ascend to the power that was rightfully his, he would have to remove the Volantes from his path. There were many hands that were willing to assist in such an enterprise, but Bones had been judicious. He didn't involve anyone he could not later eradicate. Bones was never a suspect. If he had made one mistake, it was sparing the life of the baby Dominique. Little did he know that she would grow into a polished assassin. Fortunately, Pascal Langella had a reputation equal to the task.

Bones stood up and rang a small brass bell for his fitness coach. A tall, muscular brunette answered the ring and assisted him out of his silk pants and helped his frail body into the wonderful, relaxing warmth of his Jacuzzi. Once in the bubbling water, he thought of DiMarco: an expendable pawn. Bones had not told anyone in the organization about Tremain's fortune for good reason. Soon he would have DiMarco's jet and all the money that the nigger Tremain had stolen. He would have it all to himself. Bones reminded himself to send fifteen thousand dollars with a note of thanks to Tavio Vazzi. His brother Mickey had been indispensable. Joe Bones sank deeper into the bubbling water. It seemed to take the ache out of his tired, old muscles.

Sunday, July 4, 1982

The evening sky was filled with splashes of color from distant fireworks as the taxi jerked and bounced over the rough cobblestone pavement of the bridge leading into Algiers. It was a warm and humid summer night. Serena sat huddled in the darkness of the backseat. The sweltering shadows of the cab's interior provided a cozy haven of security for her. This trip was her first foray away from her hotel room since she was brought in from the funeral in a semiconscious state. She had stayed in her room, living off room service without opening the curtains or lifting the blinds for nearly a week. She hadn't even turned on the lights at night. She had wanted to stay wrapped in darkness. The light garishly revealed too many past mistakes. She felt the burn of acid in the back of her throat. Her stomach was upset, as it had been much of the time since the funeral. As she looked southward a particularly bright and colorful firework exploded across the dark blue of the heavens. Just as the sparkling colors faded, a low, rumbling thunder rolled past. It sounded to her like the earth itself had indigestion.

The taxi pulled up to the curb in front of a rundown hotel. The hotel's unlit marquee was so weathered and worn that Serena could not read it in the darkness. The cabdriver, a short, stout, white man with a porkpie hat, got out and went up to talk with two black men who were lounging around the hotel's entrance. The driver returned to the taxi and got in behind the wheel. While he turned the cab in a U-turn he explained, "Sorry, missus, Sister in Desire this day. I take you now. I take you direct."

Serena stared out the windows at a passing landscape that was totally foreign to her. Although she had spent her youth in New Orleans and its surrounding environs, she was totally unable to orient herself to the ways the city had changed in the fifty-plus years since she had last visited. Unfamiliar neighborhood passed after unfamiliar neighborhood, but she could tell when she entered the colored area of the city. She was surprised to see that electricity and neon lights were everywhere, even in the colored quarter. The taxi drove into a dark, narrow alley behind an old tenement. There was one street light at the entrance to the alley and that light did not illuminate the unlit doorway to which she was directed by the driver. Before she paid him, she asked him to wait for her, but he shook his head. He told her that the neighborhood was too dangerous and that she should call a cab when she was ready to leave.

She paused a moment before she handed the driver the fare, wondering if perhaps she should discontinue her quest and return to the relative safety of the hotel. But she realized that she had no choice and pushed money into the man's hands. She was on the verge of madness.

The full weight of her past decisions had fallen upon her and crushed her to the floor, leaving her listless and vulnerable to the predations of every ghost borne of vengeance. She had spent five terrible days trying to stay awake because the moment her eyes closed she was transported to some horrible place where she was surrounded by angry crowds that shouted and screamed hateful words at her. That dream would have been bearable had she been able to relegate it as simply a figment of her unconscious mind, but she couldn't. Everything she experienced had the look and stench of reality.

She dreamed one night that she had to sit immobilized while her brother, Amos, lined up every adult and child in the mob to walk by and slap her. The next morning the left side of her face was raw and sore, and she had trouble moving her jaw. Several times she had awakened and caught herself screaming at the spirits in the emptiness of her hotel room. Her waking hours were not much better. King was able to visit her in her conscious moments while the rest of the menagerie had to wait until fatigue delivered her back to them. King was enough. He was merciless, pointing out her every mistake, deriding the smallness of her intention and ridiculing her vanity. She found herself arguing furiously with him, talking aloud as if he were actually standing before her in the flesh. The colored hotel maids who came to clean her room were afraid of her. They whispered in her presence. One of them had even flashed a gris-gris several times when she thought Serena wasn't look-

ing. Serena recognized it as a charm against harmful spirits. She had inquired if the maid knew of Sister Bornais. The maid had nodded. Sister
Bornais was very famous and she was still alive. Serena knew right then
she had to see her. She had to find out if there was some way to escape
the pain, a way to escape the creatures of her guilt. As the cab pulled
away from the curb, Serena turned and walked into the darkened doorway.

A large, solid wooden door barred her entrance. In the dim light, she
saw an iron knocker in the middle of the door and used it to announce
her arrival. She waited several minutes and there was no response. She
pounded the door with a second, more sustained effort and the door
swung open. A large, beefy, dark-skinned man with gold front teeth
stood in the doorway. He put a beer bottle up to his lips and drained
half of it then looked at Serena. His gaze was not inviting when he
asked, "Yeah?"

"I'm here to see Sister Bornais."

"It's July fourth! It's a holiday! She ain't working today!" The man
started to shut the door.

Serena was nearly frantic as she pleaded, "Please! Please! Ask if she'll
see me! I'll pay her generously for her time!"

The man made a gesture of reluctance and asked, "What's yo' name?"

"Serena Tremain! King Tremain's wife!"

The man closed the door partway while he whispered to someone
who was behind it. There was a few minutes of muffled give and take
and then he opened the door again and said, "Jes' a minute. We gon'
check if she seein' anybody today." He took another gulp of his beer
then pushed the door shut until there was barely a sliver of light coming through the doorway.

Several more minutes passed as Serena stood quietly in the darkened
doorway. She was praying that Sister Bornais would see her. She could
not afford to be sent away. There was no one else to whom she could
turn. She heard faint laughter from somewhere behind her in the darkness. She recognized the voice. It was King Tremain's. The problem
was that she couldn't tell if the sound originated in her head or if there
was really someone behind her who just sounded like King. She turned
and stared into the dim shadows of the street. With only the distant
streetlight at the end of the alley for illumination, there was not much
to see. She heard some rustling sounds punctuated by loud squeaks

around the garbage cans across the alley. She shuddered. It sounded like foraging rats. She held her purse in front of her chest and turned back to the door.

The door swung open and the man with the gold in his teeth beckoned her inside. As she started through the door a garbage can lid across the alley slid off and clanged to the pavement. The man pushed past Serena and shouted, "Goddamned rats!" He threw his beer bottle in the direction of the cans. Serena heard it shatter amidst loud squeaking and then saw the dim, humped-back shapes of large wharf rats scurrying into the darkness.

Serena was led up some rickety stairs and down a hall to a large room in which a pungent incense was burning. The room was lit by one standing lamp with a large, conical shade which stood next to a small round oak table that was placed in the center of the room. There were two high wingback chairs on opposite sides of the table. Along the walls were couches covered with knitted throws and all the windows had heavy, dark-colored curtains. Serena was seated in one of the chairs and left to await Sister Bornais's arrival. Serena stared around the room. Since the lamp focused most of the light on the table in the center of the room, the walls and periphery were dimly lit, but Serena could discern that there were numerous ornate astrological charts on the walls. Other than the charts, there was no evidence that a voodoo woman was in residence.

Sister Bornais was rolled into the room in a wheelchair by the same man who had met Serena at the door. He took the other wingback chair and put it against a wall next to a couch. Sister Bornais was wheeled up to the table and into the light. The years had been kind to Sister Bornais. Even though she was reputed to be over a hundred years old, her face was relatively unlined and her eyes were still sharp. The man stood beside her and waited for a signal. She gave him a quick nod and he backed away from the table and left the room. Sister Bornais said nothing. She studied Serena, nodding her head as she did so as if she was confirming her intuition.

Serena grew uncomfortable in the silence, which stretched into many minutes. She attempted to explain. "You may not remember me. We met at the—"

"I remember you," the old lady interjected in a trembling voice. "You was King's woman. It was almost sixty years ago, but I remembers you."

"I c-came be-because I need—"

"I knows why you came! I could feel yo' haints while you was at the front door. You got both the unborn and the dead followin' you, 'cause you didn't listen to me. You didn't follow my advice. You spurned my gift of seein' then, and now you come for help when it's too late. You want to close the door after the demons done got free. They visit you every night, don't they?"

Serena mumbled, "Wha-what do you mean?"

Sister Bornais smiled and her dark eyes flashed. "Every time you close yo' eyes, you got somebody talkin' to you. You can't find no rest in sleep, 'cause all them peoples you wronged wants they day in court, huh? You got chil'ren that was never borned talkin' to you, don't you? They wants to make sure you know what you done, ain't that right?"

Sister Bornais's insight completely disarmed Serena. She could do nothing but nod in confirmation.

"They yo' brother's and sisters' chil'rens. They numbers was picked, but you canceled they turn to live. 'Cause they had a right to life, they gon' get some of that through you. They gon' live in yo' mind and yo' thoughts."

Serena began to sob. She dabbed at the tears with her handkerchief. She pleaded, "What can I do? They're talking and screaming at me all the time! I'm going crazy! It's too much! I can't take it! It's too much weight. Please tell me, what can I do?"

"The problem is, you can't undo! You had a chance and you didn't take it. More'n that, you broke an oath you done signed in yo' own blood, and 'cause of that you done doomed some more of yo' kin to an early grave. They gon' die soon too. You can't undo what's been did. It's done."

A young woman entered the room carrying a small tray with two teacups. All that Serena really noticed about her is that she had her hair braided around her head into the shape of a horn. The woman set the tray on the table and departed as quickly as she had entered.

Sister Bornais gestured to the cup. "Drink yo' tea. It'll steady yo' nerves."

Serena's hand trembled as she picked up the cup. There was a pleading look on her face when she asked, "Isn't there something? Some way? I would give my life to correct what's been done."

Sister Bornais snorted with indignation, "Yo' life ain't worth nothin'!

You done lived it! Used it up! Yo' milk done curdled; can't nobody drink it! You ain't got nothin' to trade with! You think you gon' trade moldy bread for fresh with demons?"

Serena was incredulous. She set her cup down. She stared at the old woman, who returned her gaze with an unblinking eye. Serena had never given any thought to the possibility that there was no escape from her situation. She thought of all the clamoring voices that populated her sleeping hours and shuddered. She held her handkerchief to her mouth and gasped, "You mean there's nothing I can do? There's no hope for me? I was told that I was going to live a long time! Over a hundred! I still have plenty of life left!"

"Drink yo' tea! I'll tell you what I see in yo' leaves."

Serena picked up her cup again. Her hand was unsteady. She had to grasp the cup with both hands to get it to her lips. The hot liquid had a sweet, mint flavor and it coursed down her throat, suffusing her with warmth. She drank the whole cup in a few gulps and set it down.

Sister Bornais reached a wrinkled hand across the table and pulled the cup to her. She stared into the cup for several minutes then demanded, "Let me see yo' hand."

Serena offered her hand and was surprised at the strength of Sister Bornais's grip. The old lady's claw of a hand held her palm up in a tight clasp. She studied Serena's hand intently, then looked back and forth between the cup and the hand several times.

Sister Bornais released her and said, "You is gon' live a long time, but it's a punishment. Yo' life is gon' be lonely and unhappy. You ain't gon' have no family to speak of 'round you. You gon' be sick a lot. You gon' sink into yo' grave bit by bit. Wouldn't surprise me if you ended up in some kind of crazy house. It's gon be bad."

The air seemed to go out of Serena as she wilted and put her head in her hands. Minutes passed in silence. She could not speak. A hell beyond her worst fears loomed in front of her. In the background, faint sounds of distant conversations wafted toward her. She didn't know if they were real or a product of her unconscious. She knew only that she was on the road to madness and that she was helpless to stop the disintegration by herself. Sister Bornais had offered no buoy or beacon to help traverse the sea of darkness in which Serena now struggled. Serena prepared to leave. She pushed back from the table and said with sad politeness, "Thank you very much, Sister Bornais, for seeing me on such short notice. I have money to pay for your time. Just tell me the figure. I'll pay up and leave you to your holiday."

"I ain't doin' this for money and I ain't doin' it for you!" Sister Bornais declared haughtily. "I'm doin' this for King's seed. If you can straighten things out, it'll be better for all y'all."

"But-but, you said there was nothing I could do to change things. How can I straighten things out?"

"There's always a way out!" Sister Bornais snapped. "The problem is, it's a hard and windin' road. It's a path that goes through courage, generosity, and compassion. Travelin' that road ain't only about bein' strong and stubborn. You got to be pure in yo' intention, like the Bible say, with generosity and compassion. Can't be no pretendin'! It got to be real!"

"Tell me what to do and I'll do it!"

"That's the problem! Ain't nothin' as unpredictable as the human spirit when it comes to learnin' and doin' right. I can always see the bad 'round the corner befo' it comes. I can sometimes see good too, but the path of true generosity and compassion is always cloudy. I can't tell you what to do. You got to find it for yo'self! Only you know what's real in yo' heart. That's what makes it so hard a road to travel. Ain't no signposts. Ain't no maps. Only yo' heart can find the way and yo' heart got to be pure."

"How do I show my heart is pure?"

"Can't tell you that neither. You just got to be ready when the times comes. If'en you's up to it, you'll make it; if not, yo' life gon' be a livin' hell!" Sister Bornais rang a little bell on the arm of her wheelchair and the young woman who had served the tea came into the room and waited for direction. Sister Bornais gestured that she should be wheeled out and the woman moved to do her bidding. Before she was wheeled away, Sister Bornais said to Serena, "There ain't no charge for my services. I'm repayin' my debt to King Tremain. You wait downstairs and Junior will give you a ride back to yo' hotel." The woman pushed the wheelchair out the door without waiting for a response from Serena.

Serena stood up slowly. She was exhausted. She didn't know what she was going to do. She was alone in Bedlam and only ghosts walked the floor of her cell. There was no thought of going home. She was afraid to return to California in her delicate mental state. She didn't want anyone, particularly people she knew, to see her in her present condition. She had resolved that she would remain in New Orleans until she had matters under control. As she walked down the stairs, she realized that she might even die without ever returning to the Bay Area. She sat down on a small bench by the door and saw the woman with the braids come down the stairs and go into a room where a television was blaring some sports event. There was a muffled conversation, then she heard the man with the gold teeth exclaim angrily, "Why I got to take her? It's in the middle of the damn game!" More muffled conversation ensued. Then another explosion from the man: "She gon' have to wait. I ain't leavin' to carry nobody nowhere right now! Shoot! This the playoffs and they be bowlin' for thirty thousand dollars! It's the ninth frame! This here high yella' gal done got the chance to win it all! Shoot!"

The woman came out of the room shaking her head. She walked over to Serena and said, "Junior is going to give you a ride back to the hotel. You may have to wait a bit. If my great-grandmother wasn't resting right now, she'd make him take you this instant. Can you wait until Junior comes to his senses? I don't dare disturb her unless it's an emergency."

Serena had no energy to move at all, much less stand. She nodded, indicating that she could wait. The woman turned around and went back up the stairs and disappeared. There wasn't a moment of silence before she heard King's voice.

"Guess you found out there ain't no easy way out, huh?" His words were said right into her left ear, as if he were standing directly behind her. She would have turned around if she had not been sitting with her back to the wall. He spoke into her ear again. This time she could smell his cologne and his cigars. She could even feel the breath of his words on her skin as he said, "You havin' it easy. It ain't got rough yet. Wait till all them folks you robbed of life find a way into yo' wakin' moments. They lookin' for a way in right now. They's rippin' and runnin', lookin' hither and yon. They gon' find the way too. When they get here, you won't be able to tell day from night. They gon' put you in a loony bin."

Serena reacted without thinking. She replied out loud, "There's a way out of this! Sister Bornais said so."

She could feel him leaning over her shoulder as he spoke into her ear again. "Don't waste time tryin' to escape, there ain't no way out for you! You too small to find the way! I'm gon' walk with you until you's as

crazy as a road lizard in the desert sun. I'm gon' escort you all the way
into hell and we takin' the slow, scenic route." She felt the heat of his
breath on her neck as he laughed. Involuntarily she turned to make sure
that he hadn't somehow materialized behind her, but all she saw was a
wall covered with red-striped wallpaper.

Serena attempted to collect her thoughts. She swallowed. Her throat
was dry. She took a deep breath. She had to concentrate on what she
could see. She had to ignore sounds which didn't originate from a visible source. She focused on breathing deeply and regularly. King's laughter interrupted her thoughts. He was right in her ear again. If her eyes
had been closed, she would have sworn that he was standing right next
to her. "You think you got the key to sanity?" He chuckled. "Look up at
the top of the stairs. I brought somebody with me." Serena didn't want
to look, but she couldn't help herself. Slowly, her eyes climbed the stairs
until they came to rest upon a little girl. She was six or seven years old
and dressed in a white gingham dress with red bows. She was light-
skinned and had chestnut-colored hair, which was braided with rib-
bons. It was a scene that would have made Serena smile, if she had not
seen the look of pure hatred on the girl's face.

The girl started speaking as she slowly descended the stairs step by
step: "I would have been eight years old in May, if I had been born. But
I wasn't born because my mother wasn't born. And she wasn't born because of you. You made sure we wouldn't ever live!" The girl hopped
down two of the steps then raised up a crudely made doll in her right
hand. "I hated you so much, I made a doll of you out of your own hair.
And when I get so angry I could just pop, I stick the doll with this pin,
like this!" The girl pulled a long hairpin from her braids and pushed the
pin deep into the doll. Pain lanced through Serena's chest and abdomen. The little girl stopped and smiled evilly. "Did that hurt? What
about this?" She pulled the pin out then thrust it through the doll's
head.

Serena stumbled to her feet. The pain in her forehead was blinding.
She had to get out of the house. She had to escape the demon child.
She pulled open the door and staggered out into the darkness of the alley. The door slammed behind her and she was in complete darkness.
Initially, there was silence and Serena welcomed it, but then as her eyes
began to adjust to the darkness, she heard the rats again. They were
rummaging in the garbage. She turned back to the door, but decided

that she didn't want to go back inside. Once again, there was silence. Serena turned and saw the large rats sitting and staring at her. One of them took a few steps into the alley and tested the air for scent. Serena waited no longer; she stumbled out into the alley and made her way toward the streetlight.

Monday, July 5, 1982

"Are our lives still in danger?" Sandra Shue asked Jackson. She pushed her long black hair back from her face and stared at him; the slant in her dark brown eyes gave her a penetrating look. She was sitting on an ottoman in front of her husband Lincoln's overstuffed chair. "Should we expect more attacks?"

Jackson was standing, resting an arm on the mantel, pausing a moment to seek the best manner in which to answer her question. Although he had requested this meeting of his friends at Dan's house, he had not looked forward to it. He began carefully. "At this point, I'd have to say yes. Although I confronted the guy who sent out the Lenzinis, I can't guarantee they'll stop their depredations." He looked around the room at his friends. "I'm sorry about this."

"You're sorry?" Sandra shook her head. "Think about Wesley!"

"Hey," Dan boomed. "We started this meeting off on the basis that it wasn't about blame. We've got to keep it on that note."

Sandra explained. "I'm having a hard time with this. I've been pretty upset since we heard about it. How did we get involved in all this?"

Jackson shrugged his shoulders. "The only reasonable explanation is that they're seeking hostages."

"Why?" Dan's wife, Anu, shook her head. "Why do they want hostages? And why us?"

"I guess they think if they have one of you, they can force me to sign over my grandfather's estate."

"Why don't you just give it to them?" Sandra blurted out, her voice beginning to rise. "Give it to them and get them out of our lives! We have children and they are more important than any amount of money."

Jackson exhaled. "I wish it were that simple. It appears that there are a couple of different groups operating here and they want different things. I don't know that even if I were to turn over everything, that would stop them from attacking you. I know—"

"Why not?" Sandra interrupted impatiently. "You said that they wanted you to sign over the estate. Just sign it over!"

"Whoa!" Dan stood up and made a placating gesture with his hands. "We're jumping all over the place here. Jax is not the enemy. Let's give him a chance to explain. Why don't you take it from the top, Jax? Why are they coming after you?"

"According to the papers I've been reading, my grandfather wanted to make sure that I wasn't killed immediately after his death. . . ." Jackson went on to explain the origin of the lost certificates and how his grandfather had leaked their existence to his enemies.

After he finished, Anu declared, "You can't say that the old bastard wasn't smart."

"How much money are we talking about?" Dan asked.

"I really don't know yet, but it may be somewhere between seventy and a hundred million dollars."

Dan exclaimed, "Holy shit!"

Lincoln asked, "Exactly where are these certificates?"

"They were left in the basement of one of my grandfather's Western Addition apartment buildings."

Pres said, "I thought those had all been torn down years ago."

Jackson nodded. "There's a plaza over where the buildings once stood."

Sandra was confused. "How do you retrieve the documents then?"

"You have to go through the sewers," Jackson replied. "I guess you find the point closest to where the building stood, then drill through the sewer walls and hope that you can strike the subterranean vault of the old building."

"The atmosphere in a sewer is a mixture of carbon monoxide and methane," Lincoln concluded thoughtfully. He looked at Jackson. "How do you propose to get the certificates?"

"I don't. I'd rather let my grandfather's enemies fight for possession of them."

Lincoln said dryly, "If they were only fighting for possession of the documents, we'd have nothing to worry about."

"Let's not fool ourselves," Dan said from his easy chair. "We know

what they want! They want those certificates and they want to kill Jax."
There was a long silence after Dan finished speaking.

"I think Dan hit the nail on the head," Jackson conceded. "Unfortunately, it seems they don't care how many other people they kill in the process. That's why I'd like you folks to take my offer of one hundred thousand dollars and take a month-long vacation. I think things should be resolved by then."

"That sounds good to me," Dan exclaimed. "We sure could use the money."

"Just a minute," Anu said as she gave her husband a long steady look. She was a tall, solidly built Samoan woman who, despite giving birth to four children, was still shapely. She turned to Jackson. "What do you expect for this money?"

"Nothing," Jackson replied. "I'm giving you the money to go away, to get out of danger."

"Not all of us are interested in taking a vacation," Pres stated. "I'm interested in who these people are and what you plan to do to deal with them."

"Pres is right," Lincoln agreed. "I think we all could benefit from having the full picture and then we can make an informed decision. Who are we dealing with?"

Jackson took a deep breath. "There are three independent groups. The first are the DuMonts and they want to kill me because the Tremains and the DuMonts have been killing one another for over a hundred years. And then there is Paul DiMarco, the guy I confronted yesterday who threatened to kill me in his restaurant."

There were exclamations around the room.

Lincoln asked, "Is this DiMarco related to the attorney, Michael DiMarco, the mayoral candidate in San Francisco?"

"One of his nephews," Jackson answered.

Pres declared, "They're involved in organized crime. According to the *Bay Guardian*, the DiMarcos are connected to crime families in Las Vegas. The guys who attempted to kidnap me and the ones who attacked Rhasan are all working for the Mob!"

"Why can't you go to the newspapers or the police with this information?" Sandra asked. "Wouldn't that get these people off our backs?"

Jackson shrugged his shoulders. "I have no proof of their wrongdoing. I can't even link DiMarco to what happened to Pres or Rhasan."

"Who is the third group involved in this?" Dan asked.

"It's John Tree, the drug dealer."

Lincoln was incredulous. "You mean the guy who ran Tree's pool hall where we used play pool when we were in high school?"

"Goddamn!" Dan exclaimed. "These are some tough customers. Just how are you going to deal with them?"

"I don't know yet. I'm still collecting information. None of these people have made an effort to speak with me or express their desires, so I can't truly say that I know what will appease them."

Pres stated, "The last time we spoke, you were ready to walk away from it all." He paused for a moment then said slyly, "Do you want to hold on to your grandfather's estate now?"

Jackson reacted testily. "Nothing's changed! I'd walk away from it, if I could be sure that the hostilities would be over."

Anu was leaning against the doorjamb when she asked, "Have you told them that they could have the entire estate?"

Jackson shook his head. "No, I haven't. No one has contacted me! Truthfully, I don't know that I could trust them even if they did contact me. They killed Wesley before I went to Mexico. Then they assassinated my grandfather. During that time they tried to kidnap Pres and attempted to kill my nephew Rhasan. They don't appear to have a very high regard for human life. I can't be sure that even if I turn over everything, they won't try to kill me afterward, and I don't know what they could say that would make me trust them."

"This is the crux of the issue!" Pres challenged. "You aren't ready to give up a damn thing! You want to keep the money!"

"Who wouldn't?" Dan argued. "Hey, I don't think I'd trust these people either! And I sure in hell wouldn't give them a damn thing! Let's vote on the offer!"

"Let's not be precipitous," Lincoln cautioned. "I want to go back to how Jackson is going to deal with these people." He turned to Jackson and asked, "Are you trying to deal with all these thugs by yourself, or do you have help?"

Dan interjected, "He's got brothers. He knows he can call upon us if he needs to."

"Now wait a minute!" Anu declared angrily to Dan. "Your family needs you. You're not helping anyone fight thugs and criminals!"

Jackson said, "Don't worry, Anu, I'm not asking for that. I have my grandfather's organization to assist me. I just want to get you folks out of danger. I'll deal with these people once you're clear."

"How do you plan to stop them?" Lincoln asked Jackson.

"I'll do whatever I have to do, but I'll try talking first. The DiMarcos are in the middle of an election campaign, I'm sure they don't want their criminal activities to come to light. Tree doesn't have a large organization. Once he knows we're on to him, I think he can be brought into line."

Pres chimed in, "Are you prepared to kill?"

Jackson gave Pres a smirk then answered, "I'll do what I have to do, but you won't be part of it! That's why I recommended that you all take vacations until I get this cleared up."

Pres barked, "I don't want a damned vacation! I can't take a vacation! I've got to transfer the whole broadcast trainee project to this new radio station within the next month. I have to set up a schedule of meetings with the station executives and governing boards. I couldn't leave here if I wanted to. I won't let fifteen years' work disintegrate or dissolve because of this."

Jackson answered grimly, "Then be prepared to be on the alert and watch your back! Use the money for a bodyguard!"

Pres replied, "This money comes at a high price. This is blood money! You described it that way yourself. I think your decision goes against everything we've said we stood for. People will be killed before this is resolved. It doesn't matter what side they're on or who started it—someone will die. I'm asking you, don't make a decision that will domesticate your conscience! Because once you start down this road, you're going to have to tell your conscience to roll over and play dead. It's an unclean feeling that you can never quite rid yourself of! I'm telling you this from firsthand experience!"

Anu said, "You know, I listen and I listen, and it sounds like Jax didn't have much choice in all this! He said he'd give the money up if it would keep us out of danger. Nobody's contacted him. I think it's time to figure out whether we are going to accept his offer."

Lincoln disagreed. "Just a minute. We've got two teenagers and in the best of times they worry the hell out of us by roaming all over the city. We definitely need to discuss some type of security measures. Let me make sure I understand what you said earlier. You're offering us a hundred thousand dollars each to take a month-long vacation. Can you be sure this situation will be resolved in a month? We have kids in year-round private school. We can't keep them out of school if this situation drags on for any length of time!"

Jackson shrugged his shoulders and said, "I don't know what to tell you. I can't guarantee that it will be resolved. All I can say is that after a month, whatever you need to make your homes safe and your children secure, I'll pay for."

Dan said, "I think taking the vacation is the key for those of us with children. Anu and I have talked for years about taking the kids to Washington, D.C., then going down to Myrtle Beach to visit my mother's family. Now, we'll do it. Until we leave, we'll keep our pistols by the bed."

Pres interjected, "If we accept this blood money, we accept the karma that comes with it! This is a dangerous decision."

"Pres, you're a do-right brother and I love you," Dan said impatiently. "But sometimes you're really just out of the box! All money is blood money! There are a hundred tragic tales for every bill in your wallet."

Anu punched her husband in the shoulder and said in a softer tone, "I understand that you are speaking from your heart, Pres, but me and Dan could use the money. We got four kids, one starting college this September. He's going to San Francisco State because we can't afford to pay his tuition and board at Morehouse. Our other three would do better in private schools. Our house needs a new roof. And we're not even talking about the money we will need if Dan is to find a good nursing home for his mother. We're definitely interested in the offer that Jax is making."

"Sandra and I want to take it too," Lincoln added. "You know we've often sat around discussing what we would do if we had a little money. It appears to me Jax is offering us the opportunity. He's not asking us to kill anybody. We don't have to break any laws. All we have to do is stay on the alert until he can clean up the situation. I say it's a great and generous offer even though it comes with some risk."

"Don't forget," Anu said, shaking her finger, "a paid vacation. A four-star hotel with room service. We haven't stayed at a first-class hotel since the eldest was born!"

Pres stood and said with resignation, "I'll do what the majority decides, but bad karma comes with this money. And these are bad people. I've seen them up close."

Lincoln asked, "Are you referring to the ones you left tied together in that house down the hill from Jax's place?" Pres nodded.

"Ohhh." Anu pointed her hand at Pres. "I saw the article on those two in the Oakland paper. Whatever made you pull their pants and underwear off before you tied them together?"

"I wanted to discredit them to their own people, and I wanted to make sure it got into the newspapers. Did you see that one of the guns found on them was used in a murder last year? These guys are killers!"

"Yeah," Lincoln agreed. "That's what makes me concerned about leaving Jackson here."

"You're not thinking of helping him!" Sandra protested. "He said he's got help—"

Lincoln put up his hand. "You don't understand, honey. Jackson saved my life. I owe him big-time."

Sandra sputtered, "Whe-when was this?"

"Fifteen years ago, one night after Pres's sister's wedding."

"The Titans!" Dan exclaimed. "I've done my best to suppress that memory. But the truth is, he and Wesley saved all our asses that night. I was sure we killed some of them, but there was never any mention of it in the papers, nor any police investigation."

Pres shook his head. "It's a mystery I'm sure we'd all like to forget."

"Not me." Lincoln leaned forward in his chair and looked Jackson in the eye. "I've never forgotten that night and I want you to know if you ever need me, I'll be there. You can count on me." Sandra started to protest again, but Lincoln quieted her with a look.

Jackson was moved. "Thank you, bro. I hope never to have to ask you, but thank you."

"Let's vote and get finished," Anu said with a clap of her hands. "Talk, talk, talk! Talk is cheap when there is still so much to do like laundry, cooking, checking summer-school project assignments! We know what we will do already! We take the offer!" Anu looked around the room and received nods from Sandra, Lincoln, and Dan. She gave Pres a challenging smile and said, "That's that! Discussion over! Take a vacation, Pres."

Pres was resigned. He raised a hand in a gesture of concession. "If this is the will of the majority, so be it."

"Good!" Anu declared. Then she looked around the room and demanded, "Is there anything more that can be decided now?"

Pres admitted with reluctance, "I guess not."

"Then life must go on! Chores must be done! No more talking!" Anu clapped her hands. "No one else has four children! The Strongs must be organized big-time! Let's go!"

Everyone got to their feet and good-byes were being said when Anu called out, "Just because I rushed you all doesn't mean that I don't love you."

Lincoln waved from the door as Sandra said her good-byes, then the Shues went out to their car.

Anu said to Pres, who was standing by the door, "You, I worry about. Please be careful." She gave him a swift hug.

Pres returned her hug. "Thanks, Anu. I love you, too."

Jackson called out to Pres, "I gave you my number. Call me if you want a place to stay."

"I'll call you in the next day or so. But remember: Using violence to resolve a problem is like taking a strong medicine with side effects that are so immense they alone could kill you!" With that Pres waved and walked out into the evening air.

Anu squeezed Jackson's shoulder. "I must get the children to laying out their clothes for tomorrow. You be careful too." She gave Jackson a kiss on the cheek and turned back toward the kitchen, leaving Jackson and Dan standing at the door, talking.

Jackson said, "Your wife's got spirit!"

Dan rubbed his arm. "She moves too fast sometimes! She doesn't know how to hold back. I'm thinking about putting the old girl on Valium."

"You did real well not to interrupt Pres during his karma lecture."

"You saw that? I wanted to punch a few holes in Pres's goody-two-shoes speech."

"I liked what he said. Pres has a good heart!"

Dan put his hand over his mouth and belched. "I love him, but I swear to Buddha, whenever he starts bringing in Eastern religions to make his point I feel the forces of flatulence pressing on my abdomen."

"Everything gives you gas," Jackson observed.

Dan dismissed Jackson's observation with a wave of his hand. "By the way, whatever happened to Elizabeth?"

"She hasn't returned my calls."

"I knew when she just walked away at the shooting range that things had gone to shit. What are you going to do?"

"Nothing. What can I do?" Jackson answered with a shrug of his shoulders.

"Oh," Dan said as he recalled a forgotten point, "Wesley's funeral is next Sunday, and you know his mother has no money and his brothers are useless. I talked to the guys and we're paying for all the funeral costs, but Wesley was paying for all her in-home care. Without his help, she's going to be forced to move into some type of home. We thought you—"

"Not even an issue," Jackson interjected. "I'll take care of everything. She still has other sons who will be there for her."

"That's what makes you my brother."

"I love you too, man. I'm just so sorry that it had to come down this way." Jackson turned away with a wave and walked sadly to his car. The full weight of Wesley's death was just beginning to sit upon his shoulders.

Dan shouted to him as he drove away, "Take care of yourself, bro, and keep your pistol cocked!"

Tuesday, July 6, 1982

Jackson awoke from a restless night's sleep. He had been dreaming of the last summer he had spent with his grandfather. It was not a pleasant dream. It always started the same way. His ears were filled with the sounds and images of gunfire and explosions. Laid on top of that were the wailing screams of people in pain. He was in a darkened room in which a hand grenade had exploded. He was stepping over the mangled bodies of women and children, and despite the darkness he was able to see their bloody faces. Thus did his night continue until the soft light of early morning brought him a tired but grateful wakefulness.

The demon faces of the dead departed with the sun's arrival, but they left a sense of foreboding which oppressed him. Trying to shake off his distress, Jackson moved steadily through his morning routine, but the malaise clung to him like a wet suit. Wesley's death and the attacks on Pres and Rhasan had shaken him. Yet he really couldn't focus on those issues, because he was distracted by thoughts of Elizabeth. She had departed the shooting range without a word. She hadn't returned any of his calls. Every time he thought of her he felt a pain in his chest as if it were being squeezed by a vise.

He turned on the shower and got into it before the water had warmed up, hoping that the coldness of the spray would bring the alertness and clarity that he seemed to lack. Instead, the cold water merely confirmed his sense of foreboding. After his shower and shave, he donned his sweats and went down to the kitchen to get coffee.

Carlos, also dressed in sweats, was sitting at the table staring out the window at Alamo Square Park when Jackson walked into the kitchen with a towel, drying his hair.

"Is there any coffee left?" Jackson asked as he rubbed the towel over his head.

"There's the end of the pot." As Carlos watched Jackson pour himself some coffee he said gruffly, "I wish you'd stop acting like you're playing a game. These people are killers. You think you can go around counting coup and it will mean something. These assholes will shoot you right off your horse just like they did the Indians. I go out of town for a few days and you do something stupid!"

Jackson sat down across the table from Carlos and replied, "Carlos, you can't kill everyone. This isn't Mexico. All I did was tell DiMarco to stop bothering my friends. His family is in the midst of an election, what can he do?"

"It's a good thing you didn't try the same thing with John Tree. You might not be standing here now. Let me tell you the only reason your enemies haven't done more is that they don't trust one another. We don't want them to coordinate their actions. We want to catch them unawares." Carlos looked Jackson in the eye and said, "Anyway, I'm more concerned about your mind-set and your strategy. You've weakened your position."

"How?"

"You've given DiMarco information. He knows now that you are someone to contend with. He will be more careful, more guarded. If I knew exactly what you said, I could probably point out more information you gave away. And as important, you have blown the element of surprise."

"I thought I'd make him consider his actions more carefully."

Carlos rebutted, "We don't want him to consider his actions more carefully! We want him to feel secure, that there is no one to challenge him. Overconfidence self-destructs against a prepared opponent. You gained nothing. Making yourself known to him will not stop him. The only thing deterring DiMarco is the election. Understand you're being hunted now. They know that you are the only one authorized to sign over ownership of the documents and that this can only be done at the Central Bank in downtown Oakland. They're working hard trying to find you."

Jackson nodded his head. The logic of Carlos's words was irrefutable. He stared out the large window that overlooked Alamo Square Park. He remembered when the thought of going to the park filled him with anticipation. Sounds emanating from the kitchen interrupted his musings. The banging of pots and pans seemed strident. He had not yet grown used to having Theresa perform all his domestic chores.

Jackson stood up tiredly and said, "I've got to make a phone call." Theresa smiled at him when Jackson went past the kitchen sink to use the phone in the living room. He called Elizabeth and left a message on her home phone, then rejoined Carlos at the breakfast table.

Carlos smiled and asked, "You called the woman? The one you're dating?"

Jackson countered, "Is everything your business?"

Carlos smiled even more broadly and said with a tilt of his head, "Only when it comes to your safety. You must know that this is a dangerous time to get involved. You might be jeopardizing her life as well. Have you thought this out?"

"I haven't thought anything out. But it doesn't matter. She and I are over. She doesn't want to see me again. She won't return my calls. It seems that the criminal aspects of my new life aren't appealing to her. I can't say that I'd be thrilled to get involved with a woman who admitted to me that she had killed in the past and might kill again in the future. I'd be looking for the door before she got my address."

Carlos studied Jackson and observed, "You really like her, eh?"

"More than I knew. She sort of stays on my mind."

"Well, let's change the subject," Carlos said with a sigh. "You ready to work out?"

Jackson said, "You really want to do this knife stuff seven days a week, Carlos?"

"Fate rewards preparation. It punishes those who underestimate the level of will and discipline it takes to survive and win." Carlos paused to let his words sink in, then asked, "Are you ready to work out now?"

Jackson nodded his head resignedly and stood up. He followed Carlos down the stairs to the basement workout area and showers. The workout space was a large, open room with weights and boxing equipment similar to that located in the house in Mexico City, but the room was larger and had a fifteen-foot sparring ring in one corner. After some initial stretching, they entered the ring. Carlos handed him a large rubber Bowie knife and they began going through the patterns of the various thrust, slash, and parry positions. Carlos spent the first hour working on overhand attack movements. The second hour was spent on full-contact in-fighting, using arm and hand blocks. Jackson's wrists and forearms were sore and he was sweating when they finished.

Carlos, who looked surprisingly fresh, clapped him on the shoulder and said, "You're getting it. Don't be impatient. It takes practice. It takes time. We'll work on underhand attacks and parries all of next week. Your martial arts training gives you a good basis to build on."

Later, as Jackson grabbed a couple of towels off the shelf and tossed one to Carlos, he asked, "Where did you learn knife fighting?"

"Your grandfather sent me to Brazil to learn how to use a seven-inch blade. I worked four hours a day with a master for nearly six months. Then the next year I trained with a man in Miami for a couple months. After that I used to go back to Miami every year or so until he died."

"Have you had cause to use this skill?"

"Many times. Too many times." Carlos shrugged as he put his towel around his neck. "But you only have to need it once to cherish it."

"My grandfather sent you to learn this? Were you training to be a bodyguard?"

Carlos suggested, "We can continue this conversation while we eat." He led the way upstairs into the kitchen. As if their entrance were a signal, Theresa put two large, steaming plates of shredded pork with eggs and cheese cooked in a red sauce on the table. Then she brought over a warm stack of handmade tortillas. The two men fell upon on the food and did not stop to talk until their plates were nearly clean.

Jackson pushed his plate away. "I had no idea how hungry I was." Theresa came and collected his plate with a nod of approval. Jackson waved his hand in salute. "Thank you, Theresa; that was excellent." She acknowledged his words with another nod and busied herself in the kitchen. "So talk to me, Carlos. Were you training to be a bodyguard or what?"

"The year after El Indio was killed in the raid on El Jaguar, Federico Ramirez was killed during a dinner by an assassin who posed as part of the catering crew. He had a knife as his only weapon, yet his skill was such that he killed three of our men before he was subdued. I was responsible for setting up security that day. It was a lapse on my part; I didn't check out all the staff sufficiently. Guilt made me want vengeance. I wanted to search out those behind the attack and kill them all with knives." Carlos made a fist as he finished speaking and seemed to sink into a reverie.

Jackson said nothing. He had never heard Carlos speak with such intensity. For a moment, Jackson had an uncharacteristic view deep into Carlos's interior and saw a boiler room with blazing flames rather than the austere fluorescence of a cold fusion system he had presumed would be there. It made Jackson realize how little he actually knew about Carlos. He asked, "And did you exact revenge?"

"Yes, all blood debts are paid. I killed all three men with the blade."

"Damn, if you don't sound like my grandfather!"

"Your grandfather understood my need for revenge, that I needed to spill the blood of these men to atone for my mistake. He told me that before I could get his approval for such a mission I would have to train with a master."

Theresa put a bowl of fruit on the table and two glasses of water then said something in Spanish to Carlos. He translated to Jackson, "She says leave your laundry on the floor like you always do and she'll get it later, but now she has to hurry to her English class."

Jackson laughed ruefully. He had to admit that Theresa was a competent, organized housekeeper and other than her coffee, an excellent cook. It was the fact she had assumed responsibility for organizing everything that happened under his roof that occasionally grated upon him. She acted like she was family. And for all intents and purposes she was, for there was no way he could terminate her employment. He waved his thanks. Theresa gave him a big smile and left the room.

Carlos stared after her and said, "You are very fortunate to have Theresa. She works hard and she is loyal and courageous. Plus, she likes you. If you treat her right, she might even serve you in bed." Carlos smiled. "She is a solid woman with a nice body, no?"

Jackson shook his head, "Sometimes you are too eloquent to be a simple security specialist. She is attractive in her own way, but I have someone in my heart already."

"Who said I was simple? I run a major security service. I make pitches and presentations to major corporations. The vast majority of my clients are American corporate executives who live overseas, particularly South America. Your grandfather asked me to handle this particular assignment personally and I was happy to do it. Of course, he paid me well. He left me the security business."

"My grandfather ran a security business?"

"Not originally; it was something he built up over the years to protect himself. He had a pretty good network when I came up with the idea to sell our services so that we could keep the good people full-time on the payroll."

"Does security work always entail the physical elimination of the opponent?"

"Only occasionally. I could have as much work as I wanted, if I wanted to do removals. Cash in a suitcase, no questions asked!"

Jackson shook his head in disgust. "I don't need or want to know any more. I want to get through this and be finished with it."

"Your life is changed now; you can't ever go back! If you want to live to a ripe old age, like your grandfather, you've got to develop an alertness, a consciousness of your surroundings and the people in it."

"Don't you get it?" Jackson barked. "I don't want my grandfather's life! I can't think of anyone who I'd like my life patterned after less!"

"Why not? He lived a full life and did what he wanted. He was a man who took no word of insult from any man no matter his color at a time when it was dangerous for black men to be publicly defiant. He stood tall among all men. When he died, he was tired of living. What better way to live a life? He was generous with his wealth and assistance and as a result had many friends, people who would risk their lives for him. As I said, he stood tall among men."

"You make it sound like he was a Good Samaritan. That's not the man I remember. I remember a hard man who gave no quarter and expected none. He was feared and then respected."

"Maybe he learned something since that last summer you spent in Mexico," Carlos suggested. "Maybe we all did."

Jackson nodded, then changed the subject. "Tomorrow's the last day of my family death leave. Bedrosian granted my leave under duress. I'll be fired if I don't return to work."

Carlos said, "We need to talk strategy before you make any plans to go back to work. And we need to discuss what we're going to do in response to these attacks on your friends. These actions can't go unanswered. The enemy must not think that they can act with impunity."

"What do you propose?"

Carlos answered, "It's what you propose that must be examined."

"I need more information. I don't even know who all my enemies are yet."

"That's a good place to start. We need to pick up one of their operatives and question him a bit."

"Is that a euphemism for torture?"

"You must be prepared to do whatever is necessary to survive. Believe me, they will torture you if they are fortunate enough to capture you alive. They will only keep you alive until they have the stock certificates in hand; after that, you'll be history."

"Okay, how do we get one of their operatives?"

"We use bait. We show them something that they really want."

"What type of bait?"

"You. We show them you. That's the reason you'll return to work."

"Isn't that dangerous?" Jackson asked. "Won't they try to kill me on sight?"

"You were planning to go in to work anyway, weren't you?" Jackson nodded. Carlos continued, "Then we'll just plan to have a security force around when you go. Their first desire is to capture you alive. They will only kill you if they can't capture you."

"I feel so much better now, knowing their preference is to capture me and torture me first."

"When do you want to return to work? We need to start setting up the surveillance squad."

"Thursday."

"All right, now tell me how much you told your friends." Jackson recounted the discussion of his proposal then waited while Carlos pondered his words. After a moment, Carlos nodded his head. "A hundred grand is a good offer. Did you ask them to get involved in any way?"

"No. I might have done it fifteen years ago, but not now. They lead different lives now. Fifteen years ago it was—"

"I know all about what happened fifteen years ago between you and your friends and that street gang. You boys were sloppy drunk. You left clues and didn't get rid of the bodies. I had to step in and dispose of that evidence. That's why there was no police investigation."

"You know about that?"

"It's why your friend Presenio enlisted and Dan transferred to Howard. If you boys hadn't been drunk it probably wouldn't have happened at all."

All Jackson could muster was "Damn!"

"It's best to leave the dirty work to me and my associates," Carlos observed. "That way, it will be handled by professionals. Let your friends help you recover the stock certificates. It's much cleaner this way. Professionals have no conscience nor any desire to tell the whole truth in order to cleanse their soul. Oh, and I don't think it's a good idea to mention me either. Unless they come on board to fight, I'll be a nameless employee. Let them consider me domestic help like Theresa."

"That was a joke, right?" Jackson asked. "You're not serious?"

"It's best that they know nothing about me. This way, if one of our opponents' disappearance makes the paper, there'll be no face to connect with the action. Total disclosure is only valuable in situations where the rules are being followed. When lives are in the balance, the less known the better.

"In my business you meet many people, all sorts of people who will do certain jobs for money. Your grandfather used to keep a stable of them. They were independents. Such arrangements can still be made and I can handle any such arrangements as you will approve."

"I get the feeling you could handle this whole matter by yourself. That I don't really need to do anything."

"Maybe I could handle this for you, but what would you truly learn? You would not be ready for the next time. This is a harder test than catching and killing game in the ravines and gullies of Durango. If you live, you will make enemies, enemies who will be patient about getting their revenge. You need a certain level of alertness and offensive spontaneity that you have yet to develop. I'm here to help you through this period. When you find the stock certificates, the full wealth of your grandfather's estate will be at your disposal. You will need considerable vigilance to hold on to it."

"From the papers I couldn't figure out how much the estate is worth. Many of the properties were bought back in the twenties and thirties and haven't been evaluated since."

"Your grandfather owned properties and businesses in California and Mexico, New York, Louisiana, Oklahoma, and New Mexico."

Jackson paused, awed by the possibilities, then he asked, "How do I find these certificates?"

"Through the sewer system. Your grandfather used to use the sewer a great deal. He knew his way underground around most of the city. It was one of the ways he used to move from place to place without being seen. But I wouldn't waste time looking for the certificates until we have taken care of your enemies."

"Good, but I can't say that I'm thrilled about the prospect of obtaining an in-depth knowledge of San Francisco's sewer system."

"Well, you've got about a hundred million reasons to learn."

Tuesday, July 6, 1982

The sky was cloudless and the morning sun beat down upon the humid environs of New Orleans with a slow, throbbing intensity. Everywhere it was not paved, the water-sodden earth baked and steamed under the blaze of the sun. Waves of heat caused distant objects to become indiscernible, shimmering images.

Pug DuMont leaned on his cane as he stood inside his wrought-iron security fence and watched as the carpenters removed the bulletproof shutters from windows on both the first and second floors. His wife, Zenia, had complained about the heavy shutters for years. She had said many times that they destroyed the curb appeal of the house. Pug had ignored her protestations until he received information that King Tremain had finally been killed. The war that had dragged on for over a hundred years was at long last over. The day he heard the news he wanted to jump in the air for joy. A hated enemy had been vanquished. Pug took off his straw hat and wiped the perspiration that was dripping down his bald pate with his handkerchief. He wheezed as a slight coughing spell shook him. He knew he was dying, but he was happy. He was seventy-eight years old and for the first time since his adolescence, he was standing in front of his house without fear.

Zenia called from the house, "Pug! Just tell those men to take all those shutters off and then let them alone! Come on in here and let me make you lunch!"

Pug didn't bother to answer. Zenia was his third wife and although she catered to his every need, she grew tiresome with her constant prodding. He waved a dismissive hand in the direction of the house and limped over to the crew chief of the carpenters. He asked, "You think you can have them shutters off and the scaffolding down by next week? Me and my wife is plannin' a party next Friday."

"No problem, Mr. DuMont," replied the man just before he yelled at one of his employees directing the hoist. He excused himself and ran over to supervise the operation himself.

Pug saw his son's black Mercedes pull into the driveway and frowned. His son never came with good news. He started back toward the house. A pain lanced up his leg and made him stop. It was an old injury and it was getting worse. Still, he was alive while the man who had robbed him of so much was dead. He hobbled into the house and the air-conditioned interior provided a welcome change from the heat of the sun. He was seated at the kitchen table eating a tuna sandwich when Xavier walked in.

Xavier was a brown-skinned man of medium build in his early fifties with wavy salt-and-pepper hair. The animus of his presence entered the room like a blast of hot air. He ignored Zenia at the kitchen sink and confronted his father without a greeting. "What the hell is going on? You're having them take down the shutters? Are you crazy?"

"I done told you before, watch yo' mouth when you come into this house," Pug warned. "You ain't with yo' pals! You be respectful in front of Zenia!"

Xavier snorted with contempt. "Why? She's just your glorified nurse! A gold digger! I don't want to waste time talking about her! I heard that you laid off some of the security people I've hired. Are you getting senile? What could you possibly be thinking?"

"Don't be comin' in here talkin' 'bout my wife like that, boy! You lettin' yo' mouth write checks yo' ass can't cash! I still run this family! I won't be scolded by you or anybody!"

"You run this house, Papa, but you haven't run the family or the business in ten years. I run the business. I'm the one at the office in the morning. I sign the checks. And as for running the family, there aren't that many of us to run. You, me, and my son, Deleon, are the only men still alive that have DuMont as their last name."

Zenia brought Pug a glass of lemonade and advised, "Don't let him upset you, Raymond. Remember what the doctor said."

Xavier looked at Zenia in her garish red lipstick and tight leopard-skin pants and thought, A forty-year-old woman shouldn't dress like that. She was a money-grubbing cunt as far as he was concerned, and if it were left in his hands, he would treat her just like she deserved. Fifteen years ago she had been his fiancée. She was a nurse at the time and when his father started needing around-the-clock assistance with his medicines, Xavier had suggested Zenia apply for the job. Within six months her relationship with Xavier had fallen apart and six months after that she married his father. Xavier had been devastated and angry. He felt that he could never love anyone else like he had loved her. The utter desolation and bitterness that he felt when their affair ended was the primary cause that made him leave the Born Again Church of Jesus Christ. He just could not resolve how God could allow something so cruel to happen to a man who had spent years on his knees praying to the glory of the Almighty. His experience with Zenia made him feel that in the struggle for souls, his problems did not rate divine attention. Her betrayal never faded. His anger never dissipated. It soured and settled like uncorked wine.

Her marriage to Pug had driven a wedge between Xavier and his father; not that they had ever been close, but it destroyed whatever had existed. Where before there was a resentful tolerance, there was now open hostility. And Zenia seemed bent on driving the wedge deeper. She even seemed to have an influence with his son, Deleon. It always amazed him how she had woven herself so tightly into a family that had, prior to her, only loose associations with one another. She was a cunning beast, but he had her number now. Her time was coming.

"Zenia right! I ain't gon' let you run up my blood pressure," Pug wheezed. She patted him gently on the back. "Whatchoo come here fo'?"

Xavier straightened his tie, adjusted his suit, then ran his hand over his straightened, salt-and-pepper hair. It was his way of calming himself. He was trying to focus on issues rather than his emotions. He said, "To advise you it's not wise to cut security at this time. We should keep up our forces until we negotiate an official truce."

Pug scoffed, "Why? King's dead! There ain't no one else to worry about. Them grandsons of his ain't nothin' to be scared of."

"I wouldn't be so sure, Papa. I think we ought to keep up our security until we can work out some kind of settlement. Shouldn't be a problem once we sit down together. There's no need to keep up the hostilities now. It isn't good for business. We need to declare this feud over and finished."

Pug angrily knocked his glass of lemonade off the table. The glass hit the floor and shattered. He growled, "It ain't over as long as one of them Tremains is alive! I want them all dead befo' I go to my grave! The pickin's easy now! We just need to finish the job!"

"Now, now, lovebird," Zenia clucked as she got down on the floor and began to wipe up the lemonade. "You're letting him get you angry. Remember to breathe deeply when dealing with annoying people!"

"Shut up, bitch!" Xavier shouted, losing control of himself. He pointed his finger at her. "This is between my father and me! You have nothing to do with this!"

Pug laughed wheezingly. "Look like he ain't forgave you yet, honey!"

As she finished cleaning up the floor, Zenia said, "What do you expect from him? Someone who would be rude to a woman in her own home!"

"Let me tell you something, Papa," Xavier said through gritted teeth as he sought to get back on track. "The people who killed King were found dead. Their organization's building in Mexico City has been blown up and two of their top people have been assassinated within the last two weeks. The grandson who went to Mexico has disappeared. Whoever is behind this isn't easy pickings. They're dangerous."

Pug turned to his wife and grinned. "You was right, honey. He is scared. I thought I raised him better than that."

"Are you listening?" Xavier demanded. "Haven't you learned anything? The reason there are so damn few DuMonts is stupid decisions like this! Why underestimate an enemy that has consistently kicked our butts over the years? We should have negotiated an end to the feud twenty years ago!"

Pug's face contorted into a snarl. "You the one ain't been listenin'! I lost five older brothers, my father, and I don't know how many cousins to the Tremains! This ain't over till the last one of them is dead! You ain't gon' negotiate a goddamned thing! They gon' pay with they lives! They gon' pay in blood! I was made a cripple when I was young because of them! I got the courage to finish the job, if you don't!"

Now Xavier laughed. "The man responsible for all of that is dead. You lived in fear of him all your life. I heard how he found you under the bed when he came looking for his son. How you begged for your life! Pleaded with him not to kill you! My mother told me all about it. She said all the DuMont women were ashamed. She said that his shooting you in the crotch shouldn't have made a difference in your life since you never had any balls before that. Don't talk to me about courage!"

Pug's face was apoplectic with anger, but he said nothing. The silence was thick with tension. Xavier had struck on a tender spot and Pug hated him for it. Yet, Pug still had an ace to play. He snarled, "At least Deleon been listening. He understands the importance of blood and finishin' this fight."

Now it was Xavier's turn to display anger. "What the hell are you talking about? What type of misinformation have you been feeding my son?" Deleon was a sensitive subject. The rare times that Deleon came to the office, Xavier would turn around and see his son staring at him with a look of absolute loathing, and it would make him feel extremely uncomfortable; more than that, he felt unsafe. As a result, Xavier had started making regular overtures to mend fences with his son, but every act was coldly rebuffed. Every time he saw the cold hate in his son's eyes, Xavier was frankly shocked. What was the big deal? So he punched the kid a few times, just to get his attention! Kids needed reminding of what's what! He never broke any bones, at least none that he remembered. Anyway, it was no worse than he had taken from his own father. Xavier demanded, "Where is he?"

Pug smiled. "I talked to him in Frisco this mo'nin'. He gon' make sure Braxton doin' what we want and I told him if he get the chance to do one of them grandsons, do 'em."

"What?" Xavier exclaimed. "You dumb-ass, short-sighted old fool! You may have sent him to his death! You don't know what's happening out there, yet you risk his life!" Xavier looked in his father's smiling face and cursed the fates which permitted his son and his father to have a better relationship than Xavier had with either one of them. He enunciated slowly, "I thought we agreed that after he got out of jail this last time, he wouldn't be sent on any more illegal jobs. What happened to that? Don't you care about your grandson? Don't you care about his future?"

"This here assignment mo' impo'tant than any one man in the family!" Pug replied haughtily. "This is how we gets revenge for all them that's been killed! Blood for blood! That's the way it's been, that's the way it's gon' be! By the time we party next week, there ain't gon' be no mo' Tremain men left! We gon' be revenged! All the pains I's suffered will be paid for in blood!"

"You'll use anyone as an instrument to do your bidding!" Xavier shook his head in disgust. His father always spoke about avenging the family name, but what family? There was hardly anybody left. His father was caught up in a battle that time had passed by. The soldiers were old, toothless, and doddering. The philosophies they spouted and the causes they fought for had long been forgotten. Even their weapons and strategies were outdated. Xavier pointed his index finger in Pug's face and sneered, "You dumb, old fool, what you don't realize is that we have other irons in the fire. We understand that King's complete holdings in stock certificates are hidden somewhere in San Francisco. The grandson who went down to Mexico is the key. If Deleon kills him, you may have cost us millions of dollars' worth of unsigned stock certificates."

"You said you wanted to negotiate!" Pug challenged. "So what if we kill 'em? We'll find the certificates later!"

"The money goes to charity if he's killed! Didn't you read the material I sent over here? Let him inherit, then kill him afterward if we have to. We're interested in money, not blood. Nobody wants to spend his life like you had to, ducking in and out of cars, looking over his shoulder all the time, avoiding open windows. It isn't necessary! You can destroy people financially and that's perfectly legal. That's why I'm recommending until we've negotiated a cease-fire, that we all maintain our level of security. Once we get the cease-fire, then we can lead normal lives."

Zenia tapped Pug's shoulder and once she got his attention she shook her head as if to indicate nothing but caution could be expected of Xavier. Pug smiled and nodded in agreement.

"We takin' down the shutters at this house!" Pug announced. "We cuttin' security 'cause it ain't necessary no mo'! We ain't gon' live like we scared! We gon' enjoy ourselves. We gon' have a party next week and invite the neighbors."

Xavier shrugged. "Whatever you want to do around this house is up to you, but I'm keeping the security high around my home and the office building. And understand this, Papa, you've given your last order. You're retired. You have no further say. By sending Deleon to San Francisco, you've forced me to make a move so that I have something to trade in case they capture him."

"Whatchoo got to trade?" Pug asked skeptically.

"Serena Tremain."

Pug sat up straight. "You got Serena Tremain?"

"Not yet, but she's in town and I'm close to finding out the hotel she's staying at. I've got a couple of men ready to pick her up. I'll have to hold her as a hostage until I'm sure Deleon is safe. This is the kind of thing that complicates negotiations. This is why I don't want you freelancing from home. I wouldn't have to do this if you hadn't sent Deleon off on this stupid assignment."

"Ain't stupid," Pug answered sourly. "Blood for blood ain't stupid!"

"There, there, lovebird," soothed Zenia, rubbing Pug's shoulders. "Some people can only say nasty things. You can't let them upset you."

Later that evening while Zenia was watching *Jeopardy!* in the bedroom, Pug sat on the second-story balcony sipping a cold beer and listened to the quiet noises of his residential neighborhood. He could hear children laughing as they splashed in the pool next door. A pizza delivery truck chugged by in front of his wrought-iron security fence. Off in the distance, there was a sound of an emergency siren. The sky was clear and the stars twinkled brightly overhead. It was a warm and balmy night. Raymond 'Pug' DuMont was feeling quite good. He stretched his arms expansively then breathed deeply with only a little rattle in his lungs. It was a new experience for him to sit out on his balcony at night, and he found that he liked it. He was going to do many more things now. King was dead and he was alive. He called Zenia to bring him another beer.

She came out on the balcony and chided him again, "Remember to tell Deleon when you talk to him that we need the grandson who went to Mexico alive! We need him alive! Remember to tell him!" She set the beer on the table and returned to her television program.

Pug sighed. The damned woman wasn't happy unless she was nagging him. This was at least the fifth time she had reminded him to tell Deleon which grandson was needed. He could remember without all the nagging. He remembered to have Braxton set up an additional safe house for Deleon and remembered to open a new bank account for him as well. He damn sure wasn't senile. Only problem was that he had no way to contact Deleon and he wasn't due to talk to him again for several days.

If Deleon killed the wrong grandson, too bad. It was another Tremain in the grave and that was all to the good. Pug sipped his cold

beer and exhaled slowly and thought about what he would do to Serena
if he had her in his possession. He chuckled to himself. Yes, Lord, he
was going to have full vengeance before he died.

Thursday, July 8, 1982

Jackson Tremain boxed up the last of his personal belongings in his office and looked at the clock on his desk. It was nearly six-thirty in the
evening. He had spent the whole day preparing his city department assignments for transition to another deputy city manager. His request
for an extended leave had been denied by Bedrosian, who was practically beaming when he delivered his denial. Bedrosian had informed
Jackson that if he could not return to work by the week's end, he would
have no choice but to terminate Jackson's employment with the city.
His smile was only dampened by the fact that Jackson had refused his
offer to resign. He had even offered to place a positive reference in
Jackson's file if he would voluntarily terminate, but Jackson had rejected
it and informed Bedrosian that he wanted his attorney to receive an official denial of Jackson's extended leave request along with any papers
concerning termination. By the time Jackson left Bedrosian's office, his
request for official documents had Bedrosian frowning.

Jackson took little pleasure in causing Bedrosian discomfort. His
mind was too preoccupied with concerns related to securing the safety
of his friends and family. He was plagued with the worry that he would
receive a call informing him of another casualty. Every time the phone
rang his imagination flashed through horrifying scenes like cheap fire-
crackers firing on a single fuse. He attempted to preoccupy himself by
studying the reports that were received daily regarding the illicit activities of his enemies. He now knew the whereabouts of Tree's crack-
processing warehouse, where he conducted most of his business.
DiMarco was more difficult to uncover, but an accountant who had au-
dited DiMarco's restaurant for a bank loan was providing some very interesting information. Progress was being made on many levels.
Nonetheless, in his unguarded moments, Jackson had found himself
anxiously pacing the floor of the Fulton Street house.

He looked around his office and saw that there was still much to do. He forced himself to continue packing his possessions. He didn't examine whether he wanted them or not. It was too difficult to concentrate. As if he did not have enough on his mind, Rhasan was now a source of anxiety. Just yesterday evening Jackson had called Samantha to find out whether she and Rhasan were taking a vacation as he had suggested, and she had informed him that her son had expressed an intention to help Jackson and that he was unwilling to go anywhere without first talking with him. Samantha was both upset and frightened. She begged him to talk some sense into her son. There were sharp, fragmented tones of desperation in her voice and they penetrated into Jackson's very soul. He had scheduled to meet Rhasan the next day for lunch, but he was at a loss as to how he would explain to the young man the events that had taken place.

How could he rationalize to someone else what he hadn't been able to rationalize to himself? How could he explain that he was spending two hours a day practicing with an eight-inch blade? That he was spending hours during the week pulling pistols from different holster positions? The words he thought to say seemed like smoke above a small fire; they seemed formless, semi-transparent, and their substance dissipated under inspection. Yet Rhasan had been attacked. He deserved to hear the truth. Jackson hoped by the time that he met with him he would have developed some concept as to what shape that truth should take.

At a quarter of seven there was a light tap on the door to Jackson's office and Corazon stepped into the room, looked around at the clutter, and said, "It's not going to be the same without you. There won't be anyone concerned about the clerical and minor administrative staff now. Howard will be placed in charge of us again."

Jackson paused in his packing as he was drawn out of his reverie. He nodded and said, "Yeah, I hate the thought of that. He'll prize ass-kissing above all." He put several large binders in the last box to be filled and noticed that the cardboard was extremely dusty. He rolled up the cuffs of his white shirt, exposing dark welts on his wrists and arms.

Corazon asked, "Why are your forearms so discolored? Are those bruises? This is not from your new girlfriend, I hope."

"Martial arts workouts," Jackson explained. "I'm going to stop at a drugstore on the way home and pick up some liniment or salve for muscle soreness."

"That must be a hard workout. Say, did your grandmother ever contact you while you were in Mexico?"

Jackson shook his head and felt nausea and revulsion rise in the back of his throat. He said grimly, "No, she didn't, but someone else contacted me because of her."

Corazon saw that it wasn't a subject to be continued and patted his shoulder. "I just came in to tell you how grateful I am that you gave me a chance three years ago and hired me in an administrative capacity. The clerical staff and some of the interns asked me to speak for them. We have all appreciated your support over the years. We are deeply grateful, and as a token of our gratitude we got you a going-away present." Corazon stepped forward and put a large, flat package on his desk. She urged, "Don't open it here! Open it when you get home. One of the things inside is an old municipal calendar with an office picture of us all that we all signed. Don't forget us!" She stepped quickly around his desk and gave him a hug, kissed him on the forehead, then left the room.

Jackson sat in his office for several minutes in silence thinking about all that he was leaving. He looked at the walls, at the lighter square and rectangular silhouettes where his pictures, certificates, awards, and calendars had hung. His sweat and the air he had exhaled had helped create the darkened patina on these walls. It had taken him fourteen years to get to a deputy position in the city manager's office. He had made many sacrifices in the process: taken on additional assignments and worked longer hours than most, attended seminars and training at his own expense, but most of all he had held his tongue when he had stared into the face of racism, incompetence, and envy, and kept a smile on his face. Now, to walk away when he had not attained the pinnacle of city manager left a hollowness.

The telephone on his desk jangled. Jackson picked it up and talked with the security guard, who informed him that he was escorting three men up to Jackson's office to help him remove his possessions. Jackson hung up the phone. Back to the real world. It did not matter what his desires were; the world had pivoted and he had somehow lost his place.

In the midst of all the madness was Elizabeth. Everywhere he turned in his mind, she was there: the expressiveness of her eyes, the fullness of her lips, the warmth of her smile. Jackson could still feel the black, velvet softness of her skin against his chest. The image of her lithe, naked body moving through the shadows of her darkened bedroom had the power to arouse him even in afterthought. But there was still no contact. The door had been slammed shut. With unremitting sadness he suppressed the thought of her once more.

There was a knock on the door. Carlos and two of his associates walked into the office. Jackson directed the men as to the boxes and objects he wanted to take. With the security guard's assistance he was able to get all his things in one trip. Everything except Jackson's briefcase was loaded into a van that pulled to the curb as they waited. Carlos offered to give him a ride to his vehicle, but Jackson declined, saying that his car was only across the street in the municipal parking lot.

He headed down into the second-level parking lot toward his car, looking neither left nor right. He was lost in thought as his briefcase banged against his leg. He did not see the man following him, nor did he pay attention to the footsteps.

Fletcher Gilmore watched as Jackson, followed by Jesse Tuggle, came down the stairs of the parking garage. Gilmore had parked the brown Cadillac in such a way that Jackson would be facing away from him as he approached his vehicle. He and Jesse were in luck; it looked like Jackson was preoccupied. When Jackson began unlocking his car, Gilmore silently urged Jesse forward. Jesse moved quickly for a big man. He had crossed the space that separated them by the time Jackson got his car door open.

Jackson saw Jesse's reflection materialize in the car door's window and spun to face him. As soon as he saw Jesse, Jackson recognized him as the man from Angel Island. He put down his briefcase and prepared himself to fight.

Jesse stood in front of Jackson and said, "Someone wants to see you."

Jackson demanded, "Who wants to see me?"

"I ain't got time to fuck with you," Jesse warned. "Are you coming easy or is it going to be hard?"

"Generally, when it's hard, coming is easy," Jackson said with a smirk. The man in front of him was about his height and a little beefier, but Jackson was undaunted.

"All right, motherfucker, you asked for it!" Jesse grabbed Jackson's arm and attempted to muscle him.

Jackson resisted him momentarily, then snapped his head forward, smashing it into Jesse's nose and mouth. Jesse staggered backward from the pain and the power of the blow. Jackson followed him and kicked Jesse hard between his legs. Jesse groaned and dropped to his knees. Jackson clasped his hands together above his head and brought them down like a club on the side of Jesse's face. The force knocked Jesse flat. Jackson drew back his foot to deliver another kick, but a voice stopped him.

"Hold it right there, unless you're ready to die," Gilmore warned. He pointed a revolver in Jackson's direction.

Jackson turned to face him and saw a small, brown-skinned man with rimless glasses wearing a derby hat walking toward him. "I remember you," Jackson scoffed. "You're the second part of the team. Are you the guy who wants to talk to me?" It was strange. He didn't feel fear. He felt anger. His grandfather and Carlos were right: These people wouldn't leave him alone until he killed them.

"Just shut your mouth and stand back over there." Fletcher waved his gun in the direction that he wanted Jackson to move. Jackson obeyed and stepped back. "You all right?" Fletcher asked Jesse as he got to his feet slowly.

Jesse groaned and mumbled, "I'm going to kill that motherfucker." He staggered in Jackson's direction.

"Come on, you sack of shit," Jackson taunted. "I'm ready to die kicking your ass!"

Jesse started to say something, but Fletcher cut him off: "Don't let this guy provoke you!" He turned to Jackson. "Listen, asshole, I'm going to shoot you in your legs and arms if you don't get in the car. It's your choice." Fletcher pointed the gun at Jackson's knee.

"All right," Jackson acquiesced. He walked toward Jesse.

"Stay away from him!" Fletcher warned Jackson. "Just walk on down there to the Cadillac. Go lean against the car."

Jackson walked toward the car as directed and stood quietly while Jesse frisked him thoroughly from behind. When he finished the search, Jesse punched Jackson between his legs. Jackson had been expecting some sort of retaliation, but the pain which exploded in his groin made him see dancing lights. He doubled over involuntarily and felt Jesse's fist smash into his cheekbone. He bounced off the Cadillac's open door and fell backward. Jesse swung again and his left caught Jackson flush on the mouth as he fell backward into the car. The blow knocked Jackson flat on his back on the seat.

Jesse looked at Fletcher confidently and said, "This gon' be easier than it was with that chump with the red sports car!" He came forward to pull Jackson out of the car. Through the numbing haze of pain Jackson concentrated on fighting back. When Jesse got close, Jackson put all his strength into kicking the man between his legs again. Jesse was not expecting any more resistance and the kick surprised him as it slammed against his testicles. It doubled him over, and when he looked up, Jackson kicked him forcefully in the face with the heel of his shoe. Jesse tumbled backward and fell hard onto the cement floor. Jackson slowly pulled himself out of the car and stood up. He was not thinking about his pain; there was only one thought on his mind: These men worked for the organization that killed both Wesley and his grandfather. A blinding rage flared within him. It blocked out any thought of danger. He wanted to feel the big man's bones break. He wanted to spill his blood.

Warily, he looked in Fletcher's direction and saw that Fletcher was standing with his hands at his sides and that Carlos was holding a gun to his head. Fletcher's gun was lying on the hood of the Cadillac. Jackson threw back his head and laughed, but it was an animal sound. He was free to exact his revenge. His face was contorted when he turned and advanced toward Jesse, who was staggering to his feet.

Jackson attacked, utilizing his kicks to strike at Jesse's legs. He made contact with a knee and felt it hyperextend. Jesse cried out as his leg slowly collapsed underneath him. It was the opening that Jackson had been waiting for. He waded in with his fists, connecting with several blows to the face before Jesse went down. Jesse rolled on his side in an effort to get up, but Jackson, utilizing his full weight, dropped his knees onto Jesse's rib cage. There was a sharp crack that all could hear. Jesse screamed out and twisted in agony. Jackson slammed his fist into Jesse's temple, knocking his head against the cement. The thrashing stopped and Jesse lay still. Jackson stood up and dropped his knees again onto Jesse's rib cage, letting his 220 pounds of weight crack the bones. Jesse's body twitched then lay still. Jackson stood over Jesse's unconscious body and growled, "Yeah! That's for Wesley!"

There was a clacking sound of footsteps descending down the stairwell on the opposite side of the lot. Jackson grabbed Jesse under the arms and dragged his body behind the Cadillac. Carlos hit Fletcher sharply across the back of his head with the butt of his gun and Fletcher fell like a stone. Jackson picked up Fletcher's revolver off the hood and put the gun in the waistband of his pants then closed his suit jacket.

Jackson turned to Carlos and hissed, "I'm happy to see you! Feel free to appear like that anytime!"

"That's what providing security is all about," Carlos replied.

A woman in high heels emerged from the stairs at the far end of the garage and she clicked across the cement to her car. After she drove off Jackson and Carlos rifled through Jesse's pockets, searching for car keys. Once they found them, they loaded his body into the trunk of the brown Cadillac. Carlos used some duct tape that he found in the Cadillac's trunk to bind and gag both Jesse and Fletcher. Jackson removed a sawed-off shotgun and slammed the trunk shut. He found a rag and wiped off the shotgun before putting it on the floor of the front seat of the Cadillac. He removed the revolver from his waistband and cleaned it with the rag and placed it alongside the shotgun. He then wiped the backseat and fenders of the car to erase any prints and then locked it. Carlos went and retrieved his car and they dumped Fletcher into its trunk.

"I've radioed my men to come and get this car. I want you to drive out with us. We don't know if these are the only two on the job."

"Do you think I killed him?" Jackson asked.

Carlos observed, "He isn't dead, although with those broken ribs, he may not live much longer."

"Good! He's one of the bastards that killed Wesley!"

"Then you recognize that both these men must die?"

"These bastards deserve to die!" Jackson paused and shook his head reluctantly. "Damn! It's not even been two weeks and I'm turning into my grandfather. I need a break. I need to think. I have to have a couple hours before we do anything else."

"Take your time. I'll meet you at the boat at eleven o'clock. We'll take care of these details then." Carlos tapped the trunk with his knuckle. "I want you to follow my car until I give you the all-clear, understood? When we get out of here, take care of your face. You look like you've been in a fight. Remember that there may be more of these men around. And that they intend to kill you."

"Let me take one of your men and I'll stop by my house in the Oakland Hills and then I'll come back."

"Don't go home! There may be another team there waiting for you. I tell you what, you go to some restaurant or bar and think. I'll take these boys down to the Seventh Street house. We'll ask them a few questions and be ready for our boat ride by eleven. Here come my men now." The van pulled up and two men got out.

Jackson sniffed the air. "You smell that?"

Carlos turned to him. "Smell what?"

"That cigar smoke! Smells like my grandfather's cigars!"

Carlos took a couple of sniffs. "I don't smell anything."

"Maybe I'm just going crazy, but it smells pretty strong to me."

Carlos patted Jackson on the arm and said, "Just stay alert!" He had a muffled conversation with his men, then waved Jackson into his car. Jackson picked up his briefcase, straightened his clothes, and got into his car. He adjusted his rearview mirror and saw that his lip was bleeding and the area around his right eye was turning a nice purple. He put on a pair of sunglasses and drove his car toward the exit. When he got to the exit booth, he planned to cover his mouth with a tissue and pretend that he had a serious cough. He still smelled a trace of cigar smoke even when he drove out of the parking lot.

Thursday, July 8, 1982

After Jackson's car and the brown Cadillac had disappeared up the ramp, Deleon DuMont stepped out of hiding and walked over to his car. His shirt was dirty and his pants had oil on them. He had his leather jacket cupped under his arm to cover the scope and barrel of his 30-30 rifle. He opened the car's door, put the rifle with its silencer on the floor of the backseat, and dropped his jacket over it. He walked over to where Jesse had lain after Jackson had dropped his weight on him. There was a trail of blood drops leading from there over to the site where the Cadillac had been parked. As he walked back to his car, he concluded the situation required a drastic change in strategy. He pulled a brown herringbone jacket out of the backseat and put it on. He was in no hurry. He didn't want to leave the parking lot too soon. He figured that one of Jackson's men would be assigned to get the license numbers of all the cars that left the lot within half an hour of the incident with Jesse.

Deleon had almost made a mistake that could've ended him up in a trunk. He wouldn't make a second. He had followed Jackson and Jesse into the parking structure and when he discovered that Jackson had parked on the same floor as he had, he went to his car for his rifle. Deleon had had Jackson in his crosshairs more than once, but a hunch, a feeling, caused him to delay. Instead of pulling the trigger and listening to the soft plink of his silencer, he had watched to see what the two bumbling fools would accomplish and, in so doing, had saved his own life.

Deleon had been lying between two cars at the far end of the lot with his rifle set up on a rest made of his leather jacket. He had been watching Jesse getting his butt kicked when he heard whispering voices behind him. He'd picked up his rifle and rolled under a car just before two men walked behind where he had been laying. If he had not heard their whispered exchange, he would be dead. The stealth with which they moved made him know these weren't casual parkers. He didn't dare fire once the men passed because he had no desire to see how good the security team was. He would wait for another shot at another time. He satisfied himself with watching the events unfold from underneath a parked car.

As he witnessed Jackson brutally finish off Jesse he had wondered how good he was with a knife. It might be interesting to see how long he could last in a blade-to-blade battle. Deleon liked going up against larger men. It gave him pleasure to cut them down to size. His musings were interrupted when two additional men joined Jackson's party. Deleon had been too far away to hear any of the words exchanged, but he had seen Jesse and Fletcher's bodies get loaded into the trunks of the cars and it was clear that neither of those two were destined to live to a ripe old age. The man who first came to Jackson's assistance looked like a Colombian drug enforcer and his associates all appeared to be professionals. This grandson obviously had control of King's organization.

Two women came down the steps and walked to their vehicles. Deleon gave them a perfunctory nod and waited for them to pass before opening up the driver's-side rear door of his car. Their cars were driving up the ramp as he tried to slide into the backseat. He wanted to fix his rifle firmly in its clip beneath the back upholstery of the front seats. The problem was he couldn't open the door wide enough because a black BMW was straddling the line separating the two parking spaces. Deleon pushed the back door of his vehicle open until it scraped hard against the side of the black car. He didn't care about the car he was using, he would steal a new car by morning. The clip he had devised for this car wasn't holding the rifle firmly and he had to really push it in to seat it. He had nearly gotten the rifle seated when he was interrupted.

"Hey! What the hell are you doing to my car? Did you hear me? I'm the city manager, goddamn it! I'm talking to you! Get out of that car and give me your license!"

Deleon saw the man's pale, bespectacled reflection in the door window out of the corner of his eye. There were no other voices. The man appeared to be alone. Deleon had to be cautious. The stock of the rifle was clearly visible on the floor, but Deleon blocked the man's view of the weapon with his body. Deleon was pondering what to do when the man had the audacity to put his hands upon him and grab him by his shoulder. The man's act made things easier for Deleon. He resisted momentarily, freeing the rifle completely, then he spun around using the man's strength to add speed to his effort. The rifle butt shot out from under Deleon's left arm and hit the man across the bridge of the man's nose. There was a muffled yelp of pain as the man staggered backward holding both hands to his face. Deleon followed him, using the rifle butt like a club. He delivered several more hard blows to the man's head, but the man was able to block the first few blows with his hands and arms. Deleon kept hitting the man until he drove the butt through the man's guard. He hit the man until he stumbled and fell behind his car. When he did not move, Deleon smiled then returned to seating the rifle. Once he got it firmly in the clip, he started his vehicle and drove out of the parking lot.

Deleon smiled again as he drove along toward Fourteenth Street toward Lake Merritt with his car window down. It was a beautiful balmy night. The stars were twinkling overhead. Once he was successful with his current assignment, the other grandson could be taken care of at his leisure. His grandfather had promised him he could take over all of King's businesses after he had completed his tasks, but Deleon had politely declined. He wasn't interested in that life. He cared nothing about having a great deal of money. He already had sufficient to buy a nice home and live modestly while he studied and painted. The

path he intended to travel required the use of pastels, oils, and acrylics
on a blank surface. He sometimes dreamed of spending his mornings
stretching canvas for new paintings in an island villa that overlooked an
unending azure expanse of the ocean. All he had to do was stay focused
on his current tasks. Deleon knew that he would have another chance
at Jackson, perhaps even this evening. He and San Vicente had both
been in the lobby and had overheard Jackson ask the security guard for
the nearest pharmacy. The guard had directed him over to Eighteenth
and Lakeshore. Deleon figured that if Jackson went to the pharmacy at
all, it would be after some defensive maneuver designed to lose any tailing traffic. San Vicente was the one appointed to follow Jackson in his
car. Deleon smiled even more broadly. He might even beat San Vicente
and Jackson to the pharmacy. He could be perfectly situated when
Jackson arrived, then *plink!* That would be it.

Thursday, July 8, 1982

Jackson pulled into the parking lot of a large drugstore located a couple of blocks from Lake Merritt. After he parked and turned the engine off, he sat in his car with the window rolled down. There was a
light breeze blowing off the lake. The hour was early; families with
young children could still be seen in the store's parking lot. Sounds of
horns and traffic, human voices, dogs barking, a distant siren: all noises
of a normal evening, but this was not a normal evening.

He adjusted his sunglasses, got out of his car, and walked into the
store. He needed liniment for his arms, some salve to put on his lip, and
ingredients for a poultice for the area around his eye. Yet as he entered
the store he felt surprisingly comforted to be around people, regular
people who went from home to work and back without worrying about
being kidnapped and killed. People who felt free to be preoccupied, or
to have their children by their side. Jackson envied their sense of safety
and security. He picked up a basket and went immediately to the aisle
that contained first-aid supplies.

As he stood looking over the possible alternatives, Elizabeth, wearing a form-fitting teal and lavender Lycra workout suit, stepped in front of him and demanded, "What happened to your face? Oh, look at your lip." She moved closer to him. "You're really banged up!"

"The other person looks worse," Jackson answered tersely. Elizabeth was not the person he wanted to see this evening. He didn't want to involve her in his problems. He said by way of explanation, "I've got to find some stuff and get out of here."

"Let me help," she offered.

"Honey," how he had wanted to call her that, but this was neither the time nor place, "I'm telling you that you don't want to be involved."

She responded, "If I didn't want to help, I wouldn't have volunteered. I've been worried about you and it's driving me crazy!"

The closeness of her, the smell of her hair, the brownness of her eyes weakened Jackson's resolve. He knew he should just walk away from her, but he couldn't. He wanted to steal any moments that he could to be with her. He asked, "Why did you leave without saying good-bye? Why haven't you returned my calls?"

Elizabeth looked him straight in the eye and said evenly, "You know the answer to that." When Jackson had no reply, she touched his cheek where Jesse's fist had landed and Jackson winced. "Let me see your lip," she said, standing on her toes in front of him. She pulled his lip down gently to see the extent of the damage. "Hmmm, it's cut, but I don't think it needs stitches. Why don't you just wait here and I'll get the things that I need to fix you up."

Jackson asked, "How do you know what I need?"

"You forget that I was a beat officer who worked patrol for four years! I've had my share of scrapes and bruises."

Jackson watched admiringly while Elizabeth took his basket and walked down the aisle picking various items from the shelves. He could not help appreciating her beauty.

It was clear to Jackson that she didn't understand the gravity of the situation. He was risking her life simply because he didn't have the willpower to walk away. When Elizabeth had gotten everything she needed and was ready to go, Jackson grabbed her arm. His words issued in a coarse whisper: "Elizabeth, these clowns tried to kidnap me tonight. I had to fight them off. I'm not yet finished with them. They were going to kill me. I can't get you involved in this. This is serious."

Elizabeth gave him a long look then said, "I've had a line drawn in my mind, a line that I said to myself that I wouldn't cross. I thought that we could share a few moments, then when the line was crossed, I'd let you go. I didn't know then that I was going to fall in love with you. There hasn't been a day that I haven't been worried."

There were no other words that Jackson would rather have heard. He wanted to hold her in his arms, but now his desire to protect her was stronger. "I love you too, but I can't endanger you. We've got to go our separate ways."

She laughed humorlessly and resisted his efforts to take the basket. "I risked my life as a police officer so many times trying to make an arrest. Sometimes I knew that the suspect would be out on the streets before I finished the crime report, but I went forward nonetheless. I did my job. If I was ready to do that for work, what do you think I'm ready to do for love? I want to know what's going on. You can come to my apartment this one time and tell me the situation while I fix you up."

"What difference will this discussion make?"

"I'll at least know what's going on."

"I don't want to endanger you. Let me call you later."

"I can't concentrate on my work. I can't sleep! I want to know now!" She moved closer so that her face was inches from his. "So because of that, nothing is as important to me as finding out what's happening with you."

This was the last thing that Jackson wanted at the moment, but the smell of the woman was filling his nose. He couldn't afford to let himself get distracted. He stepped backward. "We can't talk about this now!"

Elizabeth stepped forward. "There is no other time to talk about it!"

Jackson was momentarily flustered. He fumbled for words, "Alex . . ."

"St. Clair." Elizabeth grabbed the lapels of his jacket and gave them a yank. She looked directly into his eyes and whispered, "I need this! Do this for me. Come to my apartment now!"

They stood eye to eye. The proximity of her filled him with a desire to take her in his arms. More than anything he wanted to walk away from his problems and just be with her, make love to her every night, make her laugh, be part of her smile; the list went on and on. "All right," he conceded, looking back into her eyes. They walked to the cashier and stood briefly in line. Their items were tabulated and Jackson paid.

"I'll see you at my apartment," Elizabeth said as she headed toward her car.

Jackson made one last effort. He grabbed her arm and swung her around. "We're back in the real world now. I don't want to involve—"

Elizabeth turned to face him, impatience on her face. "Didn't we already cover this? It's a done deal! Now, let's go!"

Jackson saw the determination in the set of her lips and the spirit in her flashing eyes, and realized that she would not be satisfied unless he went with her. He simply nodded to her. He watched as she walked to her car. This was going to be a painful conversation and he knew it.

Elizabeth had a spacious apartment with hardwood floors on the top floor of the five-story building which overlooked the lake. Her place was decorated principally with African art in terms of both carved figures and paintings. Her furniture was modern, but comfortable. She had fresh flowers in vases throughout the apartment. The ambience was very pleasing.

She came out of the hallway leading from her bedroom; she had put on an apron over her running suit and had an armful of articles including towels. She beckoned Jackson to come and sit at a small breakfast table.

He walked toward her. "What's all this?"

She took his suit jacket off and pushed him down in the chair before she answered, "This is basic first aid, buster. Now, be quiet and let the master continue her work." She pressed an ice pack to Jackson's bruised and swollen cheek and then grabbed his hand and placed it on the ice pack, saying, "You hold it."

Despite himself Jackson felt at ease. He wanted to be pampered and cared for by her. Only Elizabeth had the power to make him feel that way.

"Hold the ice pack higher!"

Jackson bantered, "You're bossy as hell. I can't imagine what you'll be like once you think you know me. Alex the Hun?"

She chuckled in response and said, "More like Zulu Woman! Get used to it, St. Clair! I'll be this way as long as you know me." She picked up a pair of gleaming, long-bladed scissors, then moved up and stood between his legs. She informed him, "These are the sharpest pair of scissors I have. Relax, I've done this a lot. I used to be a cop."

"Is this how you interrogated suspects who invoked Miranda?"

"When someone on my squad got injured on an assignment and it didn't require a doctor, I generally patched them up. Now, you've got a bit of skin hanging off your lip. I was just going to cut it off."

She pulled down his lip before he could react and snipped the skin with one clip of the scissors. "There, now let me put some antibiotic on it." She reached over to the table and took some gauze and poured some alcohol on it and then dabbed his lip. Jackson gave no outward indication of the pain, but the alcohol created a sharp, stinging sensation. Elizabeth patted his face and said, "Don't say anything for a couple of minutes. I want that salve to sink in." She checked his ice pack, then picked up her first-aid articles and left the room.

Jackson stood up and walked around. He saw some photos on the wall of the corridor leading to the bathroom and went to inspect them. There were several pictures of a stout, dark-skinned man in a police uniform. One picture consisted of the man and his family: a woman, three daughters, and a son. The oldest daughter bore a strong resemblance to Elizabeth.

"That's my dad," Elizabeth said over his shoulder. "One of the first black captains on the Detroit Police Department."

"Your dad wanted you in law enforcement? Is that why you became a police officer?" Jackson asked.

"Not hardly; my father was one of the original sexist pigs. He thought a woman's place was in the home."

"Why did you become a police officer?"

"My father was killed in the line of duty. I wanted to get his killers."

"Were you close with your father?"

"No, but we loved each other. When he discovered that he was destined to have only one son, he was extremely disappointed. I tried to make up for it by being a tomboy, but that didn't coincide with his sexist philosophy. My father and I were like fire and water: One could not exist in the presence of the other without being either extinguished or evaporated. We weren't even talking when he was killed, but I knew he did his best for me."

Jackson stood up and pulled her into his arms and said, "I've missed seeing you." He held her close against him. He felt her breasts and pelvis press against him, then he felt the smooth warmth of her cheek against the crook of his neck.

Elizabeth stood on her toes and whispered into his ear. "Just a hug. I can't handle anything more! I need to ask you a few questions."

"Ask," Jackson replied as he began to pull away.

Elizabeth held him tight and would not slacken her grip. "I don't want you to go anywhere. I want you to stay close to me. I want to feel your breath on my neck when you answer my questions."

"Sure!" Jackson nodded as he put his arms around Elizabeth's waist. He rubbed his cheek against hers while letting his head slowly fall to the crook of her neck. "In position," he whispered.

Elizabeth tightened her arms around him and said, "Tell me everything that's happened since I last saw you."

"Not much has changed, except for tonight."

"Tell me everything including tonight."

They stood and held each other while Jackson recounted in her ear the events leading up to and including his departure from the parking lot. When he had finished, they stood in silence for several minutes before he discovered that Elizabeth was crying. When he pushed away to look at her, her arms fell limply to her sides. Tears were streaming down her cheeks.

"Why are you crying?" he asked.

Elizabeth looked at him and said, "It won't be self-defense when you kill the second man, will it?"

"What can I do? Let him go? He'll be back with more of his cronies. I have no choice. When these men attacked me tonight, they intended to kill me after they got what they wanted."

Elizabeth shook her head. "I love you, but I have to walk away now. I can't see you again."

"Why did you invite me over here? I told you things were serious. That they tried to kill me."

"Realistically, I had no reason to expect things to be different. I just hoped and fantasized . . . I just wanted to see you."

Jackson paused a moment and gathered his thoughts then said, "You're important to me. When I saw you this evening you lifted my heart. Maybe when this is over I can earn my way back into your good graces."

"Don't you see, St. Clair, we can never be together! We're on opposite sides of the law!"

"Tell me what I can do! I will do anything to keep this relationship alive! You haven't offered me any alternatives!"

"There are no alternatives now!"

Jackson exhaled slowly and said, "I love you. I hold you in my heart. Your voice echoes in my ears. The silky smoothness of your skin makes me long to touch it. I want you! And when this is over, I will come back to ask you to be my wife!"

Elizabeth grabbed the collar of his shirt and shook him. "Don't say that! I don't want to hear that!"

"Why? Why can't I say what's in my heart?"

Elizabeth composed herself and stared up into his eyes. "Because I don't want you to come back! You'll never be able to walk away and I'm not strong enough to see you again. Please leave now and don't call me!" She turned and walked away.

Jackson was left standing by himself. He waited a few minutes then walked out the door. There were no good-byes, only silence.

After leaving Elizabeth's, Jackson's ride across the Bay Bridge had a tragic beauty. The evening winds had swept away all traces of clouds and fog. The night sky had settled to a dark, purplish blue. The glistening stars were sprinkled across the heavens like gleaming seeds thrown by a celestial hand. The sprawling, dark arms of the land surrounding the bay were twinkling with lights from Marin to San Jose. The majestic, nighttime skyline of San Francisco was a geometric pattern of lights and rectangular shadows, stretching dark cement fingers forty stories above the bay's rippling surface. At the mouth of the bay where the darkness of the sky merged with the blackness of the sea, the lights of the Golden Gate Bridge spanned like an incomplete connect-the-dot puzzle, the last line of man's construction before the vast, untamed Pacific.

As Jackson came off the bridge and headed for the Fell Street exit off the freeway, the majesty and the beauty of the city faded like a cheap illusion under close scrutiny. The burden of his conversation with Elizabeth weighed heavily upon him and as he drove up Fell Street he wondered whether he would ever see her again.

July 1961

The voices of men shouting and arguing filled the hall. There were conversations in both Spanish and English. It was the night of the long-awaited dogfight. Two champion males were to meet in the pit for a winner-take-all bout. There was excitement in the air and it was reflected in the large amounts of pesos and dollars that were being wagered.

Tall and gawky, fifteen-year-old Jackson stood at the edge of the pit watching two *campesinos* below him sweep the hard clay floor of the pit with coarse brooms. He had a thousand dollars in his hand. He was accepting bets for his grandfather.

A fat German man in a Hawaiian shirt ambled over to Jackson. "You taking bets for El Negro?" the man wheezed in his thick, German-accented English.

"Yes," replied Jackson as he studied the man in front of him. The German, whose name was Klaus, had small, beady brown eyes which sat in his fat cheeks like raisins. His lips were unusually red, almost as if he wore lipstick, but it was a natural coloring. He looked somewhat like a clown, but Jackson knew him to be a shrewd gambler.

"He doesn't think that this American dog can beat Diablito, eh?" Klaus wheezed.

"No," Jackson answered simply. He didn't like talking to Klaus. Every time Jackson heard him wheeze, he wondered if he had contagious tuberculosis.

"He taking bets on the number of turns?" Klaus asked.

"No, my grandfather says that they're both strong dogs. The fight could go for two hours easy. All he's willing to bet on is the final decision."

"What odds?" asked the German, licking his lips.

"Two to one under five hundred, even money above."

Klaus bet three hundred dollars. Jackson took his money and wrote his name and the amount in a small book. Three more people came to him to place bets. One was a tall, wiry Mexican with a weather-beaten face whom Jackson recognized as a dog handler. It surprised Jackson, because the local handlers generally bet the same way his grandfather did. The next two bettors were American tourists who had heard about the fight through a small-time hustler. Their pale, white skins made them look anemic and out of place compared to the sunburned faces of the locals, but their money was good. Combined, they bet over a thousand dollars.

"Jax!" It was his grandfather's voice. Jackson turned to face him. His grandfather was standing down in the pit. "We're closed for betting. How much you got?"

"Twenty-six hundred, but fourteen hundred is at two to one," Jackson said, leaning over the barrier to hand his grandfather the money and the notebook.

"Good. Good. Here, keep fifty for travelin' money," he said, quickly rifling through the money and handing Jackson back a few bills.

"Thank you, Grandfather," Jackson said, stuffing the money into his pocket. "Do you want me to get the guns?"

His grandfather took a look around the hall and said, "Yeah, you better. There are a lot of people here who don't know us. If we win tonight, we may have to show that we know how to keep our money. Did you clean them guns like I told you?"

"Yes, sir, but I think that the .357 Magnum has had it. There's too much play in the cylinder."

His grandfather laughed without humor. "Damn! That's what I get for letting you experiment with your own loads! Bring me my forty-fives. Can you handle that forty-four Mag?"

"Yes, sir, I think so."

"Thinkin' so ain't enough. Can you handle it?"

"Yes."

"Good." His grandfather turned away without another word. He walked across the pit and disappeared in the crowd on the far side.

Jackson checked to make sure that his money was firmly in his pocket and ambled through the mass of bodies. Occasionally, he could hear over the general noise of conversation vendors calling out in Spanish, *"Carne asada y frijoles!"* or *"Maíz con jalapeño!"* As he moved through the crowd, he nodded to people that he knew or stopped to exchange brief greetings with friends of his grandfather. Near the entrance to the hall, Jackson saw Reuben and Julio Ramirez waving at him. He waved in return and headed in their direction.

As Jackson negotiated past a group of men who were bickering aggravatedly among themselves, a squat, barrel-chested man blocked his path. "You still takin' bets?" the man asked in English with a thick Mexican accent.

"No, we're closed," Jackson said carefully. The man in front of him was Esteban Tejate, the father of Juan Tejate, a person he was sworn to fight. The Tejate family was almost pure-blooded Indian; it showed in their straight black hair, their broad, brown faces with high cheekbones, and in their glittering black eyes as well. They were known to be unscrupulous dog handlers. Jackson had heard that they would even use rabid dogs. They were the lowest of the low.

Jackson was in the act of stepping around Esteban when he heard Juan say loudly in Spanish, "Don't waste your time on the little Negro, Father. He doesn't have the balls to bet with us."

"Fuck you, Juan!" Jackson retorted as he swiveled to face a taller, thinner version of the father.

"Any time you want to try, sissy!" Juan sneered in English, his accent as thick as his father's. Juan's black eyes glinted in the hall's lights. He was seventeen, two years older than Jackson, and had a reputation for being tough. Although Jackson was over four inches taller and outweighed him by a few pounds, Juan looked more physically mature. He had the musculature of a man, while Jackson still looked like a gangly boy. But looks were deceiving. Jackson could deadlift his own weight and pull himself, hand over hand, up twenty feet of rope. He was not afraid of Juan; in fact, the prospect of fighting him excited him.

A horn blared, signaling that the dogfight would start soon. Jackson turned on his heel and resumed making his way through the throng of fight fans. He had to get the guns. He heard Juan jeer something in Spanish and then heard Esteban's crude laugh, but the words were lost in the milling sounds as people began making their way to their seats. The crowd was mostly men, however there was a significant number of women interspersed among them. At the door, he stopped and spoke briefly to the Ramirez brothers and then he went out into the darkness to his grandfather's truck.

When he returned the dogs were already in the pit. Their handlers were walking them up and down, building the dogs' excitement. The American dog was a big, chestnut-colored Staffordshire bullterrier. His broad head and shoulders bespoke the centuries of breeding that had developed his tremendous physical strength and fighting heart. His coat gleamed in the stark lights of the pit. His ears were cropped and they stood up like little triangles on his head. The dog pranced lightly beside his handler, eager to be at the other dog. The American dog's name was Prince and Jackson thought he looked like one. He was the most handsome pit bull that Jackson had ever seen. He knew that if he had such a dog, he would never put him in the pit to fight, but of course, he would never put any dog in the pit. Jackson only attended dogfights because of his grandfather.

His grandfather had seats in the first row above the pit. Jackson sat down next to him and passed him his pistols wrapped up in an old sweater. His grandfather took the sweater and casually slid one gun into a holster that he had sewn into his jacket; the other pistol he pushed into his waistband.

The second dog was named Diablito. He was a thickset mongrel terrier. His coat was black and his muzzle and neck were covered with scars from previous pit battles. He looked like a mix between an English bullterrier and the American Staffordshire. He was built stockier and closer to the ground than Prince.

Unlike Diablito, Prince had no scars visible on the chestnut sheen of his coat. When Jackson mentioned this to his grandfather, his grandfather said, "His owner got class; he only fights him twice a year."

The dogs were brought to the scratch lines. Diablito's handler shook the carcass of a dead cat in front of the dog to excite its blood lust. A referee stepped forward and announced that the fight would be conducted under standard rules. Then everyone cleared the pit except for the handlers.

A horn blared and the dogs were loosed on each other. Diablito shot across the pit. It looked as if the fight would be over in seconds, for Diablito was within inches of Prince's throat. With sheer power and heart, Prince fought off the wall and forced Diablito back to the center of the pit. The crowd roared its approval at Prince's effort.

Despite himself, Jackson found himself transfixed by the snarling, guttural action in the pit. It soon became apparent why Prince had such a horde of supporters: The dog had both speed and strength. After the initial clash, Prince began to elude Diablito's short, quick lunges and began making parrying attacks himself. In the first five minutes, it was obvious to all observers that Prince was quicker than his adversary, but he did not possess Diablito's massive strength.

Fifteen minutes into the fight, the first turn occurred. Prince, in an attempt to avoid Diablito's lunging attack, leaped against the pit wall and was immediately pinned by Diablito. Diablito gained a head hold and Prince's head was turned. The dog handlers entered the pit at once and separated the dogs. Prince was bleeding from the muzzle and Diablito's head and shoulders were a mass of oozing cuts.

The fight crowd, which had never been quiet, roared to life. People shouted across the pit to their friends. All around the hall, people were marveling at the power and courage of the dogs. It was a good fight:

speed and youth against age and strength. Everyone knew that this was a fight which would be talked about for years. It would set the standard for the future.

The dogs were brought back to the scratch line and the horn blared again. The fight commenced. Diablito shot across the pit again, but Prince had learned his lesson; he was not there. As if he had taken advice from his handler, the American dog's strategy had changed. He began to make serious counterattacks after every lunge by his adversary. Prince was not striking for the head, but at his opponent's legs and feet. After several near misses, the crowd, sensing a change in the fight, sat forward in their seats. It was not long in coming.

Diablito, with his tremendous fighting heart and great strength, had never learned to adjust his fighting tactics. He would keep charging at his opponents until they were dead or he was killed. Prince was a dog of a different kind. He owed his unblemished coat to the fact he had both speed and the ability to learn. It was a question of time. Coordinating his movement with Diablito's lunge, Prince struck. His powerful jaws closed around Diablito's right foreleg and there was a loud snap that was heard all around the pit. Diablito's inertia caused him to flip over on his back as Prince kept a hold on his leg. Prince struck for the throat, but Diablito, being a crafty veteran of many battles, twisted away in time and Prince missed. Diablito's head was twisted back and another turn was called.

The handlers rushed into the pit. The dogs were separated again. The crowd waited in hushed silence for Diablito's handler to make the decision as to whether his dog could continue or not. Jackson was on the edge of his seat as well. He watched Diablito standing on three legs down in the pit. He was a mass of confusion. He wanted his grandfather to win, but he also felt that the chestnut dog was superior and if the fight continued, Prince would eventually kill Diablito.

After checking the condition of Diablito's leg, his handler stood up and looked at Jackson's grandfather. The two of them exchanged hand signals and then the handler went to talk with the referee.

Jackson's grandfather stood up and took out a large wad of money from his pocket and said loudly for all to hear, "Five thousand dollars on Diablito!"

There was a shocked silence, then pandemonium. People in the crowd had trouble believing their ears. Jackson could not believe it himself. He couldn't understand his grandfather's thinking. Was the bet some kind of ploy? he wondered. Jackson hoped that his grandfather did not still think that Diablito could win. People began to reach across him or lean on him in an effort to bet their money with his grandfather. He shook someone off his shoulder angrily and stood up. Men were jostling around his grandfather as he was taking bets.

Jackson asked, "Do you need me, Grandfather?"

"No, I got it covered, boy."

"I'm going outside for some air, if that's okay with you," Jackson said, stretching slowly.

"Just stay close when it's time to collect the money. I may need you," his grandfather said without taking his eyes off the money he was counting.

Jackson walked away through the crowd. Outside under the dim light of the stars, he bought some skewered meat that an old woman was cooking on a brazier. The meat was hot and juicy and very spicy. His grandfather called it "losing dog" meat, but Jackson liked it. Lots of others had followed him out into the coolness of the night air. The old woman at the brazier was doing a booming business. People stood around in its flickering light, pulling hot pieces of meat off the skewers with their teeth. Everyone was talking about the amazing bet that El Negro had just placed. One man said loudly that El Negro was throwing money away, but someone close to him pointed out Jackson and the man fell silent.

The horn blared. People began to rush back into the hall to get to their seats. Jackson ambled to the door, but he did not want to go inside. This was the part of dogfights that he disliked the most: Both animals were bloodied and tired, yet still fighting on courage and instinct, ready to die in order to vanquish their rival. He felt particularly badly during this dogfight, because he didn't think Diablito stood much of a chance before his leg had been broken. Now, with that impairment, Jackson thought that it was extremely cold-blooded to let the fight continue. It was like sending Diablito to his death with no veneer of fair play. Whatever his grandfather's motive, money seemed to be a poor reason for Diablito to die.

Inside the crowd roared and then roared again. It sounded as if death was close. Jackson went back in the hall and returned to his seat. The scene that he saw shocked him. Diablito had a death hold on Prince; how that had happened was unimaginable to Jackson, yet here it was in front of him. Prince was fading fast. Diablito had a firm grip on his throat. Inside his head, Jackson pleaded for the fight to be stopped. He started to get up and go back outside, but his grandfather grabbed his arm and gestured for him to stay seated. Jackson closed his eyes and begged the invisible gods to intercede on Prince's behalf. As if fate had only been waiting for this entreaty, a towel was thrown into the pit by Prince's handler. The crowd roared its approval, signaling that others thought that the fight should be stopped as well.

After the dogs had been taken out of the pit, Jackson stood at the edge of the pit once again, watching as it was being swept with coarse brooms. His grandfather was counting his cash. He had done quite well, more than quadrupling his original money due to several late side bets. People were beginning to file out of the hall. Everyone was talking about the spectacular turnabout in the fight.

Jackson still did not understand how his grandfather had known that Diablito would win. When Jackson asked him, all he would say was "To gamble, you got to know how to judge the heart in both man and beast."

Across the pit, Jackson saw Juan Tejate walking out with one of his brothers and his father. Juan saw him as well and made an obscene gesture, which Jackson's grandfather witnessed.

"You havin' trouble with the Tejates?" his grandfather asked curtly.

"Looks like Juan and I have a few things to work out," Jackson answered.

"Can you kick his ass?" his grandfather asked, still counting his money.

"Yes." Jackson nodded. "I think I can, anyway."

"What did I tell you about the difference between thinkin' and doin'?"

"I can whip him," Jackson said with more certainty.

"You ready to try it now?" His grandfather measured him with a steady look.

"Yeah, I guess so," Jackson said, slightly confused. "But where?"

"Down there." His grandfather indicated the pit with a nod of his head and continued to count his money.

"Down there?" Jackson questioned, not particularly pleased at the prospect of fighting in the same arena as the dogs.

"Better down there in the open than in some alley where him and his brothers jump you and maybe kill you."

There was a certain logic to it, Jackson had to admit. "Okay," he said hesitantly.

"Then call him out," his grandfather said in a matter-of-fact tone.

Jackson turned and shouted across the pit in Spanish, "Juan Tejate, you're a cowardly dog and a bastard! If you have any balls at all, you'll meet me in the pit. Then we'll see how tough you are, you homosexual thief!"

His grandfather looked at him without emotion and said, "I hope you can fight better than you can curse."

Jackson leaped down into the pit and waited. Juan entered the pit through one of the gates. He was livid. It appeared as if Jackson's awkward insults had hit the mark. Juan strode across the pit with the clear intent to start fighting as soon as he was close enough to punch.

Jackson's grandfather's voice boomed across the pit, "Hold it, Juan!"

Juan paused midstride. It wasn't that he was afraid of El Negro, but he knew that it wasn't wise to unnecessarily irritate him. El Negro was acknowledged by all who knew him as an extremely dangerous man. That is what made the little Negro's challenge so sweet. Juan's father had pointed it out to him on the way to the pit. This would be the one time that he could beat the little Negro until he fell without risking the wrath of El Negro. Any other time and El Negro would come seeking blood, even if there was no hint of foul play. However, here in front of the world, he could give the Negrito a real beating and his grandfather would be unable to take any action. His hands would be tied by his own stupid sense of honor. It was a gift from the gods. Juan almost laughed as he turned with a swagger to face El Negro.

People began returning to their seats. There were muffled conversations as the word of what was happening rippled through the crowd.

El Negro said loudly, "This is hand-to-hand gambler's rules. No weapons allowed! No guns! No knives!"

Jackson heard his grandfather's words and realized that he still had the .44 Mag in his waistband. He opened his jacket and pulled out the big revolver, which he handed up to his grandfather.

The crowd gasped as they saw the big gun emerge from Jackson's clothing. Their attention shifted back to Juan; everyone was waiting to see what type of weapon he would produce.

"I don't have no gun," Juan said in Spanish. There was a nasty smile on his face.

Someone cried out from the crowd, "What about the knife in his boot?"

A shot rang out. The bullet ricocheted in the dirt between Juan's feet and thudded into the wall behind him, splintering the wooden walls of the pit. The barrel of the .44 Magnum in El Negro's hand was smoking.

There was a sudden quiet among the onlookers. It was obvious to all that there was no love lost between the families of the boys in the pit. Juan knelt quickly and removed the knife from his boot and handed the weapon up to his father, who now sat on the opposite side of the pit from El Negro.

People began jostling one another, trying to get good seats. It was a fight crowd and they could smell blood. Everyone knew that El Negro was a tough, vicious fighter who was good with a knife and an excellent shot with either pistol or rifle, but his grandson was an unknown quantity. Juan, on the other hand, was known. He was building a reputation for himself as a tough, hard-nosed kid. He had already assisted his father with several enforcement actions, and it was commonly known that the victims of those actions were dead.

Jackson was unable to concentrate on anything other than Juan. All the sounds of the crowd—catcalls, the shouts of support—blended together to produce a noise similar to the static of poor radio reception. Even his grandfather's voice was difficult to distinguish. The lights, the faces, the bright-colored clothing all swirled and spun into a kaleidoscopic vortex and at the center of this tunnel of color stood Juan. No one else was real. Only he and Juan existed. There was an eerie peace in their isolation, but it was not relaxing. The tension seemed to grow with each passing minute. Jackson shook himself, trying to loosen up his muscles and reduce his nervousness. He was not concerned with winning, but with fighting bravely. There was no shame attached to losing if one fought courageously. And, if one fought with courage, that commitment alone often carried the day.

A referee was selected and the fight began. Juan and Jackson circled each other slowly, looking for openings. Juan carried his hands low, confident of his strength and ability. Jackson's stance was that of the classical boxer: hands high protecting his head, and elbows in close to his body. Juan made the first attack by lunging in with a big, roundhouse right. Jackson eluded it easily and gave Juan two stiff jabs for his effort. Twice more Juan tried this approach with the same result except the third time, Jackson followed the jab with a hard right cross that opened up Juan's cheek. The crowd cheered at the first sign of blood.

Juan felt the blood trickle down his skin and grimly faced his taller, thinner opponent. The little Negro was quicker than he expected; not that he was in doubt about the final outcome, but Juan realized that he would have to change his strategy and get under the guard of his enemy. He saw an opportunity when Jackson got his legs crossed avoiding a feint and he rushed at Jackson with his head down, aiming for the hips. Juan felt solid contact as he hit Jackson waist high and drove him back to the wall of the pit. With satisfaction he heard Jackson exhale sharply as the air was forced out of his diaphragm. Juan dropped low and tried to grab Jackson's legs to sweep his feet from underneath him, but Jackson's speed helped him again and he stepped out of Juan's grasp. Juan did not let him back into the center of the pit. He kept Jackson pinned against the wall, choosing the spots where he would press his attack. At one point he lunged and Jackson met him with a two-fisted defense.

Throwing uppercuts and hooks, it looked like Jackson was going to drive Juan back across the pit; he was landing solidly to the head and the body. Then Juan struck, once to the head and once to the body. Jackson's knees buckled and he nearly went down, but he caught himself. Jackson took several hard blows on his arms and shoulders before he was able to escape to the center of the pit.

The fight crowd, which had started out in a noisy, jocular mood, had grown quiet. As the fight wore on, its mood grew even more somber, as if the crowd realized that there were larger issues at stake than in the dogfight which preceded it. The onlookers sat with the collective silence of a giant predator, watching the ebb and flow of the action. The only sound in the hall was made by the boys in the pit.

Jackson was hitting Juan three times for every punch Juan landed. He had opened up cuts over both of Juan's eyes with hard, snapping combinations and was continuing to land solid punches, but he was unable to stop Juan's forward progress. With each exchange, it grew more obvious who hit the hardest. Juan had staggered him twice and had backed him up consistently throughout the fight. Jackson had speed and technique and Juan had stopping power.

There was an air of déjà vu about the fight; people in the audience began to mention it among themselves. Jackson had the flash of Prince and Juan was the relentless Diablito. There were many who thought the result was inevitable: Diabito would win again. There were even a few who stated to whoever would listen that both boys had proven their courage and the fight should be stopped. Needless to say, these few were a very small minority. To the gamblers, the odds were based upon whether they thought three of Jackson's punches equaled one of Juan's.

The fight was fairly even until Jackson made a foolish mistake. He allowed Juan to lunge underneath his guard. Juan did not stop to throw a punch, but instead continued his rush, using his head like a battering ram. Jackson swiveled to avoid the butt; however, he misjudged Juan's momentum. Juan's head hit him on his left jaw and he was driven, spinning, to the wall by the impact of Juan's body. Unable to get his hands up in time, he hit the wall face first. The inertia of his spin caused the brunt of his collision to be taken on his arms and shoulders, but when he came away from the wall a tooth fell out of his mouth and blood dripped down his chin. He was stunned and out on his feet. Juan was ready for him. Juan hit him with a straight left on the chin and Jackson dropped to the ground like he had been shot. The right, which Juan had also intended for him, glanced off the top of his head and thudded into the wall. As Jackson got to his knees, Juan kicked him in the stomach and Jackson fell over in the dirt.

The crowd roared its disapproval. Kicking an opponent who was down was taboo in gambler's rules. If someone was knocked off his feet, he was given a leisurely count of ten to get off the ground and stand up. If he wanted to continue, the fight went on. El Negro stood up and many noticed that his hand gripped the pistol in his waistband. People began to move away from where the Tejate family was sitting.

Jackson fell in a heap, hearing bells. He rolled to his knees and pain exploded in his stomach, knocking the air out of him. He fell back in the dirt. Despite the pain in his side, he noticed that his vision was clearing. He saw the referee bending over him and realized that he was still lying on the ground. He got to his feet by the count of eight. Over the referee's shoulder, he could see the dark, piercing eyes of his grandfather. Jackson nodded his head at his grandfather, indicating that he was all right. The referee asked him if he wanted to continue. Jackson looked again at his grandfather, saw the glittering eyes, and said yes.

When it became clear that Jackson would continue, people began to shake their heads knowingly; the boy was cut from the same material as the grandfather. For the first time there was doubt among some of the audience as to whether Juan would win or not. A Tejate supporter began shouting repeatedly in Spanish, "Stop the fight! Juan is the winner! Stop the fight! Juan is the winner!"

A voice cut through the general chatter. It was El Negro and he said, "You better say joe, 'cause you sho' don't know! Ten thousand dollars on my grandson!"

There was a collective gasp. Ten thousand dollars was a small fortune. In an area where people often killed for less than one hundred dollars, it created awe.

"Tejate," El Negro yelled across the pit to Esteban. "Where's your money?"

Once again the hall grew quiet. El Negro had thrown a direct challenge to the Tejates. Esteban had to match the money or lose considerable face. Esteban made no move to respond. It became obvious to everyone that Tejate was not going to gamble his money on his son winning. Now, even if his grandson lost, El Negro had cast shame on the Tejate family, which far exceeded any honors that would be earned from the beating of his grandson. There were those in attendance who stated that it was disgusting that anybody would allow their kin to fight in a pit designed for dogs, but to bet on it was truly a sin. These people spoke quietly and addressed their remarks in confidence to their friends. But the gamblers and regulars knew that El Negro had found his heir.

Jackson knew that his grandfather had not placed the bet just to win more money, but that it was a message for him. It was a vote of confidence. His grandfather thought he could win, but even if he lost, he knew he had earned his grandfather's respect. This understanding made Jackson feel invincible. His pains were not forgotten, but they were in the distant background. He was eager for the fight to begin. He felt light, almost buoyant.

Juan's right hand was swelling rapidly and hurt when he moved either his fingers or his wrist. It did not feel broken, but it hurt all the way to his elbow. He had hoped that the little Negro would not come to scratch, but he was disappointed. The fight was begun and he noticed that Jackson was fighting like he had been rejuvenated. Juan's right hand was useless to him and for the first time, he found himself backing up. He tried another battering-ram-like lunge, but his opponent was too quick. Juan received several hard punches to the back of his neck and kidneys. He threw a flurry of punches to drive Jackson back, but Jackson caught him on the chin with an uppercut as he was closing with him. The punch snapped Juan's head back and staggered him. As he fought to maintain his balance, a hard right crashed against his temple. His legs were rubbery as he fought to remain upright.

Jackson saw this opening and attacked. He drove past Juan's faltering guard and hit him on the jaw with a vicious right hook. The blow propelled Juan backward. His head hit the wooden wall of the pit with a loud crack. He bounced off the wall and stumbled as he began to fall. Jackson met him with another hard right, which snapped his head back. Juan fell in a pile at his feet.

Jackson looked up at his grandfather and saw him clench his fists in front of him and roar, "That's my blood! That's my blood!"

Jackson looked down at the crumpled form at his feet and felt the power of victory flow through him. With blood trickling down his face, Jackson threw back his head and roared his triumph. He was tired, but he was jubilant, for he had proven himself before the sternest of judges. He was still shouting when his grandfather led him away.

Thursday, July 8, 1982

Mamie, the forty-five-foot motor cruiser, nosed its way through the bay's choppy waters with an easy rhythm. The powerful engines purred as Jackson Tremain let the throttle out halfway. Other than the few recent daylight test runs he had made on the bay, it had been nearly twenty years since he had piloted the big motorboat, but the memory was only hazy, not forgotten. He checked the charts and knew that if he stayed within the main channel, he would not have to rely on the banks of navigation instruments on the panel in front of him. He touched his cheek involuntarily where Jesse had hit him; it was aching and sensitive to the touch.

The night was dark and moonless and the pale light of the distant stars cast no reflection on the dark and rippling waters of San Francisco Bay. Jackson kept his eyes on the radar screen, watching the image of an oil tanker headed toward the entrance of the Golden Gate. The tanker appeared to be going about twenty knots an hour and bearing down fast. Jackson did not want to be near the tanker when it rushed through the Gate. The cabin was lit solely by the green and yellow lights of the navigational instruments. Jackson touched the teak panel and thought of his grandfather. The old man seemed to have thought of everything. For nearly twenty-five years King had paid to maintain this same motor cruiser in the estuary between Oakland and Alameda. Jackson had reviewed the maintenance and dry-dock reports and had approved: Five years ago the cruiser had been refitted with new engines and drive assemblies, and during the time it was dry-docked, the hull was refinished and painted. The fittings glistened and the teak paneling gleamed, an indication of time and attention. Jackson felt comfortable in the cabin's dimness. He pushed the throttle higher and felt the boat surge forward. The cruiser's hull skimmed the surface of the bay, slapping against the waves in a complex staccato rhythm. He could see the navigational beacons in the darkness at the base of the Golden Gate Bridge. The stanchions of the bridge rose like dark shapes against the lighter darkness of night, up to a distant halo of lights. He recalled from his many boating and fishing trips along the north coast with his grandfather that there were dangerous shoals on the north side of the Gate.

The cabin door slid open and Carlos came in carrying two mugs of hot soup. A cold breeze, bringing the taste of the salt sea, entered with him. Carlos shouldered the door shut. "How much farther out do you want to go?"

Jackson took a mug of soup, set it down, and said sardonically, "Whenever I have to dump a body, I like to do it far enough out so that they don't float back in before I dock."

"They won't float for long," Carlos said with a laugh. "I've got them weighted down with old truck batteries."

"Carlos, you've been like a combination uncle and older brother to me since the first year we met. There's never been a time when I didn't like who you were. But the way you accept killing as part of life is disturbing. I don't want to get used to it. And it was unnerving to see you torturing that man. Hell, it made me think of death squads."

Carlos walked over to the seat next to the captain's chair and sat down. He noisily slurped his soup and said nothing. Jackson gave him a long, serious look then gestured with his hand, asking for a response.

"We needed his information," Carlos said tiredly. "He would not have given it without persuasion. I had to persuade him."

"I guess euphemisms are important when you torture and kill people," Jackson said.

Carlos gave Jackson an understanding smile. "I used to feel as you do. I let men who wanted to kill me get to their feet. Time has since taught me the stupidity of such decisions. That man's pain saved us time and perhaps our lives. We now have the name of a third man that wasn't on your list. Life will be simpler now with this information and these men will be consumed in the coldness of the sea."

"Is it really that simple?" Jackson asked.

"Yes!" Carlos said with an emphatic nod of his head. "I've always lived on the edge of civilization, where life is cheap and death is good if it comes without torture. I didn't create that world, I just lived in it."

The cruiser slewed to one side briefly before Jackson got it back on course. "We're going through the Gate," Jackson explained. "The current always gets a little crazy here." He looked at Carlos's features, tinted green by the panel lights. "If you know the world you live in is that bad, yet you have alternatives, why continue to live in it? There are ten thousand worlds."

"I guess really only one reason." Carlos slurped his soup. "Almost everybody that I cared for lived in that world. It was El Indio and El Negro's world. Now it's ours."

"No, it's not. I don't want to live my life taking other people's lives. I've lost the only woman I've ever truly loved because of this crap. I'm prepared to fight because I have to, but I don't want this. I don't want to have to check for enemies when I walk out of my house, or carry a gun ten years from now."

"Then hire bodyguards," Carlos answered. "There can be no return to your past existence. You can't turn back the clock. This is your life."

"Elizabeth said the same thing when I saw her this evening."

"She sounds like a wise woman."

"Wise enough to tell me that she never wanted to see me again." Jackson picked up his mug and drank his soup.

"That tanker is gaining fast," Carlos observed, watching the radar screen. "She'll be on us within five minutes."

"We'll be out of the way by then," Jackson answered. "I couldn't go through the Gate at top speed; the current is too unpredictable. We'll clear the shoals and then we'll veer off to the right."

The waters outside the Gate moved in larger swells and the cruiser rose and dropped accordingly. Along the San Francisco coast, lights twinkled and in the clear, cloudless sky the stars gleamed balefully. The wind had picked up; Jackson could hear the intermittent gusts whistling past. In the darkness ahead he saw a final beacon, dancing on the movement of the sea. It was two minutes away. He would clear the beacon well before the tanker overtook him.

"You know what I think your problem is?" Carlos mused.

"I'm sure that you're going to tell me," Jackson answered.

"I think that you're afraid of yourself."

"What the hell does that mean?" Jackson asked, exasperated. "That could be the answer for damn near everything."

"It *is* the answer for damn near everything," Carlos asserted.

"Then it's meaningless!"

"Only if you choose it to be so," Carlos answered. "Why don't you let me make my point and then you can make your decision as to whether it's meaningless or not."

Jackson nodded his head. "Okay."

"I think that you realize that you have the capacity and willingness to kill."

"Under the right circumstances, so does everyone," Jackson countered.

"Ah, but yours is close to the surface. You have a lot of El Negro in you and it comes out when you least expect it."

"Explain," Jackson demanded.

"The man that you beat in the parking garage; you intended to kill him—"

"Whoa! That was self-defense and anger. I didn't go looking for trouble. He and his buddy started it. I fought back, that's all."

"When you dropped your weight on him, I knew that the spirit of El Negro was not dead."

"I only meant to disable him," Jackson said defensively.

"You weigh, what—two hundred and thirty pounds? You dropped on him twice on the chest. You must have meant to kill him. You cracked his ribs and probably drove them into his lungs."

"He was still alive when we put him in the trunk," Jackson protested.

"Don't waste time rationalizing; he's dead now. What I want to get through to you is that ambivalence leads to hesitation. You must be committed to maximize your reflexes. You will need to have quick reactions. Don't fight yourself!"

A blast from a foghorn warned them that the tanker was close. It could be seen three hundred yards to their stern, a towering, dark shape with numerous running lights, churning out of the Gate. The last beacon was just off to the starboard. Jackson turned the boat slightly to the right, angling away from the path of the tanker.

"We should drop them here," Carlos suggested. "Maybe they'll get sucked into the propellers of the tanker."

Jackson shivered. It seemed so heartless and cold, but on the other hand, if he was committed to killing, what difference did it make? "If we drop them here, you'll have to do it by yourself, Carlos. We're still too close to that tanker to stop; the wake alone will wash over us."

"No problem," Carlos said. He got up and left the cabin, leaving Jackson with his thoughts.

The sound of wind swooshed through the cabin door and then stopped abruptly as the door was slid closed. Off the starboard beam, Jackson could see whitecaps as the waves rushed over the shoals. It was definitely rougher outside the Gate. The boat now pitched up and down with each succeeding swell. Jackson wanted to make sure that he had sufficient distance from the tanker and had the boat facing in the direction of its wake. He didn't want water washing over the low stern of his motor cruiser. As he turned the cruiser, it fell into the trough of a wave with a loud smack and a burst of spray. He throttled back slowly until the boat rode the waves without drifting toward the shoals. He braced the wheel and went out to drop the sea anchor, then he turned to help Carlos.

Jackson and Carlos labored in darkness as the spray of waves washed over them. Jesse's body went over the side first. The two large batteries attached to his legs caused him to disappear with little more than a splash. Fletcher was more difficult since he was conscious and he struggled. Carlos and Jackson wrestled his body up the gangway. The pitching motion and the wet deck of the boat hindered their efforts. Jackson grabbed Fletcher's legs, which had been tied together with rope tied to the coarse webbing that held the heavy truck batteries. Even in the darkness Jackson could see the panic on his face. Tape had been placed across his mouth to prevent him from screaming, but it did not prevent him from grunting and groaning as he fought to break free from Jackson and Carlos.

The tanker gave another warning blast as it headed out into the open sea. From the stern of the cruiser, it looked like a five-story building passing in the night. The bow of the huge ship cut through the water with hardly a roll. The wake caused by the passage of the tanker caused the cruiser to pitch and roll with even greater height and frequency.

Carlos lost his footing and fell heavily as a swell hit the side of the cruiser, spraying icy salt water over the three of them. When he regained his feet, Jackson shouted, "We've got to throw him over the side now. I can't be sure how far we've drifted." The cold, moisture-laden wind whipped the sound of his voice away. Carlos nodded and lifted the bundled batteries with a grunt and tossed them overboard. Almost immediately the rope that was connected to Fletcher's legs grew taut. The boat fell into a trough and another wave smacked against the side, dousing them anew with cold spray. Jackson grabbed Fletcher under the arms while Carlos got a grip on his legs. They lifted Fletcher's body together and waited for the cruiser to ride the swells and pitch in the right direction. Even though the man's hands were tied and lashed against his waist, he clutched at Jackson's coat sleeve and begged. His words were garbled and indistinct due to the tape, but Jackson understood him. The man was pleading for his life. Yet he felt nothing. This was one of the men who had killed Wesley.

They waited for the next swell to pass and when the cruiser rose, lifted by the swell, they tossed the writhing man overboard. His head bobbed momentarily on the surface and then disappeared under the water's darkness.

Friday, July 9, 1982

Jackson sat back in the comfortable executive chair and stared across the table at Delbert Witherspoon and his attorney. Delbert had taken his black felt fedora off the table and was now kneading it in his hands. His nervous eyes blinked rapidly and every few moments there was a twitch in his shoulders. There was a scared look on his narrow face, yet it was hard for Jackson to imagine him with any other kind of expression. The blatancy of the man's fear made Jackson feel uncomfortable, but Delbert was the first cog in the line that he had to strip until he brought his enemies' criminal machinery to a screeching halt. Jackson had discovered there was currently about four and a half million in drug profits being laundered through T&W Construction. He had the money impounded and had filed an injunction against further transfers. He had also started proceedings to freeze the target accounts as well.

Jackson opened the thick file in front of him and took out a copy of a contract. He took a deep breath and asked, "Do you know why you're here, Mr. Witherspoon?"

Witherspoon looked at his attorney before answering. When his attorney gave him the go-ahead nod, he answered, "Uh, I received some sort of writ and, uh, lots of legal notices about, uh, injunctions you've filed."

"Do you know why I filed them, Mr. Witherspoon?"

Delbert's attorney, Barney Phillips, retorted tiredly, "Do you expect him to read your mind?" After he finished speaking, Phillips pulled the cuffs of his shirt out of his suit jacket and checked his nails. He was a stocky black man who had his head shaved and wore a beard precisely trimmed in the Van Dyke style. He did not appear to be greatly interested in what Jackson had to say.

Jackson slid the contract across the table. "Have you ever seen this? This is the founding legal document outlining the contractual arrangements under which T and W would operate." Phillips snatched up the contract and began to read it.

Jackson gave Witherspoon a smile and continued. "This contract spells out the ownership and the means by which the revenues of T and W Construction will be distributed."

Delbert blanched. "That—that was signed with King Tremain. He's dead. That contract can't still be legal. When he was declared a wanted felon, all his property that they could find was confiscated."

Phillips jumped in. "Clearly, a wanted felon would not be able to keep property gained as a consequence of criminal activity and certainly that would be one prong of our attack should this ever get to court."

Jackson chuckled. "It's too bad you're not more familiar with your

client's case, Mr. Phillips. You see, King Tremain sold his investment in
T and W to Rockland United in 1951, three years before he was declared a wanted felon." Jackson pulled another contract from the folder
and slid it across the table. "Your father also signed this transfer of ownership in front of a notary public. This is a legal document."

Jackson watched Witherspoon fidget in his seat while Phillips hastily
reviewed the new document. Jackson thought that if he could separate
Witherspoon from his attorney, there might be a greater chance of success in getting him to understand that Jackson was not after him. "Mr.
Witherspoon, I requested this meeting so that we could talk informally
and without attorneys because I thought that we might be able to work
out an arrangement that might serve us both well."

Phillips scoffed, "You called this meeting in a law office. My client
has no desire to meet with you without legal representation."

"Although I have contracted the services of Johnson, Wyland and
Johnson, I'm in this room by myself. I convened this meeting in their
general conference room because they are a prestigious law firm and I
wanted Mr. Witherspoon to know that everything that I will do will be
legal and aboveboard. I didn't want him to be afraid."

Phillips stood up huffily. "How dare you! My client isn't afraid! Unless you've got something else, this meeting is over! We'll see you in
court!"

"Before you go, let me give you a statement of my commitment. I am
prepared to spend ten million dollars in legal fees to win this case and in
the process I'll prevent T and W from moving one piece of equipment.
This company won't work for at least two years. I'll freeze the bank accounts. I'll have auditors poring over the records. According to your
IRS filings, T and W made twenty million last year, but your individual
taxes were only a hundred and fifty thousand. Where did all that
money go? It's not showing on the company's books."

Phillips nudged his client. "Let's go, Mr. Witherspoon."

"Go ahead," Jackson chuckled humorlessly as he pointed at Witherspoon. "But you'll be the fall guy. Your buddies will leave you out to dry.
And how do you think they'll treat you when they see you're of no
more use to them? You know too much. You're a loose string. And you
know they don't like loose strings." Jackson tapped his chest. "I'm your
only hope and if you help me, you might even walk away with the company."

Phillips sputtered angrily, "How dare you! How dare you attempt to intimidate my client! You'll answer for this! I'll slap a libel suit on you so fast you won't know what hit you!"

Jackson laughed. "You're small fish, Phillips! I told you I'm willing to spend ten million dollars to win this case. I can crush you for a million and a half. I'll bury you in litigation. You're just a bug on the floor. Mr. Witherspoon, on the other hand, has an opportunity to free himself of parasites."

"I won't stand here and be threatened! I'm surprised that Johnson, Wyland and Johnson would put up with this type of chicanery! Let's go!" Phillips attempted to hurry Witherspoon from the conference room.

Jackson ignored Phillips and directed his remarks at Witherspoon. "It'll cost you nothing just to sit and listen to my proposal. You don't have to say anything, just listen."

Phillips grabbed Witherspoon's arm. "We've heard everything he has to say!" Several times Witherspoon looked questioningly over his shoulder at Jackson and appeared to be on the edge of saying something, but his courage failed him. He was led away without comment.

After Witherspoon's departure, Jackson spent another forty-five minutes with his attorney reviewing the legal actions that had been prepared. He left the office with the understanding that litigation would commence the next day. He had struck his first blow against his enemies. There were a number of other actions that he planned to undertake over the next few days which would flush them farther out of their holes. When Jackson left the law offices through the building's service entrance, an unmarked black van was waiting for him. He got into the back of the van and directed the driver across the bridge to the East Bay. The van was set up like a limousine, with a closure for the driver, executive chairs, telephone, writing table, and fold-down benches for extra riders. His grandfather had two of the vehicles built to unobtrusively move men around the Bay Area. Carlos had suggested that Jackson use one for his own errands and tasks.

The day was overcast and grim. A northwesterly wind gusted through the Gate as gray and silver clouds preceded a dark, charcoal formation that was billowing ominously just off the coast. Jackson hadn't listened to any weather reports, but it looked as if the day's climate had no relation to the day before.

Jackson picked up Rhasan outside the Oakland museum. When he got into the van, Rhasan began to chatter away immediately about his run-in with the Lenzinis, but Jackson waved him to silence. "We can talk about all of that when we get to where we're going. Tell me about your plans to leave for college."

Rhasan looked at Jackson intently and said with youthful fervor, "I was thinking about passing on those plans until we dealt with the problems caused by my great-grandfather's death."

"What's this 'we' stuff?"

Rhasan was shocked by Jackson's question. He tapped his chest and said through gritted teeth, "I'm going to help you. This is a family fight. Plus, I want to kick that fat guy's ass! We'll show them not to mess with the Tremains!"

Jackson did not respond immediately. He began mulling over how best he could harness Rhasan's desire to help in a manner that would keep him out of danger. He didn't want the added anxiety of worrying about his nephew. He watched the expressions cross Rhasan's face as he inspected the inside of the van.

Rhasan turned to him. "This ain't bad, Uncle Jax. Is this one of Great-grandfather's rides?"

"Yeah, he had two like this."

"Man, oh man! This is cool! One of his attack vehicles, huh?"

"You might call it that."

"Does he still have that motor cruiser you used to tell me about? I'd like to go sailing on it sometime."

Jackson nodded and said, "We'll see about that."

"So, what are we going to do today?"

"We're going to talk. You and I. I want you to be clear about your role."

"That sounds like you've been talking to my mother!" Rhasan retorted, an angry tone entering his voice. "Listen, I'm not a kid anymore! I'm an adult! I know it's hard for you older types to cut the apron strings, but I'm a man. And I'm prepared to take on a man's responsibilities!"

"Good! There are plenty of adult responsibilities related to getting your life on track and they should occupy all of your time."

"What are we riding around for?" Rhasan demanded angrily. "There's no need for discussion! You've already made up your mind! You want to treat me like a child too! If you don't want to include me, that's okay, but I'm not running away! I can get some protection from Fox. I got friends who'll cover my back!"

The implications of Rhasan's statement were not lost on Jackson. Eighteen was a period in life when rashness often crossed all the way over into stupidity. He couldn't afford a war of the wills with his nephew. "All right! All right," Jackson conceded. "Why don't we do this. Ride with me over to Muir Woods. I'll listen to whatever you have to say regarding what you think your participation should be and you'll listen to my response. Okay?"

"Why go all the way over there? We could talk right here!"

"I want us both to have ample time to think about what we're going to say and I want us to say it in the most constructive fashion possible. This is not a game! People have been killed! Are you prepared to take time and formulate your thoughts before we discuss?"

Rhasan was so full of ideas and thoughts he was about to burst, yet he swallowed down his words with an effort and said, "I know what I think right now!"

"Well, good for you. I don't. You are important to me and I don't want to present my ideas poorly. Are you willing to give me until we get to Muir Woods?"

"Why Muir Woods? Why can't we go to a restaurant like Edie's like we used to?"

"I think the quiet force of nature has a calming effect on troubled souls."

"I don't have a troubled soul!" Rhasan protested, and turned toward the window with an attitude just a few shades above a pout.

They sat in silence for the thirty-five minutes it took to reach Muir Woods, each left to his own thoughts. The passing landscape gradually changed from urban to rural as the van wound its way through the hills of western Marin. A low-lying thick, milky fog drifted in off the Pacific and blotted out the sky. The passing trees, made indistinct by the thickening fog, stood slope-shouldered like grim, shadowy presences. Few cars were passed. The road was desolate and the views were limited to occasional breaks in the fog. When they finally pulled into the parking lot at the entrance to the park, there were only ten other cars. Jackson had a few words with the driver then got out with Rhasan. They paid the fee and entered the brooding darkness beneath the park's towering redwood trees.

Rhasan and Jackson walked for about ten minutes along the paved paths in and around the gigantic redwood trees, some of which were more than twenty feet in circumference. They passed a group of German tourists with teenage children who were bickering among themselves. The harsh and guttural sounds of their language seemed strident against the background of the moist, dark green, dripping silence of the trees. They were soon just disembodied voices swallowed by the thick fog that was flowing down the valley walls of the Woods. The drifting fog combined with the shadows cast by the huge trees and the lush undergrowth to create a shifting, ephemeral darkness around the base of the towering giants.

Rhasan complained, "Man, this place is cold and damp! Why would you want to come to a place like this?"

"I like to feel the fog on my face. It refreshes me."

"Leave me out of your next trip."

When the path was clear of other hikers, Jackson turned to Rhasan and said, "Tell me everything about your experience with the Lenzinis."

Rhasan responded in animated fashion and told the story from the point where he and his friends arrived at the house to the moment they left the men in the construction site down the hill from Jackson's home. Jackson listened with only an occasional question. After Rhasan completed his tale he spent a few minutes talking about how he would like to get revenge for the beating he took.

Jackson asked, "What is your understanding of the situation I'm involved in?"

Rhasan turned his smooth brown face toward Jackson, and for a moment Jackson saw the child he used to be. Then the teenager returned. A look of cunning crossed Rhasan's face as he said, "You're fighting Great-grandfather Tremain's enemies."

"Do you know what is at stake?"

Rhasan thought a minute then answered, "No. I just know they're real interested in talking with you."

"Did you know that six people have been killed so far?"

A look of shock flashed across Rhasan's face before it hardened into a frown. He scoffed, "That doesn't worry me. I can take care of myself!"

"This isn't about you. This isn't about me. They want your great-grandfather's money and organization. Once they get ahold of it, we become unnecessary nuisances. Then they'll get rid of us as well."

"What are you going to do about it?"

"The first thing I've got to do is make sure that all my noncombatants are off the field, that all my family is secure and safe."

A smirk crossed Rhasan's face. "Oh, I know where this is headed!"

"Do you? Do you know that eventually I want to turn this whole thing over to you?"

Rhasan's eyes widened in surprise. "Wha—what?"

"Yes, I want to be able to turn this all over to you, but first you need training and education. You aren't prepared or ready yet for this level of responsibility."

"How can you say that? I've done what you've asked me. I've done better! I finished high school as the class valedictorian! You said all along that eighteen was the entrance to manhood. Now I'm here, you don't want to treat me like a man! What's up with that?"

The certainty and fervor in Rhasan's voice made Jackson feel old. He stared off into the tangled undergrowth of ferns, hawthorn, and poison oak. "My nephew, you're at the entrance of manhood, and although you're more man than many who are older than you, there are still many lessons you have yet to learn, lessons which will temper your ardor and your anger, your confidence and your anxiety. This job is for the tested." Jackson moved on down the path.

Rhasan hurried to walk alongside. He declared, "People my age are sent to war all the time!"

"That is true and for the most part, they are used as if they are dispensable. We cannot afford to use our family members in such a manner."

"How do I get to be tested, if you keep on sheltering me?"

"After you have completed your education, you will have many opportunities to defend the family. Your main job will be to oversee the transition to legitimacy."

"So, you don't want my help now? Is that what you're saying?"

"How can you help? What are you trained to do? Communications? Reconnaissance? What?"

"I, er, I . . ." Rhasan was momentarily at a loss for words, then he blurted out, "I can fight! I can definitely fight!"

"You can fight? Against professionals?"

Rhasan smacked his chest. "I've proved myself in the streets!"

Jackson watched Rhasan's posturing and decided to change his tactics. He stood face-to-face with his nephew and said, "Stop me from grabbing your throat." Not waiting for Rhasan to fully comprehend his statement, Jackson made a couple of half-hearted grabs toward his throat.

Rhasan backpedaled, blocking Jackson's efforts with his forearms. "What? Come on, Unc. You know you're no match for me."

Jackson saw the opening that he was looking for and burst into action. He rushed forward, stepping on Rhasan's right foot, preventing him from retreating, then he forcefully knocked Rhasan's hands aside and grabbed his throat in a tight grip.

Rhasan was totally surprised. When Jackson released him, he protested, "That's not fair. You stepped on my foot!"

"This is a fight to the death! Everything is fair! Right now, you would be a dead man and I'm nowhere as good as a professional."

A look of delight and excitement entered Rhasan's eyes. "Can you teach me stuff like that? Can you teach me to fight like a professional?"

"Why would you want to learn? Be smart! Your responsibilities should be in an office. You can buy people to fight for you, if the need arises."

"I want to be tough like Grandpa Tremain! I want to be able to defend my family and my businesses however I need to!"

"You realize you're talking about potentially killing people and risking being killed yourself?"

"All my life I've heard stories about Grandpa Tremain and how he took you and made a man out of you, how he taught you to live off the land, how he taught you how to shoot and throw a knife. I want to learn all of that! There's nothing more that I want in my life than to someday be the head of this family and I want to be a powerful man like him. Like he used to be. No disrespect to you, Uncle Jax, but you're laid-back. I mean, you're always talking about avoiding violent situations and not getting in trouble and stuff. Sometimes, I thought you'd just turned into an old fuddy-duddy, that you were trying to walk away from everything that Great-grandfather gave you."

Jackson walked along in silence for a minute thinking that Rhasan was correct. He *had* tried to walk away. He had not taken to his grandfather's teachings with enthusiasm. He had learned his lessons dutifully, but without joy. He looked at Rhasan out of the corner of his eye. Maybe his nephew was King's rightful heir and Jackson was just a caretaker until Rhasan assumed control. The boy certainly evinced an excitement that Jackson had not felt.

"You were trying to walk away, weren't you, Uncle Jax?"

"Yes, I was. Your great-grandfather's life wasn't all butter and cream. There was a lot of discomfort and a lot of violence. He left a trail of dead people. His life didn't seem all that good to me."

"But you're in it now, aren't you? And his training is helping you, isn't it?"

"I'm only in it because his enemies give me no choice. They'll kill all of us if I don't fight back."

Rhasan persisted, "The training he gave you is helping you, isn't it?"

"To some degree," Jackson grudgingly conceded. "Although I don't intend to leave you in the circumstance he left me."

"Unc, can you really guarantee the situation will be different? That a DuMont won't come looking for revenge? That these Mob guys won't ever try again?"

Jackson stared at Rhasan, surprised that he had so much information. "Did your mother tell you all this?"

Rhasan nodded. "Yeah, she told me a lot of stuff when she was trying to scare me and persuade me that you didn't need my help."

"She's right. I don't need your help now." When Jackson saw the frown spread across Rhasan's face he continued, "And I don't want your help until you've been educated and trained." Jackson saw two burly white men over Rhasan's shoulder coming toward them. He looked around quickly and saw there was a bench off the path that would require both men to face him if they were intending harm. "Rhasan, step around behind me and let's go sit on that bench." Rhasan looked over his shoulder and saw the two men. He immediately followed his uncle's direction and joined him on the bench.

As the two men drew abreast, one of them turned to Jackson and asked, "Do you know if the trail over the hill to the coast is open?"

Jackson kept his hands folded in front of him. He forced a smile on his face and replied, "Don't know. You might check at the ranger station at the entrance to the park."

One of the men reached quickly under his jacket, fumbled for a moment, then pulled out a map. After a moment of reviewing the map, he suggested to his companion, "Why don't we try it anyway? It's too far to go back to the entrance."

The second man shrugged. "Okay with me." They both nodded to Jackson and Rhasan and continued on the path.

Jackson waited until the men were out of sight then slid a small .45 automatic back into the holster under his arm.

Rhasan asked in a shocked whisper, "You're carrying a gun, Uncle Jax?"

"An unfortunate but necessary precaution."

There was awe in Rhasan's voice when he said, "Uncle Jax, you are so cool."

Jackson retorted, "Why, because I'm carrying a gun? That's not cool! Having to carry a gun means that I haven't taken care of the business that I needed to."

"No, Uncle Jax, that's not it. It's just that I never figured you to do something like this and you do it so cool and unbothered, like it happens every day! Forget what I said about Grandfather Tremain, I want to be like you! Low-key and as cold as ice! When that guy reached under his coat like he had a gun, you didn't even budge. Yet you were prepared all the time. Uncle Jax, when will you start training me?"

"Let's get out of the park alive first. Come on, let's head back to the car."

"Okay, but when do I start?"

"The training is rigorous. You have to really want it. Nobody is going to force you to continue."

"*Okay!* When do I start?"

"You start now. Keep an eye out over your shoulder for those men. We don't want them following us!"

"Okay! Okay, but when do I really start?"

"You'll start in Atlanta, where you're going to college. I'll get someone to start you off in judo. You'll have to set aside a minimum of six hours a week for two years. You'll do this while you're taking a full load at college and your grades have to be maintained at a B or better. I will loan you the BMW for as long as you maintain your grade level. After judo, you'll switch to jujitsu for a year, then in your senior year you'll switch to aikido. Every summer, depending upon your grades, I'll send you wherever you want to vacation. If you're still interested in more martial arts training when you graduate, I'll send you to Brazil to learn how to fight with knives."

Rhasan had trouble containing his excitement. "That's great! What about shooting, huh? Do I get trained in that too?"

Jackson smiled. "You'll get that too, if that's what you want."

"You won't be sorry, Uncle Jax! You won't be sorry you took me under your wing! I'll make you proud! I promise!"

His nephew's fervor brought a smile to Jackson's face. He put his arm around Rhasan's shoulder as they headed back to the car.

Rhasan walked alongside him for several minutes then asked, "Uncle Jax, can I ask a favor? Can we go out on the motor cruiser today?"

Jackson pointed at the sky. "It's not good weather for sailing today; maybe another day."

Rhasan persisted, "Can I at least see the boat today?"

Jackson nodded, unable to deny his nephew's youthful exuberance.

The rain started to fall as they entered the parking lot. Within minutes a heavy downpour began and fell steadily as the van headed back to the dangers of civilization. Outside the van's windows, visibility was poor. Jackson saw a parallel with his own inability to see into the future. The shape of things to come was blurred and indistinct. As the van drove over the Richmond Bridge, Jackson was pondering just how he would explain his decision to train Rhasan in the ways he had been trained to Samantha. He hoped that he had chosen the right path, that Rhasan would never be the subject of a late-night phone call.

Monday, July 12, 1982

Jackson and Carlos were sitting around the table, drinking coffee and discussing Braxton when the phone rang. The jangle surprised both men. No calls were ever received at the house, but were arranged on various pay phones throughout the city. The house phone was reserved for emergencies. Carlos gave Jackson a questioning stare then went to the phone. He picked it up and said, "Good morning." He listened for a few minutes and then said, "You can talk to me. I am empowered to speak for him." Several more minutes passed then he handed the phone to Jackson. "It's Deleon DuMont. He says he's kidnapped Elizabeth."

Jackson was on his feet instantly and snatched the receiver out of Carlos's hands. "This is Jackson Tremain!"

The voice that issued out of the phone had a soft, southern twang.

"Deleon DuMont here. Nice to speak to you at last. I'm looking forward to meeting you, but I don't want all the men in the parking garage around when we meet."

"I beg your pardon?"

"You know, the parking lot where you killed Jesse. I'll bet both Jesse and Fletcher are dead now, aren't they? Can't say that I miss their bungling asses much."

"What do you want?" Jackson demanded. "Do you have Elizabeth? If I don't hear her voice in the next minute, I'm going to hang up!"

"Don't be hasty. She's here and still in good health for now."

"You bastard, if you harm her, I'll kill you. I'll spend my life tracking you down! Let me talk to her now!" The phone went dead. Jackson turned to Carlos and said in an incredulous tone, "He hung up!"

Carlos stared at Jackson for a moment before he spoke. "Are you thinking at all? Have you given thought to the consequences of your words?"

Exasperated, Jackson asked, "What did I do now?"

"You gave away information again. After your outburst he knows now that he truly has a valuable commodity to bargain with and that she has the power to make you react without thinking."

Jackson threw up his hands. "There's too much to think about! I'm not a robot! This woman is not a commodity to me! I love her! I'm prepared to risk everything for her! Everything!" He fell silent as he was suffused with a terrible fear that he might not ever see Elizabeth alive again. When he began speaking again, his eyes were hard and his voice was cold. "I'm ready to risk everything! And I'm prepared to kill lots of people to get her back."

Carlos nodded then said, "Then you must use your mind even more. You must control your emotions. I told you before this is not a game. If you rescue her, you're going to have to kill this man and everyone he has working with him. Everything you do should be consistent with that goal. Remember, you are at war and you cannot rest until the enemy is dead."

Jackson said nothing. The logic of Carlos's words was unassailable. When he thought of the way he had acted so carelessly, he was embarrassed and angry. He recognized that he had never fully subscribed to the fact he was in a war. He had acted as if Carlos's words had originated from a radio station that he couldn't turn off. Now for the first time, he truly tuned in to the message and he was ready to carry the conflict forward. No matter the cost in human life, he was determined to rescue Elizabeth or die trying.

He turned to Carlos and said slowly and clearly, "I ask you to continue to help me. I apologize for my stupidity and my foolish reluctance to take your advice to heart. I was wrong. That is all changed. This is war. I accept that and I want to win it. I swear to give your counsel the attention and respect it deserves." Carlos nodded, a smile slowly spreading across his face. Jackson continued, "The most important thing to me right now is getting Elizabeth back. I'll need your help and advice on the best way to do that."

Jackson stopped, suddenly overcome with emotion. Tears formed in his eyes. Then anger welled up and turned his expression into a snarl. He growled, "If anything happens to her, I swear on my grandfather's grave, I'll leave a wide trail of blood!"

Carlos wondered aloud, "I wonder how he got this number? It looks like we have a hole in our security and we better plug it fast."

"I gave Elizabeth this number to call in case of emergency. *I'm* the goddamned hole in the security! And I've really fucked up! DuMont was in the garage when I fought Jesse! I must've led him directly to her apartment from the drugstore. What a fool I've been!"

Carlos came over and put his hand on Jackson's shoulder and said, "We will get your woman. When he calls again, I want you to try to keep him on the phone as long as possible. Maybe we can get some help from one of our technicians at the phone company to trace the call. Take a moment and compose yourself. When he calls again, find out exactly what he wants. Under what circumstances might he release the girl. Make sure you write down the location and times of any meetings he proposes. Don't let him provoke you. Keep your cool. Now, tell me exactly what he said when he spoke to you."

Later that afternoon, in a house on a hill in San Francisco's Noe Valley, Jackson sat at the window and looked out over Twenty-fourth Street. He leaned forward and opened the window so that he could hear the sounds of the street. His thoughts wandered back to Elizabeth. He was thinking about the last time he had seen her at her apartment in Oakland, the night Jesse and Fletcher were dumped in the bay. The images of that evening floated slowly across Jackson's mind, changing shape and meaning like clouds pushed by a strong but sporadic breeze.

He recalled her tears of sadness and disappointment. He knew without being told that she would never be released alive, whether the papers were handed over or not. Dark thoughts of fear and guilt soared around him like vultures. He was responsible for her capture. He had not acted with the forethought that the situation warranted. If he lost her, he would have no one to blame but himself.

The sounds of giggling children wafted up to him from the street below. He looked out the window again and saw a bunch of kids between the ages of eight and twelve playing dodgeball against the garage door of a neighboring house. Their rich and infectious laughter only increased the somber weight on his shoulders. He had made a lot of stupid mistakes since his grandfather had died. He could almost see the old man looking up from hell and shaking his head disgustedly. Jackson had undermined the strength of his battle position. He remembered his grandfather saying countless times as he was growing up, "Never underestimate the doggedness of the enemy!"

Deleon had not called back until it was nearly noon. In the intervening hour and a half, Carlos had his contacts set up a trace on the phone. Then he mobilized both Jackson and Theresa to pack all personal possessions and prepare to move. He reasoned that once the DuMonts had the phone number, it was merely a question of time before they had the address.

When the call was received, Jackson was in the midst of packing. He picked up the phone and heard Elizabeth's voice scream out in pain. The sound cut into him like a knife. Yet Jackson controlled himself and gave no indication of his seething anger. Deleon asked a number of questions about the certificates and corporation papers. Jackson answered as if he had the papers in his possession. A meeting was arranged for Thursday. Despite Jackson's urging for something sooner, Deleon would not move the date. When he hung up, Jackson threw back his head and roared out his frustration. He wanted to pound Deleon's face until he beat him senseless. After giving voice to his anger, Jackson stood panting, breathing deeply to fill his lungs, energizing the hatred he was beginning to feel. Then he returned to the task of packing with a cold dedication. After the trucks arrived, the Fulton Street house was vacated within the hour.

The silent turmoil of his thoughts was once again broken as peals of giggles and laughter rose from the children on the sidewalk below.

Jackson leaned out of the window so that he could watch them play. They aroused thoughts of the family that he wanted to have with Elizabeth. In order for those dreams to be realized, he had to rescue her.

The only opportunity to save her lay in surprising the kidnappers. He needed to attack their headquarters within twenty-four hours. He began pacing back and forth. For the strike to be a success, every detail had to be worked out to the letter. There could be no mistakes. He had to be ready to kill without hesitation. The monstrosity of the task before him was daunting and he knew that the odds against his achieving his goal were high. There were more squeals of laughter and giggling from the children, but the carefree sound of their play now tore at his heart. He closed the window, shutting out the sounds of joy that were still rising up from the street below.

He thought of Braxton, Tree, and DiMarco. They wanted war. He would give them war. There would be no quarter. He would kill them all. Immediately after hanging up the phone with Deleon, Jackson had told Carlos that he wanted some DuMont hostages. Following a brief discussion, Carlos agreed to dispatch a couple of men to New Orleans to kidnap Deleon's father. Next, Jackson wanted to question Tree and Braxton to determine whether they knew where Deleon was hiding, and he made it clear that he wanted the questioning to be prompted by pain. Carlos contacted his men in the field to find out where those two men were.

He strapped on his grandfather's two-gun shoulder holster. He checked the slides on both pistols and ensured they had full magazines before he chambered a bullet in them both. The holster had loops for four additional magazines, which he filled. He saw his grandfather's Bowie knife, but decided against it as being too large and chose a knife with an eight-inch blade similar in size to the one he used in his practice sessions with Carlos. When he walked out of his bedroom, he was ready to leave a pile of his enemies' bodies after each encounter. The animus of King Tremain would rise and walk the earth again.

Wednesday, July 14, 1982

Elroy Fontenot was from the old school. He believed in the Old Testament, that the culpable should be called to answer. That belief was part of the reason he had been a good policeman and it was the reason he had come to New Orleans. He adjusted his earphones and stared through the side curtains of his rented van at the mansion across the street, which stood behind a high wrought-iron fence. He turned to his bank of electronic-monitoring equipment and saw one of the meters oscillating. He fiddled with a few dials. A speaker squawked and static followed, then with more fine tuning, Elroy was able to distinguish voices. He listened for a moment and determined that the telephone conversation was between two women and concerned an impending shopping spree. He turned another dial and switched to a different monitoring system, where he heard a radio blaring its call letters over disco music. He cycled through his various monitoring pickups and was unable to find another human voice. He turned down the sound and slipped behind his spotting scope, through which he studied the building and its surrounding grounds. He saw the two guards making their appointed rounds. They functioned like clockwork, down to the time they took their breaks. After five days of watching, Elroy knew their schedules to the minute.

His last ten years in the San Francisco Police Department Detective Division performing surveillance work had stood him in good stead. Over the years he had collected a considerable amount of electronic equipment and he was intimately familiar with its repair, deployment, and limitations. Once he had made his decision, it didn't take but a couple of hours to get the information he needed. It had not been difficult for him to obtain the necessary addresses through his network of law enforcement associates with whom he still maintained a relationship. He had gotten on the plane that very night with all his equipment. After checking into a nice motel, he rented two different-colored vans and had three different sets of detachable signs painted for their sides. He bought a good sleeping bag, an air mattress, urinals, and a small portable toilet. He spent two days tracking down errant addresses and then—success. He had found the home of his quarry, seen him preening in his front yard as if he didn't have a care in the world, a wrinkled, limping old man who thought he had outlived his enemies.

Fortune was with Elroy. When he first arrived on the scene the street corner closest to the mansion was under construction. There were a number of different utility vehicles from several different companies parked up and down the street. Men in work clothes were all around. His vans fit right in. The first day of surveillance he scaled a telephone pole and tapped into the mansion's phone line. The second day, he posed as a utility field technician and entered the property and had one of the guards take him around to the main power meters and then escort him through the mansion while he checked for gas leaks and possible electrical shorts. The guard was an uninterested fool. He paid no attention to Elroy's actual activities. Everywhere he thought was a good site, Elroy had left a small electronic bug.

The ease and facility with which everything had been accomplished was disturbing. It appeared that once he had made the decision to kill Pug DuMont and any other male DuMonts who chose to fight, Lady Luck was at his shoulder. It seemed too easy. Elroy was not used to having luck in his pursuits. He continually ran afoul of the world, which he thought should run with the organization and efficiency of an orphanage. He had understood distance, order, and routines. He had not understood emotions and the messy way people spilled out of their personalities, losing all shape and form. He hadn't solved the mystery of nurturing until it was too late. Success in a family required the very things he had not experienced, and as a result the very things he was unable to pass on to his children.

Elroy had come to Louisiana to avenge himself. As a police officer he had done a number of things that, strictly speaking, were illegal, but he had held and still held that they were acts done in the best interests of the community. So what if a damned killer, child molester, or a dirty, drug-dealing weasel occasionally didn't get a fair trial? Or for that matter, didn't even make it to jail sometimes. So what? Those men had been vectors of evil. He had seen the effect of their crimes. So had he, first-hand, seen the results of Pug DuMont's crimes. He read the file that Jackson had given him straight through the first night he had received it. Even though it brought tears to his eyes, he could not put it down. The narrative held him with a destructive fascination. He was trembling with anger and hate when he finished reading it. The mother that he had dreamed about on countless, lonely nights in the darkness of the orphanage had been passed around from man to man for the sick pleasure of causing her pain. Then the DuMonts had left her in the swamp to

die. The file revealed that in 1935 King had tracked her down in Mississippi. He had personally gone to visit her and discovered that she
had never regained her senses. He had paid for her institutionalization
in a good facility from 1935 until she died in 1960. At this point, Elroy
had to put the file down for a while. His mother had been destroyed by
the DuMonts' desire to get back at King Tremain. Not only had they
violated his mother, but his own life with his family had been forfeited
because of their treachery. It affected not only who he was, but who he
wasn't.

Elroy stared at his equipment, which he had either built from kits or
purchased at his own expense, and shook his head sadly. The equipment reminded him of his years within the San Francisco Police Department. He had retired as a detective sergeant after twenty-five years
of service. He had been passed over for promotion countless times even
though he scored in the top percentile on the written test. He had been
a vocal foe of the racism he experienced in the department, and that
had not won him any friends in management. The only reason he had
received the promotion to sergeant in 1967 was because he had hired
an attorney to sue the city for failing to comply with their own rules.
The city chose to negotiate rather than go to court. He was promoted
with much defamatory innuendo from the rank and file and a clear lack
of support from the captain of his division. It was the captain's unwillingness to distribute funds and resources equitably to Elroy's squad that
caused him to start building and collecting his own equipment.

Elroy could not say that he ever grew used to the blatant discrimina-
tion that was manifest in his department, but he did develop patterns
for dealing with it. Early in his career his method was to meet aggression with aggression, insult with insult, violence with violence. In the
paramilitary lexicon of the police, he became labeled as a Negro with a
chip on his shoulder, a troublemaker who was hypersensitive about
race-related issues. It was often said that he couldn't take a joke. Yet
when he looked back, from the height of his years, he realized that
some of the whites' allegations were true. He had been bitter. He did
have a chip on his shoulder.

His anger had actually begun to take shape in his first year on the
force, beginning with the one time that he had met King Tremain. It
happened long before he knew that King was his father, but the memory of their meeting was still as clear in his mind as if it had happened

yesterday. He had risen early that morning. It was in the summer of 1954. He'd kissed the picture of his fiancée that he kept on his bureau dresser and thought they could now start planning their wedding since he had a steady job with benefits, vacation, and a pension. He had a breakfast of grits with sugar and milk as the rays of a pale sun, partially obscured by clouds, came through the window of his kitchen. He had a nice view of the shipyards and the East Bay from his Quonset hut on Hunter's Point. He liked gauging the weather from his window while at breakfast. It was his way of determining what type of day it would turn out to be. That particular day all the fog and low-lying clouds had been swept away and the views of the East Bay hills were startlingly clear. He had judged it to be a good day. June rains had been showering the city for days on end and any abatement had to be a positive sign.

His police uniform was nice and clean. Elroy had been selected to participate in an experimental effort by the mayor to allow five Negro officers to hold permanent positions on the force and exercise the full range of the law. Prior to this program San Francisco's only colored police were in temporary status and most of those had been hired during World War II, when many of the whites had joined the army to fight overseas. Elroy had been very excited when he was first selected. He realized that he and his four colleagues were pioneers of a sort, blazing the way for others to follow. He had looked forward to bearing up to the charge, but as the months wore on, the constant barrage of invective, derisive remarks and cruel practical jokes by white officers began to take their toll. When the whites returned from the war in the mid-forties, the original colored officers who had been hired during the war had either been terminated from their temporary public safety positions or allowed to transition to turnkey positions in the jail. The turnkeys were limited to billy clubs and the colored section of the jail. These men who were no longer allowed to carry guns were taken as the standard for Negro achievement. Elroy knew his white counterparts hated the way he pushed against the department's racist restrictions, but he felt he had earned his rights in the war.

After six months on his new assignment, Elroy returned the hostile acts of the white officers in their own coin. He once fought one of the strongest whites in the department at two o'clock in the morning at the Polo Grounds. The fight was attended by officers and turnkeys. Elroy had always been good with his fists, and his years as a foot soldier in

World War II had only served to polish his skills. The man's brute strength was no match for one who had fought many times hand to hand for his survival. Needless to say, Elroy slowly beat the man to the ground.

As the first year passed, through demonstrations of bravery and physical effort, the five slowly earned the grudging respect of some of the rank-and-file patrolmen. However, the majority of the whites never fully accepted working with Negro officers. Despite all the hostility to which he had been subjected, Elroy was unprepared for the way events had unfolded on the day he met his father.

He arrived at his station near city hall punctually and had been informed by the white sergeant over his unit that he was assigned to work with a strike force that was responsible for stopping racketeering activities in the nonwhite areas of the city, like Chinatown, Hunter's Point, Mission Street, and the Fillmore. Everyone knew the real purpose behind the strike force was to shut down any Negro, Chinese, Filipino, Mexican, or Japanese gangster who was growing too powerful in his community. The detective division had received information from a reliable informant that one of the major figures in the extortion and protection rackets in the Fillmore had his bank in the basement of an apartment building on O'Farrell between Scott and Pierce streets.

Elroy and his four colleagues reported to the assignment room and learned that they were going after King Tremain. He remembered shaking his head and laughing cynically. Everyone in the room knew that King Tremain was involved in gambling and had nothing to do with extortion. His real crime was standing up to the Italians who were trying to push heroin in the Fillmore. There had been several murders in the Fillmore, then another spate in North Beach and more murders in Napa. The North Beach and Napa murders caused considerable outcry in the papers and radio news. One whole branch of the DiMarcos had been wiped out. There was no evidence to link King to those deaths, but many people knew he was responsible. The Mob had decided to pay the police to take King out and the department was happy to do it. Tremain was considered to be a nigger who had outgrown his britches and there were many officers eager to cut him down to size. Elroy looked out the department's second-story window and saw storm clouds once again amassing above Twin Peaks. More rain was on its way.

When the police deployed around the apartment building, Elroy and his colored unit, wearing plainclothes, were sent in first. The unit entered through the main lobby and cautiously descended the stairs into the darkness of the basement. Each man was alert as he moved into the shadows. They knew that King was a dangerous man and would not willingly submit to arrest. They had their guns at the ready and were prepared to fire at the first sign of movement. The basement was divided into a parking area and a walled-off corridor which led to a row of rooms near the back of the building. Elroy and Tyree Washington chose the corridor while their three companions entered the dimly lit parking area. There was one bare lightbulb lighting the corridor as the two crept toward the closed doors in the rear. They passed several darkened rooms with open doors; a quick search revealed there was no one in them, but near the end of the hall they heard noises coming from a room whose door was partially ajar. Tyree and Elroy gathered themselves and burst into the room. Elroy rolled in on the floor and came to his feet ready to fire his gun. Tyree followed him closely. They saw Sergeant Dale Thurmondson standing over a body.

Thurmondson turned his pink face toward them and brushed blond hair out of his eyes. He smiled. "Glad to see you boys finally made it, but we didn't get here in time to save old Riley Turner. Looks like that nigger Tremain killed him."

As Elroy rushed to Turner's side, he could feel there was something wrong with the scene, but he couldn't put his finger on the source of the feeling. Turner's dark brown face stared sightlessly up at the ceiling. He had been shot in the chest at close range; there were powder burns on his uniform. Elroy closed the man's eyes and felt a deep sadness. Turner was one of the original officers, a senior man who had continued to encourage him to stay on the force. It was his recommendation that caused Elroy to be selected for the new unit.

As he passed the sergeant, Tyree asked, "How long you been here? We didn't hear no shots! We were supposed to be the first ones in here! What happened? Where's King Tremain?" He knelt beside the body and took Turner's limp hand in his own.

"Turner was all right for a colored," Thurmondson said as he ignored Tyree's questions. He lit a cigarette and as he exhaled he said, "He knew his place, not like some of you niggers."

There was something in his tone which caused Elroy to turn toward him. He found himself staring into Thurmondson's pistol. He realized then that he and Tyree were going to be killed just like Turner and it would be blamed on Tremain. He should have known from the very moment he set foot into the room. Thurmondson was one of the sergeants who had been very vocal and active against the new Negro unit. He was uniformly disliked by all the Negro officers. Muffled gunshots erupted in the parking area but through the walls they sounded like someone was beating on a distant kettledrum.

Thurmondson smiled broadly. "Sounds like your three nigger pals have gone the same way that Turner went, huh?" Tyree made a sudden move and Thurmondson's pistol discharged. The bullet spun Tyree around and drove him back to the wall. The pistol swung back in Elroy's direction. Thurmondson was distracted by the sounds of more shots originating from the parking area. He kept his gun on Elroy, but he backed up to the doorway and glanced down the hall.

"Maybe your boys weren't successful," Elroy chided. "Maybe there's a few of them lying on the floor now with bullet wounds!"

Thurmondson stepped back into the room and growled, "The only reason I don't kill you now is I've decided to save you for Harmon Mueller. Take your gun out of your holster slowly. Grab the handle by your fingertips. That's it! Now lay it down on the ground. Good, now step back. Harmon hasn't forgotten that beating you gave him at the Polo Grounds. He wants to kick your ass before he kills you and I'm going to watch!" Thurmondson began to guffaw loudly. He was still laughing when a tall, brown-skinned man in a Stetson and a double-breasted overcoat appeared in the doorway behind him. The man had a big forty-four-caliber Magnum revolver in his hand.

Although Elroy had never seen him before, he knew immediately that the man in the doorway was King Tremain. He nodded to him and said, "How do you do?"

Thurmondson's pistol didn't waver as he snorted, "You don't think I'm going to fall for that trick, do you? Anyway, anybody who would help you is dead by now!"

King Tremain answered, "You better say joe, 'cause you sho' don't know!" Thurmondson swiveled but King fired two shots before he finished his turn. The slugs knocked Thurmondson sideways across the room, spinning him so that he fell to the floor on his face. King walked over and put another bullet in Thurmondson's back then turned his gaze upon Elroy. "Yo' name Elroy?" he asked.

Elroy nodded but said nothing. His hand trembled as he thought about his own .38 revolver that was still lying on the floor close to his feet. His eyes strayed to the gun.

King warned, "Don't do it, son. I don't want to kill you. Them white boys done killed enough colored coppers this day. I don't want to add no more colored men to their count." He watched as Elroy relaxed and stepped back from his gun. King knelt and exchanged guns with Thurmondson. He pressed Thurmondson's finger around the revolver's grip. He stood and casually wiped off the pistol then checked the magazine. He pulled back the slide and chambered a round. There was a moment of silence then he said, "Seems to me like these boys been plannin' this little deal for a while and they was intendin' on doin' all of y'all! 'Course, they wasn't figurin' on me really bein' here! They was just gon' blame yo' deaths on me!" King held up the pistol he had taken out of Thurmondson's hand. "Yep, this is one of mine. My wife must've given it to them to set me up." He laughed; it was a cold sound without humor.

Why King's wife would set him up was a mystery to Elroy and the truth was, he didn't care to solve that mystery. He just wanted to get out of the building with his life. He heard King's chilling laughter again and asked, "What are you going to do with me?"

King stepped out of the way of the door and said, "You's free to go. If you want to live, you best skin on out the back. If you goes out the front, you gon' have a mess of explainin' to do about the dead white cops that's in this buildin'. Yo' three buddies was killed with one of my guns, but I done all the white boys with one of their own hog legs. I figure it come out about equal."

Elroy walked over to where Tyree had fallen and saw that he was still breathing. He turned to King and asked, "My buddy's still alive. Can I carry him out of here with me?"

King nodded and pointed to the third body. "Is that Riley Turner? Damn! The son of a bitch killed Riley! That's a damn shame!"

"You knew him?" Elroy was surprised.

"Riley and me go way back, son. You got to carry him out of here too. He don't deserve to burn in this place and I'm about to set fire to this dump!"

"What about the residents in the building?" Elroy demanded.

"They didn't tell you? Ain't no residents! This buildin' been condemned! This was a setup from the git." King went over and picked up

Elroy's revolver. "You gon' need this to get yo' story right." He handed
Elroy his gun. "You and yo' buddy best get yo' stories together. They
gon' be a big investigation over this."

"I know." Elroy shook his head. "Because I'm alive, I'll be a prime suspect."

"You ain't fired yo' weapon, but that won't matter if they really want
you. 'Course, if I was to leave my guns here, it might take some weight
off you. It would look like a shootout took place between yo' boys and
me. You could say you saw me shoot yo' pal as I was escapin'. 'Course,
you got to fire your weapon down the hall a couple of times to make it
real. When they bring the other white cops up, just tell the truth: You
don't know how they died. Say you and yo' unit got split up in the darkness. You never saw no whites but this sergeant and he was already dead
when you got here. You carried yo' buddies out the building just as it
caught fire!" King laid his pistol back on the ground. "Go ahead and fire
your gun down the hall to the left."

Elroy raised his gun and fired four shots. He holstered his gun and
asked, "Why are you doing this? Why are you trying to help us?"

"You's part of that new permanent colored unit, the ones that's allowed to carry guns, ain't you?" Elroy nodded. King said, "We need
more of you boys. Colored folks deserve the same protection as whites.
Ain't no reason why you boys shouldn't have the same authority as
them white boys. You is pavin' the way for other colored folks. You
doin' somethin' important. Just stay on yo' toes and don't let nobody do
you. But if'en you wise, you gon' quit workin' for this particular police
department and find yo'self a job policin' somewheres else. They done
killed every colored officer but you and yo' buddy. And if you stay, they
gon' get you. Best get on out of here now, I'm gon' start some fires."

Elroy was in shock as he lifted Tyree up onto his shoulder. "Why are
you going to burn the building?"

"To confuse the investigation. Ain't no reason to give 'em a clear-cut
path. So long, son." King waved as he left the room.

Elroy staggered out of the room with Tyree on his shoulder. He adjusted the heavy weight of his friend and made his way hurriedly to the
stairs leading to the back door. Once out in the open, even though
there was a slight drizzle falling from the gray, overcast sky, the brightness of daylight shocked him. In the darkness of the basement, he had
forgotten that it was the middle of the afternoon. He laid Tyree out

carefully. He had been shot in the shoulder. Elroy checked to see that he was breathing easily before he went back into the building after Turner. He saw King pouring the contents of a gasoline can along the baseboards of the corridor walls as he went back into the room where Thurmondson had been killed. The acrid, stifling smell of the liquid was already filling the hall. When he picked up Turner's body, he noticed that Thurmondson had also been doused with gasoline. He hurried back down the hallway as fast as his burden would permit. He heard the first blasts of the gasoline igniting as he was leaving the building. The rain was falling heavily when he laid Riley Turner out on the cement pavement. Elroy headed off through the pelting rain to get some medical assistance. He hoped there wasn't going to be a problem getting an ambulance. St. John's Hospital, one of the few that served coloreds, wasn't too far away. As he walked along the side of the building and felt the cold rain dripping down his collar, he realized that King was correct; he would have to quit because if he stayed on, eventually he would be killed. Another dream not just deferred but crushed. There was no doubt in his mind that the day had turned absolutely to shit.

That was the last and only time Elroy had ever seen his father. Two months after the death of Riley, Elroy got a job as a police officer in a small town with a large black population near Monterey and adjacent to the army base. He worked there until the early sixties, when San Francisco once more made an effort to hire black police officers.

Elroy straightened out his left leg, which had been beginning to cramp, and set it on the portable toilet. It was hard to find a comfortable position after spending endless hours in the van. He took a folded letter from his breast pocket. It was one of the last items in the file that Jackson had given him. He opened it and read it for perhaps the thousandth time.

To my lost son, Elroy Fontenot,

I must be dead if you're reading this. These here are my words, but I had somebody else write this letter for me. Getting old, the fingers don't work so good. But this ain't about me, it's about you. I didn't want to pass from this world without telling you a few things.

You was a wanted child. I didn't choose for you to grow up in no damn orphanage. Some other people made that decision for me. I near killed off every male DuMont who was of fighting age after you and your mother was took. I made everybody who was responsible pay. I was a man going around taking names, but I couldn't kill Serena. She was my wife for better or worse. Still, I done found a way to pay her back too. But ain't nothing can make up for snatching a child from the arms of its family, no matter how many die. No way to make up for them lost years. No way.

I want you to know I never gave up looking for you. When first I found out where you were, I went down to Port Arthur looking for you, but you was seventeen and had already left for Chicago. I kept on searching and I spent a pretty penny following up the wrong leads. I learned you had joined the army in Chicago and I then lost touch with your whereabouts until you was discharged and moved to San Francisco. By then you was a man, making his living as John Law. It's a laugher, I spent so long looking for you, but I never thought what I'd say to you when I found you. Truth to tell, I didn't know what to say. We was on different sides of the law and I couldn't do nothing about it, because I still had enemies to kill. I didn't know what kind of man you were, but I knew a copper didn't need a father like me.

Because I didn't tell you I was your father don't mean I didn't care about you. I want you to know the only reason I came to the building that day we met was to save your life. A couple of white friends in the department let me know what was in the wind. I had been keeping in touch with your life through Riley Turner. I didn't have no opportunity to give you nothing while you was growing up. I thought if I could do a little something to make up for all the things we missed, if we ever met as father and son, you'd remember me in a good light. I wanted to do something for you and have you know it's me who's doing the doing. I wasn't in time for your buddies or Riley, but I was there in time for you.

You my blood, but because I didn't have a hand in raising you I don't know you as a son. Frankly, I ain't had much reason to like boys I ain't raised, so I'll let my grandson, Jackson, figure what your inheritance is. You'll find he's a fair man, just like I am. I had a hand in raising him. He's a Tremain through and through. Make friends with your nephew Jackson. You got things in common. Both his daddy and his mama died before he was nine. He could use an uncle who cares about him. Become part of the family. You both have Tremain blood.

I ain't much of a praying man, but I done got down on my knees a time or two about you. I've prayed for you to be a strong, responsible man, able to keep kith and kin together. As I think about this, I regret now that we didn't talk face-to-face about all this. I see that I made a mistake about not hooking up with you and *now I'll never hear the sound of your sons laughing. Grandchildren I've never met. Damn!*

Just know I'm still praying for you, son.

King Tremain
October 1975

Elroy folded the letter neatly and put it back in his pocket. It was amazing to him that King had written the letter seven years before he died. It was like he had seen into the future and known that Elroy would one day read these words. The letter answered questions that had been gnawing at Elroy for most of his life. His father had cared about him. He did have a real family. A family that was, if he chose, in his future. The letter was a slender thread connecting Elroy to the dream that he never knew.

Elroy heard the loud, coughing engine of an old truck pull up to the gate of the mansion. He stared through his scope as the truck chugged through the gate and pulled around to the side of the building. He watched as a gray-haired old woman was hustled from the truck into the house. He turned to his monitoring equipment and began adjusting the various dials. Within minutes he was picking up the sound of excited voices.

Saturday, June 22, 1964

Mexico City, sprawling under a haze of smog, lay in a highland basin surrounded by mountains. As his plane prepared to land at Benito Juárez Airport, Jackson could see the two extinct volcanoes rising above the miasma of pollution to the east. The plane swerved around to land into the wind and the western rim of mountains came into view, their uneven peaks reaching up like fangs through the man-made murk. It didn't look pleasant. Eighteen-year-old Jackson wondered again why he had decided to come and visit his grandfather. He had not seen the old man in two years, not since the old man's last trip into the United States, and that was not a good memory. Jackson stared out the window as the plane sank into the gray-brown smog and wondered if anything positive would really be achieved in his visit.

The plane landed smoothly and Jackson passed through customs without more than casual inspection. He was carrying his bags toward the exit leading to the curbside taxis when a man wearing a cap and uniform came out of an unmarked door in the right wall of the corridor. The man walked directly over to Jackson and grabbed his arm firmly. It was Carlos.

"Go to that door just ahead on our left, Diablito! You are being followed! Hurry! The door will open as soon as we draw near!" Carlos pressed him into a quick step. The door opened as Jackson reached out to grab its handle. In a matter of seconds they were through the door and it was locked behind them. Jackson was led down some dark stairs to a waiting jitney. They took off across a vast interior parking lot that housed the vehicles which were used to maintain, service, and restock the aircraft. The jitney turned into a broad, two-lane tunnel running the length of the airport. Periodically, they passed driveways leading out to the tarmac and daylight.

A third man was driving. Jackson didn't recognize him. He was a different man from the one who had opened the door. Jackson shook his head ruefully; another escape orchestrated by his grandfather. The jitney pulled to a curb behind a black limousine. Jackson's bags were transferred to the trunk and he climbed into the backseat. Carlos joined him and the limousine made a couple of turns then pulled out of a long line of limousines that were waiting to pick up passengers. The dark-tinted windows dimmed the surprise of moving out into the sunlight.

"It's been two long years, Diablito! Too long. We need to hunt and cook our food over an open fire and get to know each other again. Maybe go up to Gomez Palacios and hunt pig! A good idea, eh?"

"I'd love to spend some time trekking through high-desert country. I haven't fired a gun or eaten game in ages."

Jackson and Carlos exchanged pleasantries for nearly twenty minutes as the limousine made its way through the afternoon traffic. After a break in the conversation, Jackson turned to Carlos with a serious look on his face. "Who was following me?"

"Two men. If you were more observant, you might have seen them."

"Why? I've never been followed in San Francisco!"

"How little you know. I followed you last summer for nearly two months. You had a girlfriend who lived off of Portola, but you used to like to sneak over and see that big Samoan girl in the Mission. Her sister's going out now with one of your friends, a big football jock. Isn't that right?"

Jackson was shocked. He had no words, he merely nodded that Carlos was correct.

Carlos continued, "The reason they leave you alone is because if they bother you, or anyone in the family, they know your grandfather will attack and kill as many of their family as he can. There is a truce as far as families are concerned. Still, they want to kill him. They continue to look for him. If they find him, the truce is over."

Jackson had become distracted; he did not hear the grim tone in Carlos's words. The limousine was now driving down the street that led to his grandfather's villa. He was staring out the window like a child, trying to catch the first glimpse of the house.

The vehicle stopped in front of heavy wrought-iron gates that blocked the opening of a high stucco wall. Two men ran across the interior courtyard to pull the gates open and the car drove inside and stopped near the stairs of a three-story stucco mansion with a red-tiled roof. There were wrought-iron balconies jutting out over the courtyard for the rooms on the second floor. Jackson's bags were taken inside. There was no sign of his grandfather as he walked into the cool darkness of the house.

As soon as he stepped into the foyer, he smelled his grandfather's Cuban cigars, a woody, pungent smell. He called, "Grandfather?"

"No use to shoutin', boy. I's in my den. Come on in!"

Jackson pushed open a door on his left and saw his grandfather sitting at his desk with a pistol disassembled in front of him. There was also the odor of cleaning fluid mixed in with the cigar's aroma. His grandfather stood and walked toward him. There was still a bounce in his step and fire in his eyes even though he was in his sixties.

"I's happy to see you, boy." The old man stuck out his hand.

Jackson returned the firm shake and said, "I'm glad to see you too, Grandfather. You don't look like you've aged at all."

"Nobody resists the force of time. You just done forgot what I looked like, but I ain't forgot you! I sho' see that you changed. You done filled out in the chest and arms. You got beard hair on yo' chin and you done graduated high school. You gon' be a college man! I'm proud of you, boy! I knows it was easier to quit and give up. I knows you been unhappy with yo' grandmother, but you hung in there, youngblood! You hung in there!"

Through the open door, his grandfather saw someone standing in the hall outside the room and beckoned them to come in. Two women entered the room quietly. One woman was in her late thirties or early forties, the other appeared to be about the same age as Jackson. Both women possessed beautiful large, hooded dark eyes like the actress Delores Del Rio and had long, flowing black hair. The Indian blood was strong in their veins. Their skin was a coppery tone and their faces had the prominent cheekbones and the broad flatness of the pure-blooded inland people.

"This here is Alma," his grandfather introduced the older woman. "You may remember, she had just started working for me when you was last here."

Jackson didn't remember her, but he smiled and nodded his head in greeting. She gave him a warm smile in return.

"And this is her niece, Maria. Maria, this is my famous grandson, the one in all the pictures you see around the house."

Maria turned her eyes to Jackson and immediately dropped her gaze bashfully. There was a trace of a smile on the edge of her lips. When she looked up at Jackson again, her large, dark eyes seemed full of emotion. It added a vulnerability to the smooth skin and even features of her face. For fear of falling into her eyes, Jackson merely nodded his head in greeting and looked away. She was the most beautiful woman that he had ever seen.

He mumbled, "Nice to meet you," and picked up his bags and took them to his room on the second floor. The room had the smell of lemon oil. It had been recently dusted and the wooden furniture had been polished. Heavy metal shutters had been pulled open to let the breezes through the screened windows. Over his dresser was the stuffed head of a bighorn sheep that he had shot when he was eleven. His .308 rifle was hung just beneath it. An old sombrero and a serape hung on the wall over his bed. On the nightstand beside his bed was a glass jar filled with dirt from the pit where he had fought Juan Tejate. It was a room filled with grim mementos and memories.

Later that afternoon, he joined his grandfather, who was working out in the gym next to the dog kennel. His grandfather appeared to be in excellent health as he worked out on the heavy bag, landing hard punches with a savage regularity. Jackson began with stretches and then started on the speed bag. No word was spoken. The two men worked out together for nearly an hour until his grandfather took a break and sat down on the weight bench. The old man was perspiring and breathing heavily. Jackson went to the linen chest and took out a couple of towels and threw one to his grandfather.

"You all right, Grandfather?" Jackson asked as he watched his grandfather breathing deeply.

"Sho, boy! I's just a little winded. It's what happens when you gets this side of sixty." He gave Jackson a long, penetrating look and asked, "You up for some huntin'? Maybe go up Durango way and get some pigs? What you say?"

Jackson returned his grandfather's look and asked, "Aren't you going to ask me why I haven't come down here since I was sixteen? Shouldn't we be talking about that? It seems like everything important in this family is covered with a veil of silence."

King Tremain gave his grandson a long, evaluative look and said, "What's to talk about? I know why you ain't been down here. Ain't no mystery to me."

"You know? Don't you think we should talk about it?"

"What's to say? You didn't like me killin' that man in front of you! I told you it had to be done. I knew it was right, you thought it was wrong. What's to say?"

"You shot him in cold blood, Grandfather! I knew you killed people, but I never thought I would have to witness you taking an innocent man's life!"

"Don't get it twisted, boy! He weren't no innocent man. I knew him. He knew me. He was there to kill us both. Ain't no mercy in war."

"What war are you still fighting, Grandfather?"

"The one you gon' be fightin' when I'm dead! What you don't understand is, I done carved out something here that a black man in my day weren't supposed to have the chitlins, much less the brains, to think about. Ain't s'posed to have it today neither. Yet I got it. I'm a rich, independent black man, boy, at a time when there ain't too many of us around. I knows you gon' say that there's plenty ways to get rich without killin', but I ain't just rich, boy! I's feared and respected."

"Respected? Grandfather, you're in Mexico because in the United States there is a warrant out for your arrest, a warrant for the murder of four policemen. Let's be real!"

"Just 'cause I'm wanted for them murders don't mean I did 'em!"

"Probably the only four people who've been murdered on the western seaboard in the last ten years that you haven't killed!"

His grandfather stood up and said with a slow smile, "You gettin' smart mouth with me, boy? I ain't ready for smart-mouthin'!"

Jackson stared at his grandfather. For the first time, he was eye to eye with the old man. A long silence began as the men separated by a generation evaluated each other. Jackson was slightly taller, but not as heavy or filled out as the older man. He had youth and speed, but he had seen the story of youth and speed vying against strength and wisdom played out in the pit many times. He broke the silence with his own smile and asked in a playful tone, "Would you kill me over this, Grandfather?"

King Tremain's face cracked into an even larger smile. He retorted, "No, but ain't nothin' wrong with a decent ass-whippin'! Sometimes an AW administered at the right time makes the world look different!"

"I don't want to have to fight you, Grandfather, but I want to be able to speak my mind. I deserve at least as much respect as you give the people working for you."

"You got plenty ways of sayin' what you mean without gettin' smart mouth. My rules ain't changed. They're the same for every man-jack walkin'!"

"Okay, Grandfather, that's straight up. I can deal with those rules."

"Good! Now when you's finished yo' college work and got that big-time degree, what degree you gon' have? You gon' be a doctor, a lawyer, a scientist, what?"

"I haven't exactly figured that out yet. I'm pursuing a liberal arts curriculum. I'm thinking about possibly majoring in African history or social psychology. I haven't made up my mind as yet."

"What the hell you gon' do with African history? What do that got to do with the price of beans or the problems black folks is facin' in the States? And social what? What is that? Has these white folk done messed yo' head up already? What you think America is, a free country? You better get yo'self some practical learnin'! Only way a man can be free is by usin' what he know to make his own decisions. The more he know the more choices he got, the freer he is!"

Jackson attempted to be patient as he explained. "There are many learned people who believe that those who do not know their history are doomed to repeat the mistakes made in the past. Black Americans don't know that they descended from princes and kings. We need to teach our people their history so that they can be proud of their heritage."

"They ain't teachin' the real history of Africa! They's teachin' what the whites want you to know. Shit, even in Africa there was a whole lot more peasant folk than there was princes and kings! Damn few of us descended from royalty and it don't matter a damn anyway! A man can only feel pride in who he is by what he does in the here and now! That's the secret! You are what you earn! Whatever a man's ancestors had is just a fart in the wind unless they kept it in the family. I ain't met nobody who wasn't dealin' with the problems of the here and now. Them folks who got a sense of this royal history don't seem to have no better handle on life than the rest of us. Hell, sometimes they even got less a grip!"

"Why are you cutting me down, Grandfather?"

"Boy, I ain't disrespected you. I done spoke my mind. I's tellin' you my experience. You want to spend yo' time doin' somethin' important? There's only two ways you gon' do somethin' important: It happens because you is true in following a purpose, or it happens because you love what you doin'. Them's the only two ways you put the necessary dedication on the line to do somethin' important. Ain't no reason to play fragile. This ain't no storm. I'm just sayin' what I think."

"I don't know what I want to do with my life yet, Grandfather. I chose liberal arts because I would have the broadest range of options and choices. I don't know where the path leads, I just want to follow it for a while."

"If you don't know where you's goin', what does it matter which way you go?"

"If you don't like my selection, you don't have to finance it! I am prepared to pay my own way!"

"You's way too thin-skinned, boy, for one that likes to throw a dig in every now and again. I ain't decided nothin'. I just wants to hear yo' reasonin' and get an understandin' of yo' commitment. You my only grandson! I'm gon' give you all the help you want to get through college. You don't have to do what I say for me to help. Money ain't nothin' but Vaseline, it just make things slicker. It don't help with no real problems.

I ain't gon' play no money games with you. I done already put five years of tuition in yo' bank account. I'll send you the same amount next year whether we talk or not!"

Jackson breathed a sigh of relief. He had only a partial scholarship and he was happy that he could rely on his grandfather's support. He would not have asked for it, but he was willing to accept if it was offered.

"Thank you for your support, Grandfather. I am very grateful."

"Good! Now, can we talk about huntin'? I built me a pig-sticker roaster in the back of the house and ain't got no pig to stick in it. I would dearly love to bring back a couple of them peccaries from Durango."

"Sure, Grandfather, when do you want to go?"

"I needs a couple of days to take care of a few things first. Them boys that followed you need some talkin' to. You's welcome to join me if'en you wants to find out how they knew you was coming on that particular flight. It won't be pleasant, but it'll be real. I knows you don't want no part of this life. I's offerin' 'cause I wants you to know what's goin' on. Ain't no disrespect if'en you wants to pass."

Jackson shook his head. "I don't want any part of it." Sometimes his grandfather seemed too incredible to be believed. After all that had passed between them, his grandfather still had the gall to invite him to watch two men being tortured. The old man was as persistent as the tide, washing away bits and pieces of his grandson's protective coastline with each assault. Jackson had to renew his resolve regularly.

His grandfather nodded his head then said, "You and Carlos could go up to the huntin' lodge outside of Nombre de Dios in Durango and make sure it's stocked with vittles. We gon' need at least a week's worth of supplies and I'll have some men bring up the horses we gon' need."

"You're planning to hunt peccaries on horseback?"

"It ain't as dangerous as on foot and it be more sportin' than a vehicle. Gives the pigs a bit more of a chance and sho' do test how well a man can sit his horse!"

"I thought we were just going to hunt." Jackson didn't like the thought of a herd of thirty or forty outraged pigs chasing him, while he, astride a horse, attempted to escape them in the twisting arroyos and canyons of Durango's high desert. One fifty-pound pig could be savage enough on its own, but the prospect of facing a whole pack was quite frightening. The local folk in the hills of Durango called them *javelina*, because of the shape of their sharp tusks. "I'll drive the jeep for cut-off or pickup."

King Tremain accepted his grandson's offer with a wave of his hand. Doing pickup for a peccary hunt was sometimes more dangerous than the hunt itself. Peccaries had a highly developed social structure and were tremendously loyal to other herd members. Sometimes they would lurk out of sight in the bush for hours before abandoning the fallen individual to desert predators and scavengers. The unsuspecting person who alighted from his horse to field-dress a peccary kill sometimes paid with his life.

"Maybe we'll just use the horses to flush 'em out, but if they're back in some of those steep and narrow ravines, we gon' hunt 'em where they be. May not be able to get the jeeps in there at all."

"I'll work whatever you assign me, Grandfather. If we have to go down into the ravines after the pigs, I'm with you."

"Good! I talked to Alma and Maria and they want to get out of the city for a while. So they'll join us at the lodge. It'll be better this way, because we'll have someone concentrating on the cooking the whole time. We'll get coffee and hot food in the mornings and when we return. Can't beat that with a stick! You folk could leave tomorrow morning and be in Durango by late tomorrow night. We could be set up for our first scoutin' party by Wednesday."

At four-thirty the next morning two four-wheel-drive vehicles pulled out of the courtyard of King Tremain's Chapultepec house and headed north out of the city. The larger vehicle, a station wagon with a fully packed roof rack, was driven by Carlos, and the smaller, canvas-covered jeep was driven by Jackson. Alma rode with Carlos while Maria rode with Jackson. The station wagon led the way along broad boulevards, past numerous plazas, and finally through the broad streets which led out of the city. Even at five in the morning, Mexico City's vehicular traffic was a snarling, cacophonous experience. The trucks and cars swerved in and out of traffic, seemingly unconcerned that there were painted lanes to direct the flow of motorized vehicles.

Once they were free of the city, the two cars headed north across an upward-sloping plain toward a pass in the mountains which ringed the basin in which Mexico City was located. They passed irrigated fields which were a luminous green in the first shafts of sunrise. The sun ap-

peared as an orange disk above the eastern edge of the two extinct volcanoes. Even outside of the city, the polluting haze distorted and
dimmed the outlines of the surrounding purple mountains.

It was nearly midnight when they drove into the city of Durango.
They spent the night at a *taberna* in which King had purchased a half
share. The other owner, Pablo Guzman, was a longtime friend of both
King and Rico Ramirez. He was a chubby, jovial, brown-skinned man
with a shaved head and heavy black eyebrows and an even thicker
black mustache. He greeted his guests with smiles and laughter and led
them to their rooms. After they had washed the travel dust from their
faces, he took them down to a large kitchen, where bowls of steaming
rabbit stew awaited them.

Jackson was exhausted from the drive; he ate the spicy stew and then
went to his room. He fell into a deep sleep and dreamed about Maria.
Mostly he dreamed about their long drive northward. There was a tension between them that confused him. It was not an uncomfortable tension, but for some reason he thought and rethought everything that he
wanted to say and then when he attempted to say it, he became
tongue-tied. She did not seem to be affected by the same affliction, but
she did not talk much. She spent a lot of time watching him, staring at
his face.

Since Carlos did not stop for meal breaks, they ate as they drove. At
one point along a two-lane stretch of highway, as the two vehicles were
passing slower farm vehicles and heavily laden trucks, Maria had
brought out lunch, which consisted of meat and beans loosely wrapped
in tortillas. Jackson could not handle the food and drive at the same
time, so she had fed him. She moved so close to him that her breast
grazed his arm and he could smell the soap she had used.

Her touch had given him an erection, which was further titillated
when she picked the crumbs out of his lap. After they finished eating,
she did not move away but stayed next to him. By the time they drove
into Durango, she was asleep against his shoulder. When he woke her
to go into the *taberna*, the sleepy smile she gave him warmed his heart.

The next morning the clean, cool, dry breeze of the high desert
greeted them as Jackson drove Alma and Maria to the marketplace on
the edge of Durango. In the distance, the Sierra Madre Occidental
raised their brown and gray peaks skyward. The city of Durango
sprawled across the foothills of the Sierras like a drunken man lying on

a low sofa. Below the city the Mezquital River wound its way placidly to the Sea of Cortez. From the outdoor market which was between the river and the lowest area of town, the rest of Durango could be seen rising gently above it, rows upon rows of white buildings interspersed with the beige, brown, and clay of adobe structures. At the edge of the market the bells in the spire of an old church tolled out the hour, joining the churches farther up the hill, calling the faithful to prayer.

Alma, Maria, and Jackson walked down the main aisle of the market. There were rows of brightly covered wooden stalls where vendors displayed their neatly stacked wares and produce. It was a typical farmers' market to be found on the edge of comparable cities in countries throughout the world. Most of the produce was grown locally by the extended families of the people working the stalls. Even though it was Sunday morning, the market was rippling with vitality and color. There were hundreds of passionate exchanges and conversations being conducted in Spanish as buyers and sellers argued over prices and quality, and somewhere in the distance came the braying of a burro. Jackson passed booths festooned with wreaths of green and red peppers. Other booths had bright yellow bananas, green tomatillos, and red tomatoes. Maria and Alma occupied themselves haggling with the vendors over prices while Jackson performed the manual labor of carrying the large woven basket into which the purchased goods were placed. Since his assigned task required little thought, Jackson allowed himself to be distracted by the color and sights around him.

If Jackson had been more alert he might have seen Juan Tejate standing between two booths staring at him. Juan had grown no taller since he had last met Jackson, but he had filled out into a solid, muscular man. Juan pulled his stiletto from his boot and tested the nine-inch blade for sharpness by sawing through a leather scrap. His black eyes gleamed as he watched Jackson moving through the market assisting the two women. Juan had not forgotten the beating that he had received at Jackson's hands. He had spent many days and nights dreaming about his revenge. Now, after three years, the opportunity was in his hands. Only this time, it would end in death for El Negro's grandson. Juan held the knife so that the blade was up his sleeve then stepped out into the crowd.

Wednesday, July 14, 1982

The old panel van rolled silently to the curb a quarter of a block from the corner of McAllister and Octavia streets and turned off its lights. It was parked in the shadows down the block from the corner streetlamp. Three men dressed in black got out of the back of the van and melted away into the night. Jackson rested his arms on the steering wheel, took a deep breath. He felt uncomfortable and restricted in his bulletproof vest. He tried to adjust it unsuccessfully, but it was beneath his shirt and wouldn't budge. After a few futile efforts he gave up and looked at Carlos in the passenger's seat. Carlos acknowledged Jackson's look with a nod then took a silencer out of his pocket and screwed it onto his machine pistol. He gestured that Jackson do the same. Jackson took his .45 Colt from its holster, secured the silencer, then pulled back the slide, chambering a bullet. He holstered the gun, patted the hilt of the knife in his back sheath, and took another deep breath to steady himself. He was nervous and edgy, and no matter how many deep breaths he took to calm himself, he couldn't seem to reduce the pounding speed of his heart. He picked up a long, black sports bag containing a pair of dark goggles, a flashlight, a compact twelve-gauge shotgun, and a cane machete, and got out of the driver's side of the van. Carlos got out of the other side with his own sports bag and checked to ensure that all the van's doors were locked. He and Jackson then synchronized their watches before heading off into the darkness. They turned into a street in which there were a couple of garages, a number of different repair shops, a cabinet shop, and a lighting store. All of the businesses were closed and the street was surprisingly dark. There were only two streetlights at either end of the block.

They were headed for a converted two-story garage in the middle of the block that John Tree used as the headquarters for his heroin and cocaine distribution. The first three men out of the van were responsible for securing the building's roof and perimeter. Carlos carried his machine pistol, dark goggles, a couple of flash grenades, and a cloth-wrapped packet containing various instruments of persuasion in his sports bag. He signaled a halt and stared at the roof of the old garage, waiting for an all clear. They waited several minutes and then saw two bright flashes from the top of the building. Carlos led the way at a run to the front door of the building. Underneath an old painted sign that read USED FURNITURE there was a heavy wooden door that was partially ajar. Carlos slipped inside. Jackson followed him into the darkness then scuttled out of the doorway and squatted down against the wall. He wanted to give his eyes a chance to adjust to the interior of the building's gloom and shadows. The only illumination came from windows high on the walls that caught the weak, ambient gleam of distant streetlights. Carlos closed and locked the front door and joined him against the wall. As Jackson's eyes adjusted, he saw that they were in a large hall filled with dining table and chair sets, couches, end tables, and lamps. On his left, above a small office, there were stairs leading to an upper level. There was movement in the darkness and his heart jumped in his chest. He almost pulled his gun, then he saw that it was one of Carlos's men, Tavio Lopez, dragging a body into the little office. Tavio came out of the office and waved the all clear. Carlos led the way up the darkened stairway.

Jackson was trying to be alert and attentive to his surroundings, but the truth was that he could barely hear anything over the pounding of his heart. They reached the top of the stairs. A hallway illuminated only by the thin slits of light which glowed underneath a couple of closed doors. They headed to the first door. Jackson's gun was now in his hand and his trigger finger had a terrible twitch. He was concerned that if he kept his gun in his hand he was going to inadvertently shoot himself in the foot. He was concentrating on controlling himself when a door swung open on his right and light flooded the hall. A tall, dark-skinned man in a dashiki walked through the doorway and Jackson fired on reflex. The gun puffed and jerked in his hand, but there was no sound. He put three bullets in the man's torso before he knew what he was doing, and the bullets hitting the man's body made more noise than the silencer, thudding, splattering sounds that seemed to ring in his ears. The man staggered backward through the door and fell against a chair then landed on the floor with a crash.

"What the fuck is goin' on out there? Can't you assholes keep it quiet?" The growling voice originated from a room farther down the darkened corridor.

Carlos rolled into the room with his gun at the ready, but the room was empty. Jackson stood in the hallway, panting and nervous. He stared down at the man he had shot and it was not a pretty sight. There were big, red holes in the man's chest and there was blood puddling slowly beside his body. A smell of bile filled his nose. It was sickening, yet Jackson could not tear his eyes away from watching the man's last twitches and movements before the life left his body. Killing the man did not make him feel powerful; instead it nauseated him because he realized that he himself could be killed just as easily; he too could be killed by a stranger who merely reacted out of fear. Carlos tapped him on the shoulder and gestured to a door farther down the hall. Jackson followed Carlos and focused his thoughts on Elizabeth because he knew that he would kill a roomful of men to get her back.

Tavio went into the room where the man had fallen and closed the door, leaving Jackson and Carlos in darkness as they continued down the hall. The doorway whence the growling voice had originated was cracked open. Looking through the crack, Jackson saw four men sitting at a long collapsible table. A fifth chair had a jacket upon it, but it was unoccupied. Two of the men had their backs to the door, while two were facing it. Carlos pushed open the door and Jackson followed him into the room. It was a big bright room, lit by overhead banks of fluorescent lights. All along the walls were stacks of folding tables and chairs. This room with its smooth hardwood floor had served as Tree's prep and bag room, and when in operation it had been a busy place with more than forty employees. It was where pills and tablets were pressed and counted, where freebase rock cocaine was cooked, and the heroin was cut. However, since Tree had shut down his action, the room was not in use.

The conversation between the four men at the table stopped and the two men who were facing away from the door turned and looked over their shoulders. Jackson was ready for any sudden action. His trigger finger was twitching again. He was determined not to die at the hands of these fools; he would kill them all first. An overweight, heavyset man with a disfiguring scar across his face pushed back from the table and growled, "What the hell you motherfuckers want? You here to jack me up for some dope?"

Jackson was not in the mood to answer questions. He demanded, "Where does Deleon DuMont live? Where can we find him?"

Jackson recognized the bald-headed man to the left of the big man with the scar as the attorney who had represented Delbert at Johnson, Wyland & Johnson the week before, but he couldn't remember his name. The attorney nudged the man with the scar and said, "That's him, Tree! That's Tremain!"

Tree guffawed. "You mean to tell me he was fool enough to walk in here? Well, ain't he a cherry for pickin'?" He turned to one of the other men at the table and said, "Dwayne, go get my cherry picker. The shiny one!"

Jackson warned, "Stay where you are!" He pointed his pistol directly at Tree's head. Fletcher had identified John Tree as one of the men who had had a hand in the death of Jackson's father. That thought kept flashing across his mind. He was filled with such unanticipated anger that briefly he considered pulling the trigger and blowing off the top of Tree's head, but it did not seem penalty enough.

Carlos patted them down for weapons as Jackson stood guard. Tavio entered the room and assisted Carlos. Two revolvers and three knives were confiscated and the guns were emptied of bullets. Tavio went and stood at the rear of the room next to two closed doors.

Jackson walked over to the table and studied the four men. He forced himself to look into each one of their faces. He and Carlos had agreed beforehand that he would take the lead and Carlos would speak only if absolutely necessary. Jackson said to the men, "This can be easy, or it can be difficult. Frankly, I don't care which it is. I need some information. Where can I find Deleon DuMont? Who knows where he's staying?"

The attorney smiled and fingered his Van Dyke as he said, "We shouldn't be talking with guns in our hands. We should be sitting down and negotiating."

"What's to negotiate?" Jackson asked, pacing around the table. Another one of Carlos's team entered the room and conferred with Carlos. Carlos turned to Jackson and tapped his watch. Jackson nodded in response and repeated, "What's to negotiate?"

The attorney smiled as if he had caught Jackson asking a trick question. "I think there are a wide spectrum of issues that—"

Jackson interrupted impatiently, "I know who you are, you sleazy bastard! So don't give me your bullshit! There are only two issues I want you to focus on and that's where is Deleon and where is Braxton?"

Jackson saw the fourth man at the table glance involuntarily at the jacket on the unoccupied chair next to him. Jackson walked over and checked the jacket's pockets. He found a wallet in an inside breast pocket and when he flipped it open, it was Braxton's. A strange excitement suddenly filled him. The one who had masterminded the attacks against his family was also close at hand. He turned to Carlos. "Braxton!

He's here somewhere! Watch these men. I want to find him. Tavio! Diego! Check all the doors in the hallway. Don't take any risks. Spray the walls with bullets; that may encourage him to give up easily. I'll check behind the two doors at the rear of this room. These walls don't seem that thick," Jackson commented as he pointed his .45 waist high at the rear wall and fired measured shots into it every four feet. The smack of crushed Sheetrock and the splintering of wood drowned out the soft bark of his silenced weapon. He was halfway across the rear wall when he heard commotion behind the door on the right.

All vestiges of hesitation were gone. Jackson emptied the rest of his magazine into the walls around the door behind which the sounds had originated. He dropped an empty magazine on the floor and popped in a new one. Once he had chambered a bullet, he opened the door cautiously. He let the door swing open all the way and with his gun at the ready, he entered a short hallway which led to an office. It was a small office with a heavy wooden desk and cheap leather furniture. Other than the dim light which flowed through the doorway that he had entered, the office was unlit. Jackson checked the iron-grille-covered door on the far side of the desk and the small toilet and shower which adjoined the office. It was only when he stood examining the huge padlock that was still locked tightly on the grille door that he noticed the window behind the curtains. It was a large double-hung window which had its lower section pushed open. He saw that there was blood on the windowsill and that the window's outer metal grille was unlatched and opened. He leaned out the window and saw in the shadows of the unlit alley fifteen feet below a dimly outlined pile of black plastic garbage bags. He thought he saw a human leg sticking out of the pile, but when he pointed his gun down toward it, he saw a police car stop at the end of the alley and focus its spotlight down the length of the alley. Jackson pulled the window's grille closed and stepped behind the curtains.

Frustration and anger swept through him. So close, yet so far. Momentarily, Jackson considered firing his gun into the pile of plastic bags, but he could not be sure that the flare of his weapon's discharge wouldn't be seen. He did not want to arouse the suspicions of the men in the patrol car. He waited by the window listening for sounds of a human scrambling to his feet, but there were none. The police car remained parked at the end of the alley, although it turned out its spotlight. After a few minutes Jackson shut the window and walked back through the hallway to the main room, slamming doors behind him. "The bastard must've jumped out the goddamn window!" he explained to Carlos. "I think he's still down there, but a police car is sitting at the end of the alley."

The attorney interjected, "You don't have a lot of time now! If you want to—"

"Shut the fuck up!" Jackson growled, pointing his pistol in his direction.

The attorney forced a frightened chuckle. "If you kill me, you'll never find out what you want to know!"

Jackson stared at him for a minute, saw the smirk on his face, and thought, I don't have time for this bullshit! He did not hesitate; he pointed his pistol and shot the attorney in his left foot. The man screamed and bent over the table. Jackson was getting angrier and angrier. These men were wasting his time, and in doing so they were preventing him from getting to Elizabeth. A new and different feeling was welling up within him and it was eagerness. He wanted the men to take some precipitous action that would justify the infliction of pain. He watched unsympathetically as the attorney gasped in agony, then he demanded, "Do we have a failure to communicate? Have I focused your attention, or do I have to shoot you someplace else?" Jackson moved around to shoot the other foot that was under the table.

The attorney panted, "Yes! Yes! I'm focusing! Please, no more!"

Tree growled, "You mighty brave when you got all this backup! You gon' be this brave when the police get here?"

Jackson had difficulty looking into Tree's face because every time he did, he wanted to kill him. There was no conscious thought about it. It was simply a desire that originated somewhere deep within him. He had to restrain himself from filling the man's chest with lead.

Tree suggested with a smile, "Them police boys is probably coming for their weekly payoff!"

Jackson turned and looked at Tree. "Before he died, Fletcher told us all about you. You're the one who always brags about setting my father up, aren't you?"

Tree's eyes narrowed. "You know where Jesse is?"

Jackson smiled. "Good old Jesse. He and Fletcher are feeding the fish."

"You done killed my nephew?"

Jackson confirmed, "Damn straight!"

The man sitting across from Tree stood suddenly and shouted at Jackson, "You goddamn motherfucker!" Tavio shot him before he was all the way erect. The man jerked as the bullet hit him then crumpled to the floor. Tavio walked around the table to make sure that he had made a killing hit. The man was still breathing, but not for long. The bullet had just barely missed his heart. This time neither the body nor the blood held any fascination for Jackson. He felt no remorse for this man. He was ready to move on to the next. He began to pace around the table once more. "Once again, where is Deleon DuMont? Where can I find him?"

"You fuckin' pieces of shit killed Dwayne! I ain't tellin' you a goddamn thing!" Tree declared. His face, with the scar tugging at the right side, was a lopsided snarl. He pointed at Jackson and taunted, "You just a jive-ass punk with a gun! Shit, if I was to go hand to hand with you, I'd eat you up like I did yo' daddy! Whachoo think of that, punk?"

He could not be sure at what point he stopped hearing Tree's voice. Jackson had never considered the anger he might feel toward a man who had actually participated in his father's murder. The heat of indignation flared out across his thoughts, filling his mind with blazing color, like flames rising in the wind above a raging fire. He had no sensation. All he knew was that his fingers were tingling and his mouth was dry. He turned and stared at Tree, who was mouthing some words which Jackson could not even hear. Jackson had no conscious awareness of when his hearing returned, but suddenly he smelled cigar smoke and was back firmly in the room with his enemies. He glanced around the room for the source of the smoke and then his gaze fell on Tree.

For the first time in his life Jackson felt true hatred. He tasted its bitterness and it completely erased any thoughts of compassion and sympathy. Suddenly, everything that his grandfather had said became clear to him, and with that realization came the understanding that he would be the one to collect on the family's debts. But more than that, he now *wanted* to be the one to collect. He went over to where the confiscated weapons lay on the floor and picked up one of the knives. It was a switchblade. He tossed the knife at Tree's feet. "Get up, asshole!" Tree said nothing. He looked down at the knife but made no move toward it. Jackson prodded, "You're going to die one way or the other! I'm giving you a chance to die with a weapon in your hand!"

Tree stared around the room at Carlos, Diego, and Tavio. "Yo' peoples is just gon' shoot me if'en I gets up!"

Jackson shrugged. "If you're afraid to fight me, you can die by torture."

Tree bent down and picked up the knife, flicked it open, then launched himself right at Jackson. The knife flashed in his hand as he stabbed for Jackson, but his fifty-two-year-old body could not match the reflexes of the younger man. Jackson was prepared and eluded his charge easily. He held up his hand as a signal for Tavio and Carlos to hold their fire.

Tree, who had landed on the floor, got to his feet slowly and bellowed, "I'm gon' kill you like I did yo' mama and yo' daddy!" He brandished the thin, six-inch blade in his right hand.

Jackson handed Carlos his gun and turned to face Tree. "Come on out here where there's some open floor," he beckoned to Tree as he backed away from the table.

"Not a good idea. We don't have time for this," Carlos admonished.

"Give me two, three minutes," Jackson replied. He knew that Carlos was warning him again that a bulletproof vest wouldn't stop a knife thrust. Jackson didn't care. He had already palmed the knife like his grandfather had taught him and had the blade hidden in his grip. He felt the primal call of revenge; it spoke to the core of him, the tribal man, and its fundamental intensity swept him away. Everything that the old man had taught him came rushing to the surface. It was a ritual. He would repay this part of the debt with the spilling of Tree's blood. He would stare into Tree's face as he delivered the killing stroke and watch death take him. He beckoned Tree closer.

Tree was hesitant. He looked from Carlos to Tavio, but they backed out of his way. He came toward Jackson more confidently. He carried his knife underhanded so that it was positioned out in front of him. He gave Jackson a toothy grin. "It's just you and me now, ain't that right?"

Jackson circled to his right, so that his left shoulder was turned toward Tree. "That's right, just you and me." Tree feinted then slashed at Jackson, who stepped out of danger with minimal effort. He was watching Tree's footwork as he adjusted his position. Tree trotted forward, hoping to cut off Jackson's evasive action. Jackson seemed indecisive. Tree charged, thinking that with his greater weight he would drive Jackson back against the stacks of furniture, but Jackson feinted a move to his right and when Tree swerved to cut him off he evaded Tree again by moving quickly to his left. This time Jackson did not try to move away but stayed close. Tree turned suddenly and slashed at Jackson, who instead of evading stepped in and blocked the knife arm. Jackson smashed Tree in the nose with the hand that was carrying his knife. It was a heavy punch and it knocked Tree on his heels. Jackson followed it with a hard left hook to the side of Tree's head. Tree staggered into a stack of chairs and fell to his knees.

Jackson waited until Tree regained his feet then closed with him again. Tree was staring down at Jackson's right hand. He had seen the big-bladed knife in Jackson's hand just before the punch arrived. For the first time there was concern on his face. He now knew that Jackson knew how to fight. Unless he was able to lure Jackson into something, he was a dead man. In his day, Tree had been good with a knife, but in the last ten years he had slowed down considerably. He pretended to have hurt his leg and limped toward Jackson. His intent was to get close enough to fling himself upon Jackson and with his weight bear him down to the floor. Jackson accommodated by stepping in front of him. Tree lunged, holding his knife arm back, seeking to grab Jackson with his left hand. Surprisingly, Jackson did not move away.

Tree started to smile as he reached for Jackson's collar, but his hand got knocked away. The inertia from the lunge caused him to lose his balance. He stumbled but didn't fall. Jackson had stopped his lunge with a shoulder then had grabbed his knife hand in an iron grip. Tree tried to turn to face Jackson but a tremendous pain seared through his abdomen. He looked down as the long, bloody blade was withdrawn from his stomach. Then he felt more numbing as the knife was stabbed through his intestines. He stood for a moment, the world hazing over in red, the pain ringing in his ears. Then Jackson stabbed him again in the stomach. Even though he saw the knife enter his flesh, Tree could not feel it. Jackson loosened his hold and stepped away. Tree could not control his legs. He couldn't stand up. He sank to his knees. He saw a foot come up and shove his face backward. He fell over on his back and lay looking up at the ceiling. His vision was darkening around the edges and the darkness was increasing rapidly. He saw Jackson's smiling face as if it were on the other side of a tunnel of shadow. He wanted to shout curses at the face, but he couldn't speak. He could not turn his head.

Jackson stood over Tree's body and felt the exhilaration of a victorious gladiator. It was a primal feeling which coiled like a spring within him, giving bounce to his step. Yet there was more than that: He felt as if he had truly tapped into the meaning of blood and the obligations that came with it. It was not the death of Tree that was important, but that a wrong done to Jackson's family had been avenged and that vengeance had been wrought by a Tremain. It was the ancient way of balancing the scales. He felt intuitively that the souls of his mother and father could now rest easier in the ether knowing that retribution was being meted out for the injustice of their deaths. He looked down at the body at his feet and spat on it. He raised his bloody knife to the ceiling and shouted, "I hear you, Grandfather! Everything will be paid in full! Everything!"

Jackson turned and walked over to the table and looked at the attorney and the remaining man. He stabbed the knife deep into the table's plywood. "Who's next?" he growled.

Both men flinched when the knife was stuck into the table, but neither said a word. Jackson motioned to Tavio. "Bring my machete! I feel like chopping some parts!"

The man who sat across from the attorney began babbling. "I-ain't-a-part-of-this!-Whatever-it-is!-I-just-do-a-little-coke-and-some-crank!-I-don't-know-nothing-about-why-you-killin'-peoples!-I-works-here-baggin'-doin'-final-cleanup-and-checkin'-the-final-tally-each-night-but-I-don't-know-nothin'-about-no-guns!-Shit,-I-use-my-knife-to-line-out-coke-or-to-cut-hash!-I-ain't-thinkin'-about-stabbin'-nobody-with-that-knife!-But-I-do-remember-a-dude-name-DuMont-I-think-I know-where-he-he-he—" The man fell silent and his eyes grew bigger as he watched Jackson pry his bloody knife out of the table.

"Speak slowly and go back to that part about the dude named DuMont," Jackson said as he pulled his knife free. He walked over to the attorney and wiped both sides of his blade on the man's face, then checked the sharpness of the blade by cutting open the breast pocket of the man's herringbone jacket. "Start talking!" he demanded as he continued to clean his blade on the attorney.

"You talkin' to me?" the man asked as he touched his chest. "My name Harold! If you talkin' to me all you got to say is Harold and I be johnny-on-the-spot! If you talkin' to me!"

Jackson pointed his knife at the man and ordered, "Talk, Harold!"

Jackson went back to cutting pieces off the attorney's jacket. Every time the knife came near the man's face he flinched.

"I made a delivery of some keys to a DuMont. I remember 'cause he cursed me out for coming there. He was yellin' that Tree should've come himself. I couldn't do nothin' about that! Tree sent me, so I went!"

"What's the address? What part of town?" Jackson demanded.

"It was out in Potrero Hill. I don't remember the name of the street, but I could show you. I remember the place because the guy had three, maybe four Doberman pinschers behind a high chain-link fence."

Jackson demanded, "What were the keys for?"

"Uh . . . uh . . ." Harold looked guiltily at the attorney.

Jackson kicked his chair. "It's me you have to worry about, not him!"

"Uh! They was keys for another house. Mr. Phillips here, he leased the house for that DuMont fellow. He know where it's at!"

Jackson turned to Carlos. "Bring the van around. I want to be out of here in fifteen minutes."

Carlos replied, "We've got cleanup problems to deal with first. We need to cover our tracks and you need to make a decision regarding these two." He gestured in Phillips's and Harold's direction.

Jackson pointed at Phillips and said, "Find out everything he knows, including all of the different bank accounts. There is no reason Tree's estate should have any money, when we could give it all to some organization that's doing solid community work! Take your time torturing him, then we'll give him the old ride out the Gate."

"You don't have to do this!" Phillips pleaded. "I'm sure we can work out something amicable. All we have to do is talk!"

"What's the address?"

"It's 5757 Lawton, just off Dolores Street! You see? I can tell you lots of things!"

Jackson nodded and smiled. "You'll talk! You'll do *all* the talking! When you're screaming think of me!" Jackson turned to Tavio. "Tape him and roll him!"

"Noooo—" Phillips's scream was cut off as a gag was forced into his mouth.

"What's gon' happen to me?" Harold wailed.

"If this is the right house, I'll set you free."

"Not a good idea!" Carlos countered.

"I'll take the risk," Jackson averred. He turned to Harold. "Furthermore, if you show us where Tree keeps his money and his stash, I'll let you take half of his stash. We'll burn the rest to make it look like a drug deal gone bad. What do you say?"

Harold nodded enthusiastically and asked, "Can I get up? I'll show you where it is. I even know where he keeps the numbers to his safe. Sometimes he gets so loaded, he can't remember the number, then I get it for him."

"Lead the way."

Wednesday, July 14, 1982

Pain was the only sensation. It was so severe that Braxton could not tell where in his body it originated. He knew only that every time he tried to move, there was agony. Colors appeared before his eyes and there was a loud ringing in his ears. It hurt so badly that he couldn't tell whether he was lying, sitting, or standing. Yet he knew he didn't dare scream out. He didn't want to bring attention to himself. His only chance of escape lay in avoiding detection. Fear caused him to lie quietly.

He opened his eyes wide with an effort and saw darkness. Then after a few moments he realized something was pressing against his face. He pushed with his arms. There were sharp stabbing pains, but as he moved there was the barest glimmer of light coming from behind him. Something was on his back. He had to get his legs moving. He pulled up his knees and pain exploded in his left leg. Involuntarily, he moaned. It hurt so bad that his face burned and he began to perspire. He lay quietly for a few minutes, gathering his strength. He had to get away from the building. There would be people checking the alley for him and they would be coming soon.

He remembered now. He had jumped into a pile of black plastic garbage bags to escape Tremain's grandson. He turned over gingerly and pushed the plastic bags off him, then bent down to check his left leg. It was swollen and throbbing. He couldn't touch it without igniting explosions of pain. It was too dark to make anything but a general assessment, but from the way it was bent it looked like he had a compound fracture in the lower shin. Still, he had to get moving.

Cautiously, he looked out around the bags and saw a policeman from a patrol car pissing on a telephone pole. He made no effort to call him. He could not afford to be linked to Tree, not while he had all that drug preparation paraphernalia stashed in his building. The policeman finished urinating and returned to his car. Braxton got to his knees and crawled in the direction of the patrol car, but he kept in the shadows. By the time he had crawled twenty feet to the fence at the back of an auto repair garage, he knew that he would have to find another way to move around. There were too many foreign objects on the ground. His hands and knees couldn't take it. Plus, even if his left foot just barely brushed something it was excruciating.

The patrol car at the end of the alley turned on its siren and roared off to some crime or emergency in progress. Braxton sank back into the shadows behind the repair shop's garbage cans. Once the police were gone, Tremain was sure to come looking for him; a quick death would be the best he could expect. He wedged himself into the darkest corner he could find and pulled a newspaper over his head. A large cockroach fell off the paper and landed between his legs. It scuttled away while he watched it. He sat absolutely still and forced himself to take light, shallow breaths. He didn't have long to wait. He heard the sound of people coming down the alley toward him. He heard the sounds of the garbage bags being thrown aside. Some trash cans were moved around then there was silence. Braxton was cautious. He remained where he was for nearly thirty minutes after they had gone.

He pushed the paper off his head and pulled himself erect using a fence as support. He could see flames in Tree's second-story window. He figured if they had set the building to match, they would be long gone and he had better follow suit. He didn't want to have to answer a whole lot of questions from law enforcement. Plus this was surely going to be an arson as well as a homicide case.

Lying by the fence was a long piece of plumbing pipe. Braxton bent down and picked it up. Holding on to it with two hands, he was able to use it like a crutch. He pushed his sixty-six-year-old body to the point of exhaustion, but he made it to Gough Street by the time Tree's building blew up in a rush of flames. Sirens were blaring on nearby streets when he finally got a cab to take him to a small private hospital which he had used often during the years of his medical practice. As he lay on a gurney in the emergency room waiting to have his leg tended to, he began making plans. The reality was, if he needed surgery, he wouldn't be able to travel for some weeks. Plus, it would take that long to get his finances straight. It was likely that they would be watching both his home and his office. Once he was released from the hospital he would go down to his secret weekend hideaway on the coast near Half Moon Bay. From there he could arrange to transfer his bank accounts and set up his departure.

His first problem was how was he going to replace his identification and credit cards, which had been left in his jacket at Tree's? It was too much to worry about. He was exhausted. The tremendous pain in his leg throbbed, sometimes causing him to shiver involuntarily. Braxton knew now that he had underestimated Jackson Tremain. In the back of his mind there was a grudging respect for King Tremain. Even though King was in the grave, his plans for protecting his family were unassailable.

Braxton fell into a drug-laden stupor as he was wheeled into surgery. The last thing he remembered seeing was King Tremain's evil smile.

Thursday, July 15, 1982

Fisherman's Wharf was crowded with people attending an evening street festival. Several streets were blocked off and strung with lights. Booths were selling a variety of crafts, jewelry, paintings, and food. Costumed clowns, jugglers, and magicians strolled through the crowds giving impromptu performances. There was even a small stage set up on the green slope of Aquatic Park near the cable car turnabout. A five-piece band had just finished playing a set of loud rock music and were in the process of packing up their equipment.

Jackson and Carlos sat alone in a private banquet room at a large table next to a window overlooking the Hyde Street cable car turnabout and the adjacent Aquatic Park. The table was loaded with a variety of different Chinese dishes. Although Carlos was nibbling on some appetizers, the food was not the reason they were in the restaurant. The private banquet room, which had been reserved for three thousand in cash, had an excellent view of DiMarco's restaurant on the wharf and also had its own separate means of egress.

Jackson asked Carlos, "Was someone there at Tree's smoking cigars last night? I smelled cigars when I came back in the room after losing Braxton."

"This is the second time you've asked about cigar smoke. No, I didn't smell any cigars. But since you brought up last night, what was that foolishness with Tree? You could've been killed!"

"Honestly, I don't know what came over me. I just got real angry and wanted to make him pay. I can't explain it."

Carlos leaned forward and stated firmly, "Don't think that your month of working out with a knife makes you anything more than an amateur with a few moves. There are people out there who've been practitioners for years. Don't let anger make you take chances that you don't have to take."

"I hear you," Jackson conceded with a wave of his hand.

Carlos continued, "Another thing, and I know I've mentioned this before, but you need to hit San Vicente's operation in Mexico. He has to know there's a penalty for his actions. Just give me the okay and I'll set it up. It would be wise to start gathering information now about his bases, in case Elizabeth gets taken across the border."

"Whatever you need to do, do it! After I get Elizabeth back I'll still need to deal with him and the DuMonts. The more information I'll have, the better."

Carlos nodded and returned to tasting some of the hot dishes. Jackson stared absentmindedly out the window and contented himself with watching the steady stream of pedestrians going back and forth between the street fair and Ghirardelli Square. He and Carlos were waiting for DiMarco's to close for the night, but during the time that they had been watching the restaurant, they had noticed Paul DiMarco leave by the kitchen door several times to meet with some men whose cars were parked down the street from the restaurant. The men DiMarco spoke with never got out of their cars, nor did they leave when he had finished speaking with them.

"It looks like DiMarco is up to something," Jackson surmised. "You think those are just his bodyguards?"

"Hard to tell," Carlos replied, staring through a pair of binoculars. "We'll just have to keep an eye on them."

The crowds attending the street festival began to abate around tenthirty in the evening. As they waited Jackson and Carlos conducted a rambling conversation.

Jackson was not aware of exactly when he stopped hearing Carlos and fell into the deep well of his thoughts. He had the vague impression that he was suspended in the dark far below his consciousness on a terribly thin hawser as angry images came boiling up beneath him and dominated his thoughts. His actions of the night before had not saved Elizabeth. It had been close, but she was still in the hands of his enemies. He didn't even know if she was still alive. They had gone to both houses that Harold had identified. The first had been vacated and the second had been guarded by Dobermans. The dogs gave the alarm before they had gained entry to the house and a firefight had ensued. It had been a strange battle. Both sides used silenced weapons and bullets were whistling in every direction making more noise when they hit than when they were fired. It had been brief and intense, lasting less than five minutes. During that time Jackson's team killed three dogs and one man. Deleon and the rest escaped.

Jackson and his team had little time to go through the house before the police arrived. It was a mad search for clues that might lead them to the next hiding place. In one of the bedrooms Tavio Lopez found some plane tickets with names on them, and one of the names was Francisco San Vicente, the Jaguar's grandson. The dead man's identification indicated that he was a resident of New Orleans. There was no clear evidence to indicate where Deleon and San Vicente might land next. As Jackson was driven from the scene, a disappointment had settled upon him like a cold fog off the Pacific. He could only hope that Elizabeth was still alive. Although he felt he had no right to ask God any favors, he prayed for Elizabeth's survival, that he might hold her in his arms once again and know the soft caress of her skin.

When his thoughts were not inundated with images of Elizabeth, Jackson pondered his other sources of frustration and disappointment. It appeared that Braxton had gotten away clean. Although men were assigned to watch both his house and his office, there was no sign of him. Jackson could not even be sure he was still in the state.

Jackson had to wait for more information to be gathered, yet while he was waiting he planned to take whatever action he could to destroy his enemies. With Braxton on the run and Tree dead, DiMarco was next in line. Jackson intended to take the three kilos of heroin that he had removed from Tree's and stash it in DiMarco's office and then he planned to start an electrical fire to burn just the dining area of his restaurant. If everything went correctly the drugs would be found by the authorities. As he reviewed his plans, he wondered what had become of the person who had thought his grandfather had been a cold-hearted brute. Even as he searched his soul, Jackson could not find remorse for the lives that he had taken. Was he really any different from his grandfather?

Jackson's ruminations were interrupted after midnight when Carlos tapped his arm and said, "Looks like we got some action going on. That maître d' you talked about is being followed by the men in those cars."

Jackson looked out the window and saw Dominique making her way up Hyde Street. The festival was over, the crowds were gone, but there were still a few pedestrians. Dominique was coming toward the restaurant in which he and Carlos were sitting and it didn't look like she was aware that she was being followed.

Looking through his binoculars, Carlos commented, "Those guys following her are carrying. I can see bulges under their jackets and it looks like they mean business."

Jackson stood, buttoned his own jacket, and said, "Well, I'm going to throw a wrench into their plans."

"Not a good idea," Carlos advised. "Let them do their business and then we'll do ours. No reason to put them on guard."

"I'm not going to sit by and let them kill that woman."

"You don't know what they're going to do," Carlos challenged. "Why get into it? What's she to you? Are you willing to jeopardize our plans to save her?"

"We can always burn that goddamn restaurant!" Jackson retorted. "If not tonight, some other night. From this point on, I don't intend to let one of their plans come to fruition if I can stop it. I know you think this is foolishness, so I won't ask you to join me. But I have to go." Jackson turned and walked toward the exit, which had its own private staircase to the street. He was not operating purely out of enmity. He had mentioned to Pres that he had met Dominique and Pres had evinced a strong desire to see her again. He did not want to see the look on Pres's face if he had to tell him that he had done nothing to save her from harm. Jackson walked out the door and descended the metal fire escape into the darkness of a small alley. Keeping in the shadows, he was walking toward the thoroughfare when Dominique entered the alley coming in his direction. Jackson figured that she must be headed toward the parking lot where the employees of the surrounding businesses all parked. He stepped into the darkness of a recessed doorway.

Dominique was now walking fast, looking over her shoulder every few seconds. It was obvious that she knew she was being followed. She was a quarter of the way when two men followed by a large sedan without headlights turned down the alley. The men following Dominique broke into a run. Dominique started to run as well. She was going to run right past where Jackson was standing, but he grabbed her arm and jerked her into the doorway beside him. It was a sudden move that took her by surprise and it was only due to Jackson's daily training with Carlos that he was able to knock her knife away from his throat.

"I'm on your side!" he hissed as they struggled briefly in the darkness of the doorway. "I'm Pres's friend!"

Dominique stopped struggling once she recognized his face. "What are you doing here?" she demanded.

"Keep your voice down! I'm after your buddies, and if I happen to save your ass while I'm at it, so much the better!"

"Well, you better have a gun because they're coming!"

"No problem!" Jackson replied, pulling his pistol out with its silencer attached. He looked around the corner of the doorway and saw in the dimness that the two men had slowed down their approach. Jackson pointed his gun at the nearest man and fired two quick shots. One of his bullets hit the man in the shoulder and spun him around.

The man cried out, "I'm hit! The bitch has got a gun!" His companion sprayed the alley with bullets from his machine pistol. He too was using a silencer and the slugs that ricocheted down the length of the alley made more noise than his weapon.

Jackson waited for a pause in the zinging bullets; then, while the man was changing magazines, he fired back. The man with the machine pistol was wearing a light-colored shirt which stood out even in the darkness of the alley. Jackson aimed for his torso and kept firing until the man fell with a scream.

The headlights of the sedan suddenly turned on, flooding the alley with bright light. The car screeched to a halt beside the injured men and its doors were flung open as they were helped inside. The car started forward, but a hail of bullets from above knocked out one of its lights, tore through the vehicle's hood, and ricocheted off its bullet-proof glass. The sedan jerked into reverse and backed out of the alley with a screech of tires.

From above and behind him, Jackson heard Carlos call, "You all right down there?"

"Yeah, we're okay. Thanks for the backup. I'll be up in a minute."

Before he went back inside Carlos said, "Remember, we still have a job to do."

Dominique looked up into Jackson's face. "Who the hell are you?"

"Jackson Tremain, an enemy of the DiMarcos. Who the hell are you? And why are these clowns after you?"

"A family vendetta," Dominique answered tiredly. "I'm a Volante. The Volantes and the Minettis have had problems for some time. This evening was planned by the Minettis."

"A revenge hit before the election?"

"They expected it to be easy. Once I was down they would've taken my body somewhere else and dumped it."

"You're mighty calm about all this."

Dominique raised her eyebrows quickly as a "so what?" expression flashed across her face. She said, "A girl's gotta do what a girl's gotta do." She straightened her jacket and waved her hand in farewell. "Thanks for 'saving my ass,' as you say, but I've got to be going. I've got things to do."

"Well, don't worry about coming to work tomorrow."

"I wasn't planning on coming in, but why are you saying that?"

"I'm going to burn it down."

"You've done me a favor, I'll do you one: Don't burn the whole place. Just burn the kitchen and leave the safe open; the arson investigator will have access to both sets of his books."

"That's good, but how do I get the safe open?"

"The combination is on the bottom of his blotter on his desk and the extra key is in the peppercorn jar in the spice cabinet by the fridge. Oh, and the burglar alarm code numbers are the same as the address." Dominique looked both ways down the alley and stepped out of the doorway.

Jackson asked, "What do I tell Pres? He sure wanted to see you."

Dominique pushed her long black hair out of her eyes and looked at Jackson. "Tell him it's bad timing. If I'm still here when all this is over, I'd love to see him, but until then I don't intend anyone to find me."

"Why don't you take the number of my answering service, just in case." Jackson took out a piece of paper and jotted a number on it then handed it to her.

Dominique took the piece of paper reluctantly and asked, "In case of what?"

"In case you want to talk to him or you need help."

"Why should I need help?"

"You needed it tonight!"

"Don't fool yourself! They weren't going to get me!" Dominique pulled a small-caliber pistol from her handbag. "I was just leading them to the darkest part of the alley."

"Whatever you say," Jackson said, stepping back. "Good luck."

"Good luck to you. Or should I say, 'Burn, baby, burn'?" Dominique turned and walked away into the darkness of the alley.

Jackson watched her until she disappeared in the shadows then made his way back upstairs to the private dining room. Strangely, he felt close to Dominique, as if she were a long-lost sibling. It seemed they were fathered by the same events. When she had mentioned the family vendetta, Jackson understood all that her statement implied. It was a small consolation to know that he wasn't the only one twisted and turned on a lathe, and cut to a template that was made long before his birth.

Jackson was not a particularly religious person, yet he found himself again calling on the Lord as he entered the banquet room, praying that he would find Elizabeth unharmed and that he would vanquish all who stood against him. He had no concept of how much he had already changed.

Friday, July 16, 1982

The phone's insistent, high-pitched ring was shrill in Paul DiMarco's ears. As much as he wanted to, he could not ignore its sound. He rubbed the sleep from his eyes and looked at the clock on his bedside table. It was three o'clock in the morning. Who the hell can this be? he wondered as he pushed himself to a sitting position. His irritation increased when he discovered that his wife had moved the phone back to her side of the bed. He thought briefly about clambering over her body, but he didn't want to deal with her screaming. He got up and walked around the bed. Just as he got to the phone, his wife reached out and picked up the receiver.

"Hello?" she asked sleepily.

"Give me the phone, Camille!" Paul demanded.

She ignored him and asked into the receiver, "Who's calling? Do you know what time it is? Didn't your mother raise you better?"

"Give me the goddamned phone!"

Camille did not hand him the phone and she evinced no fear when she turned to him and demanded, "How come you got people calling you in the middle of the night? You were supposed to give everything up!"

Paul snatched the phone out of her hands, then pointed his finger menacingly at her as he spoke into the phone, "This is DiMarco, who the hell is this? . . . Okay, it's you, Mickey. Why you got to call at this hour in the morning?"

Mickey Vazzi sounded winded and a little frantic and when DiMarco heard his news he understood why. Two hours earlier Joe Bones's penthouse apartment had been bombed with him in it. Joe Bones had been whacked two days before he had planned to come to San Francisco. Mickey didn't have to say any more. A hit on Bones was a hit on the Las Vegas Mob; there would be retribution exacted. Bones held such a high position that all the likely suspects might just get whacked to send a message.

Vazzi's voice dropped to a whisper. He asked, "You didn't have nothing to do with it, did you?"

Paul exclaimed, "Are you crazy? Never! Why would you ask a fool question like that?"

"People are going to think it's you because I just left there, after delivering the jet. Everybody knows you weren't happy about giving up the jet. I'm worried somebody is going to come looking for me to answer questions and I ain't got no answers!"

"Me either! I don't know who did it. This is really fucked! Thanks for calling me and telling me, Mickey. You're a friend." Paul was about to set the phone softly back on its cradle when Mickey said, "That ain't all the news either."

"What the fuck more can there be?" Paul demanded.

"There's lots more. Somebody burned down part of the restaurant."

"What? When?"

"Sometime this morning. They must've come in after we closed. They left gas cans everywhere. Whoever did it wanted it to look like arson."

Paul exploded. "Goddamn it!" This was all he needed. More complications. He figured that the fire must've been set by Tremain. Still, it was not the end of the world. He calmed himself with an effort and asked, "How did you hear about all this?"

"Langella called me around midnight. He needed a place to take an injured man and a place to dump a body. I was going to go by the restaurant and get the keys for the apartment we keep for out-of-town visitors when I saw the fire department and the police picking through the wreckage of the fire."

Paul looked around at his wife and saw that she was watching him and listening. He asked, "So at least everything went well with Asti, huh?"

"No, she got away."

Paul couldn't believe it. "What? Then who's the stiff?"

"One of Langella's men. That bitch led them into an ambush. Langella would've been killed if the car hadn't had bulletproof glass."

Paul almost dropped the phone. It seemed that his whole world was on the verge of crashing around his ears. All semblance of a normal life for him was over. He had the Mob on one side and a freelance assassin on the other. He tried to gather his thoughts. He needed money. A lot of money. "Listen, Mickey, I need you to go back to the restaurant and get into the safe—"

"I can't!"

"Listen, damn it! I'm going to give you the combination!"

"I'm trying to tell you the safe was already open when I got there.

The police department was taking stuff out of it as evidence. They found three kilos of heroin in it."

"What heroin?" Paul was nearly apoplectic. "Where did that come from?"

"I don't know. I guess somebody set you up."

DiMarco was stunned. "How did the safe get opened? Did the police take the money as evidence?"

Mickey's voice dropped. "I couldn't get real close, but I don't think there was any money in there. I think all they got was the heroin and your books."

Paul put the phone back on the hook. There was nothing more to say. He had underestimated both Asti and Tremain and now he had to pay the piper. He felt hollow, slack, like a sail without wind. The fact that Joe Bones had been hit at the same time that the arson was committed was an extremely crafty move. Somebody had made a trap for him and it looked airtight. The legal case against him was open and shut. The heroin combined with the fact his two sets of accounting books were in the hands of the authorities would give them all they needed. There would be a trail of millions of dollars for which his restaurant could not account. He would be charged with drug dealing and it would make the papers. The DiMarcos would be publicly forced to repudiate any connection or link with him and organized crime, but behind the scenes they would expend every effort to show the Mob that they were in control of their city. No stone would be left unturned in rooting out the perpetrators of the hit on Bones. Paul, the rogue DiMarco, was expendable. He would be thrown on the sacrificial altar to show that the DiMarcos were sincere and thorough even if it meant one of their own family was involved.

Paul couldn't go back to sleep now. He had to make plans or he would never see another sunrise. First thing was he needed money. He was walking out of the bedroom when his wife's voice interrupted him.

"What the hell is Mickey Vazzi doing calling here at this time of the night? I thought you were warned to stop all business until after the election!"

Paul's initial reaction was to ignore her, but he thought better of it. He answered simply, "Someone whacked Joe Bones!"

"Oh my God!" Camille sat up. She knew what his news meant. "You didn't have anything to do with it, did you?" Paul shook his head.

Camille's hand trembled a bit as she took a cigarette from a pack on the bedside table and lit it. She inhaled deeply then asked, "But you're a suspect, aren't you?"

"Yep. But that ain't all. Somebody burned down part of the restaurant and left three kilos of heroin in my office. I've been framed like a picture. Set up like quail under glass."

"Oh God!" Camille stood up and put on her robe. "They'll be coming here!" Paul knew that she wasn't referring to the police when he nodded in agreement. Camille puffed her cigarette nervously as she continued, "I've got to get the children up! If I go to my mother's will I be endangering her?"

Paul shrugged and replied, "I don't know."

"Will they . . . will they kill all of us?"

"Fuck if I know! It might be best if you and the kids went up to my sister's in Reno. She ain't part of the life. It'll take 'em a month to find you there, by that time—"

"Can't you do something? Can't you find who did this?" Camille's voice was pleading. Gone was her indignation. She was a mother begging for the lives of her two male sons. She knew all too well the consequences of a hit on one of the bosses. Her own father and two brothers had been killed after just such a hit. Tears had now joined her words. "Can't you do something?"

Paul started to say "Everything's going to be all right!," but he couldn't bring himself to lie. He shook his head and left the bedroom.

Friday, July 16, 1982

Pug DuMont's party was well under way when Elroy pulled up to the mansion gates with his van filled with trays of pastries. He straightened his uniform and reviewed his cover story as he waited for the gate to open. Elroy wanted to enter, take care of his business, and leave with the least commotion and fuss. He didn't want to hurt anyone unnecessarily. Therefore, his disguise had to be good enough to pass a close inspection. He had rented a third van and had assembled the metal racks upon which the trays of pastries were loaded himself. He had fastened new signs to its sides which read ROYALE BAKERIE. He prepared his own employee identification card and had it laminated with his picture. He wore a starched white apron over his white uniform and even wore a chef's hat. Then, after all his preparation, the man guarding the gate didn't even ask for identification, just waved Elroy inside.

Elroy drove the van around to the side entrance and parked next to a large catering truck. He got out and went to the back of the van and un-loaded a metal cart. He slipped on some latex gloves and slid three pas-try trays into grooves on the cart's legs. There was a metal drawer in the top of the cart that Elroy covered with white linen and placed a fourth tray on top of it. He made sure that he could access the drawer. Inside the drawer were three pairs of handcuffs, a coil of rope, an unregistered .357 Magnum revolver, and a hypodermic needle filled with a fast-acting poison. Before he had left San Francisco, he had reconciled him-self to the prospect of death. He wheeled his cart into the house. He was going to cast his lot with fate and let the devil take the hindmost.

He knew that the party was being held in the main wing of the house, but he had heard over his receiver that Pug had left the party and had gone to the sitting room, where they were keeping Serena. It seemed that Pug took unusual pleasure in taunting her with threats of the things he was going to do to her. Although he had little sympathy for Serena, Elroy respected her for not breaking down or acting fright-ened. It was obvious that the old girl had some grit. Elroy rolled his cart past the hallway that led to the sitting room, but there were two body-guards lounging by the door. Elroy didn't want to go into the kitchen; the possibility that he would be challenged by one of the catering staff or, at the minimum, be put to work, was too great. He rolled his cart into an alcove and slid out a tray and carried it down the corridor into the main ballroom. He saw a group of waiters in white coats conferring near the door and asked where he should leave the tray of pastries.

"You way too late," drawled a lanky, dark-skinned man. "I'm bussing dishes now!"

"You ain't too late!" countered another man. He pointed to the far side of the room. "None of the people at table fifteen got any dessert. Take the tray over there."

Elroy followed the man's direction and walked around the room crowded with people sitting at round tables. There was a convivial din as people laughed and conversed between tables. There was an eight-piece swing band tuning their instruments and checking microphones on a small temporary stage. Elroy dutifully set the tray on a sideboard and made his exit. When he returned to the alcove, he noticed that the bodyguards were still in the hall leading to the sitting room. He sighed and took another tray of pastries into the dining room. At the door, the same waiter who had told him that he was too late took the tray and hurried to a nearby table to serve its occupants. The band began to play "Stardust" and the sound of the brass reverberated through the room. Before he could turn and leave, two other waiters asked him to bring more trays of pastry. Elroy went back to the alcove and saw that Xavier DuMont was leaving the sitting room followed by his bodyguards. Elroy rolled his cart out of the alcove and headed for the dining room ahead of Xavier.

Xavier's commanding voice called out behind Elroy, "You there! Hold up! Stop!" Initially Elroy kept walking. He didn't want to talk with Xavier and he didn't think that Xavier was addressing him. Xavier called out again, "Goddamn it! I'm talking to you!" Elroy looked around to see if there was anyone else in the corridor and there wasn't. He stopped and turned to see what Xavier wanted.

Xavier, followed by his bodyguards, came up and slapped Elroy across the face. "When I call you, you obey! Goddamn it! If you ever want to get another catering job in this city, you better clean out your ears! I'm going to report you to your superiors! What's your name and who do you work for?"

Elroy covered his anger and affected a southern drawl. "My name Clarence Renfro. I work for Royale Bakerie down off of Desire."

Xavier turned to one of his bodyguards. "Write that down! I don't want to forget it!" The man awkwardly rummaged through his pockets looking for a pen. He found a ballpoint but didn't have any paper. Xavier was exasperated. He looked at Elroy and demanded, "Do you have a business card?"

"Naw, suh. I ain't got nothin' like that."

Xavier looked over the tray of pastries and sneered, "These look like shit! Let's see how they taste." He picked up an eclair and bit off the end. He chewed a few times then spit it out. "This is shit! Let's try another." He bit into a flan tart and shortly afterward spit it out too. "This is all shit! I won't let you serve this to my guests!" Xavier pushed over the cart, spilling the contents of the trays onto the floor. He pointed to the floor and ordered Elroy, "Clean all this shit off my floor! Jasper, you stay here and sees that he does it!"

As he watched Xavier walk away with the other bodyguard, Elroy was furious. The lower legs of his pants and his shoes were covered with rich pastry filling. He was not used to taking umbrage without some sort of response, but he focused on his objective and swallowed his pride. He got down on his knees and began putting the overturned pastries back on one of the trays. He then picked up his cart and set it on its wheels.

Jasper took two strides and kicked the cart over again. He pointed to the floor covered with custard, flan, and cream and said, "The boss, he say clean this shit up!" Elroy could not keep the anger off his face. Jasper saw his expression and challenged, "Whachoo gon' do? You feel froggish? Let's see you jump bad."

Elroy lifted the cart again and set it upright on its wheels. He turned his back to Jasper, put his hand in the top drawer, and pulled out the gun. He backed up, rolling the cart out of the mess on the floor.

Jasper threatened, "You need another slappin'? You better get down on yo' hands and knees and clean that crap up!"

"I don't think I will," Elroy retorted defiantly. He turned to face Jasper. "I think you should clean it up!"

"Well, ain't this some shit!" Jasper exclaimed as he walked toward Elroy. "Clarence, you done fucked with the wrong man!" Jasper feinted with his left, then threw a right at Elroy's head.

Elroy blocked the punch with his own right and then backhanded Jasper across the face with the butt of the pistol. A gash opened over Jasper's right eye as he stumbled backward in pain. Using the butt of the pistol as his weapon, Elroy followed him and clipped the top of his head. Jasper fell back against the wall and attempted to pull out his own gun, but Elroy hit him in the mouth, knocking out a few teeth. Jasper dropped to the floor, stunned. His eyes were just focusing as Elroy bent over him with his arm raised to deliver another blow.

Jasper cried out in fear, "Don't kill me over this shit!" He raised his arm to protect his head. It was no defense. The butt of the pistol landed on his head with a sickening thud and Jasper lost consciousness.

Elroy stood up and went back to the cart for a pair of handcuffs and the rope. He handcuffed Jasper's hands behind him then dragged him into a side room. He deposited him behind a couch then tied his feet together and pulled the rope taut through the handcuffs so that Jasper's legs were curled behind him. Elroy tore a piece of curtain and made a gag, which he tied over Jasper's mouth. He returned to the cart and after getting his hypodermic and the other two pairs of cuffs, he pushed the cart once more into the alcove. He knew there was another entrance to the sitting room through a bedroom at the end of the hall. He decided that entry better suited his purposes, because then he wouldn't have his back to whoever came down the main hall. The bedroom door was open. Elroy entered and locked it behind him. He could hear the sound of Pug's raspy voice coming through the partially opened sitting room door. Elroy moved quietly to the door and waited. He wanted to determine the number of people in the room before he entered.

"You say you don't remember me, huh?" Pug scoffed. "You remember when my brothers Chess and Eddy was kilt by yo' no-good husband? I was the one that got away. I sho' remember you. How 'bout this, you remember when yo sons was kilt? I do, 'cause I'm the one that planned it! You shaking yo' head, huh? You don't believe it? Well, you know Billy DuMont Braxton? He's my sister's boy. I used him to set up both killings. Yo' oldest boy was the easiest. All Billy had to do was lie and tell him where King had his money stashed. Yo' fool of a son went and dressed up like King and when he went to the address we gave him, them Eye-talians shot him up good."

"I'm sorry to bother you, sweetie pie," Zenia's voice interrupted. "You're way past due to drain your bladder. Let's step—"

"Goddamn it, Zenia! Can't you see I'm busy with somethin' important? I ain't got time for that now!"

"Oh, honey, you know if we don't keep to the schedule you'll get sick. I just don't want you to—" Zenia stopped talking as she saw Elroy enter the room with a gun in his hand.

Pug turned around and stared at the intruder. It took him only a second to recognize Elroy as one of King's descendants. He exclaimed, "It's a goddamn Tremain! Walkin' in here like he got a right!" Pug raised his voice and shouted, "Xavier! Xavier!"

Elroy smiled and said, "Even if he comes, he won't be able to help you!"

Zenia held up her hand placatingly. "Please don't hurt him. He's in ill health—"

Pug's face turned purple with rage. "Goddamn it, Zenia! Don't beg from a Tremain! We DuMonts got pride! If he got the balls to kill me in my own house, let him try it!" Pug tried to get out of his chair and stand. "Shit! If I was ten years younger, I'd . . ." The exertion was too much and he fell back into his seat. The effort caused spasticity to set off in his legs and soon his whole body was jerking with spasms. He snarled, "Kill me! I ain't gon' beg for my life! Kill me!"

"Please, mister," Zenia pleaded. "I need to drain his bladder. Can we leave the room for a minute?"

Elroy shook his head. "Whatever you have to do has to be done here!"

Zenia nodded and set about her task. She opened a small plastic kit, donned a pair of gloves, and took out a length of clear plastic tubing. She squeezed some lubricant on it and pulled up Pug's shirt, exposing a plastic cap. She pulled off the cap and inserted the tube down the surgically implanted canal. When the tube was two thirds inserted, pale urine began to dribble into a urinal, which she held.

Elroy watched the whole operation and was sickened. It was obvious to him that Pug was a sick and dying man who was just holding on to life by a thread. There was no pleasure in the revenge that could be gained from killing him. In truth, Pug was already dead; hate was the only thing keeping him alive. Elroy felt tremendously disappointed. There was nothing that he could do to Pug that would ease the pain and sadness that he himself felt. There was no balm in Gilead. Elroy was destined to live with the darkness and waste of his life until he lived no more. He could not even remember what he hoped to achieve in killing Pug. The anger and indignation he had felt when he entered the room drained away, leaving only the stains of its existence and a vast emptiness. He shrugged and set the hypodermic down on the table beside Zenia.

"What's that for?" she asked.

Elroy gestured at Pug. "It's poison. It was for him. I came to kill him for what he did to my mother, but his life is already over. Nothing I could do would be worse than letting him continue to live like this."

Pug looked at Elroy through bleary eyes and urged, "Kill me, you bastard! Go ahead, I ain't afraid!"

Elroy pointed to the hypodermic and suggested, "Kill yourself. I don't want to dirty my hands with you. You're not worth killing. You're just a piece of trash that will blow away with the next strong wind." Elroy turned and looked at Serena. "You don't deserve it, but do you want to leave with me?" Serena looked at him with lifeless eyes and shook her head. Elroy shrugged and headed for the door leading to the main hall.

Pug shouted, "Kill me! Kill me!" He was a man raised in the ways of the feud. He had hated the Tremains ever since he could remember and in the strange dynamic of warfare had measured himself against them. Now these same enemies whom he had pitted himself against all his adult life didn't even feel that he was worth killing. It was the greatest insult that he had ever experienced. He begged, "Kill me! Kill me!"

Elroy refused to even look his way as he walked toward the door.

Xavier and the remaining bodyguard opened the door and entered the room while Elroy was still ten feet from the exit. There was a momentary tableau as Xavier and his hireling stared at Elroy.

Pug shouted, "Kill him, Donnell! He's a Tremain!"

The bodyguard started to reach beneath his jacket, but Elroy raised his gun. "Don't do anything foolish," he warned. "I don't want to hurt anybody. I just plan on walking out of here."

Xavier threatened, "Donnell, if you want to keep your job, you better kill this asshole!"

Donnell looked back and forth between Xavier and Elroy, then made a sudden move to pull out his pistol. Elroy shot him twice in the chest. The bullets knocked Donnell backward against the door, which slammed shut. When Elroy didn't see blood he figured that Donnell was wearing a bulletproof vest, so he shot him in the head. Donnell fell to the floor and lay still.

Elroy advanced on Xavier, who was cowering now by the door. He snarled, "You were a big man when you had two bodyguards. How tough are you now?"

Xavier was like any other bully. He folded when he saw that he didn't have the upper hand. He sputtered, "Please, we have money. You can have it all, just don't hurt me."

"I don't want your money," Elroy replied as he walked up to Xavier. "But payback is a bitch!" Without warning he hauled off and slapped Xavier hard across the face. Xavier fell backward and bounced off the wall. As he came off the wall, Elroy slapped him again, this time knocking him to the floor. Xavier drew himself up into a fetal position and pleaded, "Please, no more! Please, I'm sorry!"

Elroy ordered, "Get up! Get up!" When Xavier refused to get to his feet, Elroy began kicking him. *"Get up!"*

Xavier wailed as he was kicked. "Please! Please, don't hurt me any-more!"

Pug watched his son and was filled with embarrassment. "Don't beg, Xavier! Goddamn! This is a Tremain! Be a man, Xavier!"

Xavier did not heed his father. He begged, "Please, I'll do anything. Please don't kill me! I'll do anything you want!"

Elroy looked down at Xavier's quivering body without sympathy and demanded, "You'll do anything, will you?"

"Yes, just don't hurt me anymore."

"All right, I've got a mess for you to clean up! I want you to lick my shoes clean of all that pastry crap you spilled on them!"

Pug was appalled. "Don't do it, Xavier! Don't do it! At least die like a man!"

Xavier crawled over to where Elroy stood and began licking his shoes. Elroy watched him for a moment then looked at Pug. He asked, "This is your son? This is your legacy? You really are dead!" Elroy knew he could strike no more telling blow to Pug than abasing his son in pub-lic. He lifted his shoe and ordered, "Lick the bottoms too!" Xavier didn't argue. He began licking the sole of Elroy's shoe.

Tears were running down Pug's cheeks as he shouted at Elroy, "Kill him! Kill him! He ain't no son of mine! He don't deserve to live! Take him out of his misery! Kill him! Save me from killing him!"

Elroy stared down at the man who was licking his shoes and thought, Cowardice like yours causes the worst cruelty. Your father is right, you *do* deserve to die. He bent down and put the barrel of the gun against Xavier's head. When the cold metal touched his skin, Xavier screamed, a high, wailing keen. Elroy stepped back, surprised that such a sound could come from a man's body. Then he noticed the smell of feces. He looked with disgust down at the trembling figure at his feet, then he glanced at Pug. "You smell that?" he asked. "Your son just shit on him-self!"

Pug shouted, "Kill him! He ain't no son of mine! He ain't a DuMont. He ain't got no backbone! He just a worm!"

"You're begging me to kill your own son?" Elroy looked at Pug and shook his head. "You raised him! You do it! I'm finished here!" Elroy turned and walked over to the door. He pulled Donnell's body out of the way, swung the door open, and continued down the hall to where he left his cart. The music of the band was loud and filled the hall.

As soon as Elroy had left the room, Xavier pulled himself into a sitting position and wiped the tears from his face. He stared at Elroy's retreating back then looked around and saw the butt of Donnell's gun sticking out from under his jacket. Xavier quickly crawled over to Donnell's body and pulled the gun from its holster. Using Donnell as a rest, he aimed the revolver at Elroy's back and fired. His shot went true. The bullet hit Elroy high on his back and he fell to the floor as if he were dead.

"I did it! I did it!" Xavier shouted with surprise. "I killed him! I killed a Tremain!"

"Good," his father retorted. "Now use the gun on yo'self and kill yo'-self! You ain't got nothin' worth living for! You just scum! Cowardly scum!"

Anger flashed across Xavier's face. "What do you mean? I killed him!"

Pug waved his hand dismissively. "Yeah, you shot him in the back after he made you lick his shoes and shit on yo'self. You ain't nothin' to be proud of. Why don't you save Deleon the trouble and kill yo'self!"

"What do you mean, 'save Deleon the trouble'?"

Pug actually smiled. "Me and Deleon got us a deal. When he finish killin' King Tremain's grandsons and setting things to right, he gon' come back here and kill yo' cowardly ass! I told him if'en he did right in Frisco, I wouldn't stand in his way when he came to do you."

Xavier was irate. "You goddamn bastard! You set my own son against me?"

"You the one who did that by smacking him and his mama around!"

"I didn't do anything to him that you didn't do to me!"

"Guess he got way more backbone than you, huh? Which ain't sayin' much 'cause you ain't got nothin' to keep yo' back straight!"

An old anger bubbled up in Xavier. He was being ridiculed by his father again, despite the fact he had just killed a Tremain. A family enemy. He should've been lauded and complimented. But no, once again he wasn't good enough. With eyes filled with rage, Xavier stared at his father. "Nothing I do is good enough for you, is it?"

"Oh, go change yo' pants!" Pug dismissed Xavier with a wave. "I can smell yo' shit from here. Deleon be doin' all of us a favor when he kill this one. Can you smell it, Zenia?"

Zenia nodded. "He's stinking up the place as usual."

Rage swept over Xavier. All his life his father had derided him. He was tired of it. He wasn't going to take any more ridicule. He got to his feet and pointed the revolver at his father. "I'm through taking your shit, you old bastard. You best shut the fuck up!"

Pug cackled. "I don't need to give you shit. It look like you got plenty in yo' pants! Ain't that right, Zenia?" Zenia nodded in affirmation.

"I'm warning you!" Xavier threatened, waving the pistol for emphasis.

"Oh?" Pug said with feigned surprise. "You got enough guts now to shoot somebody that's lookin' at you?"

Involuntarily Xavier pulled the trigger and the gun discharged. The bullet hit Pug in the chest and knocked him out of his chair.

Zenia screamed and rushed to kneel down by Pug's fallen body. She checked and there was only a trace of a pulse. She pulled him into her lap, but he was dying quickly. When Pug stopped breathing, Zenia turned to Xavier and cursed him. "You killed him, you sniveling little cowardly dog! Pug was right, you're just scum! I hope Deleon takes his time with you! I hope he takes you apart piece by piece!" She laid Pug down carefully, stood up, and returned to her seat.

Xavier pointed the gun at Zenia. He had not considered killing her, but now it seemed a good idea. He would be getting rid of a hostile witness and he wouldn't have to share his inheritance with her. He only needed one thing from her before she died. He walked toward her. "What's the combo to the safe, Zenia?"

"Why should I tell you? You're going to kill me anyway!"

"Because I'll shoot you in your feet and your legs and then I'll shoot you in your hands and arms. You'll tell me one way or the other!"

"All right. Come closer and I'll tell you."

"Why? Tell me from here!"

Zenia sneered, "Oh, the little boy is afraid of me; even having a gun doesn't make him feel secure."

"I'm not afraid of you!" Xavier protested, walking over to stand in front of her.

"Well, lean down and I'll tell you the combination."

Making sure that he had a firm grip on the revolver, Xavier bent down to hear the list of numbers. Zenia made a sudden movement and Xavier felt a sharp pain in the side of his neck. He fired his gun as a reflex as he staggered backward. Zenia was slumping to the floor when he fired a second bullet into her body. He reached up and pulled a hypodermic from his neck. He examined it briefly then threw it on the floor beside her lifeless body.

Serena spoke for the first time. "Kill me too. I'm a witness. If you don't kill me, I'll testify against you."

"I'll get to you in a minute. I got to figure my angle first." Xavier went and sat down for a moment. He needed to think. He had to get a plausible story together to explain all the bodies. After a few minutes he had developed a plan. He would blame all the deaths on the Tremain lying in the hall. All he had to do was shoot Serena, then claim that Tremain had killed everyone then dropped the gun as he left. Xavier nodded. He would explain that he merely picked up the gun afterward and shot Tremain before he escaped. It was so simple.

Xavier pushed himself erect and almost fell. His legs were unsteady and there was a severe pain in his neck. His vision seemed to be blurring. He had to blink several times to focus. His legs felt like they were made of lead. He had trouble lifting his feet. He fell as he tried to walk toward Serena. It was strange; he didn't even feel it when he hit the floor. He tried to stand up, but was only able to get on his hands and knees. He started crawling toward Serena. He had to kill her. Once that was done, everything would be his. Absolutely everything. He would be living in clover. He—

Serena sat in the chair and looked around her at the dead bodies and wondered how it was that she was still alive. She could not imagine what more could be squeezed from her. Wakefulness had become nearly as terrible as slumber. She had been begging for death and her pleas had been denied. She remained sitting in her chair. She had no energy and there was no place she wanted to go. She might have gone on sitting in the chair until the police arrived, but she smelled a trace of cigar smoke and opened her eyes. King Tremain was standing beside her.

"What do you want?" she demanded. "What more can you do to me?"

King smiled and said, "Yo' heart is just a dried prune, but the rest of you is flesh." He turned to the doorway and called, "Lakeesha! Come on in here, girl." The little girl that Serena had seen at Sister Bornais's house walked in the room carrying her doll. King said to the girl, "Why don't you show her how you done learned to use yo' needle?"

The look on the girl's face was so filled with hate that Serena shuddered involuntarily. The girl pulled a long needle out of her hair and wiggled it slowly through the head of the doll.

A piercing pain exploded in Serena's skull. She screamed and fell out of her chair. She put her hands to her head, but the excruciating pain would not abate. Serena begged for it to stop. She pleaded, but it didn't cease until King said, "Okay, Lakeesha. I think she got the idea now. You can go."

Serena sat up with difficulty. She could barely open her eyes. The pain had been so great that the mere memory of it caused her to wince.

King puffed on his cigar and said, "There's a whole mess of her kin-folk just waiting for you outside. If it wasn't for me, they'd be in here now makin' yo' life hell. They done already divided you up. Each one of them is ready to cause you enough pain to drive you out of yo' mind."

Serena didn't have the strength to argue. "Just tell me what you want me to do."

"You know who that is lyin' out there in the hall?"

"I know who it is." Serena nodded. She knew it was Elroy. The one who had begun it all. She had recognized his facial features from the moment he first entered the sitting room. "What do you want me to do?"

"I want you to get off yo' ass and go out there and take care of my son! Like you should've done when he was a baby! I want you to call an ambulance and get him some medical attention! You do that and maybe I'll keep them off you."

Serena stood up and moved woodenly to the phone. "Put some speed on!" King prodded. Serena hurried up and called an ambulance and the police. King then directed her to remove the pistol from Elroy's hand and place it in Pug's. When the police and paramedics arrived Serena was kneeling beside Elroy. She had covered him with a blanket and had attempted to stanch the flow of blood. She watched the paramedics start an IV and connect telemetry wires to Elroy. Once he had been stabilized, they went on to see if there was anyone else alive among the carnage. Serena's mind was a thousand miles away. She thought about the boy Elroy had been and the evil she had perpetrated on him. Now more than fifty years later, he was lying injured on the floor in front of her. She knew there was no way she could atone for what she had done.

A detective interrupted her reverie and asked her for a statement which she gave exactly as King had coached her. It included her saying that Elroy was her son. Her explanations seemed to satisfy the officer's questions. After scheduling an appointment at police headquarters the next day, the officer allowed her to assist in getting Elroy out to the ambulance. As he was lifted into the vehicle, one of the paramedics asked if Elroy had insurance because if he had none, he would be taken to County Hospital. Serena climbed in the ambulance and told the man to drive to the best hospital in the city. She would take care of all the bills. When the paramedic told her that only family could ride with the patient, she replied without hesitation that she was his mother. She was strapped in beside Elroy's gurney, but before the paramedic closed the rear doors, Serena looked out and saw a crowd of people standing by the side entrance of the mansion and they were all staring at her. These were people whom no one else seemed to notice. Law enforcement personnel moved through them without ever stopping. The caterers moved trays and food warmers through their midst without a word. They were silent watchers, but in their silence was an ominous hatred. It was palpable. She looked down at Elroy and for a moment thought she saw King lying in his place. The doors were slammed shut and the siren began blaring as the ambulance pulled out into traffic. Serena stared out the small rear windows as the watchers and the mansion disappeared in the distance.

She looked down at Elroy's face again. She saw how she had briefly mistaken him for King. The Tremain genes were strong. She could see pieces of Jacques and Jackson in his face. She took his hand in hers and studied it. It was the large, callused hand of a working man. Although she knew nothing about his life, she took comfort in holding his hand. He was the son of the only man she had ever loved. She could've made him her son as well, but she had lacked the wisdom to make such a decision. She sighed. The past could not be undone, but perhaps she could be of use to him now. She resolved to get Elroy the very best doctors and the best medical care money could buy. She recalled that hospitals were terribly lonely places at night. Perhaps she could even provide him companionship. As she was pondering other ways that she could make a difference for him, she realized that the heavy cloud that had hung over her since the funeral had risen noticeably. She felt a sense of purpose that she had not experienced in a very long time. She squeezed Elroy's hand gratefully. She thought, If I am to go crazy, at least let this one not be on my conscience. As the ambulance drove through the streets with its siren blaring, Serena held his hand and prayed out loud, "Please, don't die! Please, Lord, don't let him die."

Sunday, July 18, 1982

Pres set his coffee cup down and leaned both elbows on the table. He looked across at Jackson and said, "I really appreciate you allowing me to stay here. Last night was the first sound sleep I've had. I've been sleeping in my car and staying at motels for the last couple of weeks and that has really been a bear."

"No problem, bro," Jackson replied, sipping his own coffee. "That's what friends are for. If you'd told me about your living situation earlier, we could've made arrangements. There's money for you to live in the best hotels if you want it. And wherever I have a roof, you always have a place to stay."

"I didn't want to ask you, particularly after all I had said against taking the money and getting involved in this war. But I've realized that you never had any choice. And now that your woman has been kidnapped . . ."

At the mention of Elizabeth, Jackson put his head in his hands. He had not been able to sleep the last couple of nights because of his concerns for her safety. Each day that passed without word from Deleon caused him to get more depressed. He doubted the wisdom of his attack on Deleon's house and he regularly cursed himself for failing to save her when he had the chance.

Pres watched his friend with concern and said, "I'm sorry to remind you of her."

"The thought of her is never out of my mind. I wish I could stop worrying."

"I've only seen you like this once before, that time you came home from Mexico talking about that Mexican girl. What was her name?"

"Maria. Maria Cervantes."

"Well, seems this woman has gotten under your skin in the same manner."

"This is different. I was a boy with Maria. I love Elizabeth as a man loves a woman. And I never told her how much I truly love her."

Theresa came with two steaming plates of food and set them down in front of Jackson and Pres. Jackson pushed his away. He wasn't hungry, but Theresa wouldn't hear of it. She pushed the plate back in front of him and said, "Eat! Must be strong! Eat now! Good food!" Jackson merely shook his head. An expression of worry spread across Theresa's brown face. She put her hand on Jackson's shoulder and said forcefully, "We get her! Everybody looking! We get her!"

Jackson patted Theresa's hand and mumbled a few words of gratitude as he looked down and studied his plate. He picked up his fork and pushed the food around.

"How long has she been gone?" Pres asked.

"I don't really know. We got a call from them on the twelfth and haven't heard from them since we hit their hideouts."

"From what you told me, it sounds like you've been leaving no stone unturned. The papers are full of news about the fire at DiMarco's restaurant. The heroin that was found has created an uproar and it looks like Paul is now under investigation for drug dealing, racketeering, and tax evasion. The family has disavowed all knowledge of his activities and are distancing themselves from him too."

"Yeah," Jackson said with a grim smile. "His neck is in a pretty tight noose."

"I read something else in the paper." Pres looked into Jackson's eyes. "It seems that Bedrosian was beaten severely in the same parking lot on the night you fought those two thugs."

Jackson answered with an uncaring shrug, "So?" and returned Pres's gaze without blinking.

Pres merely smiled and returned to his original line of thought. "There was a big spread in the afternoon papers on the death of John Tree and his gang. The papers are saying that it was a professional hit because the building was blown up with some high-tech form of plastique. You've been busy."

"Not as busy as I'm going to be!" Jackson said through gritted teeth. His expression took on a hostile cast. "I'll kill every one of those assholes that I can find! They've awakened the wrong person! My grandfather had the right idea all along!"

Pres studied Jackson's face with a thirty-year span of familiarity. He could read the nuance in the movement of the lips and the height of the eyebrow. Jackson was in every way but blood his brother. They had grown into men together. It was Jackson who had reached out and held him without judgment in the bad times after he returned from Vietnam. It was Jackson who took two years out of his career and enticed him to go to Spain and live the libertine life of an expatriate. Pres credited

those two years as a major factor in the reclamation of his sanity. Even
if he did not agree with everything that Jackson was doing, how could
he not join him? This was his brother and this was the time that family
really counted. Pres reached his hand across the table and grasped Jackson's hand. He said, "I want you to count me in on whatever plans you
make to rescue her! I've got your back!"

Jackson gripped Pres's hand. "Thanks, bro, but this isn't your fight."

"I'm making it mine! You're my best friend. What concerns you, concerns me. I'm going to the mat with you! I'm in all the way to the top of
my head! And I know what that means!"

Carlos walked in with a sheaf of papers. "Pardon! Didn't mean to interrupt." He gave Jackson a nod. "Do you have a moment?"

"Just a minute please, Carlos," Jackson replied and turned to Pres.
"Are you really in? This is what you want to do?"

"To the top of my head."

Jackson turned to Carlos. "He can hear whatever we have to talk
about. Pres, this is Carlos. The one I've told you about."

Carlos smiled and said, "I wondered how long it would be before you
started bringing them in. I've been expecting you, Pres. Let's get down
to business. There's news."

Jackson burst out, "Elizabeth?"

Carlos shook his head. "It'll take them at least a week to get relo-
cated. We won't hear from them for a while. Don't worry, they need her
alive and well if they intend to trade. That would be the only purpose
in taking her hostage."

Jackson answered, "I wish I could believe that."

"All you can do is hope. . . . Well, we got a call from Delbert Witherspoon. He wants to talk with you as soon as possible. He left a number.
Good day or night."

"That's good," Jackson said. "That's real good. DiMarco must be putting some pressure on him about those transfers we froze."

"There's more news. The maître d' called. She complimented you on
a job well done. She also said she'd like to take you up on your offer of
assistance. She says she has something in mind that will benefit you
both. And she left a number."

Pres asked, "Are you talking about Dominique?"

Jackson nodded. "That's your girl."

Carlos said to Jackson, "If your description of her actions was accurate, this woman is not just a maître d'. This woman is an assassin."

"Dominique?" Pres questioned in an incredulous tone. "When we were in Spain I told you she was tough, but an assassin? I don't think so."

Jackson countered, "She was mighty cool about almost being killed."

Carlos tapped the table to get attention. "Let's make sure of certain things. I don't want to trust her with any of our information. I don't want her to know where our safe houses are. And if we do something together, I don't want her covering the exit behind us. We clear?"

"Sounds reasonable to me," Jackson said, standing up. "I'll get on these phone calls now."

"Wait! There's more news from New Orleans."

Jackson turned to Carlos. "Do we have a hostage to trade for Elizabeth?"

"No, and it won't be possible to get one. Pug DuMont, his wife, and his son, Xavier, are all dead."

"What? That wasn't our plan! What happened?"

"It appears that your uncle, Elroy Fontenot, got there before us. From the reports I've received, which were based on articles in the local papers, it looks like he went in to save your grandmother, who had been kidnapped out of her hotel by the DuMonts. A gun battle ensued and he was seriously wounded in the effort."

"Serena Tremain? What was she doing in New Orleans in the first place? Why would Elroy risk his life for her? That doesn't make any sense!"

"There's a big investigation going on behind this. My people can't get through the police cordon. I'm afraid we'd have to go there to make sense out of it."

"We don't have time for that!" Jackson replied. "What we can do is make sure that the best surgeon in the United States is brought in."

"According to the papers, your grandmother has already taken care of that. She has assembled the best team of doctors she could find in the area. She's even sent for some doctors from Johns Hopkins."

"My grandmother? That doesn't even sound like the old bitch!"

Pres offered, "People change, sometimes for the better. Maybe that's true for your grandmother too."

Jackson scoffed, "Unlikely! This is the same woman who sold me and my grandfather out less than three weeks ago. I don't see her changing, ever."

Pres persisted, "Why not? You are."

Jackson gave Pres a look that conveyed his incredulity and stood up. "I'll make those phone calls now."

Later that afternoon, around four o'clock, Jackson and Pres took a drive up to Twin Peaks. They parked and got out of the car. There were a number of other cars and a tour bus. Pres and Jackson started walking slowly through the tourists toward an unpaved area away from the crowds. The city of San Francisco was spread out below them, discolored and blurred by a low-lying haze. The bay beyond the city was a brownish gray and was dotted by sailboats laboring with weak and inconsistent winds.

Jackson asked, "Remember when we used to come up here when we were kids?"

"Yep. To drink Spañada, Red Mountain, and Mad Dog 20-20 and make out with our high school honeys."

"The world was simpler then. Lancers and Blue Nun were high-class wines and there was a clear demarcation between right and wrong."

"There still is, if you want to see it."

Jackson turned to his friend with a frown on his face. "What's right, Pres? Do you think that if I went to the police I'd ever see Elizabeth again? What is right in this situation?"

"You'll find the right answer eventually. You always have, after some brief detours."

"Man, you don't know about detours. I've been places lately that were way off the road! Not even on the map of the civilized world!"

Pres confirmed with a trace of sarcasm, "You've been very busy."

Jackson retorted angrily, "I had to take some kind of action. I couldn't let these people run roughshod over my friends and family!"

"Face it, Jax, you're doing exactly as your grandfather wants you to do and trained you to do."

Jackson smiled sadly and shrugged. "You're probably right. He knew I wouldn't run, that I'd stay and fight."

"Stop using past tense. Use present tense. Your grandfather's alive in you! You'll follow his code. You'll attack like him. You'll kill like him. You'll be as cold-blooded as he was."

"If I'm acting like my grandfather, why are you joining me?"

"You're my brother and you're in trouble. They've kidnapped your woman. You're being drawn deeper into the shit." Pres chuckled then said, "I'm going to go along with you to fight for your soul."

"If you're going with me, get ready to fight for your ass as well as my soul!"

Pres shook his head then asked, "You don't sense that there have been some drastic changes in your character? You've got to admit you've changed."

Jackson, tiring of this line of questioning, responded angrily, "All I know is that I will be happy when all this is over and I have Elizabeth back."

Pres shook his head. "It'll never be over. Even when you get Elizabeth back, it won't be over. The cycle of violence gains momentum with time. You can't kill everybody. Even your grandfather couldn't kill everybody and he tried. Anyway, every time you kill somebody, you make a new enemy. They have a brother, wife, son, cousin, nephew, lover, somebody! I bet there are people still being killed in Vietnam for things done during the war."

"Oh, there's a way out of this!" Jackson declared. "And I intend to find it, but my first priority is finding Elizabeth. While I'm waiting for information to come in about her, I'm going to cause as much havoc for Braxton and DiMarco as I can."

"Your actions haven't stopped them from continuing to try to get a hostage. Your house in Oakland was burnt to the ground. Lincoln's was broken into and ransacked. Yesterday Anu's brothers chased some white guy out of their backyard until he turned around and starting shooting at them!"

"All I can do is continue to apply the pressure and I think tonight's meeting will be very fruitful in that regard."

"You're going to meet with Dominique this evening?"

"Yes, she says she's got some information that will please me."

"I told you I want to come along. Did you tell her about me?"

There was an eagerness in Pres's tone that made Jackson smile. He knew that Pres had really cared for Dominique when they had first met in Spain, but the war had made him too crazy to deal with any commitments. It was obvious that he was over any such reluctance now. Jackson answered casually, "Yeah, I told her about you."

"What did she say?"

"She asked if you were the same and I said worse, so she said bring you along."

"You know this woman is important to me. There's been no one since I was with her."

"What if Carlos is right and she's an assassin?"

"I'll adjust to it. Look, I've adjusted to your new incarnation."

On the ride back to Noe Valley, Pres discussed how he had successfully placed his training program at a local junior college. But his problems had arisen when Atlantis Broadcasting sought a legal injunction to prevent him from moving the training program, over which they claimed they had proprietary rights. Pres didn't have the money for a protracted legal battle, so he had been trying to get support from a number of elected leaders with varying degrees of success.

Jackson patted him on the shoulder and asked, "How much do you need?"

"I'm guessing but the legal fees could run as high as fifty thousand."

"You got it. Do you want cash or check?"

"You're serious? You really have that kind of money?"

Jackson nodded. "Took ten times that out of Tree's safe. Since you're in the mix, you might as well take the money."

"You'd give me Tree's money? Let me ask you, how does it make you feel to have taken his life?"

Jackson gave Pres a hard look then said firmly, "I don't feel anything. It was Old Testament justice. I don't think twice about it."

"That's harsh, isn't it? To take a life and feel no remorse."

"Yes, I took his life and I watched him die! You may not understand this because he wasn't responsible for the death of both of your parents! I'm not sorry! He deserved it and I'd do it again! Does that surprise you?"

Pres shook his head as he watched the passing traffic. Faces behind the transparent shields of glass, physically so near but in reality a million miles away.

Jackson turned the car down upper Market then pressed his question. "Are you surprised?"

Pres watched more faces in cars zipping past then answered softly, "It's a different Jax speaking than the one I used to know, or thought I knew!"

BOOK IV

The Resolution

Sunday, July 18, 1982

There comes a time when presumptions, intentions, and dreams must be put to the test, when opportunities must be seized or cast aside. At such times even men like Deleon DuMont must confront the inner reality, must discover whether there is sufficient substance to their hopes and desires to withstand the tide of fate's design. For years Deleon had dreamed of a future in which he spent every day, for as long as there was natural light, trying to find his own path across canvas after canvas after canvas. This was his one dream that rose above his origins; the oasis where his thirst for color and composition was quenched; where his whimsy was allowed to flower. Thus, when he received the news that both his father and his grandfather had been killed, he was faced with choices.

Deleon sat in his hotel suite after returning the telephone receiver to its cradle. He was stunned by the information he had received from his family's office in New Orleans. The news explained why there had been no answer at his grandfather's house. Deleon sat still trying to decipher his feelings. He could not say that he loved any of the people who had been killed, but he did feel a sense of loss. It was the only family he knew. His mother's upper-middle-class family had disowned her when she married Xavier and they weren't the least bit interested in any offspring that resulted from the match. Pure and simple, when it came down to it: He was a DuMont. It was the only name he could claim.

There was a moan from the second bedroom in the suite. Deleon pushed himself to his feet and walked past the couch into the room. Elizabeth was lying on the bed. Her hands and legs were taped together and her mouth was gagged. She was just awakening from the drugs that had been used to quiet her during the most recent move. Her

eyes opened hazily then focused on him. He saw a look of pure hatred
as she stared at him. He smiled. He respected a fighting spirit. Deleon
said, "We'll only be here a short while. If you need to use the toilet,
grunt now. The same rules apply. If you make noise or try to escape,
you'll get the taser again. Do you want to use the toilet?"

Elizabeth shook her head. She tried to contain her metabolic urges
until she could resist no longer. She hated having to relieve herself before the watchful eyes of her captors. If there was any way she could reduce the number of times she was abased, she was going to try it. And
as always, whenever she was not drugged, she was going to stay alert.
She had reason to hope. She knew Jackson was searching for her, that
he had nearly saved her, but her captors had taken her and escaped out
the back door. She had struggled despite her bonds to be a difficult burden, but at the top of the back stairs she had been injected with some
drug and she remembered nothing further. Now, whenever they moved
her they drugged her first, and when she awakened she checked herself
for soreness to determine whether she had been violated again. The
first time after her capture that she had awakened, she knew immediately that she had been both raped and sodomized. And Deleon Du-
Mont had admitted to being the culprit. She studied the lines and
surfaces of the man's brown face, committing every detail to memory.

Deleon moved around the bed checking to make sure that none of
Elizabeth's bonds was too tight. He examined both her legs and her
arms for sores. Her wrists and ankles were chafed, but her soft, black
skin was intact. Deleon allowed his eyes to travel over her body. She
was a long-legged woman with a nice figure, but he was not attracted to
her. The only reason he had raped her was to make a statement to both
her and Jackson, should she live long enough to tell him. Sex with men
was actually more exciting for him, but she was the first woman he'd
had in a long time and in that regard it was all right. It hadn't bothered
him that she was unconscious when he had entered her. Half the men
he had sex with in prison had been unconscious at the time. Sometimes
it was the easiest way. It was not an act of intimacy for him, it was an animal function. When he had finished his business he got up, leaving his
victim often still lying unconscious on the ground. However, more and
more lately, he found after he was spent, he nonetheless remained unfulfilled. Something was missing from the act. Something he could not
identify. And its absence was preventing him from truly enjoying sex.

He noticed her hateful glare studying him. He stopped his rumina-tions and realized that he no longer had to concern himself with her. He could walk away and never see her again. There was nothing to hold him to past obligations. Deleon returned Elizabeth's stare, but his thoughts were elsewhere. He was the last male with the DuMont name. He knew that was significant, but he didn't know really what it meant.

Deleon turned away from Elizabeth and walked back into the sitting room. He was feeling a strange giddiness. With the death of his father and grandfather, he was suddenly freed from further tasks. All past ob-ligations were no longer relevant. He could walk away and go straight to the Caribbean and paint. He could drop the whole escapade with Jackson Tremain and retreat to some hilltop villa where he would serve his only true master: the blank canvas.

The nearness of realizing his creative desires filled him with a light-ness until he began to consider the pitfalls of such a decision. The truth was that he didn't know whether it was safe to walk away without fin-ishing the job. San Vicente had not forgotten his two Cubans. Then there was Jackson, who had already shown that he was not an easy mark. The hit on Deleon's father and grandfather was the move of an implacable enemy, an enemy that was willing to risk the death of the hostage to send a message. Tremain was saying he had only two choices: a quick death or a slow death. Deleon's gang in prison had sent many such messages. It was the language of professionals; no hostage was prized too greatly.

Deleon sat down at the desk and began to doodle on some hotel let-terhead. The woman still had some value. As long as Jackson thought she was alive he would be moving as fast as possible, so fast that he might make a mistake. Her presence could force him to be intemperate. What was the best way to lure Jackson in? The Bay Area would have to be vacated. It was Jackson's stronghold. He had access to more services than Deleon. Deleon had to find a safe, secure place from which to op-erate. He knew too many people in New Orleans to stay out of sight for long. That was not an option. He knew San Vicente was heading back to Mexico to his fortified mansion. That would be the ideal place, if it were not for the enmity that existed between him and San Vicente. Deleon had caused him to lose face with his Cuban connection and it was an act that a drug dealer could not ignore. San Vicente was duty-bound to try to kill him. Even if Jackson was to accept a truce, which he wouldn't, San Vicente would continue to search for him until he could collect his pound of flesh. The more Deleon thought about it, the more certain he became that Mexico was the best place to resolve with both his enemies. He would take up residence in the eye of the storm.

Later that afternoon, Deleon sat in a bar with Francisco San Vicente and discussed his decision. San Vicente looked at him as if he were totally mad.

"You would come to Tijuana with me? You think this is wise, climbing into the spider's web? Surely you must know that I have to kill you. The business between us is not finished."

Deleon had to smile. He had been duly warned. "I know only that you, like me, need to deal with Tremain before you can turn your mind to other things. At least in this one area we are allies. Our positions can be strengthened by our cooperation."

"There is much to what you say, but I don't think this is the time to continue our battle with Tremain. He is not a simple man acting alone. He has an organization of significant size. The day after he missed us on Potrero Hill, his people attacked my old house in Victoria. They killed my older brother, his wife, and two of my cousins. I think it would be safer to wait six months then attack again when his guard is down."

"Do you think he'll let you wait six months? Tremain will be coming before that."

San Vicente laughed smugly. "So? Even if he finds me, he would not be foolish enough to attack me in my fortress in Mexico. I have the police, the federales, and everyone of importance in my pocket. By the time he took his second shot he would be surrounded."

"But that's what we want! We want to lure him someplace where we are safe and secure. We want him to think that there is a crack in our armor. If we can get him to come to your turf, we'll have the advantage, but we have to get him moving with a sense of urgency."

"The woman? You'll use her as bait?" San Vicente rubbed his chin as he contemplated Deleon's proposal.

"She's the catalyst to keep him moving fast. As long as she's alive and well, he'll keep on making flash raids, trying to find her."

"This is quite a proposition you are making. It sounds good, but I'm left with a lot of questions." San Vicente sat silent for a few moments then asked, "Why are you offering this to me, particularly at the risk of your life? Why not take her back to New Orleans where your family is strong?"

Deleon smiled. "I want you and me to finish our business. If we both go to Mexico, it'll be easier to conclude."

A look of surprise flashed across San Vicente's face, followed by one of understanding. "Oh, I see. You think that you can come to my house and then leave. And if you are alive, I would have to be dead. I see. Hmm, that is very bold thinking."

"The only thing that I'm going to ask is that we agree not to begin our personal dispute until Jackson Tremain is dead. We each get a chance to see his body before any action is taken. Once he is dead, we will finish our business."

San Vicente nodded. "I can agree to that, but this you should know: Killing you is not an affair of honor for me, it is business. I do not have to kill you myself for the deed to be done."

"We understand each other," Deleon replied. "Business is business. There will be no hostile action between us until we have viewed Tremain's dead body. Is that agreed?"

"Agreed!"

"Let's shake on it!" Deleon extended his hand and San Vicente shook it. Both men knew that this was an agreement made to be broken, yet each also knew that the other intended to honor the agreement as long as was reasonable.

"My people will be here with transportation this evening," San Vicente advised, studying Deleon intently. On the face of it, he had the clear advantage over Deleon once they were in Mexico, yet Deleon appeared confident and unperturbed. Was it possible that Deleon already had a team in Mexico or had infiltrated his organization? Once they were in Mexico, San Vicente would concentrate on finding answers to these and other questions. Still, it was a good idea. If he used Deleon as the front man, Tremain would never know that he was involved. Tremain would think he was only dealing with the DuMonts, and if a meeting could be set up in San Diego, where the San Vicente organization was strong, all debts could be cleared with one stroke. He would send Deleon's head to the Cubans, then he would take Tremain's heart back to Mexico and bury it beside his father and grandfather. Yes, it was an excellent idea. One thing was for sure. He would wipe the smug smile off Deleon's face. He asked, "You will bring the girl with us?"

Deleon nodded. "Yeah, she's coming with us, but I want it agreed that nothing happens to her until we get Tremain. She doesn't get passed around; none of that. I want her in top condition in case he wants to trade."

San Vicente shook his head. "If I had her, I would have cut off her hand and sent it to him."

"Then he would assume she's dead or about to be killed and he would make his plans more thoroughly. If we want to end this quickly, we'll keep her alive and in one piece. He will only become more dangerous with time. I want to kill him now!"

Deleon finished his statement with such emphasis that San Vicente looked at him with surprise. "This was just a job for you. When did it start turning personal?"

"I guess I was speaking as a DuMont. Maybe I was remembering all the blood that's been shed." San Vicente seemed to accept his words, but Deleon knew that he was suspicious, that he would be watching closely everything that Deleon did.

When San Vicente got up to finalize their travel arrangements, Deleon remained in the bar, nursing his drink. There were simpler, less dangerous ways to accomplish his objectives than going into San Vicente's stronghold, but he had discarded them as too time-consuming. It was now important for him to kill Jackson. Jackson had robbed him of the opportunity of exacting vengeance against his father. At first, Deleon had not understood how crucial that was to him. Since he was eighteen he had lived with that one goal in his mind. It had made all the sacrifices seem small in comparison. All the years and nights of broken dreams and troubled sleep had been endured without complaint for that one purpose. Then to have that cherished moment snatched away just as he was going to experience it was too much to bear; to have it stolen by a rival Tremain made it a personal affront. Jackson would now take the place of his father and Deleon would not rest until he was dead. San Vicente would be killed whenever Deleon was sure that Jackson had taken the bait.

As he sipped his drink, Deleon thought about his grandfather. His grandfather would've been proud of his decision to go to Mexico. It was a wonderful endgame move, luring one opponent into a web while striking deep into the heart of another. The old guy must be smiling in his grave. There would be a battle between the last DuMont and the only Tremain that mattered. There was no doubt in Deleon's mind that when it was all over, he would be the one left standing. With his ene-mies buried, he could begin his life as a painter. Perhaps he would go to St. Vincent, or Trinidad. He would buy a nice villa overlooking a beau-tiful coastline. He would have a studio filled with northern light. He could almost see the swirls of red that would dominate his first canvas.

Sunday, June 23, 1964

Juan Tejate had come to Durango with two companions to do some collection work for El Jaguar. The independent truckers were balking at paying the necessary tariff when they drove through areas controlled by El Jaguar. Two truckers had been caught, tortured, and their trucks were burned, but a third man had been prepared with a group of his friends. Juan and his companions had barely escaped with their lives. In fact, one of his companions had been seriously injured before they got separated during their escape. Juan had come to the market to recon-nect with his companions.

He was following Jackson, who was acting as blind and unaware as a tourist. It would be easy to kill him, but Juan wanted to make sure that he did not get caught. He wanted to make his attack at a busy intersec-tion in the market, where there were several aisles providing different avenues of escape. They were coming close to the main axis of pedes-trian traffic. All he had to do was close the distance between them. He could almost hear the sound as the point of the knife penetrated cloth-ing and flesh. Juan stayed behind a fat man who was ambling in Jack-son's general direction. Juan pulled his straw hat lower over his eyes and started toward his victim.

Someone called out in Spanish, "Tejate! Tejate, over here!"

Juan immediately dropped to one knee and pretended that he was adjusting his boot. He didn't want Jackson to see him.

The man who had called Juan's name stepped out of the crowd and demanded in Spanish, "What the hell are you doing kneeling down there? We got to get out of here! Those damn truckers may have fol-lowed. Did you hear me? Let's go now!"

"Not now, Perez! I've got an old score to settle," Juan said, rising to his feet. He stared at Jackson's inviting back. "I'll be with you in five minutes."

"We don't have five minutes!" Perez argued. "Garcia needs medical attention now! He's got a bad knife wound. It's going to take both of us to get him out of the hotel. You can't be running your own game and help him too."

"Damn!" Juan ejaculated with frustration and pointed to where Jackson and Maria were talking. "I got King Tremain's grandson ready for the taking. I could kill him easy and I wouldn't mind taking his girlfriend along with us either."

"We don't need any trouble with King Tremain right now. We've got enough problems!" Perez put his hand on Juan's shoulder. "Hold it a moment! I've seen that girl before. That's Maria Cervantes! Tigre Melendez's niece! Remember about two years ago, she was taken from Linares in a raid? Tigre's younger brothers were killed and her father, Armando Cervantes, El Jaguar's accountant, was taken."

"Yes, I remember," Juan said with a nod of his head. Tigre Melendez was one of El Jaguar's top captains. Juan mused, "A lot of money was supposed to have been transferred out of El Jaguar's American accounts because of that raid."

"That's right! Let's go!" Perez said with a satisfied grunt. "This is news that Tigre will reward us handsomely for. Come!"

"Wait! We don't know how long they will be here," Juan argued. "We should follow them and maybe we can tell Tigre exactly where she is."

Perez nodded his head. "Good idea, but first things first. We must get Garcia into the car and get him to a doctor. Plus, those truckers may have organized a search party by now."

Juan gave Perez a twisted smile. "What's more important to you, Tigre's gratitude or Garcia's life? If we didn't have to get him to a doctor, we might be able to follow them to where they're staying. Put it this way, what will be more important to Tigre, this information or Garcia's life?"

While Juan was asking his question Jackson was standing in front of a booth watching an old man pare iced prickly pears for him. Jackson gobbled the first one, swallowing the pits and feeling the cool, soft flesh slide down his throat. Before he had finished the third, Maria came over and told him that they were ready to return to the *taberna*. The woven basket was so heavy that Jackson had to hoist it to his shoulder in order to carry it. Since they were buying provisions for nearly ten people, both women were also loaded down with bags when they returned to the jeep. Wisely, Jackson had parked it in front of the church to discourage theft and vandalism. He started the jeep and drove up the steep and winding street which led back to the *taberna*. If he looked into his rearview mirror, it was only for traffic purposes.

At the *taberna*, he assisted Carlos in packing the station wagon and after they finished Carlos turned to him and said, "I'm going to lead the way out of town. When we turn off Highway Forty-five toward Nombre de Dios, I'm going to drop behind you. You'll stay on the road for Nombre de Dios until you see a sign on the left that says 'Ocho Conejos.' You'll take the next unmarked road to your right. Drive until you see a man on horseback. He'll lead you the rest of the way."

Jackson asked, "Will I know him?"

"Hernando de Jesus. You'll remember him. He's a big fellow. He and Esteban Muñoz were the ones who first taught you to ride a horse. His father, Esteban de Jesus, was an old cubano friend of your grandfather's. No more talk! We need to be out of here in ten minutes."

The drive to the lodge happened without incident. Hernando de Jesus greeted Jackson warmly and directed him on the roads and turns to take and they arrived at the lodge in forty-five minutes. The lodge was a large, square, two-story stone structure that sat among some trees on a small ridge. There was a broad covered porch which ran along all four sides of the lodge, providing an excellent view of the surrounding countryside. Lower down the ridge behind the lodge was a large stable with an attached garage for three cars built of the same stonework.

After unloading the vehicles, Jackson went down to the stable to look at the horses. He hadn't been riding since the last time he had visited his grandfather. There were six horses in the stable, including his grandfather's bay gelding, Suerte. Jackson was looking at the horses to determine which one he would prefer to ride. In the last stall there was a large roan with white feet. The horse flicked back its ears and snorted warningly as Jackson stood at the entrance to the stall. The horse's name was Sangria. Jackson had been told about this horse and knew that he was temperamental and high strung, but that he also possessed great speed and stamina. Jackson had learned to ride on such horses. He went over to the bin where his grandfather kept the oats and grabbed a handful and returned to Sangria's stall. The horse snorted suspiciously several times, but nonetheless ate the oats from Jackson's hand.

Sangria looked over Jackson's shoulders and his ears flicked backward again. Jackson turned and saw Maria standing behind him. Even in the semidarkness of the stable, her big eyes seemed to shine.

She gave him a smile and said, "El Negro said that you would want to ride Sangria. He said that you helped foal his father."

Jackson nodded. "That would be Peligroso. I must have been twelve or so when that horse was foaled. My grandfather, the vet, and I spent all night waiting for him. He didn't want to come into this world; we had to pull him out, and ever since then he and all his offspring have been unpredictable, skittish animals."

Maria moved up so that she was standing beside him. "I would like to go riding, but Carlos told me that I could not go alone." She looked him in the eye. "Would you go with me?"

Unable to resist her invitation, Jackson answered, "Sure! Which horse will you ride?" He watched as she walked back along the stalls. She had changed into riding garb. She was wearing a loose white blouse which was tucked into a faded pair of blue jeans that showed off the shape of her hips. Jackson could tell by the way her breasts jiggled under the blouse that she wore no bra. Maria stopped in front of a stall that had a black mare.

"I'll ride Chaquita. She knows me."

The afternoon sun blazed in a cloudless blue sky and baked the rolling foothills of the Sierra Madre Occidental. There was no breeze. The only respite from the sun that could be found in the arid landscape was under the occasional stand of scrub oak that grew in the creases and folds of the surrounding hills. The horses moved languidly through the dry, golden grass which covered the land to the horizon. Jackson was headed toward a creek which originated high in the Sierras and joined the Mezquital River below the city of Durango. High above the riders, hawks circled, riding thermals over the golden landscape.

The horses sped up when they smelled water and began to move toward the gorge in which the creek ran. Jackson guided Sangria up to a high tree-covered ridge above the gorge. The ridge provided a panoramic view of the surrounding countryside. The creek, in midsummer, was little more than a stream and it meandered through the trees and dropped into the gorge. Large oak trees covered the ridge and offered a welcome relief from the sun.

Under the shade of the trees, Jackson alighted from his horse and tied the reins loosely to allow the animal access to water. He pulled a Winchester lever-action rifle from its scabbard and held it in the crook of his arm. A red fox and her kits barked warningly from a den across the creek and disappeared into the bushes.

Maria slid off her horse and stood beside him. "Did you see that? Those little foxes were cute."

"Foxes, coyotes, and wildcats are the only predators left in these hills. The wolves and mountain lions have been hunted to extinction and so have their prey, the mule deer and bighorn sheep that used to live in these mountains."

"You know this country well?"

"I wouldn't say that, but I've been coming here since I was about ten, ever since my grandfather bought this place. There were a hell of a lot more game animals around then."

"Are you hungry? I brought us lunch."

"That's great! I'm glad you thought of it. All I brought was two canteens of water. There's a flat rock under that big oak where we can sit." Jackson tied Maria's mare alongside Sangria. She pulled two packets out of her saddlebags and walked to the rock.

A red and gold centipede scuttled for its burrow then Maria and Jackson had the rock to themselves. She laid out a small cloth and set out a block of cheese, a loaf of bread, some cold, baked chicken, and a large bunch of grapes. Jackson leaned the rifle against the rock, put down the canteen, pulled his Bowie knife from its sheath, and began slicing the bread and cheese. Maria prepared him a sandwich of cheese and chicken and then made one for herself. They ate in silence for nearly twenty minutes. From the rock they could see the rolling low-lands falling away to the distant town of Nombre de Dios and the mountains rising in the west.

It was very calm and peaceful. Neither Jackson nor Maria spoke. They were both comfortable simply enjoying the majesty of the landscape. Every once in a while they would look at each other and smile. Other than the occasional snort of the horses, the buzzing of insects, and the distant cry of hawks there was no sound.

"This is very beautiful. This is very much like where I was born," Maria said in a dreamy voice. "My mother used to take me out to a grove of trees on a hill behind our house and we would sit there and talk about our dreams."

"What type of dreams would you talk about?"

"My mother would always talk about freedom. If she had been born into another family, she would have been a poet or a singer, or even a dancer. It was a cruel thing that she was born in a family that thought of women only as laborers and breeders of children. She had such a tender heart that she would never kill anything. She used to say, 'If God gave it life, who am I to question his decision?' She was always tending orphans and strays. She once found an injured young fox pup when she was walking home from the store and nursed it back to health, but that ended badly, like so many other things. My father was mean to her and over the years, I saw her slowly die like a plant that doesn't get enough water. She died a heartbroken woman."

Jackson was silent for several minutes after Maria finished speaking. He didn't know what to say. It was only because he felt that he had to say something that he said, "I'm sorry. That sounds awful. It must have been very painful for you."

Maria nodded her head. "It was, but I am stronger than my mother. I would not let pain kill me."

"What happened to the fox cub? You said that ended badly."

"My mother's brother, Tigre Melendez, kept a kennel of fighting dogs, like your grandfather. When the fox was well enough to be released, he took it and threw it in the kennel."

"Damn!" was all Jackson was able to muster.

"Yes." Maria looked at him and there were traces of tears at the corners of her eyes. "I know it goes against the laws of God and church, but I hate my family!"

"I know that feeling!" Jackson said with a nod of his head.

"You hate your family?" Maria stared at him with astonishment. "I was told your parents were dead, that you only had your grandmother and grandfather."

"There are many different ways to be cruel."

"Your grandfather, cruel?" Maria asked with disbelief. "He is a great man who is loved by many. He has given me hope. At my aunt's request, he rescued me from my father's house and brought me to live in Mexico City. He is the one who encouraged me to go to college. I am a student now at university. He even taught me a poem, the first poem I ever memorized."

"I bet I know that poem!" Jackson declared.

"You know this poem? How so?"

"He only knows one poem! It's 'Invictus.' I know because he made me memorize it when I was eight years old. He used to poke me hard in the chest with his index finger and tell me that I had to learn the words so well that I believed them."

Maria leaned forward and asked, "Do you still know it?"

Jackson recited from memory, the words flowing out of him as if they were his own:

"Out of the night that covers me,
Black as the Pit from pole to pole,
I thank whatever gods may be
For my unconquerable soul—"

"That's it!" Maria interrupted. "Say the last stanza. I like that one best."

"It matters not how strait the gate,
How charged with punishments the scroll,
I am the Master of my fate:
I am the Captain of my soul."

At some part during his recitation Maria joined him and they finished the last line together. There were tears in her eyes. She grabbed his hand and said, "With this poem, I could live even in my father's house and not be beaten down! It was an act of love that made him teach it to you!"

Jackson admitted, "I never thought of it like that."

Maria still gripped his hand tightly as she said, "Don't you see? He has given you something that can never be taken away! You are lucky that someone would love you so much that they would teach you things to make you strong. After my mother died I was alone until your grandfather entered my life. No one in my family wanted to teach me anything. They just wanted to use me."

Jackson just nodded his head in response. The fervor in her dark, hooded eyes moved him. She seemed even more beautiful than before, but what affected him most was the feeling that he had been invited inside of her own personal hell, that the door had been cracked and he had been allowed to look into the flames and flickering shadows of her painful past.

The tears streamed down her face. She rubbed away the tears but still they came. "I am foolish to cry," she said, using the towel that Jackson handed her.

"No, you're not!" Jackson protested.

"It is because I feel comfortable with you," she explained. "Your grandfather has told me so many stories about you, I feel that I know you. When I heard you were coming, I was happy. I knew that I would like you! I felt it in my bones!" Maria dabbed her eyes and looked at him. "Have you ever had such a feeling?" Jackson shook his head. Maria took his hand again. "When El Negro told me about your parents, I knew that we shared some of the same pain. Do you not feel this bond?"

"Yes, but I didn't know what it was. I thought it was because you're beautiful and attractive. I don't know that I've ever been so close to such a beautiful woman before."

Maria laughed and gripped his hand tighter. "You're being kind, no? Even if you are, I love this little lie."

"I'm not lying or even exaggerating," Jackson said, feeling the calluses on her hand. He turned her palms up and observed, "These are not the hands of a student. These are the hands of a worker."

"Yes! Your grandfather pays for everything: my clothes, my education. I would not have him think that I am using him. He has been too kind! I work hard around the house so that he will see that I appreciate everything. Is it that my hands are not feminine?"

Jackson did not say anything. He was staring down into a small arroyo where he had seen a flickering of sunlight. He stood up and went to his horse and got a pair of binoculars. He spent several minutes scouring the countryside until he found the source of the flickering light. It was a man on horseback. Jackson studied the man for several minutes and discovered the source of the reflection: The man also had a pair of binoculars, and he was searching for something. Jackson saw that the man rode Indian-style, without a saddle, and carried a rifle with a scope. It caused a warning bell to go off in Jackson's mind. He knew that most people in the surrounding area were poor; if they owned a gun, it was an older model and rarely had a scope.

Jackson pulled Maria back into the deeper shade of the oaks and informed her that they had to vacate their spot. She acquiesced reluctantly. She gathered their lunch and rewrapped it.

As she was packing her saddlebags, he brushed past her and she swiveled to face him. They stood for a long moment staring into each other's eyes. Her breasts were grazing his chest. Jackson bent down and kissed her lightly on the lips. She stood on her tiptoes and kissed him back, then they stood looking at each other again. No words were spoken. They kissed again, this time more passionately. She pressed herself against him. He probed the unresisting softness of her lips with his tongue and felt the nipples of her breasts harden against him. He felt himself grow aroused and hard, full of desire for her. When the kiss had traveled its tumultuous course, they stood for several minutes in each other's arms, her face pressed against his chest. Her head fit right under his chin. He could smell the cleanness of her thick, black hair.

"We have to go," he whispered. He didn't want to leave, but he had a greater fear of appearing foolish in Carlos's and his grandfather's eyes. Nothing would be said, but the looks that they would give him would be damning.

"I know we have to go," she answered, squeezing him tightly. "I hope that we can go riding again tomorrow."

He pushed away from her and said with a smile, "I don't see why not. Let's head toward home now. We'll have to take the back way. We don't want that rider to see us."

They crossed the stream and headed down a small ravine on the other side of the gorge. They flushed a bevy of quail as they entered a section overgrown with madrona and piñon, but other than that they saw nothing except the soaring hawks until they arrived back at the lodge.

Jackson had ridden all the way back to the lodge with an erection. It had grown quite uncomfortable, jiggling against the saddle horn and the confines of his jeans. Fortunately, it had grown limp by the time they trotted up to the stables. Carlos walked down to the stable as they were alighting from their horses. Jackson reported the sighting of the rider to Carlos and he sent out two men to investigate. Maria was needed in the house to help prepare the afternoon meal, so Jackson unsaddled the horses, watered them, then curried them down as he had been taught. The grooming and care of the horses helped distract him from the thought of Maria's firm and voluptuous body. When he finally headed up to the lodge, Jackson had regained control of his thoughts.

After dinner Jackson went to sit out on the porch, where Carlos was giving out assignments to the five men who had joined them for dinner.

Jackson had been introduced to all of them, but he didn't remember their names except for Hernando de Jesus, the man who had given him directions to the lodge. Most of the men were mestizos, short in stature, but lean and desert tough. One man was pure-blood Indian like Carlos, and Hernando clearly had African ancestry. As Jackson watched, Carlos began talking about sentry duty assignments.

"I'll take one," Jackson volunteered. Carlos smiled and the men around him nodded their heads in approval. It was only right that El Negro's grandson assume some responsibility for the safety of the group. Hernando clapped him on the shoulder and pulled him into the circle.

Jackson was given the first four-hour shift on the interior perimeter, which consisted of the stand of trees which circled the house, the stables, and the two outhouses. The outer perimeter of the surrounding hills was patrolled by two men who routinely reported in by flashlight. Jackson armed himself with a short, double-barrel shotgun that slid into a holster across his chest and his Winchester 30.06. When Carlos pointed to the shotgun questioningly, Jackson informed him it was his "pig gun."

Jackson began his shift at eight o'clock and made his rounds every fifteen minutes or so. There was a cool breeze coming off the western mountains, but the night sky was clear and filled with stars. Other than the gentle rustling of the trees, there was no sound. Jackson found himself enjoying the silence and peace of guard duty. The Big Dipper, the belt of Orion, and the Milky Way appeared particularly bright in the moonless sky and brought to mind Jackson's feeling that the glistening stars overhead promised adventure to all those who could escape the gravity of their daily lives.

At midnight Jackson was relieved from duty but he could not go to sleep. He sat on the steps of the porch and studied the night sky and the quiet countryside. He heard the porch creak behind him. He turned and saw Maria standing there. She wore a gingham dress with a shawl over her shoulders. Her large eyes glistened in the dimness of starlight. She sat down beside him on the steps.

"Is it all right if I join you?" she asked in a soft voice. "I couldn't sleep."

"Of course," he replied. "I'd rather have your company than anyone else's."

She touched his face. "Are you always so kind? You seem even nicer than I imagined, so unspoiled, almost innocent."

Jackson chuckled. "I wouldn't call myself innocent, but I do try to be nice; of course, that's no struggle with you. You're easy to be nice to. I've been thinking about our ride all day." He could feel the heat of her body even though he was not touching her. The tension of his desire was strong and he felt himself grow aroused.

Maria bit her bottom lip and said, "I've been thinking about the way you touched me and kissed me. I have never been held so tenderly." She edged over next to him, so that their knees were touching. When Jackson said nothing, she asked, "Am I too forward?" Her eyes were filled with concern and unspoken pleas.

"No, I'm glad to hear that you feel the same way as I do. I've been thinking about you too. I wanted to touch you more, but I wondered if I was too forward."

A breeze gusted up the steps and blew Maria's dress up to midthigh, exposing her long, brown-skinned legs. She did not pull her dress down again, but instead stared at Jackson's face. He returned her gaze then stared down at her exposed legs. He could not deny his desire. He placed a hand on her bare thigh and felt the soft, unresisting skin. She watched his hand as he gently pressed her legs apart and pushed it slowly up between her legs. Jackson contented himself with caressing the softness of her inner thigh. He did not want to be too pushy and risk her rejection. But nonetheless, his desire was growing and hardening into an unquellable force.

He kissed her and she responded with lips and tongue. It was a long, passionate kiss. Jackson's hand moved up higher between her thighs and probed the dampness between her legs. She arched her back and gasped in reaction to his touch then she grabbed his hand.

"I must tell you something," she whispered in a husky, aroused tone. "I am not pure! You're the first of my choosing, but you are not the first. My uncle used to use me whenever he wanted and sometimes he gave me to other men. I don't want you to think you're getting something unspoiled. I want you to know the truth; then, if you still want me, I want you!"

The truth was that Jackson was so aroused that if she'd told him that she'd been with the entire Mexican Army, he would not have been dissuaded, but he felt strangely touched that she should volunteer such information. He was totally disarmed. "I am the first that you wanted to be with?" She nodded silently. Jackson smiled. "Then it's the first time."

Tears seeped from her eyes. "Thank you!" she sobbed. "I have dreamed about this moment for nearly a year. I knew that I would want you! Please hold me!"

Jackson put both arms around her and held her until her tears subsided. He could smell the smoke of the cooking fire in the thick, silky blackness of her hair. He felt her hand slowly make its way up to the crotch of his pants. He could not ever remember being as aroused as he was at that moment.

Maria raised her head. "Where can we go?"

"There is a hayloft above the stable," Jackson suggested.

Maria stood up and offered her hand to him. "Let's go."

They walked to the stables in the darkness and climbed the old ladder into the hayloft. Between bales of hay, they lay kissing on a pungent carpet of drying fodder. It did not distract them in the least. Jackson pulled down the shoulder of Maria's blouse and exposed her nipple, which grew hard as he sucked on it. He felt her tremble and put his hand back up into the dampness between her legs. She pulled up her dress and took off her underwear. She pressed him down on his back and unfastened his jeans, pulling them down around his knees. She straddled his thighs and guided him into her wetness. She rocked on top of him until she felt release come in the tremors of her climax. She collapsed on top of him. He was still hard inside of her. He put his arms around her and thrust deep into her with a slow and ancient rhythm. Each time he entered her, he felt the spasms as she contracted around him. When he finally came, he felt that he had reached a peak that was unique and rarely revisited.

They lay in each other's arms until they heard someone enter the stable. Whoever it was, the person was attempting to be quiet. Jackson quickly pulled on his pants. He had no weapons and he cursed himself for being lax. Jackson crouched, ready to throw himself at the ladder should the interloper attempt to climb it.

"Diablito? Are you in here? Is Maria with you?" It was Carlos's voice.

Jackson took a deep breath and felt embarrassed. "We're here, Carlos. Is something wrong?"

"Not now," Carlos answered with a chuckle. "Be ready to ride early in the morning! We'll be scouting pigs!"

"Don't worry, Carlos. I'll be ready!" He lay back down in the darkness of the loft. He saw the dark outline of Maria raise herself on one elbow. He thought he saw a smile on her face.

Maria said, "You shouldn't have told Carlos that you'll be ready."

"Why?" Jackson asked, feeling her hand slowly traverse up his pants leg.

"Take off your pants," Maria murmured. "We're not finished here. Take them all the way off this time."

Jackson wasn't ready the next morning when Carlos came for him, but he pulled himself into his clothes and climbed down from the loft. He was alone. Maria had departed some time during the night. Jackson rubbed his eyes and tried to focus on the source of the voice. He had hay in his hair and clinging to his clothing.

Carlos looked at Jackson and laughed and said, "Wolf cub! Wolf cub! You look like she fucked the daylights out of you! Are you sure you can sit a saddle?"

"No problem," Jackson replied, making halfhearted attempts to brush the hay from his hair and clothing.

Carlos looked at Jackson carefully. "You know this girl has lived a hard life. She is no angel, although she may look angelic to you. She is no fool either. She does things for reasons; be aware."

"What are you saying?" Jackson challenged, suddenly angry that his woman should be given such short shrift. Unable to rub the sleep out of his eyes, he squinted at her detractor.

"You need some cold water! I said 'be aware,' not 'beware'! I'll get you a clean shirt and some pants from the house. Meanwhile, you better wash yourself into a high state of alertness and get that fodder smell out of your hair. I had soap and towels along with a couple of buckets of water put behind the stables for you." Carlos turned and walked away.

Even the cold water in which he washed could not detract from the warmth that Jackson felt. Maria was the most beautiful and exciting woman that he had ever been with. Soft and sensual, warm and wise, she seemed to be the answer to his silent prayers. He wondered whether he was already in love with her. He wanted to spend as much time as he could with her. Perhaps all his fears and doubts about visiting his grandfather had been unfounded. Maybe this visit would be truly a pleasurable experience. He whistled happily as he finished rinsing in the frigid water.

Wednesday, July 21, 1982

Paul DiMarco sat in his rental car and studied the construction site through binoculars. The first and second floors of the community center had been walled in, but the third still had steel beams visible. Most of the construction crew had left when the Klaxon had sounded at five, but there were still two cement trucks in position to pour the last of the interior floor and foundation for the building and there was a team of five men waiting to work with the cement. Even from the distance where the car was parked, the ambient noise of the construction site and the surrounding industrial park was considerable. One could hear the grind and clank of heavy cranes and construction equipment, and underneath that the steady background roar of machinery from a nearby factory that extruded plastic along with the regular beat of its giant presses which printed plastic wrappings. Weaving through those sounds was the clatter and jangle of small business metalworks and body shops.

Mickey Vazzi, who sat in the passenger seat, took a long pull on his cigarette, his pitted face displaying the pleasure he took in the taste of tobacco. He blew a smoke ring and asked, "You see anything fishy?"

Paul shook his head. "Not yet. Those cement trucks are dumping their loads now. When they pull out and those men down there finish packing it down, we'll go down and see if that nigger Witherspoon brought everything he was supposed to."

"You really think he was able to get his hands on five hundred thousand in cash? You only gave him a day and a half."

"Sure! Braxton and me, we used to keep in his safe a floating cash reserve fund of a million and a half for small buys, housing, bail, and legal incidentals. We haven't taken any money out of it since we paid that Vietnamese gang a million for the hit on Chinatown's big two. There should still be at least half a million in there. You'll get two hundred thousand. That should allow you and your family to disappear for a year. By then I'll have worked out something."

Vazzi exhaled smoke and nodded. "That's mighty generous of you."

Paul affirmed, "Mickey, you're my right hand. I've trusted you with the most important jobs and you did what I needed. You're a good soldier. I'm sorry that you got to go on the run because of me." Paul picked up his binoculars and studied the jumble of warehouses and small industrial businesses that made up the surrounding area. He saw nothing that was glaringly out of order. He had no reason to believe that anyone knew that he and Mickey were meeting Delbert at the community center construction site, but there was now a price on his head. Caution was crucial. The reason he had only Mickey with him was that he didn't trust any of the other people on his payroll. Delbert himself posed no threat, but there was always the possibility that some of Braxton's muscle might be nearby. He could not be too sure of anything. Paul studied the perimeter of the construction site for what seemed like the hundredth time.

Paul had scheduled to meet Delbert Witherspoon at six in the evening, but he had arrived at three-thirty to scope out the scene. The previous Friday he had spent several hours reconnoitering the site, so he had some idea as to what normal activity looked like. He saw Delbert's car arrive at a quarter after five and pull up to the gate. There was a brief exchange with the security guard, then Delbert drove through the hurricane fence topped by barbed wire and disappeared around the corner of an extra-wide trailer that was being used as an administrative office. Paul waited until the two cement trucks had pulled out of the gate before he started his car and drove to a point a block away from the construction site. He intended to enter the site through a slit he had cut in the back of the fence the day before. He and Vazzi were wearing stained coveralls over bulletproof vests. When they donned their hard hats and sunglasses, they'd blend in with the majority of workers in the industrial park. They left the car in an alley behind a Dumpster and walked a circuitous route to the site. All around them was the ambient noise of large machinery grinding through its repetitive motions.

They entered the slit without problems and began to make their way through a maze created by a series of towering stacks of building materials, many of which were covered with a thick translucent plastic. DiMarco and Vazzi were working toward the trailer when two men passed in front of them. DiMarco and Vazzi were not seen because they ducked down behind a stack of cement blocks, but they were close enough to overhear the discussion between the two men.

One of the men asked his companion, "What time is he due?"

"Don't you worry about that!" retorted the other. "You just hurry and get the entrance covered!"

The rest of the conversation was inaudible because the men moved away. DiMarco muffled a curse and turned to say something to Vazzi and noticed that Vazzi was immediately behind him and that there was a wild look in his eyes. The look on Vazzi's face was unsettling. Fortunately for DiMarco, his pistol was in his hand. He backed away from Vazzi and demanded in a whisper, "What's going on?"

Vazzi stammered, "Uh, nothing, boss. I'm just worried we might get into some gunplay and never get the money."

At that moment DiMarco knew that Vazzi had set him up. DiMarco wanted to kick himself. He should've seen it coming. It was the smart move. He would've made the same decision in Vazzi's shoes. Briefly he considered turning back then discarded the idea. Despite the dangers, he had no choice but to go ahead. He needed the cash in order to set his family up safely. He would not be accessing his bank accounts until he had set up some type of front to throw off his pursuers. He looked at Vazzi and anger filled him. Just because it was logical didn't make him happy with Vazzi's change of allegiance. He had always hated people who betrayed him. He gestured with his gun. "You go in front and if there's any shooting, I'll be right behind you."

Vazzi didn't stop to plead or question. He stepped past DiMarco and led the way across the open ground to the trailer. Before they were halfway to their goal, a voice called out, "Hold it right there, Paul!" It was Edward's voice. Paul jerked around looking for the source of the words. "Don't waste time looking for me! I've got three semiautomatic rifles aimed at your legs. If you try anything now, I'll make sure you die a slow, painful death. Get his gun, Mickey!"

Three men armed with automatic weapons stepped out from behind some of the stacks of equipment as Vazzi turned to face DiMarco. Vazzi looked into DiMarco's eyes, shrugged, then reached for DiMarco's gun. DiMarco let him grip the barrel then twisted the gun and fired through Vazzi's hand into his armpit. The gun's discharge was loud even against the background noise of the surrounding businesses. Vazzi stumbled backward and fell to the ground, blood quickly covering his side. DiMarco wanted to fire another round into Vazzi, but he knew better than to push his luck. He dropped the gun and put his hands over his head.

"You're a real bastard!" Edward commented as he stepped out from behind a plastic-covered stack. "Mickey was going to be a made man, but you fucked that for him."

Paul spat on the ground. "He got what traitors get!"

Edward scoffed, "What should you get? You're a traitor too, aren't you? You've jeopardized your family's political plans! Despite all the warnings we gave you! Bobbie, Duke, drag Vazzi's body inside!"

Duke bent down over Vazzi and heard a gasp. Duke looked up at Edward. "He ain't dead, boss."

Edward answered, "He will be soon. He's shot through the lungs and he isn't one of ours. Drag him inside."

"I see you're treating him like a traitor too," Paul sneered.

Edward looked at Paul and smirked. "Vazzi came to us after you killed Joe Bones. He thought you implicated him by killing Bones shortly after he left Las Vegas."

"I didn't kill Joe Bones!" Paul protested. "Vazzi went to Las Vegas to deliver the jet, nothing more. It was a gesture of respect!"

Edward chuckled disbelievingly and turned to the two other men. "Vince, Pascal! Take Paul inside the building too. If he tries anything, shoot him in the legs. Try not to kill him. We need to turn him over alive. Then I want to take a quick look around for this money. What happened to that wimp Witherspoon? We've got to find him and squeeze him until he tells us where the money is. We've got to hurry. We don't want the cement to harden too much. Witherspoon and Vazzi have to be stuffed into it!"

Vince moved his big body forward and grabbed Paul's arm. He pushed Paul none too gently toward the trailer. Tall and lean, Pascal Langella stepped out from his hiding place and walked on the other side of Paul. Pascal had a long, pale, cavernous face, heavy with five o'clock shadow, and when he looked at Paul, he gave him a cold, saturnine smile.

Paul, anxious not to show fear, bantered with Pascal. "Hey, Pascal, did you ever catch up with Dominique? She's a pretty tricky little bitch, isn't she? When do you think you'll nail her?"

"Forget about it!" Pascal retorted, shoving Paul roughly. "I ain't got time for your fucking questions! You probably told her I was coming to town!"

Paul straightened his jacket defiantly then sneered, "If I had told her, asshole, you'd be lying dead like the rest of those bozos you brought with you."

Without warning, Langella hit Paul on the back of his head with a sap. Paul stumbled forward and fell against a stack of culvert pipes. He didn't lose consciousness, but his legs went stiff and he was dazed and disoriented. He leaned against the pipes a moment to gather himself. When his eyes were able to focus, he turned to face Langella, who was preparing to hit him again. Before Paul could set himself, there was a rush of air and something hit him numbingly hard in the chest and careened off. He did not get a chance to see what it was because the force of the blow knocked him off his feet. The pain in his chest was immense, but there was no blood. He pushed himself to a sitting position and discovered he couldn't breathe. He coughed and choked, then inhaled. With each breath, shafts of pain shot across his chest. Out of the corner of his eye, he saw Vince coming toward him, firing his pistol. Two bullets hit the pipes to the left of his head and caromed off. Paul ducked down. The pain in his chest was making him dizzy. He heard Vince shout in his gravelly voice, "The goddamn bastard! He set us up! I'll kill him myself! The fucking—!"

Paul didn't want to be shot cowering, so he sat up with an effort. He saw Vince fall over backward, the top of his head blown away. Whoever was shooting was somewhere behind him and was a very good shot. From where he sat, Paul could see Langella's body. He figured that Langella couldn't be alive with his legs and arm bent like that. Bobbie was lying in the middle of an aisle, his eyes wide open and unblinking. Duke and Edward had taken cover. Paul didn't have the strength to move. A bullet had glanced off his bulletproof vest. Considering its power, had it been a straight-on trajectory it would have penetrated his vest and he would probably be dead. The pain in his chest was still debilitating. He had to limit himself to shallow breaths; anything deeper was pure agony.

Edward called out, "Who do you have shooting at us, Paul?"

"Damned if I know!" Paul wheezed, wincing from the effort. "It could be her! It could be Dominique!"

"Well, whoever it is, you better call them off!"

Edward's demand almost made Paul laugh. "Why? What are you going to do, kill me?"

"Yes, but slowly." A shot rang out and the toe of Paul's shoe disappeared. It took everything he had not to scream. The pain was now so great that he had to grit his teeth just to breathe without moaning. From what he could see, at least two of the toes on his right foot were gone.

Blood and bits of flesh blocked any further examination. He tried to crawl out of view, but there was no way he could find cover for his legs.

Paul called out as loud as the pain in his chest would permit, "These aren't my people! I don't know who's shooting at us! I swear on my mother's soul!"

"Can you believe this fuck, Duke? He's bringing up my aunt! Like that will help his situation! Shoot him in the other foot!"

Another shot was fired and it hit Paul's ankle. He experienced another sudden flaring of unbearable pain, then he passed out.

Jackson's voice called out, "Come on out, Edward! If you want to live, it's time to talk!"

"Who the hell are you? You must not know what you're mixing in! My people will hunt you down if it takes all your life to catch you!"

"Your people won't do shit! And you're about to be alone!"

There was a barrage of whizzing bullets. Duke grunted and rolled out into the aisle. Edward stared at him, looking for signs of life. There were none. His chest and stomach were covered with blood. Edward took a deep breath. Duke had been wearing a bulletproof vest. Whatever ammunition they were using made vests irrelevant.

"There's your last man, Edward. You came with four and now there's none. You want to die there, or do you want to talk?"

Edward quickly reviewed his options, which were extremely limited. He knew he was dead if he remained where he was. He moved, trying to back out of his position, but bullets kicked up dirt in the place he was trying to move to.

"You either throw down your weapon or plan on dying where you squat!"

Edward threw out his gun and stood with his hands up. "Okay! Okay, I'm coming out!" He stepped into the aisle. Jackson and Dominique advanced to meet him. He knew Dominique, but he stared at Jackson for a moment then demanded, "Who the fuck are you?"

"Jackson Tremain, King Tremain's grandson. Your foolish cousin thought he was going to run over me, but he'll be going to a secret graveyard now along with your goons."

Edward was confused. He had only thought that he was dealing with Paul. He didn't see the connection that would cause Jackson to insert himself in a family altercation. "What the fuck do you want?"

"Edward, you're a businessman." Jackson gestured to Dominique.

"We're both businesspeople too. You're trying to go legitimate, so are we. You have an election to win, we can help you."

"How?"

"We can make sure that certain information never comes to light. For example, your father and your sister used to own several holding companies which appear to have received nearly three million dollars from Paul's Bahamas bank account. This money seems to have made its way into your father's campaign coffers, although it was never declared to the IRS in any personal returns."

A man came up and spoke in Jackson's ear. Jackson carried on a brief conversation with the man then indicated the bodies with a wave of his hand. The man bent over Paul's supine body and said, "This one's alive. A bullet must've hit his ankle gun, because it looks like his own gun shot off his foot."

"Good," Jackson replied with a cold smile. "Throw some water on him and when he wakes up prod him about our friends from Louisiana and Mexico. One way or the other, he's going into the cement. Have him taken inside." The man nodded and beckoned to two other men who were awaiting his signal to appear. They brought large pieces of heavy, translucent plastic in which to drag the bodies and immediately set to moving them into the building. Jackson turned to Edward. "Why don't we go inside. My cleanup team needs space to operate."

Edward was still confused. He was trying to figure out who Jackson really was. It appeared that he had a professional team that was used to dealing with both the killing and disposal of their enemies. He was not sure he wanted to go inside. The thought that he might be tortured made his stomach turn. Stalling for more time to reconcile his thoughts he demanded, "How do I know you've got proof for any of these allegations?"

Dominique held up a ledger. "Paul wrote down everything. And it looks like he had you sign some of these transfers. Plus, we've got the signed statement of an accountant regarding some of his questionable money transactions. There's no doubt that there are sufficient questions raised by the records found in the fire that if these are added to it, the whole election could be jeopardized."

Jackson interjected, "Your whole family could be arrested and that doesn't even include the crime of murder."

"Murder? What murder?"

"Alive or dead, when you leave here, your fingerprints will be all over the weapons used here this evening! And the location of these weapons will be kept secret until such time as they are needed."

"And if that's not enough," Dominique added, "there's Joe Bones. Rumor has it Paul did the job for you because Joe was making a move on the DiMarcos. It would really be terrible for your family if evidence should come to light that revealed there was animosity between Bones and you."

Edward barked, "You have such information?"

Jackson ignored his question and gestured toward the community center building. "Shall we?"

Edward felt his heart sink as he turned to walk in front of Jackson and Dominique. An investigation into financial wrongdoing could be tied up in the courts for years, but murder was a different matter. His political future was now compromised, but potentially he could lose even more. If there was evidence linking the DiMarcos to Bones's murder, there would be Mob retaliation. Edward might have to be sacrificed for the family's greater good.

They entered the building through a double door and walked into a huge, cavernous room illuminated by large halogen lights. To the right of the door along the wall there was a long rectangular pit about four feet deep. As he watched, the bodies of his men were being rolled into the pit. It sickened him. It had taken him nearly a decade to assemble four men he trusted and now in one night, they were gone. A man who had no trusted cadre had no one to perform dangerous errands or protect his back. Years of work down the drain. Jackson interrupted Edward's thoughts.

"Have a seat." Jackson pointed to some metal folding chairs around a similarly constructed folding table.

Edward did as he was bidden and took a seat facing Jackson. He kept the malevolence off his face, but in his heart he was raging against Jackson. Somehow this particular Negro had just stuck out his big, black feet and squashed everything that Edward had been working for. His life now would have to be lived in relationship to his enemy's power over him. He did not fancy the prospect of future dealings with Jackson, yet he knew there would be many.

Jackson and Dominique sat down across from Edward. Jackson said, "I've worked hard to make sure your family seems to have considerable involvement in Paul's drug business. For example, we left a few things in your cousin's safe that will implicate him in the hit on John Tree. There is also a note from your father's campaign committee thanking Paul for a sizeable donation. There should be a number of different agencies interested in investigating whether Paul was acting alone, or whether he was representing your family."

"So it was you who started the fire at the restaurant?" Edward questioned and Jackson nodded in response. He had been baffled at the connection between Jackson and Paul, a connection that would cause Jackson to burn down the restaurant, but now he was remembering vaguely the explanation Paul had given him and Vince about Tremain's grandsons. It was obvious, contrary to Paul's description, that he had aroused a very dangerous man, a man who had both the means and the willingness to conduct a costly war. Edward needed time to think. He was ready to promise anything for his life. He would consult with his father later and develop a plan of action. He asked, "What do you want of me?"

Dominique said, "I want the restaurant. I'll pay five hundred thousand cash to his wife and kids through an attorney or under the table. However they want it. I'll take it over and run it right, and you'll do a campaign fund-raiser there when I get it rebuilt."

Edward asked, "Is this the money that Paul was coming here for?"

Dominique pushed her long black hair out of her face. "Someone had to take it."

Edward looked back and forth from Dominique to Jackson then asked, "What more do you want from me?"

"We want your jacket. We'll bury that with one of the bodies to tie you to the scene. As for the deed to the restaurant, deliver it tomorrow to the law offices of Johnson, Wyland and Johnson. If anything happens to Dominique or myself, not only will all information make it to the press and relevant law enforcement agencies, but a full-scale war will begin against your family. It will be scorched earth and everyone will be considered a combatant. If your father wins the election, he won't live long enough to enjoy it!"

"I don't have the authority to make this deal."

Dominique smiled sweetly. "Call your father! We know he's waiting to hear from you."

"Better yet, take a few days," Jackson suggested. "Oh, here come the weapons. It's time for you to show off your grip. After that, you'll spend a couple of hours at a nearby motel with friends then you'll be released. By the way, not all of the bodies will be buried here. We may want a few of them more accessible just in case."

Edward asked though clenched teeth, "How do I contact you?"

Jackson replied, "We'll call you at your father's campaign headquarters." He turned and waved to one of his men. "Let's get that last cement truck pouring now."

Paul DiMarco never regained consciousness sufficiently to answer any questions regarding Elizabeth's whereabouts. His life was ended when the suffocating cement flowed over his mouth and nostrils and covered him.

Friday, July 23, 1982

The stench of human waste, mold, and dampness dominated the small, spare, low-ceilinged basement room. The walls were stained and cracked, unpainted plaster. In some places the interior lathing was exposed. There were stains on the walls that looked like blood, and even in the dimness it was clear that the scratches in the plaster were made by human hands.

Elizabeth ached with hunger as she paced the room's cement floor for what seemed like the millionth time. She had lost count somewhere in the twenty thousands. Back and forth, past the foot of the cot, from the casement window on the exterior wall across to the heavy, wooden entry door and back again. She had estimated that her prison was around ten feet square. Five hundred twenty-eight laps made up almost a mile. She liked pacing. It was a mesmerizing exercise that seemed to free her mind from the monotony of her hunger and her imprisonment. She had been locked in this particular cell for the last three days. The only sound other than her regulated breathing and her footsteps was the muffled broadcast of a Spanish-language radio station from the other side of the heavy door.

Every detail of the dingy, pallid little prison had been memorized and filed away: the low-wattage bulb hanging on a wire from the ceiling; the weak rays of light which filtered through the dirty pane of the casement window; the military-issue cot; the chipped porcelain sink and the portable orange plastic toilet. She had given particular attention to the two doors leading into the room: the heavy, wooden door, through which all traffic entered and exited, and the second, a narrower door, similar in size to those for small closets and pantries. Both doors and the window were locked securely. There appeared to be no escape.

She was permitted to leave the room once a day for the noontime meal, which was the main meal of the day. She was taken upstairs to an old hacienda-style kitchen with a wide-open hearth and a heavy, cast-iron cookstove and ate her food alone at a rough-hewn wooden table while her guards watched. The peasant women working in the kitchen did not look at her. They wisely kept their heads down and talked in whispers. The only serving of meat she received, if she received any at all, was at that meal. Dinner consisted of a plastic container of water and a small serving of beans wrapped in a couple of corn tortillas, and there was no breakfast. While she had never considered herself a big eater, by the time lunch came around, she was pretty hungry.

She stretched her arms over her head as she paced the cement floor and winced at the strength of the odor her body gave off. Although the room's temperature was only eighty degrees, its stuffiness caused her to perspire profusely. Elizabeth took pains twice a day to wash up in the small sink with the rough rags and harsh soap they had given her, but that did nothing to mitigate the smell of her clothes. Unconsciously, she put her hands up to check her hair. There was no mirror but she could feel the unraveling of her miniature braids with her fingers. It had been nearly two weeks since she'd washed her hair. She felt like she was wearing a filthy cap. She had been allowed to shower only once since her capture and that had been in full view of Deleon. From her years in police work she knew that debasement and degradation were the general lot of kidnap victims, that she should consider herself lucky that she had been raped only once, but the realization brought her no comfort. She took a deep breath and increased the speed of her pacing. Resolution was the key. She had to focus her energies on staying strong so that she would be ready to take advantage of any opportunity that came along.

Elizabeth had deduced from the look of the peasant women, the Spanish-language newspapers she had seen in the kitchen, and the snatches of Spanish that she had heard spoken that she had been taken south across the border to Mexico. Her deduction made her heart fall for she knew it lessened the chance of Jackson finding her, much less rescuing her. She would have to rely upon her own ingenuity. She had established a workout regimen to stay in shape the first day that she was released from her bonds. She started her morning with a stretching routine then jogged thirty-two hundred laps. In the afternoon she paced out four thousand laps and worked on her push-ups. At night she spent hours trying to pick the lock of the narrow door with one of her few remaining large bobby pins. It was an old-fashioned lock which was opened by a round-stemmed key. A couple times she had thought the tumblers had rolled over, but the door had remained locked. She wished she had paid better attention while attending police seminars on the methods and implements of breaking and entering. She could only hope that her perseverance would eventually pay off.

She had no memory of her journey to Mexico. Much of it she had spent in a drug-induced stupor. The first time she awakened in this room the floor had been cold and hard. She could not tell whether the room was lighted or not. She had been blindfolded, bound, and gagged. She had fought back the fear that squirmed deep in her chest. She tried to lie quietly and reserve her strength, but fear was an adrenaline-pulsing entity that hurled itself against the confines of her rib cage. It was a force in her mind that sent her thoughts scattering in confusion like bowling pins hit by a well-placed ball.

She picked up her pace, losing herself in the rhythm of her steps. Time passed slowly, interminably, seconds ticking as if slogging through a sea of molasses. She thought about her life before her capture and shook her head in amazement. Her whole worldview had been wrong. She remembered the angst and concern that her work at the district attorney's office had caused her, how she had felt that her life wasn't fulfilling. Now such feelings seemed to be the petty concerns of a sheltered fool. The truth was, she didn't know how good she'd had it. She had been living a life of cherries and cream. How could she have been dissatisfied with her career? Then there was Jackson. She realized now that, instead of being guarded and cautious, she should have taken every second of the time she had with him and enjoyed it to the fullest. How easy it was to see now that neither love nor life was guaranteed. The sounds of voices outside the wooden door halted her reverie.

The door swung open and a voice commanded, "Move away from

the door and stand where we can see you!" Elizabeth did as she was ordered. Deleon, followed by Alejandro, Tercero, Simon, and San Vicente, entered the room. During Elizabeth's imprisonment she had learned each of the men's names. Alejandro, Tercero, and Simon were her guards. They were the ones who emptied her plastic toilet and escorted her to the kitchen.

San Vicente ordered, "Bring her a chair!" Simon immediately left the room and returned with a wooden chair, which he placed in the middle of the floor facing the door. With a gesture, San Vicente directed her to take a seat. He gave her a cold smile, his sunglasses reflecting the harsh light of the bare bulb. "Now that we've gotten our security set up, it's time we were introduced formerly. I am Don San Vicente. These three are my men. And you know Señor DuMont already. You are now my prisoner. Señor DuMont has relinquished control over your well-being to me." San Vicente's men moved around behind Elizabeth.

"Why am I here?" Elizabeth put a submissive whimper in her voice. She hoped to make her captors underestimate her.

"You don't ask questions here." San Vicente tapped his chest. "I ask the questions. Where are the stock certificates?"

"The—the what?" Elizabeth sputtered. "Why would I know about stock certificates?"

Someone behind her stepped forward and slapped the back of her head hard. She cried out as the sting of the blow spread across the back of her skull. "You don't ask questions!" Tercero declared from behind her in a thick Mexican accent.

San Vicente continued, "I ask you once again, where are the stock certificates?"

Elizabeth hunched down as she replied in a whining voice, "I swear I don't know anything about any stock certificates! No one ever talked to me about that! On my father's grave, I swear! What stock certificates?"

Someone else slapped the back of her head hard and said, "You don't ask questions!" Elizabeth bent over with pain and screamed.

Deleon turned and confronted San Vicente. "Goddamn it! This wasn't the agreement! We need her in good shape!"

There was an ominous quality in San Vicente's words when he replied, "We are partners, yes? But you are not master here, DuMont! Watch how you speak!"

Deleon answered, "I'm just saying what you're doing isn't smart. We have a phone call scheduled in thirty minutes. We want her to be able to talk to him. Why mess up the hostage before that if it isn't necessary?"

San Vicente didn't bother to oblige Deleon with an answer. He studied Elizabeth, his eyes hidden behind his dark glasses. He walked around her chair. No one spoke. Only his footsteps echoed in the room. After making a complete circuit around her chair, he turned to her and said, "I believe you. I don't think Tremain would be stupid enough to tell you anything either. Of course, I have ways of finding out if you are lying. But these ways will change the way you look, the way you move, even the way you think—if you live. But for now, we will just keep you prisoner and see what your boyfriend will do."

Elizabeth did not let her facial expression change. Since her captors were Jackson's enemies, she was only valuable to them as bait. Once Jackson was lured into their trap, she would be expendable. She set her mind to thinking about her options. No one would know where she was. She would have to manufacture her own route to escape. Surprise was her only weapon. She must continue to present a weak and frightened facade, but not too weak and not too frightened.

San Vicente walked over to Elizabeth and let a finger brush her cheek. "You are dark but pretty. Some of my men want to bed you. It might go easier for you if you share what you have between your legs. Do you want that?" Elizabeth kept her head down and shook her head. San Vicente pointed to Deleon. "He has had some, no? Why not share it with my men too?"

Deleon challenged, "That's not what we agreed upon! Stick with the agreement!"

Deleon's words and tone angered San Vicente and his men. There was some shuffling of positions as if a couple of the men were preparing to attack Deleon, but San Vicente held up his hand. When he spoke to Deleon there was no warmth in his voice. "This is the last time I'll warn you! Watch your tone and your words!" San Vicente paused then smiled evilly. "We both know, don't we, that agreements are made to be broken. You are fortunate I am a honorable man." Tercero and Alejandro laughed at the way their boss was toying with Deleon. San Vicente's smile was gone when he turned to Elizabeth. He grabbed her jaw in a firm grip and growled, "You are my prisoner, not his. You will live by my rules or not live at all. You are fortunate that I do not like dark women because I would take you whether you wanted it or not. But since I do not desire you, you only have to obey my commands. The penalty for disobedience will be harsh. It would be a shame to mark your face unnecessarily because you will bring a good price once you're broken."

Elizabeth trembled and she did not have to pretend. The coldness of the man's tone left no doubt in her mind that San Vicente would torture her and kill her should his plans to exchange her for the certificates go awry. She wondered if there was any way she could play on the obvious tension and enmity that existed between San Vicente and Deleon.

San Vicente stepped back and asked in a more kindly tone, "Are you hungry?"

Elizabeth knew that, despite her loss of appetite, she should eat. She nodded her head meekly, keeping her glance downward.

San Vicente said, "Well, after I show you escape is impossible, we'll take you to the kitchen and you'll get a good meal from old Sonja."

Deleon interjected, "It might be best not to give her a tour, so that she doesn't know her way around."

"You think she can escape here?" San Vicente demanded angrily. "From Playa Rosalía? With my dogs? I think she should see one of her guards. I think it will take any idea of escape from her mind. Bring in Rex!" There was a moment's pause and none of the men moved. San Vicente stared around angrily. "I said bring in the dog!"

Alejandro, a tall, muscular man who wore his black hair in a ponytail, stepped from behind Elizabeth and said, "He's chained up, boss. Can't nobody but you and the trainer loose him." By his voice Elizabeth figured him to be the second one who had slapped the back of her head.

San Vicente laughed and walked swiftly out of the room. He came back in less than a minute with a large-boned brown Doberman. The dog's ears were cropped to short, triangular points above its head. San Vicente signaled the dog with a hand gesture to stand beside the chair in which Elizabeth was seated. The dog obeyed. San Vicente made another hand signal and the dog sat on its haunches. San Vicente ordered Elizabeth, "Pet him!" Elizabeth looked at the dog and recognized that it had received training on par with police dogs, but she was nonetheless hesitant to touch the dog. It could easily take her hand off at the wrist. "Pet the dog!" San Vicente ordered.

"Pet the dog!" Alejandro reiterated and slapped the back of her head again. The dog turned in a single movement and tensed to attack him. Although its teeth were bared, no sound issued from its mouth, for it had been taught to attack without warning.

Only San Vicente's shouting "Sit, Rex! Sit!" prevented the dog from leaping on Alejandro. The dog swiveled and returned to sitting on its haunches. It awaited its next command. San Vicente laughed again and said, "You must be careful, Alejandro. Rex doesn't like you and I've told you many times, do not make sudden moves around the dogs."

San Vicente turned once more to Elizabeth and directed her to pet the dog. With great reluctance, she reached out and petted the dog's head. "You see," San Vicente said with a nod of his head, "the dog is well trained, eh? Come, let us go to where he is chained." He patted his hand against his thigh and the dog went to heel by his side. Elizabeth was pulled erect and pushed to follow San Vicente through the door. She was taken into a long rectangular room with a cot and a telephone and a radio sitting beside a bureau. At the end of the room was the staircase leading up to the first floor. San Vicente took the Doberman over to the wall next to the staircase and chained the dog to the wall. He pointed to a painted line on the floor and told Elizabeth, "Stand there!" Elizabeth moved to the spot indicated. "You just petted him, no?" San Vicente asked. Elizabeth nodded her head meekly. San Vicente pointed at her and commanded, "Attack!" The dog hurled itself straight for Elizabeth's throat.

Involuntarily, she stumbled backward, trying to escape the teeth that seemed destined to be sunk into her neck, and fell to the floor. Only the strength of the chain had kept the animal from tearing out her throat. The dog's move to attack was so quick that it was frightening. Even though she was lying on the ground far beyond the reach of its chain, the animal did not stop hurling itself at her until San Vicente commanded, "Heel!"

Alejandro lifted Elizabeth roughly to her feet and as he did so he intentionally grabbed her breast. She pulled angrily out of his grasp and stood trying to compose herself. She was shaken by the dog's speed and ferocity.

San Vicente smiled. "Are you still hungry?"

Elizabeth knew the more that she saw of the facility in which she was imprisoned, the better. She nodded meekly.

"Good!" San Vicente said with a nod of his head and led the way up the steps. He stopped a third of the way up and pointed to the dog. "Stay!"

Elizabeth was pushed toward the stairs by Tercero, a lean, wiry man with a full, black mustache. She noticed out of the corner of her eye as she began to climb the stairs that the dog's chain was long enough to reach to at least the bottom three steps. She would not be able to escape while the dog was on guard. She heard some jostling behind her on the stairs and felt someone's hand thrusting between her legs. She turned without warning and slapped the offender hard across the face. She put her whole weight behind the blow and it nearly caused Alejandro to fall backward on his companions who were following him. Elizabeth shouted, "Keep your filthy hands to yourself!"

Everyone laughed but Alejandro. There was a look of anger on his face when he started up the steps toward Elizabeth, but he never reached her. Deleon pushed past her and confronted him. Deleon challenged Alejandro, "You forget what your job is already? We don't want marks on the merchandise! She's got to be left alone until we hear about the stocks! Do I need to explain it differently?"

Alejandro stared at Deleon and it was clear that had he had his way, Deleon would be his meat, but he looked over Deleon's shoulder and saw a signal to calm down from his boss.

San Vicente laughed. "I'm sorry, but he's right, Alejandro. Right now she is very valuable to us. If you persist, I'll have to give you to either DuMont or the dogs."

Tercero guffawed. "Don't give him to Rex! He'll give the dog indigestion!" There was a round of laughter as Tercero's joke broke the tension.

Elizabeth followed San Vicente up the stairs and entered a long hallway which led to another flight of stairs. She was being taken into parts of the mansion where she had never been. The tour lasted twenty minutes. First, San Vicente showed her his state-of-the-art security and communications center with its bank of monitors which had cameras in all the major hallways and entries. The communications center was separated from the main house, but was linked by a second-story catwalk constructed over a cobblestone courtyard with a large fountain. San Vicente introduced the two men staffing the center. "This place is run by Angel and Jesus." He laughed. "With them in charge, you might say I have divine protection. With my security system, I do not fear attacks from even the strongest of my rivals." He pointed to a green phone and said, "This is a direct line to the police station. All we have to do is pick up the phone and they answer." San Vicente asked Jesus to turn on a suitcase-sized shortwave radio and tune in the police bandwidth. San Vicente explained that he had people with shortwave radios all over the region who regularly reported the arrival or movement of unusual groups of men. He pointed out the window to his huge satellite dish and bragged that it was larger than the one the federales had. The last thing he showed Elizabeth was a red switch which he said sent out a recorded radio alarm on all the police bands. If his compound was ever attacked, the red switch would be flicked and police from the surrounding areas would respond. From there Elizabeth was taken back across the catwalk to look down on the dog kennel, where there were five other Dobermans like Rex. She was informed that the dogs freely roamed the grounds during the early evening hours; otherwise they were used to augment regular two-man patrols of the house and perimeter wall. As they walked down the stairs back to the main floor, she kept her facial expression blank, but her fear was growing. The likelihood of rescue was growing more and more remote. It was beginning to appear that the best she could hope was to die quickly.

San Vicente led the way down a different set of stairs into a broad, high-ceilinged hallway. The hallway emptied into a large domed room with a twenty-foot ceiling. Thick carpets lay upon the floor, the walls were lined with heavy, embroidered drapes, and a long wooden table stood in front of a huge stone fireplace. Elizabeth stopped and looked around the room. This was the center of the mansion. She was trying to remember everything she saw.

San Vicente misunderstood her interest. "It's nice, huh? Like a mansion in Europe or the States." Elizabeth nodded and continued to look around. San Vicente went on proudly, "This compound is built on five acres of landscaped grounds, all of it surrounded by ten-foot stone walls."

Deleon reminded San Vicente, "It's time to make the call." San Vicente did not like being interrupted and there was a frown on his face when he went to the telephone. Before he picked up the receiver, he turned to Elizabeth and said, "Make no mention of me or of where you think you are. If you attempt to give your boyfriend any clues, I will chop you up into pieces after I have passed you around to my men!" He dialed several numbers and began speaking in rapid-fire Spanish; after several pauses he handed the phone to Deleon.

Deleon spoke into the receiver, "Hello? Mr. Tremain? Mr. Jackson Tremain? Deleon DuMont here. Yes, we haven't talked for a spell. Who? Oh, she's fine. You'll get to talk to her in a moment if you'll just calm down. Hey! No need for threats! That's better. She could've been back home by now if you hadn't attacked my house. Look, all we're interested in are the stock certificates. If you bring the certificates to the San Diego Hilton at two-thirty this coming Tuesday afternoon, we can end this thing amicably. I know you want to talk to her, but don't threaten me. . . . Let me show you what I think of your threats! Bring the bitch here!" Tercero and Alejandro wrestled a struggling Elizabeth in front of him. Deleon pivoted and punched her viciously in the stomach and she fell to the floor with a cry of pain. He spoke into the phone, "I don't have to tell you what will happen to her if you don't show, do I?" Then he dropped the phone on the floor by her head and nudged her body with the toe of his shoe. "Be careful of what you say!"

Elizabeth pushed herself to a sitting position. She did not even attempt to get up. She picked up the receiver and held it to her ear. She heard Jackson's frantic voice. "Hello! Hello! Elizabeth? What the fuck has he done to her? I'll kill him! I swear to God, I'll kill all of them!"

Elizabeth inhaled deeply a few times to catch her breath then said softly, "I'm here." The pain in her stomach prevented her from speaking more loudly.

"Elizabeth? Is that you? Are you all right? What did that bastard do to you?"

"I'm all right! I just miss my life! I miss you."

"Listen to me, Elizabeth! I love you! I love you with all my heart! Just be strong and know that I love you! Don't let them break your spirit! Just stay focused on staying alive! Come hell or high water, I will find you! Believe in me! I will find you! No matter how long it takes!"

Elizabeth heard Jackson's voice break as his words, filled with brittle emotion, shattered in his throat before he could fully formulate them. She forced herself to speak in a strong, clear voice. "I am all right. Don't be foolish! I am—"

Tercero stepped forward and knocked the phone out of her hands. He growled, "You were warned! Watch what you say!" He raised his hand to slap her. Elizabeth cowered on the floor before him, waiting for the blow to fall.

Deleon intervened. "I think that's enough rough stuff for today. Hang up the phone."

Tercero looked at San Vicente for direction, who nodded in agreement with Deleon.

San Vicente mused, "I wonder whether he will come. I think he knows this is personal and has nothing to do with business. If you were on the other side, isn't that the conclusion you would draw?"

Deleon paused and after a moment nodded. "Yes, but I would not expect to rescue anyone. I would come for vengeance only."

"So would I. But I think that Tremain is different. I don't think he has the *cojones* to come."

Deleon shook his head and said with a slight smile, "It is not wise to underestimate your enemies."

San Vicente looked at Deleon for a second then broke out into a belly laugh. He pointed to Deleon. "You are warning me, eh? In my own house! You know if it weren't for those Cubans, I think I could like you, Señor DuMont." San Vicente laughed some more. He waved his hand in a grandiose gesture to Deleon. "Shall we go to the kitchen for lunch? Old Sonja has made pork tamales and refried beans."

Elizabeth got to her feet slowly. Her stomach still ached from the blow that she'd received. She stood for a moment, trying to orient herself, trying to remember how she had been led into this great hall. Despite all distractions, she needed to commit the layout of the mansion to memory. She stared up at the huge chandelier which hung from the center of the ceiling. She wondered whether she would be alive to see this chandelier in the coming week.

San Vicente saw Elizabeth staring up at the chandelier and came over to her. "It's beautiful, isn't it?" Elizabeth put her head down submissively and nodded. "My grandfather built this hacienda the year before the depression. This chandelier was his most prized possession. He imported this chandelier from France the year before he was killed by Tremain."

Deleon questioned, "I thought you said King Tremain never attacked this place?"

"He didn't!" San Vicente's voice changed; a hard edge entered into his words. "My grandfather and my father were killed in Tremain's raid on my grandfather's house near Ciudad Victoria the year after this chandelier was put up." San Vicente turned to Elizabeth and stabbed one of his short, stubby fingers at her. "They were killed by your boyfriend's grandfather. And I understand that your boyfriend was along for the ride at the time. You know anything about that?" Elizabeth shook her head. San Vicente nodded. "I thought not. You see, your boyfriend, DuMont, and me, we all have history. Our lives were tied together before we were born. I have been waiting to meet Tremain for years. I will keep him alive for weeks before I kill him!"

"Wha—what will happen to me if he doesn't come?" Elizabeth stammered.

San Vicente replied, "Oh, we'll wait a couple of days then we will contact him again. We will give him an additional forty-eight hours to produce the certificates. If we don't hear from him, we will send him a few of your fingers and toes. No more than two fingers; we don't want to jeopardize your sale price. A big girl like you could bring as much as thirty-five thousand dollars in Japan or the Middle East."

Monday, June 26, 1964

It was a long day in the saddle for Jackson. He, Carlos, and a man named Culio left the house at eight in the morning and returned at two in the afternoon. They rode over some steep and unforgiving terrain: through canyons, up arroyos, down ravines, and over ridges. The landscape had changed from rolling hills with gold-colored grass to the dry red clay and brush country of the high desert. There were few trees and the saguaro dwarfed those in height. Jackson was getting tired and saddle sore by eleven o'clock. Sangria was a major factor in his fatigue, for the horse could not be ridden carelessly. The stallion nearly threw him several times with his sudden shying and rearing. Jackson was forced to stay alert and keep his knees tight around the animal's body. He said nothing of his discomfort. He knew that his companions did not want to quit until they found pig sign.

After they had stopped for a lunch of jerked meat and tortillas and had climbed back into the saddle, their luck improved. Through his binoculars Culio saw fresh tracks leading out of a box canyon. It was decided that Culio would go down to check if the feces were fresh. He returned in fifteen minutes, nodding. "This morning, a large herd, maybe fifty," he called out.

Carlos nodded. "The pigs return to the canyon in the evening for shelter. The sides are too steep for anything but a mountain lion. We will find them here tomorrow." The scouting party headed back for the lodge.

Jackson fell asleep as soon as he found the way to a bed and slept until dinner was served. When he awakened both his thighs and his behind were extremely sore and caused him to move slowly and cautiously. Yet once he arrived at the dinner table, he discovered that his hunger was such that his pain was barely a distraction. He ate heartily without conversation. He was careful not to look at Maria too often as she was bringing in the platters of food. He focused on his plate and did not speak unless spoken to directly. Part of this noninvolvement was his decision and part was that most of the conversation was being conducted in rapid-fire Spanish. While a surprising amount of his Spanish had been reawakened, it was not sufficient to participate in the staccato exchanges that were flying back and forth. Hernando was telling a long joke that had most of the table laughing with each stage. Maria came up to Jackson and nudged him with her hip, indicating that she wanted him to make room for her on the bench next to him. He slid over gingerly. His body ached.

As Maria sat down she glanced at him and asked quietly, "You were gone a long time. Are you sore from the saddle?"

"Yes, I think I about rode my butt off. I may need a transplant."

She whispered in his ear, "El Negro has some liniment. I'll rub you down after you finish sentry duty. Maybe we can ease some of the pain before you go back out tomorrow."

"That sounds good, but I don't know if I can stand that prickly hay tonight."

"Don't worry!" Maria assured him. "Carlos has given us one of the large front rooms. We sleep on a bed tonight and I'll be there when you wake up tomorrow morning. All your things have already been moved."

Laughter exploded around the table at Hernando's punch line. Jackson stood up and left the dining room. He needed some air and he wanted to give his behind some relief from the sitting.

He walked around to the back of the lodge where he had sat with Maria the night before. The stars were just beginning to shine in the darkening sky. There was still a line of gold edged with purple along the tops of the western mountains as the sunset moved through its final cycle of colors. All around him Jackson heard crickets chirping out the temperature with their mating calls. He turned and discovered that Maria was standing behind him.

Her face seemed to gather the last stray beams of sunlight and glow in the growing twilight. Her heavy-lidded, glistening eyes reflected the endless depths of the night sky.

Jackson was speechless. She was the most beautiful woman he had ever made love to. He realized that all of his previous sexual encounters had been with girls. Maria was his first real woman, with a woman's appetite and understanding. His legs without his conscious will moved toward her. He took her in his arms and kissed her. She responded without restraint and soon her breast was exposed for his lips. They kissed and touched until Jackson pushed her away and said, "I'll see you after my shift. It'll be the longest four hours I've ever spent."

Maria brushed his lips with her own and gave him a big smile. "Think of the pleasure we will have later. Now, we both must work. *Hasta luego, hombre mío.*" She straightened her dress, grabbed his arm, and walked with him along the darkened porch toward the side door that led into the pantry and kitchen.

Later that night after Jackson and Maria had finished their first session of lovemaking, Jackson lay propped up on his elbow, looking out the window at the pale, beige sliver of a new moon crossing over the vibrant nightscape of the Milky Way. Maria lay behind him on the bed. He could hear the soft, even breathing of her slumber. He couldn't sleep. His feelings would not allow his mind to be dormant. He fervently wanted to experience the same level of companionship and sensual pleasure that he had with Maria every day of his future life. He didn't know if it was love or not, but he had never wanted a woman more. He wondered whether they should talk about marriage. Then Carlos's words came back to haunt him: "She is no fool. She does things for reasons." Those words made Jackson wonder whether he was being played like an instrument. She herself had said that he was unspoiled, almost innocent. Did that mean too dumb to see the larger game? He knew Carlos, who only had his best interests in mind, had warned him for some reason.

Maria stirred behind him and nestled the warmth of her body next to him, sliding her hand under his arm and across his chest. She kissed the back of his neck. "What are you thinking about?" she asked in a soft voice.

"I'm wondering whether I am being foolish to care so much for you. I mean, I don't really know who you are and I think I'm falling in love with you. It seems so stupid. I've only known you a few days."

"Don't worry," she said, kissing his neck. "Your heart is safe with me." Jackson grunted in acknowledgment but said nothing. There was a long silence then Maria said, "There is something bothering you. What is it?"

"Carlos said that you 'did things for a reason.' I'm wondering if there was some premeditation on your part."

"Premeditation? I don't know that word."

"It means calculated. Planned. Like did you plan our relationship before you ever met me?"

"Yes! I told you I did! I have thought about it for more than a year!"

Jackson turned around on the bed to face her. It seemed strange to him that in the darkness of a room lit only by the light of the stars and a pale moon, her eyes could still glisten. "Why? You hadn't even met me. How could you know that you would make love to me?" he asked, his questions driven by self-doubt.

Maria answered as if she was stating common knowledge. "You are El Negro's heir, his grandson. If I am with you, I don't have to bed with or tolerate approaches from the other men. Plus, if I treat you well and you like me, El Negro will have greater cause to treat me well. He is a powerful friend to have."

"Then you are just using me." Strains of anger and disappointment began to creep into his words. "This was only a practical decision; it had nothing to do with whether you liked me or not! I see now. I guess I didn't know how innocent I truly was!"

"You are disturbed? Why?"

"Damn straight I'm disturbed! Your decision to have sex with me was a business decision, it had nothing to do with me! And I thought you liked me! *Me*, Jackson Tremain!"

"You see nothing! Your anger is in the way! I do like you! I like you very much, more than I thought possible. I have tried not to lie to you. I don't want to hurt your feelings, but the truth is not always kind. It is true that I made the decision to make love with you before I ever met you. But when I actually met you, you gave me many reasons to be with you. I feel good with you. I can speak my heart and you will listen. I wanted to enjoy myself with you and I do. I don't have to pretend that you give me pleasure."

She put her hand on his face and caressed his cheek tenderly then continued, "You don't understand, but for a poor woman life is very hard in this country. This is a man's land and if a woman is considered attractive she may be taken young unless she has family to protect her. That type of life can squeeze blood from the body. After a time it is like an artery is cut and your spirit drains away! A woman who is not yet thirty can look sixty years old if she does not make smart business decisions.

"I have survived by making decisions with my head that I could not afford to let my heart make. You have felt the ridges on the skin of my back?" She waited for Jackson to respond. His dark silhouette nodded in response to her question. She continued, "They are the scars from being whipped with a riding crop! I was whipped until the blood ran! I was not always obedient, but I could not afford to be stupid! I do not wish you to marry me or even take me back to the United States with you. All I wanted was to avoid being passed around and to have favor in El Negro's eyes. Now, I have more than I ever expected to have. We are friends and lovers, no?"

"I guess," Jackson answered, the darkness hiding the confusion on his face.

"I want to give you pleasure and be with you as long as you want to be with me. Is this wrong?"

Her large, dark eyes stared at him with a trace of fear. He suddenly realized that she was afraid of displeasing him. He shrugged and shook his head. "I don't know. Who's to say what is right and what is wrong? But your story is very chilling."

She asked in a soft voice, "Do you still want me?"

Her question totally disarmed him. It gave him a sense of her vulnerability and it made him feel ashamed that he had challenged her motives. It made him want to protect her. He reached out and put his arms around her and pulled her close until their bodies were touching. "Yes, more than ever," he murmured into her ear. She pressed herself against him and he grew hard in the grip of her hand.

Jackson's grandfather arrived midafternoon on Tuesday and he greeted his grandson with a hug and a handshake, but Jackson saw appraising eyes behind the actions and felt immediate resentment: He didn't realize that he was doomed to live by his grandfather's standards until he developed his own. The sight of El Indio, who had come with his grandfather, washed away any ill feelings he had. Jackson hadn't seen the old Indian since he was fifteen. A flood of warmth flushed through him. He rushed over and gave El Indio a hug, which was returned.

El Indio pushed Jackson away and held him at arm's length. He nodded his head as he looked him up and down. "Much time has passed."

Jackson nodded, noticing the gray hair that sprinkled El Indio's once jet-black mane and the sun-weathered and wrinkled face. Only the black, flat-brimmed hat with the white, black-tipped feather stuck in its band and the glitter of the dark eyes remained the same.

El Indio smiled and said, "Diablito returns to us as a man! Soon, we will have to find another name for him! A man's name!"

El Indio's announcement pleased Jackson. Although he never gave it credence consciously, his grandfather and the men around him were extremely important to him. He would rather risk death than appear weak or foolish in their eyes.

After dinner a map was laid on the table and the hunt was planned. Once again Jackson begged off horseback assignments, explaining that his behind was still sore from the previous day's six hours in the saddle. Amid laughter and a few coarse jokes, he was assigned to drive the jeep and carry supplies. Only Culio, Carlos, El Indio, and Hernando were going to join Jackson and his grandfather on the hunt. Tomas would head the three-man team assigned to stay behind and guard the lodge. The departure time for the hunt was six in the morning.

After his shift of sentry duty, Jackson lay in bed with Maria basking in the warm afterglow of passionate lovemaking. He knew he should be trying to rest, but sleep was far away. He was thinking about returning to the United States. The prospect filled him with dismay. He didn't want what he had with Maria to stop. He had begun to think about asking her to leave Mexico and return with him. Doubt assailed him and his uneasiness increased as he considered the possibility of asking her. He knew that she was awake as well, for she was caressing his back slowly.

"You should sleep," she urged softly. "Tomorrow will take all your strength."

He turned to her and stared at her dark outline against the white sheets. In the room's darkness, he couldn't see the expression on her face, but he could feel the warmth of her body. "What if I told you I didn't want this to stop, that I want to be with you?"

"I would love it," she answered with a sigh.

"I don't want it to stop," Jackson declared.

"Neither do I," she whispered.

"Would you come to America with me?"

"I would go anywhere with you! To go to America would be like a dream come true, a fairy tale come to life!"

"We've got to figure out how we'll do it!"

"You just ask your grandfather! He will do anything that you ask. He complains often that you never ask him for anything. He says that he gives more to other people than he does to you."

"Maybe it's easier for them to ask than it is for me."

"If you truly want to take me with you, I promise that I will do everything to please you! You will never regret this decision!"

"Well, I've got to find a way to tell my grandfather," Jackson said with obvious trepidation.

"Perhaps it's time for you to rest and leave that for later," Maria suggested. "Hunting the *javelina* is dangerous work. It requires alertness and attention. I'll worry about you if you don't get enough rest. Let me hold you." Jackson lay down and entwined himself with Maria and tried to let the silence and darkness bring sleep, but it did not come. The first light of morning found him still awake.

Jackson and the five horsemen started out before the sun rose on Wednesday morning and arrived at nine o'clock at the top ravine leading to the box canyon where the peccaries sheltered during the night. The animals had already left the canyon to forage for tubers in an arroyo where a small creek still ran.

Jackson's grandfather rode his horse alongside the jeep into the valley at the mouth of the canyon. His grandfather explained the strategy behind the hunt and what Jackson would be expected to do. At the end of his explanation, he gave Jackson a long look and said, "I see you with Maria. She ain't what I'd call a good girl, but she's got a good heart. She a hard worker and a straight shooter. And she got gumption too! You could do a whole lot worse. If'en you treat her right, you can't have a better friend."

Jackson didn't say anything. He couldn't. His lips couldn't form the request to ask to take Maria back to the States with him, and those were the only words he wanted to say. It was fear of the look that would cross his grandfather's face that kept him from asking. He decided it wasn't the right time. After the hunt would be better.

Jackson assisted Carlos in building a barricade across an intersecting ravine. They didn't want the pigs to avoid the trap and circle around behind the waiting hunters. They stretched red dyed canvas across the ravine and collected dried branches and small boulders to heap behind it. The barricade would not stand an assault, but they thought the appearance of a new obstacle would frighten the pigs and keep them on their regular route to the box canyon. Jackson was positioned in the jeep above the barricade so that he could warn the hunters of any breach. He didn't much care for his location because he was at the top of a steep ravine with no easy way down unless he reversed and went back a half mile. If the pigs climbed up to him, he had no ready escape. The low sides of the jeep would present no challenge for the enraged pigs.

Jackson checked and rechecked his guns, ensuring that they were in full working order. He had the short, double-barrel shotgun in a holster across his chest and his 30.06 Winchester in the seat next to him. He settled down to wait as he had been taught. He positioned himself so that he had a view of the direction in which the pigs would come and pulled his straw hat down over his forehead. The essence of hunting was absolute stillness. Only the eyes were allowed to move. Soon his thoughts were drifting toward Maria and her luscious body.

The sky to the west had grown dark above the mountains and there were flashes of lightning among the dark gray clouds. Distant rumblings foretold thunder. It looked like a rare summer rainstorm was moving in their direction. Jackson had experienced a few of these summer thundershowers and knew them to be extremely dangerous because of the tremendous forces that could be unleashed. A summer shower might only last an hour, but the amount of water which fell upon the cracked and thirsty earth was staggering. It could rain so hard that one could not see farther than thirty feet in any direction. The lightning would branch across the sky like the crooked finger of God and smite the earth with the thud of a giant fist.

A shot echoed across the landscape. The pigs were coming. Jackson put two fingers in his mouth and gave out a loud, high whistle. He heard a whistle in response and turned on the jeep's engine. He wanted to be ready to go. The sound of thunder rumbled more distinctly. The storm was moving fast. The herd appeared coming out of a jumble of sagebrush and tumbleweed. He saw them through his binoculars. The pigs were running hard, but not at top speed. They were scared but not pressed. There were about twenty to thirty animals in the group led by a couple large adults. The wind was blowing toward him so he could smell their gamey odor, but they could not pick up his scent. He sat without movement. Waiting.

The first part of the pack passed in the ravine below him, high ridge-backed bodies, covered with short, bristling brown fur. Their grunting and the sound of their hooves pounding on the hard clay filled the air. His grandfather, El Indio, and Carlos awaited the pigs at the entrance to the box canyon. Their plan was to shoot the first five pigs that spilled out of the ravine. Generally, killing the leaders would turn a pack, but if that failed the three hunters had found a steep path of retreat up the far side of the valley which lay at the mouth of the box canyon. Jackson put the jeep in gear and bumped along on the rough and uneven terrain that lay along the brink of the ravine, trying to keep the pigs in sight. They were outrunning him. The last of them disappeared around the curve of the ravine.

Jackson maintained the highest speed the broken land would permit. He had to circumnavigate a landslide leading steeply down to the bed of the ravine. A fusillade of rifle fire rang out amid the loud squealing of peccaries. Several more rifle shots echoed through the twisted maze of gorges and arroyos. Then there was the sound of a horse shrieking in pain. Jackson drove the jeep around to the end of the ridge and climbed up on the hood. Below him on the far side of the valley lay his grandfather's horse on its side, waving its legs frantically. His grandfather was not visible. Jackson picked up the binoculars and saw that his grandfather was still in the saddle and that his leg was caught under his horse.

Behind him he heard the squealing of more pigs. He turned and saw the rest of the pack hurtling down the floor of the ravine straight toward his grandfather. They were about a quarter of a mile away and closing fast. Jackson couldn't get a good estimate of their number as they ran through the brush, but it looked like the herd was in excess of twenty animals. He had no time to go back and find a suitable way down; he had to go straight down the steep side of the ravine. It was thirty-five feet deep, and the sides were about a sixty-degree slant. He realized he stood a good chance of killing himself, but he sat down in the jeep, fastened his seat belt, and drove it directly over the lip of the ravine. First there was a momentary free fall, then the jeep bounced lopsidedly down the slope, slowly turning sidewise. Jackson gunned the accelerator and got the nose of the vehicle leading his downward plunge. The front tires hit the hard bed of the ravine and Jackson's forehead banged hard against the metal frame of the windshield and the jeep bounced across the hard clay surface and came to rest within twenty feet of the downed horse and rider.

Blood ran down Jackson's face and there was a strange drumming in his ears. The pain in his head was so severe that it was numbing. The sensation in his hands seemed to be gone. The edge of his vision was filled with exploding black and red dots. Then he heard a new drumming sound in his ears. The pigs were three hundred yards away and running hard. Jackson pulled the shotgun from its holster and cocked both barrels. The herd was coming right toward him, but at least the jeep was blocking his grandfather. He waited. At twenty yards he would fire both barrels into their leaders and if they didn't turn perhaps he would have time to reload once.

Rifle shots reverberated along the walls of the ravine. Jackson saw pigs falling, but still the herd came on, a juggernaut on a sea of sand. He waited until he could see the animals' beady eyes and their tongues lolling out of their mouths. He fired both barrels. The sound deafened him. The gun kicked high. He hit the release and popped it open, discarding spent shells and loading two more in their place. There was a loud thud as a pig's body collided against the rear fender of the jeep. Jackson waved his gun around seeking a target, but in the time it took him to reload the herd had turned and escaped into the brush. Culio, El Indio, and Carlos rode down into the ravine. Carlos was off his horse before it stopped and he ran to El Negro.

When Jackson's grandfather had been pulled from beneath his horse and he had dispatched the animal with a pistol shot, he came over and stood in front of Jackson. He pointed to his grandson and shouted to the other men, "That's my grandson! That's my blood. That's my goddamn blood pumping in that body! He's a man's man! Ain't a lot of steam to him, but there's a hell of a fire in the boiler!"

Both Culio and Carlos nodded knowingly as if to say they expected no less, he was El Negro's heir. El Indio took the feather out of his hat and walked over and handed it to Jackson. The act was done without affectation, but everyone knew it was significant. To earn a feather in the field, a man had to show uncommon courage and daring. Jackson was extremely moved. His grandfather was smiling and stalking around like a proud, old rooster. Jackson took off his hat and put the feather securely in the band of his hat. The hat seemed heavier when he put it back on his head.

The men collected nine pigs and concluded that they could take no more. They decided not to field-dress the pigs until they had cleared out of pig country and left the land of arroyos and flash floods behind. It took them an hour and a half to reach the rolling foothills of the mountains. Even though the storm was pressing, his grandfather decided to gut and butcher the pigs away from the hunting lodge. The pigs were hung in a stand of trees ten miles from the lodge and Hernando was sent to bring Alma and Maria to assist with the butchering.

Jackson was digging a hole in which to bury the entrails when Hernando rode off. Culio was building a small, smokeless fire while Carlos, El Indio, and his grandfather moved from pig to pig, gutting each animal. Jackson noticed there was a difference in the way the men treated him. He had earned respect independent of his grandfather. It wasn't so much his act of bravery that they respected, but rather the nerve he had demonstrated in waiting until the last moment to fire upon the stampeding pigs. El Indio had called him *muy macho* and he had received many claps on the back from the men in the hunting party. Since he had performed a deed that had even earned his grandfather's grudging acknowledgment, Jackson decided that he would ask him about taking Maria back with him when they returned to Mexico City; that way it would not seem so impetuous a decision. He glanced around at the surrounding countryside, the rolling hills covered with the gold of dried grass. Even with the dark charcoal and gray sky above it, it seemed to be one of the most beautiful spots on earth.

Jackson was not aware of when Hernando had returned, for he had become engrossed in carrying shovelfuls of offal to the hole he had dug. Jackson was concentrating on not letting the slimy, bloody mess get on his clothing. However, he heard the notes of urgency in the voices, then he heard his grandfather barking out orders in Spanish. Jackson dropped his shovel and went to find out what was causing the stir.

Carlos was coming toward him as Jackson ambled over. "What's going on?" Jackson asked. He saw Hernando's horse and looked around for Maria and Alma, but there was no sign of them. "Where's Maria?" he asked.

Carlos hesitated a moment then said without inflection, "The lodge was attacked! Tomas and the rest of the guards are dead. Alma's been killed and we think that they have taken Maria."

Jackson was aghast. "What? Attacked? By who? Who would attack women?"

"El Jaguar. He left his signature on the walls."

Jackson could not believe it. "Why? Why would he attack women?"

"It was a raid on El Negro. The women were secondary. They took Maria because she is the niece of Tigre Melendez. He is one of the Jaguar's captains and probably the successor to his throne."

Jackson looked around and noticed that the men were packing up. "What's going to happen now?" he asked, knowing the answer.

"We're going after them. But first we need to go to the lodge and take care of some business. We'll probably be on the road by six this evening. I figure that gives them about a six-hour head start. El Negro wants to know if you want to come along."

Jackson asked, "Shouldn't we let the police handle this?"

"The police will only get in the way! Whether they'll help depends on who paid them last. The best way is to bury the dead. Then deal out our own justice. Do you wish to come?"

Jackson said nothing. If he said yes, he would voluntarily be participating in one of his grandfather's wars, and once he agreed to that, where would it stop? If he said no, he would be abandoning Maria and the likelihood was that he would never see her again. Why would she want to be with a man who didn't have the courage to try to rescue her? It was this thought which caused him to nod affirmatively.

Carlos was studying Jackson's face. "You have proven your courage," he said with a thoughtful tone. "No one will think ill if you choose not to come. There is a difference between hunting men and hunting animals, and we will be hunting and killing men. If you choose to come along, know that there will be no mercy shown to our enemies. We intend to kill the Jaguar and Tigre, but in the process we will also kill as many of their people as we can."

"What about Maria?"

"She is your responsibility. If in our other efforts we rescue her, good.

But that is not our objective. We intend to wipe out the Jaguar's organization."

Jackson sputtered, "That shows no loyalty to her!"

"She is not family. Her family kidnapped her and took her back with them. She does not expect us to save her, or to risk lives in the search for her. Of course, if she means enough to you for you to join us, we will assist you in every way."

"You are extorting my participation! If I don't help, you won't seek to rescue her! That's not right! I expected more from you, Carlos!"

"I didn't say that we wouldn't seek to rescue her, but that rescuing her was not our objective. There is a difference. I don't feel strongly enough about her to risk my life to find her. But I feel strongly about you! If you are willing to risk your life to find her, I will join you."

"Let's go, men!" King shouted as he led his horse into a clearing. "We got to get the radio workin' befo' this storm hits! You comin', Grandson?"

Jackson looked at Carlos then answered, "Yes, Grandfather. I'm coming!"

King mounted the extra horse that Hernando had brought back from the lodge and ordered, "Then let's get to steppin'! I'll see you at the house!" He, Hernando, and El Indio rode off at a gallop.

Carlos and Culio cut down the six pigs that had been gutted and wrapped them in a canvas tarp. The wrapped meat was placed in the back of the jeep. The remaining three pigs were left hanging in the trees. The fire was put out and then they left the grove.

As Jackson drove away, he glanced back at the grove of trees, heavy with the smell of blood, and wondered what he had thought was so beautiful about the little, depressing stand of trees.

When he arrived at the lodge Hernando and Culio were erecting a thirty-foot radio antenna. He pulled down to the stable and helped El Indio unload the pigs and hang them on racks in the smokehouse. Then Jackson was sent out to dig a large grave at the edge of the trees behind the outhouses. Hernando joined him and they picked and dug a four-foot-deep trench in the hard-packed red clay. Culio rode up to the grave site with the bodies of three strange men tied to a travois. He had rigged the device to drag behind his horse. He untied them and rolled the bodies off the travois and into the trench.

"We got four more to bring here," Culio announced. He rolled himself a cigarette. "They must've come with a pretty big party to lose seven!" He lighted his smoke and guided his horse back toward the lodge. Hernando picked up a large plastic container and shook out white, powered lime across the bodies.

It was strange, depressing work burying human corpses. It made Jackson feel queasy, particularly when he threw lime on the face of one of the dead men whose eyes were still open. The eyes stared upward as if there were still a will to see. Slowly, shovelful by shovelful, the bodies were covered with rocks and dirt. Then he and Hernando covered the grave with large rocks which had been originally collected to build a fence. Jackson returned to the lodge with the image of the dead man's eyes burning in his mind.

Alma and the three men who had died defending the lodge were placed in graves across the valley from the lodge. It was more difficult for Jackson to see the bodies of people who he knew and liked. Even though they were recognizable, their faces seemed robbed of a vital identifying feature. He was beginning to understand that death was a thief of essence. Their bodies now were merely empty husks, relics of what once was living. They were placed in their separate graves in silence. It seemed a particularly bleak day to die. The sky was dark with nature's fire and vengeance. Thunder rumbled solemnly while flashes of lightning illuminated the charcoal sky. His grandfather intoned words of prayer over the graves.

As Jackson bowed his head he thought of Maria. She was gone. Stolen away. Her sweet, wonderful smile was gone. The soft feel of her skin was gone. He felt a hollowness in his stomach then he felt anger. She was a victim in one of his grandfather's wars. He studied his grandfather's face and thought his grandfather must have intoned the ritual of last rites many times. He wondered if it mattered whether words of sacrament were said over a grave if the man saying them was a man who having sent so many to a premature death appeared to have little or no appreciation of God.

Saturday, July 24, 1982

S erena sat tiredly on an uncomfortable, metal-framed plastic chair in
the hospital hallway, watching the white-garbed medical staff walk
up and down the halls. She rubbed her eyes. She had just come out of
the darkness of Elroy's room, and the unremitting glare of fluorescent
lights in the hall was forcing her eyes to adjust to brightness. If there
was anything in the hospital she really disliked, it was the lighting,
which seemed to be the antithesis of a healing environment with its cold
chemical luminescence. The banks of fluorescent tubes always seemed
to bring out the blue-gray pallor of illness even in healthy people.

A young nurse stopped in front of her. "Mrs. Tremain, why don't you
go home for a while? You've been here twenty-four hours a day since
your son was brought in. He seems to be resting easily now since his
second surgery. I'm sure you'd be more comfort to him if you took care
of yourself."

Serena looked up into the nurse's concerned face and shook her
head. She thought, I have no place to go and no place where I'd rather
be. For her nothing mattered more than Elroy's health. She felt that if
she could right any part of the wrong that she had done, she would rest
easier. If she had any doubts, all she had to do was walk down the hall
to the elevators and there waiting for her were the ghosts. While she
remained in the hospital with Elroy, they left her alone. It was the first
peace she'd had since Amos's funeral. There was no doubt in her mind
that if Elroy should die, she would have no respite from the wraiths that
now waited for her.

The nurse, concerned by her silence and the faraway look in her
eyes, asked, "Are you sure you don't want me to call you a cab? If you
stay here any longer we may have to hospitalize you."

"I'll be all right, dear, as soon as my son is out of danger."

"He's out of danger now, otherwise they wouldn't have released him
from intensive care. If he keeps improving the way he's going, they
should release him some time in the next two weeks, provided that he'll
get good home nursing care."

"He'll get everything that money can buy and a supportive family
can provide."

The nurse smiled. "Mrs. Tremain, I wish all parents cared as much as you do. Your son is a lucky fellow. I may nominate you for Mother of the Year."

Serena's smile acknowledged not the compliment, but its misplacement. "That's kind of you, but I don't deserve it."

"And humble too?" The nurse shook her head appreciatively. "You're pretty special, Mrs. Tremain. All the staff on this floor think so. Well, I've got to clock out. I'll see you tomorrow and I hope that you'll get some rest between now and then."

Serena thanked the nurse and watched her walk down the hall toward the nursing desk. She had no doubt that if Elroy's full story were known, the nurse would think differently. She stood up slowly and discovered that she was stiff from sitting in the uncomfortable chair. She walked back to Elroy's room and entered into the welcoming darkness. She heard intermittent snatches of speech coming from his bed. She crossed over to him and stood beside the bed in the semidarkness, watching him. Elroy seemed to have fallen into a delirium again. In the past few days he'd had several bouts of semiconsciousness in which he often mumbled and sometimes shouted. As far as Serena could tell, most of the time he was remembering some military or police-related experience. The nurses had told her that these bouts were nothing to worry about unless they were attended by a fever. He was tossing and turning as much as his injuries would permit. She leaned down to feel his forehead as he began muttering.

His voice was whispery and emotional. "Papa! Papa, why is them white men burning down our house? It's burning to the ground! Mama got out, didn't she? Oh, God, Papa, is that Ruthie all burned like that? She smells like barbecue, Papa! Please, God, don't let that be Ruthie! Judah, Papa been shot! Oh, no! No, please, God, don't let him be dead! What we gon' do? Don't hit me, Judah! I'm running for all I got! I hear them bullets whistling! Which way, Judah? Judah?"

Serena watched as Elroy's voice tapered off, but she saw that he was still deep in his delirium. His head twitched back and forth on his pillow and he began panting loudly, making a gurgling sound deep in his chest. Serena was alarmed. This was new behavior and it didn't look good. She moved to the head of his bed and searched for the nurse call button. Elroy did his best to shout in his whispery voice, "Judah? Judah, don't play now! Please, don't be dead. Oh, God! Please, God! Don't let Judah be dead!" The force with which he spoke caused him to cough

and gasp, but still his words were distinct. Serena heard them clearly;
each word burned through the casing of her heart, striking deep within
her, like molten metal falling onto solid ice. She was beginning to have
trouble breathing. She traced the call button's wire, finally locating it
under his pillow, and pushed it.

She stepped back away from the bed. Was there no escape? Was she
going to be continually confronted by her crimes? Serena sat down in a
chair to catch her breath. She knew the story of the Caldwell family.
She had been contacted by the nuns when they were first thinking of
adopting Elroy. Using the mother superior as her go-between, Serena
had sent a message to the Caldwells through her attorney that she
would assist in the education of all their children should they decide to
adopt Elroy. The Caldwells declined her offer, saying that they chose
Elroy because of what was in his heart. At first, Serena had thought her
worries were over, but Tini's subsequent death and Della's continued
miscarriages eradicated that presumption; then four years afterward,
the orphanage contacted her again and informed her of the circumstances surrounding Elroy's return. Now, forty-nine years after the fact,
she was hearing his firsthand account of the tragedy.

The nurse, a stocky Filipino woman, pushed open the door and entered the room. "Something wrong, Mrs. Tremain?"

"Well, he's in some sort of delirium and he's moving pretty wildly!"

The nurse walked over to Elroy's bed and reached down and grabbed
Elroy's hand. She said firmly, "Push the red emergency button!"

Serena did as she was bidden. She asked anxiously, "He's not in danger, is he?"

"No, he's torn out his IV and it's making a bit of a mess, but I think we
want to sedate him right now before he does any more damage to himself. I need some help. Your son is a big guy. Might be better for you to
wait outside when the other nurses get here. We're going to need to
change the linen on this bed."

Serena stepped out into the hall as the reinforcements arrived. The
brightness of the corridors accosted her eyes once more. She returned
to the same uncomfortable chair that she had sat in before. She inhaled
deeply. Her chest had gotten tight as she had listened to Elroy's memory of the Klan attack. Serena put her head in her hands and began to
cry. There was no sound, the tears just began to flow. They dripped
down her face leaving the streaks of their passage. One of the nurses

stepped out of Elroy's room and saw her. The woman came quickly to her side.

"You shouldn't worry, Mrs. Tremain. Your son is all right. It was just a bit of thrashing. Why don't you go and rest. We've replaced the cot you've been using with a real bed. Why don't you go lie down. We'll have someone check on him every hour. I wish all our patients' families were as supportive as you are."

The nurse helped Serena to her feet and guided her back into the room. Serena lay down on the bed provided and she remembered no more until she awakened in the wee hours of the morning. Restless dreams and a full bladder caused her to get up and make her way into the bathroom. On her way back she stopped by Elroy's bed and saw that he was sleeping calmly. In his face at rest, Serena again saw traces of King. There was no doubt it was predestined that he would be a part of her life. She felt abashed and humbled by the forces which had caused her to finally accept him.

Serena had been a churchgoer, but had never spent much time in prayer. She had always been more concerned with the appearance and impact of her own presence rather than devotion. However, she felt this was a good time to reestablish her relationship with the Almighty.

Serena got down on her knees and began to pray out loud. "Lord, I know it's been a long time and maybe I don't have the right to ask, but I'm asking you to help this man back to life. I don't know whether he's a sinner or a saint, whether he's lived a just life or not. But I'm asking you to lighten his load and help him to heal because I've sinned against him. I've wronged him and I'm asking you to help me right that wrong. I can't undo the bad that I've done and I know there is no atonement for me, but maybe you can do something to put a smile in his heart and a spring in his step. Help him find joy in life." Serena fell silent as she pressed her face against the cold metal of Elroy's bed rails. She began praying once more. "I know I'm a sinner, Lord. I've done terrible things to people that I loved. I've stunted the lives of my sons and destroyed my family's ability to bear children. I look back on my actions now and there seems no justification for them. I know that hell awaits me and I do not seek to turn away from it. I ask nothing for myself. I ask only that you look kindly on the family that I have nearly destroyed and help them find peace and joy—" Serena heard movement in the bed and looked up. Elroy was lying on his side, staring at her. She was embarrassed, as if she had been caught undressed. She dipped her head to him and said, "I'm sorry if I awakened you."

Elroy said nothing, he just looked at her. Serena exhaled slowly and began to pull herself to her feet. As she stood up, Elroy asked in his whispery voice, "Why did you leave me in that orphanage?"

Serena looked down at the floor and shrugged helplessly. "I was a petty, jealous woman. I was afraid for my oldest boy, LaValle. He wasn't tough like his brother Jacques, like you. He was a weak boy who, through my ignorance, I helped turn into a weaker man. I knew it was wrong, but once I got on that road I couldn't get off. I know you can't forgive me and I won't ask you. But I will ask you to get well and not waste your life like I have. Don't waste time hating me. The Tremain family is your family and they need you. They need someone to help pull them together. I can't do it, but you could do it. You've always been part of this family; I was the one who prevented you from being included. Now I'm begging you, please come and help us. Help us be a family."

"Is that why you're here? To ask me this? Why now? Why after all this time?"

Serena started to cry again. "I'm so sorry for the wrongs I've done you. I needed to apologize to you in person and be of assistance to you in your recovery. I just want to do anything I can that will be of help to you. I've ruined so many people's lives. It's hard to live with the weight of it."

Elroy didn't reply immediately. He was silent for almost five minutes. Serena began to fear that he would ask her to leave. She started to turn away when he began to speak. "I know that you've been here all the time. I remember seeing your face each time I woke up. The nurses told me that you brought in a surgeon from Johns Hopkins to operate on me. I guess I owe you something, maybe even my life." Elroy paused to catch his breath. When he continued his voice was a bit stronger. "I say, let the one without sin cast the first stone. Sorry is all you can say to God. I accept your apology."

The tears welled up in Serena's eyes. She reached hesitantly for his hand and gripped it lightly. "Oh, thank you. Your willingness to forgive me means so much. I can't tell you. Thank you." Serena stood in silence by the bed, gratefully holding Elroy's hand. The irony of the situation was not lost on her. She was receiving comfort from the original one she had wronged so long ago and out of all of her family, he was probably the only one who would accept her apology. She squeezed his hand gently and asked, "Can I stay here with you?"

Elroy nodded, closed his eyes then said, "I thought I wanted revenge. I thought killing those responsible would make me feel better. That's why I went to the DuMonts', but when I saw him I knew I could kill a million like him and it wouldn't change a thing in my life. The cruelty was committed a long time ago and the years have covered it with dust. It's time now to leave all that behind and leave the dust undisturbed."

Serena dabbed at her tears with the back of her sleeve. "I'm so grateful that you allow me to stay here with you. I've been so stupid and petty that no one in my family cares about me or wants to spend time with me. I can't even look into their faces without feeling shame." She put her free hand to her face and covered her eyes.

Elroy watched her for a moment then said, "I know what it is like to mistreat those you love. I tried to make my sons tough. I was hard and demanding with them. I let my oldest son go to Vietnam and I never told him that I loved him. When I got the telegram telling me he had been killed, I felt like an absolute fool, like I had thrown away a divine gift. I was no better with my youngest son. I knocked him down when he was sixteen and he never forgave me. I haven't seen him in over ten years and he's nearly twenty-eight now. I'm no winner either." Elroy swallowed hard and continued, "I know what it's like to find out you're going down the wrong road and being unable to make yourself turn back. To know you're wrong, but keep doing it anyway. I've been there. I did it with my wife and my boys. Not once, but over and over again. I'm talking about brutality, hurtful things. Don't get me wrong, I never raised a hand to my wife or my oldest son and I only hit the younger one once, but that doesn't excuse me from being a brute. Sometimes I knew I was standing right on their hearts, squashing them flat. Sometimes I even thought I could see them shrivel inside, but I never stopped what I was doing. I didn't keep doing those things to be hurtful, I kept doing them because I didn't know any other way. I look back on those times now and I see that I had a thousand other ways to accomplish my goals. Now, I got nothing. My life is as blank and empty as that hospital wall. You see, you're asking the wrong guy to help you pull your family back together."

Serena knew intimately of what he was referring to when he mentioned being a brute. She knew all about being brutishly correct and coldly perfect. She had played those hands in spades. She knew of the emptiness. The fearful shape of darkness. The silence of a still house, a silence broken only by paid staff. There was no living person that she could point to whom she had given her love. Money she had given, and she had made all who had received it pay dearly for that gift. She had squeezed out her pound of flesh before gratitude could flow of its own accord. The unfortunate thing about a pound of flesh was that it could not be stored. Once it was pressed from the unwilling victim, it disappeared, leaving nothing but resentment. She who had dreamed of a joyous house knew that she herself was the reason that no fire could bring warmth to her still hearth.

Elroy began speaking again. "I've been here thinking about whether I want to live or die, whether there was anything worth living for. I even relived pieces of my life over again searching for clues. I never got anywhere close to a clear-cut answer to those questions, but I did get clear on a couple of things. First, I've spent my life blaming somebody for leaving me in that orphanage. I blamed all the things I didn't know on being raised in an institution. When I read about you and Pug, I hated you, hated you both. I blamed you for everything, like I didn't have a thing to do with my life. That's all a lot of bull! I realized when I was lying there in DuMont's house, with my blood trickling onto the floor, that I had no one who I could call, that I had lived my whole life and didn't have a friend or relative that would gladly come to my assistance. It occurred to me then that I was responsible for that. I'm the one responsible for my life. I had every chance to learn the things I didn't know and I ignored those lessons and kept ignoring them until it was too late.

"When I get out of here, I'm going to change my life. I know I want people in my life. I want to find my remaining son and try to develop a relationship with him. He may not need a daddy, but maybe he still needs a father. I'll look for a larger apartment when I get back, so he and his girlfriend can stay with me. And maybe, just maybe I can be an uncle to your grandson Jackson. He looks just like my oldest boy, Denmark. Maybe I can show him the love that I was too foolish to give my own sons. But the first step in all of that is taking the weight and blame off of you. My shoulders are broad enough to carry the weight of my life. If I have any power to forgive, then let it be known I forgive you. I forgive you! Let's go on from here."

With her lips trembling Serena said, "Thank you!" She blinked back tears and slowly reached out again and took Elroy's big callused hand in hers. She began speaking tentatively: "I have a big house, er . . . with lots of room. While you're recuperating maybe you could stay with me. I could make sure you get all the medical attention you need and physical therapy. I've got people working for me who can assist you when you need it. Your son and his girlfriend would be welcome. Please, think about it. You don't have to answer right away. It would be no problem, in fact . . . in fact it would be the best thing that has happened to me in years." Tears began streaming down Serena's cheeks. She didn't bother to wipe them away. She held his hand in both of hers and said, "If you would stay with me, if you would allow me to take care of you, it would be a gift to me. Because . . . because I could really use a son right now. I could really use a son."

Saturday, July 24, 1982

Deleon, San Vicente, Alejandro, and Tercero pushed through the glass doors of Big Boy Bob's on Agua Caliente Boulevard in downtown Tijuana. Big Boy Bob's, called "El Big" by the locals, was an informal meeting place of Tijuana's power merchants. On any given evening, one could find representatives of all the local drug kingpins, the mayor, the commander of the regional federal police force, the municipal police chief, and the head of the state police. Among this bejeweled and mustached assembly were also the heads of the various gangs that trafficked in smuggled flesh; these men, who, when it suited them, raped, robbed, and murdered, were completely at home with their proximity to Tijuana's law enforcement. After all, everyone who had authority with a badge had been paid off. In fact, for the right amount of money, almost anyone could hire law enforcement bodyguards to protect their criminal activities. Deleon had been told all this in the car while en route to town from San Vicente's mansion. He sensed that things were perhaps a shade too joyful. Something wasn't right. This feeling was separate and apart from his unexpressed judgment that it was dangerous to go into Tijuana to see a jai alai match days prior to their scheduled meeting with Jackson. Then, if that wasn't obtuse enough, San Vicente's waltzing into a place like Big Boy's, announcing to everyone that he was on the scene, was utter stupidity. San Vicente had the kind of arrogance that would lead to an early death. It was a weakness that Deleon felt gave him the edge.

As soon as they pushed through the door, heads turned in their direction. A green-uniformed waitress grabbed several menus and deferred to San Vicente's choice of tables. San Vicente led the way to a corner booth as he waved to groups of men along the way. Deleon was offered the opportunity to sit next to San Vicente, so he slid across the padded, red plastic upholstery behind the beige Formica table. Without inquiring of his companions' desires, San Vicente ordered hamburgers and shakes for everyone.

"You see those three people, the two men and a woman sitting by the door," San Vicente said, nodding his head vaguely in the direction they had entered.

Deleon followed his gesture and replied, "Yeah, one of the men has gray hair?"

"They are journalists," San Vicente said with a frown, as if the word *journalist* caused a bad taste. "They are here every night. Sometimes they write their columns about extortion, murder, assassinations and never leave here."

Tercero chuckled. "They don't chase news. It comes to them."

San Vicente continued, "Those four men in the booth across from them are federal police."

Tercero scoffed, *"Pelotón!"*

"What's the Pelotón?" Deleon asked.

San Vicente answered, "It's an organization within the federal police that does dirty work for the Arellanos organization."

Tercero spat, "They kill women and children! Anybody! They don't care."

"They seemed friendly to you," Deleon observed to San Vicente. "They waved and smiled at you when you came in."

"Well, I've hired them to provide security next Tuesday in San Diego for the meeting with Tremain."

Deleon said nothing. He was remembering the hard look he had received from one of those men as he had passed their booth. It all came clear to him. San Vicente had contracted out the hit on him to the Pelotón. He would be taken care of after the meeting with Jackson.

A bald-headed man with a thick black mustache from a nearby booth called to San Vicente, "Hey, Cisco! Carnal! I knew you would be in town. It's jai alai night tonight! El Palacio Frontón hasn't had such a lineup in years. We have ten of the top twenty players in South America here tonight for the opening celebration of Fiesta Santiago. Betting money is flowing like water. I'm putting ten thousand dollars on Nestor Esquival to win it all! I might have a couple of thousand extra for a side bet with you, because I know you're a supporter of García Lomas, the man from Sinaloa."

San Vicente responded enthusiastically: "Aburto, I've got twenty-five thousand in my pocket that says Lomas walks away with everything! And I'm willing to put more money on that new boy, Reynoso, from Mexico City! He will come in second ahead of your Esquival."

Aburto sat silent for a moment doing some mental arithmetic, then he asked, "How much are you willing to put on Reynoso?"

San Vicente retorted, "How much cash do you have?"

"What does it matter?" Aburto shrugged. "You know I'm good for it! I'll give you a check if I lose."

San Vicente shook his head. "The banks will be closed tomorrow and on Monday for the national holiday. Cash bets only. You know your brother still hasn't made good on the IOU he wrote to me. If I see him, I may have to show him how displeased I am about that." San Vicente's tone carried a hint of threat. Aburto shrugged in response and said nothing, but his silence seemed to cover anger.

Further conversation was halted due to the arrival of the shakes and burgers. Throughout the eating of their meal, San Vicente pointed out to Deleon the various tables and booths in which members and henchmen of the drug cartels and human smuggling rings were sitting. As he was munching on a french fry, Deleon asked, "Who's the guy who wants you to accept his check for a bet?"

San Vicente smirked. "He works for the Gaxiola clan, part of the Gulf drug cartel. They've been trying to move in on my territory since spring. I'll take care of them after I deal with Tremain. I've got something planned for those *chenchos!*" Tercero and Alejandro laughed nastily, as if they knew what was in store for Aburto. San Vicente said to Deleon, "You notice even with my enemies sitting ten feet away, I do not carry a handgun. Only bosses who are afraid and insecure carry such weapons! I know no one who is foolish enough to attack me in Tijuana. But even if there were such fools, I would not carry one." San Vicente gestured to Alejandro and Tercero and the members of the Pelotón. "My people would deal with them." He pulled his knife and set it on the table. "If the attackers are close, I will take care of them myself. This blade has taken many lives and will taste the blood of many more." Deleon merely nodded in response. There was no more conversation. The food was finished in silence.

When they left the restaurant, San Vicente waved cheerfully to Aburto and stopped along the way to talk with the men in several other booths and tables. From the way he was greeted it was obvious that San Vicente was among his own and was respected. Deleon filed the information away as he sought to figure out the best method to upset San Vicente's intended plans.

The drive to El Palacio Frontón took five minutes, more because of traffic than due to distance. Bumper to bumper, the cars moved at a stop-and-go pace, while the sidewalks were filled with pedestrians, many of them dressed in traditional folk attire. There were small vendors with propane lights above their stalls and carts, calling out their wares, and strolling mariachis and groups of costumed *folklórico* dancers all drawing approving crowds. When Deleon asked what was going on, he was told that it was the eve of a national holiday, the Feast of Santiago. Tercero said that every campesino between Mexicali and Ensenada would be coming to town tomorrow dressed in their best clothes to participate in the festivities. The crowds would be much greater tomorrow when there was a *chareada* (a Mexican-style rodeo) scheduled in the Plaza de Toros. Alejandro added that it would be a day of drinking and feasting, that he would drink until his bottle was as dry as the Tijuana River.

San Vicente's driver dropped them at a side entrance of El Palacio Frontón which allowed them to enter the huge, Moorish-looking structure without waiting in line. An usher led them through boisterous, milling crowds directly to San Vicente's private box on the second-floor balcony. The box had an excellent view of the jai alai court. San Vicente ordered a bottle of añejo tequila and some cold beer, then began talking over the side wall to the people in the neighboring box.

Deleon sat down in a chair and focused his thoughts on developing a plan of his own. A preliminary jai alai match was already under way. Distractedly, he watched the two players, men in helmets with huge wicker scoops on their right hands, catch and fling a speeding ball against the three-walled court. The crowds cheered every point, some of which were not obvious to Deleon, but he really didn't care. He was assembling all the facts that related to his predicament and shuffling them around. The tequila arrived, along with an ice-cold bucket of bottled San Miguel beer. San Vicente poured shots of tequila for everyone and they toasted to a great night of jai alai. Deleon joined in with a smile. He had developed a plan. He would have to wait until the big matches with the star players began before he initiated the first step.

Esquival and Lomas were playing a hotly contested match when Deleon asked where the toilets were located. San Vicente gestured absentmindedly back toward the stairs that they had ascended. Deleon walked through a crowded hallway toward the stairs, stepped into an alcove, and turned his reversible jacket inside out, from white to blue. Within two minutes, he saw Alejandro looking for him. There was a line of men waiting to get into the second-floor rest rooms. Alejandro, disgruntled at having to leave the box during an important match, walked down the stairs pushing people out of his way. Deleon followed him through the crowds at an appropriate distance. Alejandro made his way to the first-floor rest rooms, which were located next to the food and drink concessions, and stood looking around. Deleon watched Alejandro from the foot of the stairs, trying to determine the best way to lose him. He needed to use a phone and he could not afford to have Alejandro see him using it. A sweaty-faced, fat, barrel-shaped man accidentally lurched into Deleon as he trundled toward the bar. The man looked at Deleon and continued on his way. His look indicated that Deleon didn't merit an apology. On any other evening, Deleon would've been the last person the fat man would ever bump into, but this evening he had bigger fish to fry.

There was a roar from the crowd, then another. The contest between Lomas and Esquival was heating up. People started rushing away from the concessions, heading back to their seats. Alejandro stopped looking around for Deleon and went to stand by the tables overlooking the first-floor seating which had a clearer view of the match. Through a break in the milling people, Deleon saw that Aburto and three tough-looking men were sitting at a nearby table. He saw Alejandro and one of the men exchange glances and saw Alejandro make a derisive gesture to him. Deleon smiled. He now had the means to distract Alejandro. There was another roar and people began shouting in support of their favorite. Deleon looked around and saw the fat man who had bumped into him hurrying with a cardboard tray filled with plastic cups of beer directly toward where Alejandro was standing. When the fat man bustled past him, Deleon stuck out his foot and gave the man a slight shove. The fat man stumbled and barreled right into Alejandro, who in turn was knocked onto Aburto's table.

Deleon didn't wait to see the results. He turned away immediately and went to the bank of phones that he had seen next to the betting windows. There appeared to be one on the end that was unoccupied. Deleon stepped into the phone booth and before he could close the door completely, a tattooed young tough in his early twenties wearing a baseball cap backward and a Dixie flag T-shirt pushed open the door and said, "Hey, gringo, you want to use the phone, you pay me first!"

Deleon smiled. He was pretty sure that this was a straight robbery attempt. He replied, "Sure, step in here. I don't want everyone to see my money."

The tough grinned in response. He squeezed into the booth, shoving the door shut behind him, and stuck his hand in his pocket, probably reaching for a knife. Deleon moved so quickly the tough never had a chance. Deleon hit him in his testicles and when he bent over in surprise, Deleon grabbed his head and snapped his neck. The youth slumped to the floor without a sound. Deleon took his cap and put it on. He then dialed Jackson's number in San Francisco. An answering service answered and Deleon left a message with the booth's phone number. As he waited, he studied the now peaceful face of his victim. The young man had a nice face and a lean, muscular body. Had Deleon seen him while in prison, he would have marked him for sex, and he would've had him, conscious or unconscious. He looked at his watch; at most he could wait safely in the booth for ten minutes. His eyes returned to the body on the floor. The young man would've made an interesting model. He had the heavy-lidded eyes of a Diego Rivera figure. It occurred to Deleon that he hadn't thought about painting since he had come down to Mexico. Further thoughts were interrupted when the phone rang.

Deleon picked up on the second ring. Jackson's voice demanded, "DuMont, is that you?" Deleon smiled and answered, "Glad you could get back to me. I've got a proposition for you."

"I'm listening."

"I'm down here with San Vicente and he is planning to kill both you and your girlfriend."

"How does that differ from you?"

Deleon chuckled. "Why, I only want to kill you. I don't give a damn about your girlfriend. Once you arrive, she can go free as far as I'm concerned."

There was a pause, then Jackson inquired, "If that's the case, why don't you bring her someplace that you and I arrange?"

"Can't do that. Since you drove me out of Frisco, I had to turn her over to San Vicente. He's got her in his mansion at Playa Rosalía."

"What's your proposal?"

"If you attack San Vicente's mansion tomorrow night, I'll help you. I'll knock out his electricity and take care of his security system."

"To what do I owe this generosity? Why would you do that for me?"

Deleon laughed again. "Because San Vicente wants to kill me too."

"Why tomorrow night? That's cutting it close."

"Because tomorrow is a Mexican national holiday. The roads are busy. People will be coming in from the countryside. It's a festival with lots of drinking and carousing. Your arrival and movement will be less obvious then. You should know that San Vicente has people all over this province on the lookout for strangers."

"You'll let Elizabeth go once I arrive?"

"I didn't say that. I don't know if I can free her, but I do know that if you wait until next week it'll be worse for her. She'll be passed around among the men. Her overall chances will be better if you come tomorrow."

"What time?"

"After ten at night; by then everybody but security staff will have gone home, and those that remain will be feeling no pain."

"What assurance have I that you're just not trying to lure me in?"

"None! You'll just have to take my word. Oh, if you want to increase your chances of success, you'll hit the Gaxiola clan before you attack San Vicente. Along with the holiday festivities that should provide enough of a diversion for the authorities."

Jackson said grimly, "I'll be seeing you tomorrow."

Deleon smiled and said, "I look forward to it." He hung up the phone and looked down at the tough. He wrestled the body into the seat then propped it up against the wall. He took the phone off the hook and nestled it on the dead man's shoulder. He touched the man's cheek regretfully. He would've liked to have had sex with him before he killed him. Now that he was dead, it was too late. Deleon had had sex with dead men a couple of times while in prison and had found it to be thoroughly unsatisfying. Unconscious was one thing, but dead was just cold, unresponsive flesh. He reversed his jacket to white and whistled as he walked through the crowds away from the booth. Tomorrow was going to be very interesting.

Saturday, July 24, 1982

R hasan was standing in the kitchen eating Theresa's chile rellenos when the call from Deleon came in. Since his Muir Woods meeting with his uncle, he had gotten in the habit of coming by the house and occasionally spending the night. He was enthralled by all that his uncle was involved in and he loved Theresa's cooking. The chile rellenos were the best he had ever eaten, but he stopped chewing to listen to the ensuing conversation between the men in the dining room.

"What did I tell you. I knew that San Vicente would be in Tijuana!" Carlos declared after Jackson related his conversation with Deleon. "Everything leads to his hacienda at Rosalía Beach!"

Jackson conceded, "Okay, you were right, but how do we mount any kind of effective effort in one day? My grandfather used to say, 'Only fools and dead men rush in.' How do we prevent ourselves from being caught in a trap?"

Pres interjected, "I thought your grandfather had an organization. Can't you utilize that?"

Jackson shook his head. "When you go after big-time drug dealers, you can't use mercenaries or people other than those you trust on the deepest level. The money that cartels can pay for information or collaboration can allow a person and his whole family to retire for the rest of their lives. Plus, we don't have the time to set anything up." Jackson turned to Carlos. "How many trusted people can you field by tomorrow?"

Carlos sighed and responded, "I've sent three men to New Orleans. I can't reach them until they check in, so including the Ramirez brothers and Esteban, I have five and that's not enough to attack a fortified position. Actually, I have seven, but I'll use Tavio and Diego for cutting the phone lines around San Vicente's compound, then I'll have them hit the Gaxiolas with rocket launchers. That's a two-man job and nobody else knows the roads and terrain around Tijuana."

Jackson nodded. "A diversion."

"It's the smart move," Carlos agreed. "As for our attack force, I'm counting you and me in that seven as well. With more time I could have fifteen men, but not within twenty-four hours."

Pres asked, "Are you counting me?" Carlos shook his head. Pres tapped his chest. "Three and a half years in Vietnam. I've been in firefights and hand-to-hand combat!"

Carlos conceded, "Okay, we can use you."

Pres continued, "How many would be enough?"

"Ideally, I'd like fifteen, but we have a good chance of success with twelve."

Pres stated, "I can get you at least one more."

Jackson frowned. "Who?"

"Dominique. She's probably a better shot than any of us."

"She would come in on this?" Jackson questioned. "You talked to her?"

"Yeah, she told me to tell you that you can count on her in any effort to save Elizabeth. She feels she owes you."

Jackson glanced at Carlos for his opinion. Carlos nodded and said, "She's a professional. We can use her."

"What about Dan and Lincoln?" Pres suggested.

Carlos waved his hand in dismissal. "They're not trained. They aren't field tested. We're talking about killing people, we're not talking about shooting targets."

Pres replied, "Lincoln is a black belt in aikido as well as a crack shot with a rifle. And Dan's a better shot than he is. Dan is better with a rifle than Jackson. He hunts every chance he gets and he always brings something home."

Jackson asked Carlos, "Can we do this with less people?"

"No! From what I know of San Vicente's layout, we need at least seven to go in, two to remain outside with rocket launchers to stop reinforcements, and one to guard our vehicles."

Jackson frowned. "How did you come up with these numbers?"

"I studied San Vicente's layout before. Your grandfather was considering putting a hit on him and his two brothers about five years ago until a truce was worked out. I had aerial shots taken of his place at the time, and I bet he hasn't done much to change things since then."

Carlos picked up a lined tablet and began to sketch. "We'll get better plans before the attack, but here's what I remember of the layout. Guard towers are here. His communications center is here and his power generator is here. After we cut all the phone lines in his area, we'll use the rocket launchers to take out his communications center and satellite dish. Two of our force will go inside, situate themselves here, and take out his power plant and generator. Two others will take this position to destroy his guard towers and give us covering machine gun fire. These four will be responsible for keeping any extra men in the barracks pinned down. The remaining three will go down inside, blow his arsenal, and find Elizabeth. I'd rather have six of us to go inside; that way we could make certain that we killed both Deleon and San Vicente in the process." Carlos sighed. "Three will have to do."

"We still only have nine people," Jackson observed with some frustration. "Your plan requires twelve. If we can't do it with less men . . ." He put his face in his hands.

Pres asked Carlos, "Only the three that are going in the main house are going to be moving around, right? The other four are stationary? If that's true, why can't we use Dan and Lincoln in these stationary positions? They're good shots. They could do this!"

Jackson wondered, "Are they still in town? They haven't left yet?"

Pres answered, "Dan doesn't join Anu in D.C. until next Friday and Lincoln and Sandra can't get out of here until next week."

Carlos asked, "Is this something they would do?"

"All we can do is ask," Pres replied with a shrug.

"Even if they accept, we still have only eleven," Jackson observed. "Where are we going to get the other person?" Carlos pointed behind Jackson to Rhasan, who was standing in the doorway with a pleading look on his face. Jackson shook his head. "I can't do that. If he got hurt, I would never forgive myself. He's not ready for this. He doesn't know what he's getting into!"

Rhasan argued, "You said I was a man, that you'd treat me like a man."

"This isn't about being a man!" Jackson retorted. "Killing people has nothing to do with manhood or anything respectable! The reason I don't want to take you is that you are untrained!"

Rhasan sputtered, "You were eighteen when you went after the Jaguar!"

Jackson turned to Carlos. "You told him about that?"

Carlos shrugged. "I told him the history behind this conflict. You said don't lie to him. I didn't lie."

"Did you tell him that from the time I was eight until I was eighteen I was trained to use guns and fight? Did you tell him that despite that training, I was responsible for the death of El Indio and the wounding of Esteban? That I almost jeopardized our escape route? That I punked out and didn't finish the job? Did you tell him all that?"

"No, because that is not what I remember. No wonder you were so angry with your grandfather. You have held yourself responsible all of this time? That is strange. I remember you being more man than you knew you were. There was never a time that you did not make your grandfather or the rest of us proud. You have his heart, his will, and his courage!"

Jackson was moved by Carlos's confirmation. He looked down at the floor and said, "You look on me more kindly than I deserve."

Carlos replied, "Put aside your memories; they do not do you justice."

Jackson exhaled. "Whether my memory serves me or not, I still cannot agree to let Rhasan join us—"

Rhasan interjected, "When do I become a man? When do I have a say about how I will live my life? Will you be watching over me, sheltering me forever?"

Jackson asked with an air of fatigue, "What about our agreement, the one we discussed at Muir Woods? After you finish college, you'll join in."

"Circumstances have changed! You need me *now!*" You are my uncle, the only man who has ever reached out to me and been there when I needed him! Now, you are telling me that I can't be there for you? What's up with that? I know this is dangerous, but it is important to me to be called upon and be used when my family needs me. What kind of man would I be if I didn't feel this way?"

Carlos stood up and suggested, "Why don't you see if your other friends will join us? Then if they agree, make your decision about

Rhasan. I'd recommend we give him a flak jacket, an Uzi, and let him guard our vehicles. He can handle it. He's a tough kid just like you were, and there should be only limited danger. Now I have to make arrangements for our travel and contact people in Mexico." Carlos left the room.

Jackson looked at Rhasan for a long moment and was about to speak when he was interrupted by Pres. "I'm going to get Dan and Lincoln on the phone. Where do you want to meet?"

"East Bay. We can meet at the Dock of the Bay in an hour."

Pres nodded, "I'll get on the horn now."

After Pres left the room Jackson reluctantly said to Rhasan, "If they agree to come along, I'll need you. But you'll have to do exactly as you are told!" Rhasan ran to his uncle and gave him a bear hug. Jackson protested, "Don't hug me! I'm not doing you a favor!"

"Yes, you are, Uncle Jax! Yes, you are!"

"Well, I hope I don't regret it."

"You won't!"

Carlos came to the door with a yellow pad in his hand. "Good. Now that that's settled, Rhasan, I need you to go by army surplus. I've got a list of things we're going to need." Rhasan jumped up enthusiastically to do Carlos's bidding.

After Rhasan left the room, Jackson walked into the kitchen and watched as Pres hung up the phone. He said, "I hope this decision to let Rhasan join us doesn't come back to haunt me."

"Only God knows and only time will tell." Pres stood up and walked over to Jackson. He put his hand on his friend's shoulder and said, "Let's roll."

As they walked out the door, Carlos advised, "If your friends decide to come along, tell them to be at Moffit Field by four tomorrow morning." He handed Jackson the sketch of San Vicente's compound. "This should help explain what they will be required to do." Then he whispered in Jackson's ear.

Jackson looked at Carlos, then a smile spread across his face. "Of course," he acknowledged. "Of course!"

The meeting with Lincoln and Dan did not last long. As they sat around a table in the nearly empty bar, Jackson laid out the plan of attack and emphasized that the plan could not be undertaken without their assistance. No one spoke after he finished. Finally, Jackson prodded them, "What do you think?"

Dan shook his head and said, "I love you and you're my brother, but

I think this is some crazy shit! I can't do this! I'm not a soldier! Even if I wanted to, I'm out of shape. I get exhausted going for pizzas!"

"Oh, come on," Pres protested. "You're always bragging about how you had to hike ten to fifteen miles away from your truck to bag an elk. How bad a shape can you be in?"

Dan explained, "There's no pressure in hunting. I take my time. And believe me, if elk had high-powered weapons, I wouldn't be hunting them! Anyway, I wouldn't be an asset for this mission. I'd just get my fat ass shot off!"

"This is not a suicide mission!" Jackson declared. "I love Elizabeth and I will do everything in my power to rescue her, but I will not needlessly risk your lives. Rhasan is also coming with us. If I didn't think we had a high probability of success, I wouldn't allow him to come and I wouldn't ask you. This is a solid plan and we'll have an update on any changes in fortifications before we commence. Flak jackets will be issued to everyone and we'll have the element of surprise on our side."

Dan shrugged. "I appreciate that, but can't you get somebody else? I mean, hire real professionals?"

Jackson shook his head. "Not by tomorrow." Then he looked at Lincoln, waiting for his response.

Lincoln took a deep breath and said, "I owe you and I want to help you. I would come to you if something like this happened to Sandra, but I've got some serious concerns. Going to Mexico to attack a drug lord on his home turf doesn't sound smart, I don't care what kind of holiday it is. No matter how well planned you have this, there is a real possibility one or more of us could be killed! They have rocket launchers too!"

Jackson nodded. "I wouldn't lie to you. This is dangerous. I wouldn't ask you if I didn't really need you. All I can say is we'll surprise them and hit them hard before they can mount a defense!"

"There's another concern I have," Lincoln continued. "Neither Dan nor I has ever killed anyone. We—"

"Wrong!" Jackson corrected. "Have you forgotten the Mission Street Titans? My grandfather's head of security disposed of three bodies that night: the one that Wesley clocked with that lead pipe, the one Dan knocked down those stairs, and the one you drove over when we were trying to get away."

There was another period of silence, then Dan barked, "They really were dead? We weren't just drunk?"

Pres surmised, "So that's why it never made the papers."

Lincoln tapped the table and said, "Even if that's true, we have never killed anyone with premeditation. And I for one don't know that I have the nerve to do that!"

"I'm not worried about your nerve," Jackson replied. "I'd trust you with my life."

"That's what scares me," Lincoln admitted.

Dan asked Pres, "You're going, I take it?"

Pres nodded and replied, "Got to be there for my village."

Dan looked at Lincoln then pointed to the sketch. "Go over the plan again and tell me exactly what I have to do."

Jackson recounted the plan once more and once again was met with silence. There were a few questions then more silence.

Dan shook his head. "I don't know about this, man."

Lincoln asked, "Once we're inside the compound, we don't have to move? We shoot from cover?"

"Like you're hunting from a blind," Jackson confirmed. He watched as they studied the sketch and when he thought he saw a weakening in their reluctance he said, "Let me sweeten the pot. As managers, you guys made between forty and fifty thousand last year, am I right?"

Lincoln and Dan nodded, but Pres scoffed, "I wish!"

Jackson stated, "I'll give you five million dollars each if you come with me! You'll get the money whether we rescue Elizabeth or not. You can live quite well on the interest of the principal. Even if you only get six percent a year, that'll be more than six times your annual salary. You can have the lives you've always dreamed about!" There was another silence.

"Five million dollars!" Dan grunted. "That's a lot of money! It would solve a lot of my problems, that's for sure." He looked intently into Jackson's eyes, seeking to plumb their depths.

"Go ahead and accept," Jackson urged, meeting Dan's stare with a smile. "I know you love me and I know you want to help me, but I also know this is a dangerous thing to ask."

Lincoln interjected, "You're offering us money to come with you? We're not mercenaries! Five million dollars can't buy our lives!"

"I know it can't!" Jackson retorted. "I'm in a tough situation right now. If I had time I'd use the total resources that I had at my disposal and I'd probably spend fifteen to twenty million dollars hiring the best professionals and equipment I could find to mount this assault. But I don't have time. So the money that I would pay strangers, I'm offering to the people I love. It will serve as a form of insurance for your families should the worst happen."

"You really have access to that kind of money?" Dan asked. "That's fifteen million dollars sitting around this table!"

Jackson confirmed with a nod of his head, "Twenty million, counting Wesley's family. Yes! I have it!"

Lincoln was also studying Jackson and when he spoke he pushed his words as if they were pawns on a chessboard. "There is no doubt, five million dollars would change the quality of our lives. But if I go with you, it won't be for the money. It'll be because of our relationship and I trust that you have a good plan."

Jackson nodded. "Understood."

Lincoln continued, "You told us the bulk of your grandfather's estate was in those lost certificates. Does your offer depend upon finding these certificates?"

Dan concluded, "Suppose no one finds the certificates?"

"The answer to your questions, gentlemen, is that your families will be taken care of whether we come back or not. My grandfather has enough property and other assets to pay this agreement in full whether the certificates are ever found or not. I will draw up a letter indicating these amounts as the legal debt that I owe each of you. I'll get the appropriate language from my attorney and get it notarized tonight. You'll have your notarized statements before we take off."

Lincoln pushed back from the table. "I need to talk with Sandra. Can I get back to you in an hour?" Jackson nodded.

"I don't need to talk to Anu. She'd never agree anyway," Dan said with a shrug, then a grim smile spread across his face. He stuck his thumb up and said, "Five million dollars buys a lot of gumption. I'm definitely in. And there ain't no discussion on that."

"Thank you! Your participation means the world to me!"

Lincoln stood up and said to Jackson, "We're going to be placing our lives in your hands tomorrow morning. I'm hoping that your intelligence work is accurate."

Jackson stood up as well. "The best that money can buy."

When Pres and Jackson returned to the house, they sat discussing the logistics of the raid with Carlos.

Carlos explained, "The plane will be here at two-thirty tomorrow morning. We'll leave for Ensenada around six in the morning. We don't have a definite takeoff time yet, but everyone should be at Moffit by four. We'll meet up with the Ramirez brothers when we arrive. Tell people to wear black and just to bring one change of clothes and toiletries. Weapons, flak jackets, and everything else will be provided. We'll go over the plan of attack and everybody's assignment while we're in the air. We'll go over it again when we arrive and make whatever changes are necessary."

The phone rang. It was Lincoln confirming his participation.

Pres concluded, "I guess we're a go. Okay, we'll be there by four. See you tomorrow morning."

Jackson and Carlos were left in the dining room looking over Carlos's hand-drawn layout of San Vicente's mansion. Jackson asked, "How do we keep the police out of this? From what you've told me San Vicente is pretty well connected in Tijuana."

Carlos smiled. "One of my cousins, Tomás Zacatecas, works in Tijuana in a police outfit called Grupo Beta. He's going to help us."

"Grupo Beta? What's that?"

"They primarily spend time protecting illegal immigrants from getting raped and robbed by thugs and other police agencies; sometimes they even have shoot-outs with other police. He's one of the good guys and he hates San Vicente. He'll put out the word that San Vicente is going to war with Gaxiola; that'll keep the federales and the police out of it for a while. Unless they get paid up front, they don't generally get involved in drug dealers' wars."

"How much time will that give us?"

"Max? Maybe an hour from the time we fire the first shots. And we only have that much time because San Vicente's mansion is pretty far out of Tijuana and almost everybody will be celebrating the holiday. Get that map of Mexico off the shelf. I want to go over with you our possible escape routes and the weapons we'll need."

Jackson retrieved the map and said forcefully, "This is different from eighteen years ago. There'll be no stopping this time until I've rescued Elizabeth and I've killed them all!" It was no longer his grandfather's world in which he had become entangled, it was now his own. The men he was fighting were his enemies and the responsibility for success lay firmly on his shoulders. As he bent over the map and focused his attention on Carlos's discussion there was no doubt in his mind that the name Tremain would once again instill fear.

Wednesday, June 26, 1964

The rain began as they left the lodge and it fell as if a hole had opened in the heavens. Sheets of water traveled across a darkened landscape like waves rushing an unknown coast. The rain drummed on the canvas top of the jeep with the roar of a drum corps playing an eternal funeral march. Visibility was extremely poor, but all Jackson had to do was follow the taillights of the vehicle in front of him. There were periods of straight highway, but for the most part the road was tortuous as it curved around the foothills of Durango. They drove without a break for two hours. It was six-thirty in the evening and the rain had ceased by the time they drove down into a small valley which contained an isolated dirt airstrip. As he got out of the jeep, Jackson wondered whether Maria was still alive.

A twenty-passenger plane waited at the end of the airstrip next to a small hangar. Five men were already on the plane waiting when they boarded. No sooner than they had fastened their seat belts, the plane was airborne. Jackson was introduced around. The only man that he had known previously was Esteban Muñoz. He was one of the men who had taught Jackson how to ride and take care of horses when Jackson was ten years old. Esteban greeted him warmly and acknowledged that Jackson had grown into a strong young man. Jackson nodded in response, but said nothing. The seriousness of the situation inhibited light discussion. The flight lasted three hours. The plane landed at another airstrip identical to the first, except there was no hangar. Jackson rubbed his legs to get the blood circulating and exited the plane behind Carlos. Night had now fallen and with it came a cold and gusting wind. Jackson was unprepared for the chill and force of the gusts. It nearly blew his straw hat, with El Indio's feather, off his head.

"Give me the feather," said Carlos, leading Jackson around the plane's wing toward the luggage bay. "I'll put it away for you, so you'll be able to take it home with you. The hat you can lose."

A large, metal-paneled truck pulled up to the edge of the runway. Jackson helped Carlos carry a heavy box that had BAZOOKA stenciled on its lid. He teamed with Carlos until all of the plane's baggage had been loaded into the side compartments of the truck. Jackson noticed that they unloaded considerably more equipment from the plane than they had taken on. He had seen boxes containing short-barreled trench mortars and automatic rifles being loaded into the truck along with numerous wooden boxes of ammunition.

Jackson was watching the lights of the plane as it taxied and lifted off into the overcast night sky when his grandfather clapped him on the shoulder and handed him a sheepskin coat and a bandolier of shotgun shells. His grandfather gestured to the bandolier and said, "That's for your 'pig' gun." The old man turned and walked away before his grandson could respond. Jackson watched as his grandfather continued to bark out orders and direct traffic.

There was no doubt in Jackson's mind now, he was participating in a war. He had little time to ponder this thought, for the call was given to climb aboard. He followed Carlos into the back of the truck and pushed past a heavy woolen curtain into the bright atmosphere of fluorescent lights. The truck's interior had been converted to a control center. There was a bank of shortwave radio equipment sitting on a counter at the far end of the compartment and fold-down padded benches were situated along the sides.

Carlos waved Jackson to a seat and went to stand beside El Negro, who was sitting next to Hernando at the radio. Hernando was wearing earphones and flipping switches on the bank of radio equipment. Jackson felt a surge and a slow rocking as the truck turned and got under way. Culio sat down next to him and indicated that he should fasten his seat belt. The ride was rough until they reached a highway then it was easygoing. After they had been driving about half an hour, foil-wrapped packages of soft-shell tacos were handed out along with big bottles of Fanta soda. Jackson gobbled his tacos down. He had forgotten how hungry he was. There was no taste to the food, it merely satisfied his hunger. He could not savor it.

The pins and needles of anxiety began to prick Jackson's consciousness. He wondered how he would react to killing a human, whether he would experience a guilt greater than any he had previously known. And sometimes, in moments of confusion, he let his thoughts drift to Maria. He had tried not thinking about her, to stifle his concern for her, but his will was not equal to the task. The fear that she was already dead was strong and he could not rid himself of its clammy logic.

The truck pulled off the road and Jackson's grandfather led a briefing on the attack. The plan involved a direct assault on the Jaguar's home base, located in an isolated area fifty miles outside of Linares. El Negro stated that the Jaguar had sent a party of at least twenty of his top men in the attack on the hunting lodge, and according to the radio transmission from the spies that Carlos had planted, the party had just returned within the hour. The report indicated that there were many injured among the survivors, which meant that the number of trained men left to guard the base would be significantly reduced.

King declared that the element of surprise was on their side because the Jaguar didn't expect any assault until the next morning, but that there wasn't much time because reinforcements had been sent for from Linares and surrounding towns. The additional men were expected to arrive in the next three hours. Jackson listened as his grandfather, El Indio, and Carlos discussed the strategy of the attack and gave out assignments. He did not hear his name mentioned. He was both relieved and concerned. He was not sure how he would react under fire, but he didn't want to be left out of the action. Wooden crates were hauled out of the side compartments and carried into the truck. Carlos broke them open with a crowbar. Machine pistols with silencers and extra magazines were distributed. Out of another crate bulletproof vests were issued. From a third crate military-issue, thick-barreled M16s were handed out. The truck was abuzz with activity as men strapped on their vests and checked out their weapons.

King walked over and sat next to his grandson.

"This is a pretty fancy rig, Grandfather," Jackson said nervously, gesturing around to the truck's compartment.

"Yeah, we got a couple of these trucks. It's a good way to command an operation. We keep in touch by shortwave. Carlos brought this idea from one of his security seminars." King looked around at the rest of the men checking their guns and asked, "We're about ready to hit it. You ready for this?" He stared at Jackson's face.

Jackson took a deep breath and exhaled. "I think so."

"Thinkin' ain't enough, boy! There can't be no hesitation! This is life and death! Is you ready?"

"I've never killed anyone before, Grandfather. I don't know."

"Killin' folk is the easiest part. Just squeeze the trigger. It's how you react to them tryin' to kill you that matters. People is different from pigs. They find a way to fight back."

"I'm not coming with you because I want to kill, Grandfather. I'm coming along because I want to rescue Maria. I want to take her back to the States with me."

His grandfather chuckled with surprise. "That girl is smarter than I thought! Got yo' nose open in four days! Many a man done lost his life over a triangle of hair. It be a hell of a thing to lose yo' life just for some pussy. You sho' this is what you want? You prepared to kill to get her back?"

Jackson stared at his grandfather's dark, glittering eyes and retorted in clipped tones, "She's not just some pussy to me and I'll do whatever's necessary to get her back."

"Then we's in business, ain't we? You come with me and El Indio, but let me tell you straight up, Grandson. Here's what's necessary: Kill everyone you see, otherwise you gon' put yo'self or somebody else in danger. If we want to leave here alive and uninjured, there can't be no hesitation or mercy. This is for keeps! You ready?"

"I'll do what is necessary, Grandfather," Jackson replied in a flat, tone-less voice.

"I'll take you at yo' word. Let's shake on it." His grandfather stood up and held out his hand. Jackson rose and took his grandfather's hand. The old man turned and called to Carlos, "Toss me one of them vests for my grandson, and he needs an M16 too."

Jackson put the bulky vest on underneath his sheepskin coat and waited for his orders. El Indio came over and knelt in front of him. By the light of a flashlight, he drew a diagram in the dirt and explained Jackson's assignment. After everyone was briefed, they loaded back in the truck and rode to the point of disembarkation.

The wind whistled as it blew over the dark and broken landscape of the mesa, rustling the leaves and branches of the desert vegetation. The night sky was overcast and grim, hiding the moon and the stars with a dense layer of dark, moisture-filled clouds. Jackson turned up his sheep-skin collar against the wind and followed El Indio up the steep incline of a brush- and scrub-covered ridge. In the darkness, he could barely see the ground beneath his feet and caught several branches across the face as he hastened through the underbrush to keep El Indio in sight. The old Indian was a silent silhouette moving quickly through the inky darkness. They reached the crest of the ridge and followed it until it peaked and descended to the mesa.

A small, darkened guardhouse stood on the edge of the ridge, over-looking a large, walled compound. As he neared the small building, Jackson saw his grandfather drag a man's body by the feet around the back of it. Jackson shifted the M16 to the crook of his arm and checked its operation quickly. It was a customized weapon fitted with an extra-thick barrel which served as both a silencer and flash protector. Once he satisfied himself that all was in working order, he walked over to where his grandfather and El Indio stood waiting for a signal from Carlos. The compound consisted of a high wall surrounding a jumble of stucco buildings around a larger fortlike structure in the back of the compound. Jackson estimated that the buildings within the compound could easily house more than a hundred people. Three quick flashes of light emanated from the far wall of the compound and were repeated.

"That's him!" King declared. "He's cut the phone wire and disabled the radio antenna!"

Another light flashed twice and was repeated. This signal originated from the nearer wall of the compound. "That's Hernando. He's taken care of the two sentries guarding this side of the wall. We've got ten minutes to get over the wall before the outside patrol comes around again. Let's get to steppin'!"

They started down the darkened hillside at a trot, occasionally sliding through the brush on the hard clay and laterite of the slope. Jackson kept his automatic rifle in front of him to protect his face from being lashed by branches in the underbrush. At the foot of the ridge there was about a fifty-foot strip of cleared ground to cross before the walls could be reached. Jackson waited behind a low-lying thicket for his grandfather's signal. When the three quick flashes came from the edge of the wall, all three men ran full throttle across the security zone. Jackson was the first one to the wall; the two older men were close behind but breathing heavily. A ladder made of rope was thrown over the wall and the men used it to enter the compound. They dropped down into an unlighted alley between buildings.

Carlos led them through a maze of alleyways until they reached the base of the fortlike main house. They stopped at a small door opening down into a cellar. "This is the way in behind the bar. The passageway up to El Jaguar's chambers is off the main room. We've got machine gun lanes set up at both ends of the street fronting on this building. Once you take care of the bodyguards in the bar, there should be no further resistance."

King looked at his watch and asked, "How long do we have before the mortars start fallin'?"

Carlos answered, "Ten minutes. Then you have twenty minutes to get the Jaguar and get out. We'll open fire on this building with the bazookas in thirty minutes from now. The truck will be waiting around the back of the compound."

"What about Maria?" Jackson demanded.

Carlos said, "If she's alive and in this compound, she'll be in this building. Tigre has a small apartment underneath the Jaguar's suite."

King opened the door and said, "Let's hit it and quit it! The clock is ticking!" He stepped down into the darkness of the cellar and with the narrow beam of a flashlight led the way to a flight of stairs. Turning off the flashlight and using only the light which issued from under the door at the top of the stairs, he motioned to Jackson to stay behind him and stealthily ascended the steps. At the top of the stairs King pushed the door open a crack. He peered through the crack for a couple of minutes before signaling to El Indio to follow him. The two men squatted down and pushed through the doorway behind the bar.

Sweat was running down Jackson's face as he climbed the stairs after his grandfather. The bulletproof vest and the sheepskin coat weighed heavily on his shoulders and obstructed his movements. Conversely, the rifle felt light as a toy in his hands. He pushed open the door and crawled to a kneeling position behind the long, wooden bar. There was no sign of either El Indio or his grandfather. The coarse sound of men laughing and telling bawdy stories in Spanish floated over the bar. Jackson did not know which direction to take around the bar, so he sat still and waited. His heart was pounding and the sweat fell in streams off his brow. He kept swiveling his head in opposite directions, trying to keep both entrances behind the bar in view.

A chair scraped at a table and a man's voice said in the thick idiom of the local people of Linares that he wanted mescal, that he was tired of tequila. His boots trod unevenly toward the bar. Jackson could hear chairs being pushed aside as the footsteps came around from the left side of the bar. Jackson pulled the slide and fed a bullet quietly into the chamber of his M16 and waited. The man staggered into view and frowned confusedly when he saw Jackson on the floor. He swayed back and forth for a moment as he attempted to focus his alcohol-soaked mind on the image before him. The frown changed into an expression of anger and he reached for something in his belt. Jackson fired a burst into the man's chest, sending him backward across the table behind him.

Voices of alarm were raised. Jackson heard some men get to their feet. Then he heard the soft, puffing noise of the machine pistols, followed by the sound of bullets chipping and glancing off adobe walls. There were groans and cries of pain as men fell to the floor dead or wounded. Jackson stayed on the floor behind the bar. He was afraid to stand up amid the whizzing of bullets.

A door across from the right entrance to the bar opened timidly and a head poked out. Juan Tejate and Jackson Tremain were staring at each other. Tejate rammed the door all the way open and sprinted to a long stairway leading to a level beneath the bar. Jackson was on his feet immediately and flying after Tejate. When he reached the top of the stairwell, bullets zinged past like miniature jets. Tejate had pulled a revolver and was firing up the stairs. Jackson reached around the corner and returned the fire with two blasts of his pig gun. He heard Tejate yelp in pain and fall down the stairs.

When he looked cautiously down the stairwell, Jackson saw a bloody Tejate pull himself to his feet and limp out of view. Jackson reloaded his pig gun as he descended the stairs. From the foot of the steps he saw Tejate at the end of a short hall struggling to open a heavy, wooden door. There was debris on the floor blocking the door's passage, but Tejate only tried to kick it out of the way as he strained to open the heavy door. He had gotten the door cracked when Jackson put on a burst of speed and flung himself against the door. He hit the door full tilt with his shoulder, causing it to slam shut.

Tejate screamed as the fingers of his right hand crunched in the heavy vise of the door and the jamb. Jackson slammed the butt of his rifle into Tejate's chest and the man fell backward onto the floor. Jackson pointed his pig gun at Tejate and demanded, "Where's Maria?"

Juan pulled himself to a sitting position against the wall, holding his crushed hand in front of him. He was bleeding steadily from wounds in both his side and back.

"Who?" Tejate asked with a humorless laugh. "You want to know about that *puta?*"

Jackson threatened, "Watch your mouth, you bastard, or I'll blast you where you lay!"

"Oh, you like her, huh? I'll tell you about her, *maricón.* She was still tight and sweet when I had her, but I was one of the first. A friend told me that by the time he'd had her, she was all loose and bloody! She was useless, didn't put any effort in it. Some women forget where they come from! I think somebody shot her in the head and left her on the side of the highway."

The hand holding the pig gun fell to Jackson's side. The air was taken out of him. He could not have pictured worse news. Images of Maria flashed across his consciousness, reminding him that he would never have her company again, or lie sated from lovemaking in a darkened room with her. She was dead.

Out of the corner of his eye, Jackson saw Juan fingering his boot with his good hand and felt a sudden rush of anger. Here was one of the vandals who had robbed Jackson of his dream, this man who had no other purpose in life but to destroy the things he did not have the class to possess. Jackson fired both barrels into Juan's body just as Juan pulled the knife from his boot. The acrid smell of cordite filled the small space. Jackson did not give Juan's bloody body a second glance before he turned away.

Jackson reloaded his pig gun as he slowly climbed the stairs. He felt no regret at having killed Tejate yet he was despondent. He stepped out from behind the bar and saw carnage all around him. There were perhaps ten dead men lying about on the floor and the smell of their blood was sickening. From the other side of the compound he heard the explosion of mortars. The blasts shook the walls and rattled the windows. He picked up his rifle and climbed the stairs that led up to the Jaguar's chambers and Tigre's apartment. He went through Tigre's rooms to ensure himself that Maria had not been hidden away, then continued up to the Jaguar's suite. As soon as he walked through the doors of the lavishly furnished suite, Jackson heard someone screaming in agony.

He heard his grandfather's voice growling out questions; there was a pause then more screams. Jackson pushed open the door slowly and saw El Indio's gun pointing at him. His grandfather was standing over an old, bald-headed man with a pair of bloody shears. The bald-headed man was trembling on his knees with pain. Jackson's grandfather looked at Jackson and said, "You don't want to see this! I got twenty minutes to kill this fool and I'm gon' take all of it! El Indio, take him out of here and cover the machine guns' retreat."

Jackson protested, "Is this why we're here, Grandfather, to torture old men?"

"This is the Jaguar! This man gave the orders to attack my home and family! He will pay with what little he has left as slowly as I can make it! I should have killed him years ago!"

El Indio led Jackson away as the Jaguar gave out a long, high shriek; it was a piercing and grating sound of terrible pain. Jackson knew he would remember the sounds the Jaguar made before he died; that and the sound of the wind howling over the tortured hills would hold the essence of this visit for him.

El Indio told Jackson to guard the alley leading to their departure point. Jackson climbed up on a roof to get a better view. The far side of the compound was ablaze and the fire was spreading fast. Jackson could hear the panicked screams of women and children amid the shouts of men's voices as people mobilized to fight the fire. He saw a figure with clothes aflame run out of a burning house and fall in the street. Jackson was suddenly nauseous. He bent over and retched until he had nothing more in his stomach. He had come to find Maria. He had not come to kill everyone he saw or torture old men. Now that Maria was dead, Jackson had no further interest in participating in his grandfather's wars. He wanted to throw his gun down and just leave the compound, but he understood that others were depending upon him to protect their line of retreat. He exhaled slowly and tried to focus on his responsibility. He stared out into the dark areas of the compound that were unaffected by the fires now raging on the far perimeter. He saw dark shapes frenziedly running back and forth in the distant shadows but did not shoot because he didn't want to kill anybody else, and in particular he didn't want to fire on women and children. Whoever they were, he figured that if they weren't threatening the line of retreat, there was no need to kill them.

Waiting quietly on the roof was proving difficult. He was growing increasingly nervous and impatient. For the first time in many years, he knew that he would be happy to see his grandmother's house again. Salty sweat ran into his eyes and caused a stinging sensation. He put down his rifle and rubbed his eyes frantically, wiping away the sweat. He kept his face in his hands for a moment, trying to calm himself. Soon the whole thing would be over and he would be on his way back to the States. This was the last trip to Mexico to visit his grandfather that he would ever make.

Jackson looked up and saw a bare-chested man with a machete slip across an alley into the shadows. Jackson picked up his rifle and stared into the darkness. He cursed his stupidity for allowing himself to be inattentive. He searched the jumble of alleys and buildings looking for the man. Then he saw fire reflected in the gleam of the machete's blade as the weapon rose out of the shadows and chopped downward swiftly. A man stumbled out from between the buildings and dropped to his knees in the street. The man's hat slipped off his head and fell to the ground. Even in the darkness, Jackson could see El Indio's black, high-domed hat with the wide brim lying in the dirt. The man with the machete stepped into view and raised the weapon for the killing shot. He never finished his swing.

Jackson emptied his clip into the man's body and the machete fell from his hands as the impact of the bullets knocked him out of view. Out of the corner of his eye, Jackson saw the flash of a gun and ducked down. That reflex action saved his life. A fusillade of bullets raked the stucco just above where he was lying, throwing particles and dust in every direction. Jackson was protected by the raised edge of the roof, but he was pinned down on his back. The barrage of bullets continued for what seemed like hours, chipping away the veneer of stucco and exposing the building materials beneath.

Jackson tried to shimmy on his back out of the line of fire, but the combined bulk of the sheepskin coat and the vest beneath it prevented him from moving rapidly. Still, he struggled to get deeper into the shadows. A loud explosion shook the walls of the compound and lit the buildings and surrounding landscape with its incandescence. Several other lesser explosions followed upon the heels of the first. Jackson lifted up and tried quickly to roll over the lip of the roof down into the safety of the alley, but the lower hem of his sheepskin coat snagged on a nail along the edge and left him dangling a foot or two above the ground. He fought to free himself from the coat, but he could not drop out of it. He tried raising his arms and kicking his legs. Fear caused him to struggle frantically.

On the periphery of his vision, Jackson saw the shape of a man break from the shadows and run in his direction. He tried to bring the M16 around to bear on his assailant, but he had begun to slip out of the coat and could not get the weapon pointed in the right direction. He saw the gleam of a machete blade flash toward him and then felt the sensation of falling. He landed awkwardly on one leg and fell on top of his rifle. He pulled his pig gun from its holster and rolled to a sitting position, ready to fire. Hernando shoved the machete back into its scabbard and saluted Jackson before he ran back to his post.

Jackson stood up slowly and shrugged out of the coat. He took his M16 and followed Hernando. At an intersection of two alleys, Hernando waved him into the shadows. Five men were running up the street toward the Jaguar's residence. When the men were almost abreast, Hernando opened fire. Jackson followed his lead, but the M16's magazine was empty. Jackson didn't fumble with changing magazines, but pulled the pig gun free and fired both barrels at the enemy. Four of the men crumpled and fell before the onslaught of lead and Hernando fired a few extra bursts into their bodies to ensure that they would pose no further threat, but the fifth man, firing a machine gun over his shoulder, limped around the corner of a building.

Hernando gestured that Jackson should track the man down and kill him. Jackson loaded another magazine into his M16 and hurried after the man as he shoved two more shells in his pig gun. When he got to the corner, he dropped to his stomach and peered around it searching for his quarry. The man stumbled out of the shadows farther up the street, heading for an entrance to one of the buildings. Jackson fired a burst at the man and saw his body jerk, but the man still made it to the doorway and was able to get inside just before bullets from Jackson's gun raked the place where he had been standing. Staying in the shadows, Jackson crept up to the doorway. He kicked the door open and jumped to the side. A hail of bullets blew past him. Jackson took out his pig gun and fired both barrels around the corner of the doorway into the building. He was loading his pig gun for another blast when he heard the screams of children and women originating from within the building. His stomach knotted. His shots had injured women and children. He sat back against the wall, overcome with remorse. Perhaps something could be done for the wounded, something to correct this terrible wrong. He pushed open the door and entered the darkness of the building with his gun over his head, apologizing loudly. He hoped his show of peacemaking would allow the injured women and children to receive medical attention. He could see nothing but shadows and deeper darkness. He stammered, "I—I—I'm sorry! I'm so—sorry! Let me help you!" He heard a noise from the depths of the darkness. He turned toward it. A woman came flying out of the shadows. He didn't even see the knife in her hand until it started to descend toward his chest. The blade never touched him because Hernando knocked the woman down with the butt of his automatic rifle. Hernando dragged him out of the building and pushed him up against a wall, then he pulled two hand grenades out of a pouch and prepared to throw them into the building.

"Wait! Wait!" Jackson protested. "There are women and children in there!"

Hernando nodded sadly and replied, "The cost of war. There is also a man with a gun in there and this is the path we will use to leave. We cannot have enemies between us and our exit."

Jackson argued, "You can't kill women and children! They are not soldiers!"

Their conversation was interrupted by a call from Carlos. "I need help here! Culio and Chico are pinned down by a sniper on the roof!"

Hernando looked at Jackson with an exasperated expression then pushed the grenades into his hands. Hernando took off running in the direction of Carlos's voice. He was almost to the covering shadows when a rifle shot rang out. Hernando was hit. He fell on the ground and began crawling, trying to reach the protection of the shadows. Jackson was horrified. The shot had originated from within the building that Hernando had wanted to grenade. Another shot rang out, kicking up dirt by Hernando's shoulders. Not hesitating any longer, Jackson pulled the pin and threw the grenade into the open doorway. After a momentary pause, there was an earthshaking explosion from within. Tears formed in Jackson's eyes as he pulled the pin of the second grenade and threw it into the building. With the second explosion, pieces of adobe fell off the building into the street. Roofing tile fell and shattered around him. He stood against the wall, stunned by his own actions. He kept telling himself that it was the "cost of war."

He was still mumbling to himself when Carlos appeared at the end of another alley and shouted, "Time to get to the truck!"

Jackson awakened from his stupor and waved to get Carlos's attention. He ran toward him. "El Indio! El Indio has been hurt!"

"I know," Carlos answered without emotion. "He's dead."

The guilt rose up in Jackson's throat and nearly gagged him. He blurted out, "It's my fault! I should have been more alert. I didn't see the man until the last minute! I was thinking about myself—I'm so sorry! I—"

"Get to the truck!" Carlos ordered. "We don't have time for this now!"

"What about Hernando? I got him injured too!"

Carlos grabbed Jackson's collar and growled, "Get back to the truck! Culio and Chico are helping him! Worry about yourself! Get going!"

Esteban led Jackson over the wall and across the cleared band of ground to the truck, which was waiting in a thicket of scrub oak and madrona. Culio was sitting on top of the vehicle with a bazooka on his shoulder. When Jackson's grandfather and Carlos clambered over the wall and were crossing into the thicket, Culio fired. A trail of yellow fire followed the rocket to its destination. The Jaguar's residence exploded and a wall fell down into the street of the compound. Culio fired two more rockets and the residence was ablaze.

The truck rolled away in the darkness without headlights. Under the truck's interior lights Esteban and Carlos worked on stemming the bleeding from Hernando's leg wound. There was silence in the compartment as the men slumped in their fold-down seats. El Indio's body lay on the floor wrapped in a tarp. No one had anything to say. There was no mood of joy or sense of achievement. No victorious smiles. A friend had fallen and there was nothing that could offset the sadness. Jackson stared down at the floor of the truck. This night was an experience that would be branded in his memory like the night of his father's death. The silence of the men in the compartment could not subdue the screams that echoed in his ears or dampen the turmoil in his heart.

When the truck reached the highway and the ride leveled out a man named Tovares went to the radio and began contacting other stations. Carlos joined him and directed his efforts. King sat quietly, staring at the motionless mound of the tarp on the floor. No one could tell the thoughts he was thinking by looking at him. His face was impassive and his eyes were dark and glinting. The force of the man was submerged beneath his guarded exterior.

Carlos came over and sat down next to King. "A plane will pick us up outside of Gómez Palacio and will take us to Tampico. We'll take Hernando to the doctor and El Indio to the crematorium there. Rico and Octavio Ramirez will meet us afterward. Then after we finish with Tigre, we'll fly to Chiapas and spread El Indio's ashes over the hills around his village as he requested. We'll be at the airstrip in two hours."

Jackson could not believe his ears. His grandfather wanted to kill more people? "I don't want to go!" he declared angrily. "Haven't we killed enough? Isn't your lust for blood satisfied?" Jackson gestured to his throat and said, "I'm filled up to here with all of this! And I'm through with it!"

His grandfather did not raise his voice, but when he spoke his words cut through the tension like a blade through flesh. "A friend is lyin' at my feet killed by the Jaguar's men. Our lives been tied together for nearly forty years and I won't let his life pass without retribution. He deserves to have his death avenged. I'm gon' cut a wide path through the heart of the Jaguar's organization. He will not die alone!"

"He didn't die alone! I avenged him!" Jackson shouted. "I killed the man that killed him! And you killed many more! Has everybody got to die before this is over? When does it all stop?"

King's voice did not rise in volume, but it stabbed through Jackson like the barbed point of an arrow: "You ain't got nothin' you care about more than yo'self, so you can do whatever you want. You ain't got to go along."

"How can you say that?" Jackson demanded. "People that I loved are dead! Maria and El Indio are dead! I killed people tonight! We left at least thirty people dead back there, including women and children! When is enough?"

"When the debt is paid in full!"

"There isn't enough blood in the world to pay all your debts, Grandfather!"

"You talk good, boy; let's see where your heart is. The Jaguar told me that Maria was alive, that she was taken by Tigre back to Mante del Nord. And I know for a fact he wasn't lyin'. That's where we goin' now. What you gon' do? Do you really love her, or was it jus' childish talk?"

"Oh, no, Grandfather! I came with you to rescue Maria and all I have to show for my effort is the blood on my hands, blood that I will never stop seeing! I'm through!"

"When you grow up you gon' learn, boy, that you got to be hooked into something larger than yo'self. It's all about family and who you make yo' family; that's really what makes life worthwhile. Ain't nothin' else important. That's why you go to the mat for yo' family and yo' friends. That's the way you show yo' love and loyalty. Talk don't mean shit unless it's backed up by action!"

His grandfather's words poured out of his mouth like acid and etched themselves on Jackson's heart. He stood up, surprised to be fighting back tears. "If I haven't earned your respect by now, you can let me out here. I'll make my own way back! And don't worry, I'll never come down here again and shame you with my childishness! We're through, Grandfather! As for your money, I don't want it because I never want to see you again!"

Jackson was left on an empty ribbon of highway. The truck's taillights disappeared around a sloping shoulder of the rising terrain and left him in darkness. Jackson was alone with his thoughts and the gusting wind. He started walking along the side of the highway, heading toward a little town fifteen miles distant called Casas de Piedras. Carlos had informed him that a bus passed through the town traveling to Durango. There was no other traffic in sight. The sky and the landscape merged in gray and black shadows. Distant clouds shimmered with lightning and the wind howled along the open corridor created by the winding asphalt highway.

Jackson pulled up the collar of his grandfather's second sheepskin coat and kept striding down the shoulder of the highway. He was not afraid as he walked through the dark and desolate high mesa country. He kept one hand underneath his coat on the butt of his pig gun. Just because he didn't want to kill didn't mean that he was willing to be prey. He discovered that the time seemed to pass more quickly if he chanted the mantra, "I'll never kill again for you, Grandfather! I will never kill for you again!" He repeated it for over four hours until he entered the town limits of Casas de Piedras.

It took him nearly three days to get to the Mexico City airport. He hitchhiked rides and rode buses where possible and spent two nights huddled on the side of the road. When he finally boarded the plane, he was dirty and unwashed, but happy to be headed home.

Three members of the four-man team that his grandfather had assigned to follow him south to Mexico City reported that Jackson was safely in the air. The fourth member was seated several rows behind Jackson on the aircraft.

Sunday, July 25, 1982

E lizabeth awakened to hands between her legs. Alarmed, she sat up immediately and was shoved roughly down on the cot. It was Alejandro. He pulled a knife from his belt and held it to her throat while his other hand traveled roughly over her body, squeezing her breasts and jabbing his fingers between her legs. She lay quietly and offered no resistance. Fortunately, her workout suit had no easily accessible openings for him to stick his hands into, so after a few minutes he stood up and gestured with his knife for her to get up.

Concerned that this was the moment in which she would have to fight for her life, Elizabeth hesitated.

Noticing her reluctance, Alejandro guffawed, "What? You don't want lunch? Ain't you hungry? Or do you just want to stay down here with me?" He grabbed his crotch suggestively. "I got something real big for you! You ain't ever had it like I'm going to give it to you!"

Elizabeth got up from the cot and walked around Alejandro. As she passed him heading out the door, he pinched her buttocks hard. She kept walking as if nothing had happened. Alejandro laughed and followed her out of the room. Adolfo, the dog handler, was kneeling at the bottom of the stairs unchaining Rex for his patrol of the grounds. Rex was sitting quietly while Adolfo brushed his gleaming coat. Elizabeth halted, afraid to walk past the dog and climb the stairs. Alejandro came up behind her and pinched her buttocks again. This time Elizabeth swung and punched him full in the face. It was a hard blow, but it only knocked Alejandro back a few paces.

Elizabeth shouted, "Keep your goddamn hands off of me!"

Alejandro, who still had the knife in his hand, started for Elizabeth. His face was contorted with anger as blood dripped from his lips. He raised his hand to slash her with his blade, but Rex leaped at him. It was only Adolfo's grip on the dog's chain that kept Rex from reaching him. Elizabeth ran up the stairs. Alejandro wanted to follow her, but the ferocity of the dog blocking his way momentarily disconcerted him. He unleashed a torrent of angry Spanish at Adolfo. Adolfo only smiled in response and gave Rex a little more chain to move around. Alejandro backed up and fell silent as he faced the enraged dog. He looked to Adolfo for help.

Adolfo said in English, "You got to remember, he's trained to attack anyone with a weapon in his hands! Plus, he don't like you in particular. I think it's because you fed him those burritos with those goddamn jalapeño peppers!"

"You just keep that fucking dog off of me or I'll kill him!"

"You'll kill who?" Adolfo let out a bit more chain. "You'll kill who?"

Alejandro glanced up the stairs after Elizabeth then back at Adolfo. He said placatingly, "Hey, I'm supposed be guarding that bitch! You got to let me pass!"

"I hear you're supposed to be keeping your hands to yourself too. I'm sure Don San Vicente wouldn't like to hear about the way you're guarding her."

Alejandro's bravado disappeared. "Hey, this is between you and me, huh? I mean, we both work for the same boss. We're friends, ain't that right?"

"No, we ain't friends and if you fuck with another of my dogs, I'll let Rex loose on you!"

Alejandro conceded with an exasperated tone, "Okay! I made a mistake. Can I pass now?"

Elizabeth had waited at the top of the stairs when she heard the men below begin to speak in English. She needed as much information as possible if she was going to escape. However, once Alejandro was allowed to pass by Rex, she pushed open the door and headed for the kitchen. She was seated at the table waiting for her food when Alejandro entered the room. He started toward her, but Deleon and San Vicente entered the kitchen. Deleon sat down next to her while San Vicente went over to talk with the cooks. Alejandro sat at a different table, watching her.

Deleon asked her, "How's it going?"

She wanted to respond, "How do you think, you sick fuck? I've been kidnapped, raped, and threatened with being sold into slavery!" Instead she said quietly, "Alejandro tried to force himself upon me. Only the dog handler's presence stopped him."

A frown passed across Deleon's face. He got up and went to speak to San Vicente. There was a brief interchange during which San Vicente nodded and then Deleon picked up an aluminum pot and walked over to the refrigerator, which was behind Alejandro. Alejandro watched Deleon but did not turn when he went behind him. Without warning,

Deleon turned and hit Alejandro on the side of his head with the pot. The pot clanged off Alejandro's head as he fell to the floor, dazed. Deleon growled, "You were warned about touching the merchandise!" He raised the pot for another blow, but San Vicente stopped him.

"That's enough of a lesson. Don't hit him again. I need him for guard duty tonight. Half my men are off because of the national holiday." San Vicente watched Alejandro pick himself up slowly and observed, "You'll be more careful now. Won't you, Alejandro?"

Alejandro nodded silently, but Elizabeth noticed that his eyes were filled with evil intention. She knew that if he had his choice, her death would be painful and unpleasant. She continued to eat and could not taste the food. She was ushered back to her imprisonment without incident, but knew things were only going to get worse. She had to work out a plan. She got out her bobby pin and dedicated herself to opening the room's other door. She had no idea what was in the room on the other side, but she hoped to find some implement or tool that would serve as a weapon. Despite the fact her fingers were cramping and sore, Elizabeth continued working on the lock. Afternoon passed on into evening, and after she had eaten her nightly tortilla and beans, she returned to her task.

When her fingers could no longer grasp the pin, she rested, then after a brief respite she began again. She wiped the sweat off her forehead and looked at the darkness outside the dirty casement window. It had been dark for many hours. She had moved the tumblers a number of times, but the bobby pin was simply not stout enough for the task. She looked around the room seeking an alternative as she had a thousand times, but there was nothing in the room but the cot, the sink, and the plastic toilet.

On a whim, she turned the cot over and examined its metal frame. There was a narrow supporting strut that was loose on the corner, held only by one rusty screw. The strut would fit in the old-fashioned keyhole. Fortunately, the screw was not rusted solid. She removed the strut and returned the cot and mattress to their upright position and went back to the lock. Although the strut fit into the lock, it would not move the tumblers. She needed to affix the bobby pin to the strut in such a manner that it would move the tumblers. She looked at the mattress and saw that it was hemmed with a heavy twine. Within twenty minutes, she had ten inches of the twine, which she had unraveled and bitten off the mattress. She opened the bobby pin and then wrapped it around the strut. She then bound the twine around both strut and bobby pin as tightly as she could manage. The finished product was still a bit loose, but it was serviceable. She returned to the lock. The strut was just narrow enough that she was able to turn it in the lock a third of a turn. She could feel the tumblers. She bent the bobby pin's prongs at an acute angle and jiggled the strut, then heard a click. She became excited. She kept moving the strut back and forth in the lock. Every few minutes she would hear another click, but the door remained locked. Finally, out of patience and frustrated, she jammed the strut into the lock and bent it in the process of trying to turn it and the door swung open.

She was so surprised that at first, she thought someone had opened the door from the other side, but there was only darkness and silence awaiting her. She peered cautiously into the room's interior, into shadows which were cast by the indirect light of the bare bulb. She saw boxes of American soap powders, aerosol cans, and bottles of fluid sitting on shelves. On the floor was an old canister vacuum cleaner, a rug steamer, and an assortment of mops and brooms. She entered the room after waiting for her eyes to adjust to the dimness. It was simply a storeroom used for housecleaning supplies and equipment. It was about the size of the room in which she was imprisoned. She picked up a heavy string mop. The wooden handle was thick enough for a weapon, but it was too long and unwieldy for her to use effectively. She had been trained with a police baton, not a quarter staff. At the far end of the room, she saw creases of light around a closed door. She knew right away from its position that it must open very close to where Rex was chained. She would not venture near it for fear of arousing the dog.

She continued searching, returning every ten or fifteen minutes to her room and listening at the door for movement from the guard. All seemed peaceful. The guard was probably asleep. After an hour of looking on shelves and through dusty boxes, she found a hacksaw. Wrapping it in rags, she immediately began to saw off a four-foot section of the mop handle. She took her time, stopping every few strokes to listen. It took her nearly twenty minutes, but at the end she had a club that could easily break a man's forearm. The only other useful item she found was an aerosol container of Black Flag. The directions on the container indicated it could shoot a solid stream of insecticide a twenty-foot distance. She hid both the aerosol can and the wooden club under her mattress, then, using a piece of rag, she wedged the door to the storeroom shut. She dropped onto the cot totally exhausted and fell into a deep, dreamless sleep.

She had not been asleep long when she was awakened by an explosion. The walls were trembling from its force. The first explosion was followed quickly by three others, more powerful than the first. Even in the isolation of her room, she could hear the sound of automatic weapons being fired. Suddenly, she was filled with hope. She prayed that it was Jackson coming to rescue her. Then reality hit her. Whether it was Jackson or not, this might be her only chance of escape. She had to be prepared. She pulled out her club and can of aerosol from beneath the mattress. She stood up and knocked out the bare bulb above her head. She set the aerosol can by the storeroom door and settled down in the darkness behind the door to wait. The only light in the darkened room came from the dirty casement window and it was very weak. Even as her eyes adjusted, all she could see in the darkness was the dim outline of the cot. Another explosion shook the building then the door of her room opened, sending a shaft of light across the floor. She heard Alejandro's voice, "What the hell!"

Elizabeth threw her full weight against the door, slamming into Alejandro. The force of the door knocked him off his feet and she slammed it shut, hoping that she had an advantage in the darkness. She saw him warily get to his feet and she waded in with her club. Unfortunately, he heard her coming and was able to avoid the first blow, which would have probably ended the fight. Elizabeth was forced to follow him. She hit him a glancing blow on the arm and a gun discharged; the bullet whistled past her head. She swung again and connected hard to his body. He fired two more shots wildly, which chipped the plaster walls behind her. She saw the silhouette of his gun in front of the casement window and hit the barrel of the gun, knocking it from his hands. The gun clattered as it hit the floor and disappeared in the darkness.

Another series of explosions rocked the building, several of which were close enough that their detonations actually cast quick glimmerings of light through the casement window. Alejandro turned toward her and snarled, "I see you now, you black bitch! I'm going to cut off your tits!" He charged her.

Elizabeth swung the club with both hands, putting every ounce of her weight behind the blow. The club smacked the top of his head, but his inertia carried him into her. She was knocked backward as he fell across the tops of her legs. She tried to break her fall, but in the darkness she couldn't see where she was going to land and hyperextended her left elbow when she fell against the wall. She cried out in pain as she crumpled to the floor. Alejandro groggily reached for her. She began kicking frantically, trying to get him off her legs. The club had fallen somewhere in the darkness. She got one leg free and kicked him in the head. He rolled off her other leg with a groan.

"You *puta!*" he growled, still slightly stunned. "I'm going to kill you! I'm going to cut you into little pieces!"

Elizabeth scrambled to her feet and ran to the storeroom door. She stooped, seeking the aerosol canister. She found it where she had left it and picked it up. She waited in silence by the door, hoping to squirt the insecticide into Alejandro's face and blind him. Her left arm was practically useless. The insecticide was her only weapon. She had to wait until she had a clear shot. She heard him get slowly to his feet then stumble into the cot and fall to the floor again.

Alejandro cursed, "Goddamn you, bitch! Goddamn you!"

Elizabeth heard him get to his feet again. He moved cautiously to a wall and made his way to the exit door and opened it. A bright shaft of light fell onto the floor of the room, illuminating it. She saw him standing in the light. There was blood dripping from the top of his head. He turned to look around the room for her. Elizabeth knew she was now visible. It took him a moment to focus on her. Still she waited. She wanted a full frontal shot before she used the insecticide. She would have only one opportunity.

"I see you, *puta!* I see your black ass now!" Alejandro started toward her, his knife glistening in his hand.

Elizabeth waited until he had taken several steps then aimed the canister at his face. A stream of foul-smelling liquid hit Alejandro just above his left eye.

"What the fuck!" he exclaimed. Then the toxic fluid dripped down into his eye. "You bitch! You tried to put out my eye! Oh, you fucking bitch!" He wiped his eye with the sleeve of his shirt.

Elizabeth squirted him again, hitting him in the forehead and arm. He staggered toward her, slashing his knife wildly in front of him.

Elizabeth waited no longer; she turned and ran into the darkness of the storeroom. There was no place to hide. She ran past the shelves, went to the far door, and opened it, hoping that Rex had been taken out on patrol. The dog hit the door with the power of its seventy-pound body. If Elizabeth had not braced the door with her shoulder before she opened it, Rex would have been inside with the force of his charge. The dog was only able to force its sleek head through the opening and it was struggling mightily to squeeze its whole body into the room. With only one arm Elizabeth was having trouble keeping the dog out. It tried to nip at her. She sprayed its muzzle with the insecticide. The dog snorted and shook its head a couple of times then backed out of the doorway. Gratefully, Elizabeth slammed the door shut, but it trembled as Rex threw himself against it again and again. She leaned against the door to catch her breath. While she was recovering, she saw Alejandro enter the storeroom through the other door. He held his knife in front of him as he searched the darkness for her.

"Where are you, *puta*? I've got a little present for you! Come out, come out, *puta!*"

Elizabeth knew that the light coming under the door would eventually reveal her presence. She waited until he was halfway into the room and squirted him again, but as soon as he heard the sound of the aerosol can he turned away. The insecticide fell harmlessly on the side of his head.

"I know your tricks now and I see where you are!"

"Then come and get me, you useless piece of shit!" Elizabeth taunted. "Let's see how tough you really are!" She had to lure him closer.

Alejandro ran toward her. "I'll kill you! I'll kill—"

Elizabeth waited until the last possible moment then opened the door and Rex burst into the room and saw Alejandro. The dog leaped on the man, who was unable to stop his forward progress. Both man and dog fell in a tangle of legs and arms and fur. The dog's ferocious snarls filled the little room. Elizabeth slipped out the door and unhooked Rex's chain then ran up the stairs. She pushed open the door and slammed it behind her. She heard the sound of running feet coming toward her and slipped behind some heavy drapes that hung beside a tall window. The footsteps ran past her and faded in the distance. The sound of machine-gun fire was much louder on the first floor. Elizabeth knew she had to get out of the building. There were shouts and cries of pain coming from outside. She didn't know what or who was out there, but she knew she could fare no worse with them than with San Vicente.

She headed to the stairs that led to an upper-floor walkway, hoping against hope that Jackson would be there.

Sunday, July 25, 1982

Jackson stood at the prow of the *Sampson*, a seventy-five-foot motor cruiser, as it rocked slowly back and forth on gentle waves. A soft summer breeze rose out of the west. The distant coastline of Baja California lay to the east like a thin layer of chocolate icing on the shimmering blue of the temperate sea. It was a warm and easy twilight. The red-orange sun had just set on the shining, magenta horizon of the Pacific Ocean. The sky was cloudless, yet filled with shades of red and purple. A pale half-moon rose in the southern sky. Jackson leaned over and studied the rolling water, lapping in rhythm against the cruiser's hull. He was lost in thought. What if each one of these waves had its own individual sentient, pulsing life and not one had a clearer picture of its destiny than a mortal human? The waves could no more change their direction than he could. He wondered whether he shared the same destiny, whether his life too would break apart on some foreign shore. He chuckled to himself. So be it. He could not turn away this time and abandon the one he loved. If death should come, he asked only to die bravely.

The trip from San Francisco down to Playa Rosalía had been long and arduous for him. The private plane had taken off from Oakland at five-fifteen in the morning, which had been particularly ungodly because he had been unable to sleep at all the night before. He had spent his sleepless time taping pairs of M16 magazines together so that when the first was spent the second could easily be flipped around in its place. Then, because they were taking over eighteen hundred pounds of guns, ammunition, and equipment, he and Carlos had to be at the airport at three-thirty to make sure everything was loaded properly. The flight to San Diego had taken ninety minutes, at which point they had transferred all of their gear to the *Sampson*, which was anchored in the yacht harbor. Tavio and Diego, who had flown down the night before, met them on the tarmac by the plane with a truck and a small bus. All the equipment was offloaded into the truck and driven to the harbor, where it again was picked up and hauled aboard the motor cruiser. The *Sampson*'s captain and his two-man crew had the cruiser nosing out of the harbor and heading south toward Baja California at eighteen knots before eleven o'clock.

At twelve o'clock the attack team had a two-hour briefing on assignments over sandwiches. Jackson laid out the general plan of attack. The raid was designed to take a maximum of forty minutes. After that time had elapsed, everyone would be transported back to the boat, with or without Elizabeth.

At five-thirty Jackson came out on the prow to be alone and to think. He directed his thoughts to Elizabeth, to the times that they had made love. He remembered the unending softness of her dark brown skin, the firmness of her lips, the flashing brightness of her large, brown eyes, the rise of her breasts, the flatness of her stomach, and the strength in her legs; but the most consuming memory was the sense of exaltation and completeness that he had felt as he rested in her arms after they had both climaxed. Further thoughts were interrupted by the sound of powerful outboard engines drawing near.

When the motorboat drew alongside, Jackson went down to greet Julio and Reuben. He exchanged hugs with both men and afterward, Julio leaned over and whispered in his ear, "Blood bothers until we die."

Jackson replied, "Let us hope that when our time does come, we're as old as my grandfather and tired of living." Jackson led the way to the conference room and introduced the Ramirez brothers to the rest of the team. There was a brief overview of the plans once more and then the equipment was offloaded into the motorboat. The darkness of night had finally settled and the thirty-minute ride to the coast was guarded over by millions of stars twinkling overhead. Jackson was reminded of his first boat ride as a child to see his grandfather, yet other than the presence of the stars there was no similarity.

They docked at a dilapidated pier in a small, dark, deserted cove. While they transferred their equipment and gear to the waiting panel trucks, two dirt bikes for Tavio and Diego were rolled out of the back of one of the trucks. As the men donned their motorcycle helmets and strapped bags holding the rocket launchers to their backs, Jackson thanked them for their assistance and wished them luck. Shortly after they roared off, the trucks got under way. Jackson rode up front with

Julio while Carlos and Reuben drove the other vehicle. A mile from San Vicente's mansion, Julio pulled off the road and drove to a construction site. When he got out Jackson slid over behind the wheel. He watched Julio walk over and climb up on a big bulldozer. Once Julio had the big machine started, Jackson pulled the truck back on the main road and followed the other truck to San Vicente's mansion. Within a half mile of their objective, the headlights were turned off and the remainder of the way was driven in darkness.

San Vicente's compound was a quarter of a mile off the main road and was built on a small knoll behind shrub-covered ridges of low, rolling hills. The main house sat on the apex of the knoll while the perimeter walls were built around its base. From a distance, its lights made it look like a small Mediterranean city. The trucks turned onto a narrow, rutted road and drove into a small gully, where they parked. Guns were checked and plans were gone over once more while they awaited the arrival of the bulldozer. They climbed the small hill, making their way through the thatch and brush carrying crates of rockets and ammunition. Once they reached the crest of the hill, three pairs of binoculars were passed around as time was spent studying the compound, which was three hundred yards away. In the far distance colorful fireworks could be seen exploding in the night sky.

Carlos crouched down and began drawing a diagram of the compound in the dirt with a short stick. A particularly bright firework flared briefly. He commented, "It looks like they're partying even in the suburbs of Tijuana."

"Let's hope they're partying as heavily at San Vicente's house," Pres replied as he knelt down beside Carlos. "Where do you want us to fire the rockets from?"

"Right here would be good, but remember, they have rockets too. Once you get off four or five quick shots, you've got to move. You've got to cover the distance between here and the outer wall in three minutes. If you don't hit the tower by the arch above the gate, they'll turn the exterior lights on you. If that happens, you may not have even three minutes. Make sure your second round of shots hit the antenna and the satellite dish."

"Don't worry," Dominique said as she hoisted her rocket launcher. "We won't miss. I've used these before. We'll take out the tower and the whole front side."

"Good!" Carlos said with a nod. He pointed the stick at the diagram.

"We'll come in from here and hit the barracks, the power plant, and the communications room. We don't want to be hit by your rockets, so confine your targets to this area until you enter the gates and see where we are."

Pres nodded, "No problem! Once we get inside the gate, we'll provide a crossfire for whoever needs it."

Reuben walked over and asked, "How are you planning to handle the dogs?"

Jackson, who was stooping over Pres and Carlos, questioned, "How many are we talking about?"

Reuben exhaled. "I've heard he has as many as ten and they are all trained killers. In fact, he brags about setting his dogs loose on people who've crossed him or just generally pissed him off."

Jackson began, "Well, if they're in a kennel—"

"We'll make sure that no one lets them out!" Dominique concluded firmly.

Dan said in a subdued voice, "Sounds like the 'dozer is close."

Carlos stood up. "All right! Let's get to our positions!"

Jackson said, "Just a minute!" He stretched out his hand, palm down, and asked, "Please put your right hand on mine!" Pres clapped his hand down on Jackson's with a smile. He was followed by Carlos, Lincoln, Reuben, and the rest. Once all hands were in, Jackson put his other hand on top and said with a determined tone, "We don't know what this evening brings. So I swear you this oath now, to each and every one. No injured will be left behind! We come together. We shall leave together. May God smile upon us and may this evening's end see us all rejoicing!" There was an emphatic pressing down of hands, and members of the team turned away to move through the shrubbery toward the south gate.

Dan, followed by Lincoln, walked up to Jackson and Pres, who were shaking hands, and Dan said, "I love it when you speak that urban Shakespearean shit!"

Jackson put his arm around Lincoln and Dan's shoulders and said, "Alamo Square Rangers forever!" The men released and turned away.

The attack began as planned. Pres and Dominique destroyed the first guard tower, the antenna, the dish, and the front wall with their rockets. The bulldozer broke through the south gate. Julio and Reuben fired their rockets into the power plant, reducing it to rubble within minutes.

Next they turned their fire on the second guard tower and knocked it out of commission with direct hits. Things were moving on schedule until a large-caliber machine gun began firing down from the roof. No one had foreseen that San Vicente would mount a heavy machine gun in one of the attic dormer windows. In the darkness, the continuous discharge of the big gun could clearly be seen. The sounds of explosions, the whistling of bullets, and the deep ack-ack of the heavy machine gun filled the air. The heavy gun covered the interior of the compound and it poured an endless stream of bullets down on the Caterpillar which ricocheted off its raised shovel blade. Bullets were flying everywhere, kicking up the dirt, deflecting off the walls and chipping away their stucco finish. All seven of the attacking party were pinned behind the Caterpillar for precious minutes by the south gate until Pres and Dominique were able to hit the dormer window with rockets. A huge plume of flames flared into the air as the roof exploded.

The covering dark of twilight was now gone. The moon, half full and bright, had risen above the dark horizon, and it cast its pale light, making visible what had previously been hidden. The precious minutes lost had given the men in the barracks time to get their weapons and make a stand of it, and allowed snipers to take their positions on the roof.

With Dan and Lincoln providing covering fire, Julio and Reuben began firing rockets at the outlying buildings. Jackson, Carlos, and Esteban left the cover of the bulldozer and headed across the open courtyard. Bullets kicked up grass and sod around them. They crossed over into a cobblestone plaza and had to take cover in the shadows behind a large, imposing fountain. Despite the fact they were in the shadows, bullets still pinged off the cobblestones near them while errant shots whizzed over their heads as San Vicente's men fired from their barracks.

Carlos crawled over next to Jackson. "Keep your head down! They've got our range!"

"How the hell can they tell where we are? I can barely see the roof from here!"

"Infrared! We can't stay here! They can move around and get a clear shot of us!" Carlos pulled some objects from a pouch and said, "I've got a couple of flash grenades. They should cover our run to the house! Put your goggles on!" Carlos pulled the pins and lobbed them at the other side of the fountain. As soon as they exploded all three men were up

and running. There were a few shots, but the bullets caromed harmlessly off the cobblestones. They made the sheltering cover of the
eaves and stood against the exterior wall of the main house out of the
way of the heavy tile and pieces of the roof, which were still falling on
the cobblestones from the rocket blasts.

Jackson was removing his goggles when a man carrying two machine
pistols burst through a door. Esteban hit him in the chest with a burst
from his automatic rifle. The man fell down and then struggled to his
feet firing his pistols, spraying bullets in all directions. Esteban, Jackson, and Carlos hugged the wall behind a jutting facade as a fusillade of
whistling lead sped past them. The bullets stopped suddenly as covering fire from across the square centered on the man. Carlos pulled the
pin and threw a hand grenade around the corner in the man's direction.
The explosion shattered windows and rattled the door through which
the man had come. There was more fire from across the square and then
silence.

Jackson poked his head around the corner and was heading for the
door when he heard a piercing whistle. He looked across the square
and saw Dan pointing above him to an upper balcony of the main
house. Jackson started to move away from the building to get a better
look.

Carlos warned, "Don't step out there!" and he grabbed Jackson's arm,
pulling him back close to the building. "Do you want to give them a
clear shot?"

Jackson questioned, "What was Dan pointing at?"

"You'll live to see it, if you remember caution is the first step in all
things. Oh, damn!" Carlos gestured across the square. "What is your
friend doing? He's making himself a target!"

Jackson followed Carlos's hand and saw that Dan was climbing a partially destroyed spiral staircase to get on the catwalk between the ruins
of the communications center and the main house. No sooner had Dan
started across the catwalk than automatic-rifle fire started chipping
away the stucco around him. He ducked down behind the stucco walls.

Carlos exhaled. "He's in a death trap up there. They don't even have
to know where he is. All they have to do is continue to spray bullets up
and down that catwalk and eventually a ricochet will find him." As if
signaled by Carlos's statement, a hail of bullets raked across the catwalk, pinging off the stucco. The bullets were answered by rifle fire and

rockets from the rest of the team. There were more explosions along the roofline. Falling pieces of smoking debris and roofing tile shattered on the ungiving cobblestones.

Jackson started for the doorway again, only to be stopped once more by an exclamation from Carlos.

Jackson looked back across the square to see Rhasan climbing the stairs leading to the catwalk. Several shots splintered the wall near him as he continued up the stairs. It was useless to call to him amid the sound of automatic weapons. Jackson studied the length of the main house, searching for the source of the bullets firing on Rhasan. He saw the discharge of a gun from an upper window in a projecting wing of the house. He hefted his rifle to his shoulder and waited a few seconds then emptied his magazine into the lower part of the window. He popped the clip out and flipped it around and plugged home its unused partner. He waited for more shots from the window, but there were none. There was now only the intermittent firing from across the square.

He heard Rhasan shout, "Elizabeth! She's here! But she's pinned down by a sniper on the roof!" Jackson turned immediately and ran into the main house followed by Carlos and Esteban. There was a flight of narrow stairs leading to the second floor, which he took three at a time. Under the dim light of a bulb on the landing, he took a quick look around then pushed the door onto the balcony open a few inches and peered out. He saw Elizabeth crouching down in the shadows under an eave. He searched the roofline for the sniper but could see no one in the darkness. Then he saw the outline of a man's torso as he was preparing to make a throwing motion. As Jackson swung his rifle up, a shot rang out across the plaza and the man fell backward. An explosion blew the man's body into the air, flinging it off the roof down to the cobblestones below.

Esteban pushed past Jackson. "Let me go first! There may be more snipers."

Jackson grabbed his arm. "Thank you, my friend, but this is my job." He slipped out the door, staying in the shadows under the eaves. "Elizabeth? Elizabeth, are you all right?" When she heard his voice she sprang to her feet and ran into his arms.

Elizabeth laid her head in the crook of his neck. "God! Oh, God! I hoped and dreamed it was you! St. Clair!"

Jackson gripped her fiercely and growled, "I told you I would come!

Only divine intervention could've stopped me! You mean everything to me! There is nothing without you!"

Carlos tapped his shoulder. "Let's get out of here! We don't know how many soldiers are left. We wait too long, they could regroup and then we'll be fighting to get out of here. Then, of course, the police will come eventually." There were three long blasts of a whistle. Everyone looked across the square to see Julio and Reuben waving the all-clear sign as they ran toward another entry into the main house. Lincoln was climbing the sagging stairs to the catwalk.

"What about San Vicente and Deleon?"

"We'll have to hit them again, but I'd rather do it with a force of professionals in three or four days. We were very lucky tonight. I think we have minimal injuries, unless your friend Dan took a serious hit."

"Where are Dan and Rhasan?" Jackson asked, turning toward the doorway, moving with his arm around Elizabeth.

Esteban pointed down toward the other end of the main house. "They were on the catwalk and there's a door across from it."

Carlos interjected, "If you have to spend time looking for them, I'd better check out the interior and give support to Julio and Reuben." Esteban started to follow him, but Carlos gestured for him to stay with Jackson.

Jackson saw Carlos's gesture and asked Esteban, "Would you please see Elizabeth to one of the trucks and stay with her?" Exasperated, Carlos threw up his hands and pivoted away, entering through the same door that they had exited.

Esteban gave a quick nod of his head. "If that is what you wish."

Elizabeth pulled out of Jackson's arms. "That is not what *I* wish! I'm not going anywhere without you! When you leave, I leave! And give me a gun!"

"It's dangerous! Why risk any more?"

Elizabeth spat, "Dangerous! Where do you think I've been the last few weeks? I wouldn't mind killing a few of these assholes myself! I know you're carrying two pistols; give me one!" She stuck out her hand. "Let's find Rhasan! I'm going with you!" Jackson knew it was useless to argue. He pulled a .45 from its holster and handed it to her. As she quickly pulled out the magazine and checked the chamber, she looked at the black outfits of Jackson and Esteban and asked, "All the good guys dressed like you?"

"Pretty much," Jackson replied. "Everybody, including the one woman, is dressed in black."

Elizabeth's eyes flashed as she clicked home the magazine. "One woman, huh? Now you've got two."

Jackson shook his head and turned toward the catwalk and moved swiftly to the door. He called out, "Dan? Rhasan?"

There was a loud explosion at the other end of the mansion as San Vicente's arsenal detonated. The building's floors above the explosion slowly collapsed with a tremendous rending of wood and metal, and debris fell into the courtyard below. There were fires throughout the compound and bodies littered the plaza.

Jackson's heart was in his mouth when he called out again, "Rhasan! Dan! Where are you?"

Sunday, July 25, 1982

Deleon was sharing an expensive bottle of single-malt bourbon with Angel and Jesus in the communications center when the first explosion occurred. Angel leaped up immediately to look out the window, knocking over his bourbon-filled paper cup in the process. "What was that?" he demanded. The first explosion was quickly followed by several other, more powerful ones. The communications center was rattling from the force of the detonations. Angel turned to Jesus. "The front tower's been blow away! Get on the phone! We're under attack!"

Jesus picked up the phone and listened for a second, clicked the receiver button a few times, then returned it to its cradle. "The line's dead! Let me get on the radio!" As he finished speaking, the power went out and the room was plunged into darkness.

"Don't worry," advised Angel. "The generator will kick on in a few seconds then we'll get the alarm out!"

Deleon stood up, pulled his twenty-two-caliber pistol out of his jacket, and moved behind Angel. Another explosion, closer this time, broke a nearby window and caused some objects to fall off the shelves. Deleon shot Angel in the base of his skull. The sound of his small-caliber pistol didn't even register amid the din of automatic gunfire which could now be heard. As Angel fell forward across his desk, Deleon shouted to Jesus, who was across the room twiddling knobs on the radio, "Damn! It looks like Angel has been hit!"

"What? How?" Jesus questioned as he stood up and went to help his companion. As soon as Jesus saw the blood flowing from the back of Angel's head he turned to Deleon, but it was too late. Deleon fired point-blank into his cheek and then followed it up with another shot in the temple. Jesus collapsed without a sound.

Deleon looked at his watch. It was only nine-thirty. Obviously, Jackson didn't want to wait until the time he had suggested. A hum emanated from the banks of equipment, and the monitors and the emergency lights came back on. Deleon stepped over Jesus's body and went over and flipped the red switch on the radio which sent out the recorded alarm over the police band. He figured that with the holiday festivities, he had at least half an hour to forty-five minutes to finish his business before the first police arrived. He left the communications center and heard the clatter of a heavy machine gun firing from one of the dormer windows of the main house. But no sooner than Deleon had located it, it was destroyed by rocket fire and the resultant blast blew off a large section of the roof. There were more rocket explosions throughout the compound. The attackers had already destroyed much of San Vicente's security system. Both guard towers were destroyed. None of the security beacons were lit, vast parts of the complex were in darkness. As he started on the catwalk that led across to the main house he saw pockets of defenders in firefights with the attackers; several of the guards were pinned down in their barracks. He didn't give a moment's thought to helping either side. He had his own agenda.

He was halfway across the catwalk when he saw a rocket's fiery tail heading directly for the center. He threw himself down as the rush of hot air from the explosion blew bits of debris over him. He got up into a stoop and hurried for the safety of the main building. Once in the shadows, he moved to the guard wall of the balcony and took stock of the situation. Jackson's team and their rockets were overwhelming the defenders. San Vicente's men were giving way rapidly. Deleon's only fear was that Jackson was winning so quickly that San Vicente would make his escape before Deleon could deal with him. He knew that if San Vicente was able to get away and gain the protection of the police then his own life would be forfeit. Down below on the ground at an entrance midway toward the other end of the house, there was machine-gun fire followed by a small explosion. He saw the dog handler, Adolfo, staggering toward the kennel to unleash the dogs. Adolfo made it to the gate, but before he could open it he was cut down by a burst from an automatic weapon. Deleon shook his head. Things were going fast.

He went into the main house, heading directly toward San Vicente's quarters. Earlier in the evening, he had heard San Vicente tell his men that he was bringing in a woman. He hoped that San Vicente was sufficiently distracted that he hadn't had time to empty his safe and escape. The interior of the house was dark, only intermittently lit by emergency lights. Deleon stayed close to the walls and made as little noise as possible as he hurried through the wide halls and down the broad, swirling stairs. He expected that some sort of resistance would be set up to stop the invaders, but strangely he saw no one. In sharp contrast to the din outside, the interior of the house was as silent as a tomb. It was almost eerie. He had to be cautious. He didn't want to rush into an ambush. San Vicente had a small arsenal in his bedroom and his most trusted men would make their way there to defend him.

As Deleon turned into the shadows of the corridor that led to San Vicente's bedroom, he heard the sound of footsteps coming toward him. Deleon faded back into the darkness next to curtains along the wall. As the man came abreast of him, Deleon saw that it was Tercero. He was carrying a machine pistol and was moving cautiously. Deleon waited until Tercero had moved past him, then he stepped out silently behind him and sprang upon him, pulling back his head and cutting his throat before he could utter a sound. He grabbed the pistol as it slipped from Tercero's helpless hands and eased the body to the floor. Moving quickly, he dragged the body close to the wall. He thought a moment about keeping the pistol, but it was an unfamiliar make and in the darkness, he couldn't see much but the trigger. He decided that it was better to use weapons he knew and left the machine pistol by the corpse. He made no effort to move farther up the corridor for he heard more footsteps coming in his direction.

"*Tercero? Tercero, venga aquí! Venga!*" San Vicente moved cautiously down the corridor whispering, "*Hombre! Dónde está?*"

Even in the darkness, Deleon could see that he was carrying a heavy strongbox and an automatic rifle. Had Deleon kept the heavier caliber

machine pistol, he might've considered shooting San Vicente and end-
ing it right there, but the truth was he wanted to kill San Vicente up
close and personal: He wanted to kill him with his knife. He waited until no more than three paces separated them before he rushed his adversary. San Vicente heard him after his first step, but his ability to turn
was slowed by the weight of the strongbox, and by the time he swung
his rifle around, Deleon easily blocked it with a chopping blow, knocking it out of his hand. San Vicente dropped the strongbox and tried to
defend himself, but Deleon was too quick for him. Deleon thrust his
blade into San Vicente's chest, but it was deflected by a metal object under his bulletproof vest. San Vicente fell over his strongbox and
sprawled on the floor. In the darkness, Deleon could not risk continuing his attack. There was always the chance that San Vicente might
have a handgun. He pulled his pistol and waited until San Vicente regained his feet.

San Vicente pulled his own knife and challenged, "You want knives?
I've got a knife and I'm facing you! And Tercero is somewhere behind
you!"

"Tercero won't be coming to help," Deleon answered as he judged
the distance between himself and his prey.

"You killed Tercero?" San Vicente asked incredulously.

"Just like I'm going to kill you," Deleon answered as he started
toward him.

San Vicente circled to his right and suggested, "We can both leave
here alive, and I'll call things equal between us."

Deleon stopped for a moment and laughed at the ridiculousness of
the idea then replied, "You'll never leave here!"

San Vicente tapped his chest and growled, *"Entonces mátame!* Kill me if
you can!" He charged Deleon, who easily ducked under his slashing
blade.

Deleon closed quickly with him again, ignoring his feint, and thrust
past his guard. This time there was nothing to deflect his knife. He
drove the blade up to its hilt into San Vicente's stomach, twisting it up
and to the right. As he was falling San Vicente tried to counterattack,
but Deleon blocked his knife with his forearm and head-butted him
hard across his nose. San Vicente fell backward and hit the floor heavily. "Now things are equal between us!" Deleon said as he wiped his
blade on the hall curtains.

San Vicente gasped, "You black fuck! You didn't keep our agreement!"

Deleon chuckled. "You were the one who said agreements were made to be broken."

San Vicente growled, "I'll be waiting for you in hell!"

"See you there." Deleon walked over to him and fired his .22 into San Vicente's head. He turned away and picked up the automatic rifle. This was a weapon he knew. He checked the chamber to ensure that it was loaded and headed for the basement. Outside the gunfire had fallen silent. Deleon deduced that if the police hadn't come by now, they weren't going to show up at all. No police involvement meant that Jackson was in control of the compound. It also meant that the possibility of his leaving the compound with his life was minimal. Surprisingly, that did not disturb him. If he could get Elizabeth then he could perhaps trade her for safe passage, but he didn't really want safe passage. He wanted a face-to-face with Jackson Tremain to repay him for stealing his opportunity to kill Xavier. He wouldn't mind dying if he could take Tremain with him. Plus, it all had a poetic, Shakespearean quality: the last DuMont and the last Tremain who mattered dying together. His mood was light; he almost smiled as he opened the door to the basement.

As soon as Deleon had partially opened the door, Rex's head surged through it and bit his left hand, the hand in which he was carrying the automatic rifle. The rifle clattered to the floor as Deleon put his weight against the door and slammed it hard on the dog's head. The animal loosened its grip with a yelp and Deleon was able to force the door shut, but his thumb, index, and middle fingers of his left hand were torn open and bleeding. His left hand was useless. He picked up the rifle one-handed and fired a burst through the lower part of the door. He reopened the door and saw the dog lying midway down the stairs. Deleon fired another burst into the dog and stepped over him as he descended into the basement. There was only one emergency light illuminating the basement at the bottom of the stairs. As soon as Deleon saw the door to her room open, he knew Elizabeth was either dead or had escaped. He went on and searched her room anyway. Deleon stumbled over Alejandro's mangled body, but there was no sign of Elizabeth. Frustrated, he turned and retraced his way up the stairs.

He needed a plan B now, but he didn't have one. One thing was for sure, he had to get out of the building. If Jackson had Elizabeth, Deleon figured that he would blow the compound to rubble from a distance. Deleon cut a long piece of backing off one of the curtains and wrapped it tightly around the fingers and thumb of his left hand. Holding one end between his teeth, he tied the bandage securely. He opened the injured hand with a grimace. At least with his fingers wrapped together he would be able to grip objects with his left hand. He went to the next staircase and began making his way to an upper story. Perhaps he could find a hiding place from which he could shoot Jackson. He would probably have to expose himself in order to get off a shot. With limited use of one hand, the rifle was unwieldy and his pistol wouldn't provide a killing shot from any distance.

As Deleon started up to the second floor, he heard voices, voices speaking English. He climbed the stairs slowly and silently. He heard two men's voices; one was groaning in pain while the other was trying to soothe him. Deleon dropped down into a crouch. He had not dared hope for such luck, but it looked like fate was now smiling upon him. He stopped four or five steps from the top of the staircase and listened. The muffled conversation sounded as if it was originating in the vestibule of the second-floor entrance, a large room off the hall. There were no other sounds in the hallway. Using all his guile, he moved catlike up the remaining stairs and across the hall. Keeping to the wall, he tiptoed to the vestibule's doorway and listened.

"I've got the tourniquet as tight as I can, Dan," Rhasan said with concern. "I can't get it any tighter."

Dan gritted his teeth. "Try and give it another half turn, Rhasan. The blood's still oozing out! Oh, shit! It's looks like I've lost a quart already. Where are vampires when you really need them?"

Rhasan made a face. "I don't think we can stop it. The bullet went clean through your thigh and the hole in the back is pretty big."

Dan lay back flat on the floor. "I'm getting groggy. Hard to stay awake . . ."

To Deleon, it sounded like there were only two men in the vestibule. He peeped around the corner and saw that he was correct and both men were faced toward the outside door, away from him. They were on the floor next to a low coffee table beside some heavy wooden chairs. He moved quietly into the room, relying on stealth to get as close as possible before he made his presence known. He was within ten feet before either man noticed him.

It was Rhasan who saw Deleon first. A questioning frown crossed his face then he demanded, "Who are you?" He started to reach for the Uzi, which was a couple of feet behind him.

"Don't!" Deleon warned, pointing the barrel of his rifle at Rhasan. "Not if you want to live another minute!" Deleon moved forward swiftly and kicked the Uzi across the room.

Dan lifted his head, but he couldn't focus on the voice. "Is that you, Jax?"

Deleon didn't answer. He walked around Dan to make sure that he had no weapon. Dan's face was sweaty and he was starting to tremble a bit. Deleon told Rhasan, "He's beginning to go into shock. If you want to help him, tear down one of the curtains and cover him. But don't make any sudden moves, or it'll be you lying on the floor with bullet holes in you!" Rhasan got up obediently and pulled down one of the heavy drapes that lined the wall. He made sure the tourniquet was still tight then tucked the drapes around Dan's body.

Deleon studied Rhasan. The boy had a bit of a goatee, but his brown skin had the smooth softness of youth. In prison he would be considered a virgin fuck. Such a boy would be reserved only for the most powerful gang leaders. He was a real prize. Deleon regretted that he did not have the time to sample the boy's flesh, but his thoughts gravitated to the business at hand; destiny was pressing and it required all of his attention.

Rhasan said to Deleon, "Whoever you are, you can still escape. My uncle will be here soon. He'll be coming to check on us!"

Deleon smiled. "You're Jackson's nephew? Good. Very good. I want to see your uncle."

"What do you want with him?" Rhasan demanded. A look of alarm spread across his face.

"That's my business. I want you to call him."

Suddenly Rhasan understood. He pointed at Deleon and exclaimed, "You're a DuMont! You don't just want to see him, you want to kill him!"

"You answered the sixty-four-thousand-dollar question. Now, go and call him!" Deleon's voice was cold and hard. "Do it now!"

Rhasan pounded his chest with youthful bravado. "You can kill me! I don't care! I'll never call him!"

Deleon snorted at Rhasan's foolishness. Rhasan was too valuable to injure immediately. Deleon merely pointed his rifle at Dan's supine body and said, "I'll put a bullet in him for every time I have to ask you!"

Rhasan put his hands up, pleading, "Don't shoot him. It's me that's disobeying you. I'm the one that's not going to call!"

"I'm going to fill him up with bullets then I'm going to start on you. What do you bet that when I make you scream, your uncle will come in here anyway? And, boy, I *will* make you scream! This is time number one. Go to the door and call your uncle!"

Voices from outside precluded Rhasan's response. "Rhasan? Dan?" It was Jackson's voice.

Deleon shouted, "Your nephew's in here! He's in here along with one of your friends! If you want to see either one of them alive, you'll come in here by yourself! This is Deleon DuMont speaking! I've been waiting to meet you! And I warn you, don't do anything foolish! The boy will die first! If anyone else comes in, I'll kill them!"

Outside on the balcony Jackson started toward the door, but Elizabeth yanked him back. Her eyes were filling with tears. She shook her head. "No, you don't! Don't throw it away after all of this! How do you know he just won't kill you?" Jackson tapped his vest, to which Elizabeth replied, "All he has to do is knock you down with a few shots, then he can take his time killing you!"

Jackson touched her face. "How can I not go? Both Dan and Rhasan came here as a favor to me." He pulled out of her grip and said to Esteban, "Don't let anything happen to her!"

They heard Deleon's voice shouting, "I'm waiting in here! And I'm getting impatient!"

Jackson walked to the edge of the door and demanded, "When I walk into the room I want you to release Rhasan and Dan!"

"And if I don't?"

"We'll assume the worst and come in firing!"

Deleon laughed cynically. "Sure thing! I'll let them go! I just love agreements!" Standing behind Rhasan, he pushed the barrel of his .22 into the base of his skull, pressing the sharp blade of his knife under the boy's chin to keep him from trying to escape. Deleon hadn't decided whether he would kill the boy or not; it depended upon the whim of the moment as well as circumstance.

Jackson stepped into the room with a pistol in his hand. Immediately he saw the gleam of the blade at Rhasan's throat. He stepped out of the doorway and moved along the wall. He said in a quiet voice, "I'm in here. What's the shouting about?"

"Put down your gun and I'll show you!"

"I'll put the gun down when you let Rhasan go. Otherwise, kill him now. There's no way I'm putting this gun down until he's released."

"You fool! You must think I'm playing! Your friend will pay!" Deleon turned the .22 on Dan's unconscious body and saw a movement from Jackson out of the corner of his eye. It made him hesitate and hunker down. That movement saved his life. Jackson fired off two quick shots. The first clipped the barrel of his pistol, knocking it from his hands, and the second whizzed a quarter of an inch over his head. He felt its passage. Deleon switched the knife into his good hand and ducked down behind Rhasan.

"Let Rhasan go and I'll put the gun down!"

Deleon knew that Jackson was too good with a pistol to play out his situation too long. If he killed the boy, Jackson would kill him. It wasn't a fair exchange. At best, it was a knight for a king. The game would be over. Jackson started pacing on a horizontal to where Deleon was holding Rhasan. Deleon tightened his grip on the boy and growled, "Stop right there! I'll kill him! I may not kill you, but I'll definitely kill him!" Jackson stopped moving. He stood still, the pistol pointed obliquely in Deleon's direction. Despite the pain Deleon stuck the fingers of his left hand into the boy's nostrils and pulled the boy's head back roughly then dragged the edge of his blade around the boy's throat, cutting just the first thin layer of skin. He held the point of his knife against the side of the boy's neck. From this position, he could throw his knife with deadly accuracy should Jackson move within ten feet. He would've played a waiting game with Jackson had he not heard the soft, shuffling sound of someone moving on the stairwell. He had no time. He had to let the boy go. He had to gamble that Jackson was stupid enough to believe that he had to honor the agreement to put his pistol down. Deleon gave Jackson a big smile and said, "All right, I'll release the boy, then you put your gun on the floor."

Jackson smiled back. "I'll put my gun on the floor when he and Dan are out of the range of your knife."

Deleon frowned and said, "I'm going to trust you this time. Get out of here, kid!" He let go of Rhasan, who fell to the floor and scrambled away.

Jackson ordered, "Rhasan, get Dan under the arms and drag him out of here!"

Rhasan stood up slowly. He put his hand up to his neck then saw his fingers were covered with blood. He gave Deleon a look of pure rage. Jackson interrupted his thoughts.

"Rhasan! Get Dan out of here now! He needs medical attention!" Rhasan turned to the task as ordered. Deleon shifted his position casually, trying to get a better angle on Jackson while keeping in throwing range of Rhasan. Jackson stopped him with a warning. "Move any farther and I'll start shooting!"

Rhasan dragged Dan's unconscious body out the door. Jackson called after him, "Tell everyone to stay out!" He knelt and put his gun on the floor.

Deleon figured there were three and a half strides between him and Jackson. If the gun were farther away, Deleon could be on him and kill him before he could squat down to pick it up. Deleon opened his hands to show that all he possessed was his knife. "Kick the gun away! It's just you and me now." Jackson did as requested. Before the gun had skidded to a stop Deleon took off for him. He had made two strides before Jackson had even decided how he would react and then he only dropped down into a defensive crouch with his hands low. Deleon landed on his third stride and launched himself at Jackson, changing the attack line of his blade from low to high at the last minute. He was aiming for the throat. Then suddenly Jackson's foot shot up, striking for his head. With a torque of his body Deleon contorted out of the way so that the shoe only grazed his ear. He slashed at Jackson's unprotected belly as he continued past him and struck home, but the blade of his knife was unable to slice through the Kevlar netting of the bulletproof vest.

Deleon rolled to his feet and began another quick attack. This time he intended to stab directly through the vest. He shifted to a low striking position, hoping to bring Jackson's hands down. He made several flashing stabs for the thighs and Jackson gave ground. Then without warning he leaped forward, stabbing for the stomach, which surprisingly Jackson blocked. Using his opponent's arm as a pivot, Deleon slashed for the neck and the blow was blocked again. Deleon was about to make an arm cut when he saw a blade slashing for his face. Deleon had to contort his body again to avoid the blow. He broke with Jackson and cursed himself. He had been too arrogant. With two hands the fight would've been over, but with only the use of one he should've started gradually and determined Jackson's skill level. The palmed-blade technique was old school. Jackson had obviously trained some-where.

Deleon started another attack. This time it consisted of a series of rapid stabs and parries, checking out Jackson's defenses. Their blades clashed in the block and parry. Deleon noted that there were opportunities to inflict various cuts on Jackson which would eventually wear him down. However, Deleon needed something more immediate. He hadn't forgotten those noises in the hall, plus using his left arm in close blocking was extremely painful. Several times his arm almost gave way because of the pain. He needed a mortal thrust. Deleon kept his blade flashing through the attack patterns, seeking his opening. He had seen that Jackson responded to a right-handed overhand throat attack by not fully side-stepping, but blocking it with his left hoping to come under it with his own blade. Yet he gave way to the right when attacked from the left.

Deleon used this information to back Jackson toward the low coffee table. He made several low lunging attacks then came up quickly with a throat thrust. Jackson was only able to avoid the blade by leaping back-ward, but the table caught the backs of his legs and he went sprawling. Deleon did not wait for him to land fully on the table before he launched himself. He had his knife high behind his head and he was striking for the heart. Jackson saw him at the last moment and raised his left hand to block, but Deleon drove his blade through Jackson's hand and tried to put the weight of his landing behind the thrust. Strangely, he wasn't able to drive the blade into Jackson's heart. The tip of the knife only penetrated the vest. Deleon scrambled to get his weight behind the blade of his knife while trying to keep a grip on Jackson's knife arm.

The blade had gone through Jackson's hand so fast that he didn't recognize it until the tip of the knife penetrated his chest. He realized that he was moments away from death. Deleon was trying to reposition himself, to put his weight behind the knife. Jackson's left hand couldn't take much more. Then suddenly he looked up and saw his grandfather staring down at him. The old man was wearing his white Stetson and smoking a cigar. The old man kicked him in the side and growled, "Get up, goddamn it, and stop playing around! I got mo' things for you to do!"

Jackson was so outraged by his grandfather's words, he exploded. He didn't quite know what happened next but he twisted his blade hand out of Deleon's grip and then drove his knife up to its hilt into Deleon's heart. He twisted the blade savagely until Deleon's body went limp and his eyes closed. Jackson rolled the dying body off him and stood up. He pulled Deleon's knife out of his hand. The pain caused him to bend over in agony. He dropped the knife on the floor and looked around for his grandfather, but he was gone. There was only a trace of cigar smoke in the air.

When Jackson twisted his knife out of the weakened grip of his left hand, Deleon knew that death was coming. He was not even surprised when the blade entered his chest. There was only momentary pain then all was numb. As his eyes closed for the last time, his dying thought was that the swirling red painting he had dreamed of was being done in his own blood.

Jackson looked down at Deleon's body and realized that the last debt had been paid. He threw back his head and roared. The sound came from deep inside of him, beyond the world of logic and ideas. It was the raw, primal energy of an animal that had conquered a bitter rival. It was the sound of victory.

Wednesday, August 25, 1982

Serena hummed a gospel song to herself as she looked over the plates of hors d'oeuvres and made adjustments to the table decorations. She particularly liked the three large bouquets of red and pink roses that Gabriel Fontenot and his wife had brought. There was laughter coming from the living room. She also heard the sound of Elroy coughing. Concerned, she went to the door and looked in to see if he needed any assistance. Elroy was in the midst of telling a funny story. He was surrounded by Samantha, Rhasan, Jackson, Carlos, Reuben, and Julio, along with his own son, Gabriel, and his wife, Nora. Elroy saw her in the doorway, smiled, and gestured that he was fine, then continued with his story.

Serena turned back into the dining room. She was beaming. It had been a stroke of luck to have located Elroy's son in Sacramento. All Elroy had known was that he worked as a structural engineer for a large development corporation. Serena had called in a few favors from her real estate contacts in Sacramento and within a week she had found him. Gabriel and his wife were only too happy to come down once they heard about Elroy's injuries. Gabriel had given Serena quite a shock when he had come through the door, because he looked like Jackson's father, Jacques. Tremain blood was there through and through. Serena's thoughts were interrupted by more laughter from the living room. The sound of it swelled her heart. It seemed a century ago that she was sitting in a quiet, still house contemplating death. She felt that she had journeyed into the bowels of hell itself and had been blessed with a miraculous reprieve. She would not waste this second chance on anything less than happiness. Whatever little time she had left, she wanted it like this, with a laughter-filled house.

Mrs. Marquez entered from the kitchen carrying a sweet-smelling, partially sliced glazed ham on one of Serena's fine porcelain platters.

"You've outdone yourself, Mrs. Marquez. That looks wonderful."

Mrs. Marquez smiled. "Thank you, but it is your recipe. I only fix it like you say. The chickens, they come, oh, maybe five minutes. They look beautiful too." She chuckled and glanced over the table and put her hand to her mouth. "Oh, I forgot the deviled eggs!" She began to scurry toward the kitchen

Serena laughed and said, "Take your time, Mrs. Marquez. In a week, you'll be retiring from this job of twenty-five years and you're the grandmother of a college-bound high school graduate."

Mrs. Marquez paused momentarily before going through the kitchen door, as if Serena's words had somehow stabbed her painfully in the back. When she returned with the platter of deviled eggs, her head was down and there was a leaden movement in her gait.

Serena asked with concern, "Did I say something? What's wrong?"

When Mrs. Marquez looked up there were tears in her eyes. "I'm sorry! So sorry to cry at your party! I go now! Maybe talk later! Please forgive! I come back with chickens!" She turned away, heading toward her quarters.

"Please, Mrs. Marquez! Please can't we talk now?"

Mrs. Marquez turned, tears staining her cheeks, and said, "Please, Mrs. Tremain, I need to take back my resignation. I need my job here with you. I can't retire."

"Mrs. Marquez, of course you can have your job back. There's no one else I'd rather have. But I thought the severance package of twenty-five thousand along with your retirement plan was enough."

"You are very generous. It was enough, but my grandson, he . . . he . . ." Mrs. Marquez started to cry.

Serena put her arm around Mrs. Marquez and walked her into a small sitting room and closed the door. "What's happened to your grandson? Tell me."

Mrs. Marquez dabbed at her eyes, took a deep breath, and said, "He had motorcycle accident. He and his girlfriend. They are both in County Hospital in Oakland. He is paralyzed from the neck down and she has head injuries. They have no medical insurance and they get treatment like they are homeless. There aren't enough nurses. The doctors are always in a hurry. Only one person can visit at a time. The hospital security act like we're thieves. I will give everything I have to see that he gets a good doctor. I worked too long and too hard to see my only grandchild have no future. I can't retire while he is in need."

Serena hugged her and said, "You don't have to come back to work for me to help you get medical attention for your grandson. I'd be happy to—"

Alarm spread across Mrs. Marquez's face and she pulled away. "I no ask you for charity! You been very generous! You have helped much already. If you let me come back, that is help enough! I no ask you for anything but the job. Please, don't think me like that."

Serena touched Mrs. Marquez's cheek softly. She had discovered that she liked touching people, that she needed to touch those she cared about. She said, "I have learned that there are many things that money can't purchase: loyalty, love, trust, hope, joy, just to name a few. But this—this can be purchased! I think we can get the very best medical attention for your grandson and his girlfriend."

"This cost big money, maybe fifty thousand dollars."

"We have big money! Your grandson will get the best!"

Tears began to stream down Mrs. Marquez's face, then she rushed forward and hugged Serena. "Thank you! Thank you! You give me so much! You give me hope! It is blessing I work for you. Thank you so much! You are saint!"

"I'm no saint, Mrs. Marquez; I can assure you of that!"

Mrs. Marquez started to say something more then she clapped her hands to her face. "The chickens!" She turned to rush out of the room.

Serena said, "To hell with the chickens! We're talking here!"

Mrs. Marquez gave her a look of surprise. "I never hear you curse before! But I must get chickens. I no let your party be ruin because of me." She hurried out of the room.

Serena followed her into the kitchen. "I want to talk to you more about this later. But I want you to know you don't have to come back to work."

"No, I must work," Mrs. Marquez said as she took a tray with two brown chickens on it out of the oven. "I cannot pay for this great blessing, but I can show my gratitude this way. I work for you. I will work hard because I am thankful. It is my way."

"I shall be happy to see you, but when you need time off I want you to take it. And if you find that for some reason work gets in the way of your helping your grandson, I want you to tell me. Right now, I want to check on Elroy. He's been sitting up a long time."

Mrs. Marquez nodded. "He is nice man. Always telling jokes and laughing. You are very close with this one who has been gone, no?"

"Yes. We are very close. We had a trip to the edge together. We looked deep into the abyss of hell, and were in danger of falling all the way in, but we climbed back out with each other's help. He is my long-lost son and I owe him my life."

"Your lost son! Is wonderful you find him. Things have been different since you have returned with him. The house used to be cold and dark. I used to wear my sweater all the time. Now, there is light and warmth. People come to visit. The house is alive with laughter. It is easier to work here now. I think I come work for you again even if not for my grandson. I like my job and I love my boss. She is saint, but doesn't know it."

"Mrs. Marquez, you touch my heart," Serena said as she walked out the door. She was feeling expansive as she went into the dining room.

Franklin and Victoreen were picking over the hors d'oeuvres as she walked by.

"We need to talk," Franklin said to her as she passed him.

Serena exhaled. Franklin was tiresome, but he was her grandson. She nodded and said, "I'll be right back. I want to check on Elroy." She walked into the living room and now Jackson was telling a story. He stopped when she put her hand on his shoulder. "Pardon me, Grandson, I just want to check on our patient."

Elroy smiled and waved. "I'm all right. In fact, I'm feeling great. Surrounded by family is the only way to be."

Gabriel said, "Don't tire yourself out on our account, Dad. We only live eighty miles away."

Jackson teased, "I'm more worried about him tiring us out with these shaggy-dog stories."

Julio pointed at Jackson. "You're as bad as him, maybe worse."

Samantha stood up. "Take my word for it, Jackson is much worse. Do you need a hand in the kitchen, Grandma?"

"Please, dear, if you don't mind." Serena, placing a hand on his shoulder, bent down and asked in Jackson's ear, "Will you say grace and carve the chickens and the roast?"

Jackson turned toward her and suppressed a look of surprise. He was unaccustomed to her touch and her closeness. "Of course, Grandmother, when do you need me?"

"In twenty minutes or so. And please, I'd appreciate it if you'd call me 'Grandma'; it's much less formal. I've begun to like informality in my old age." Serena smiled and gave Jackson a kiss on the forehead. She walked into the dining room arm in arm with Samantha.

Franklin was waiting for her with a frown on his face. "What's all this stuff with that stranger? You take him in like he's family! Hell, he acts like he's king of the roost here!"

Serena replied without rancor, "He is. He's a Tremain. He's my son."

Franklin was incredulous. "What? I don't understand you all of a sudden! As far as I know, you had only two sons and both of those are dead!"

Serena sighed. She didn't want to slip back into her old habits of condescension and sarcasm, but it was difficult with Franklin. She said in a kindly tone, " 'As far as you know' is an apt description of your knowledge in this area. Let it go, and accept him as your uncle."

Franklin sputtered, "He's no uncle to me! I'm not taking in some stranger and all his children!"

Serena was exhausted with the discussion. She said more firmly, "You don't have to take him in, and if you don't like what's going on in this house, you don't have to stay. You're free to go."

At this point, Samantha interjected, "I'm going into the kitchen to help Mrs. Marquez. Victoreen, would you like to lend a hand?"

Victoreen sucked her teeth and said haughtily, "I don't do kitchen work! I got my nails to think about!"

As she headed into the kitchen Samantha retorted, "Too bad your brain isn't held in the same esteem as your fingers."

A frown crossed Victoreen's face. "What did she say?"

Franklin ignored his wife and continued with his grandmother. "This new attitude of yours is going to make it difficult when we file our legal suit against the will."

Serena was surprised. "What suit? I don't plan to file any suit!"

Now it was Franklin's turn to be surprised. "You mean the way that Jackson got everything doesn't bother you? I mean, he had all his friends here. His friends! And he promised them millions of dollars! He's giving money to Chinks and—"

"That will be enough! I won't have that type of language spoken in my house!"

Franklin laughed sarcastically. "This isn't your house! The reading of the will gave the house to Jackson!"

Serena drew herself up and said politely, "I told him that I wanted to continue living here, so he gave the house to me."

"You're going to live here? In this mausoleum? This is too big for you!"

"Elroy and I both plan to live here. This will be the family seat. All the major gatherings and holidays will take place here, as I first imagined it when King and I bought this house."

Franklin was aghast. "But I thought my family would take it over! It would be perfect for us and the three kids!"

Serena looked at Franklin with both love and sadness. The world could not be changed. Franklin was going to be like his selfish, self-centered father. He was doomed to run afoul of the stronger members of his family. She said softly, "I was under the impression that Pacific Heights was where you wanted to be."

"This Fulton Street neighborhood is coming back now, and I wasn't able to buy the size I needed over there."

Victoreen added, "Once they move the nigger element totally out around here, the prices will skyrocket. We'll be sitting pretty then."

"Well, you will never be living in this house now! Accept it and go on. And Victoreen, don't ever use that word in this house again!"

"Don't you see?" Franklin was excited. "We don't have to accept the will. We file a suit and tie up everything for years. He'll have to settle with us!"

"I told you and it's final! I don't plan to be a party in any suit! I will not challenge the will!"

A look of cunning spread across Franklin's face. "What else did he give you? How did he buy you off?"

"How dare you! This conversation is terminated." Serena started to turn away but Franklin's next remark caused her to turn back.

"I know people who want to get rid of him permanently! They came to me! I guess I'll have to contact them now."

Serena walked over and stood face-to-face with her grandson. "Don't you understand that for the will to be read in this house, all of King's enemies had to be dead? Jackson has disposed of every one of them! If you start something like that with him, I won't be able to protect you. And believe me, if he turns on you, you won't be here long! Take my advice, accept things the way they are."

Franklin's greed spurred him on. "What about Braxton? He said he knew people that would take him out!"

Serena nodded then said with resignation, "Try and find him, then, if that's what you want to do. But understand, you're digging your own grave." Serena turned away and walked down the hall to her bedroom suite. She needed a moment's respite. She had been tempted to tell Franklin that Braxton would never be seen again, but that would've revealed too much. Serena went and stood in front of her bathroom mirror and touched up her makeup. Her trip out to Half Moon Bay two days ago was a secret that no one knew. She had learned of Braxton's whereabouts from Samantha in casual conversation several days earlier. Samantha had indicated that the woman she was seeing worked as Braxton's secretary and they had planned a trip to Yosemite together, but had to cancel because Braxton needed her to make arrangements for a long trip overseas. Samantha had, with some apprehension, revealed that Braxton was being unusually secretive about his being in Half Moon Bay. But the key for Serena had been when Samantha had mentioned that Braxton wanted large amounts of money transferred.

Serena picked up a vial of perfume and dabbed traces on her wrists and neck. She studied her face in the mirror. It looked no different from the way it had a few days earlier. It was lined with her mistakes and fears, but her dealings with Braxton hadn't changed it. She had known from the very moment she heard about the money that Braxton was trying to escape and regroup. She knew that she could not let him make another attempt to destroy her family. Serena liked and valued what she now possessed and would give her life to maintain it. With Elroy in the house, Jackson and Elizabeth had started dropping by regularly and often they stayed for dinner. Sometimes she and Elizabeth joined Mrs. Marquez in the kitchen to prepare a specifically requested dish, and they would end up laughing and talking, almost forgetting what they had wanted to prepare. It was the most joyous time Serena could remember since her early days in Oklahoma. However, with this joy came the intuitive understanding that she could've had this same feeling decades earlier if she had but made a different decision. It had taken a life of tragedy, but she had truly learned that life was worth nothing without the investment of time and love in family and friends.

If Braxton escaped there was always the chance that he would make another try to destroy her family. To forestall such an occurrence, Serena had taken the nickel-plated .357 Magnum that King had given her out of its box. She hadn't picked up the gun since she had first taken Jackson to Mexico all those years ago. It was heavy in her hand as she had carried it to her car.

The drive to the coast had been rather arduous. Frankly, neither her eyesight nor her reflexes were up to the task, but she had arrived safely. She had been to Braxton's house in Half Moon Bay many years ago and, surprisingly, she remembered the way without problems. There was shock in Braxton's eyes when he had first opened the door. He almost dropped his crutches. He didn't even bother to beg. He just stepped back from the door. Serena entered the house and closed the door behind her. She pointed the gun at Braxton's chest and fired once. Braxton had fallen over backward. Serena walked to see where she had hit him. It was a messy wound just under the heart, but it was clear that Braxton was not going to survive the injury. Serena had stood over him and uttered, "That was for the Tremain family! For King, LaValle, and Jacques!" Then she had turned and driven back to San Francisco. She had taken the gun that had been used once and once only and given it to Jackson to discard. He didn't ask her any questions, he merely nodded and said he would take care of it. Serena knew she wasn't a saint, but she was ready to make any sacrifice to protect those she loved.

Jackson was standing by the mantel listening to Nora Fontenot tell stories to the gathering about her experiences as a public health nurse when Carlos came over, tapped him on the shoulder, and whispered, "They're ten minutes away. Can we meet downstairs?"

Jackson nodded and walked out to the hallway. He opened the dou-

ble doors that led down to his grandfather's old office in the basement.
The room was unchanged from the time Jackson was a child. There was
still a full-sized bar and pool table at the back, and a huge rolltop desk
in an alcove opposite the stairs and a large card table surrounded by
chairs up near the front of the house. It had its own entrance in the wall
adjacent to the alcove. As they descended the stairs Jackson asked, "Are
these people aware that I don't want to continue selling guns and ammunition?"

"No, and I didn't see any reason to tell them. They sent a substantial
down payment three months ago. There have been some delays in delivery and now their representatives want to meet the man who took
over El Negro's organization. All you have to do is assure them that
everything will be done to get them their shipment as soon as possible.
The meeting will be quite short."

"Is that true? Everything's being done?"

"I wouldn't tell you if it wasn't. Lying isn't part of my business."

"Okay, I'm ready to go. Let them in when they get here."

Carlos put his hand on Jackson's shoulder and advised, "You might
consider getting a place in Atlanta since that's one of the major airports
that we ship out of. It would help you keep better tabs on the operation."

Jackson shook his head. "Why? I don't want to get any more involved with running guns than I have to."

"Maybe I ought to tell you that our principal competitor is Oswaldo
San Vicente, Francisco's older brother."

"The one who's sworn to kill me?"

"The very same. He's watching you for signs of weakness. He's afraid
to move on you now because of what happened to his brother, but like
your grandfather used to say, 'he's talking smack' in underworld circles."

Jackson asked, "Well, I can't afford to lose business to him, can I?"
Carlos shook his head and stared back at him meaningfully. Jackson
winnowed his intent and asked with resignation, "Will I have to kill this
San Vicente too? When will all this be over?"

"It'll never be over. The San Vicentes have allies and as you grow
stronger, more enemies will appear. Then there's the Gaxiolas. Oswaldo's been telling them that it was you that attacked their compound.
And don't forget the DiMarcos, because I assure you they haven't forgotten you. You need to remain strong and maintain a trained and dedicated corps of soldiers."

"A dedicated corps of soldiers? You've mentioned this before. Isn't it expensive?"

"That's why your grandfather was in the military-hardware business. It's the only thing outside of drugs that can pay that type of money. It's your major revenue generator."

Jackson conceded, "Okay, I'll find a house in Atlanta. At least the Du-Monts are no more."

"Don't count on it! El Negro thought he had wiped them out two or three times. It's a big family. That's why the feud has lasted over a hundred years."

"You're full of bright news."

"It's my job."

There was a tapping at the exterior door and Carlos went to answer it. Tavio and Diego ushered in two men from southern Mexico. Introductions were made and then everyone sat down at the card table. Jackson produced a bottle of añejo tequila and poured shots around. He reiterated what Carlos had said and gave his word that their shipment would be given the highest priority. He was a little surprised when they stood up to leave after one drink, but they thanked him respectfully and were escorted to the door by Tavio and Diego. Before leaving one of the men shook his hand and said, "Gracias, El Negro."

Jackson gripped the man's hand and merely nodded in response. After they had left he commented to Carlos, "That was quick."

"I told you they just wanted to see you. Now they will go back to their people and say you look just like El Negro and their money is safe."

"How do they know?"

"You forget, you have history in Mexico. Francisco San Vicente's demise is widely discussed. Plus, there are many who remember the fight in the pit and many more who have heard about it. They know you are El Negro's heir, that you will honor his memory. That is why he called you El Negro."

"I never thought of myself as ever taking my grandfather's place, much less honoring his memory. But I have to admit that my opinions have changed regarding the old man. Well, Carlos, I guess the last thing to do is figure out how get ahold of those lost certificates. I'm certainly not looking forward to going into San Francisco's sewer system. I wonder why there was no mention of it in the will."

"Now that the will has been read, I must give you something and it may answer your questions about the certificates." Carlos stood up and went to an old leather satchel and pulled out a wooden box with an envelope taped to the top. He brought it over and handed it to Jackson.

"Portugas cigars! My grandfather's favorite! I don't know why, but lately I've been thinking about smoking one of these."

"Before you open the cigars, you should open this first." Carlos handed Jackson a smaller box made of highly polished cherry wood.

Jackson took the box and gave Carlos a questioning look.

"Open it," Carlos urged.

Jackson pulled off the cover and there, lying on blue velvet, was a white feather tipped with black. Jackson was speechless. He looked at Carlos.

Carlos nodded and said, "Yes, it is the same feather that El Indio gave you so many years ago. I have kept it for this moment. Now you have earned it twice."

Jackson exhaled. "This is quite an honor, to have this gift from El Indio. I don't know what to say."

"Say nothing, just continue to act in a manner that the old ones would respect. You are El Negro now." Carlos nodded to the envelope on top of the cigar box. "That's the last letter your grandfather dictated before he was killed."

Jackson pulled the tape off the box and held up the envelope. "I bet there's a bombshell or two in here." He shook his head as he studied the envelope. "I don't know if I even want to read this! Let me enjoy the feather for a moment." He laid the envelope down on the table and shook his head again.

The door at the top of the stairs opened suddenly and there was the sound of steps descending rapidly. Rhasan burst into the room. "Man, my mother's gone crazy! I have to live with you! I can't stay with her!"

Jackson put up his hands. "Whoa! What's this all about?"

"She's nagging me all the time! I'm beyond all that, I'm eighteen now! I'm a man! I want to move in with you. She's wacko!"

Jackson studied his nephew then inquired, "I have to ask, are you dealing with all your responsibilities? Or is she having to do your share?" He put the box containing the feather in the rolltop desk.

Carlos stood up and said, "I'll go upstairs while you finish this discussion." He turned and headed for the stairs.

Jackson looked at Rhasan. "Are you doing your share?"

Rhasan frowned and shook his head. "Why do you always start off as if I'm in the wrong?" Rhasan rapped his chest. "Why do you question me?"

"Because your mother is a fairly sane, logical person who's just trying to get you to carry your weight. Isn't she trying to get the house ready for sale? Isn't there a lot of packing still to be done?"

Rhasan growled, "How do you know I haven't done my share? I—"

"Watch your tone!" Jackson warned. "We are here to discuss, not argue! There'll be no raised voices or angry intonation! This is family; you bring your best skills to the discussion."

"Just answer me: Why do you think I'm always at fault?"

"If you want the truth, it's because you've been getting pretty full of yourself since we've returned from Mexico. You want to act like you're the equal of men who've been tested many times."

Rhasan tapped his chest. "I only respect those who respect me!"

"Respect is valuable, but it isn't given freely. It must be earned. You haven't earned it. You haven't done anything worth the stature you've given yourself. And let's examine the way you're dealing with your mother. Isn't it true that when your mother asked you to assist with the packing, you told her to hire someone?"

"She told you, huh?" Rhasan exhaled then he turned jaunty. "Well, we got money, why sweat the small stuff? We don't have to do the packing ourselves now!"

"All the money you have was given to you. You haven't earned any of it and it isn't yours. Yet you feel free to spend it in lieu of your work."

"You talk all this family stuff, you say I'll lead the family one day, then you say the money isn't mine! What's up with that?"

Jackson stared at Rhasan then asked, "Do you really want to be part of the family business? And if you do, how much do you want it? Truthfully!"

"I want it more than anything!"

"Then you have to prepare yourself. You must be willing to learn all the lessons of leadership. But most of all you must be willing to work and take your responsibilities seriously. We're not going to let the power to ruin or improve this family fall into the hands of a fool. Otherwise, we'd give Franklin control. He's family too. You don't get anything until you have shown that you have the discipline and focus to guide this family's fortunes."

"What do I have to do to show that I have that?"

"Be willing to work hard in all family-related matters. Complete your college degree with a B or better grade point average and get your nose out of your ass. Treat your mother with the respect that she deserves. Do more than your share of the work."

"Okay! Okay! But I'm moving out! I'm not going to live under her roof ever again!"

"Where will you live?"

"You won't let me live with you?"

"No!"

"Well, Fox has some room—"

"If you do that you'll throw away your future. You better move in here."

Rhasan's eyes got big with excitement. He looked around the room. "Move in here? Sure!"

Jackson continued, "You can take my old room. But you'll observe all the rules of the house, including whatever chores are demanded, being here for dinner every night, and the hours of curfew. You fail to comply, you lose the BMW."

"Curfew?"

"You heard me right. Unless you've received permission from Grandmother, you're home by the time the house closes up."

"Do I keep getting the training in self-defense?"

"As long as you show that you've got your eyes focused on the family's long-term goals."

"Okay. I can do that."

"One last thing. Don't ever come down here without knocking and requesting permission first."

"But I thought—"

"This matter is not open to discussion. You are not part of the business until you've completed college. Another thing, until you head the family you cannot bring anyone in here without permission. Not your friends. Not anyone. This room is sacrosanct. Don't ever violate the rules concerning this room!"

"Okay, but can I come down here and play pool if no one is here?"

"As long as you don't touch anything else and you clean up after yourself."

Rhasan nodded his head and said, "That's cool. I can live with that."

"Good." Jackson turned toward the rolltop desk, but his nephew stopped him.

"Say, Uncle Jax. I know I don't have the right to ask this, but if it wasn't important to me I wouldn't ask for it."

Jackson faced his nephew. "Go ahead."

"Ever since you brought Diablito home, you know he and I have been tight. I've been taking him everywhere and you encouraged it."

"Yes, I've noticed that you and he seem to have bonded."

"You know I've never had a dog before and I've always wanted one. Well, Diablito is my dog now and I don't want to leave him. When I come home from college next summer, he won't be a puppy anymore. I don't want to miss that time."

"But you're living in a dorm."

"I know, that's the problem, Unc. So I was talking to Terry Strong—"

Jackson interrupted. "Dan's son?"

"Yeah, he's going to Morehouse now. And we've been talking about getting an apartment, but we need some help with the money so . . ."

Jackson's first reaction was to tell his nephew that he hadn't demonstrated sufficient responsibility to live off campus or have a pet, but as he thought about it, other ideas sprang to mind. He had to get a place in Atlanta anyway. Why not let it serve multiple purposes? He gave Rhasan a long look, then said, "Your schedule, including your studies and your martial arts training, is going to be pretty rigorous. Are you sure you want to add the pressure of a dog? Pit bulls in particular need a lot of attention and must be taken to obedience school. It's dangerous to have one that isn't trained. Are you sure you have the vinegar and commitment to do all this?"

Rhasan considered Jackson's question a moment then nodded. "I think I can do it."

"What did I tell you about the difference between thinking and doing?"

Rhasan affirmed, "I can do it. I'll make you proud."

"All right. I have business in Atlanta, so I'll buy a house in which you and Terry can stay. Further, I'll send Theresa out there to watch over things and make sure you get at least one good meal a day."

Rhasan was exuberant. "You'll send Theresa too? Uncle Jax, that's the bomb! Wait till I tell Terry. Thank you! Thank you!"

"Understand Theresa is not there to be your maid and I'll be visiting often to check on things."

"No problem. I intend to be a man of my word like you and Great-grandfather. Can we shoot a game of pool to celebrate this?"

"You go ahead, my nephew. I have a letter to read."

While Rhasan racked the balls on the pool table, Jackson lit a cigar and opened the envelope. The letter it contained was one page, type-written. It read:

Well, Grandson,

If you're reading this, you've done almost everything I wanted you to do. Congratulations!

I guess I should clear up a few things so I got somebody to write this letter for me—the hand ain't steady now. First, there are no blank certificates. It was all a ruse to keep my enemies from killing you before you were ready to fight. Sampson Davis gave his life to set up the ruse. He was dying of cancer anyway. (Make sure he was buried right.) Like me he wanted to go down fighting rather than die piece by piece in a hospital. Your name has been on everything for years. You own everything that I possessed. If you want a full account of all your holdings, contact my attorneys (Goldbaum & Goldbaum) in New York. Ira Goldbaum is dead, but his son, Noah, is an able and honest man.

I know you're probably wondering why I didn't tell you this following item while I was alive. Well, I didn't tell you because then I wasn't sure you had the stuff to deal with it successfully. But now that you've proven yourself, here it is. There's a boy in Tampico who'll be around eighteen as you read this and he looks just like you. I never saw him myself, but my sources say it's clear he has Tremain blood. He's Maria's son. To protect him, she let another family raise him. He's working in a shoe factory. The one problem about going to get him is he's in the middle of San Vicente's turf. They don't know exactly where he is, but they know he's somewhere on the northeastern coast of Mexico. They haven't really looked for him, but they probably will now. You've got to beat them to the punch, otherwise they'll take him hostage. Then they'll torture him and keep him alive for years waiting for you to come and get him. Understand, there's no way you can get him without spilling blood. When you go after him, plan it well and know that you're going to be in a fight. Just by the by, Maria died in 1975 of pneumonia.

I want my ashes spread in the Sea of Cortez, the San Francisco Bay, and wherever you buy land to build a family house. Until then keep my ashes behind the bar in my office in the Fulton Street house.

One last thing: I don't ever want Franklin to inherit or be given any part of my estate. He is not of my blood and I don't want him benefitting from my sacrifice and my sweat. I know you have become attached to Samantha and

Rhasan. My feelings toward Franklin do not apply to them. From what I hear,
Rhasan acts like a Tremain. Take him hunting. Train him like I trained you.
And with that in mind, you should train all the young Tremains. One day you
will need the strength of their arms, the will in their hearts, and the quickness of
their minds.

I just want you to know that I feel comfortable leaving the family's future in
your hands. My only request is that you do everything in your power to make
our family strong! Help build the family spirit. Maybe buy some rural acreage
with a lot of trees and build a big house where all the family can gather during
the summer. All your big decisions should be made based on what's good for the
family, not on what you personally want. Don't make my mistakes! I judged
harshly and I didn't forgive easily! That was one of the many ways I went
wrong. I did what I wanted and I let the devil take the hindmost. That isn't the
way to build a family. If you choose correctly, you'll bring the Tremain family
together as it has never been before and you will fulfill the legacy prophesied by
Sister Bornais. Do right, my grandson, and there will be a Tremain standing at
the scratch line for as long as there is a race of men.

You are my blood and my heir.

Jackson put down the letter and wiped the sweat off his forehead.
Suddenly it was quite warm in the room. He got up and walked out of
the exterior door. He stood on the paved walkway on the side of the
house and felt the cool breeze blowing across his face. He had a son. A
son that he had never seen. Jackson let his cigar go out as he reread the
letter. How long had his grandfather known of the boy's existence?
Why was everything so byzantine with his grandparents? Jackson began thinking about how he would mount a rescue effort. There was
never a moment's doubt whether he was going to go after his son. He
would not knowingly abandon a child of his blood, particularly when
that child was in danger. Jackson was angry when he turned back into
the house. Why did his child have to pay this price? Eighteen years
lost! Another Tremain raised by strangers. He needed to talk to Carlos,
to plan.

Rhasan leaned on his cue and looked around the room. It seemed like
he was in a dream. He was shooting pool where his great-grandfather
had stood. All the stories he had heard, now he was standing here him-

self. The future was laid out for him. All he had to do was perform and one day, he would be a man like his uncle Jackson; one day he would lead the family and he would be the one explaining the rules of this sacrosanct room. His chest was filled with pride. His family was one of the toughest that walked the earth. Not only was there King Tremain and Jackson, but his great-uncle Elroy was something too! Rhasan had wheedled the story out of him about how he had walked into the den of the DuMonts and held a gun to old Pug himself. He knew that there were real men in his family and that there was nothing he wouldn't do to earn their respect.

He broke the rack and followed the cue ball down to the other end of the table. He had sunk half of the balls when he heard footsteps coming down the stairs. He stopped and looked up, expecting Carlos. He was surprised to see Franklin step into the room. Rhasan returned to his pool game without a word. He had never gotten along with his snooty uncle Franklin and he had nothing to say to him now.

"Well, I see that Grandmother opened up this old room. It looks the same as I remember. Is that cigars I smell?" Rhasan continued shooting pool and did not respond. Franklin declared angrily, "I'm talking to you!"

"Oh, I thought you were talking to yourself."

"I was talking to *you*! Was someone smoking cigars?"

"Yeah, Uncle Jax. He's got a box of them on the table."

Franklin went over to the table and exclaimed, "Portugas! These are some of the best Cuban cigars! I'll take a few of these!"

"You better ask Uncle Jax, they belong to him!"

Franklin retorted, "The way some people talk, he owns every damn thing! Hell, I'll take the whole box! He has enough money to buy more!" Franklin scooped up the box and turned toward the stairs.

Rhasan repeated, "Those don't belong to you!"

"You young punks are so disrespectful! You better watch it or I'll have to teach you a lesson! You use that tone with me again and I'll knock you down!"

Rhasan looked at Franklin and said, "You may knock me down, but I will get up!"

Franklin started toward Rhasan. "You little punk—" His harangue and forward motion were stopped by Jackson's entrance.

"What the fuck are you doing down here?" Jackson demanded as he walked toward Franklin.

Franklin drew himself up and retorted, "I've got as much right to be here as you do!"

Rhasan volunteered, "He's stealing your cigars, Uncle Jax! And he was going to try to slap me around!"

Franklin declared, "He needs it! I won't tolerate insolence from street thugs!" He turned toward the stairs.

Jackson quickened his step and intercepted Franklin before he reached the bottom of the stairs. When Franklin spun around to face him, Jackson did not hesitate: He hit Franklin with a hard right on the side of the head. Franklin went sprawling on the floor and as he started to rise, Jackson kicked him hard in the gut. Jackson put his cigar in an ashtray, stepped back, and growled, "Get up, Frankie. It's time for another ass whipping! Come on, I only have one hand!" Jackson held up his bandaged left.

"Wait! Wait!" Franklin pleaded as he pulled himself up. He discovered that he was standing next to a rack of cues. He pulled one off the rack. His face filled with anger as he clutched the cue like a club. "I'll show you who's going to get their ass kicked!" He swung wildly at Jackson, who gave ground around the pool table.

Franklin was swinging the cue so hard that he was uncovered after every swing. Jackson timed him after one particularly wild swing and rushed him. Jackson did not even bother to grab the cue. He aimed for Franklin's throat but caught his chin with his right fist and knocked Franklin down again.

This time Franklin did not get up. Blood was running from both his nose and mouth. He screamed out, "Help! He's trying to kill me!"

"Shut the fuck up!" Jackson ordered. "If I wanted to kill you, you'd already be dead!"

Franklin screamed again. "Help! He's—"

Jackson kicked him hard in the stomach and cut off his air, then stooped down and dragged Franklin to his feet. He slammed Franklin into the wall at the bottom of the stairs and growled, "I know you are a traitor! Samantha told me about you calling Braxton's office every day this week! I know all about you, but you don't know me! If you ever do anything against me again, I'll have you killed!" He jammed his elbow under Franklin's chin, pressing it against his throat. "Do you understand me? You can be dead tomorrow!"

Serena heard the front doorbell and went to answer it. She was feeling happy and could not keep the smile off her face. Elizabeth stepped

in when she opened the door and gave her a warm hug, which she returned. Serena walked arm in arm with Elizabeth down the main hall.

Elizabeth asked, "Did the reading of the will go well?"

"It went as expected. Everyone but Franklin is happy. Jackson's
friends and their wives all seemed pleased. And I am extremely happy.
Jackson gave me this house. So Elroy and I will continue to live here.
For me this is the happiest period in my life in a long time. I'm looking
forward to spending my remaining years in the bosom of my family. I
must say I was a little surprised that you weren't here for the reading."

"I had a doctor's appointment."

Serena stopped walking and turned to look into Elizabeth's face. "A
doctor's appointment? Is there something wrong?"

Elizabeth was about to answer when the sound of a muffled scream
came through the closed door that led to King's old office. Both women
rushed to the door and opened it. Below them at the bottom of the
stairs, Jackson was pressing his forearm against Franklin's throat.

To Serena it was déjà vu. It was the powerful slope of Jackson's shoulders and the angry frown on his face. It was the fear in Franklin's eyes
and the blood that was dripping onto the floor. She had seen many such
scenes before. Everything that had been gained seemed on the verge of
being destroyed. Without thinking, she screamed out, "King! Please,
don't hurt him!" Franklin looked up at her with pleading in his eyes, but
Jackson's concentration on Franklin was unbroken by the sound of her
voice. It looked like he intended to kill Franklin. She turned wordlessly
to Elizabeth, begging for assistance.

Elizabeth called out, "St. Clair! Let him go! St. Clair!" For the first
time, Jackson looked up the stairs, then he backed away. As soon as
Franklin was released he scrambled up the stairs, happy to escape.

Jackson warned him, "Don't ever come down here again!" Franklin
did not stop or turn around. He pushed past the two women and ran
down the hall.

Serena was so thankful, she grabbed Elizabeth and gave her a hug.
"Thank you, dear. Thank you!"

Elizabeth kissed her cheek and said, "For nothing, Grandma T. Let
me go down there and corral my man."

Serena nodded and closed the door behind her. She rested for a moment against the wall. Everything was not going to be milk and honey.
The family still needed the help of a kind and gracious God. Serena

knew intuitively that her primary duty in her remaining years was to keep Franklin from doing something stupid that would cause Jackson to kill him. She had seen the look on Jackson's face and realized that King was not absolutely dead. His presence was alive and well in his grandson.

Elizabeth went down the stairs to Jackson, who stood waiting for her at the bottom. "What was that all about?" she asked.

Rhasan blurted out, "That slimeball was trying to steal the cigars that Great-grandfather Tremain had left Uncle Jax and he was going to try and slap me around for telling him that he was stealing! But Uncle Jax took care of him but good!"

Jackson turned to Rhasan with a smile on his face and asked, "Would you mind going upstairs and letting Elizabeth and me have a moment of privacy?"

"Sure thing, Uncle Jax, but can I ask one question first?" When Jackson nodded, Rhasan asked, "Were those rules you told me about this room the ones you had to follow?" Jackson nodded again in response and Rhasan smiled and said, "I knew it! That is so strong!" He put his cue in the rack and ran up the stairs two at a time. At the top of the stairs he turned and said, "I picked up the cigars and put the box on the table." He went through the door and closed it behind him.

Elizabeth looked at Jackson and said, "For a moment there, it looked like you thought you were back in Mexico."

"Funny you should mention Mexico. I am back there, but more on that later. What did the doctor say?"

"I was right. I *am* pregnant."

"And you're sure that it's Deleon's child?"

"There's no doubt. It's in the very early stages." Elizabeth paused and looked into Jackson's eyes. "Don't worry, I scheduled a date for an abortion."

Jackson studied the smooth skin of Elizabeth's face then said, "But you said you never wanted to have an abortion."

Elizabeth looked down at the floor and sighed. "It gives me problems, but I never thought I would be raped by the enemy of my fiancé."

"Can you have more children after this? Will there be any complications?"

"No, the doctor said that things should be pretty routine. She doesn't foresee any problems."

Jackson walked over to the table and sat down. He picked up and relit his cigar. Elizabeth joined him at the table. He puffed on his cigar
and blew a smoke ring then said, "I've been thinking hard about this
since you first mentioned it and I've reached a different decision. I think
you should have this baby. I don't want our marriage to start with any
more deaths. This baby isn't an enemy. This baby is going to be a
Tremain. Maybe the only way to truly end the feud is to raise this child
as my own. I will not make the mistakes that my grandparents made.
This will be my child in every way and he or she will never know any
other father."

Tears filled Elizabeth's eyes. "You don't have to do this."

"I know I don't have to do this, but that's what makes it a good decision and a right decision."

Elizabeth grabbed his hand and said, "Then you need not worry;
Tremain blood will be flowing in this child's veins because I am a
Tremain. And all my children will be Tremains. In my life I will have no
other last name. I am your wife, your lover, your partner until the heart
stops beating in my chest."

Jackson kissed Elizabeth's hand. "I love you, woman, particularly
when you're dramatic."

Elizabeth smiled and her big eyes flashed. "You sound like Dan. Tell
me about you being back in Mexico."

"A letter that my grandfather left informs me that I have an eighteen-
year-old son living in Tampico, and that the San Vicentes are looking
for him. If they get him first, he will be used as a hostage and tortured
until I come for him."

"A son! You have a *son!* When do we leave?"

"Hey, you're a pregnant mother. We don't want to endanger either
you or this child."

"St. Clair, you're not going anywhere without me. Understand that!
Where you are, I am. We're a set."

"Honey, please—"

"Honey nothing! I'm going! Don't waste time arguing."

There was a knock at the door at the top of the stairs and then
Rhasan's voice, "Grandma T says you should come on up, it's time for
dinner."

The dinner table was set for eleven when Jackson and Elizabeth entered the dining room. Elizabeth went immediately into the kitchen to
help with the serving. Serena was seating Elroy at the head of the table.

Jackson asked, "When do you want me to start carving, Grand-mother?"

Serena answered, "Thank you, but Elroy and Gabriel took care of it. I'd like you to say grace, though." She gestured for Jackson to take the chair at the other end of the table.

Jackson asked, "Where are you sitting?"

Serena tapped a chair at the center of the table. "I'll sit here, com-fortably in the middle of my family. You and Elroy are the heads of this family. You two will sit in the end chairs. Everyone else will sit where they choose." She waved Carlos, Julio, and Reuben to sit down. Nora and Gabriel sat next to Elroy. Rhasan was sent into the kitchen to help bring in the food.

"Where are Franklin and Victoreen?"

Serena gave Jackson an arched eyebrow and replied, "They saw fit not to join us this time. I hope that will change in the future."

Elizabeth and Samantha came in from the kitchen bearing platters of sweet potatoes, pot roast, and chicken. Elizabeth said to Jackson, "Save me a seat next to you." She set down her platter and returned to the kitchen.

Once the food was on the table and everyone was seated, Serena nodded to Jackson.

Jackson looked down the table at Elroy and said, "I defer to my uncle Elroy."

Elroy nodded and said, "I do want to say a few words of thanks, but the grace is still on you, young blood." Elroy looked around the table then bowed his head. "Lord, I haven't been too big on prayers in my life, yet right now I feel truly blessed. I'm sitting here at a table piled high with food and I'm surrounded by family. My own family! I want to thank you for letting me live long enough to learn something from my mistakes. I want to thank you for my son and daughter-in-law being present. I admit I wasn't much of a father to him or his brother. I was hard and I was cold. Lord, I'm so thankful that you have let this son grow large enough to forgive me my shortcomings and my faults. I can take no credit for his manhood. He is a good man and a good human being in spite of me. I love him with all my heart and will do everything I can to earn a place in his life. My only regret is that I didn't have the wisdom to say these words to his older brother.

"Lord, I want to thank you for my mother, Serena Tremain. We found each other at the right time. I needed her and she needed me. I thank you because she is the mother I always dreamed of and wished for. Thank you for this miracle! To my nephew Jackson and the rest of the family, I am happy to be a part of the Tremain family. I am committed to earning a place in each of your hearts and becoming a pillar that can be leaned on. In Jesus' name, I say thank you."

There were more than a few wet eyes around the table when Elroy finished. Serena was weeping openly. Samantha was dabbing her eyes, as was Elizabeth.

Jackson cleared his throat and said, "I don't think anything that I can say will be more gracious or grateful than what Uncle Elroy has just said."

Elizabeth squeezed his hand and said, "We still need a grace, St. Clair."

Jackson took a deep breath and said, "Well, let's get some family business out of the way first. Rhasan wants to move out of his mother's house. I have recommended that he move in here, Grandmother, if you don't have a problem with that."

Serena could not speak.

Jackson continued, "He will comply with all the house rules and in the summer, this is where he'll return until he has completed college. Is that all right with you, Grandmother?"

It took Serena a moment to gather herself, for she was emotionally overcome. She turned to Jackson and said through her tears, "To recommend him to my care, this means you must think that I—that I have done something right, that I have something of value to give! Oh, my grandson, you have truly touched me this moment! This is what I have dreamed of my whole life! To have my house filled with family, happy family." Serena stood up and put one hand high above her head. "Lord, let me be the one to say thank you, for I am the true sinner in this gathering! I am the one who lost her way! And I am the one who has caused those she loved so much pain! This day you have given me blessings I do not deserve. I have been petty. I have been envious. I have been small. And through these things I have destroyed those I have loved and lost others that I never knew. Yet in your beneficence and grace, you have given me back the family that I thought I had driven away completely." The tears began in earnest and Serena choked up. "Lord, I'm overwhelmed with your generosity, with this gift, with this miracle! I am so grateful! Thank you! Thank you!" Serena collapsed in her chair.

Elizabeth and Samantha immediately went to her side and held her. The emotion had flowed back and forth across the table like a riptide, sucking everyone in its path under its roiling forces. It took a moment for all at the table to regain their composure.

Mrs. Marquez, teary eyed, came in with a tureen of gravy. She said to Jackson, "This is the best dinner ever for Mrs. Tremain. The best!" She returned to the kitchen wiping her eyes on her apron.

When Jackson stood to say grace, he knew that he would lead the family out of the madness that had torn and separated them for so many years. He did not know whether he would be able to end the violence and death of his grandfather's wars, or whether he would merely continue them. The only things that he promised himself were that there would be no more secrets and half-hidden truths. It was his desire to bring all the family, perhaps even Franklin, but definitely his children, to the table, to be sharing and supportive of one another, so that none of the children now being raised would ever look back on a haunting, distant summer with fear and trepidation.

He bowed his head and began, "Thank you, Lord, for all the blessings . . ."

GUY JOHNSON is the author of the novel *Standing at the Scratch Line*, and a book of poetry, *In the Wild Shadows*. After graduating from high school in Egypt, he completed college in Ghana. Johnson managed a bar on Spain's Costa del Sol, ran a photo-safari service from London through Morocco and Algeria, and worked on oil rigs in Kuwait. Most recently he worked in the local government of Oakland, California, for more than ten years. He lives in Oakland with his wife and son. He is the son of Dr. Maya Angelou. To learn more about Guy Johnson and his work, visit his website at www.guyjohnsonbooks.com.

ABOUT THE TYPE

This book was set in Weiss, a typeface designed by a German artist, Emil Rudolf Weiss (1875–1942). The designs of the roman and italic were completed in 1928 and 1931 respectively. The Weiss types are rich, well balanced, and even in color, and they reflect the subtle skill of a fine calligrapher.